CW00855623

Extreme Prejudice

•

WAYNE KEESEE

•

Cover Illustration by
MS. DIANE D. DAIGLE

PUBLISHING™

• Canada • UK • Ireland • USA •

© Copyright 2005 Wayne Keesee.

All rights reserved. No part of this publication may be reproduced, stored in a retrieval system, or transmitted, in any form or by any means, electronic, mechanical, photocopying, recording, or otherwise, without the written prior permission of the author.

Note for Librarians: a cataloguing record for this book that includes Dewey Decimal Classification and US Library of Congress numbers is available from the Library and Archives of Canada. The complete cataloguing record can be obtained from their online database at:
www.collectionscanada.ca/amicus/index-e.html
ISBN 1-4120-6470-8
Printed in Victoria, BC, Canada

Printed on paper with minimum 30% recycled fibre. Trafford's print shop runs on "green energy" from solar, wind and other environmentally-friendly power sources.

TRAFFORD
PUBLISHING™

Offices in Canada, USA, Ireland and UK
This book was published *on-demand* in cooperation with Trafford Publishing. On-demand publishing is a unique process and service of making a book available for retail sale to the public taking advantage of on-demand manufacturing and Internet marketing. On-demand publishing includes promotions, retail sales, manufacturing, order fulfilment, accounting and collecting royalties on behalf of the author.

Book sales for North America and international:
Trafford Publishing, 6E–2333 Government St.,
Victoria, BC v8t 4p4 CANADA
phone 250 383 6864 (toll-free 1 888 232 4444)
fax 250 383 6804; email to orders@trafford.com
Book sales in Europe:
Trafford Publishing (uk) Limited, 9 Park End Street, 2nd Floor
Oxford, UK ox1 1hh UNITED KINGDOM
phone 44 (0)1865 722 113 (local rate 0845 230 9601)
facsimile 44 (0)1865 722 868; info.uk@trafford.com
Order online at:
trafford.com/05-1381

10 9 8 7

DEDICATION

I dedicate this book to all the brave Americans that served in Vietnam and in particular to the Air Force crews I flew with while I was there. To a man, they all performed with distinction and valor, and I consider it an honor to have known and worked with them.

I especially want to dedicate this book to my wife, Kim. She has faithfully stood by me through all the happy and sad times, and she has endured the aggravation and frustration that I have leveled at her during the writing of this manuscript. Without her support and patience, I would have never finished it. She is my best friend.

I offer special thanks to all the veterans I interviewed during the course of my military and airline careers. Their insights and experiences proved invaluable during the writing of this book.

Also, the *Dictionary Of The Vietnam War*, by Peter Bedrick Books of New York, edited by James S. Olson, was a valuable source of information on Vietnam. I thank Mr. Olson for his efforts.

MT. WASHINGTON, NEW HAMPSHIRE
AUGUST 4, 1964

The cool mountain air had given way to afternoon heat. The sky was a hazy blue, and the sun's rays beat down on everything below. Humidity was high in the White Mountain National Forest in central New Hampshire.

The middle-aged couple had been climbing Tuckerman's Ravine for most of the day, and they were almost at the summit. The forest that shaded the gentle trail at the beginning had gradually thinned, and the trail near the top was open to the elements. They were well above the tree line, and the path to the top was steep and dangerous to the unwary.

"Let's take five, Ben." Sally wiped her brow with the heel of her hand and leaned against a boulder.

"Okay." Ben was a big man, towering over others half his age. At forty-five, he was in excellent physical condition. He sat on a rock outcropping and took out his canteen. "Here." He handed it to his wife and stared across the wilderness.

She saw the sad and distant look in his eyes. "A penny for your thoughts."

He looked at her. "We've been coming up here for a long time,

Sally. It's been hard without him, but now I think it's time to move on."

"Yes. It is." Her heart went out to him. There was a moment of silence, then she said, "Let's walk in the sand next year, Ben. It's about time you started treating this old doll with respect. I'm not a pack mule you know!" She wanted to lift his spirits, especially today.

"That's the best offer I've had in months. Besides, I'm ready for the old man routine anyway." He grinned at her.

"What? Ben, have you been holding out on me? I thought I'd have to fight to get you to move to a warmer climate where the biggest mountain is a kid's sand castle."

"Nope. Just wanted you to say uncle first."

"Get moving before you rust!" She handed the canteen back to him.

"Hey, you're older than me, remember?" He laughed and started up the hill.

"Never mind that. You're still a dirty old man."

"Thank you."

It had been ten years since their only son had died while hiking Tuckerman's Ravine, and they had consoled themselves since then by hiking the mountain annually on the anniversary of his death. Upon reaching the top, they would hold hands and say a silent prayer. Their annual trek up the mountain served as a soul cleansing, and on this day, they would lay their son's memory to rest for the last time.

Reaching the ledge near the east summit, they removed their packs and sat on a large boulder. After a short rest, they walked hand-in-hand to the monument that stood a silent vigil to the memory of their lost child.

A metal plaque was attached to the flat side of a large granite boulder. The inscription was a dedication to their lost son—a lasting tribute to his memory.

The two men descended from the weather station at the top of the mountain, and they handled the rugged terrain with the agility of mountain goats. They were experienced hikers, enjoying the outdoors, away from the nearby rat race of Boston. Reaching the ledge of the east summit, they looked across the great expanse to Sebago Lake, Maine. Noticing the couple standing next to a giant boulder, they decided to introduce themselves.

"Hi, folks. How's it going?" the first one said.

Ben turned towards the voice. "Hi, guys. Good day for a hike, ain't it?"

"Perfect."

The larger of the two men stood beside Ben while his partner stood silently behind Sally. After a minute the first man walked to the monument and read the inscription. "Hmm, guess someone didn't make it." Still looking at the sign, he said, "This is a nice touch, putting this here in memory of their kid."

"He was our son," Sally said, looking across the ravine. "Today is the tenth anniversary of his death." Her words were strained.

They also confirmed the couple's identity.

The targets had been found.

After a moment, the larger man said, "It can be dangerous up here. I'm sorry about your son." He extended his hand to Ben.

Ben was touched with the gesture, but he was totally unprepared for what happened next. The assassin twisted Ben's hand, forcing him to the ground. "What the—?" Before Ben could recover, the assassin kicked him in the head. At that same instant the second assassin grabbed Sally from behind, restraining her in a head lock. He glanced at his partner and nodded; it was the signal to proceed.

Holding Sally in a strangle hold with one arm, he reached around with the other and sharply twisted her head. Her neck snapped instantly, and she dropped to the ground.

Ben began to fight back. Summoning all his strength, he kicked his assailant in the groin. The man doubled over in pain. Ben was almost up when Sally's killer struck him from behind with a blackjack. Ben dropped to his knees, stunned from the blow.

Ben's attacker was more enraged now than hurt. "This one is difficult. This was not expected. We finish this now."

"*Da.* We must hurry before someone comes. Push them over the edge. It must look like an accident," the second man said. "We will escape down the ravine."

The two assassins picked up Sally's body and threw it over the edge of the cliff. They then positioned themselves at opposite ends of the semi-conscious man on the ground. They picked him up and moved cautiously toward the edge. Ben's attacker held him up by hooking his arms under Ben's armpits, allowing Ben's head to rest on his chest—a fatal mistake.

They swung his body into the air. In that last instant before they released him, Ben reached up and wrapped his arms around the neck of the startled man holding him. Ben knew he was going to die, and he was determined to take one of them with him. The momentum was too great to overcome, despite the assassin's frantic efforts to escape. They went over the precipice, locked in mortal combat. Neither man made a sound as they fell to their deaths.

The remaining assassin stood motionless, staring down the steep palisade. He looked around, making sure that he was alone. He quickly threw all the equipment over the cliff. Picking up his own pack, he made his way down the same path that Sally and Ben had ascended earlier. He disappeared into the wilderness.

Gulf of Tonkin
Vietnam
Same Day

"Coming down like cats and dogs, ain't it?" Yeoman Tom Bast said from his position on the port side of the *USS Maddox*. It had been raining for several hours, and the seas were ten feet and rising.

"Standard stuff, man." Gunner's Mate Luis Sanchez approached carefully with two cups of coffee. "This ain't nothing. Wait til your first typhoon."

"First what?"

"Typhoon, *Amigo*. Pacific hurricane. Some of 'em been known to wipe out entire villages."

"Sounds pretty bad," Bast said. "Guess this could be worse."

"Yeah, like more of those zipper-heads coming for another visit. They come back, and the old man's gonna fire up the big guns. Blew two of 'em all to hell the other night. Pricks got what they deserved. Hell, they won't—"

CLANG-CLANG-CLANG! The noise of the crashing waves against the ship was abruptly broken by the shrill klaxon announcing General Quarters. The two seamen dropped their cups and ran to their battle stations without having to think about it. The *Maddox* had come under attack two days earlier by at least two North Vietnamese torpedo boats. The crews on the *Maddox* and the *C. Turner Joy*, her sister ship, were nervous and trigger happy. The radar on the *Maddox* had been malfunctioning, and positive identification of enemy ships was not possible. It appeared that another attack was underway.

The Combat Information Center aboard the *Maddox* reported several targets closing fast, and the crew assumed them to be North Vietnamese patrol boats. The *Maddox* and *Joy* maneuvered into defensive positions and prepared to fire. *Joy* opened fire first when reports of torpedoes in the water came in. The *Maddox* was ordered to fire, but the head of the gunnery department refused until he heard from *Joy*. It was probably a wise decision, considering the confusion at the time.

Fortunately, cooler heads prevailed since the *Joy* turned out to be the target of the *Maddox*.

By dawn the commander of the *Maddox* began to have doubts as to whether the ship had in fact been attacked at all. Neither the *Maddox* nor the *Joy* had reported any actual contact with enemy ships. In retrospect, the captain of the *Maddox* felt that no actual attack had taken place, and he reported his findings to his superiors at Pearl Harbor.

The President ignored the reports of his Navy commanders. He believed that the attacks did occur, and he used the episode as the basis for his speech before Congress that resulted in the *Gulf of Tonkin Resolution*. The President asked for and received support for the Resolution on August 5, 1964. Congress agreed with the President, and the resolution passed, giving the President the power to "… take all necessary measures … "

PART ONE

CHAPTER 1

AUGUST 5, 1964

"Damn this all to hell!" Jack Wilder rubbed his temples while watching the newscast.

"... and the resolution was passed by an almost unanimous vote of the Congress," the commentator droned.

Colonel Jack Edward Wilder, US Air Force, Retired, turned down the volume and dropped wearily into his chair. A former Air Force intelligence officer for twenty-five years, and now the Director of Operations for the Central Intelligence Agency, he knew what the ramifications would be. He was not happy.

The intercom buzzed. "Yes?"

"Jack, your brother-in-law is here. I'll send him in right away. You're now officially gone for the day, if anyone asks."

"You read my mind, Linda. Thanks." Wilder closed his eyes and smiled to himself. He was thankful for friends he could count on.

The Director of the National Security Agency entered the room, glanced at Wilder, and walked to the bar. "Seen the news?" Bruce Spencer poured two glasses of whisky and handed one to his brother-in-law and friend.

"Yeah, and I don't like it. Johnson's been given *carte blanche* to start his own little war. He's creating a monster and he has no clue. This could get real nasty."

"Agreed." The NSA chief studied his drink. "Nothing much changes. Nobody listens to the on-scene commanders. The skipper of the *Maddox* was adamant about not being attacked. Made that point perfectly clear."

"Yeah, and those self-serving pellet-heads in Congress didn't listen either. It's called political boot-licking of the first caliber." Jack Wilder always called a spade a spade, political correctness be damned, and many said that he was passed over for Flag rank because of it. He believed it was better to be honest and to call things the way they really were, rather than to agree with the gnomes elected over him for the sake of a promotion. It was easier to remember the truth than to remember a lie. He raised his two sons to be the same way.

Aside from the obvious, Jack Wilder had his own reasons for regretting American involvement in Vietnam. As a former intelligence officer, he had seen action in World War II and Korea, and he was familiar with the Oriental mind. As an entity, it was persistent and patient. It would wait. Because of it, the American effort, however noble, would fail, and he feared that his boys would become victims of that failure.

His oldest son was named after him. Nicknamed Little Jack, he was an F-4 pilot on the *USS Ticonderoga*, currently on duty in the South China Sea. His younger son was a high school senior. Bill was bound for college, Wilder hoped. Either that or the draft.

Spencer stared at him. "Jack, I know what you're thinking, and it's not healthy to keep it inside. I love those boys, and I don't like what's facing them anymore than you do."

"But what can we do? Little Jack's already there. And Bill's coming up on his eighteenth birthday. Do you have any idea—"

"Yes, I do, Jack. Look, your wife is my sister, and I look at your kids like they're my own. I'm not going to let anything happen to them if I can help it. You know that."

Wilder looked out the window towards Disney Land East, also known as Washington, DC. He closed his eyes. *Why is this happening? I paid my dues, didn't I?* He thought of his oldest son. He looked at Spencer and said, "I got a call from Mac on the *Ticonderoga* earlier today. Says that his carrier group is running air strikes around the clock."

"Isn't he Little Jack's skipper?"

"Yeah, but Mac's no grandmother to him."

Spencer smiled at Wilder's remark. They both knew the "skipper" of the *Ticonderoga* personally.

"Mac" was Navy Captain Thomas Franklin McIvor, commander of the *USS Ticonderoga*. Several years earlier, he had served with Wilder and Spencer in the Pentagon and had become good friends with both. Spencer was married to McIvor's sister until she died from cancer. The couple was childless.

"How does Little Jack like being an F-4 jock on Mac's boat?"

"Bruce, the kid loves it. I tried to talk him into going into the Air Force, but you know him."

"Yeah, stubborn like his old man."

"I'll take that as a compliment," Wilder said ruefully.

"What about Bill? He still wants to go to VMI?"

"He does. I hope he gets accepted." The alternative was unacceptable.

"He will, Jack." *Time to change the subject.* "Hey, how's my sister? You treating her right or what?"

"Liz is fine. She wants you to come for dinner, by the way. How about it?"

"Sold. Let's go."

The two men left the CIA building in Langley, Virginia, and headed to Franconia. It was time to put the today's events behind them. Elizabeth Wilder always kept and extra plate for her brother.

American involvement in South Vietnam began to escalate almost overnight. On October 1, 1964, the US Army Fifth Special Forces Group, later known as the Green Berets, arrived in Vietnam to train the South Vietnamese Army. On November 1, Vietnamese communists attacked Bien Hoa Air Force base near Saigon, destroying several B-57 bombers and damaging many more. Four American military advisors were killed, while thirty others were wounded. On Christmas Eve, Vietcong agents exploded a car bomb beneath the

Brinks Hotel in Saigon, killing two American officers and wounding fifty-eight.

These events served as a wake up call to the Johnson administration, and Jack Wilder made the point at every opportunity. He observed that, first, the Vietcong (VC) and the North Vietnamese Army (NVA) had the ability to move at will anywhere within the region, including the capital city of Saigon, without detection. Second, he pointed out that the South Vietnamese government was unable, or willing, to protect its own citizens or its allies. Americans would have to be afforded some measure of protection if they were going to succeed in their training capacity. He told military planners and government officials that, based on this assessment, no one was completely safe from VC terrorism. He hoped that the administration would then decide to withdraw all Americans from Vietnam. Unfortunately, his remarks had just the opposite effect. President Johnson ordered the speeding up of the movement of American personnel and equipment to Southeast Asia.

By the end of 1964, there were 23,300 military personnel in South Vietnam.

CHAPTER 2

DECEMBER 23, 1964

"Answer the door, Jack. I'm busy in the kitchen," Elizabeth Wilder shouted.

"Okay." *Damn holy-rollers. Probably have their hands out again.* He opened the door.

Standing in front of him was a younger version of himself. An overgrown, underweight kid, barely out of his teens, grinned back at him. "Hi, Pop! Not chasing spies today? Thought I'd drop by for a day or two and drain a few with you. Gonna let me in or what?"

"Little Jack!" Wilder grabbed his son and desperately hugged him. His eyes misted over but he didn't care. He was happy to have his young soldier home, and he wasn't ashamed to show it. "What a surprise! Boy, am I glad to see you. When did you get in?" He picked up his son's bag and slapped him on the shoulder.

"Just got off the plane at Andrews. Didn't call because I wanted to surprise you guys."

"Well, you sure as hell did, Jack." Wilder yelled at the kitchen door. "Lizzy, your boy is home from the South Seas."

The kitchen door flew open. "Little Jack?" Elizabeth ran across the room and grabbed her son. "It's really you!" She burst into tears. "Oh, Jack, I'm so glad you're home. What a wonderful surprise." She hugged him for almost a full minute then stood back and studied him. "Let me look at you. Jack, have you lost weight? Are you eating right? How do you feel? How are they treating you? Are you—"

"Relax, Mom. I'm fine." He relished his mother's fussing over him, but he didn't want it to show. "You guys look great." He looked around the living room. "Sure is good to be home."

"Sit down, Jack. Let me get you something. A glass of milk?"

"Thanks, Mom, but I'd prefer a beer." Little Jack laughed. His mother still thought of him as a child.

"A beer?" Elizabeth was uncertain.

"That's what the boy wants, Lizzy."

"Well, ... okay." In her eyes, Little Jack was still a boy. She hugged him again and hurried into the kitchen.

Wilder looked at his son, a thousand questions racing through his mind. He wanted to learn about Vietnam through his son's perspective, but he had to be careful not to overwhelm the boy. He wished more than anything that Little Jack would not have to go back.

Elizabeth returned with two beers and a cup of coffee for herself.

"So, Jack, tell me all about your shipmates."

"Let the boy unwind, Liz. He just got home."

"It's okay, Dad. I'll tell you all about it over the next two weeks." Little Jack looked around again at the familiar surroundings. "Great to be home."

"Yes, it is." Wilder smiled at his wife.

They spoke of things that families talk about when separated by war, and their coming together gave them a chance to deal with their emotions in a positive way. This was an especially good time to be home; it was two days before Christmas.

"Hey, where's that runt brother of mine?" Little Jack asked. "Still doing that chop suey stuff?"

"You know he took first place in the nationals last month. Sixth degree black belt now." Wilder smiled. "I don't think I'd call him a runt. He's bigger than you, Jack."

"He's that all right." Little Jack finished his beer. Looking at the empty bottle, he said, "This sure hits the spot." He looked at his parents. "By the way, has VMI come through yet?"

"Soon, I hope," his mother said. The draft was always on her mind.

"Indications are good, Jack. He'll be a shoe-in. How about another beer, son?"

"Jack, I don't think—"

"He's earned the right, Liz."

"... I suppose so."

"You guys stay put. I'll get it." Little Jack hugged his parents again and headed for the kitchen.

"I'm so proud of him, Jack." Elizabeth's face beamed. It was the first time Wilder had seen his wife this happy since Little Jack finished flight school in Pensacola.

"Me too."

The front door flew open. "Hi, guys."

"Bill, how was your workout?" Wilder smiled at his younger son.

"Great. Learned some new techniques today." He dropped his gym bag on the floor and looked at his parents. He knew by their expressions that something was going on. "Okay, what gives?"

"We have a surprise for you," Elizabeth said.

"What?"

"Go look in the kitchen," his father said.

"You guys are up to something." Bill winked at his parents and walked across the room. Pushing open the swinging saloon doors, he entered the kitchen. He saw his brother grinning back at him.

"Hi, runt! You expecting Raquel Welch or something?"

"You navy puke!" The two brothers hugged each other. "Man, am I glad to see your mug, Jack-O! You look terrific. How long you gonna be here?" Bill hugged his brother again.

"Couple weeks." Little Jack studied his younger brother. "Damn, you're big now."

"Yeah, been eating my Wheaties." Bill noticed the beer in his brother's hand. "Hey, got one of those for me?"

"Why not? I don't think they'll mind." Little Jack pointed his thumb over his shoulder towards the living room. "But just one."

"Right." They both laughed.

The Wilders had always been a close knit family. Elizabeth and

Jack did their best to set the proper examples for their sons. The kids were as close as two siblings could be. Although Bill was six years younger than Little Jack, the two were inseparable. Bill had always looked up to his older brother, and he took it hard when Little Jack left for duty in Southeast Asia.

As a child, Bill was small for his age. Quiet and reserved, he never called attention to himself. When he was five years old, he was attacked by three older kids and severely beaten over a bag of candy. Little Jack, then eleven, ran across the field and drove the bullies away with a shovel, breaking two noses in the process. After a day in the hospital, the youngest of the Wilder children spent the next week in bed. Little Jack never left his side.

The Wilders decided that the child had to learn to defend himself. The following month, Captain Jack Wilder was transferred to Seoul, South Korea. Shortly after the family's arrival, Bill began his martial training.

Now, at eighteen, he was both a national and international *Tae Kwon Do* champion, and he had multiple black belts in several of the martial arts to show for his efforts. No one ever picked on him again.

"What's it like over there, Jack?"

"The flying's great, but the war ain't." The smile left Little Jack's face. "Things are heating up, Bill. I like what I'm doing, and I believe in it, but I sometimes think that people back home don't."

"Huh?" Bill didn't understand.

"Don't you watch the news, boy?"

"No. Should I?"

"Yes, you should, Bill, although I sometimes wonder what side the press is on. Uncle Sam sugar coats things, but I know what people think. A lot of them don't support us."

"That's crazy. I support you, Jack."

"I know, Bill, but not everyone does. It's complicated, Bro." Little Jack looked at his brother and a sad feeling came over him. "Look, I don't want to get into it right now. Do me a favor, kid. Just keep your eyes and ears open and watch what's going on, okay? Then you can form your own opinion."

"Okay." Bill worshipped his brother, and he took Little Jack's words to heart.

"Hey, that's enough of this heavy stuff. Let's go visit the folks in the other room." Little Jack slapped his kid brother on the back.

"Okay."

Vietnam was left where it belonged—on the other side of the world. It didn't exist while Little Jack was home. It was the best Christmas the Wilders ever had.

CHAPTER 3

MAY, 1965

The *USS Ticonderoga* was an *Essex* Class aircraft carrier that had seen duty against the Japanese during World War II. Decommissioned in January 1947, she was refitted for jet operations and commissioned again in 1954. In 1964 she saw her first action against the North Vietnamese in the Tonkin Gulf.

Lieutenant (junior grade) "Little Jack" Wilder was an F-4 pilot assigned to the *Ticonderoga*. Although the captain of the ship knew young Wilder through the boy's father, he didn't show any favoritism. Carrier duty was difficult at best, and Captain Thomas McIvor took pains to show fairness to all his men, regardless of family ties. He was well respected in return.

Lieutenant Wilder was what was known as a short-timer. He was in his last month of duty aboard the carrier, and he was due to rotate back to the States after his last mission. He greeted each morning with a grin and grease pencil to mark off the days on his helmet. He had earned the respect of his peers, and they took every opportunity to poke fun at him. "Hey, EL-TEE, you gotta be short... I can't see you... Must be walking under your shoes." He was the envy of everyone aboard the ship.

Many of Wilder's fellow pilots had not been so fortunate. Some had been shot down. Most had been rescued, but others either died or became prisoners of war, captured by the North Vietnamese. Everyone remembered Lt. Everett Alvarez, a fellow Navy pilot, and the first American POW. Some considered that a fate worse than death.

Vampire One Flight, a formation of six F-4 Phantom aircraft, had just taken off from the *Ticonderoga* and was rendezvousing with an Air Force KC-135 tanker aircraft off the coast of North Vietnam. Little Jack was leading the formation.

"Texaco One-Three, this is Vampire One. Flight of six approaching the IP. Angels two-five thousand. ETA 1125 Zulu."

"Roger, Vampire One. Have radar contact. Authenticate Sierra Bravo."

"Authentication is November."

"Roger, Vampire. That checks. Cleared to the pre-contact position." The tanker pilot recognized Wilder's voice, but he still had to go through the formalities. *"Block altitude two-five zero to two-seven zero. C'mon in guys."*

"Roger. Moving in."

"Cleared to contact. Texaco One-Three is ready."

"Vampire One ready."

Wilder maneuvered his aircraft behind and beneath the tanker. The drogue basket connected with the probe on the side of Wilder's fighter.

"Contact," the boomer announced. Wilder acknowledged with two clicks of his mike button. Watching the giant plane above him, he gently moved the controls to maintain his position with respect to the tanker. Within minutes, Wilder's fuel tanks were full and the boom operator called, *"Disconnect now."*

Both Wilder and the boom operator simultaneously pressed their disconnect buttons. The drogue disconnected and withdrew to a position just below the tanker's tail. Wilder drifted back slowly while keeping his eyes on the tanker. He maneuvered to the rear of the waiting formation as the second fighter positioned itself for refueling.

The sequence was repeated until the last fighter was done.

"Okay, Texaco, we're done here. Time to go to work."

"Roger that, Vampire. Good hunting. See you on the rebound, Jack."

Wilder transmitted to the formation. "Okay, guys, IFF's off and radars to standby." IFF stood for Identification-Friend-or-Foe. It was a device that sent an electronic signal to friendly radar to identify a specific aircraft. The signal could also be read by enemy radar, and Wilder wanted to limit the formation's electronic emissions to a minimum. "Fly loose, guys. Let's take it down." The formation descended to less than five hundred feet above the water and headed for the North Vietnamese coast.

Vampire One Flight was part of Operation Rolling Thunder, which began in March 1965. It was designed to persuade the North Vietnamese to stop warring in the south, and it started in a step by step escalation. Before May only targets south of the twentieth parallel were attacked, but now, American aircraft were striking targets as close as thirty miles from Hanoi and within ten miles of Haiphong Harbor. Anything within those parameters was fair game.

"Hi, Bill. How's it going?" Jack Wilder was pre-occupied with events in Vietnam when his son came through the door. Intelligence reports indicated that the North Vietnamese and Vietcong were moving more freely in the southern part of the country than the Americans had anticipated. Terrorist attacks had become more frequent, and the Armed Forces of Vietnam, or ARVN, had not been able to stop them. It weighed heavily on Wilder's mind.

Bill slowly waved his hand across his father's face. "Hello ... Is anyone in there?" He tapped his father lightly on the head.

"What?" His concentration broken, Wilder looked up to see his younger son grinning down at him. The challenge had been made. It was father-and-son time. "You're dead meat, boy!" He grabbed his son and held him in a head lock. Bill could easily tie his father into a knot, but he always let Dad win. The bonding between father and son kept their relationship strong, and it would serve them well in the future.

"Okay, you win—again!" Bill shouted.

"As usual." Wilder laughed and released his son after a session of *Uncle*. "How was your workout, Bud?"

"You should've been there, Dad. A little four-on-one action. Nobody could get close to me."

"Excellent. You've worked hard and done well, and we're proud of you." Wilder's tone turned serious. "But remember, no matter how good you are, there's always someone better. Keep that in the back of your mind when you're out on the street. Food for thought."

Bill studied his father for a moment. "I'll remember that."

"Now, how about that homework? Bruce is coming for dinner, and you'll want to get it out of the way before he gets here. Mom's fixing your favorite."

"Roast beast? Cool. And Bruce is always good for a war story."

"Let's get to it." Wilder stared at the empty staircase long after Bill disappeared. *I'd give my soul for a crystal ball.*

Vampire One flight streaked across the jungle canopy, its bombs and napalm creating huge secondary explosions as enemy munitions went up in flames. Anti-aircraft fire was heavy, and two fighters had been shot down. Little Jack prayed that his luck would hold out a little longer. This was his last mission, but it was the hottest in terms of enemy fire that he had seen. Naval artillery had failed to soften the North Vietnamese anti-aircraft batteries, and the bad guys were throwing everything they had at the Americans.

Because of continuing American air attacks in and around the major North Vietnamese cities and ports, the enemy had constructed a vast array of surface-to-air missiles, known as SAM's. MIG-17 and MIG-21 aircraft were added, and, as a result, Hanoi and Haiphong Harbor soon became the most heavily defended pieces of real estate in history. Anti-aircraft batteries capable of firing to 45,000 feet were often lethal, and today was no exception.

"*Vampire One, break right. Break right, NOW! Got a SAM on your six!*" Vampire Three shouted into his radio.

"Outta here!" Vampire One rolled sharply to the right and dove towards the missile in an attempt to break the missile's lock-on signal.

"Up link! Up link! It's still onto us!" the back-seater shouted into his mask microphone. "Move!"

"Pulling up," Little Jack shouted. He rolled the fighter right side up and pulled back on the control stick as the back seat weapons systems officer tried to electronically jam the SAM's radar. The aircraft rolled and dove again, breaking the SAM's radar lock. The missile exploded harmlessly at altitude.

"Break lock!" the back seater shouted. He was out of breath. "*Damn*, that was close!"

"I'm going after that son-of-a-bitching SAM site," Little Jack shouted over his radio. "Two, you got lead."

"*Roger, One.*"

Little Jack broke out of the formation and rolled left into a wide turn. He was less than a hundred feet above the jungle, speeding at five hundred knots. The SAM site had troops garrisoned nearby, and he was determined to take both of them out on this, his last mission.

He flew his craft through a narrow valley towards his target, the mountains on either side being high enough to hide his approach. He would make his first pass using napalm. Although not very effective against hardened targets, napalm would take out any enemy personnel in the area. Napalm was jellied gasoline, and its effects were particularly nasty. Exploding on impact, it would engulf huge areas, sucking up all oxygen and burning everything it touched. If it came into contact with the skin, it could not be brushed off. It was literally hell on earth. Wilder would then make another pass and drop his bombs to destroy the site itself. He was furious and he could almost taste blood. He rolled out of the turn and bore down on his target.

"… and, according to Army sources, the Vietcong attacked fire base Alpha to the west of the city of Hue. Officials reported over two hundred Vietcong and twenty-three Americans killed. It is the largest single American loss to date.

It other news, at the urging of South Vietnam's President Thieu, President Johnson has authorized more American troops and materiel to be sent to Vietnam. The escalation of the war continues … "

"Jack, do you have to watch that? It's bad enough that you have to deal with that stuff all day at work. Give me a hand with the table. Bruce will be here soon." Elizabeth Wilder dealt with her emotions by staying busy while avoiding the news or anything that had to do with the fighting, and she was annoyed when her husband brought Vietnam home from Langley.

Wilder heard the edginess in her voice. He knew how she felt, but he was hard pressed to do anything about it. He turned off the television and set the table for dinner. He promised himself that he would not mention the war or talk of Little Jack's involvement in front of her again.

Bill had taken his brother's advise and began to follow the war and events surrounding it. He listened to the news, and he quickly learned to read between the lines and to take the press with a grain of salt. He also picked his father's brain about what was really going on half a world away. Bill had never been in trouble in school, nor did he become part of the hippie movement that was taking over the country. He promised his brother that he would not become corrupted by the anti-war movement, and that he would try to keep his perspective when the subject of Vietnam came up. He would form his own educated opinion of the war and events going on around him.

Dinner was almost ready. Elizabeth enjoyed cooking for her family which, on this night, also included her brother. Bruce Spencer was a favorite in the Wilder home, and he spent the lion's share of his free time there. He would arrive with minutes.

"Bill, go check the mail, will you?" his mother asked when he came downstairs.

"Okay."

"I hope he hears something soon." Wilder watched his son go out the door.

"He will. I feel it in my bones."

A minute later, the door flew open, and Bill danced into the living room, holding an open letter in his hand. "I got in! I got in!"

"Got in what?" his father asked, already knowing the answer.

"VMI! What else is there?" Bill grinned and waved the letter above his head.

"Congratulations, Bud. I knew you'd do it." Wilder shook his son's hand.

"Oh, Bill, that's wonderful. I'm so happy for you." His mother hugged him.

"This makes my day!" Bill was on Cloud Nine. Looking at the letter, he said, "Matriculation is in September." He looked at his parents. "Will you—"

"Of course we'll be there. And so will Little Jack. Wouldn't miss it for the world," his father said.

Bill felt ten feet tall. His brother was coming home for good within days, and he was going to VMI. Life couldn't be better.

Their joy was interrupted by the door bell. Elizabeth looked at her watch. "That's Bruce. Give him the good news, Bill."

"You bet!" He opened the door and proudly held up the letter. "Looky here!" .

Bruce Spencer loved his sister's family as if it was his own. He always had a smile and joke or two when he came. But there was no smile this time. His face showed a disquieting mixture of rage and helplessness, and his eyes were red and strained. A Navy chaplain stood quietly beside him. "Bill, may we come in?"

"Uh, sure." Bill sensed that something was wrong. His uncle had never asked to come in before.

"Jack?" Elizabeth grabbed her husband's arm.

"It's okay, Lizzy." Wilder took his wife's hand and looked at his brother-in-law. Their eyes met, and Wilder understood. It hit him like a train. "Hello, Bruce." His voice almost cracked.

Spencer smiled sadly at his sister then turned to Wilder. He gestured towards the man beside him. "This is Captain Steele, the Annapolis chaplain." Spencer faced his family. "I don't know how to say this, Jack … I'm afraid I have some bad news."

"What's going on?" Bill looked at his father for an answer.

"Shhh. Listen, Bud." Wilder held his wife's shaking hand.

Spencer looked at each of them. He took a deep breath and exhaled. "Perhaps it would be better if everyone sat down."

"I'll stand, Bruce." Wilder wanted to be strong for his family, but his knees were beginning to weaken.

Bill's eyes darted back and forth between his uncle and Captain Steele. *Why a chaplain?*

"We tried to contact you at Langley, Jack, but your secretary said that you had gone home early… " Spencer noticed the place setting for him, and he wanted to hug his sister desperately.

"Please get to the point, Bruce."

Spencer rubbed temples. *How do I say this?* "Little Jack's plane was shot down over North Vietnam. We have every reason to believe that he was captured by the North Vietnamese."

"Oh, God!" Elizabeth's hands went to her face. She fainted.

Her husband caught her and carried her to the sofa. He placed her on the pillows then gently brushed the hair from her face. Holding his wife's hand while on one knee, he looked at his brother-in-law. "Are you sure?"

"I'm afraid so, Jack. Mac called from the *Ticonderoga*. It was Little Jack's last mission. I'm so sorry."

Wilder stroked his wife's brow and looked at his son. "Bud, bring me a cold cloth, please."

Bill was stunned. *Shot down? Captured?* His emotions were going in every direction, he didn't know what to do or say.

"Bud—"

"Okay." Bill went to the kitchen, unable to comprehend what he had just heard. He returned with the cloth and looked at his unconscious mother on the sofa, then at his father and uncle. The anguished looks …

It finally hit him. "Bastards!" Clenching his fists, he stood motionless. He wanted to strike out, but there was nowhere to vent his anger. Looking around the room he saw the pain and sadness in everyone's eyes. He turned and walked slowly up the stairs.

Wilder watched his son walk away. He looked at Spencer and Steele. "What happened?" The lines on his face suddenly got deeper.

"Jack, perhaps later would—"

"Now."

Spencer sat wearily on the coffee table. He looked at his brother-in-law for a full minute. His voice cracked when he spoke. "Mac said that Little Jack was running an attack against a military installation just outside Hanoi. Two fighters had been shot down when he went after the SAM site. When he rolled out of the turn for his run in, an anti-aircraft battery hit him. The plane exploded, and he ejected. The back-seater didn't make it. The other members of the formation saw his chute open, and he appeared unhurt. They tried to provide air cover, but they were bingo on fuel and had to leave. By the time the rescue choppers got there, it was too late. Jack, we feel certain that he was captured. That's all we know."

Wilder held his wife's hand and looked at her face in silence.

Spencer had never felt more helpless in his life. He looked sadly at his sister and at the table she had set for them.

Dinner was uneaten that night.

Unable to sleep, Bill paced the floor in his room until sunrise. His brother and best friend was now a prisoner of war, and life was suddenly turned upside down by events over which he had no control. Having nowhere to turn, he was confused, afraid, and angry. He wasn't one to rush into things; there wasn't anything he could do anyway. Though he didn't know it then, he was about to embark on a journey that would affect him for the rest of his life.

The Students for a Democratic Society, or SDS, was established in 1960 as a civil rights organization. By the mid-sixties, however, the SDS had become more involved in the anti-war movement than anything else. After the Gulf of Tonkin incident in 1964, the SDS began to organize against the Vietnam War. The organization circulated *We Won't Go* petitions to college students and draft age men, and it held rallies throughout the country against the government's involvement in the war. On April 17, 1965, the SDS organized a demonstration in Washington, DC, in which more than 20,000 protesters took part. It was the largest demonstration to date, and it was one of the first to become violent. Other demonstrations followed, and the violence escalated. The government tried to prevent them, but it was powerless to do so.

Families were destroyed as sons died in Vietnam. Others fled to Canada to avoid the draft. The war was tearing the country apart.

At eighteen, Bill Wilder watched the demonstrations with curiosity and interest. While he did not participate, many of his friends did. Although he agreed with them in principal, he could not understand the need for violence. Free speech and right to assemble were guaranteed by the Constitution, but he didn't believe that people had the right to destroy what was not theirs. Nor did they have the right to treat returning soldiers like dirt. Bill resented the demonstrators for their behavior, and he vowed that he would not become part of it. His energy would be directed towards other things.

He would go to VMI in September. In the meantime, he refused to let the SDS, the hippies, the drug culture, or anything else keep him from his self-imposed goal; to do as much damage as he could to the people that captured his brother. He had no love of war, but he also hated the North Vietnamese. Little Jack had been taken from his family by them, and he swore to make them pay for their mistake.

CHAPTER 4

SEPTEMBER 9, 1965

"Drop and give me twenty, mister. Now!" The cadre sergeant screamed into his ear. It was Bill Wilder's first day at the Virginia Military Institute, and it would be one of the longest days of his life. "Get up! Too slow! Drop for another twenty!"

"Yes, sir." Wilder did twenty more push-ups in rapid succession.

"Move, rat!" Wilder jumped to his feet and stood at rigid attention. Upper classmen swarmed all over him. He and the other new cadets were tormented in the hot September sun as the senior cadets barked out drill routines, demanded push-ups, and orchestrated other punishments that were designed to train as well as wear them down.

The Rat Line was a regimen that all new cadets had to undergo during their first year at VMI. It's initial purpose was to reduce a group of over four hundred individuals to the lowest common denominator. Then, over a period of months, harsh discipline and training would be imposed by the First Class, or the senior cadets. Eventually, the new cadets would evolve into a cohesive unit, a group of young men with its own identity and spirit. Through common suffering, they would learn to depend upon one another and to help each other endure the demands of the Institute. They would learn to adapt and become independent, while, at the same time, coming together as a class. This spirit and the VMI Honor Code would guide them for the rest of their lives. The essence of the Brother Rat system would form friendships that would last a lifetime.

But the process would take time, and this was the first day.

The cadre sergeants and officers, in their white starched pants and pressed wool blouses, were cool and in complete control. By contrast, the rats were sweat-soaked and exhausted. Many new cadets not only were in poor physical shape, some were totally unprepared emotionally for the intense verbal barrage aimed at them. For some the abrupt assault by the cadre was more than they could endure. Many would leave within weeks, and several more would call it quits before Christmas.

The new cadets were scared and confused; a typical reaction of young people that have been thrust into a foreign and seemingly hostile environment. The drilling and push-ups were relentless, and by the end of the first day, they were worn out. At 2300 hours, the rats were marched to their rooms by their respective cadre sergeants and told to go to bed.

The rats were housed on the fourth floor of the barracks. The rooms were hot, and with the exception of an occasional warm breeze that blew through the screen-less open windows and doors, there was no relief from the heat.

"Get those hays put together, and get this room in shape. I'll be back at 0600. That's six o'clock for you people that don't have a clue." The lights went out and the door slammed.

Wilder sat in silence with three of his brother rats. They were all too tired to move or speak. Some were scared but too afraid to admit it. One got up and walked to the sink in the corner. There were no cups or glasses, so he drank with his hands. The others followed suit. Then they sat around the table and looked at each other in the dark.

After several minutes of silence, Wilder finally spoke up. "What have we done?"

"S'um bitch. We done screwed up! That's what we've done." The ruddy-faced kid at the end of the table stood up. "Name's John Slaughter. Denton, Texas." He looked around the room. "Who are you clowns?"

Wilder extended his hand from across the table. "Bill Wilder. Franconia, Virginia. Glad to meet someone with a sense of humor. I think we're going to need it." They shook hands, and Wilder took an instant liking to the brash Texan. "Guess we did screw up a little."

"A little? Shit! This is a screw up of epic proportions! Can you believe our folks paid good money to serve up our butts on a platter to these assholes? I knew my old man wanted me out of the house, but I had no idea I was *that* bad!"

Everyone laughed. It broke the ice and helped them to relax a little.

"I'm Joey Johnson. Would you believe my dad went here and wanted me to come?"

"Your old man ain't right, boy," Slaughter said.

"Maybe not. Anyway, I'm from Richmond, although right now, I may as well be from Mars."

The last one spoke up. "Pete Bledsoe. Glad to meet you guys. We have to stop talking. They might hear us." He had been crying.

"Take it easy, Pete. My dad said he cried too, but I didn't believe it til now. It'll be over before you know it," Johnson said.

"That's right. Ain't no big deal. Hell, these pricks don't know you from Adam. Just take it a day at a time." Slaughter grinned and slapped Bledsoe on the shoulder.

"He's right, Pete," Wilder said. "Just remember that all these screamers went through what we're going through, and there will be many more behind us. Hell, in a year, you'll be barking at some poor slob yourself."

"Maybe. But let's get these hays put together and go to bed."

"When I hit the sack, I'm gonna dream about my sweetie pie back home." Slaughter started working on his bed.

"That's about as close as you're gonna get to that pie for a long time," Wilder said.

"Yep, and she's gonna miss out!"

Takes all kinds, Wilder thought. His roommates were as different from each other as they could be. Yet, they all shared a common misery, and they would have to depend on each other to survive. He thought of his brother languishing in a North Vietnamese POW camp, and that made his own predicament less than trivial. He remembered the inscription on the wall of Jackson Arch: *You May Be What You Resolve To Be.* Wilder resolved at that moment to do his best for his brother, and he prayed that Little Jack was well and that he would be released soon. He looked around the room, and a wry smile crossed his face. *It's not so bad here.* He was asleep in minutes.

1965 was a pivotal year for American involvement in South Vietnam. In March the first American combat unit, the US Third Marine Regiment, was sent to Vietnam to defend the city of Da Nang, located in the northern part of the country near the North Vietnamese border. In April President Johnson authorized US ground troops to conduct offensive operations in South Vietnam for the first time. In June the first B-52 bomber raid took place on a suspected Vietcong base north of Saigon, the capital of South Vietnam. This systematic heavy bombing was called Arc Light, and it would become one of the most feared and devastating of all bombing operations of the war. Before the Arc Light operations would end, over 126,000 B-52 missions would be completed, both over North and South Vietnam and Cambodia.

By the end of 1965, the number of American troops in Vietnam had grown from 23,300 to over 184,000.

CHAPTER 5

JANUARY 1966

Colonel Smith lit his cigar and leaned back in his leather chair. The brandy on his desk was expensive and old, and he savored the aroma before he tasted it. Rank did have its privileges. He clicked the intercom on his desk. "Send in Captain Jones." He leaned back and propped his feet on his desk.

The door opened and a young officer walked in, stood at attention, and saluted. "Captain Jones reporting, sir." He was tall and slim, and his Air Force uniform fit him like a glove.

"Relax, Jones," Smith said while looking at the file in front of him. "Let's have a *dusha-dushe*." A little talk.

"Okay," Jones said, dropping onto a wooden chair.

"Get up. Get the *hell* up!" Smith yelled. "What do you think you're doing? Do not speak to me in Russian! *Na-shto-zhaloo-yetyes*? What's the matter with you?"

"Excuse me?" *Yeb vas*. Fuck you. Jones bit his tongue.

"English is your only language. Do you understand?"

"I don't know any other language, sir." Jones stared at the overweight blob behind the desk. *Fat tub of shit*.

"Captain Jones" was, in reality, Ivan Yevgenni Petrov of the Soviet KGB. A former pilot of the Soviet Air Defense Forces, he was a spy assigned to the Fifth Directorate. This part of the KGB conducted what was known in the CIA as Black Operations, and there was no real oversight or control by the Soviet government. It was the dark side of the KGB.

"Smith" was Colonel Peytr Gregkov, Petrov's immediate supervisor. Gregkov's office was on the second floor of the dreaded Lubyanka Prison, headquarters of the KGB, in central Moscow. The Russian people feared the KGB, and they avoided going near the building or even looking at it. Unwary citizens were often "invited" in at all hours of the night. Few came out.

"Your assignment has been changed," Gregkov said. "There is another, more important task for you now."

"Yes?"

"You will go to the Hoa Lo prison in Hanoi, North Vietnam. There are American pilots there. You will learn all you can from them. They will be willing to talk, especially when you intervene in their behalf. Their treatment by those whore-mongering monkeys is pathetic, but that is not our concern. We need intelligence information. They have it. You will get it."

"There are others more qualified, Colonel Smith."

"Indeed, Captain Jones, that is true. But a peculiar situation exists that makes it necessary that *you* go."

"And that is?"

"You will be briefed soon, Captain." Gregkov picked up the file and pretended to study it. It was the signal for Petrov to leave."

"Yes, sir." *You piece of dung.* Petrov stood and saluted. He walked out and left the door open.

Gregkov was right about the Vietnamese monkeys, Petrov knew. Vietnam was a hell-hole, filled with sewer rats with no sense of purpose, other than to satisfy their own physical needs. Petrov hated the Vietnamese. They were no more than leeches, sucking on his country for support.

There were many prisons in and around North Vietnam that housed American POWs. The most infamous was the Hoa Lo Prison located near the center of Hanoi. Built by the French several years earlier, it was known by many names; New Guy Village, Little Vegas, Camp Unity, and the Hanoi Hilton.

The prison occupied a city block. Its walls were twenty feet high and four feet thick. Thick shards of glass were imbedded along the tops of the walls, along with electrified strands of barbed wire. It was hot and dank, and the prisoners, both Vietnamese and American, suffered extreme hardships at the hands of their captors.

Little Jack was in the Hanoi Hilton. His cell was nine by eight feet, and his bed was a concrete slab with metal and wood stocks at the base. A peephole in the door was flanked by small windows, which had been covered over with thin sheets of concrete. His cell, along with the others, was infested with rats, insects, and other vermin. His toilet was a bucket that was emptied once a day, if the guards felt like it.

The food was not fit to eat, and medical treatment, such as it was, was almost non-existent. Any real aim at treatment came only when a captive's condition became so serious that his life was threatened. Or when he cooperated.

Torture was a way of life. It took many forms; beatings, physical isolation, sleep deprivation, and withholding of food and medicine. When prisoners began to physically break down, psychological means were then used.

Despite preventative efforts by their captors, the POWs managed to communicate with each other through various unobtrusive means. There were networks that used Morse and tap codes. Whistling, scratching sounds, and even cadence of a sweeping broom were used.

Prisoners were frequently moved or tortured when they were discovered trying to contact each other. Their communication systems, however, could not be destroyed by the North Vietnamese. The will to survive was too great.

Little Jack had suffered a back injury during his ejection from his ill-fated aircraft, and the Vietnamese had beaten him and broken his arm soon after his capture. He had not received any medical attention. His condition had been aggravated by his captors, and he had lost thirty pounds since his capture.

He believed the American government was doing everything it

could to secure his freedom. His belief in God and his family gave him the strength and courage to go on, and he stood up reasonably well, despite his poor treatment. He often thought of his younger brother. Did Bill understand what was happening? Little Jack believed he did, but he also knew that his brother would not sit idle and do nothing. He prayed that Bill would not end up in a North Vietnamese prison like him.

April 1966

It was the last week of the Rat Line, and the upper classmen, especially the First Class, were making life miserable for the rats. At the end of the week, the rats would be recognized as an entity, and the Class of 1969 would be born. In the meantime, however, the hazing would continue unabated.

They sat at the table and labored to catch their breath. "This sucks!" Wilder groaned and rubbed his arms. Everyone was soaked after the "sweat" party that the upper classmen had thrown for them.

"Well, duh! You got a keen grasp of the fucking obvious," Slaughter said, going to the sink for a drink. They had graduated to cups now instead of their hands. He drank deeply and wiped his face with his shirt. "Those candy-asses in the Third Class wouldn't stand a chance in a fair fight. I'd give my left nut to get my paws on the cretin that lives in the hole below us. Bill, why don't you teach me some of the chow mein crap so I can kick some butt real good?"

"It's *Tae Kwon Do*, John." Wilder rolled his eyes, but he did agree with Slaughter about the cretin in the room below. He especially had made their lives miserable for seven months. "Brush it off, Animal. It's almost over. Then it's a level playing field."

"Damned right."

Animal was the nickname that Slaughter had earned during the year. He was uncouth and crude, and he had the innate ability to reduce the English language to its basest form. But he was liked by everyone. He called things the way he saw them, and there was no ambiguity about where he stood. He was always in demerit trouble, and he marched penalty tours almost every Saturday and Wednesday afternoon. It was a running joke that Slaughter was the commander of the Goon Platoon. He took it all in stride.

Wilder and Slaughter became best friends during their rat year. The Wilders welcomed him into their home and treated him like their own son. Despite his crudeness, Slaughter was polite and respectful to them, and he was a perfect gentleman in Mrs. Wilder's presence. He became their *de facto* son, taking Little Jack's place, although nothing was ever said.

John Attison Slaughter grew up on a cattle ranch in Denton, Texas. For all intensive purposes he learned to swear and shoot before he went to school. Raised in an area where frontier justice was the rule rather than the exception, he learned that if you didn't do it for yourself, someone else would do it to you, take the credit, the woman, and ride off into the sunset, leaving you with your ass in your hand. He learned to fight as a kid, and he would rather pound someone into the ground than negotiate. He spoke in terms more graphic than socially acceptable, resulting in his repeatedly being thrown out of various establishments of ill-repute.

His relationship with local law enforcement officials was one of comic relief rather than anything serious. As a teenager, he broke the nose of a hapless cowboy that made a pass at one of his girlfriends, then bought Broken Nose a beer. He was arrested and jailed for commandeering a pickup truck and giving chase to a drifter that took his mother's purse. The purse was recovered, and the thief ended up with the standard broken nose. Slaughter spent the night in the can, but the sheriff released him early the next morning so the two of them could have breakfast at a local diner.

He was an honest kid, and he spoke his mind. If someone didn't like it, that person had the right to shut up and walk away, or to have his nose broken, afterwards knowing that Slaughter was good for a beer. At eighteen, he took that attitude to VMI.

Despite his brashness, Slaughter never lacked for female companionship. He always had dates for himself and Wilder, whether Wilder wanted one or not. But the confinement and penalty tours were often a problem. He couldn't be in two places at once, and Wilder often had to juggle two women on short notice, a task often envied by other cadets.

"This crap's almost over." Wilder shook his head in disgust. "Listen to me. I'm starting to sound like you, Animal."

"You need to lighten up, you dirt bag. You're such a damned straight-arrow." Slaughter laughed at him, his hands on his hips.

Johnson and Bledsoe dragged themselves into the room. They were drenched.

"You guys look like shit. Think this is a party or something?" Slaughter said.

"Yeah. Circus is more like it," Bledsoe shot back.

"Oooo, a real bad-ass!" Slaughter flapped his hands and stuck out his tongue.

"You prick!" Bledsoe chased him around the room. They needed to blow off steam, and the consequences could be damned. They were going to have their fun.

CHAPTER 6

Little Jack's imprisonment was difficult on the Wilders. Elizabeth's health began to deteriorate shortly after his capture. There had been several doctors, but most of her problems were a result of her mental condition. She had seen countless psychologists, but nothing had helped. She kept to herself and didn't receive visitors, the only exception being Bill and his friends. Bill was the center of her life now, and John filled a void left by Little Jack. Their visits lifted her spirits, and her husband was grateful, but she continued to lapse into depression when the boys left.

Jack Wilder was at a loss to help his wife. It pained him to watch her suffer, and he did everything he could for her. The war was not going well, and the news from his field agents and foreign station managers was not good. His brother-in-law at the National Security Agency did what he could to encourage the family, but when it came to Little Jack, he was helpless.

The pressure on the Wilders was enormous, and Jack often thought of throwing in the towel and resigning. But he knew that leaving the Agency would accomplish nothing. Little Jack would still be in a POW camp, and Bill would be on his way to Vietnam if the war continued. The *if* was why he stayed. And if Jack Wilder could make a difference, then his sacrifice would be worth it. After all, Little Jack had made a sacrifice, hadn't he?

The North Vietnamese were not signatories to the Geneva Convention, which outlined the treatment of prisoners of war. The United States repeatedly protested the mistreatment of the American prisoners, but the North Vietnamese ignored the warnings, and the mistreatment continued. Jack Wilder had firsthand knowledge of the poor treatment the prisoners were getting. His operatives were often hesitant to give him hard information, however, when it concerned Little Jack. The news was usually not good.

In 1966 American casualties were alarmingly high. As a result anti-war demonstrations began to take on a life of their own. A counter-culture began to grow as a form of protest against the American government. Young people grew their hair long, dressed in *avanteguard* clothing, used drugs, and engaged in communal living and free love. The hippies were the most visible group to protest the war.

Older Americans began to question the war when casualty levels grew high and the draft began to take too many of their sons. Americans of all ages and backgrounds began to think that the war was morally wrong and that it could not be won. American lives and valuable resources were being wasted.

The anti-war movement took many forms. Students and older Americans were facing off against each other. There were pacifists, communists, church groups, liberals, and conservatives. They all protested the war in some fashion, but when their protests failed to alter government policy towards Vietnam in 1967 and 1968, these groups began to polarize into two sides.

One group advocated non-violent civil disobedience, while the other called for violent confrontation and the use of force. The Southern Christian Leadership Conference, for example, advocated non-violence, while the SDS and the Weather Underground became increasingly militant and prone to violent protests. They bombed Selective Service offices and ROTC buildings and burned draft cards in open defiance of the law. It was becoming popular to outlaw ROTC on college campuses.

By the end of 1966, 385,000 US military personnel were in Vietnam. That number increased to 485,600 a year later. By the end of 1967, 16,021 Americans had been killed in action.

1968, however, was a pivotal year for American involvement as the attitude of the US government began to change in its persecution of the war. In late 1967, North Vietnamese Regulars and Vietcong guerrillas moved into and occupied strategic positions throughout South Vietnam. The buildup took quite a while and was accomplished under the guise of a cease-fire for the Tet holidays. By the time the holiday itself arrived, the enemy had moved over 100,000 troops and supplies into undetected areas. The South Vietnamese and the Americans were both caught off guard.

On January 30, 1968, the North Vietnamese and Vietcong launched widespread attacks against the military installations in the I and II Corps of the northern and central part of South Vietnam. The attacks soon spread to many of the provincial capitals and major cities throughout the southern end of the country. The US embassy in Saigon was attacked, along with Tan Son Nhut Air Force Base, just outside the city. Both the South Vietnamese Army (ARVN) and the American forces were helpless to stop it.

Although the Tet Offensive was brilliant in its planning, the North Vietnamese and Vietcong failed in their efforts to win support of the masses of Vietnamese citizens. The ARVN managed to hold onto most of its territory, and with American reinforcements, it was able to regain all the areas lost in the fighting. The only exception was the imperial capital of Hue, where the fighting lasted for weeks. By the end of the offensive, over 40,000 North Vietnamese and Vietcong died, and they never recovered strength wise.

Even though they lost on the battlefield, the North Vietnamese and Vietcong scored a major victory with respect to the American government and public opinion. Prior to Tet, US officials and military commanders talked of how long the enemy would be able to hold out against American and ARVN forces. General William Westmoreland, commander of American forces in South Vietnam, spoke on November, 17,1967. In a televised press conference, he described the war as the "… light at the end of the tunnel." It was just a matter of time before enemy forces would be forced to surrender and bring an end to the war. Then, with the Tet Offensive, the "Light in the Tunnel" theory was dispelled. The North Vietnamese and Viet-cong, although thought to be decimated, still fought the Americans with no plan of surrender in sight. With Tet over and the enemy still fighting, American policy began to change. It went from winning to concentrating on finding an honorable way out.

"How's your mother, Jack? It's been a long time since you've heard from her, hasn't it? Would you like to write to her?" Petrov slowly circled Little Jack and glared down at him. He sat behind his desk and propped his feet on the corner. "Come on, Jack, there's no need for this. Just tell me what I want to know, and I'll do what I can to get you released. What do you say?"

Little Jack sat motionless on the stool. He was dizzy with pain from his recent torture session. He had been beaten with a bamboo cane, and his back and feet bled from the wounds. He stared at Petrov through swollen eyes. He remained silent.

Petrov studied him intently. Finally, he put his feet on the floor and placed his hands on the desk. "Jack, I know what the guards have done to you. They're disgusting animals."

Little Jack didn't move.

Petrov leaned forward. "Look, I don't want to be here any more than you do. So, let's cut the crap and cooperate with each other, okay?" Petrov's dislike of the Vietnamese was real, and he allowed it to show around the American prisoners. As long as he had to be here, he figured that he would use these little people to his advantage.

"Screw you, Petrov." Little Jack's voice was a rasp. His throat was dry and his lips were cracked, and it was difficult for him to speak.

"Tch, tch. That's no way to be, Jack." Petrov shook his head and leaned back in his chair. "I'm trying to help you, don't you see that? I know you've been mistreated, and I feel bad for you. But I am not in command here. If it was up to me, I'd make sure you got proper food and medical treatment. I've been at odds with the camp commander over this. You believe me, don't you, Jack?"

"You're wasting your, time. I have nothing to say." Little Jack tried to look around, but he was gaunt and weak from weight loss, and he had little strength. His ragged, lice-infested pajamas hung loosely on his emaciated frame.

Petrov stood and walked behind Little Jack. He put his hand on Jack's shoulder and squeezed. Jack winced, and Petrov smiled to himself. "You know what will happen if I send you back to your cell."

Little Jack said nothing.

"Let's talk of other things. I'll tell you about Russia, and you tell me about the United States." Petrov dragged his chair from behind the desk and sat beside his prisoner. "Jack, when I was a boy, I wanted to be a pilot, like you. I thought it was the most exciting thing there was. My father was in the Party, and he helped me to get into flight training. Privilege comes with rank, doesn't it?"

Nothing.

"I know that you went to the Naval Academy in Annapolis. A fine school. You and I are alike in many ways, Jack. I have a family in Moscow, and you have one in Virginia. Let's talk about your family. Your father is Colonel Jack Wilder, and you are named after him. He is very proud of you. That's good, isn't it?" Petrov waited for a response but got none. "You have a younger brother. William is has name, but you call him Bill. Your father sometimes calls him Bud. He's a student at the Virginia Military Institute. He wants to be a pilot like you, doesn't he, Jack? Only he wants to go into the Air Force."

Little Jack strained to look at Petrov. He was surprised at Petrov's knowledge. *How did you know that?* Petrov had hit a nerve, but Little Jack refused to let it show. He resumed his blank stare at the floor. It took all his strength and concentration to keep from falling off the stool.

Petrov knew that he had touched a sensitive area. He didn't want to alienate Jack any more than he already had. But he knew of Jack's father and that he was involved with the CIA, and he wanted to probe that subject as much as possible. He had to be careful. "It's good to be close to your family, Jack," Petrov said. "My father was a colonel in the Red Army, and he also worked for the KGB. Your father and mine have a great deal in common, Jack, as do we. The only difference is the color of our uniforms."

Little Jack again strained to look at his adversary. "We have nothing in common. My father and I are free men. You and your family are prisoners of your government. At least I can sleep at night with a clear conscience." He shook when a jab of pain shot up his back.

Petrov leered at him. "A free man?" He waved his hand at the room. "Look around, Jack. How long have you been here? Three years? Do you really think your government is trying to get you out of here? *You* are the prisoner here, not me." He looked at his uniform then at Jack's shabby rags. "Who's in charge here Jack? Me or you?"

"You won't get anything from me, and you know it. Give it up." Little Jack doubled over, his stomach wracked with pain. His food had been laced with an agent designed to further break him down. He fought for control and slowly raised his head. "You won't do anything for me, and we both know it. You're here because some Bolshevik asshole sent you. You're a prisoner here, same as me." Little Jack squeezed his eyes shut and tried to fight off the pain that was consuming him. He almost fell off the stool when he began to cough uncontrollably.

Petrov sneered at him and clenched his fists. He desperately needed information about the CIA and its Vietnam operations, and he was losing his patience with this cocky naval aviator. He had begrudging admiration for the American that he was loathe to admit. Wilder was fortunate to have come from such a close knit family.

Petrov's mother had been branded as a traitor and a prostitute by the Party. She had suffered from an uncontrollable drinking problem, and she was what the Party called a "loose woman." She had never been around when the child needed her, and the young boy learned to hate her when he grew older. If there was a hell, he hoped that she was there. Petrov's father had in fact been a colonel in the KGB, but his relationship with his son had been less than desirable. The younger Petrov was forced to raise himself since his father was frequently away on Party business. The young boy had grown into an angry man.

Petrov looked at the American. Though Wilder suffered physical agony, he was free in spirit, and Petrov resented him for it. *How dare you have something I cannot.*

CHAPTER 7

MARCH 1968

By their Junior year Wilder and Slaughter were inseparable. Having survived the Rat Line, they had done well for themselves since then. The other cadets knew that Wilder's brother was a POW, and they allowed for it, but not everyone agreed with America's involvement in Vietnam. It was an emotionally charged issue that Wilder would just as soon avoid. In his opinion, American involvement in Asian affairs was the domain of the talking suits in Washington. He quickly dismissed any discussion of the war, and he wouldn't entertain any disrespectful mention of his brother.

Tom Berwick was Wilder's and Slaughter's third roommate. He didn't believe that America had any right to be in Vietnam, and he took exception to Wilder's opinion with respect to Little Jack. In Berwick's mind, Little Jack got what he deserved. It was just a matter of time before the explosive issue came to a head.

"I don't care what you or Wilder think. So what if Americans get shot down? They're bombing innocent people. Wilder's brother got what he deserved, so screw him."

"Shut your mouth, you little prick! You're talking about my friend's brother," Slaughter shot back. "You're nothing but a poor little rich kid with no brothers or sisters to have to share anything with. All you think about is your own little candy-ass. You'd better shut that hole under your nose before Bill hears you. He'll—"

"He'll what?" Wilder walked across the room and tossed his hat onto the table. He stood opposite Berwick, facing him. There was controlled rage in his voice, and the atmosphere in the room was electric.

Berwick was defiant. "Don't get bent out of shape at me, Wilder. It's not my fault your brother's in a POW camp."

"No, it isn't." The hair bristled on Wilder's neck. He stood motionless, his fists clenched at his side. His breathing slowed, and he concentrated on the man in front of him.

"He knew what he was getting into. Nobody made him go over there. He bombed those people of his own free will, and he got shot down. He deserved it. He—"

A smashing palm heel turned Berwick's nose into mush. He staggered backwards and his knees began to buckle. A powerful front snap kick to the chin sent him flying backwards, and he crashed onto the table. The momentum kept him going, and he flipped over backwards onto the floor. Wilder walked calmly around the table, grabbed Berwick by the collar, and jerked his head up like a rag doll.

Berwick screamed in pain, blood gushing from his nose and chin.

Wilder put his mouth close to Berwick's ear. "Listen, asshole. My brother didn't ask to be shot down, and didn't deserve it. He was doing his duty." He pulled Berwick's face close to his. "Now, you lay here a while and think about what I just said before I show you some *real* pain." Wilder released him and stood up.

Berwick dropped to the floor and curled into the fetal position. He began to whimper.

"I'm going to say this once. I'm walking out of this room, and when I come back, you'd better be gone. Get your ass out of here before you get hurt. I'm not the only one around here that's had enough of your shit. And one more thing; if I see you in Vietnam, I'll consider you fair game. Now get the hell out!" Wilder glanced at Slaughter, picked up his hat, and left the room without another word.

Slaughter walked to the door and looked back at Berwick. "Better listen to what he said, corn pone. Be out of here when we get back, or

I'll pound you so deep into the ground that you'll have to look up to see the bottom." He walked out and closed the door.

Slaughter caught up with Wilder. They walked to town in silence.

Berwick left the Institute, and word quickly spread throughout the barracks. Wilder didn't regret his actions, but he knew there would be consequences. He didn't care. No one had the right to talk down Little Jack. Wilder's conscience was clear on that point.

The expected knock on the door came. It was the Sergeant of the Guard, Larry Cummings. He walked slowly into the room. "How's it going, guys?" He was nervous and he didn't want to be there.

"No complaints." Slaughter sat on the edge of the table and looked at Cummings.

Wilder said nothing.

"Uh, Bill, Colonel Jennings wants to see you in his office right away." Cummings was uncomfortable. "I'm sorry, Bill, but for what it's worth, I agree with what you did."

"I appreciate that. I'll take the heat—"

"Like hell!" Slaughter jumped off the table and stormed across the room. He stood in front of his friend. "We're both in on this, and I'm going with you."

"Listen, John, you didn't hit Berwick. I did. I knew exactly what I was doing, and I have no regrets. The Commandant's just doing his job. If he throws the book at me, then so be it."

"Don't be such a martyr. Everybody was in line to pound that idiot."

"Maybe so, but I'm the one that did it. You stay out of this." Wilder put his hand on Slaughter's shoulder. "John, you're my best friend, and it means a lot that you would stand with me on this. That's more than a guy can ask. But I'll face the consequences myself. Just keep one thing in mind; I'd do it again in a heartbeat."

"You're the toughest nut to crack I've ever seen." Slaughter tried to smile but couldn't.

"Don't go soft on me, Animal. You *do* have a reputation to uphold, you know."

"Yeah." Slaughter turned and looked out the window. He didn't want Wilder to see his eyes.

Wilder looked at Cummings. "I'm on my way."

Cummings stared at the door after Wilder left. "That man has steel balls. I don't envy him, but I wish I was like him."

"Me to." Slaughter continued to stare out the window.

Crossing the courtyard, Wilder thought about what he had done. Did he act out of impulse, or were his actions part of conscious thought? Certainly, his emotional state had been affected by Little Jack's imprisonment, and his mother's failing health had not helped. But did he have the right to do what he did? Berwick had been agitating him for months about Little Jack, and it was no secret that Berwick was against the war. He had the right to express his opinion of American involvement in foreign wars, but he did not have the right to insult Wilder's brother. No one could do that. Did Wilder have the right to do what he did to Berwick? *Yes. And I'd do it again*, he thought to himself. He walked purposefully to the Commandant's office.

Colonel Jay Jennings was the Commandant of Cadets. He was responsible for enforcing the Institute rules evenly and fairly for all cadets, regardless of personal or professional ties to their families. He knew the Wilders and was intimately familiar with their situation.

There was a knock on his door. "Come in."

Wilder walked in and closed the door. He approached the desk and stood at attention. He saluted. "Sir, Cadet Wilder reporting as ordered."

"Stand at ease, Mr. Wilder." Jennings returned the salute. He glanced at a piece of paper on his desk then looked at the young man. "Mr. Wilder, you know why I called you here."

"Yes, sir."

Jennings folded his hands on the desk. "One of your brother rats, Mr. Tom Berwick, resigned from the Institute yesterday. He left without talking to me. He returned home and he's not coming back. I received a phone call from his parents and this telegram." He pointed to the paper on his desk. "Mr. Berwick said that, for personal reasons, his son decided to leave and go to school elsewhere. He was not specific beyond that." Jennings waited for a reaction.

Wilder tensed but didn't move.

Jennings continued. "Mr. Berwick said that his son had been injured in a fight, but that the boy wouldn't elaborate. No names were mentioned. Would you care to read his telegram?"

"No, thank you, sir."

Jennings saw the questioning look. "The bottom line, Mr. Wilder, is that no formal complaint has been filed." He wanted to know what had happened between the two young men, and Wilder was the star witness. He knew of the torment that the young cadet was going through. A brother suffering at the hands of the North Vietnamese, and the inability to do anything about it, was like no hell on earth. His compassion for the young man was deep, and he wanted to help him.

Wilder remained motionless, afraid to speak.

Jennings walked around the desk and put his hand on the boy's shoulder. "Bill, you've not been charged with anything. As far as the Institute is concerned, the Berwick issue has officially died a quiet death." He pointed to a chair. "Please have a seat."

Wilder reluctantly sat down.

Jennings took off his tunic and hung it over his chair. He sat on the edge of the desk, wanting to put Wilder at ease. "Bill, your dad and I served together years ago. I know your family situation, and I understand how you feel. Now, speaking man to man, I think it would help if you told me exactly what happened between you and Berwick. It will not leave this room. It's time to get everything off your chest, son."

Wilder looked out the window. He could see House Mountain in the distance, and he longed to be alone up there. He looked a Jennings but said nothing.

"Take your time." Jennings patiently waited.

Wilder took a deep breath and began. "Colonel Jennings, I apologize for embarrassing you and the Institute. It's the last thing on earth I'd—"

"You haven't done any such thing. While I am concerned about the Berwick issue, he did give us an out here. He said nothing detrimental about you or anyone else. He just felt that he didn't belong here, and he left on his own accord. You can speak with a clear conscience."

Wilder leaned back and closed his eyes. He badly needed to talk with someone, but he didn't want to look like a coward, and he didn't want to say or do anything to shame his family or friends. He opened his eyes and looked straight at the commandant.

"Bill, I want to tell you something. It'll give you a different frame of reference. I was a POW in North Korea for a year."

"*You* were a POW?" Wilder sat upright in his chair.

"I was at the wrong place at the wrong time, not unlike your brother. I know what you're going through. Now, let's talk."

"I had no idea, sir." Wilder was both shocked and relieved. The weight on his shoulders had been shifted. He had someone to talk to that had been *there*. He looked at Colonel Jennings with new-found respect.

"There was no need to mention it til now. My ordeal is long since over, as will be your brother's."

Finally, Wilder spoke. "Little Jack was on his last mission when he got shot down, and he's been a POW for over three years now."

"I know."

"It's been hard on my parents, especially my mother. She's been ill for a long time, and the doctors haven't been able to help her much. Dad's stoic, but I see the strain in his face. I've tried to get him to retire, but he's a workaholic. He—"

"Don't be hard on him, Bill. I've known your father for years. Work is his way of coping. Besides, his job at the CIA is more important now than ever." Jennings sat beside Wilder. They were eye to eye. "Your father is in a position to do more for your brother than anyone outside the White House."

"What?"

"It's true. No, he can't go over there and get your brother out, but the CIA can get information on your brother and the other POW's quicker than anyone else. Your dad prepares that information, along with his suggestions, for the administration and the military. They use that information to make decisions—"

"Excuse me, sir, but with all due respect, those clowns in Washington couldn't get laid in a whore house if they had a million bucks. They're only interested in body counts and making names for themselves."

"Well, I don't disagree with you on that point, Bill, but your father is doing the best he can to influence decisions that relate to the POW's. I can't say with any certainty, but I wouldn't be surprised if there were plans in a desk somewhere to mount a rescue effort at some point.

"But getting back to you and your family, your decision to come to VMI has made your parents extremely proud, and they hope that you'll channel your ambitions to good ends. But do it for yourself, not somebody else. Don't lose sight of the big picture here. It's not your fault that your brother is where he is. He made his decision, and he stood by it. You can be proud of him for that. Make yours and stand by it."

Wilder stared at the Commandant. He slowly shook his head in agreement. "I guess I sometimes say and do the wrong things, but I can't let anyone disrespect my brother."

"And you shouldn't. Your brother is a brave man, as are all of our troops. But they have a job to do, and so do we."

"And I should give Dad more credit. I've been so consumed with my own feelings that I haven't really considered his. He's suffered in silence all this time." Bill closed his eyes as tears ran down his face. "God, forgive me for being so selfish." Bill Wilder cried for the first time in years. He poured out his feelings to the Commandant-now-friend. Jennings encouraged the young man to get everything out into the open, and he did just that. They both missed military duty that afternoon, and that was fine with both of them.

Some things were more important than others.

Slaughter placed his M-1 in the gun rack when Wilder came into the room. He watched his friend walk to the window and stare into the distance.

In his mind Wilder was alone on the top of House Mountain. His spirit was free and unencumbered. He stood motionless for several minutes. But then his face clouded over, and he looked at Slaughter. "Berwick's quit. He's not coming back."

"And?"

"He didn't mention anything about what happened. Nothing."

"I figured the asshole would sell us out. He probably got a dose of religion or something."

"Yeah, *or something*." Wilder rubbed his chin thoughtfully, then put both hands on his hips.

"I see that conniving look again," Slaughter said, scratching his head and sitting on the floor.

"It doesn't add up. That Berwick and I didn't see eye to eye was no state secret, but I can't figure why he didn't say anything about my pounding him. You'd think he'd want to get even."

"Don't kick a gift horse in the mouth. We slid on this one. Let it go."

"It's not that simple, John. Something's going on." Wilder's gaze returned to House Mountain.

"What about Jennings?"

Wilder lay on his hay, put his hands behind his head, and looked at the ceiling. "He knows my parents. He worked with Dad in Korea."

"Yeah?"

"He knew pretty much what happened between me and Berwick, but he didn't say anything. He understands what I'm going through."

"You were in there long enough." Slaughter knew not to pry.

"John, I listened to that man, and he listened to me." Wilder propped himself on one elbow and looked at Slaughter. "He could have thrown me out of school, but he didn't. He understood because he's been there."

"What do you mean?"

"He was a POW in Korea."

"S'um bitch!"

CHAPTER 8

The beatings, deprivation, and poor food had taken their toll on Little Jack. His wounds had not healed, and he was in constant pain. The daily torture had left him despondent, and he prayed every day that an American bomb would mercifully end it all.

Time meant nothing to him, and he didn't know if it was day or night. His sleep schedule, such as it was, was constantly interrupted by his captors. The guards prodded him with wooden rods and shot at him with empty weapons, and the single light bulb in the ceiling was switched on and off at random in an effort to deprive him of sleep.

After three years at the hands of the North Vietnamese, Little Jack's resistance had waned. His health had gone from bad to worse. Open sores covered his body, and the injuries inflicted on him during his torture had become infected. He had resigned himself to death—he looked forward to it. Anything was better than this. His faith in God and his family, however, had given him the courage not to give in to his captors. He still had not told Petrov anything.

Although he didn't go out of his way to prevent it, Petrov had not actively participated in the torture of the American prisoners. His role was to learn as much as he could from them. He was anxious to complete his assignment and infiltrate the United States. He hated his Vietnamese hosts, and he made no attempt to hide it. They were an arrogant lot, not worthy of respect, especially from a member of the KGB. If he had to "befriend" an American to get out of this cursed country, he would do it. He was willing to do whatever necessary.

"Bring in Wilder. I wish to talk to him," Petrov ordered.

"Not possible," the Vietnamese major replied with contempt. "You will interrogate the prisoners when I say. I am the commander here."

Petrov leaped to his feet, pointed an American .38 caliber revolver at the major's head, and shouted, "You listen to me, *monkey-san*. You will bring me the prisoner now, or you'll become the shit that you eat." Petrov held the gun to the major's head and cocked the hammer.

The Vietnamese major had lost face. He had been humiliated and disgraced by a Slav that had no business in his country. He hated Petrov, but he had no choice other than to cooperate with the Russian. The Soviets provided military and financial aid to his country, and the major knew it. With bile in his throat, he forced himself to bite his tongue. "Very well. Perhaps the American dog can provide us with some useful information before his is exterminated." His English wasn't as clear as Petrov's, but there was no mistaking his intent.

Wilder was dragged into the adjacent room by two Vietnamese guards who were no more than bullies. They had beaten him almost senseless. His eyes were swollen shut, and his face bled profusely. Several teeth had been kicked out, and he could barely speak. He was unable to stand. He had no idea of what time it was; the light in his cell had been on for days.

Petrov studied Wilder through the slit in the wall. *Fucking monkeys*, he thought. "You people are not making my job any easier." He looked at his Vietnamese counterpart. "You bastards can do what you want *after* I'm done with him. Not before!" Petrov held the revolver menacingly in his hand.

"This is my camp," the Vietnamese sneered.

"Fuck you, you goddamn rice-ball!"

The major went for his side arm, but Petrov had his finger on the trigger. The round from Little Jack's .38 struck the Vietnamese between the eyes, killing him instantly. Petrov slowly holstered the revolver while glaring at the dead man. He hated the Vietnamese almost as much as the hated the Americans. He would finish his assignment and get out of this hell-hole, even if it meant killing his "allies" in the process.

He opened the door and walked into the small room. It was smelly and dank, and the only light was a dim bulb hanging from a thin wire. Wilder sat unsteadily on the wooden stool in the center of the room. The guards were gone.

"Hello, Jack. It's good to see you again." Petrov stared at the nasty wounds. The Vietnamese were hateful in the extreme to the American prisoners, and Wilder had been singled out because of Petrov's special interest in him. Petrov swore to avenge himself against these low-life animals, but only after he extracted what he wanted from Wilder. After that, to hell with all of them, Americans included. "I sincerely apologize for the treatment you have received from your hosts, Jack. I will convince them to change their ways. I assure you of that."

"Bullshit," Little Jack whispered through his broken teeth. He strained to look at Petrov through one eye. "You're as bad as they are." He went into a coughing spasm and spat blood. He panted for several minutes, trying to catch his breath. Finally, he was able to speak. "Shoot me and get it over with. I'm not telling you a damn thing." He closed his eye and slumped over when another wave of pain swept over him.

Petrov studied him in silence. Then he slowly walked around the crippled American, wondering what, if anything, he could do to make Wilder talk. "Listen, Jack, I don't like what these animals are doing to you, but I have no control over them. I've protested their treatment of the Americans from the beginning, but they—"

"Leave me alone," Jack croaked. "Send me back to my cell." He shook with pain.

Petrov walked to the table and picked up a metal container. He opened it, and the aroma of hot beef stew filled the small room. He took a loaf of bread and a spoon from a bag and placed them on the table, along with the container. He sat back and waited for a reaction.

Wilder's senses were bombarded with the smell of the hot food. He had not had a hot meal since his capture, and he was starved. He strained to open one eye and looked at the food. His stomach ached, and it took all of his strength to control himself. He stared hungrily at the container, his thoughts consumed with its contents.

"Perhaps in another life, we could have been friends, Jack." Petrov looked at him for a moment then walked to the door. Turning around, he said, "Eat. Regain your strength." He turned and walked out of the room, closing the door behind him.

Little Jack was alone. The pain in his body was shadowed by the starving ache in his gut, and his willpower was taxed beyond his endurance. He slid forward, falling to the floor. He began to crawl painfully towards the table. His hands and feet were burned and bleeding, and the pain became more excruciating with each move. But his desire for the food overcame any agony he suffered, and he steadily inched forward. After what seemed like an eternity, he reached the table and slowly pulled himself to his knees. The smell assailed his senses, and he bowed his head and asked God for His forgiveness. He wept as he devoured the food.

CHAPTER 9

The Spring of 1968 was unique for both good and bad reasons. On March 16, the My Lai massacre in Vietnam saw the deaths of many innocent men, women, and children, resulting in the trials of Army Captain Ernest Medina and Lieutenant William Calley. In the short term, the massacre showed the futility and horror of war and how it could be inflicted indiscriminately and without regard to civilian rule or rights. In a broader sense, the massacre and resulting trials served to point out the blatant flaws in the Uniform Code of Military Justice and how official blame and punishment flowed down hill. On March 26, the Senior Advisory Group on Vietnam, a Washington DC based committee advising the Johnson administration, recommended that America de-escalate its involvement in Vietnam.

As a result of these events and because of the negative impact of the Tet Offensive earlier in the year, President Johnson announced on March 31 his decision not to run for re-election. His decision, however, did nothing to stop the riots and anti-war protests that were rampant across the nation. Riots began at Columbia University on April 23, and on April 26, two hundred thousand people demonstrated in New York City against the war.

On May 3, President Johnson announced the beginning of peace talks in Paris with the North Vietnamese, and on May 12, the talks formally opened.

Having completed ROTC summer camp at Randolph Air Force Base in San Antonio, Texas, Slaughter was looking forward to going to Virginia Beach with his friend. He lived in his worn out MG for three days; it was a long hot drive from Texas to Virginia.

Less than fifteen minutes from the Wilder residence, he pulled into a convenience store parking lot to buy a six-pack of beer. When he came out of the store, there were two hippies standing on the driver's side of his car. He walked up to them like a man that didn't have a care in the world—because he didn't. "Well, if it ain't Curly and Moe. Where's Larry?"

"Going somewhere, GI Joe? Like, say, Vietnam? How many babies you killed, man?" The first hippie leaned against the MG, a smirk on his face.

"Yeah, I'm going somewhere, you limp-dick!" Slaughter kicked him squarely in the groin. The hippie doubled over and fell to the ground, coughing and writhing in pain. "I'm going straight through you yahoos like crap through a goose. Then my friend and I are gonna get drunk and chase women. What do you think of that?" Slaughter was like a fireplug; fixed in place and as hard as steel. He looked at the second hippie.

"Hey, no problem, man. Be cool." The second hippie backed away, keeping his eyes on Slaughter. He climbed into his VW van and slumped down in his seat. After seeing his friend go down in a heap, the thought of messing with a human bowling ball lost its appeal.

Slaughter scanned the immediate area for any hidden surprises. Seeing none, he looked at the figure on the ground. "Screw with me again, and I'll break your friggin' nose. I'm good at it." He climbed over the door and dropped into the driver's seat. "Have a nice day, asshole!" He sped out of the parking lot.

The door bell rang. "I'll get it," Bill shouted. He looked out the window and saw the MG in the driveway. It had been two months since the cadets were let out on furlough, and they were both anxious to see each other. He opened the door.

"Hey, pecker-head!" Slaughter walked through the door and thrust a beer at his friend. "Good to see your ugly face."

They shook hands. "Welcome home from the summer games, John. Come in and take a load off." The two men dropped onto the sofa and propped their feet on Elizabeth Wilder's new coffee table. "How was your trip?"

"Boring as hell til a little while ago."

"What happened?"

"Two hippies and I had a meaningful discussion about the meaning of life when I stopped to pick up some beer." The toothy grin said it all.

Bill looked at the ceiling and shook his head. *Oh, Christ!* He looked at Slaughter. "And can I assume that you properly taught them to see the light?"

"You can."

"And how did I know you'd say that?"

"What else was I supposed to do?" Slaughter drained his beer and reached for another. "S'um bitch stood between me and my mechanical horse."

Bill's mother walked into the room. "Oh, John, I didn't know you were here. What a pleasant surprise."

"Hello, Mrs. W." Slaughter stood. "You look absolutely splendid. I hope this slug of a son has been behaving himself and acting proper around such a fine lady." He went out of his way with Bill's mother, and she loved it.

"He's been his usual self, John." She smiled and looked at her son. "Take your feet off my new table. You know better than that."

"Yes, ma'am." Bill rolled his eyes and looked at Slaughter. "How do you get away with it? She didn't catch you. Only me."

The Texan pounded his chest like an ape. "Stealth, cunning, and a superior attitude."

Why me?

"Jack is out back. I'm sure he'd like to see you, John."

"I'd like to see him too, Mrs. W. I trust that the good colonel is healthy and in fine spirits?"

"Why, yes, he is, John. Thank you for asking. How polite of you." Elizabeth smiled and headed for the kitchen. "You should learn some manners from your friend, Bill," she said over her shoulder.

"What? Animal has no manners. He's one of Pavlov's dogs. He learns from rote."

"What a disgusting name. You mustn't call your best friend an animal. Shame on you."

"But he—" .

"He's civilized. Period." Elizabeth was having fun at her son's expense, but she knew he didn't mind. The tit-for-tat exchange lifted her spirits.

Bill threw his hands into the air in mock submission. "I don't believe this." He looked at Slaughter. "She thinks you're *civilized*. Man, do you have her fooled."

"I can swoon the ladies with the best of them." Slaughter laughed.

"Your father's waiting outside. Take him a beer. It's hot over the grill."

"Okay... Hey, Mom?" Bill stopped and looked at his mother.

"Yes?"

"Thanks."

"For what?"

"For nothing in particular, and for everything in general."

Elizabeth stood in the kitchen, her eyes filled with tears. *Dear God, please watch over them.*

"Hey, look who's here." Jack Wilder waved when the two cadets stepped onto the deck. "Hey, John. Good to see you. How was your trip?"

"Passable fine. You're looking great, Colonel W. Feels good to be home."

Bill handed his father a beer. "Try this on, Dad. Cool you down a little."

"Thanks." Wilder took a long drink then wiped the cold bottle across his brow. "Whew! It's hot out here." He looked at the bottle. "This hits the spot."

"There's a story behind that beer, Dad." Bill looked at Slaughter.

"May as well tell him, John, before he hears it through the grapevine."

"Tell me what?"

"The short version, Colonel, is that I had to get physical with a couple flower children when I stopped for beer."

"Oh?" Wilder looked at the grill and turned the steaks over. "What happened?"

Slaughter told him the story without any hint of apology.

Wilder studied the steaks for a moment. "Guys, these aren't popular times for the military. Although you've been pretty much shielded at VMI, you've seen the war in the news and have had some experience with public opinion. Today was just another example. John, don't worry about it. You didn't do anything wrong, other than perhaps shoot first and ask questions second. I'd try verbal fisticuffs first. If that doesn't work, then do what you have to do. It'll happen again. You have to stand up for something. I'll tell you the same thing I've told Bill and Little Jack all their lives. First, if you believe in something, and—the *and* is important here—if it doesn't hurt you or anyone else, then stand up for your beliefs. Don't let herd mentality control your actions." Wilder looked intently at them. "Stand for what's right, make sure your position doesn't hurt anyone, and back up your words with deeds. People may not like you, but they'll sure as hell respect you." Wilder took the steaks from the grill and finished off his beer. "You've nothing to worry about, John. Considering who you were up against, I probably would've done the same thing."

"I appreciate that, sir. Thanks."

"Guys, I need your help with something."

"Name it, Dad." Bill thought that his father was the Rock of Gibraltar.

"I'm as proud of you two as I can be. You've accomplished a lot in three years, and in another year, you both will be on your way to flight school—and probably to Vietnam."

The two cadets looked at each other.

"Bill, your mother's health isn't good, although she tries to act like it's no big deal. Both of you know the stress she's been under, what with Little Jack and the war. She's petrified that you two could be next."

"We know, Dad. What do you want us to do?"

"Don't say anything to her about the Air Force, flight school, the war, or Little Jack. Try to keep the conversation upbeat. Talk about the things she likes. I know it bores you guys, but she's your mother, Bud. And she's my best friend." Jack looked away, as if something was in his eye.

Bill put his arm around his father's shoulder.

"We're with you, sir," Slaughter said.

"Thanks, guys. I knew I could count on you."

Elizabeth shouted from the kitchen window. "Bruce is here. Jack, are those steaks done yet?"

He cleared is throat. "Burned to a crisp. We're on our way." Wilder looked at them. "One more thing, guys. I guess you know that peace talks, if that's what you want to call them, have started in Paris."

They shook their heads in acknowledgment.

"Well, Liz's hopes are up. She thinks these talks will get Little Jack home before the end of the year in time for Christmas." He looked at his son. "Listen, Bud, I know what you and your mother have gone through, but I'm not going to give you any false hopes. I don't see anything happening there. The Vietnamese will not negotiate, and Washington is inert. Please don't say anything to encourage her hopes, okay?"

"Okay." Bill searched his father's eyes for an answer to the obvious question. "Can you tell me anything from the inside?"

"*Inside?* ... meaning the Agency?"

"Yes."

"You know I can't say anything, Bud. Just try to keep your chin up. Remember, the glass is half full, not half empty. Put yourself on a higher plane. You've been there before."

Bill understood. "*Moo goy.*"

"Moo who?"

"State of No Mind, John," Bill said, looking at his father.

They walked to the house in silence. The family enjoyed dinner, and everyone had a good time. Vietnam was not mentioned, and the men did nothing to rain on Elizabeth Wilder's parade.

The Paris peace talks were bogged down from the very beginning. The United States thought it had the upper hand from a military standpoint, and it insisted on a mutual withdrawal from South Vietnam by both North Vietnamese and American forces, thereby leaving Saigon in control of the country. The North Vietnamese and the National Liberation Front (Vietcong) rejected the idea out of hand. Negotiations were at an impasse. The United States stood firm in its position in order to show the Soviet Union that it could not be pushed around. The North Vietnamese refused to agree to any settlement that left them without control of the country. The total lack of progress in the talks was epitomized by the fact that the negotiating parties couldn't even agree on the size and shape of the table around which they would sit.

CHAPTER 10

Aside from the radio catching fire and their being stopped by the state police for not having a front bumper, the trip to Virginia Beach was uneventful. Wilder drove his beat up 1956 Chevy down the main drag looking for their motel, while Slaughter drank beer and made cat-calls at the women they passed. "Fear not, ladies, for I have arrived." He waved and gawked at them. For his efforts, he was equally ignored. "Poor things. They don't know what they're missing."

Wilder continued driving while looking at the motel signs. "Don't you ever think about anything else?"

"Beer."

"Aside from that?"

"There's nothing else to think about."

Wilder slowed the car. "Well, while you're thinking about nothing else, how about doing something besides taking up space? Help me look for this place. If we don't get there by six, we lose our reservations."

"What's it called again?"

"Sand Dunes."

"How original."

"Don't knock it," Wilder said. "It's cheap. You can spend the money you save on your favorite pastimes." They drove another mile before they saw it.

"There it is, on the left," Slaughter said.

"I see it." Wilder pulled into the empty lot and parked facing the building. He turned off the ignition. They stared silently at the tired three story structure. The paint was chipped and faded, and the cheap clapboard was split and falling off. The front porch was in shambles. The sand-covered sidewalk led to a broken screen door hanging at an angle by one rusty hinge. The front door itself was a dingy white that had blistered and peeled, and the lone picture window had a crack that ran diagonally across its full width. It added insult to injury.

"What a dump!" Slaughter finished his beer and threw the empty can into the back seat.

"You don't have to give it raves." Wilder regarded the organized firetrap with a small measure of disgust. "The *Taj Mahal* it ain't." He looked at Slaughter. "Guess you'll have more money to throw away on women and beer than you thought."

"Life is good."

Wilder opened his door. "Well, we didn't come here to sit on the verandah and drink mint juleps. Let's get moving." He walked to the rear of the vehicle and opened the trunk.

Slaughter jumped out of the car. "I'll get the cooler. We'll get checked in, have a few pops, and go trolling."

"Always thinking ahead, John."

"You finally got it figured out."

They checked into the hotel and went to their room on the second floor. Dropping their bags onto the beds, they took two beers and went out onto the porch. Their room faced the beach, and the cool ocean breeze blew through the door and windows. Despite the outside appearance, the motel was just what they needed. There were two beds, a radio, refrigerator, and a kitchenette that would see no use.

Sitting in two cane rockers overlooking the beach, they opened their beers and propped their feet on the rail. "Man, this is it. Just what the doctor ordered." Slaughter looked around the beach. His eyes finally settled on his friend. Wilder sat motionless, staring into the distance. Another person might think that he was day-dreaming, but Slaughter knew different. He sat quietly and waited.

When is this nightmare going to end? Is my brother coming home? Wilder thought of his mother, and he wondered how his father coped. His conversation with the VMI commandant came to mind, and he remembered what Jennings had said about the stress that his father had been under. He remembered when Little Jack rescued him as a child after being beaten. He thought of his childhood and of how his family had enjoyed their time together. There was a bond in the Wilder family that could not be broken. But the family had suffered because of the war and Little Jack's imprisonment, and he was determined to put an end to it.

Wilder stood and walked to the rail. He leaned against a corner post and looked out to sea. "I sometimes think what this war has done to my family is more than I can handle."

"We'll deal with it as it comes, buddy."

"How the hell does Berwick fit into this?" Wilder looked at his friend. "He didn't say a damn thing about the thrashing I gave him. Not a word." He looked at the sea. "There's something else going on here, and I don't like it."

"Let it go, Bill. You can't solve the world's problems, man. Your family needs you. Don't let that toad blind you to that. He's insignificant." Slaughter was rarely serious about anything, but this was an exception.

Wilder glared at him with a look that could scare the devil himself.

For the first the first time in their friendship, Slaughter felt uneasy.

"Interesting. Insignificant, indeed!" Wilder leaned forward so their faces almost touched. "John?"

"What ?" Slaughter didn't move.

"In the three years I've known you, this is the first time I've ever heard you speak using a word with more than four letters in it. I am impressed!"

Slaughter realized that he'd been had. "You douche bag! You scared the living shit out of me!" He leaped forward, but Wilder was already moving.

"Weren't you the one that wanted to chase women and drink beer? What are you waiting for?" Wilder bolted down the stairs.

Guess there's a wild man in there after all! Slaughter smiled to himself.

They had faced hardships over the past three years, and each man had dealt with them in his own way. What lay ahead was something that none could foresee. Their friendship, cast in stone, would be tested by events half a world away. But for now, it was time to cast off the baggage and enjoy themselves. They forgot about Vietnam, if only for a while.

By the end of the week they were partied out. Saturday night saw them going from bar to bar, and when they staggered to their room at dawn, they were drunk to the point of being sick. They collapsed on their beds and slept.

Wilder woke shortly after noon. His hangover was complete with the standard splitting headache, and his mouth tasted like the bottom of a bird cage. He showered, took three aspirin, and drank a quart of water. "Jesus, my head hurts," he said to the aspirin bottle. He kicked Slaughter's bed. "Get up, John. Let's go to the beach and sweat this crud out of our bodies."

"S'um bitch! My head feels like I used it for a bowling ball." Slaughter groaned and forced himself to sit up.

"You did."

"Shit." He looked around, trying to focus. The light hurt his eyes. "You want to what? Go to the beach? You're nuts."

"Quit bitching. Let's go." Wilder walked out the door.

"Man's crazy." Slaughter took some aspirin, grabbed a towel, and headed for the door.

Soon, the water, fresh air, and sun began to take effect. The headaches were gone, and the two party-goers dared to think that they would survive the night before. They swore that they would never get drunk again, at least until the next time. Right now they just wanted to relax and dry out. They lay on the beach and allowed the sun's rays to purge their bodies. They wanted no excitement this day.

"Well, check this out, dudes! Two military studs, dog tags and all." Four bikers approached them from the boardwalk. The leader was big and nasty looking. He wore a leather vest over his tattooed chest, torn jeans with a chain around his waist, and motorcycle boots with chains over the instep. He had a length of pipe in his hand and a hunting knife strapped to his calf. The others were similarly dressed. Two had baseball bats, while the last one tossed a broken bottle from one hand to the other.

"You sissies are on my beach," the gang leader said. They stood in a circle, looking down at their prey. "You hear me, you Nazi fags?"

Ignoring the bikers, Slaughter lazily got up and stretched. "Bill, do you smell something?"

"Yeah. Smells like day old road-kill." He slowly stood and walked towards the first biker. He spoke in a low voice. "May I speak, oh, mighty one of the stench?"

The biker sneered at him. "You got something to say to me, ass-hole?" He tapped the pipe against his leg.

"Yeah. Your mouthwash ain't making it, cheese-dick!" Wilder was eye-to-eye with him.

"What?" The biker went into a rage. "I'm gonna kill you, you fucking faggot!" He swung his pipe in a downward arc at Wilder's head.

Wilder's arms shot upwards in an X-block, stopping the pipe in mid-air. Grabbing his assailant's arm, he twisted the wrist, wrenching the pipe free. The attack was over before it began. The surprised man gaped at the piercing eyes looking back at him.

"Listen, mutt-face, I'm not looking for a fight. I have a five-alarm hangover, and I'm in no mood to play grab-ass with you cub scouts. So, run along home and hump your mama's dog before you find out what your ass looks like from the inside." Wilder held the pipe casually at his side.

"You ... you!" The biker lunged forward, grasping at Wilder with both hands.

Wilder kicked him in the stomach. He quickly followed with a punch to the solar plexus, knocking the wind out of his attacker-turned-victim. He faked another kick to the groin. When the stunned biker tried to block it, Wilder whacked him across the forehead with the pipe. The biker fell to the ground, his hands going to his head as blood gushed from the wound.

"Last warning. Behave yourselves." Wilder stood with his knees slightly bent, looking at his quarry.

"You're dead meat, man!" the second biker shouted. As he began to swing his bat, Wilder dove at him in a forward head-first roll. His right foot flew through the air, his heel striking the biker on the solar plexus. Dropping the bat, the man gasped and reached for his chest. Wilder didn't miss a stroke. On his back after completing the roll, he thrust his left foot into the man's groin with all his strength. The biker lifted slightly, then crumbled to the ground. He curled into the fetal position, retching from the stabbing pain. Wilder quickly jumped to his feet and faced the other two.

Slaughter picked up the bat, unnoticed by the others. When the third biker moved towards Wilder, Slaughter cracked him across the base of the back, bringing him immediately to his knees. "Dumb-ass! Gonna learn the hard way, I guess."

The last biker looked frantically back and forth at Wilder and Slaughter. Knowing that he stood no chance, he dropped the broken bottle and slowly backed away. When he was a safe distance, he turned and ran.

"Guess that twit ain't as dumb as his buddies. Quit while he was ahead."

"Yeah," Wilder looked at Slaughter. "Dad was right. We're going to have to put up with this stuff for a long time."

"I reckon so."

CHAPTER 11

Since the beginning of civilization, espionage has been part of the human condition. Be it for political, military, or industrial reasons, or just for the sake of survival, spying has played a pivotal role in the success or failure of nations.

The Central Intelligence Agency was established by the National Security Act of 1947 to fill the government's need for information on its enemies. While some have been pragmatic in their assessment that the CIA is a necessary entity, others have argued that such an organization is not only detrimental to the government and the governed, but it could, under the right circumstances, lead to a government within a government—a secret ruling class with powers that could go unchecked. That argument still continues.

Other nations formed their own intelligence organizations for reasons similar to the United States. British intelligence consists of two primary organizations that are separate but closely related. The British Secret Service and the Security Service, know respectfully as MI-6 and MI-5, operate in similar fashion to the American CIA and FBI. MI-6 is concerned with external espionage operations, while MI-5 is involved with internal security of the country. Unlike the FBI, however, this branch of British intelligence also engages in overseas intelligence activities.

The *Komitet Gosudarstennoi Bezopasnosti*, or Russian KGB, is the equivalent of the CIA, FBI, MI-6, and MI-5 all rolled into one. It is one of the most feared Soviet organizations in the world, and it has been the nemesis of American and British intelligence since the end of World War II.

Shortly after the war, the FBI and CIA uncovered the spy ring that gave the Soviets the ability to build the atomic bomb. Julius and Ethel Rosenberg were convicted of selling, or giving, America's atomic secrets to the Soviets, and after one of the most notorious public trials in history, they were executed for treason. The nuclear genie was out of the bottle.

In 1954 British intelligence was rocked by the Philby case. From 1940 to 1954 one H.A.R. Philby, a prominent British citizen, was a high ranking intelligence official in both MI-5 and MI-6. He was also a Soviet agent.

The cat-and-mouse game of espionage continued during the Vietnam War.

"What do you make of it, Jack?" Bruce Spencer looked at the document marked TOP SECRET on Wilder's desk.

"Too early to tell." Wilder gazed out the window, his long day just beginning. Shoving his hands into his pockets, he walked to his desk and stared at the document. "We haven't seen anything like this since the Philby case." He looked at Spencer. "George Paterson Ackerman. We used to work with him at NATO. Remember?"

"All too well." Both men stood in silence. A spy had been discovered by British intelligence. He was an expert on NATO's top secret military plans against the Eastern Bloc, and he was a Soviet agent.

"A mole in our midst," Wilder said.

"How long?"

"Ten years, according to Sir John Chattam at MI-6. John's a bit of a stuffed shirt; pip-pip and all that, but he knows his business. Said this guy's even had access to 10 Downing Street."

"Jesus Christ!"

Wilder looked at his brother-in-law. "Let's hope He's on our side here." He glanced briefly at the document and sat on the side of his desk. "We're working with the Brits and Interpol on this. We don't know his real identity yet, but he was picked up in Trafalgar Square when the Brits caught him passing information to a courier from the Soviet Embassy in London. We know that the embassy guy is KGB."

"It's going to be a long night." Spencer leaned against the wall, staring at the floor.

"I told Sir John and Duquois at INTERPOL to contact me the minute they find anything."

"Nothing we can do but wait." Spencer poured two cups of coffee and handed one to Wilder. Both men lapsed into silence, thinking unspeakable thoughts.

Within minutes the phone rang. Wilder grabbed it. "Yes?"

"Sir, Al Smith here. I have a secure telex from MI-6."

"Bring it up." Wilder hung up the phone and looked at Spencer. "This may be what we're looking for."

Spencer raised his eyebrows. "We may think otherwise after we've seen it."

I'm afraid you may be right.

There was a knock at the door and Smith entered. "Here you are, sir." Smith handed a folder to Wilder and looked at the NSA director. "Good to see you again, Mr. Spencer."

"You too, Al. Wish the circumstances were better."

"Me too." He turned to Wilder. "Sir, if you need anything else, I'll be in the communications center."

"Thanks, Al." Wilder opened the folder and scanned the document. He suddenly felt old. He dropped the message on the desk, leaned back in his chair, and looked out the window.

Spencer picked up the paper and studied it. He stood quietly and reflected on what he had just read. "Of all people, I would never have suspected Ackerman. He was in charge of Western invasion plans of the WARSAW countries." He closed his eyes and thought aloud. "He had access to NATO's tactical nuclear plans. He knows everything."

"An understatement," Wilder said. "We have to keep this on ice until all the facts come in. We need to—"

There was a knock on the door and Smith entered. "Excuse me, gentlemen. Another message from MI-6."

"Thanks, Al." Wilder took the document and read it silently. He looked at his brother-in-law. "And the screw turns. It seems that our friend Ackerman is, in fact, one Anatoly Dimitri Petrov, colonel of the KGB."

"Worst fears confirmed." Spencer shook his head.

"According to John, this Petrov character knew that he'd been compromised and was planning to leave the country. His handler had tickets for him to go to Moscow by way of Berlin on Pan Am. The spooks at MI-6 have been watching him for some time."

"Why didn't they pick up him earlier?"

"I don't know, but my money's on Sir John. My guess is that they wanted to catch him in the act. And they did."

"What about the NATO people?"

"Believe me, when they find out, they'll squeal like pigs. We need to keep a lid on this as long as we can. Won't be easy." Wilder skewed his face and rubbed his chin. There was something else on his mind. He scanned the documents for additional information. "It seems that the KGB, without knowing it, is helping in that regard."

"How so?"

"They're saying nothing about Petrov."

"No mention of him in their channel traffic?"'

"Not a word," Wilder said. The phone rang and he picked it up. "Wilder ... Yes, Sir John. Go ahead ... Okay ... Call me the minute anything comes in." Wilder looked at the phone for a moment before placing it in the cradle. He put his hands on his hips. "It gets better."

"What now?"

"It seems that Petrov has a son in the Soviet Air Defense Forces. Ivan Petrov is a pilot. He's also a captain in the KGB. MI-6 has been keeping track of him too. Sir John says he's a murderous son-of-a-bitch."

Spencer saw the strained look on his brother-in-law's face. "Give me the rest of it, Jack."

Their eyes locked. "He's in North Vietnam—at the Hanoi Hilton."

"We need to be careful here." Spencer was tactful if nothing else. "I need a drink."

They sat in silence, waiting the next ax to fall.

CHAPTER 12

What goes around, comes around. That saying applies to all of life's experiences, but it is especially true in politics.

In 1950 a Democratic president committed American military forces to the Korean conflict. In 1965 another Democratic president sent the first of over 500,000 troops to a conflict in Southeast Asia. Although neither of these brush wars were legally declared, they both had the same political result; the presidents in both situations did not run for office again, and their parties lost the ensuing elections.

Eisenhower's election in 1952 was generally accepted as a mandate for rejecting the "half-wars" that had claimed the lives of Americans in this century, specifically Korea. This lesson did not go unnoticed by Nixon in 1968. The half-war in Vietnam caused him to actively pursue peace talks with North Vietnam.

The presidential campaign in 1968 questioned, in part, the nation's capacity to engage in military challenges worldwide all at once. Additionally, it questioned the United States' position in world affairs. Heretofore, America's role was one of establishing and preserving the balance of power wherever it was threatened. This "Globalism" attitude led to American involvement in Vietnam. The United States, some argued, had no right to impose a Pax Americana upon the world. Rather, the nation should establish a national priority, then commit its resources accordingly; either engage totally with the will to win, or withdraw completely.

Americans' disenchantment with the war was but one facet that the administration had to deal with. Presidents Johnson and Nixon both had to come to terms with a totally corrupt government in South Vietnam.

Nguyen Van Thieu, a South Vietnamese military officer and graduate of the United States Command and General Staff College, was the American government's choice of leaders to head a government in South Vietnam and make a stand against the Communists. By 1965 Thieu and his vice-president, Nguyen Cao Ky, were ready to assume control. Ky was originally slated to be president in the new government, but Thieu outmaneuvered him to become the presidential candidate with Ky as vice-president. The Johnson administration did not want them to run against each other, and the government went out of its way to assure that both men would be on the same team, thus assuring a civilian government. The shaky coalition held, and the Thieu-Ky government took control in 1967.

The government was corrupt from the beginning. That Thieu was Catholic and the Vietnamese population was vastly Buddhist, did not help. His government did, however, oppose the Communists, and that was the only qualifying factor that the United States needed to prop up the regime. The Johnson administration could easily look in the other direction as long as its interests were supported by Thieu.

The 1968 Democratic National Convention brought the political divisions caused by the Vietnam war to a head. The Tet Offensive in February showed how vulnerable American forces were, and it caused a wholesale drop in American support for the war. When President Johnson decided not to run for re-election, Vice-president Hubert Humphrey and Senator Robert Kennedy became the front-runners for the Democratic nomination. But with Kennedy's assassination in June, the nomination went to Humphrey.

During the convention, the delegates argued bitterly about the Vietnam war and America's involvement in it. South Dakota's senator George McGovern argued vehemently against the war, but the Johnson-Humphrey forces prevailed in the end.

While the arguing went on inside, anti-war protesters became violent outside in their efforts to disrupt the convention. The demonstrations didn't sit well with Chicago mayor Richard Daley, and he ordered the police into the crowds. Later dubbed a "police riot," the resulting confrontation was seen on national television by a stunned nation. The media brought the national psyche into the open, and Americans, as a whole, were now seen as being against the war.

Captain Ivan Petrov was growing more impatient. His time in North Vietnam had far exceeded what he had expected, and he had become intolerant with his "hosts." He hated the Vietnamese and their dirty little country. That the Americans were bombing them back into the Stone Age, was of little consequence to him. The Vietnamese didn't have to regress very far in his opinion. They were belligerent and crude. That they mistreated their prisoners was an understatement, but even he was appalled at the treatment of their own kind. To Petrov the Vietnamese were nothing more than animals.

As a KGB officer he watched and listened to the American news broadcasts. He studied the collective American opinion against the war, and he used it expertly against the prisoners. He did, however, see a constant theme among the American POW's that he could not explain; although they were isolated from each other for the most part, none would break the faith of their bond. It was a bond among American military men that he both admired and despised. He could not crush their faith in each other or in their country, no matter how hard he tried. And try, he did, until he was recalled to Moscow.

"This way, Captain Petrov," the shapely Red Army sergeant said while walking down the hall of KGB headquarters.

Dostupniey Dyevochkia! Fucking whore! He would have his way with her when this pointless meeting was over. Walking behind her, he fantasized about what he would do to her this night. But as he approached the door, he pushed her from his mind and concentrated on his reason for being here in the first place. He was certain that now he would go to the United States.

The sergeant knocked on the door and waited.

"Come."

She opened the door and stood aside. She smiled when Petrov walked past her and into the office. Ignoring her, he closed the door, walked to the center of the room, came to attention, and saluted.

"Welcome home, Captain Petrov. I am Colonel Alexi Romanski, head of the Second Directorate." Romanski's flabby face was flushed from high blood pressure and an excess of the good life. His demeanor was one of a highly placed bureaucrat, set in his ways and not willing to make allowances for anything except himself. "I trust your time in Hanoi was productive."

"Somewhat, Colonel." *Condescending pig.*

"Please sit." Romanski motioned to a chair. Petrov sat and waited impatiently. Romanski opened a glass humidor and held it out to him. "Cigar? The finest from our comrades in Havana."

"No, thank you." *Get to the point, you mass of fat.*

"You are anxious, Captain Petrov."

He stared at Romanski but said nothing.

"I know that you wish time to indulge yourself in the things you have missed while in Hanoi, so I will get to the point. I'm afraid there is bad news, Captain." He waited for a response.

"And that is?" Petrov was bordering on insolence.

"Your father has been detained by British MI-6 agents in London. He was about to leave for Berlin when he was arrested."

Petrov's eyes bored into Romanski's. "How long have the British known of him, and why didn't you get him out sooner?"

"We knew the British suspected him. They have for some time."

"That's not what I asked. Why didn't you get him out sooner? Please, answer the question."

"Captain Petrov, do you question my authority or that of the KGB? We know what we are doing. Do not forget that your father was doing his duty for Mother Russia."

Petrov stood and walked slowly to the desk. Leaning over and placing his hands flat on the top, he glared at Romanski. "I don't believe you, Colonel. I don't believe for a minute that you and your minions couldn't do anything. Does incompetence rule here?"

Romanski's face flushed and bile rose in his throat. "Do not threaten me, Captain Petrov. You forget your station." He pressed a button under his desk. A side door opened, and two burly guards quickly entered the room and took their places on either side of him, weapons ready.

Petrov wasn't afraid of them, but he knew that there wasn't anything he could do. He looked around the room for something to focus his rage on. *That whore. She'll pay for this.* He looked at Romanski. Finally, he sat down, his muscles like springs under pressure.

Romanski reached into a desk drawer and took out a bottle of vodka and two glasses. He filled them both, stood, and offered one to Petrov. "I understand your frustration and pain, young Petrov. I understand you wish to lash out at someone because something has been taken from you. Your father understood the risks, and now you must also. We fought together in the Great War against the Germans. He was, and is, my friend. Salute your father and drink with me." Romanski held up his glass and smiled. "To Colonel of the KGB Anatoly Dimitry Petrov, Hero of the Soviet Union. *Na zdorovie.*" He drained his glass then looked at the arrogant young officer.

Petrov was unmoved. "I wish to finish my business here and go to America. I have a mission there."

Romanski drank the second glass and smirked at the young captain. "There is unfinished business for you in Hanoi."

"What do you mean?" Petrov's stomach tightened.

Romanski's bulk dropped into his chair. Wiping his mouth with his sleeve, he said, "There is something you should know." He savored his control over this young stallion. He picked up his cigar and put it in his mouth.

"Get on with it!"

"Patience is not a virtue that rewards you."

Petrov ground his teeth. "I've no time for it. That my father has been captured by British agents, has nothing to do with the American prisoners in Hanoi. It has everything to do with you and your people in Britain. Make your point."

"Listen carefully, Captain Petrov. Remember when your father was in Washington? He was inside America's Pentagon facility at the time. You were living in a place called Alexandria—"

"I know that. Again, your point?"

Romanski shrugged off Petrov's impatience. "Your father worked with an American army officer by the name of Bruce Spencer. Spencer knew of the tactical nuclear plans in Eastern Europe against our WARSAW allies. Colonel Petrov's cover was that he was a civilian consultant in the writing and execution of those war plans. Your father's cover name was George Ackerman. Do you remember?"

"I remember." Petrov reflected silently for a moment. "And my mother knew nothing of this. She died before we left for Britain."

"Regretfully, yes. I'm sure she was a fine lady." Romanski's voice rang hollow.

"You regret nothing!" Petrov sprang to his feet and the guards stepped forward. "You had her terminated after my father was ordered to leave America. I hold you accountable for her death as well as my father's capture."

"Those are strong words, Captain Petrov. You are counseled to hold your tongue." Although Romanski was flanked by the guards, there was a tinge of fear in his voice. "Understand that I am on your side. I am trying to give you information that may be helpful to you. Your insolence does not go unnoticed, but neither do your feelings for your father. He is the only family you have living."

"Again, your point?"

"I will make my point in time. This Colonel Spencer that your father worked with, he was married, but now he is a widower. His family is important to us—to you."

"How?"

"He has a sister. Her name is Elizabeth Wilder. She is married to a retired Air Force officer named Jack Wilder. He is the Director of Operations at the Central Intelligence Agency. He and Spencer are related, and their positions within the American intelligence arena require that they work together almost daily. They—"

"Wait!" Petrov's senses came alive. "The American prisoner in Hanoi—his father is with the CIA." Despite his disgust with Romansi, Petrov saw his point.

Romanski smiled, cocksure of himself. "Your deduction is correct, Captain Petrov. We are speaking of the same person. The father of your prisoner is related to the man that helped to expose your father." Romanski knew that Spencer had nothing to do with the senior Petrov's capture, but he was savvy enough to know that, if he played his cards right, he could secure a promotion for himself. Maybe even an exchange; one American flier for one Soviet agent. It wasn't out of the question, was it? Surely, he would be rewarded by the General Secretary if he could pull this off. Romanski thought nothing of the Petrovs or of the American prisoner in Hanoi, but if they could get him promoted, then why not used them to his advantage?

Petrov was wrapped in his own thoughts. "This Spencer... he is the uncle of the American prisoner Wilder?"

"Correct, Captain Petrov."

Petrov paced the floor, his mind racing. He faced Romanski. "Is it possible that the Americans would be interested in an exchange?"

Checkmate. Romanski had Petrov where he wanted him. "We wish to get Colonel Petrov returned safely to us, Captain. I think it may be in our mutual interests to pursue the idea. I will speak to the Secretary about it. You understand, of course, that the Soviet Union does not admit to spying. If an exchange can be arranged, it will have to be done through covert channels. Neither the Americans nor the British wish to admit having a long-time spy in their midst. The Americans want to get out of Vietnam, and they want the POW's back. I think they will work for an exchange of some sort."

Petrov stared at the bulbous face. Romanski was typical of the old men in the bureaucracy that Petrov loathed. Most had no useful purpose. They were nothing more than leeches—to be discarded and destroyed. On the other hand, he knew that Romanski would suggest the exchange idea, even if only to better himself. Petrov didn't care. If an exchange was acceptable to the Americans and the British, it mattered little what happened to Romanski. Let him have his dacha on the Black sea, his vodka, and his proclivities for young men. Romanski was expendable. Colonel Anatoly Dimitry Petrov was not.

"Return to Hanoi, Captain Petrov, and devote your time to your prisoner. You know what to do."

Without another word Petrov left the office, leaving the door open. He walked purposefully down the hall and stopped in front of the female sergeant's desk. "Eight o'clock. My flat." Smiling, he handed her a note with the address on it. "I will bring wine and caviar. Wear something ... interesting." He turned and walked out.

***

Petrov entered the dark room and closed the door. He sat a bottle of vodka on the table, removed his tunic, and threw it at the chair in the corner. He poured a glass of the clear liquid, drank it, and poured another. Sitting on the edge of the bed, he thought about his father and his recent encounter with Romanski. He hated the KGB colonel and all the he represented, but he had no choice but to work with him. He thought about Romanski's words, and he began to wonder. Would an exchange be possible, given the fact that his father knew more than any man about NATO? Why would the British and Americans give him up, knowing that he would reveal everything he knew to their enemies? Did Romanski really think an exchange could be done? One of the most effective spies the Soviets ever had for one lone American pilot? Petrov didn't think so. His anger and frustration continued to build. He hated the inefficiency of the Soviet political organs, but he hated the Americans even more.

His thoughts were broken by a soft knock on the door. He drained his glass and crushed out his Marlboro. He looked at his watch. *The bitch is late.* He walked across the room and opened the door.

She was wearing a full length Soviet greatcoat that revealed nothing. "Good evening, Comrade Captain. May I come in?" Her smile was lustful. She walked into the room and closed the door behind her. Looking at Petrov, she removed her coat. She was dressed in black. A tight sweater and a mini skirt complemented her shapely body. The seams on the black stockings ran down the backs of her legs and into the spiked heels she wore. Her blonde hair was down to her waist. Her eyes were heavily made up, and her full lips were painted with red wet-look lipstick. She looked like a high class whore, which was exactly what Petrov wanted.

He ran his eyes over her body, and a lewd smiled covered his lips. He walked to the table and poured two classes of vodka. He handed one to her. "Your name?"

"Olga," she said, taking the glass. Trained and experienced in the courtesan arts, she felt in control. *You haven't had a woman for months, have you? I'll get what I'm after and be gone.* She would do what she had to do. After all, he was only one man.

Keeping his eyes on her body, he emptied his glass and poured another. *Bitch!* His degrading hatred for women was well known in the KGB. Their only purpose was to satisfy his physical needs.

"You are the quiet one, Captain. Do you wish me to be someone else perhaps?"

"Olga will do fine."

"May I call you Ivan?"

Her words were barely spoken when Petrov viciously back-handed her across the mouth. She fell backwards over the chair and dropped to her knees. Her glass flew across the room and smashed against the wall.

An angry red welt began to rise on the side of her face, and she covered it with her hand while supporting herself with the other. She was dazed, shocked, and confused. After a minute, she began to regain her composure. She looked at him. "Why—"

"Shut up, bitch!" He glared hatefully at her. He slowly cracked his knuckles.

She had been with violent men before, and she knew their game. She sat quietly, looking at the floor. She knew that violence was compensation for their lack of manhood, but she didn't understand why he had to hit her so hard.

Petrov walked to the chair and sat down. Leaning back, he calmly looked at her. "Please, get up, Olga." His voice was almost compassionate. "Come over here and stand in front of me."

She slowly stood, her lip bleeding. She reached up to straighten her disheveled hair.

"Leave it."

She lowered her hands. Looking at the floor in submission, she walked slowly across the room and stood in front of him. She was motionless, silent, and a little frightened.

He knew that he was in total control now, and he folded his arms across his chest. Like a cat, he would play with his prey, torment it and make it submit again and again, before he devoured it. He poured another glass of vodka and quickly drained it. Dropping the glass to the floor, he looked at her legs. "What are you wearing under your skirt?"

"Nothing." She continued to stare at the floor.

Petrov leaned forward. "Spread your legs." He slid his hand up her skirt and began to rub her inner thighs. "Do you like this?"

"Yes."

He looked at her face, and his voice became hard. "You don't sound like it."

"Yes, yes, I do like it. Please do it again." She closed her eyes and moaned. She had to be convincing.

He grabbed her by the throat and squeezed until she almost fainted. He held her for several seconds then pushed her away. She fell backwards onto the floor, her hands grasping her neck. She gagged and coughed, trying to catch her breath. She was gripped with fear, and she cowered away from him.

Petrov walked across the room and stood over her. Seeing the terror in her eyes, he calmly said, "Pour me another drink, Olga."

"You—"

He pushed her with his foot. "Do it, bitch!" His eyes were suddenly full of rage, and he stood ready to strike her again.

Olga was petrified. She thought that Petrov would kill her if she disobeyed him. She struggled for self-control. "Whatever you wish," she said through her coughing.

"That's better." Petrov turned away from her and went to the closet, stripping off his remaining clothes. He took a small satchel from the closet shelf and went to the bed.

Olga slowly got to her feet. She was unsteady and her head reeled. She stole a glance at the door; it took all of her strength and courage to keep from making the attempt. She knew that she could not escape. Her hands shook while she filled the glass with vodka. She looked at the clear liquid. *Please, help me. I can't—*

She felt the garrote around her neck. Dropping the glass, her hands went to her throat. Her eyes bulged in terror as the noose tightened. She fought and kicked with all her strength, but there was no escape. Her vision darkened. Olga slipped into unconsciousness.

Petrov caught her limp body. He carried her across the room and placed her face down on the bed. He picked up his tunic and took out another pack of Marlboros. He lit a cigarette and cracked his knuckles.

As a teen young Petrov was a member of the Communist Youth

League, and he was recruited by his father into the KGB. Anatoly Petrov trained his son to become a KGB agent. When the elder Petrov, under the cover of George Ackerman, went to northern Virginia to work in the Pentagon, his wife and son went with him.

Ivan Petrov's physical features were more American than Slavic. Hi mother was Nordic with blonde hair and long features. His father was from Berlin, his lineage being German. Their son had brown hair and blue eyes, an uncommon combination. At just under six feet tall, he wasn't an overly accomplished athlete. He was, however, well trained by his mentors in the Lubyanka. He was skilled in the art of torture, weapons, and martial combat. Although not an expert in any of those fields, he made up for any shortcomings with a zealous approach to his work.

Petrov was sadistic with women. His mother had been a prostitute and was terminated by the KGB for her transgressions. Officially an accident, Petrov eventually learned the truth about his mother's demise. He was a child when it happened. He hated her for what she was, but she was still his mother, and the child needed his mother in spite of her behavior.

There was no one to help him cope with her behavior or her death, and the traumatic events tormented him for years. He suffered from extreme headaches when confronted with women, and he regarded all women as whores.

"George Ackerman" remained at the Pentagon until his son finished his schooling at Georgetown University. Then, while driving home from a weekend in the Virginia countryside, the "son" was killed in a fiery accident. The body was badly burned, and identification was impossible. Shortly thereafter, Ivan Petrov arrived in Moscow to begin his formal training. "George Ackerman" was transferred to Great Britain.

Years later Captain Ivan Petrov was assigned, on paper at least, to the Soviet Air Defense Forces as a MIG pilot in Eastern Europe. While in East Berlin on an undercover assignment, he garroted a prostitute to death. Shortly afterwards, he repeated the scenario with a streetwalker in Copenhagen. Because of his violent behavior, he was recalled to Moscow. There were some in the KGB hierarchy that wanted to dismiss him, but higher authorities prevailed. Because of his background as an "American," he was destined for bigger and better things.

Petrov sat perfectly still, staring at the body on the bed. He lit another cigarette and drank from the bottle. He felt the oncoming headache. There was only one thing to do.

Sitting the bottle on the floor, he stood and looked at the unconscious woman. Despite the worsening headache, he was sexually aroused. His demented mind shifted into high gear, and he went to work.

He took a roll of heavy tape from the satchel bag and tore off two strips. Lifting her head by the hair, he placed one strip tightly across her mouth and the other across her eyes. He removed four lengths of rope from the bag and placed them on the bed. He pulled her arms to their full length and tied her hands to the front corner posts. He stood on the bed and, with both hands, lifted her by the hips until her knees came up under her. He placed the pillows under her hips and jumped onto the floor. He went to the foot of the bed and pulled her feet down until her hips rested on the pillows.

He pulled her legs apart, taking care to leave her shoes on. The high heels and short dress excited him. He tied her feet to the bottom corners of the bed. She lay face down, spread to the four corners, her hips elevated by the pillows. Her skirt was hiked up, revealing her garter belt.

Petrov stood at the foot of the bed and stared at Olga's body. He put his hands against the sides of his head when a wave of pain shot through his skull. The vodka had no effect on his headache, but it did sharpen his unusual desire to inflict pain. His erection and his head pounded in unison. The pleasure—and pain—were almost unbearable. He was ready.

He opened a vial of smelling salts and held it under her nose. The pungent odor woke her within seconds. Momentarily dazed, she soon realized that she was bound and gagged. She tried to scream but the tape on her mouth prevented it from escaping. She jerked in vain against the ropes while Petrov watched her with quiet amusement. After several minutes, she stopped moving and began to sob.

"Your whining makes me sick, but it's nothing compared to what you're going to do," Petrov whispered into her ear. When she pulled helplessly against the ropes, he pressed her head to the bed. "Olga was my mother's name. She was a whore like you." Another stab of pain shot threw his head. He ground his teeth together and groaned. After it passed he looked at her. "You're going to enjoy this."

Olga shook uncontrollably when Petrov climbed onto the bed behind her. Straddling her on his knees, he grabbed her hips. He forced himself into her and began to sodomize her violently. Her body went rigid against his brutal onslaught. She screamed and sobbed, but her pitiful protests were muted by the tape.

The more her body jerked the more excited he became, and he went at her with such force that he bit his tongue. Blood poured from his mouth and down his chest. It mixed with hers until it covered the bed.

"Bitch! You *bitch!*" he screamed. Exploding inside her, he collapsed exhausted on top of her inert body.

Mercifully, Olga had passed out, the pain being too much to bear. Petrov lay panting on top of her for a long time. Finally, he pushed himself up and slowly got off the bed. His expression was like ice when he gazed at her damaged body. But when he saw that she was unconscious, he went into a rage. *You bitch! You'll be awake for this!* He took a straight razor out of the satchel.

He used the smelling salts. Suddenly conscious again, Olga screamed against the tape. He leaned over her and said, "You're one of the lucky ones. You will live to serve me again. But, first, I'm going to give you something to remember me by."

She didn't hear him—she was too consumed with pain. He straddled her back below her shoulders and lifted her head by her hair. He placed the razor against her neck. She cried pitifully when the blade slowly slit the skin on her throat from one ear to the other. She passed out again.

Petrov stood on the floor and looked at her. She was bathed in sweat and blood, her breathing erratic and shallow. He methodically wiped the blade on the sheet, packed his satchel, and got dressed. He rinsed the blood out of his mouth with vodka and spat it at the bed. The headache was gone, but the inner turmoil remained.

With one last look at the woman, he put on his tunic and left the flat.

Hurt, bleeding, and unconscious, Olga was still alive, the brutal evidence of her torture all around her.

Petrov returned to Hanoi, his attitude having gone from bad to worse. He was sure that the Americans would not deal and that he would never see his father again. *So be it,* he thought. He would vent his anger on the American prisoners.

He sent for Little Jack.

CHAPTER 13

While the Chicago riots disrupted the Democratic National Convention, Bill Wilder and John Slaughter started their First Class year at VMI. They were now in the "driver's seat" when it came to running things. Wilder was a cadet captain, and, as such, he was charged with upholding the rules of the Institute with respect to the lower three classes. To that end he tried to be even and fair, but most of the time his thoughts were half a world away.

Little Jack had been a POW for more than three years, and there had been no word on his condition. The Paris peace talks were a sham, but Wilder followed them closely, hoping against hope for a breakthrough that would lead to the release of the POW's. He prayed for his brother's return, but he was a realist. A release wouldn't come any time soon.

Frustrated by the lack of progress in Paris, Wilder was careful not to vent his feelings against the lower classmen, particularly the rats. He refused to add to their collective misery. He vented his aggressions through martial arts.

He was beginning his third year of martial instruction at the Institute. Neither the Rat Line nor the Class System existed in the *DoJang*.

The martial system of rank from beginner through Black Belt dominated the school's structure, with Wilder being the *Sa Bun Nim*, or master. All students showed respect to each other and gave differential treatment to the upper belts as due them from their years of training. Black Belt students deferred to Wilder. He, in turn, treated everyone with mutual respect. It was structured and disciplined, and it served them well.

"*Junbi. Charyot. Kyong Ye.*" Ready stance. Attention. Bow. Wilder opened the class, ready to put his students through their paces. The class consisted of both faculty and students from the Institute and from surrounding schools as far away as Roanoke. Every rank was represented from beginner to Black Belt.

Slaughter, now a Red Belt, stood in the front row. He had learned well under Wilder's instruction, but Wilder didn't cut him any slack. If anything, Wilder worked his friend harder than anyone else.

"Good afternoon," Wilder said, bowing to the class.

"Good afternoon, sir," the class responded in unison, bowing in turn.

"Today, we'll practice advanced kicking techniques and finish with some hand-to-hand combat drills. Please get a partner and form two lines." The drills began, and soon, everyone was drenched in sweat. *Sa Bun Nim* worked his students hard, but he was careful not to over extend anyone. Being an individual sport where everyone worked to his own level of proficiency, Wilder knew what each person was capable of. He was mindful of individual abilities, while requiring everyone to be proficient in all drills.

"Mr. Slaughter, please step forward."

Slaughter came and stood beside Wilder. The two men faced each other and bowed. "*Kyong Ye,*" Slaughter said.

"John, please face the class and stand in a normal relaxed position." To the group, Wilder said, "You're walking down the street, and someone grabs you around the neck from the rear with both hands in a choking fashion. What do you do? Mr. Slaughter will demonstrate." Wilder quietly stood behind him for a full minute. In an instant, he grabbed Slaughter around the neck and tried to drag him to the ground.

Slaughter reacted immediately. He spun to his right, swinging his right arm up, over, around, and under Wilder's arms above the elbows. Jerking his arm upwards, he broke Wilder's grip and forced Wilder up on his toes. He threw multiple palm heel blows at Wilder's face with his other hand, stopping just short of contact. He then threw several punches to Wilder's ribs, again avoiding contact. He followed immediately with a pendulum kick, knocking Wilder's feet out from under him. Wilder landed on his back. Slaughter shifted his grip and twisted Wilder's wrist. He then faked a stomp kick to Wilder's face. The entire maneuver was over in seconds, and it was effective by any measure. Slaughter released his friend, thinking that the demonstration was over.

It was a mistake that he would not forget.

Wilder was fast. When Slaughter bowed, Wilder reached up with both hands and grabbed his friend's belt. He pulled Slaughter down and faked two blows to the face. Before Slaughter could react, Wilder raised his legs and locked them around his neck, placing him in a head lock.

"S'um bitch!" Slaughter was caught completely by surprise.

Keeping a grip on Slaughter's belt, Wilder snapped his legs down. Slaughter flew forward and down, his body aimed head first at the floor. In the instant before impact, Wilder pulled his feet inward, deflecting the impending head blow and keeping his friend from breaking his neck. Slaughter landed with a thud on his back. Aside from his slightly injured pride, he was unhurt. Wilder released him and faked a stomp kick to his head that, under normal circumstances, would render an attacker unconscious. Wilder did a back roll and landed on his feet. He had to keep himself from laughing.

"The objective is to stun the attacker and get out of harm's way as soon as possible." He looked at his friend on the floor. "Isn't that right, John?"

Slaughter stood and looked around, a sheepish grin on his face. "I reckon so." He looked at Wilder and raised his hinds in submission. "Guess that's gonna cost me a beer or two." Everyone laughed.

"Better than your life, John." They shook hands and Wilder faced the class. "Never underestimate your enemy. No matter how good you are, there's always someone better. A wise man told me that a few years ago."

"Yeah, kick butt and get gone."

"In a manner of speaking, yes. Thanks for putting it so succinctly, John, and for your demonstration." The men bowed to each other, and Slaughter took his place in line.

By the end of class everyone was exhausted. "Excellent workout," Wilder said. "I see that everyone is soaked. Just remember that no one ever drowned in sweat. The word is attitude, guys. Attitude is everything. And never let defeat have the last word." He bowed and the class bowed in return. "*Ko Mop So Me Da.* Thank you for coming."

"*Ko Mop So Me Da, Sa Bun Nim.*" Everyone bowed. The class was over.

Walking back to the barracks, Slaughter said, "Bill, you never fail to whoop my ass. I really thought I had you that time."

"You did, John. The opening came when you let go, thinking that the exercise was over. Remember what I said in class. Never underestimate your enemy. No matter how good you are, there's always someone better. Dad told me that."

"Your dad was right. Thick-headed, I am. Dumb, I ain't. I'll remember next time." Slaughter shivered in the cold wind. "Sweat's turning into ice."

"Let's go." The two men ran through Washington Arch to the warmth of their room. The time between November and March at the Institute was known as the Dark Ages. There was little relief from the winds that blew through the mountains and the barracks, and each cadet dealt with the winter doldrums in his own way. For Wilder and Slaughter, martial arts helped them to forget the cold and dreariness, and each passing day brought them a day closer to graduation.

The mountains were steep and treacherous, and lush green foliage covered every inch of the rugged terrain. The steamy jungle floor was alive with snakes, lizards, insects, and vicious carnivores of every description. The extreme heat was matched with humidity, and the combination of the two was fatal to the unwary. The only saving grace, by some standards, was the fact the opium poppy grew profusely here due to the climate and the fact that the government did little except to turn a blind eye to it. The high mountain terrain was populated with unfriendly natives that jealously guarded their poppy fields and their sole source of income.

Known as the Golden Triangle, the area boarded by northern Thailand, northern Laos, and eastern Burma was rife with the opium poppy. Raw opium was processed into high grade heroin in make-shift plants that scattered the countryside. The finished heroin was ninety-nine percent pure, and it found its way through the mountain passes and jungles to the various ports along the coasts of Burma, Thailand, and both North and South Vietnam. From there the deadly substance was smuggled to the major countries of the world, includ-ing the United States. It also found its way both to the North and South Vietnamese armies and to the American soldiers in South Viet-nam.

"Dim, this shipment is ready to go?" the North Vietnamese major asked.

A nod. The Laotian "businessman" was dressed in rags. With black teeth stained from betel nut and worn from lack of care and a face that showed the weariness of having survived a dangerous life in a primitive war-torn region, the local tribesman approached the Vietnamese officer with caution. The major had one thousand Ameri-can dollars to exchange for the merchandise the Laotian held in a worn leather bag, and the Laotian was eager to complete his end of the deal and go about his business. He hated the Vietnamese because of the way they had treated the Laotians during the course of the war and before, but money was the common denominator that everyone understood. He wearily handed the bag to the Vietnamese officer for his inspection. He stepped back and waited in silence, his eyes never leaving the bag. There was a worn but completely workable Chinese AK-47 assault rifle hanging over his shoulder within easy reach.

Major Nguyen Van Trang opened the bag and inspected the con-tents. He placed a small amount on his tongue. Satisfied that the heroin was of high quality, he closed the bag and slung it over his shoulder. He handed the money to the Laotian and said, "My people will be pleased. Prepare the next shipment. I will return at the usual time." He stared at the native with contempt. He had no use for the Laotians.

Taking the bag of money the Laotian turned without a word and trudged off towards his village, his AK-47 in his right hand. The area was rife with cutthroats. Even though they were his countrymen, there was no loyalty when it came to the sums of money being passed. One thousand American dollars was a fortune in this part of the world.

This particular pack of money was worth more than most, however. On the inside of one of the wrappers, a coded message had been written. That message would make its way to Vientiane and into the hands of an operative for Air America, the CIA airline. The American Air Force Attaché in Bangkok would take it via diplomatic pouch to Langley, Virginia, and deliver it into the hands of Jack Wilder.

"Your daughter will graduate as scheduled with her class, Mr. McIvor, even though she finished her studies a semester early. But I must tell you that her behavior this past year has been less than what I would consider appropriate for a student at Boston College. As you know she has been part of virtually every protest group on and around campus, and she has openly expressed her views in the student newspaper about the Vietnam conflict. Her grades have been excellent, and I certainly respect her as an academic. She's been on the Dean's List her entire time here, and she has completed a four year course of study in three and a half. But, again, I regret to say that her behavior with respect to this institution has been less than what I expect of my students." Dean Ryan was courteous but firm. "I have asked Maggie to leave the campus until commencement exercises in May and to remain off campus until the class of 1969 graduates. She has been a fine student, and I have no doubt that she will be a fine journalist. I only hope that she can put her views second to reporting the facts."

Captain Thomas Franklin McIvor, US Navy, Retired, sighed at the dean's words. His wife saw the disappointment in his face, and she placed her hand on his shoulder. He reached up and patted hers. McIvor sank back in his chair and listened for several more minutes to the man on the other end of the phone.

"I'm sorry, Mr. McIvor, but that's my decision."

"Dr. Ryan, I appreciate your concern, but you must understand that these are difficult times for these kids. Maggie is an independent woman with her own views, and, although I don't always agree with them, they have nothing to do with her academic performance. Many of these kids have seen their friends die in an undeclared and unpopular war, and they are trying their best to deal with it. I don't share all my daughter's views, but I can't deny them to her. Her mother and I have spoken to her many times and have tried to persuade her to tone her activities down."

"I understand, Mr. McIvor. Believe me, if there was any other way to handle this, I certainly would entertain it. However, I have thought this through, and I have made my decision. Maggie is not allowed on campus until graduation. I'm sorry."

McIvor sighed in resignation. "Yeah, me too." He thought for a moment, then said, "Considering your position, I think you should award Maggie her diploma now, rather than wait until May. She would probably cause a scene, and I don't think you'd like that."

"… Perhaps you are correct."

"Then it's settled. Thank you for your time, Dr. Ryan." McIvor slowly hung up the phone. He stared at it for a minute, rubbed his eyes, and looked at his wife. "Maggie isn't allowed on campus until graduation. I suggested that Ryan give Maggie her diploma now to avoid another confrontation. Under the circumstances, I think it's the best thing to do."

Audrey McIvor looked wearily at the ceiling then at her husband. "Poor thing. She'll be so disappointed."

The Vietnam War politically devastated the Democratic Party and caused President Johnson to decline to run for re-election. Richard Nixon became the Republican candidate for President and a convert from supporting the war to actively calling for American involvement to end. Promising a new plan to end the war and to withdraw American forces from Vietnam, Nixon barely defeated Hubert Humphrey in the general election to become the next president of the United States.

Until 1967 Nixon had been a hard-liner, supporting America's involvement in the war. As the national mood changed to reflect disgust with the war, Nixon changed his position and became convinced, along with his national security advisor, Henry Kissinger, that American involvement must end. He was, however, a pragmatist. He did not want an ignominious withdrawal; rather, he wanted an "honorable" peace so that his grand design with respect to the People's Republic of China and the Soviet Union would not be compromised. He approached the office of President with these ideas in mind.

By the end of 1968, 536,000 American soldiers were in Vietnam. 30,610 had been killed.

CHAPTER 14

WASHINGTON, DC
JANUARY 22, 1969

"S'um bitch! Colder than a well digger's ass. Whose bright idea was this anyway?" Slaughter grumbled and blew into his hands in a vain attempt to warm them. His attitude reflected the general feeling of the senior class cadets as they stood in the cold, waiting for the parade to begin. The day was overcast and raw and they had been waiting for over an hour.

"Look at this way, Animal. How many people get to march in a parade for the President? You'll be able to tell your children that you marched for President Nixon. What do you think about that?"

"That and fifty cents will buy me a cup of coffee. Let's get this show on the road."

"Mr. Lynch, time to form up," Colonel Jennings said, looking down Pennsylvania Avenue. "We march in five minutes."

The First Captain gave the command, and the milling around quickly gave way to order. The regiment stood in formation with cadet officers standing line-of-breast in front with their sabers drawn. Everyone stood at ease, waiting for the march order.

As a cadet officer Wilder stood in front of his column with Slaughter behind him leaning on his M-1. "Why do you get to carry that pig-sticker and I have to haul this antique around? Ain't fair."

"Stop bitching, John. Better save your strength. You may need it." Wilder looked at the gathering crowd. Anti-war activists were everywhere, and a large crowd congregated near the cadet formation. That the cadets had never been to Vietnam was irrelevant. To the protesters the uniforms represented the military-industrial complex that was responsible for the war. The cadets, unfortunately, were between a rock and a hard spot.

The regimental band gave the signal, and the First Captain called his classmates to attention. Bayonets were fixed and weapons were brought to right shoulder arms. Finally, the command came. "Forward, *march!*" the First Captain's voice echoed, and the cadet corps began its trek down Pennsylvania Avenue.

The formation passed the reviewing stand and President Nixon stood. He clapped as the First Captain flashed his saber in a salute on behalf of his classmates. Everyone marched in step with lines straight and rifles aligned. Colonel Jennings watched from the side lines and smiled with self-satisfaction. *They always come together in a pinch.*

The parade continued along Pennsylvania Avenue to its termination point, whereupon each group turned onto a specified side street to exit the stream. The regiment turned at its designated point and marched two blocks. A bus was waiting to take the shivering cadets to Ft. Belvoir and a hot meal, courtesy of the Unites States Army.

The protesters were also waiting.

The cadets marked time in position. "Regiment, *halt!* Port *arms!*" The cadets stood at attention while hecklers shouted obscenities and threw rocks and bottles at them. Several protesters grabbed hats and tore at overcoat capes, but despite their itch for a fight, the cadets maintained discipline. The jeers and shouts grew louder.

Colonel Jennings, having been a cadet himself, understood. "Gentlemen, be at Ft. Belvoir in one hour. Mr. Lynch, carry on." Climbing into his staff car, Jennings smiled to himself. He quickly disappeared around the corner. He made it a point not to remember that something *might* happen.

Lynch faced his classmates. "*Fall out!*"

At that instant a protester grabbed Slaughter's brass breast plate.

It was a colossal mistake. The butt of Slaughter's M-1 flew threw the air, smashing his attacker in the nose and turning it into mush. The stunned man stumbled back, not yet realizing what had happened. "Fucking miscreant!" Slaughter shouted. He kicked his assailant in the groin and back-fisted him across the face. The protester fell backwards and hit the ground hard. He curled into the fetal position and screamed in pain. "Can you dig it, shortcake?" Slaughter was enjoying himself, and he lost no time in going after another misfortunate.

The protesters never stood a chance; the cadets were all over them. The First Captain ran one protester up a telephone pole with his saber. Tossing it and his hat to the ground, he climbed the pole after his prey. The cadets proceeded to reorganize both the anatomy and attitude of their tormentors. It was a long overdue release.

Wilder found himself cornered by three of them. They were big and mean looking, and they glared at him with hateful eyes. The biggest one shouted, "Hey, queer-bait, think you're cute in your little faggot suit? We're gonna kill you, you chicken-shit!" They saw that he was unarmed; his saber was on the street. They started towards him, but a seed of doubt took hold when they saw him stand his ground. They glanced at each other as if looking for support, then moved against him in unison.

"We'll see about that, flower children!" Wilder was loose, his hands moving in front of his chest. "You rose petals need a bath. But first, it's time for school. Lesson one is about to begin."

The first one jumped at him from the side, but Wilder was already moving. He lashed out with a side stomp kick, striking his assailant in the knee. The snap was sharp and loud. The knee folded sideways, the leg collapsed, and the first flower child fell screaming to the ground.

The second one charged with a knife. He shouted an obscenity and back-slashed at Wilder's face. Wilder threw a right outer forearm block, deflecting the attacker's arm. With his right hand he quickly grabbed the attacker's wrist to control the knife. He rammed his left palm heel into the back of his attacker's elbow. There was a sickening crack. Rose Petal Two screamed and dropped the knife. Wilder spun to his right and pulled the arm over his shoulder. He jerked the wrist down, breaking the elbow outwards. He rammed his left elbow rearward into his assailant's face. The man screamed again and dropped to the ground.

Wilder looked at the helpless heap then turned his attention to the last of the trio. He waved his finger, beckoning his would-be assailant to come closer.

Rose Petal Three held a baseball bat with both hands. He looked with uncertainty at his friends agonizing on the ground.

Wilder's smile was malevolent. "Lesson two. Want to see what that bat looks like shoved up your ass?"

The terrified man dropped the bat and ran.

Wilder looked at the first two unfortunates, still rolling in pain. "Looks like your buddy decided to split. He passes. You fail. School's out, boys."

Realizing they were in trouble, the protesters began to run. The cadets, on the other hand, wanted to fight. And fight they did. They wanted to even the score for the torment they had endured. But the protesters would have none of it, and the fight, such as it was, was over in minutes.

"Hey, John," Lynch shouted from across the street.

"Yeah?"

"Kinda ruined his day, didn't you?" Lynch pointed to the bloody face that resembled the butt of an M-1 rifle.

"Cretin asked for it. Grabbed me first."

Lynch looked around. The cadets were none the worse for wear, and their exuberance showed in the smiles on their faces. Lynch shouted, "Guys, let's load up and get going."

Everyone laughed, but they knew it was time to leave. Their actions were warranted in their opinions, but the DC police would think differently. By design or otherwise, the police were nowhere around. But that would soon change, and the cadets knew that it would be in their collective best interests to become scarce. They picked up their weapons, sabers, hats, and pieces of torn uniforms. Within minutes they were on the bus and on their way to Belvoir. The only evidence of their former presence on the Washington side street were several worse-for-wear protesters that, for reasons unknown, had decided to take their frustrations out on each other.

The ride from Washington to Ft. Belvoir was less than an hour.

Several cadets laughed and joked while others sat in quiet introspection. Wilder watched the scenery go by in silence. He thought about the back-door politics that went on in the marble and granite edifices of Washington, and he wondered what decisions were being made regarding his brother and the other POW's. He looked across the expanse of Arlington National Cemetery, the former home of the Confederate General Robert E. Lee, and he wondered how many of the thousands of men buried there had died in vain. How many of his classmates would end up there? How many would give their lives in a place that most people couldn't find on a map? Nor cared to?

Wilder was suddenly consumed with feelings of foreboding. It wasn't the tangle with the protesters, but something darker that he couldn't put his hands on. What was it?

CHAPTER 15

Major Charles McElroy was exhausted. His journey began in Bangkok, Thailand, in an embassy vehicle that took him for the hour drive to U-Tapao Air Force Base. He boarded an Air Force C-141 Starlifter cargo jet for the three leg flight to Travis Air Force Base, California. Having survived several in-flight crew meals that were fit for neither man nor beast, he arrived twenty hours later in much need of a shower and sleep. Within minutes of touch down, he boarded a C-135, the military version of a Boeing 707, for his final leg to Andrews Air Force Base, Maryland.

As the Air Attaché to the American embassy in Bangkok, McElroy worked closely with the CIA station chief there. Versed in covert activities in that part of the world, he had seen the dark underbelly of military operations. This mission, although removed from the combat arena, was the most difficult yet, but he had to see it through to completion. The message from the Golden Triangle had been decoded, and its contents were devastating.

The C-135 taxied to its parking spot in front of base operations at Andrews, where a blue staff car waited. McElroy walked down the portable stairs, his briefcase handcuffed to his wrist, and climbed into the back seat of the car. With a military police escort, the entourage sped through the main gate and onto the beltway, making its way to CIA headquarters at Langley.

The NSA chief entered without knocking. He'd been expected. Wilder looked up from his desk and motioned to a seat. "McElroy's on his way." He leaned back in his chair. "His plane arrived at Andrews a short time ago. He'll be here in thirty minutes." The lines in his face had grown deeper.

Spencer studied him. "Any ideas?"

"No, but it must be serious. McElroy's bringing information by diplomatic pouch, rather than sending it via secure line. And he's using Air Force planes to do it. I've known that boy for a while, and he isn't given to theatrics."

Spencer rubbed his eyes. "More interesting by the minute."

"Yeah."

Neither spoke his thoughts. They engaged in small talk, both being careful not to broach the subject that was on their minds.

The intercom buzzed. "Sir, Major McElroy is here."

Thank God. "Send him in, Linda, please."

"Jack?"

"Yes?"

"He looks like the fuzzy end of the stick. I took the liberty of having some hot food and fresh coffee sent from the mess. There's a bottle of Wild Turkey in your cabinet. Shall I call Elizabeth?"

Wilder smiled to himself. *Thank God for this woman.* "Please. We're going to be here a while. Thanks for the food. I'm sure our weary traveler can use it."

"I'm a mother too, you know. This young major is about my son's age."

"I understand."

McElroy entered Wilder's office, stood at attention, and saluted.

"Relax, Chuck. Pull up a seat and take a load off. You must be exhausted." Wilder walked around his desk and shook the major's hand. He was not one to stand on protocol, especially when the man in front of him was dead on his feet.

"Thank you, sir," McElroy said. He dropped into the chair vacated by Spencer.

"Welcome home, Major." Spencer patted the officer on the shoulder. "Here. Try this on for size." He handed McElroy a glass of bourbon.

McElroy looked at the glass then at Wilder.

"Go ahead, son. You've more than earned it."

"Thanks." McElroy drank the liquid and closed his eyes, savoring the warm fluid. After a moment, he looked at his mentors. "Is there another where that came from?"

"Certainly." Spencer refilled his glass.

Wilder was anxious to get to the subject at hand, but he knew not to push. "Chuck, I know you're tired and hungry. Linda's arranged something for you. I want you to relax and eat. Collect yourself and unwind."

At that moment the door opened and Wilder's secretary wheeled in a cart. Parking it in front of McElroy, she said, "Welcome home, young man. Here's something that will make you feel better." She looked at Wilder and Spencer and smiled. "Don't let these bullies push you around, Charles. You eat first, questions later. Understood?"

"Yes, ma'am." He responded to her warmth, feeling instantly at home. He unlocked the briefcase from his wrist and sat it beside his chair.

"I'll be in my office if you need anything."

"You should go spend a quiet evening with your family, Linda. We're legally closed for business now."

"Thank you, but I have some paperwork to do. Besides, you never know ... " Linda Mason sensed that something was terribly wrong, and she wanted to be there to help. After all, it could have been her son in that prison. She left the office and returned to her desk.

Wilder watched the door close behind her. "This place would shutdown if it wasn't for her." He looked at McElroy. The major was wolfing down his food. "Slow down, Chuck. I know this is the first real food you've had since Bangkok, but it's not going anywhere." He looked at Spencer. "How about a drink to celebrate Chuck's homecoming, Bruce?"

Spencer didn't really want one, but he poured two anyway. He figured that it would put everyone at ease. The calm before the storm.

McElroy finished his meal and sat back in his chair. He closed his eyes and collected his thoughts. Looking briefly at Spencer, he focused on Wilder. Without a word, he opened his briefcase and took out a sealed packet. He stood and held out the envelope. Wilder took it and looked at the TOP SECRET/EYES ONLY label.

"Sir," McElroy began, "the information in this document comes from our operative in Hanoi… "

The food was hot and there was plenty of it. The dreary weather outside was forgotten while the cadets indulged themselves, courtesy of Uncle Sam.

"Good groceries," Slaughter said, stuffing a buttered roll into his mouth.

"No argument there, Animal." Wilder was ravenous. The hot food took his mind away from Washington and Arlington Cemetery, his sense of foreboding long forgotten.

"How's your fist, Bill?" Lynch shouted from the next table. "Doesn't look any worse for wear." The First Captain was having a good time too.

Wilder looked at his hand. "All healed up! Imagine that." Both men laughed. The hot food and warm atmosphere did wonders to lift everyone's spirits. The cadets were enjoying themselves.

The Commandant reflected on the events of the day. He suspected that the cadets had been involved in a "tactical" event, but he said nothing. He remembered what it was like to be a cadet—and a POW in North Korea. *Some things never change.*

His thoughts were interrupted by one of his tactical officers.

"Colonel, there's a call for you from a Mrs. Linda Mason," Captain Wood whispered. "She says it's urgent."

"Who?"

"She's calling for Colonel Jack Wilder. I believe you know him."

"Yes. His son is a First Classman."

"She said it's urgent."

"Right." Jennings stood. "Where's the phone?"

"This way." Captain Wood escorted the commandant to an office in the rear of the building.

The Army lieutenant rose from behind his desk when the two officers entered. "Have a seat, Colonel. Your party is on the line."

"Thanks." Jennings' senses were alert. Jack Wilder wasn't frivolous with his time. Any call from Wilder's office had to be important. He picked up the phone. "Colonel Jennings here."

"Hello, Colonel Jennings. My name is Linda Mason. I'm Jack Wilder's secretary at Langley. I'm sorry to have to interfere with your plans, Colonel, but I have an urgent request of you."

"No problem, Mrs. Mason. I know Jack. What can I do for you?"

"I'm glad I got to you before you started back to Lexington. We need to reach Bill right away."

Jennings sensed the tension in her voice. "He's in the mess hall."

"Colonel, I need you to keep him there. His father and Mr. Bruce Spencer, NSA chief, are on their way there now. They need to see him right away."

"I'll take care of it."

Silence.

"Is there something I can do in the mean time, Mrs. Mason?"

"Say a prayer."

"It's that bad?"

"Yes, Colonel Jennings, it is."

Neither man noticed when their chauffeured staff car passed threw the main gate at Belvoir. Their thoughts were thousands of miles away, in a place where no American should be. Spencer looked at his brother-in-law. He wanted to say something, but he was at a loss for words. Perhaps it would be better to say nothing.

Jack Wilder stared out the window, not realizing that the car had stopped.

"Sir, we're here. Colonel Jennings is waiting for you," the driver said.

"Huh? Oh." Wilder's mind came back to the present, and he stepped out of the car. Spencer was waiting. "Well, let's get this over with, Bruce." Wilder seemed to slump under his emotional burden. They walked into the mess hall in silence.

Bill was glad to see his family, but the look on their faces made him feel uncomfortable. He went to meet them. "Hi, guys. Did you see the parade?" His heart was pounding.

"We did, Bud. The regiment looked great." The enthusiasm wasn't there, despite the effort.

"Your class is to be congratulated, Bill." Spencer looked around the room. "One of the best performances I've seen in years."

There was an awkward silence. Finally, Bill said, "How about some hot coffee? On the house." Bill waved his hand at Slaughter.

John was there in seconds. "Here you are, gentlemen. Hot java."

"Thanks, John," Spencer said.

Jack looked at his cup. "John, would you excuse us for a few minutes, please?"

"No problem, Colonel W." Slaughter knew something was wrong, and he knew not to say anything. "I'll be over there, Bill, if you need me."

"Thanks, John." Bill stared at his father, his mind racing. "Is Mom okay?"

"Mother's fine." Jack looked at Spencer then back at his son. "We need to talk. Alone." They walked towards the office where Colonel Jennings had called.

Spencer closed the door behind Jack and his son. He waited in the hall.

Jack sat on the desk. He was weary and tired. Bill took it as an ominous sign and stood at attention. Jack looked briefly out the window then at his son. "Bill, you—"

"Dad, we mixed it up with some protesters after the parade, but they deserved it. Are the police—"

Jack raised his hand, stopping his son in mid-sentence. "Bill, this has nothing to do with your head-banging session. Lord knows, I would've done it too. If it were only that simple. "

Bill was confused. "Mom's okay and the cops are none the wiser. What gives?"

Jack looked at his son and took a deep breath. "Bud, you've gone through a lot over the past few years, and you've had to endure more than your share of pain—"

"Dad—"

"It's about your brother."

Bill stiffened but said nothing.

Jack closed his eyes. He had suffered more than any man should have to. His wife was wasting away before him, and his family was being destroyed. How could a man do what was being ask of him now? It was the most difficult day of his life. He steadied himself and looked at his younger son.

"Dad?"

"Bill, your brother was killed by his captors in North Vietnam. I'm so sorry."

CHAPTER 16

JANUARY 23, 1969

The door flew open and slammed into the wall. "Damn him. Just *damn* him! Who the hell does he think he is? He has no right—"

"Margaret McIvor, hold your tongue! I will not have that kind of talk in this house, young lady," her mother scolded not unkindly. She knew how her daughter felt, and she sympathized with her. Audrey McIvor saw herself in her child. Twenty-two years ago, Audrey was as full of fire and brimstone as the young woman standing before her. Nevertheless, certain standards of behavior had to be maintained in the McIvor household.

Margaret Erin McIvor, Maggie to her family and friends, had inherited both her red hair and fiery temper from her Irish mother. An outspoken woman, she had no reservations when it came to expressing her opinions. It didn't matter what the subject was. She wasn't a hippie, and she wasn't interested in the women's lib movement, but she stood her ground when she believed in something, no matter whose toes were stepped on. She had stepped on several. Her views on Vietnam had caused her problems with the school faculty, particularly the dean, Dr. Jerome Ryan.

Maggie stormed across the room and threw her rolled diploma unceremoniously at the table. She dropped onto a chair, placed her elbows on her knees, and rested her chin in her hands. She looked at her mother. "Well, just what do you expect me to do? I can't graduate with my class! *'Miss McIvor, congratulations on your successful completion of your studies,'* he says. *'I wish you well in you chosen career. However, Miss McIvor, blah-blah-blah, here is your diploma. Good day.'* Well, how about that, sports fans?" She looked at her mother, tears running down her face. "Mom, do you have any idea how that makes me feel?"

Audrey McIvor's heart was breaking. She wanted to scoop her child into her arms and hold her, to comfort her like she did when Maggie was small. Stroking Maggie's hair, she could feel the young woman shaking with rage. "Honey, I know how disappointed you are. Believe me, I do."

Maggie looked at her mother, her eyes pleading. "Do you? Do you really?" Her breath was ragged. "You and Dad have been like a rock to me, and I've said and done so many things to embarrass both of you. And now I've *really* humiliated you guys by getting thrown out of school. I'm so ashamed." She buried her face in her hands and sobbed.

Her mother tried to comfort her. She softly said, "Maggie, you haven't humiliated or embarrassed anybody. Believe me. Your father and I are proud of you, and we support your right to be your own person."

Maggie looked into her mother's eyes and knew that she was telling the truth. She stood and hugged her. "Thanks, Mom. Thanks for everything." She cried on her mother's shoulder.

Thomas McIvor stood at the door; he'd seen everything from the porch. He knew his daughter was upset, and he wanted her to vent her frustration and blow off pent-up steam before he said anything. Maggie was going through a catharsis, and her mother was the best person to deal with it. He would patiently wait for Maggie to calm down, then he would go to soothe her.

He walked into the room and wrapped his arms around his wife and daughter. It had a calming effect on everyone. "It's okay, Maggie. It's all right." He patted her on the head like he did when she was a little girl. Whenever she skinned her knee or broke her toys, he was always there with a hug and a pat on the head.

She looked at him and wiped the tears away with the back of her hand. "Thanks for being there, Dad."

"Any time, my dear."

"You're not mad at me?"

"Of course not. Why should I be?"

"Dad, I made a fool of myself in there. I embarrassed you in front of the dean of the entire school."

"You did *not* embarrass me. You were magnificent!"

"Huh?" Maggie was non-plussed.

McIvor winked at his daughter. "Be back in a minute." He went into the kitchen and returned with two bottles of beer. He handed one to her and raised his bottle in a toast. "Cheers."

"What?" Maggie didn't understand. She knew that her father supported her right to her own opinion, but she never thought he would be jubilant about it. "Dad, are you okay?"

"Time for a family meeting. There's something I want to share with you, Maggie."

Audrey knew what was coming. She smiled inwardly at her husband. The McIvor clan had been having these family meetings for as long as Maggie could remember. Whenever a crisis or problem arose, a family meeting would be called to resolve whatever it was they were facing. The entire family was usually involved, including Tom Junior, but he hadn't come home from school yet. He would graduate from high school in June.

McIvor sat in his favorite chair. He looked at his wife and daughter sitting across from him. He leaned forward and smiled at his oldest child. "Maggie, there are some things I want to tell you. It may be confusing at first, but please bear with me. But before I get into it, I want you to understand that your performance in Ryan's office today was exactly what I was hoping for."

"What?" She expected her father to preach to her about her performance in front of the dean, but this was totally unexpected.

"That's right. Listen, Maggie, when you stood there and patiently listened to that old codger—"

"Tom, really!" Audrey interjected.

"Nope," McIvor said with a wave of dismissal. "Codger is the right word, Audrey." He looked back at his daughter. "Maggie, you've been vocal in your beliefs all your life. Your mother and I haven't always seen eye to eye with you, but you can rest assured that we've always agreed with each other when it came to your integrity. That you're honest to a fault is a godsend. There's too much hypocrisy in this world, and, as parents, we're proud to have a daughter that is honest, up front, and not afraid to speak the truth.

"People may not always agree with your opinions, Maggie, but one thing's for damn certain; every last one of them respects you for being honest. You pull no strings, and you're not a politician. I'm singularly proud of that. Some of the high-rollers in the Navy could take a lesson from you. God knows, there's so much politicking there, and the amount of ass-kissing I've seen would fill volumes if I ever decided to write about it. We tried to raise you kids to be honest and forthright, no matter what. I'm proud to say we succeeded.

"Maggie, when I was in the Navy, I listened to thousands of unsolicited opinions by those trying to get ahead, and most of those opinions were wrong. People didn't give their *own* opinions; they just rehashed their *commander's* opinions in their own words. World class boot-licking is what I called it. No one spoke his mind for fear that his report card would get a black mark and his career would hit the skids.

"When I was on the *Ticonderoga*, I got my orders from CINCPAC, who got his orders from the White House after all was said and done. I didn't question those orders; I just followed them. I sometimes wondered what the purpose of some of those ridiculous exercises was, but I never questioned them. God knows, I sent many young fliers to their deaths unnecessarily, and I'll never forgive myself for it. I always wondered why certain decisions were made, but I never officially questioned them. As a naval officer I wasn't supposed to. Perhaps I should have. I just don't know.

"In any event, Maggie, I see in you what I was never able to see in myself; simply the ability to question authority when you think that authority is wrong. If more people in this country, especially in the government and the military, had that quality, perhaps we wouldn't be in bogged down in Vietnam now."

Maggie was dumbfounded. "Dad—"

"Hold on. I haven't gotten to the best part yet." His face seemed to age before her eyes. "This is going to be difficult to believe, but you must. I've dragged this family all over the world, and you've come to expect certain actions and behavior from me. You know that as a naval officer, I had a job to do. Sometimes it was purposeful and sometimes not. You and your mother never questioned it, but I did."

Maggie's eyes bulged at her father's words.

"That's right, Maggie. I did question authority on occasion. Not openly, but to myself. There were many sleepless nights."

"I had no idea, Dad. Why didn't you say something?"

"Maggie, the war in Vietnam is wrong, and we as a country have absolutely no business in it. We should get out now before more American lives are wasted."

"What? I don't understand." She shook her head in disbelief. "How can the war, I mean how can you … *you*, of all people, be against the war?"

McIvor walked to the fire place. He leaned against the mantle and gazed into the fire for several moments. Finally, he said, "Maggie, in 1937 the Japanese invaded China with an army that was no match for the Chinese. Their goal was raw military conquest." He looked at her. "They butchered their way across to Nanking. At that time Nanking was one of the largest cities in China. After taking the city, the Japanese methodically slaughtered and raped thousands of innocent men, women, and children. The western nations sat on their collective asses and did nothing while the Japanese invaded, conquered, and destroyed their neighbors.

"On December 7, 1941, the Japanese attacked Pearl Harbor. As a young ensign, I was assigned to the *Arizona*. I was on shore leave when it happened. The ship sank with most if its crew. The Japanese wanted to dominate the Pacific, and the attack at Pearl Harbor was part of their master plan. Unfortunately for them, they just pissed us off.

"Roosevelt declared war on Japan and, eventually, on all the Axis powers. The British had been trying for a long time to get us into the war against Hitler, but Uncle Sam resisted. It took an attack on American soil by the Japanese to push us into the war. It was pretty cut and dry. We were attacked, and we defended ourselves.

"Vietnam is a different animal, Maggie. At the end of World

War II, the Japanese left Vietnam and abandoned any colonial ideas they had. The French, on the other hand, had been there for years, and they filled the vacuum left by the Japanese. But the Vietnamese didn't want their country divided up by the French or anyone else. As a result, the Vietnamese fought the French and finally defeated them at Dien Bien Phu."

"Dad, what does all of that have to do with you?"

"I'll get to that in a minute, Maggie. Anyway, Vietnam was divided into the North and South. The North was led by a guy named Ho Chi Minh."

"I know about him."

"I'm sure you do, but did you know that he asked the United States for help in reuniting his country?"

"What? No, I didn't."

"And our government refused."

"Why?"

"Well, a peace treaty of sorts was drafted between the North and South, but the corrupt South Vietnamese government, led by a Catholic, refused to re-united the country under the agreed terms. To make a long story short, the United States refused to back Ho because he was Communist. It didn't matter that he was vastly popular among his own people. Because he was a Communist, the McCarthy types in Washington refused to do business with him. Our government supported the regime in the South, and the war between the North and South began to escalate with American involvement growing steadily until we got into the fix we're in today.

"Maggie, my point is this; the attack on Pearl Harbor was straight forward, and it required a response on our part. Hence, our involvement in World War II. But Vietnam is a civil war, not unlike our own in the 1860's. The Vietnamese didn't attack us on our soil. We went over there and took the place of the French when they pulled out. An end run so to speak. We're fighting someone else's war." McIvor looked into his daughter's eyes. "We have absolutely no business there at all."

For years Maggie had opposed her father's position as a navy officer and his involvement in Vietnam. But now she was at a loss for words. She had no idea, until now, that her father had been opposed to the war all along. He didn't easily share his feelings, and this confession was hard for him. Maggie had a newfound respect for her father.

"Hi, guys. What's up?" Tommy walked through the front door. He dropped his book bag on the floor and flopped onto the sofa.

"Nothing much," McIvor answered. "How was your day?"

Nothing much! Maggie stared at her father.

"Same old school stuff." He jumped up and headed to the kitchen for a soda. Shouting over his shoulder, he said, "By the way, I have to register for the draft. I'll be eighteen tomorrow. Remember?"

No one said a word.

"Hey, it's my birthday!"

They didn't hear the telephone ring.

"Anybody gonna answer that?" Tommy shouted from the kitchen. "I'll get it." He picked up the receiver. "Hullo? … Yeah …yes, sir. I'm fine, sir… He's here. Just a minute." Tommy looked through the doorway at his father. "It's for you, Dad. It's a Colonel Jack Wilder in Washington."

It had been over three years since McIvor and Wilder last talked. Perhaps this call would bring good news. It couldn't be any worse than their last conversation.

"Mac here … Hey, Jack, it's good to hear from you, old buddy … Yeah, we're all fine. How's your—" His face clouded over.

Audrey watched him, afraid to move.

"Yes, Jack, I do. I'll never forget it as long as I live. I know it's been tough—" He closed his eyes. "God Almighty!" He slowly reached for Audrey's hand. She took it and stood patiently. He listened intently. Finally, his voice a whisper, he said, "Yes, Jack, we'll be there. I'll call Annapolis right away. I'll leave tonight … I understand. God bless." McIvor slowly hung up the phone. He stared at it for a moment, then looked at his wife.

"Liz?" Audrey squeezed his hand.

"She's fine." He looked at his kids then at his wife. "Remember their boys, Little Jack and Bill?"

"Yes."

"Little Jack was one of my pilots on the *Ticonderoga*."

"What?"

"Back in '65 he flew F-4's off my carrier. He was shot down on his last mission and captured by the North Vietnamese. He's been a POW ever since."

Audrey slowly sat down, her mouth agape. "Jesus, Tom! Why didn't you tell me?"

"It wouldn't have accomplished anything."

"But—"

"There's more." His face was somber. "He was just killed in that POW camp."

"Dear God!" Audrey's eyes filled with tears. "His poor mother!"

CHAPTER 17

FEBRUARY 1969

"Ladies and gentlemen, this is your captain. We're beginning our descent into the New York area now. We're descending through ten thousand feet and will be arriving at JFK International Airport in approximately fifteen minutes. New York has clear skies with a temperature of minus two degrees Celsius, or twenty-eight degrees Fahrenheit. Please fasten your seat belts and remain seated. Thank you for flying with us, and welcome to the United States. *Au Revoir.* Good-bye, and have a good day."

The seat belt sign came on, and the flight attendants began their final rounds. The passenger in seat 23B handed his cup to the pretty young woman smiling at him. "Thank you," she chirped. She had conversed with him during the flight from Paris, and she decided that it would be fun to take him up on his offer to a night on the town. He was coming back from a European ski vacation and wanted to celebrate his return. He was from Newport, Rhode Island, and he was both charming and rich. A perfect catch for a young single woman with excess hormones in her veins and gold-digging on the brain.

"Where should I meet you, Brigitte?"

"I'll wait for you outside customs, Paul. Perhaps you can ride to the hotel with us." She was excited at the prospect of bedding this rich young American.

"Actually, I have to go into the city on business first. Tell you what though; why don't you give me the name of your hotel, and I'll call for you at, say, seven tonight? That way I can tie up some loose ends, and you'll have time for a nap. You'll need your energy tonight." He winked at her.

"Perfect." She was already moist with anticipation. She hurriedly wrote down the name of her hotel and handed it to him. "See you at seven?"

"Count on it." He smiled and slid the note into his pocket.

She briefly touched his shoulder then made her way to the rear of the aircraft to prepare for landing. She was like a giddy school girl, thinking about what they would do with each other in bed.

The Air France Boeing 707 touched down on JFK's runway 31L, and the captain applied the reversers and brakes. The giant aircraft gradually slowly to taxi speed, turned off the runway, and taxied towards the Air France terminal. As the aircraft approached the gate, passengers began to move around the aisles, despite the half-hearted protests by the flight attendants for them to remain seated.

Paul Vorhees checked his passport and placed it in the side pocket of his shoulder bag. He stood after the seat belt sign was turned off and gathered his things. He glanced sideways for his *date* but didn't see her. He followed the others into the terminal and to the waiting customs agents.

The bored official opened the passport without looking up. He glanced at the picture and the name. Talking to the document, he asked, "Are you an American citizen, Mr. Vorhees?"

"Yes, I am." *It's an American passport, you idiot!*

The official glanced at him, noticing his casual dress. "Been on vacation?"

"Yeah. Been skiing in Europe." Vorhees smiled.

"Where do you live?"

"Newport, Rhode Island." *Can't read either.*

"Anything to declare?" The agent flipped through the passport and casually looked at the picture.

"No, nothing."

The customs agent stamped the passport and slid it across the counter. "Next."

"Thanks." Vorhees picked up the passport and shoved it into his pocket. He walked through the door into the cold air.

Vorhees slid into the back seat of the taxi. He noticed that the driver was not American; Indian or Pakistani most likely. Probably didn't know the language that well. Good. No questions. "Grand Central Station, please."

"Grand Central, okay," the driver replied in heavily accented English.

The taxi left the airport and joined the Van Wyck Expressway. Traffic moved smoothly for this time of the afternoon, and within fifteen minutes, they had passed LaGuardia Airport and joined the Brooklyn Queens Expressway. They crossed the East River by way of the Queens Midtown Tunnel and entered the city. The taxi made its way towards the Pan Am Building when Vorhees directed the driver to stop a block short of his destination.

"You want train, yes?" the driver asked, looking into the rear view mirror.

"No. This is fine." Vorhees paid the driver and got out of the cab. He looked around for a moment, then walked two blocks in the opposite direction. He cut over one block and walked back past the Pan Am Building for another block. He hailed another taxi to Manhattan, then took a third back to Central Park. He walked past the Omni Hotel and into Mulligan's Bar across the street.

Sitting at the end of the bar facing the windows, he had an unobstructed view of everyone that came and went. He ordered a beer and casually looked at his surroundings. He didn't want any surprises. He feigned inability to speak English when a drunk patron on an adjacent bar stool slurred at him. He wanted to concentrate his attention on the street person standing on the corner in front of the hotel.

Dressed in dirty jeans, worn sneakers, a torn field jacket, and a black watch cap, the disheveled man staggered around the newspaper stand next to the light post. He appeared to be intoxicated, and he kept scratching his unshaven face and rubbing his cold hands together. Vorhees watched him out of the corner of his eyes.

After several minutes the man removed his cap and scratched his head. He put his cap back on and pulled it low over his ears. He slowly staggered down the street towards Central Park.

Vorhees checked his watch. It was the correct time and correct signal.

He left the bar and crossed the street. He was sure he had not been followed. Still he remained cautious. He entered the hotel through the side door and approached the desk.

The clerk looked up at him. "May I help you?"

"Yes. I'm Michael Cartwright. Room 410. I need to pick up my key, and are there any messages for me?"

The clerk checked the stack of mail and the message file. There was nothing. Vorhees took the key and headed for the elevator. He went up five floors and exited, sending the elevator up to the sixth. He took the stairs back to the fourth floor.

He walked past his room, casually looking at the door with a trained eye. Going to the ice machine, he looked around. He went back to the door and inserted the key. He noticed that the fine thread was still stuck to the top of the door—it had not been opened. He quickly entered the room, closing and locking the door behind him.

After examining the room for uninvited guests and explosive devices, he took the suitcase out of the closet that had been left for him. He placed it on the bed, opened it, and examined its contents. All was in order.

He wedged a chair against the door knob, preventing the door from being opened by a would-be thief. Satisfied that the room was secure, he lay across the bed and went to sleep.

The garters were just right; black leather and lace. The stockings hugged her long shapely legs, and the seams down the back of her legs were straight. She slipped into her high stiletto heels and looked into the mirror. *Perfect.*

The telephone rang. "Yes?"

"*Bonsoir*, Miss LeFebre. I hope I didn't disturb you. Are you ready?"

"Paul! Right on time. Yes, I am ready. I'll be down in just a moment."

"Hurry, then. I can't wait to see you."

"I'm on my way." Brigitte LeFebre looked in the mirror one more time. She was feminine and a little sleazy. Just the way men like it. She picked up her coat and bag and hurried to the elevator.

She saw him standing near the gift shop. He was wearing a dark blue suit and a red tie, a cashmere overcoat over his shoulders. He had a dozen roses and a bottle champagne. She felt the heat rise in her stomach.

He heard the click of her heels and turned. "Ah, Brigitte!" He held out his arms to admire here. "You look fabulous." He undressed her with his eyes.

"*Merci, monsieur*," she cooed. She saw the way he looked at her. It pleased her that she had that effect on men. She hoped that this one would be as good in bed as he was charming.

Her white teeth and full red lips were alluring. He felt the swelling in his groin. He looked at her long legs and short skirt. *Classy looking slut.* "I trust you had a nice nap? As the French say, *Dormir*? To sleep?"

"Yes, thank you. And were you able to complete your business in the city?"

"Nothing to it. The most compelling thing I had to do was to find the right flowers for such a lovely lady. I hope you don't mind. I thought you might … " He left the sentence hanging, as if at a loss for words in the presence of her beauty.

"Oh, Paul, I love them. Thank you so much." They were the magic touch. She kissed him lightly on the lips and stroked his face softly with her fingers.

It was the response he expected. *Stupid whore.* "Hmm, guess we could leave them and the champagne with the concierge til we get back."

"No. I have a better idea. Let's go to my room and chill down the bottle. I can put the flowers in water too." Her bedroom eyes said it all.

"In that case perhaps we could enjoy some champagne right away then, before we go out." There was a sly and suggestive smile.

"Absolutely." She hooked her arm through his, and they walked towards the elevator.

A dusha-dushe, Vorhees thought. A little heart-to-heart talk. She unlocked the door and went in, holding his hand against her stomach. He closed the door and sat the flowers and champagne on the table. They rushed into each other's arms, their hands groping and fondling. Their mouths hungrily came together, and their tongues explored each other with passionate desperation.

Brigitte pulled away, panting. "Not yet, Paul. Let's take our time. I want us to enjoy this." Her mouth was open and her breathing hard. She was in heat, and she wanted him to mount her. But she also was a tease, and she would not be denied her role-play.

"Yes, we *will* enjoy this, I promise you that." He stood in front of her, rubbing his groin. He wanted her, and she knew it.

She slowly walked across the room, her eyes never leaving him. She licked her lips and said, "I'm going to the bathroom. Be right back." She closed the door behind her.

Vorhees lay his overcoat carefully across the chair and removed his jacket and tie. He picked up the champagne and took an opener out of his pocket. When she came out of the bathroom, he had poured two glasses of the sparkling liquid. He handed one to her.

"*Merci.* A toast."

"To a lovely lady." They touched glasses and drank, their eyes lusting at each other. Vorhees sat the glasses on the table, and they wrapped themselves around each other again. Her lips were all over his face, and his hands groped and fondled her legs and buttocks. She began to moan, and she pulled his hand to her groin. She ground against him feverishly.

He lifted her in his arms and carried her to the bed. He slowly began to strip. Watching him with hungry eyes, she allowed her skirt to slide above her thighs and began to fondle herself. His body was lean and hard, and she breathed heavily while looking at him. She rolled over onto her stomach seductively.

He climbed onto the bed and kneeled over her. He began stroking her thighs. She moaned and pushed back against him. He grabbed her hips and forced himself into her as hard as he could, causing her to gasp. He thrust at her, lifting her knees off the bed.

"Harder!" she screamed, pushing back at him. They went at each other for almost an hour before they both exploded in a sexual frenzy.

He glanced at the clock; it was almost nine. He slid off the bed and walked to the table. He lit a cigarette and drank from the bottle.

"You're incredible."

Vorhees was silent.

"I prefer this to going out, don't you?"

"Yes," he replied, his back still toward her.

She watched his naked body in motion, and she could feel herself becoming moist again. "I'm going for a shower. Join me?" She sat on the edge of the bed, fondling her breasts.

"I prefer the smell of musk," he said in a throaty voice. He drew on his cigarette and took another drink from the bottle.

"I like *that*," she said. She slid off the bed and approached him, unaware that he had drugged her drink.

He turned to her and handed her a glass. "To the beginning of an exciting evening."

"Exciting, indeed." She could almost feel the force behind his stare, a rush unlike anything she had experienced before. It both excited and frightened her.

"The best is yet to come." He smiled and stroked her hair.

"I'll drink to that." She drained her glass and threw it against the wall. Her eyes had that devil-may-care look.

He smashed his glass beside hers. "Cigarette?"

"No, I'm going to take that shower now." She walked towards the bathroom and looked over her shoulder. "Don't go anywhere." She licked her lips at him and closed the door behind her.

Bitch! A crazed look crossed his face. The headache had begun. He drained the champagne bottle and dropped it to the floor. He lit another cigarette and inhaled deeply. Crushing the empty Marlboro pack and tossing it across the room, he sat in a chair and waited.

"Eastern 721, Boston tower. Wind is two-three-zero at five knots. Turn left heading one-four-zero. Cleared for takeoff."

"Eastern 721 rolling," the copilot answered. The DC-9 accelerated to flying speed and smoothly lifted off the runway. The pilot made a left turn over Boston Harbor and climbed to five thousand feet initially for the flight to Washington.

Tom McIvor stared blankly at the Boston skyline while trying to cope with the day's events, especially Wilder's phone call. He knew of the horrors the POW's endured, but *this* was incredible. Little Jack *dead!*

His own problems paled in comparison. He wondered if he could have done anything different. Should he have kept the young pilot on the deck that day, or put him against a different target? His thought process was interrupted by the flight attendant.

"Sir, can I get you anything?"

He looked up. "Uh, black coffee please." She handed him the cup. "Thank you." He drank the coffee and idly thumbed a magazine but soon dropped it onto the adjacent seat in frustration. He stared out the dark window. He dozed ...

... The formation was back from its mission over the North. The arresting cable had just released the last fighter, and all the crews had returned safely. Little Jack had just completed his last mission, and an impromptu party was already underway. Mac was there with Little Jack's favorite drink. It was a time to celebrate one more short-timer going home—

"Sir? I'm sorry." The flight attendant touched his shoulder, waking him. "I need you to raise your seat back, please. We're about to land."

McIvor looked at her with a tired expression. "Okay." He rubbed his face and looked out the window. The lights of the Washington metroplex glowed brightly in the darkness. The DC-9 made its approach down the Potomac River to the south. He could see the Pentagon on his right. He slowly shook his head in disgust.

The Pentagon. There were many names for it; Fantasy Land, the Five Sided Funny Farm, Disneyland East, Bozo Barracks, Bootlicker University. There were others and they all fit, he thought. Some things never change.

The aircraft touched down on runway 18 at Washington National Airport. After turning onto the taxi way, the flight attendants made their customary announcements welcoming everyone to the nation's capitol. No one paid any attention. The aircraft soon stopped at the gate, and the captain turned off the seat belt sign. McIvor picked up his bag and followed the shuffling line into the jetway.

Jack Wilder was waiting at the door. He looked older than McIvor remembered. No surprise, considering the circumstances. "Jack, good to see you." They shook hands.

"Thanks for coming, Tom. I only wish the circumstances were different." The two men looked at each other and embraced as men-in-arms do. Nothing else had to be said.

The cold air was a welcome rush when they left the terminal. It was refreshing after the cramped airliner. They walked across the parking lot.

"How's Liz?"

"Not well, Tom. She's taken the whole thing pretty hard, and I'm afraid this may be her undoing. Thank God Bill's with her. She's been clinging to him since Little Jack's capture."

"And Bill?"

"Considering what he's been through, he's holding up a lot better than I expected. Doesn't say much though. He keeps everything inside. His martial training has taught him self-control like I've never seen, but I'm afraid something's brewing in that head of his."

"What do you mean?"

"Bill and Jack were always close. You knew that."

"Yes."

"Bill's changed since Little Jack's capture, and his death has affected Bill in some dark way. I can't put my finger on it, but my guess is that he won't be satisfied until he finds out what happened over there and comes to terms with it in his own way."

"What does *that* mean?" McIvor studied him.

Wilder looked straight ahead. "I'm not sure that I really want to know, Tom, and I don't know if anyone can stop him either."

When the crash came, an evil smile passed over Vorhees' face. He inhaled his last cigarette down to the filter and crushed the butt on the table. He stood, cracked his knuckles, and walked slowly towards the bathroom.

Brigitte LeFebre lay unconscious on the floor, the torn shower curtain in her hands. Vorhees carried her nude body to the bedroom and placed her face down on the bed. He retrieved her high heels and put them on her feet. There was a earthy excitement in them; he had to have them. He took a leather bag from an inside pocket of his overcoat and emptied the contents onto the bed. He tied her arms and legs to the corners of the bed frame, tight enough to prevent her from moving but not enough to cut off circulation. Standing over her, he lifted her body with one arm around her waist and stuffed pillows under her hips with the other. He tore two pieces of duct tape and placed one over her eyes and the other across her mouth.

Satisfied with his efforts, he sat down and waited.

They pulled into the driveway, shut off the engine, and sat in silence. Finally, Wilder said, "Let's go." The two men walked slowly to the house, dreading what lay before them.

The front door opened when they stepped onto the porch. Bill stood motionless in the light.

"Son, you remember Tom McIvor? He was Little Jack's commander on the *Ticonderoga*."

"Good evening, Captain McIvor. Thank you for coming."

"From the boy to the man." They shook hands. "It's good to see you, Bill."

"Thank you, sir." Bill looked at his father. "Bruce is here. Mom's sleeping. The doctor gave her a sedative."

McIvor noticed that Bill's conversation, although polite, was to the point and short on words. He sensed the young man's inner turmoil.

They walked into the living room. The NSA director stood and extended his hand. "Tom, glad you could make it. Been a while. Sorry about the late notice, but considering the circumstances—"

"No problem, Bruce. I just hope I can help."

"Your being here is a help in itself," Wilder said. "Have a seat." Spencer poured coffee and passed around shot glasses of whisky. The four men engaged in small talk, but the conversation was muted. Although Bill didn't know it, he was the main reason for this get-together.

***

The *Tonight Show* was on when Brigitte LeFebre began to regain consciousness. She moaned and rolled her head but soon panicked when she realized that she was bound and gagged. She thrashed and tried to scream, but her sounds were muffled by the tape on her mouth and the TV volume. Finally, out of exhaustion, she lay still, hyperventilating and choking on her own spittle.

The headache was all-consuming, but Vorhees forced all his attention on the woman. He leaned over and whispered into her ear. "I trust you had a nice rest, Brigitte." She pulled at her restraints when she heard his voice but stopped when he jerked her head up by the hair. "You had it your way. Now, it's my turn." He pressed her face to the mattress and said, "Don't move."

He placed a wire garrote and a switch blade knife on the bed beside her. Then getting on his hands and knees above her, he hissed, "It's time, bitch!" Wrapping the garrote around her neck, he mounted her. He began to sodomize her, slowly at first, then faster.

Brigitte screamed in pain against the tape on her mouth, but her pitiful protests went unheard.

Within minutes Vorhees worked himself into a frenzy, brutalizing her with increasing madness. He jerked violently on the garrote, snapping her neck and killing her instantly. Brigitte's now limp body danced like a puppet on a string when he pulled the wire. His headache was controlling him now, and he went at her until he finally passed out.

Spent and exhausted he lay motionless on top of her inert body. After several minutes he pushed himself up and looked disgustingly at the dead woman. He reached for the knife and pulled her head up by the hair. "Frosting on the cake." He drew the knife sharply across her throat.

The headache was gone.

He wiped the knife on the sheet and placed it, along with the garrote, back into the bag. He slowly got dressed, occasionally looking at the body without expression.

Ivan Petrov cracked his knuckles, picked up the bag and coat, and walked out.

***

A pregnant silence ensued. Wilder stared at his son. Finally, he said, "Bill, there's something I have to tell you." Wilder dreaded the task before him. This was the worst day of his life—again.

"Will it change anything?" Bill stood like a statue facing his father.

McIvor and Spencer knew what was coming, but they were helpless to do anything.

"Sit down, Bud." Bill sat on the edge of the coffee table. Looking at his son, Wilder took a deep breath and composed himself. "Bill, I asked Bruce and Tom to be here for several reasons. Under the circumstances, I thought it best. Bruce, being family, is here for obvious reasons. And as head of the NSA, he's officially involved now."

"Involved in what?"

Wilder hesitated for a moment then said, "Tom, as you know, was Little Jack's commander—"

"I know that. What are you trying not to say, Dad?"

"Please bear with me." This was going to difficult. "Bill, your brother was tortured in that camp along with the rest of the prisoners. But his death was by design."

The stare intensified. "What do you mean?"

"*Ch'uang tzu-chi*, Bud. Introspection. Self-control."

Bill sat motionless.

His father continued. "Bruce and Tom both know what I'm going to tell you. They're here not only for support, but also to corroborate my story." Wilder looked at each man then turned back to his son. "Not long ago, an American intelligence officer that Bruce and I had previously worked with was captured by the British while assigned to MI-6, the British equivalent of the CIA. He was in fact a Soviet spy. He was caught in the act of passing secrets to a known agent in London. Years ago he worked with us in the Pentagon on NATO and Warsaw Pact operations. He was the acknowledged expert on those areas. Unfortunately for us, he went undiscovered for years, and we have no idea yet how much damage he's caused.

"The British notified us, and a team was sent to London to interrogate him. His last name is Petrov, and he's one of the most prolific

spies of the decade. But our problems with him didn't end there."
Wilder paused to consider his next remarks.

"Petrov lived in Bethesda when he worked with us at the Pentagon. By his account his wife was sickly and required constant attention, so he kept pretty much to himself. He had a son that, according to police records, was killed in a car crash. The body was burned beyond recognition, and no positive identification was ever made. After the accident, Petrov transferred to Brussels. He made several trips to London during that time, and he was picked up on the last one." Wilder looked for a reaction. "Bill, are you with me?"

"Yes." His voice was void of emotion.

"Okay. Now it gets tricky. But before I finish with this, there's something else I have to say first." Wilder looked at Spencer and McIvor. Both men nodded. "You know that Bruce and I are involved in intelligence operations, most of which we can't talk about. I'll just say that various agencies have run extensive background checks on you and John. You'll need them for security clearances in the Air Force. But we want you and John to consider joining us."

"You mean the CIA." Bill's face was blank.

"Yes."

"I thought so."

"It's a big decision, Bill, and I want you to think about it. There's plenty of time to decide. You and John talk it over in private. Both of you still plan on going into the Air Force. That won't change, and if you decide to join us, it will be your cover."

"I'll consider it."

"That's all I need for now, Bud." *Now the hard part.* "I'm going to tell you something that's top secret, but all of us feel that you should know now. You're not to tell anyone about it."

"John?"

"He'll know in time, but it's up to us alone to tell him. Understood?"

"Understood." Bill's eyes were riveted to his father's.

"Listen carefully. We know that Petrov's son did *not* die in that crash. It was staged to allow him to leave the country undetected. The identity of the victim was never determined, and no one was reported missing. Petrov's son is one Ivan Yevgenni Petrov. He's part of the KGB's Fifth Directorate, commonly known as Murder Incorporated. They deal in wholesale killing and assassination. Black operations. Real nasty bunch." Wilder stood, looked briefly at his brother-in-law, and poured himself another cup of coffee.

Spencer picked up where Wilder left off. "Bill, this younger Petrov is dangerous. We tried to follow his movements, but he dropped off the radar. INTERPOL lost track of him shortly after his father was captured. He resurfaced in North Vietnam."

"It gets personal now, Bud, so prepare yourself," Wilder said. "Ivan Petrov went to the Hanoi Hilton because of your brother. Petrov knew that his father had been captured and that the Agency was interrogating him. He tried to get his superiors in Moscow to work a deal. His father in exchange for Little Jack.

"The Brits, of course, wouldn't hear of it. Neither would our government. The senior Petrov knows everything about NATO's plans, and the exchange was denied." Wilder hesitated, hoping for a brief respite. There was none. "We had an operative in that camp, Bill, and he smuggled out the news to us. Petrov tried to extract information from your brother by falsely befriending him. It didn't work. Then he came up with the exchange idea. When it was denied and he realized that he would never see his own father again, he took it out on Little Jack."

Bill was motionless, breathing in every word and nuance.

Jack Wilder thought his world would end with his next few words. "Son, Ivan Petrov murdered your brother. He shot Little Jack to death with his own revolver."

Deafening silence filled the room.

Bill slowly stood and walked to the bay window. He looked into the night sky. He alternately clenched and opened his fists. Shaking with rage he closed his eyes and took deep controlled breaths. Soon, the shaking subsided and he stood perfectly still.

A minute passed. Bill opened his eyes and looked straight ahead at nothing. He was on a different mental plane.

Spencer crossed the room and opened the front door. "Bill, let's take a walk. The cold air will do us good. There's something I want to share with you." They walked silently into the cold night.

Wilder noticed the frown on McIvor's face. "Tom, I know you think I told him too much, but I have my reasons."

"I'm sure you do, Jack, but this is one hell of a bomb to drop on him."

"I understand how you feel, but I'm backed against a wall here." Wilder walked to the bar and poured two whiskies. He handed one to McIvor and looked at his own glass. "Tom, when Bill decides to do something, he's usually done his homework beforehand, and there's no changing his mind. He's been like that all his life. As much as I haven't always agreed with him, I can't really fault his decisions. For a twenty-one year old kid, he's pretty level-headed."

"True enough."

"No, I didn't have to tell him about Little Jack or the Petrovs. But he'll find out sooner or later—the gun part anyway. The war won't last forever, and, God willing, those boys in North Vietnam will come home. They know what happened, and they'll tell him." Wilder sat on the table opposite McIvor. "We have two wild cards to deal with. Petrov is one, and Bill is the other. I had to tell him about Petrov because the two will probably meet sooner or later, whether we like it or not. We think Petrov will turn his attention to us and we have to prepare for it." Wilder paused and looked at the ceiling. "I sometimes wonder if I can handle him, Tom." He looked at McIvor. "Bringing him into the Agency is risky, but it may give him some measure of closure, and it sure as hell will give me a big legal handle on him. God knows I didn't ask for any of this. But it's here, and I have to deal with it the best way I can." Wilder wiped his brow with a napkin. "Is it a good idea? I don't know. But I do know that it's the only way I can control him. He'll pursue this thing to the death. This, at least, will give me legal authority over him if nothing else." He finished his drink and went for another. "God, I wish things were different."

McIvor leaned back and closed his eyes. "So do I, Jack."

The night wind blew through the naked trees and stirred the occasional snow flurry into little tornadoes. The air was cold and crisp, and it stung their eyes. Hours before, the sun had burned in the cobalt blue sky, and now the full moon washed the landscape with its haunting glow.

The scene reminded Bill of the *Taeguek*, or the Book of Changes; the Oriental philosophy that had disciplined him during his years of martial training. The wind reminded him of the *Taeguek* concept of *Seon*—being like the wind. It was forceful, yet gentle. Penetrating, yet yielding. It was pure and without evil intent. The inner turmoil caused by his father's words reminded him of *Jin*—the element of fear that occasionally enters one's life. *Jin* required the martial artist to show courage in the face of danger. And finally, he was reminded of *Gon*—the image of a mountain meaning *Top Stop*, of having the knowledge and courage of knowing when and where to stop. His martial instructor had forewarned him that one day, he would be tested to see if he was worthy of his training. He knew now that the long and tortuous test was about to begin.

Bill's mind began to evolve.

The two men walked along the deserted lane in silence, each lost in thought. They came to a hill that looked across rolling fields that were washed in the moonlight. Standing on the slight ledge they stared across the expanse, each wondering what the future would bring.

Spencer broke the silence. "Bill, if you've a mind to listen, I think I can give you some insight to the big picture."

Bill gazed into the distance. "The *Big Picture*. I used to watch that Army show when I was a kid. Been trying to figure it out ever since."

"As we all have. I don't think anyone has the *real* picture, Bill, but let me try to put things into perspective, if I may."

Bill nodded.

"When you and Little Jack were kids, I used to watch you guys ride your bikes, play ball, and all that other stuff. Since I never had kids of my own, I semi-adopted you two. I often envied your dad, and I told him so on occasion. But I took satisfaction in knowing that my sister was your mother. That made me part of you guys and that satisfied me. When your brother got accepted to the Naval Academy, it made me very happy. I was just as happy when you went to VMI. Both you boys made your parents and me very proud. But I'll tell you right now that my stomach knotted up when you guys decided to make the military a career."

Bill looked at him.

"It's true. You come from a long gray line. All the men in this family have been in one of the military branches since the beginning. They were with Stonewall Jackson at New Market during the Civil War, with Teddy Roosevelt on San Juan Hill, Pershing in Europe during World War I. They were with Patton and Eisenhower in World War II. Your father and I have spent the majority of our lives in uniform. We were both in World War II and Korea. It's a proud and noble profession, Bill, but there are a few things you need to know about the people that control your fate as a military officer.

"Politicians and bureaucrats will tell you that the American military machine exists to support national objectives. Think about that—*national objectives*. What does it mean? Ask all the politicians in Washington, and each one will give you a different answer. Ask all the generals and colonels in the Pentagon, and you'll get a different set of answers yet. Who knows? Nobody. But I'll tell you this; the military has been misused over and over, national objectives not withstanding. Vietnam is a prime example.

"This war is costing thousands of lives and millions of dollars, and the very moral fiber that holds this country together is being threatened. I think we should go over there, kick some serious ass, and be done with it. Or get the hell out altogether. Unfortunately, it's not that simple. The military can't fight when the politicians in Washington try to run things from behind their collective desks. The civilian government controls the military, not the other way around. In the big scheme of things, that's good, but it creates problems when it comes to waging war. The generals can't run Washington, and the politicians can't run a military campaign, although they try. Hell, they can't even decide where to stand on any given issue.

"Okay, enough philosophy. Now to the point. As bad as our system sometimes is, it's the only one we have, and it's the best around. If was wasn't, people wouldn't be beating down the doors to get into this country. South Vietnam, Russia, China, and all the rest are just as corrupt and more so than our own government. But defend it we must. Little Jack believed that, and he made the ultimate sacrifice because of it. He did not die in vain.

"Bill, not all of our enemies wear black pajamas and carry AK-47 assault rifles. They don't all speak a foreign language, nor do they look all that different from us. Many of them are here in this country." Spencer paused to think about his next statement. "I'm going to lay it on the line with you, Bill. You need all the facts.

"This Ivan Petrov blames *your* father for capture of *his* father. I don't understand the logic behind it, but that's the way it is. He tried to get information from your brother about your father, but Little Jack as much as told him to go pound sand. He died for it but he was defiant to the end. You can be proud of that. Like your father said, we had an operative in that camp. He got information out, and it worked its way to us. Little Jack never told Petrov anything.

"This younger Petrov is a mental case, I think. We've compiled a dossier on him that makes for interesting reading. He's a trained killer and he's good at it. He's also an American."

"What?" Bill stared at his uncle.

"We know that he was a student at Georgetown when his father was working in the Pentagon. He fit right in. He spoke perfect English, knew all the idioms, slang, and phrases. He lived here for years before leaving for Moscow. He was sent to North Vietnam specifically to work on your brother. Now that Little Jack's gone, Petrov may be looking at the rest of us."

"So, he's coming." It was a statement, not a question.

"We think so."

Bill looked at the moon. "Then it's settled."

"What's settled?"

"I'm joining the Agency."

"Be careful here, Bill. Hasty decisions will get you killed. Petrov won't show his hand any time soon because he knows we're looking for him. You've been pushed from the frying pan into the fire virtually overnight. Don't make a decision until you're ready. There's plenty of time for that."

They stood in silence. Spencer knew what was going through his nephew's mind, and he also understood youthful impulsiveness. Bill wanted to strike out at something, and it was up to his father and uncle to guide him along the narrow path. Their task would be formidable, and they would have to tread carefully.

Bill reflected on his uncle's remarks. He'd never given much thought about his father's and uncle's feelings or opinions. They were professional military men, and that was that. But now he began to understand their agony over the war and its politics. They had seen pain in their lifetimes, and he had been oblivious to it until Little Jack's capture. .

An outsider had killed his brother and was threatening his family. Now he understood the reason behind the unmarked cars near the house. Bill suddenly wanted Petrov more than anything, and he resolved at that moment that they would meet someday. Until that time, patience and perseverance would sustain him. "What does he look like?"

"INTERPOL is sending us what they have, but he's a master of disguise. An operative in Moscow gave us the best description so far, but we really don't know what to expect." Spencer watched his nephew carefully.

Bill stared straight ahead. "What about the Hanoi operative? Can he tell us anything?"

"I'm afraid not."

"Why?"

Spencer pursed his lips and rubbed the back of his neck. "He was found in the Golden Triangle area of northern Thailand. He'd been staked to the ground and covered with honey. The jungle animals took care of the rest."

Bill closed his eyes. "Christ!" He already knew the answer to his next question but decided to ask anyway. "Why is Petrov coming here?"

"To avenge his father's capture."

Bill looked into the darkness. "We'll see about that."

They stood quietly for several minutes. Spencer finally broke the silence. "Both the Agency and the Secret Service are covering your parents twenty-fours a day. They're in no danger. You don't need to worry about their safety. Finish your schooling and flight training, Bill. Life must go on, and you must accept it as it comes. You'll have plenty time to make your decision with respect to the Agency."

"I appreciate what you've told me, Bruce."

"You're now on the fast track, son." Spencer rubbed his arms and looked around. "Pretty cold out here. How about let's head back to the house?"

Bill stood on the ledge and looked into the distance. "I want to stay here for awhile. I have some thinking to do." He looked at his uncle. "I appreciate what you told me, sir. Thanks." He turned his gaze back towards the night sky. "You go ahead. I'll be fine."

Spencer looked at his nephew. The boy had indeed become a man. "Okay. You know where I am if you need me." He patted his nephew on the back and walked back to the house.

Bill sat in the Lotus position and looked across the horizon. He closed his eyes and began to meditate. All thoughts were on Ivan Petrov. *Who are you? What are you inside?* He thought once again of the *Taeguek*. He concentrated on the meaning of the Red Belt. It signified danger and cautioned the opponent to stay away. Then he thought of the Black Belt, in which the wearer was impervious to fear and unafraid of the dark, regardless of its form. The *Taeguek* was coming to fruition for him, and he focused on the future...

... Facing east, the sun was rising to greet him. It was the beginning of a new day and a new life. Bill Wilder stood looked at the red sky. He said a silent prayer for his lost brother.

CHAPTER 18

The head of the National Security Agency spoke with determination and grace to the family and well-wishers of the late "Little Jack" Wilder. His eulogy was a collection of personal thoughts about the young man and his family, as well as a statement of the fallen warrior's determination and professionalism. Bruce Spencer was saddened by the loss of his nephew, but he was honored at having the opportunity to address the audience, which included Little Jack's classmates.

The Wilders were in the front row. Bill sat beside his mother and held her hand. Jack Wilder sat on the other side of his wife and held her other hand in both of his. While the two men were stoic, Elizabeth wept openly. Her oldest son had been brutally taken from her, and she had suffered horribly since his death. Her husband and younger son did their best to comfort her, despite their own pain.

The Academy chaplain finished with a closing prayer. "… and may Little Jack fly high on the right hand of God. Amen."

"Amen," the congregation responded in unison. Everyone stood in silent respect as the Wilders and McIvors made their way to the rear of the chapel. Bill and his father had to physically support Elizabeth. She was too distraught to make it on her own.

The cars were waiting at the entrance. Captain Thomas McIvor, in full military dress, opened the door for the Wilders while his wife quietly consoled her friend.

"Audrey, I appreciate everything you've done for Elizabeth," Wilder said, choking back the tears for his wife's sake.

"No need to thank me, Jack. We're family." She smiled sadly and touched his arm. "I only wish there was something more we could do."

Wilder sighed. "It's been tough on all of us." He looked around in an effort to clear his head. He saw his son standing with Maggie by the entrance to the chapel. He smiled to himself. *The eternal hope of youth. Don't ever lose it.* "Maggie's grown into a lovely young lady. You must be proud of her."

"Indeed, we are, Jack. She's independent and proud. Reminds me of myself when I was younger." Audrey smiled. "They look good together, don't they? Bill's so mature for his age. He's a fine boy—*man*, I should say. They grow up so fast. I only hope they can put this behind them and go on with their lives. They have so much ahead of them." She gazed at the young couple with motherly affection.

"Yes, they do," Wilder said. *If you only knew.*

Audrey joined Elizabeth in the rear seat. Captain McIvor stood by the driver's door. "John, would you ride in the back with Mrs. Wilder? It would help calm her."

"My pleasure, sir." Slaughter climbed into the car and closed the door.

"Jack?"

"Be with you in a minute, Tom." Wilder approached his son. He was tired and weary but he smiled at the couple. "Bill, we're heading back to the house now. John's going with us. Maggie, your parents are staying for a few days before heading back to New England. I really appreciate your mother's help. Liz needs her right now... " His eyes wandered around the academy grounds. It was difficult to keep his emotions in check. "Look, you kids go out and enjoy yourselves. We'll be home when you get there."

They stood silently for a moment. Finally, Bill said, "Dad, what Bruce said in there was right on the money. I'm proud of my brother for what he did, and of my family."

Father and son looked at each other. There was no need for

words. They clasped hands. The bond between them was stronger than ever. Their relationship had evolved into mentor and student, a team bonded by blood and by the shared loss of a loved one. There was a common goal now; to see that justice was done. To that end, they swore a silent oath to themselves and to each other.

"Bill, you're a credit to your uniform and to the family. Your mother and I are so proud of you. If your brother was here today, he'd say the same thing."

"He already did, Dad." Bill smiled at his father.

Wilder's spirits were lifted for the first time in days. "Yeah, I guess he did." He reached out to the young woman beside his son and hugged her. "Thanks for coming, Maggie. You and your parents are more help than you know. Our home is your home."

"Thank you, Mr. Wilder. I'm happy to be here." There were tears in her eyes.

"Well, it's time for you guys to go have some fun. I'll keep John on a short leash. See you back at the house." Wilder turned towards the waiting car and waved over his shoulder. He climbed into the front seat and closed the door.

From the driver's seat, McIvor gave them a thumbs-up and started the engine. The car slowly pulled away and disappeared around the corner.

They sat in silence in his Mustang. With his coatee unbuttoned and his hands on the wheel, Wilder stared into the distance and thought about the day's events. His life was changed forever. His brother was gone and his mother's health was failing. Through it all he watched his father suffer in silence while trying to hold the family together. On the other hand his VMI friends were there for him, and he saw how his parents' friends rallied to their side when tragedy struck. And he was with a childhood friend, brought back into his life under unfortunate circumstances.

Unfortunate? Meeting Maggie McIvor again was a turn of good fortune. Her presence lifted his spirits in a way that he had not experienced since Little Jack came home for Christmas in 1965. He looked into her green eyes. "How you doing, Red?"

She looked back at him, her hand on his shoulder. "You're so considerate, Bill. After what you've been through, you ask *me* how I'm doing. I'm fine, but the question is, 'How are *you* doing?'"

"I'll be okay." He looked ahead. After a moment he turned to her. "Hey, how about a burger and a beer? There's a honky-tonk near Herndon where we hang out when we're out of school. Not much to look at, but the food's great and the beer's cold. The owner is a friend of mine. You'll like him."

"Honky-tonk?" Maggie laughed. "What's a honky-tonk?"

"You know; a road house, a gin mill." Wilder closed his eyes and rapped the side of his head with his palm. "Damn! I'm sorry." He looked at her. "I forgot. You New England blue-bloods don't have honky-tonks up there. I think *pub* is the proper term."

"Pub-schmub! Sounds like a great idea. Let's get a six-pack for the trip." She squeezed his arm.

"It may be a six-pack to you, but it's a support group for me!" She laughed at his choice of words.

He turned the key and the engine roared to life. The 1966 Mustang had been a gift from his parents and uncle for his birthday. While at the Institute, cadets were neither allowed to drive nor to have a car in Rockbridge County. As a result many cadets, including Wider and Slaughter, kept their cars at Steele's Tavern, a road house just outside the county line. Having a car gave a cadet the chance to connect with the outside world. For Bill Wilder it was a lifeline to his family—and to his sanity.

"Drive on, William." Maggie pointed ahead at the road.

"We're outta here!" They left the Academy grounds, bought some beer at a local convenience store, and settled back for the drive to Herndon.

A brown Chevy Nova pulled out from a side road and began to follow them at a distance.

They rode in silence. Wilder looked straight ahead while Maggie leaned against the passenger door studying him. *What makes you tick, Bill Wilder?* Having met during adolescence, they never really knew each other. Over the past several days she began to see a part of him that she didn't know existed. She saw a gentleman in the man next to her. He was thoughtful, gentle, and considerate. But she sensed an inner turmoil. He needed a catharsis—a cleansing of his spirit—before he could begin to heal emotionally. She knew of his martial skills and that he was lethal in his own right. But her feelings for him were strong. He was like a little boy at times, and he needed someone to help him. She wanted to be that person.

She was also falling in love with him.

The clouds soon gave way to blue skies, and the sunshine lifted their spirits. Conversation was light and they enjoyed each other's company. She was interested in everything he said, especially his martial training. They shared their views on Vietnam with each other and, although his feelings about the war weren't as intense as hers, their opinions were similar.

While Wilder wasn't the type to waste time on idle chatter, he found her engaging. She shared his grief and lightened his burden without badgering him. When she spoke she had something to say, and he found it refreshing. It was a relief from the mindless prattle he usually got from the women he dated.

They'd been traveling for a while. "Want me to drive?"

"Thanks, but I'm okay." Wilder pointed ahead. "Your *pub* is less than a mile." He looked at her with a hint of a smile. "Maggie, this place is kind of … well, it's a—"

"It's a dump."

"Uh, yeah. I guess you could say that. No point in trying to hide it." They both laughed. "The owner is a guy named Jake Newton. He's one of the good guys."

"Well, if he's anything like you or John, he must be a character. You two don't seem alike at all but I see the bond there, and you guys do compliment each other. He's really funny. I sometimes wonder if he's part animal."

Wilder tapped the wheel and laughed. "Maggie, you just hit the nail on the head. *Animal* is his nickname." He wore his feelings on his face. "John's a class-A dirt ball and he's generally no damn good, but he's the best friend I have. If I ever get in a jam, I can't think of anyone I'd rather have with me. He's a bit crude, I'll admit, but he'll give you the shirt off his back if you ask him. He's a good shit." Wilder's face reddened. "Uh, sorry."

She lightly punched him on the arm. "Not necessary, Wild Man!"

Maggie was enjoying this. "I'm sure he's a *good shit* as you say. Yeah, he's crude, but who isn't sometimes? Besides, true friends are hard to come by. I can't think of a better compliment to him than yours."

"Thanks." *Well said, lady.* "What's with the 'Wild Man' stuff?" He feigned a hurt look.

"Just what I said. You have it in you, same as John. You're just being a gentleman for my benefit. I like that but I want you to be yourself." She sat sideways and faced him. "I want to see all sides of you, *without* the candy coating. Any questions?"

He saluted. "No questions. All cards face up on the table." Wilder nodded towards the windshield. "Well, there it is, Red, for your dining and lounging pleasure." He turned the Mustang into a muddy lot, bounced over a few potholes, and parked within yards of the building. He turned off the ignition and waited for a response.

The parking lot, such as it was, was nothing more than a frozen mud hole along the side of the road. Cars and pickup trucks in various states of disrepair were scattered everywhere. A solitary excuse for a building stood forlornly at the rear of the lot. The brown paint had long since given up and peeled away, and the sagging roof appeared ready to collapse at any second. The neon lights labored in vain to ignite themselves, but an occasional flicker was all they could manage. A faded sign nailed below a cracked window read *Jake's Place.*

"What a hole! I love it!" Maggie stared at the land version of the *Titanic* disaster.

"You're so kind."

Maggie kissed him lightly on the cheek. "Let's go, Wild Man."

They walked cautiously over the ice and up the cracked steps. Bill opened the front door, taking care that it didn't fall off the hinges. Walking into the smoke-filled room, they were immediately accosted by the smell of stale beer, cheap cigars, and grease. The noise was deafening and the place was packed.

"Well, this is it. Neat, huh?"

"It's perfect, Bill."

"I'm glad the lady approves." He looked around at the familiar crowd.

"Hey, Wilder, you asshole!" someone shouted from the back of the room. "A toast to the man of the hour." There was noisy agreement. "Here's to you and your brother, man." Everybody cheered. "And to the lovely lady with you. Watch her, Bill. If you don't the rest of us will." Laughter filled the room.

"Sit the hell down, Leibecke, before you fall down," Wilder shouted from the doorway. He waved at his classmate.

Maggie looked around the room. "This is unbelievable. They're all animals. Is it safe in here?"

Wilder put his arm around her shoulder, the grin as wide as ever. "Don't worry, Maggie. These idiots don't mean anything. They'll defend you to the death because you're with me. That makes you one of the boys."

"One of the *boys*?"

"Yep. Can't get any better than that. Not many of the fair sex qualify."

"I'll take that as a compliment then." *One of the boys, indeed!* She shook her head.

"Table or bar?"

"Why, the bar, of course. What self-respecting *boy* would sit at a table?"

"Hen-pecked prick!" someone shouted from across the room. Wilder raised his social finger to the crowd behind Maggie's back. More laughter.

Maggie sat on a bar stool and looked at the crowd. "Raunchy bunch."

"They're just blowing off steam," Wilder said, looking across the room with admiration. "Most of these guys were at the Academy today. Meant a lot to me."

She saw the pride in his face when he spoke of his friends that came to pay their last respects to a lost comrade-in-arms and a kindred spirit. *This is true friendship*, Maggie thought to herself. *It doesn't get any better than that.* "My parents used to drag me to the Officer's Club at Newport every time there was a formal *you-will-show-up* function. The Navy decreed that you *will* enjoy yourself. I hated it." She looked around the room. "But this is real people having real fun. This place is—"

"A rotten pest hole! This hovel should be burned to the ground. Hell, the rats are even leaving."

Shocked at the words coming from behind her, Maggie turned to the scruffy oaf sitting on the adjacent bar stool. The face had not seen a razor in days, and the greasy handlebar mustache would have put Wyatt Earp to shame. The hair was uncombed and the shirt was either a light gray or a dingy white. She couldn't decide which.

"Uh, excuse me. Are you okay?" Maggie wasn't sure she wanted an answer.

He stood and rubbed his hands on his jeans. "Yeah, lady, I'm fine." He looked around the room. "Filthy rat hole! Always throwing some two-legged vermin out the back door. Soon as I do that, another one crawls from under a table." He looked over her shoulder at Wilder with disgust. "I'd call the low-rents at the health department, but they're afraid to show up."

"Is it really *that* bad?" Maggie was between shock and surprise.

"Worse."

"Why don't you complain to the owner?"

He took a red bandanna from his hip pocket and wiped his hands. "Lady, I *am* the owner."

"What? Oh!" Her jaw dropped. Wilder stood behind her, biting his hand to keep from laughing.

"Jake Newton, ma'am, at your service." He stroked his mustache with one hand and offered her the other. "Don't worry, you won't catch nothing. I washed it last Saturday." He smiled and winked.

Maggie knew that she'd been had and began to laugh. *Walked straight into this one, boy.* She quickly collected herself and extended her hand. "Hello, Jake. I'm Maggie McIvor. Pleased to meet you."

He bowed and kissed her hand. "Lady, any friend of Bill's is a friend of mine. Welcome to my humble establishment." He leaned close to her ear. "A word of caution. Don't believe anything that sleaze-ball tells you."

"Okay!"

He straightened up and looked at his friend. "Hey, Wilder, you useless piece of mule dung, how the hell are you? What are you doing with such a fine lady? Did you kidnap her, or are you paying her to baby-sit you?"

"Both, I guess. How's the gourmet dining business?"

"Busy as hell, especially since your buddies showed up." Newton shoved his hands into his pockets, his face serious. "Bill, I'm sorry I couldn't make it to the service, but between running this place and going to school—"

"You were there in spirit, my friend, and that's all that matters." Bill slapped him on the shoulder. "You've done a lot for my parents since all this happened, and I appreciate it."

"No, Bill, it's me that should say thanks. I owe you, man. If you ever need anything—"

"You owe me nothing, Jake. You're family." Wilder cocked his head. "I told Maggie that you had the best road-kill and coldest beer in these parts. What do you say to that?"

Newton stroked his mustache and smiled, his teeth showing from ear to ear. "Say no more, good friend." He turned to the bartender. "Hey, Sam, how about burning some scrapings for my main man and his fair lady? And some beers, please." He turned to his guests. "Nothing but the best here. On the house of course."

"Thanks, Jake, but the ink doesn't run on this wampum." Wilder reached for his wallet.

"Listen, pilgrim, I own this dump, and your money's no damn good here. You know that." Newton looked at Maggie. "Where did you find this low-life anyway?"

"Oh, I don't know. He just crawled out from under a rock." The beers arrived and she passed them out. "Cheers." She picked up her bottle and drank deeply, wiping her mouth with the back of her hand. "This is good."

Newton was pleased. "Glad you approve." He looked at Wilder. "A woman of refinement you got here."

"The best."

"Listen, you lump, let me borrow your lady for a while. I want to educate her about your heathen ways. Besides, Leibecke's been looking for you. He's in the back of the room somewhere. You'll recognize him. He's the guy passed out on the floor."

"Glad he's back to normal." Wilder finished off his beer and picked up a second. He smiled at Maggie. "Mind if I slide out for a few minutes? I'd like to see some of these ingrates. Jake will take good care of you—I think." He raised his brow at Newton.

"I'll watch her like a hungry hawk circling a rabbit."

"Don't let his gruff appearance scare you, Red." Wilder looked at Newton and winked. "He's a wimp. I'll be back in a few minutes."

"Pound sand, good friend!"

Maggie watched him wonder into the crowd. "He gets along with everybody."

"Yep. Most of these guys are his classmates, and they're all his friends." Newton looked seriously at Maggie. "Would you like to know about the *real* Bill Wilder?"

She looked curiously at her host. "What do you mean? Is there some dark secret I should know about?"

"No skeleton in his closet, Maggie. I'm the dark secret here. That man saved me from myself. If you don't mind listening, I'd like to tell you a story."

"I'm all ears, Jake." She was intrigued and she gave him her full attention.

Jake crossed his arms on the bar. He stared at his beer for a while before he spoke. "Maggie, Bill considers you family, and that's good enough for me." He looked at her. "This is just between family, okay?"

"Yes, Jake. And thanks for your confidence." Her eyes were glued to him.

"When I said that he saved my life, I wasn't kidding." His gaze returned to his beer. "When I was fifteen, I dropped out of high school. I soon got mixed up with the wrong crowd, and I was in trouble all the time. Nothing serious, just petty stuff. But I was headed for a dead end." He looked at her. "One night a bunch of us were hustling marks in the local pool hall for everything we could get. Bill and Little Jack were there, but I didn't know them then. Bill looked like an easy mark, and I beat him out of fifty bucks. Then I beat another guy out of a hundred. Beat him fair and square, but he didn't think so.

"I left the pool hall with two other guys, and we took a shortcut down an alley. But the guy who just lost his hundred bucks and two of his friends cornered us before we knew what was happening. One guy had a pool cue and another had a pipe. The guy that lost the money had a blade and he was pissed. My so called *friends* took off and left me there alone. I never saw them again. Anyway, I was scared to death and I began to cry." Jake looked at Maggie, his eyes full of tears. "I'm not afraid to admit it, Maggie. I thought I was going to die."

"Oh, God!" She began to choke up.

"I begged them not to hurt me, but they started pushing me around anyway. They said they were going to kill me. I gave them every cent I had, including the fifty bucks I took from Bill. They began to beat me and I pleaded for them to stop. I covered my face and screamed when the guy with the pipe drew back to swing at me. He was going to crush my skull. But you know what? It never came.

"When I thought I was going to get brained, I heard a familiar voice say, 'Not today, cupcake!' I looked up in time to see this guy's head snap back and his knees buckle. The pipe swung a wide arc and cracked him upside the head, and he hit the ground like a steel ball. Then the guy with the pool cue got cracked in the throat and kicked in the groin. Next thing I knew, he was spread thinner than a sheet of wet paper on the ground.

"The third guy—the one with the blade—was a hurting son-of-a-bitch. His arm got twisted like a pretzel. The knife disappeared into the atmosphere, and the guy wound up on his knees. His arm was broken backwards, and before he realized what was happening, his ribs got re-arranged. He curled into a ball and passed out."

"Jake, I don't know what to say!" Maggie's eyes were wide with disbelief.

"Honest to God, Maggie, I didn't know what to do. I was so scared."

At a loss for words, she just stared at him.

"I was afraid to move. All of a sudden it got real quiet, and this one-man army stooped down in front of me. He wasn't as big as me, but, at that instant, he was a giant. Still is in my book. He said, 'Are you okay?' I mumbled something and he held out his hand."

"Who was it?" Maggie was on the edge of the stool.

"Who do you think?"

"... Bill?"

"None other."

She stared at him in disbelief. "That's the most incredible story I've ever heard, Jake!" She looked at Wilder on the opposite side of the room, laughing with his friends. Somehow, he looked different to her now, his stature jumping tenfold.

Newton looked across the room. "That ain't the half of it."

"There's more?" Maggie was overwhelmed.

"Oh, yeah. When I looked up at him, he had a grin on his face that would put a Cheshire cat to shame. I didn't dare move. He just stood there holding out his hand. Finally, I took it and he pulled me up. I'd taken his money and he saved my life. Talk about a turn of events! Anyway, he said his name was Bill and asked who I was. We shook hands and walked out of the alley and into a new chapter in my life.

"We went to a local diner, and he bought me the first hot meal I'd had in days. I guess I was hungrier than I thought; I ate two complete meals before I realized they were gone. We talked for a long time and I began to open up to him. He was the only person that had befriended me in months. I told him about my quitting school, running away from home, and about the trouble I'd been in with the law. I guess he got the idea pretty quick that I was down and out. Anyway, when I was done I began to cry again. I was embarrassed, but I was even more scared. I suddenly realized that I had no one to turn to and nowhere to go."

Maggie pressed her fingers to her face, tears running over them. "What did you do?"

"Now, it *really* gets good. Bill got on the phone and was on it for a while. When he came back to the table, he said, 'Let's go to my place.' I had nowhere else to go, so I went home with him. The Wilders took me in and helped me get back on my feet. Bill's dad called in some favors and got my record wiped clean. He gave me a chance to start over. Bill became my best friend and he still is today.

"Thanks to the Wilders I got my act cleaned up. I made up with my parents and moved back home that summer. After high school I enlisted in the Army and did my hitch in 'Nam. When I got back, Colonel Wilder helped me buy this place. I know it doesn't look like much, Maggie, but it's a gold mine. It's paying my way through college, and it's going to help me through medical school." He winked and smiled. Pointing his thumb over his shoulder in Wilder's direction, he said, "I'm proud to say I owe that man a debt I can never repay."

Maggie was speechless. She stared at him, makeup streaming down her face. "Jake, I don't know what to say. That's the most beautiful story I've every heard. I never thought—"

"We guys have emotions too, Maggie. We ain't open about it like you gals are, but there's a silent bond there." Newton saw her tears flowing. "Hold on there, lady. No need to get all mushy! If Bill sees your face sliding off, he'll turn me into cord wood!" He gently wiped her tears with his bandanna.

"Jake—"

"Shhh! I'm proud to tell you the story. You should know." The food arrived. "Well, look at this! Two of the finest road-kill burgers on the face of the third rock from the sun." Newton slid a platter towards her. "Enjoy it, Maggie. It's really good." He gave her a toothy grin.

She looked at the platter, at Newton, and, finally, at Wilder's reflection in the bar mirror. She watched him approach from across the room. She closed her eyes. *God, this is amazing!*

"Okay, what words of wonder has this bone-head been telling you?" Wilder stood facing them with the ever-present grin.

"Nothing much. Made a pass a Red Riding Hood here but she didn't bite. Guess I've lost my charm and will have to defer to you, Bill." Newton picked up his beer and looked at Maggie. "How's the grub?"

"Uh, good." Her emotions were going in every direction. She looked at Wilder. "Bill, Jake just told me how you two became friends."

"Oh, did he now?" He looked at Newton while speaking to Maggie. "You gotta watch this guy. He could sell a refrigerator to an Eskimo."

"Yeah, and you could make him wear his ass for a hat," Newton shot back.

Maggie smiled at both of them. "You guys are amazing. I've never—"

BOOM!

The front door flew across the room, having been torn from its hinges. It slammed into a nearby table, knocking several people to the floor. Pieces of burning wood flew in every direction, and smoke quickly filled the room. Wilder reacted without thinking. He grabbed Maggie and pulled her to the floor, shielding her with his body. Newton did the same, throwing himself down between her and the explosion.

"Fire!" The bartender grabbed an extinguisher and sprayed the scattered flames. Several people raced for the gaping hole that had been the door to see what had happened.

"Maggie?" Wilder shouted over the noise. "Are you hurt?"

"Uh, no ... I, I'm okay." She was dazed but uninjured.

"Thank God." Wilder helped her to her feet and quickly looked her over. She was covered in soot and dust but otherwise uninjured. He brushed the hair from her face. He looked at Newton, already on his feet. "Jake?"

"I'm in one piece." He looked them over then turned towards the damage. "Jesus Christ! Can't be the propane tank. It's out back."

"Stay here, Maggie." Wilder turned to Leibecke. "Look after her, Bob."

"You got it."

"Let's go." Wilder and Newton ran for the opening.

Debris was blown in all directions. Vehicles were burning everywhere, their gas tanks exploding and adding to the inferno. Wilder and Newton shielded their faces with their hands, the heat too intense to allow them near the destruction. They stood on the edge of the lot and helplessly watched while the flames and billowing black smoke filled the sky. They could only watch as the fire consumed everything.

"Damn!" Newton shouted.

"Take it easy, Jake. There's nothing we can do." Wilder could hear sirens in the distance. "Fire trucks will be here in a minute." He looked around. "I hope no one got caught in this."

"Oh, hell!" Newton stared at the now destroyed Mustang.

Wilder looked at what was left of his car. The burned and twisted pieces of metal were scattered in every direction. The explosion had radiated outward from the center of his car. He stood silently, his temper barely under control. The anguish over the loss of his brother was now replaced by an anger against an enemy that had tried to kill his family and friends. The people around him were innocent victims in what had now become a personal vendetta. While everyone ran around yelling over the noise and devastation, Wilder stood motionless. He knew what had happened. And why. The explosion was meant for him.

Destroying one's enemy was an unavoidable act of war. It was expected. But the scene before him put things on a different level. Wilder felt the familiar pre-combat calm come over him, an almost transcendental disassociation between mind and body.

The hunted had now become the hunter.

PART TWO

CHAPTER 1

FEBRUARY 1969

The sky was dull and gray, the clouds pregnant with snow. A chill wind blew from the north. The attitude in Jack Wilder's office at CIA headquarters matched the miserable weather outside. He stood at the window looking at nothing in particular. He thought about all the events that had led to this day. His oldest son had been murdered in an act of cowardice, an attempt against his younger son had been made, and his wife's health was failing before his eyes. And neither the Agency nor the British authorities had been able to get a confession from Anatoly Petrov. Wilder wondered if things could get any worse.

He was a patient man when he had no other choice, and he didn't believe in extremes when it came to seeking results. But exceptions could, and would, be made. While the CIA didn't legally believe in torture, authorities and allies in other countries didn't always share the Agency's views. As a tool, drugs were often an effective option, and Wilder didn't object to the idea. He had often said as much to his brother-in-law and to his counterparts in London.

He turned from the window and looked at the NSA director. "No luck with Petrov yet, so I expect the Brits will change their approach." Both men knew what that meant.

Spencer nodded but remained silent. He sipped his coffee and watched the gray clouds slip by.

The telephone rang with urgency, interrupting their thoughts. The flasher indicated a call from MI-6. Wilder looked at it, debating to himself whether or not to answer it. But there wasn't really a choice, was there? After the third ring he picked up the receiver and held it to his ear.

"Wilder here ... Yes, Sir John ... " The one way conversation shown on Wilder's face. "Bloody hell!" He looked at Spencer, his ear glued to the phone. "When? ... You had no indications beforehand? ... Okay, I'll stay in touch." He slowly hung up the phone and leaned on his desk with both hands, his head hung low.

Spencer stared at him but said nothing.

Wilder slowly walked to the window. Looking at the dismal sky he shoved his hands into his pockets and sighed. He looked at Spencer. "That was MI-6. Petrov just hung himself."

Spencer leaned his head back against the chair and looked at the ceiling. "Are we losing control here?" He looked at Wilder. "Jack, we have to assume that Petrov told the Soviets everything. Plans are being changed—"

"I know, I know. But we have no idea how much damage ... " Wilder let the sentence hang unfinished. He slowly shook his head. Things had just gone from bad to worse. *Damn this!* Wanting desperately to change the subject, he reached for the folder on his desk. It was the lesser of two evils. He looked at the document and held it out to the NSA director. "The report on Ivan Petrov and our agent in the KGB. You know what that bastard did to her?"

"I do. How is she?" Spencer knew the generalities of the case but not the specifics.

"A gutsy woman. She's out of the hospital now, and she'll make a full recovery. But she's leaving the Agency and going back to Montana. Can't say I blame her." Wilder stared at his brother-in-law. "Do you know *exactly* what he did to her?"

"Not all the details, but I don't think it's important, do you?"

"Yes, I do. Petrov's done this sort of thing before, and maybe we can use it to track him down if, God forbid, something like this happens again."

"Let's hope it doesn't." Spencer refilled his cup from a pot on the sideboard. He turned and faced Wilder. "Okay, let's hear it."

Wilder again turned to the window. Snow was falling and it was getting dark. He related the brutal attack on his agent at Petrov's hands.

Spencer looked like he'd seen a ghost. "Jack, you're not going to believe this."

"What?"

"I spoke with John Conway this morning. He heads the FBI field office in Washington."

"I know of him."

"We talked about border patrols and surveillance at airports. During the conversation he told me about a murder in New York City recently. Seems that an Air France flight attendant was raped and murdered in her hotel room."

"Hell, that's nothing new for that city."

"Normally, no. But you just described exactly what happened to her."

"What?"

"Jack, think carefully. What kind of cigarettes did Petrov smoke in his flat in Moscow?"

"Marlboros."

"And?"

"He smoked them down to the filter. The place was littered with them. What are you driving at?"

"Conway told me that the girl had been tied and gagged with duct tape, exactly like your agent. Her throat was slashed after she was brutalized."

"The connection?"

"The cigarettes, the tape, the garrote around the neck. Jack, I think it's the same man."

Wilder clenched his fists. "It's him."

"And the explosion at Jake's. I hate to say this, Jack, but I think Ivan Petrov is right here among us."

Wilder picked up the phone. He looked at Spencer. "It's time to go to work, buddy!"

"I'll get things going on my end." With that, Spencer walked out of the office and headed for Ft. Meade, Maryland.

Federal agencies often bicker with each over other turf when it comes to joint investigations, particularly when it involves something on a national scale. In this case, however, there was no conflict. The Federal Bureau of Investigation, National Security Agency, and the Central Intelligence Agency all worked in unison, with Bruce Spencer at the helm, to find the spy Ivan Yevgenni Petrov. Having family and close friends in high places did have its advantages.

Petrov, for his part, had dropped out of sight. He knew that he was a hunted man now. He learned through his KGB contacts in Washington that his father had committed suicide, rather than succumb to British torture. That fact alone made him more determined than ever to even the score. But Petrov had a healthy respect for the American intelligence agencies, and he knew that he was no match for their collective efforts. For now he would wait and plan his next move. There was no hurry.

Jack Wilder never spoke to his wife about his job or of Petrov. She knew nothing of him, and Wilder intended to keep it that way. She was sickly and frail, and neither he nor her brother wanted to say or do anything that would cause her more anguish.

Bill, on the other hand, was fully involved in his indoctrination into the CIA and with its efforts to locate Petrov. Since his brother's death, he had begun to follow events in Vietnam in detail. In his mind he projected himself into different scenarios wherein he and Petrov crossed paths. He worked harder than ever to hone his martial skills to a fine and dangerous edge, and soon his CIA training would begin in earnest.

By the time Wilder and Slaughter graduated from the Virginia Military Institute in 1969, the total number of American military personnel in Vietnam had exceeded 543,000. President Nixon proposed a peace plan for mutual troop withdrawal. On June 8, Nixon announced the withdrawal of 25,000 troops from Vietnam, and on August 27, the US Ninth Infantry Division withdrew. The reduction of American presence had begun, but the killing continued.

By the end of 1969, US military strength had been reduced to

475,200. To date, 40,024 American military personnel had been killed. By the end of 1970, that figure had increased to 44,245.

CHAPTER 2

SEPTEMBER 1970

The Vietnamese guard was able to handle his charge easily. Having an AK-47 assault rifle also helped. "Get in there, you swine!" he shouted, shoving his prisoner into the cell. He followed with a sharp blow to the prisoner's back with the butt of his weapon. The door slammed and the bolt slid home.

Bill Wilder fell to the floor and scraped his knees. Nude and in a drugged stupor, he had no idea where he was. He remained motionless on his hands and knees while trying to regain his composure. He was disoriented and he suffered from vertigo and malnutrition. He had been deprived of normal food and rest for a month, and he was beginning to suffer from it. Slowly, he sat and leaned against the wall. Drawing his knees close to his body in an effort to stay warm, he tried to orient himself.

The single recessed ceiling light came on, casting a harsh glare. Wilder's cell was a five by five foot cube. There wasn't enough room to stand or stretch out. The walls and floor were damp concrete, and they drew away body heat. There was a bucket in the corner that served as a toilet. There was no water.

Wilder put his hands flat against his temples in an attempt to stop the spinning in his head. He remembered a trick he learned in flight school. Since he was unable to lie down, he put his arm against the wall and his hand on the door. He stared at the floor—focused on it, knowing that it was stable and that the wall it touched would not move. After a few minutes the spinning began to abate and the room stabilized. Perhaps the practice sessions learned during his physiological training were helping after all. He didn't move. He sat perfectly still, concentrating on the floor.

He was starving. Other than an occasional bowl of rice and a piece of cold fish, he had not had a regular meal since before he could remember. He tried to concentrate. How had he gotten here? Where was he? *Who* was he? Everything was cloudy, but he was determined to regain his mental composure and not allow himself to suffer from brain-rot. *Ch'uang tzu-chi,* he said to himself. Self-introspection. *Think. Concentrate.*

Exercising his mind helped to maintain self-control, and gradually things began to gel. He could not and he would not allow his captors to best him. He recalled his flight training in Georgia and the time he ejected from his T-38 trainer over the Okefenokee Swamp after flying through a flock of birds. He tried to follow events from then to now, but despite his best efforts, his recent memory was a blur.

Jack Wilder often questioned his own motives for allowing his son to join the Agency. Had he done the right thing? Clearly, he knew that Bill would pursue his own agenda, and Wilder knew that he couldn't change his son's mind once it was made up. He took some measure of comfort in knowing that he would have legal control over his son's actions, but he wondered how much *real* control he would have in the end. Wilder swore to himself that he would do everything he could to prepare his son for what lay ahead because he knew that Bill would not be stopped.

Elizabeth had been dead for six months. She had suffered from numerous ailments, but in the end, she had grieved herself to death. Her death weighed heavily on Jack Wilder's mind, and he often found it difficult to deal with the loss of both his wife and eldest son. His drinking had become excessive, and, for a while, it looked like alcohol would destroy him. His brother-in-law had been a tremendous help, but Bill's sheer backbone and determination had given him cause to reconsider his own predicament and to "buck up" under the strain. He owed his son that much. And he was determined not to fail the boy who had been thrust into an impossible situation and had become a man early in life because of it.

Bill Wilder drifted in and out of consciousness. After an indeterminable amount of time, the door to his cell opened, and the same guard entered. The angry scowl was gone and there was compassion in his expression. He sat a tray on the floor and dropped a rolled up sleeping bag beside it. "Eat this, Lieutenant. You're almost done here." He looked at the prisoner for a brief moment then closed the door. The bolt was left open.

Wilder's mind wondered. He concentrated his sight and thoughts on the food. Was this part of the good-guy-bad-guy routine he'd learned about? It didn't really matter because there wasn't anything he could do about it anyway. He looked at the tray. Instead of cold watery rice, there was a bowl of hot beef stew. Beside it sat a loaf of hot bread and two bottles of water. He stared at the food for several minutes, making sure that it wasn't a phantasm. He picked up the bowl and raised it to his nose. It smelled real, and it was hot. He began to eat the food, exercising self-control not devour it. He wanted to inhale it before it vanished, but he forced himself to eat slowly. He ate the bread and drank all the water.

He leaned back against the wall and savored the meal's warmth. The food had a medicinal effect, and his dizziness began to fade almost immediately. He looked at the sleeping bag and recognized it as US government issue. He untied the straps and rolled it out. Inside was a wool and cotton jump suit, some underwear, a pair of thick wool socks, and a pillow. He put on all the clothes, got into the sleeping bag, and zipped it closed. He was asleep within minutes. Shortly afterwards, the overhead light went out.

Wilder slept soundly for fourteen hours. He had not so much as moved. His food, although nourishing, had been laced with a sleeping agent; the intent was to allow him to sleep undisturbed while the effects of the other drugs in his system wore off.

When he awoke he suffered only from a raging thirst and the need to urinate. Although unsteady and exhausted from his month long ordeal, he felt reasonably well. The overhead light came on, and he saw a bottle of water sitting by the door. They had been watching him. It was then that the realized where he was and how he had gotten there. A slight grin crossed his face. He got out of the sleeping bag and drank the water. The door to the cell opened. "Welcome back to the world, Bill." The guard stepped into the cubicle. "Let's get out of here." The guard was actually a ÇIA field instructor and a former operative in North Vietnam. Known as Van Duc Tran in Vietnam, his American name was Charlie Hoosier, and he was a second generation Vietnamese American citizen. "You're one tough cookie, Bill. No one could get a thing out of you. Well done." He squeezed Wilder's arm and steadied him while Wilder got to his feet.

"Thanks, I think." Wilder's throat was sore from the cold and damp, and he could barely speak. He rolled his head to loosen his neck muscles.

"The ops director is anxious to see you after you regroup."

"Dad? What have you told him?" Wilder rubbed his month old beard and scratched his head.

"Nothing to tell. You were a mannequin. We got zip from you." He guided Wilder through the small door. "The medics want to check you out. Then you need some time to recuperate."

"First things first," Wilder said, stepping into the hallway. He stood up straight for the first time in a month. He stretched and flexed his muscles in an effort to regain his normal shape and to shake out some of the accumulated rust. "Number one is a hot shower and shave. Then, a seven course meal and a vintage red wine." The familiar grin returned.

Hoosier laughed. "Okay, you got it. Your seven course meal, such as it is, is waiting for you in the mess, minus the booze of course. Just remember that your eyes are bigger than your belly right now. You'll be lucky to keep down a bowl of soup."

Wilder looked at him sideways. "Maybe, but I'd like to try."

"Beer's on me tonight."

"Deal."

"Okay. Fresh clothes are in your locker. When you're done feeding your face, the ghouls in the lab want to give you the once over, just to make sure you're on one piece." Hoosier looked at him for a moment. "Sorry about the rifle butt in the back earlier. Had to be realistic. No hard feelings?"

Wilder looked straight ahead as they made their way down the hall. "My brother endured far worse."

They walked in silence. When they came to the mess hall, Hoosier said, "The hard part's over for you, Bill. Martial training comes next, but I guess you'll be more instructor than student."

"A little of both, I guess."

"Well, you know where I am. Beers later, okay?"

"Count on it." They shook hands. With that, each man went his separate way.

He stared at the food but didn't see it. He thought of his recent experience; the deprivation, drugs, and the torture, such as it was. And the games ... the never ending mind games. But as bad as it was at times, it was just training, and it would end. *Academic situation*, the instructors called it. He thought about the hell his brother had gone through, and he choked on some soup. It wasn't the food; it was the dark memory of his brother.

Showered and shaved, Bill felt almost human. Although exhausted from his month long confinement, his condition was temporary, and the lab rats had given him a clean bill of health. The drugs that had been administered during his ordeal as a "prisoner" were diluted and consisted of small doses. There would be no lasting side effects or permanent damage. He would recover completely.

He was sore from the confinement and lack of exercise. The headache was still there, despite the government APC's—military aspirin. He slowly made his way down the hall, allowing his mind to wonder. Nagging questions eclipsed his thoughts. What next? Where would events take him? Was the training worth it?

Yes, it was.

He knocked on the door, and it opened almost immediately. "Bud!" Jack Wilder practically dragged his son into his office. "I've been worried sick about you, son. Please tell me you're all right." The two men stared at each other, then the father desperately hugged his son.

Bill heard the anguish in his father's voice, and it bothered him. He had to do something to ease the tension. "Dad, I'm fine. Your guys did a number on me, but Hoosier said that I was one of the most stubborn pricks he's ever seen. *Just like you!*"

His words had the desired effect.

Relief washed over Wilder's face. "A drink to clear the cobwebs? It's not protocol, but I'm authorized to make allowances." He was visibly relieved that his son had survived in tact and was none the worse for wear.

"Sure." Bill looked around the room. "Nice digs."

"All government issue except for your leather chair. I thought you'd like to sit in it after your ordeal. Take a load off."

Bill dropped into the overstuffed chair. "Man, does this feel good!" His father handed him a glass of bourbon over ice. "Thanks." He noticed the drink in his father's hand. "Water?"

"Best thing for me these days." Wilder raised his glass. "To a job well done, Bud."

"And to you, Dad."

Enduring the *Hanoi Hilton East*, as it was called, was but one part of the total training Bill had to complete. As a CIA operative he would find himself in dangerous situations and in possession of valuable secrets, and an enemy would go to great lengths to get them. The torture aspect is what bothered his father more than anything. Wilder wondered where his son would be a year from now. Would it be Vietnam, or some other God-forsaken Third World country, trying to stay alive with no one to help him? The loss of Little Jack and the constant worry over Bill, along with the loss of his wife, had caused him to age prematurely, and the prospects for Bill weighed heavily on his mind.

Bill saw the despair in his father's face. The eyes had a forlorn sadness about them. They had seen death and destruction that Bill could only imagine. It was bad enough that his father had been through so much, but because most of it was classified, he was unable to talk about it. Bill had to do something to lighten the load on his father.

"Dad, what's going on with John? Has he finished the course on how to make friends and influence people?" The Cheshire cat grin.

Wilder looked at his son, threw back his head, and laughed harder than he had in months.

That's it, Dad. Keep it up.

"Bill, if I didn't know that boy as well as I do, I'd say he was demented." Wilder poured his son another drink and another glass of water for himself. "That poor guy. He punched out one of the interrogators and a guard. He was rewarded with leg irons, bread and water, and isolation for two weeks."

"Two weeks?"

"And this isn't the first time. He's determined to get into trouble. Have to give him credit though. He has staying power." Wilder shook his head. "He's still there as I speak, cussing like a drunk sailor on leave in Manila without any money."

Both men laughed. "Dad, don't tell him we poked fun at him. He'll kill us! Guess he'll be eating crow for a while."

"Probably wishes he had some crow right now. The bread's stale and the water's warm." They joked over Slaughter's misfortunes for several minutes, then fell silent. After a minute Wilder looked at his son and said, "I sometimes wonder if I made a mistake with him. I mean about whether or not he can handle the training."

"No, Dad, you didn't. It's his way. He knows this is training. But when the chips are down, you can count on him. I can't think of anyone I'd rather have with me when I'm in a fix. Don't worry about John. He'll be fine."

"Just wanted to make sure." Wilder turned to the window and looked out at the Tidewater countryside.

Bill looked seriously at his father. "Dad, tell me the truth about what I can expect from the bad guys, and don't sugar-coat it. I got the standard fare from the instructors, but you know more about it than they do. What are these people really like?"

"Bill, the Vietnamese are brutal, and they don't recognize the Geneva Convention with respect to POW's or anybody else. They're not schooled in the use of drugs, but they've tried them to a limited extent. They are experts at torture and pain, however. What you.recently experienced was but a taste. The idea here is to train you how to react and how to resist by using the techniques we teach. But there are limits to the amount of pain a person can withstand."

Little Jack.

"The Russians, on the other hand, are quite sophisticated when it comes to this stuff. They use drugs as freely as they drink vodka, and they'll go to barbaric extremes. You've read about the prisoner treatment in the Lubyanka?"

Bill shook his head. "Number Two Dzerzhinsky Square; the most infamous address in Moscow."

"They've been known to skin people alive then throw them into a furnace, *still* alive!"

"Jesus!"

"Quite. And this is what they do to their own people. I get first-hand reports from the field. I can't talk about them, Bud, but you get the picture."

"Anything on Petrov?"

"We know he's somewhere in the States. Right after the bombing at Jake's, we learned that he murdered an Air France flight attendant in New York a week earlier. INTERPOL and the French DGSE helped us with this one. He left Moscow on Pan Am for Berlin. Then he took an Air France flight to Kennedy. That's when he killed the girl. After the bombing at Jake's, he disappeared. But you can count on him showing his cards when the time comes."

"Can any of your foreign agents help us with this?"

"Our contacts in the Lubyanka are under suspicion, and they can't help us with Petrov. They had to break off all contact with us, for a while anyway."

"Nureyev?"

"He was made by the Soviets. We have him in the embassy now. The Russians want him back, but that's not going to happen. Remember what they do to their own people."

"Trying to get him out?"

"The KGB has the embassy surrounded, and they're armed to the teeth. Touch and go harassment, that sort of thing. No, we'll keep him inside for now. Fortunately, we got his family out before those assholes found out what was going on. So far, he's the only one that's been uncovered. The guy's a walking book. He's given us a lot of information, and we're not going to throw him to the wolves. He just became a permanent guest of the embassy staff."

"He's one of the lucky ones," Bill said.

"And there's a purge going on in the KGB right now."

"I'll pass. Who spilled the beans?"

"Well, Bud, it seems that the Ruskies had a mole in our embassy. A housekeeper. Been there for years. She told her bosses about Nureyev. He was seen talking with one of our people at Lenin's tomb. The KGB put a tag on him and he ran. Fortunately, he was lighter and younger than the cabbage-eating Bolsheviks that chased him. We grabbed him and raced back to the embassy. The Marines were forewarned and had the gates opened. Our guys raced through without so much as a dent in the fender. The score is one to nothing now, and the Russians are not good sports."

"Can't imagine why. Hooray for the good guys." Bill fixed himself another drink. The alcohol was going to his head. "Maggie's working with UPI in Washington now, and we hope to get together when John and I finish here. If we finish."

"You guys will finish. John may be a little worse for wear, but the hardest part is over. A few more weeks." The smile disappeared from Wilder's face. "Tommy's been drafted."

Bill's face went white. "When?"

"Last month. You didn't hear about it because of your confinement. He's at basic right now. Mac's been stoic about it, but Audrey's taking it hard. Maggie's beside herself. She's been after her brother to go to Canada."

"What are the kid's feelings?"

"He's too much like his dad. He signed on the dotted line."

"Where's he going, as if we don't already know?"

"I'll give you two guesses, but you'll only need one."

Bill sat his drink down and rubbed his hands together. "Damn this war to hell!"

Wilder saw the stress in his son's eyes, and his heart ached for him. Although Bill was only twenty-three years old, there were already lines on his face. Lines caused by worry, stress, and determination. He thought of Maggie and of how she had commented that Bill's features made him ruggedly handsome. Wilder was worried about the young couple's relationship. Although he dreaded the subject, he had to address it. He stood in front of his son and placed a hand on his shoulder.

"Dad?"

"Listen, Bud, there's something else we need to talk about. You know how helpful the McIvors have been over the past couple of years. I don't know what we would've done without them. They were especially helpful to your mother, God rest her soul. They're upset about Tommy being drafted, but so are thousands of other families. We can only give them our moral support because there isn't a thing we can do to keep him out of the Army. We may have some limited influence as to where he goes, but there are no guarantees. But Maggie—"

"What about her?"

"Maggie's fine, Bud. Please listen. I'm concerned about your relationship with her."

"I don't understand."

"This war has taken tens of thousands of young lives and destroyed families across the country. You know that more than anyone."

"And?"

"And as bad as it's been, it's not over. More young men are going to die before it ends, and more families are going to be affected. You lost a brother and I a son. That killed your mother more than anything else. You've dealt with it better than I ever expected, and you've been my rock of support through it all. For that, I'm grateful."

"Dad, we're in this together."

"Yes, we are, but more than you know. You're part of the CIA now. Just like me and many others you'll never meet, you'll be asked to go to places and do things that many Americans would not only find offensive, but would flat-out call criminal. You'll be in harm's way, and how you handle yourself will, in large measure, determine the outcome of your particular operation and whether or not you survive."

"I understand that, Dad, but what's your point?"

"My point is that you can't allow your actions to be clouded by emotions. You must be focused on your mission to the exclusion of almost everything and everyone else."

"Maggie?"

"Yes."

Bill stared at his father. "Am I supposed to stop seeing her?"

"No. I'm just saying that you can't become too involved with her, at least for the time being. You must understand the serious nature of what lies ahead. You'll be working under deep cover, and no one will acknowledge you. You'll be virtually unknown, except to a select few. It must remain that way. Don't misunderstand, Bill. I'm not discouraging you and Maggie from seeing each other, but I am saying that it can't go beyond a casual relationship. At least for the time being.

"Bill, we've lost people for all manner of reasons, but the overriding one is relationships exploited by foreign agents. One agent in the Middle East was compromised when his wife and children were captured by terrorists. They tortured them in front of him. He cracked under the pressure, and all of them were murdered.

"Maggie's a wonderful girl and I'd be proud to have her as a daughter-in-law. But she knows nothing of your involvement with the Agency, and if you two become involved such that someone could exploit it, then both of you would be in mortal danger, and you would no longer be a viable asset to us."

"Viable Asset? What does *that* mean? Is that government-speak for a spy that's lost it?" Bill was being sarcastic, but deep inside he knew his father was right.

"I'm sorry, Bill, but I had to say it." Wilder closed his eyes for a moment and rubbed the back of his neck. "Let me put it this way; if Petrov finds out that you and Maggie are involved, do you think that he'll go out of his way *not* to harm her? Do you know what he did to those other women?"

Bill shook his head. "No. And I don't want to know either."

"Her life would be in great danger. That's all I can say. Neither of us wants that."

Bill looked out the window while considering his father's remarks. "No, we don't." He knew that this subject would come up sooner or later, and he was ready to deal with it. "Dad, I agree with you. You can count on me."

Wilder smiled sadly at his son. "There was never a doubt, Bud." Time for a change of subject. "Now get out of here. Go get some rest. Martial training begins day after tomorrow, and I trust you'll give more than receive."

The grin returned. "A wise man once told me that no matter how good I am, there's always someone better. Let's just say there's a trick or two up my sleeve." Bill walked to the door. He turned and looked at his father, his face a microcosm of events that had shaped his life in recent years. "Half our family is gone. I won't let anything happen to the rest. I won't let you down." He opened the door.

"I know, Bud, but it was necessary to have this talk."

"Get some rest, Dad. Check you later." Bill closed the door behind him and walked down the hall.

"Be careful, son," Wilder said to the empty room. He sat in his son's leather chair and looked briefly at the bottle of bourbon on the table. He closed his eyes and dreamed of better times past.

CHAPTER 3

NOVEMBER 1970

The *Ding-How Dog* was a popular Chinese restaurant in Franconia, Virginia. The food and refreshment added to the atmosphere to make the restaurant a favorite, especially among young adults. Maggie, Wilder, and Slaughter had all been there several times, but this was the first time the three had been together in over a year. Much had happened since then, and they relished the time together.

"Good groceries." Slaughter slurped his won-ton soup. He shoved a small egg roll into his mouth and washed it down with beer. "Best chow I've had in a while."

"You have the manners of a goat." Maggie laughed at him.

"You're being kind," Wilder said. He looked at his friend and shook his head. "The poor guy doesn't know how to spell fork, much less how to use one. Forget chopsticks. Just pat him on the head and say, 'it's okay.'"

"Flattery will get you nowhere." Slaughter leaned back in his chair and belched. "Ah, that's better." He looked around the table. "When's the main course coming?"

"You act like you haven't eaten in a month," Maggie said, pushing her chicken fingers across the table to him. "Here." She pulled her hand back as if he would bite it.

"I was wondering if you were going to eat them or talk them to death." Slaughter wolfed down the food and reached for another beer. He glanced at Wilder, winked, then looked at Maggie. "You're almost right. Been camping out for a while, and I was too lazy to cook. This is the first real meal I've enjoyed in a spell."

Wilder smiled to himself. He remembered the stale bread and warm water.

The waiter approached the table with a large tray. Slaughter rubbed his hands together in anticipation. Anyone else would have been offended at his manners, but Maggie and Wilder were used to it. It amused them to watch him, and for his part, Slaughter played his role to the hilt. The three friends dined on won-ton soup, pork fried rice, shrimp, egg rolls, and cashew chicken. Slaughter guzzled beer while the other two drank rice wine and hot tea.

The food was good and the conversation light. It revolved around family, friends, and the local goings-on in Washington. Although Vietnam was next on their agenda, neither Wilder nor Slaughter gave it a thought. It was the furthest thing from their minds.

But Maggie changed all that with a few words. "I have a surprise for you."

"Let me guess." Slaughter wiped the beer from his mouth with his sleeve. "You guys are in heat and you're gonna tie the knot. Then you'll hike to Vermont, live in a tee-pee, and hug trees."

"I prefer a yurt," Wilder said, not missing a beat.

Maggie stared at them in disgust. "Don't you bottom-feeders ever take anything serious?" Her stern expression was accented by the hands on the hips, but the smile on the corners of her mouth gave her away.

"Watch out, Bill. She's gonna put the mo-jo on us." Slaughter covered his head with a napkin.

"I think she's serious, John." Wilder touched her arm. "We're just having a little fun with you, Red. So, what's the big surprise?"

Her face lit up. "UPI just gave me my first field assignment. I've been given a chance to cover Vietnam first hand."

"What?" The smile vanished from Wilder's face.

"That's right. I'm going to Vietnam with you guys on Monday

out of Dulles. We're all on the same flight. Isn't that wonderful?" Her eyes darted back and forth, looking for their approval.

Wilder's face clouded over. "Maggie, that's a dangerous place for a woman. Are you sure about this? Have you thought this through?"

She saw the doubt in his eyes, and she held his hand in hers. "Look, Bill, I've worked my tail off in the short time I've been with UPI, and this is the chance of a lifetime. A lot of people were passed up for this one, and I jumped at the chance when asked if I'd go. Just think, it'll give me the opportunity to report on the war as it happens and to tell the truth about what's going on. And it's not *that* dangerous. I'll be staying at the Caravelle Hotel in Saigon with the other correspondents. It's safe enough. Besides, we'll get to see each other ..." There was a hint of disappointment in her voice when she saw his expression.

"Is this something you really want?"

"Yes, Bill, it is. More than anything ... besides you."

"Oh, hell! Here we go again with the mush stuff," Slaughter said, lifting the napkin from his head and finishing off his last beer. He motioned to the waiter for another.

Wilder saw the hope in her eyes, and he began to realize how much this assignment meant to her. There was nothing he could do about it anyway, so he decided to at least make her comfortable with it. "You know, it might be kind of nice having you around." The grin returned. "I think this calls for drinks and a toast." He knew how hard Maggie had worked for this assignment, and she desperately wanted his approval. He didn't like the idea of her being in Vietnam, but he didn't want to disappoint her either. "Yep, it'll be nice having you around."

"Great. Just what we need." Slaughter rolled his eyes.

"What's that?" Maggie asked.

"A round-eyed mama-san looking over our shoulders."

"Don't worry, Animal. It'll take all of your short attention span just to stay ahead of the *tee-loks*. Just keep your money in your pockets and your pants zipped. You'll be okay."

Maggie laughed. "Don't worry, John, I'll only print the truth."

"Shit! That's what I'm afraid of." Slaughter threw his hands into the air. "I'm doomed."

Maggie laughed. "Okay, okay. In your case, Animal, I promise not to print anything."

"Thank God." Another egg roll disappeared into Slaughter's face.

"And what's a *tee-lok*?"

"Just some of the local talent. A lady of the evening." Slaughter took the beer from the waiter. He looked at his friends and raised the bottle. "To the first casualty of war; truth."

"In your case, John, it'll be sobriety," Wilder said while watching the confrontation across the room.

"This dung ain't fit to eat, man," the first of three punks shouted, throwing his plate across the room. He pushed the restaurant owner backwards over a chair, and the hapless man hit the floor hard. "You're no better the dog you serve up. Eat this crap yourself."

"Yeah, Chan, get your shit together." The second punk laughed at the bleeding man and turned the table over, sending dishes and glasses crashing across the floor. "Hey, this is fun!" He walked to the table across from him and shook his fist at the elderly couple cringing in fear. "What the hell are you two fossils looking at?" He glared at them, his voice filled with hate. The senior couple lowered their heads, too frightened to say anything.

The last punk pulled the injured man to his feet. "Get up, you rice-ball! We're talking to you." He violently shook his victim.

"My God! Look at what they're doing to that poor man. Why doesn't someone stop them?" Maggie was upset. "They're hurting him!" She looked desperately at her companions, her face full of fear and uncertainty.

Wilder wiped his mouth and slowly folded his napkin. He looked at his friends and smiled. "Excuse me, guys. I'll be right back." He winked at Maggie, stood, and slowly walked towards the center of attention. Everyone's eyes followed him, but the bullies didn't see him coming. They were too preoccupied with their own designs.

Maggie's heart raced. "He's by himself, John. Go help him!" She gripped his arm.

Slaughter casually looked over his shoulder. Without a word he turned back towards the table and searched for another beer. "Ah, here we go. One left." He reached for the bottle and took a drink.

"John, are you listening to me? He needs your help!" Maggie was incredulous.

He offered only a lazy smile. "Relax, Maggie. He's got 'em surrounded." Slaughter picked up the last fried won-ton, studied it, and shoved it into his mouth. "Mmm, good."

"What? Oh, Christ!"

Wilder quietly stepped between Punk One and Punk Three from behind. Placing his hands on their shoulders, he said, "How's it going, guys? I take it you don't like the food."

They turned to him in surprise. "Who the hell are you?" Punk One shouted.

"I'm the Tooth Fairy, you dick-head, and I'm going to pull your teeth out. The hard way."

"You frigging bastard!" Punk One turned and swung at Wilder.

In one rapid motion Wilder blocked the punch and grabbed the man's arm. He jerked forward and swung his left elbow across the man's face. Punk One screamed as his teeth flew out of his mouth. At the same instant, Wilder's right foot flew out in a side stomp kick, snapping Punk Three's knee. The leg folded sideways, and the man fell to the floor screaming.

Punk One's hands flew to his face. Wilder pushed him back then gave him a front snap kick to the solar plexus. He fell backwards over a chair and curled into a ball, his face a bleeding mess.

"Son-of-a-bitch!" Punk Two shouted, having turned his attention from the elderly couple. He snapped open a switch blade knife and ran at the stranger across the room, swinging the blade back and forth.

Wilder was in motion, his hands level with the knife. The first swipe came across his face. Wilder leaned back and watched the blade slice the air in front of him. In the instant the knife passed, he went into action. Two vertical forearm blocks prevented the attacker's reverse swing. He grabbed the wrist holding the knife with his right hand. Turning to the outside, he elbowed the man in the ribs with his left elbow, knocking the wind out of him. He hooked the arm over his shoulder and pulled sharply down. The elbow snapped downwards with a sickening crack, and the knife fell to the floor. Wilder released his grip, and the man dropped in agony to his knees.

Wilder helped the Chinese man to his feet. "Mr. Lee, are you all right?"

"Yes, yes. Thank you, Bill." Holding his hand to his bleeding head, he bowed slightly and looked at the three broken bodies on the floor. "I think they should leave."

"I'll take care of it." Wilder walked to the first trouble maker and jerked him to his feet like a rag doll. Looking at the ruined face, he said, "Mr. Lee, I think your food is great. Don't you agree, cupcake?" The man moaned incoherently. "I thought you would. Now, pay Mr. Lee for the damage, then you and your grease-monkey pals get the hell out. If I catch you in here again, I'll stomp you into the ground so deep that you'll have to look up to see the bottom. Got it?"

Another moan.

"Good." Wilder dropped the man to the floor and turned to his friend. "Mr. Lee, if you have any more trouble with these goons, just let me know." He winked at Lee and walked across to the elderly couple, now wide-eyed. "Sorry for their poor manners, folks. Some people just aren't very smart. They won't bother you again. Enjoy your dinner." He smiled at them and casually walked back to his table, stepping over the bodies on the floor.

Taking his seat beside Maggie, Wilder picked up his napkin. He casually looked at his food and reached for his fork. "I especially like the cashew chicken."

Slaughter leaned on his elbows and said, "I thought we agreed that you wouldn't fight."

Wilder scooped up some chicken. "Who's fighting? I just gave a class in behavior modification."

Maggie stared at him, her mouth open.

Wilder looked at her with mock surprise on his face. "Well, this is history in the making."

"What's that?" Slaughter said.

"A speechless woman."

Maggie was too dumbfounded to speak, and her two friends jokingly made the most of it. Finally, they sat back and looked at each other.

"It was a set up."

"Yes, it was, John. And they saw what they came for."

Maggie's eyes darted back and forth between them. "What are you talking about?"

"Oh, nothing. Just guy stuff." Slaughter reached for another beer.

Monday

The van ride was quiet. Jack Wilder was behind the wheel with his brother-in-law in the right seat. Tom McIvor and Slaughter were in the next seat, while Bill and Maggie were in the last row. With the long plane ride to Vietnam just hours away, each was lost in thought.

Bill was taciturn. He hadn't said two words since leaving Franconia. He had steeled himself since the incident in the restaurant days before because he knew he was being watched. That Petrov was close by irritated him, only because he could do nothing about it. The crowded van was the perfect setup and everyone, except Maggie, knew it. Hence, the unmarked escorts that were armed to the teeth. Extra security had been added at Dulles International Airport for this particular flight, courtesy of the FBI. The DC-8 that would make the flight had been secured and screened by Secret Service agents, bomb sniffing dogs, and law enforcement officials from Herndon. Bill didn't like the idea of all of them being together in one van—an opportune target—but he had no choice. Like a tiger in a cage, he sat quietly and waited.

"Hell of a place for an airport," Slaughter said, breaking the silence. "Nothing out here but woods, snakes, and taxes. Looks like they'd use Andrews instead and put the Air Force out here when they couldn't bother anybody."

"You'd think so, John," Jack Wilder said, "but that makes too much sense."

"The pellet-heads in Washington will never figure it out."

"You're smart beyond your years, John, but nothing in this town ever changes." Wilder glanced into the rear-view mirror at his son.

Bill was staring out the window, his mind elsewhere.

Wilder had to do something to snap his son out of his dark mood. He looked at his watch. There was plenty of time to spare. "Hey, guys, how about a detour to Jake's for a beer and a bite? Got plenty of time. Courtesy of the geezers in the front seat." He looked into the mirror, hoping for a reaction.

"That's a wonderful idea," Maggie said. "How about it, guys?" She looked at her father. "Dad, you'll like Jake."

"Sounds good to me," McIvor said. He turned around. "What do you say, Bill?"

"Yeah, bone-head, what say you?" Slaughter added.

Bill looked at them. Everyone was staring back at him, including his father by way of the mirror. That they were concerned for him and showed it, lifted his spirits. He grinned. "What? We're not there yet?"

Wilder smiled to himself. "Be there in ten minutes." He glanced at Spencer in the right seat, who quietly made a call on his pocket transmitter. The caravan would detour to Jake's, whereupon the building would be surrounded by a small army of crew cuts in plain Fords.

"Hot damn!" Jake Newton shouted. He circled the bar and walked across the room, his hand extended. A lump rose in his throat when he saw his friends in Air Force uniforms, but he did his best to suppress it. "Welcome, guys. You've made my day. Come in. Come in." He shook hands with everyone and hugged Maggie.

"How goes the battle, Jake?" Bill looked around the room. There was no evidence of the explosion that almost took their lives.

"Got some great news, Billy boy." Newton beamed.

"What's that, my friend?"

"I've been accepted to medical school in Charlottesville. Who knows? Maybe I'll be your doc one day and give you a shot in the ass."

"Good for you, Jake. You've certainly worked hard for it. But *pain* in the ass is more like it. And I'll settle for a shot in the arm instead."

Maggie hugged him. "I'm so happy for you, Jake. You'll be a wonderful doctor."

"My sentiments exactly, Jake," Spencer added.

"Thanks to all of you, my friends." Newton turned to the bartender. "Hey, Sam, a round beers for everybody. This calls for a celebration. And burn some road-kill, will you? The boys and girls will be dining with us."

"Coming up."

Everyone was relaxed and having a good time. Wilder and his brother-in-law looked at each other. *Coming here was a good idea,* they both thought. Wilder's son was at ease in the familiar surroundings, and Slaughter was ahead of everyone else in the beer department, complaining that the bottles had holes in the bottom of them.

Everyone enjoyed the food, drink, and conversation. Newton was a gracious host, and he went out of his way to make his friends—and adopted family—feel welcomed. Were it not for these people, he would be nowhere, and he relished the opportunity to be with them.

They finished their lunch and sat back to relax with coffee. Newton looked at Bill. *Things need to be said.* "Let's take a walk, buddy."

"Let's go." They excused themselves and headed for the front door.

"Hey, while you yahoos are picking daisies, how about sending another beer this way?" Slaughter licked his chops and reached for Maggie's uneaten fries. "Can't let these scorched earth-apples go to waste now, can we?"

She didn't hear him. Her attention was focused on the two men walking across the room towards the door.

They circled the parking lot in silence. Wilder looked at the spot where his Mustang had been blown to pieces. It wasn't the car that bothered him, it was the reason behind it that burned in his mind.

Newton was troubled. "What's the story, Bill? You're the sole surviving son of a family that's already lost one soldier in 'Nam. You know you don't have to go. Why are you doing this, man?"

Looking across the lot, Wilder rubbed his chin. "You were right."

"What? What are you talking about?"

"Plastic explosives."

"I told you that. But what does that have to do with you going to gook-land?"

"Jake, I don't expect you to understand, but this is something I have to do. Since the explosion, a lot has happened, and believe me when I say that you don't want to know about it. Just accept it on faith from a friend."

"Well, I can't live with that. You and John are off to 'Nam in a little while, and you act like it's no big deal. That place is dangerous, man, and that war is screwed up."

"You're right on all counts, Jake, and I don't like it any more than you. But there are other considerations here that I can't go into. And there's another fly in the ointment. Maggie's going with us today. She got an assignment in Saigon with UPI."

"Shit!" Newton put his hands on his hips and shook his head in disgust.

"Couldn't stop her."

"That place is FUBAR, man. Fucked up beyond all repair. That government doesn't give a hoot-in-hell about you or the other Americans there. All those crooks care about is the almighty buck."

"I know that, Jake, but that's over my pay grade. I'm not going over there to run the government. I have my reasons and you'll just have to accept them." Bill put his hand on his friend's shoulder. "Trust me on this one, buddy."

Newton snorted and nodded his head in submission. "Just some advice from and old friend; watch your six, Bill. Keep your head down, and come home in one piece."

"Count on it." They shook hands and walked back to the building. There was nothing left to say.

In less than an hour they pulled onto the road for the short trip to the airport. Standing alone in the dirt, Newton gave a final wave. He watched them disappear for what could be the last time. "Godspeed, my friends. Come home soon."

Trying to be unobtrusive, the FBI agents stood out like sore thumbs with their cookie-cutter black suits and closely cropped hair. Their eyes searched the crowd as the van pulled up to the curb.

"Dad, we'll get our boarding passes and meet you guys in the lounge."

"Okay, Bud." Wilder sat behind the wheel and watched his son walk away as if they would never meet again. "I don't know who's the most nervous, them or us."

"Me either, Jack," McIvor said. "But chins up."

"Right."

"They're not my kids, but I know how you feel," Spencer said. "Let's keep our counsel for them as well as for ourselves."

"Easier said than done, but we'll do what we can." Wilder stepped out of the van and joined the other two men. They walked silently into the terminal.

"Excuse me. We're here for the Trans-American flight to Saigon that leaves at six," Maggie said, handing their collected paperwork to the young woman behind the counter.

The bored blond took the papers, shuffled them in official fashion, and stamped three boarding passes. Handing them back to Maggie, she said, "You have seats twenty A, B, and C." Her gum popped loudly when she spoke. "The flight boards in thirty minutes. Next." She never looked at them during the entire transaction.

The trio headed towards the bar adjacent to the boarding area. "That bubble-headed moon maid doesn't know up from down. Doesn't give a shit either. She needs a good stiff—"

"Drink. That's what we need. Let's have a cocktail before we board. Your dad's over there, Bill." Maggie walked across the room and stood beside her father. "I'm so excited!" Her face glowed in anticipation.

Tom McIvor smiled, despite his depression. "You're like a kid in a toy store, Maggie. You've been all over the world, but I've never seen you this excited before."

"I was little then. Now, I can make a difference."

"Yes, you can, kiddo." McIvor hugged his daughter. She couldn't feel the hurt in his heart.

"Colonel W, what's the chow like on this tub?" Slaughter asked. "Do they give us fresh road-kill, or do we get processed food loaf?"

"Let's put it this way, John; be glad you ate at Jake's. That burned piece of beast is the best meal you'll have for a while. But I'm sure you'll survive."

"Well, just in case, this wild animal will keep us company for the trip." Slaughter patted his shoulder bag.

"Wild animal?"

"Got a bottle of Turkey in here for emergencies, Colonel," Slaughter said with a grin.

Wilder laughed despite the ache in his gut. "John, you know it's against the rules to take booze on the plane."

"Well, what are they going to do, Colonel? Send me to Vietnam?"

"I guess so, John." Wilder looked around the room. He spotted Bill standing alone staring out the window. He walked over and stood beside his son.

Neither man spoke for several minutes. Each was lost in thought over the events that had led to this day. Finally, Bill said, "Mom and Little Jack are with us."

Wilder continued to look across the airport expanse, his emotions barely under control. "Yes, they are, Bud."

Bill looked at his father. "Dad, I know what you're going through, and I wouldn't trade places with you for the world. I swear I won't disappoint you."

The years had taken their toll, and the strain showed on Jack Wilder's face. He looked at his son. "You've never disappointed me in anything you've ever done, Bill, and I know you won't now. I'm …" His voice cracked.

"I know, Dad. You don't have to say anything."

"I have to say this. Bill, I've lost half my family, thanks to this ungodly war. I don't want to lose you too. But be that as it may, promise me that you won't lose sight of your objective and why you are here. Forget the politics that put us in this situation. Keep a clear head and do what you need to do." They stared at each other. "Just come home, Bud, in one piece." Wilder's eyes were filled with tears. It was the third time Bill had seen his father cry since Little Jack's death, Elizabeth's being the second.

Bill hugged his father. The man seemed frail now, not as strong as when Bill was a child. He held his father close to him for a long time. He wasn't ashamed to show affection for this man that had lost half of his family and had bucked up under the strain to support and encourage his only remaining son.

The scene was repeated throughout the terminal as the line of uniforms prepared to leave. Spencer and Slaughter talked quietly, as did Maggie and her father. Words of wisdom and encouragement passed, along with the Torch, from one generation to the next. Mothers and fathers watched proudly and helplessly while their children boarded the mobile lounge that would begin a journey that would take them half a world away.

"I love you, son," Wilder said.

"I love you too, Dad." Bill swallowed hard, picked up his bag and walked purposefully to the boarding platform. He didn't look back.

"… and I'll make you and Mom proud of me, I promise," Maggie said, crying through her smile. She wrapped her arms around her father's neck. "I love you." She picked up her purse and ran to join Bill.

Watching her walk away, Tom McIvor felt his heart break.

"Well, it's push and shove time," Slaughter said. "We're off to the land of Little People. Keep the porch light on and don't worry. I'll keep an eye on them." He looked at Bill and Maggie, already in line. "Gentlemen, your plane leaves right after ours. My folks are looking forward to seeing you. I promise the fishing in Texas is second to none. Have a good time. See ya." He shook their hands, winked, and left to join his friends.

They were on the other side of the room now waiting to board the mobile lounge that would take them to their plane. They may as well have been the other side of the world.

The DC-8 was packed. Servicemen from all branches of the military, as well as civil service civilians, filled the plane. The faces of the younger troops were a microcosm of fear and anxiety, their lives now under the control of a nebulous being known as Uncle Sam. The more seasoned veterans heading back for their second or third tour showed nothing more than a bored tolerance for their juniors and the long flight that lay ahead. For them the flight to the other side of the world would be nothing more than an endurance run.

The trio found their row. "How'd you get the middle seat?" Slaughter sat by the aisle. "A pain worse than death as far as I'm concerned."

"Fine by me," Maggie said. Looking out the window only made her air sick, and she didn't want to be on the aisle so everybody else could bump into her. She knew the other two wouldn't stand for the center seat anyway. "I'd rather be sitting here between two known quantities than between two high school graduates with runaway hormones. That could make for a long flight. Besides, I have my man next to me." She squeezed Wilder's arm and winked at Slaughter.

"Christ, is there no escape? Am I the condemned man that has to listen to this mush for the next eighteen hours?" Slaughter unpacked the bottle of Wild Turkey. Looking at it he said, "Well, I guess it's you and me, pal. The party begins in minutes." He looked across at Wilder. "How about a snort when this tub gets off the ground? Gonna be a long flight."

"Careful, John. That bird will kick your butt if you don't watch it."

Slaughter's give-a-shit look stared back at Wilder.

"All right. But wait til the donut dollies finish cruising the aisle, okay?"

"Donut dollies?" Maggie feigned insult.

"I guess I can wait that long." Slaughter leaned back in his seat and closed his eyes. He was asleep in minutes.

Maggie looked at him and shook her head. "Amazing. That man can sleep anywhere. Doesn't anything bother him?"

"Wish I was like him." Wilder looked around the cabin.

She sensed his nervousness and tugged on his arm. "You're fine the way you are. Just sit back and enjoy the ride, okay?" She leaned over and kissed his cheek. "Who knows? You might get lucky before we get to Vietnam." She pursed her lips when he looked at her.

"Not unless you can turn yourself into a ball under a blanket. This aluminum tube is packed to the ceiling." He looked around the cabin once more, his eyes finally settling on Maggie. "I'm fine, Red. Just don't like not being in control. Pilots make lousy passengers." He kissed her hand.

"You guys are impossible. Always want to be in the driver's seat." She leaned her head against his shoulder and closed her eyes, the whine of the jet's engines relaxing her as the aircraft taxied to the runway.

The flight attendants' safety briefing was followed by a welcome from the captain. "Ladies and gentlemen, I'd like to take this oppor-

tunity to welcome you aboard ... " Few listened to the droll mono-
tone of the announcement. Their thoughts were elsewhere.

The jet lined up on runway 30, and the captain pushed the throttles forward. The engines roared to life, and the DC-8 began to race
down the runway. The nose lifted and the aircraft rose into the air.
After the landing gear and flaps were retracted, the ship turned towards the northwest and set a course for Anchorage, Alaska. Now
that the flight had begun, the passengers resigned themselves to
hours of boredom. Few words were spoken as the first leg of the long
journey to Vietnam got underway.

CHAPTER 4

SAIGON, SOUTH VIETNAM
NOVEMBER 1970

Saigon wore many faces. Originally settled by the Cambodians, it has been a major port city for centuries. It got the name from the French when they began using it as a base of operations in 1861 for their takeover attempt of the country. In 1956 Ngo Dinh Diem, the Catholic ruler of South Vietnam at that time, declared Saigon the capital city of the South. It was as corrupt as it was exotic, and one could find anything there for the right price.

Tan Son Nhut Air Force Base, located on the fringe of Saigon, was the major commercial and military airport in the region, and it handled most of the American military traffic from the United States. In 1970 the Seventh Air Force, located at Tan Son Nhut, controlled all military operations both into and out of the country, as well as "in-country" operations. The US Military Assistance Command, Vietnam, or MACV, was the headquarters of all military operations in the country, and it was also based at Tan Son Nhut. The base was often referred to as "Pentagon East" because it was the *de facto* head-quarters of the American presence in the country.

The DC-8 taxied to the commercial end of the airfield. The engines were shut down, and a Vietnamese ground crew positioned portable air stairs against the fuselage. The flight attendant opened the main entrance door and stood aside to allow her weary passengers to deplane. The oppressive heat and humidity assaulted their senses when they stepped into the harsh Vietnamese mid-day sun. They slowly shuffled off the plane and walked to the terminal where military and civilian officials waited to process them to their various units.

"S'um bitch," Slaughter growled. "Hotter than a blistered pussy in a pepper patch." He wiped his brow with a handkerchief and threw his jacket over his shoulder.

"Yes, it is," Maggie said, shielding her eyes from the blazing sun. "Guess we need to follow the crowd to the terminal." She nervously held Wilder's hand.

"I'm sure UPI's arranged for someone to meet you, Maggie. We'll get you settled then see what's in store for us." Wilder led them towards the terminal where representatives from the various military services, as well as news organizations, waited in their separate areas for the arriving passengers.

"Maggie!" A plump gray-haired elderly gentleman in a tan suit waved from the main terminal entrance leading to the tarmac. He waddled more than walked towards the trio. "Welcome, my child. Jolly good to see you again, my dear." He kissed her hand and offered a bouquet of flowers. "Orchids. They grow quite well here, you know."

"Terry! I'm so glad to see you." She took the flowers and smelled them. The nervousness evaporated. "Thank you so much."

"I trust you had a nice flight?" He beamed at the trio, his smile infectious and genuine. "Terry McAlester, from the UPI Washington bureau, at your service, gentlemen."

"Terry, this is Bill Wilder and John Slaughter. They're dear friends of mine." Maggie smiled proudly as she introduced the two pilots.

"Mr. McAlester, it's a pleasure, sir. I've heard a great deal about you," Wilder said, shaking the Englishman's hand.

"Dear me! I hope the lady didn't embellish things too much. And please call me Terry."

"She was as honest as the day is long, Terry." Wilder liked him instantly. McAlester reminded him of his uncle Spencer in many ways. He was relieved, knowing that Maggie would be secure under his watchful eye.

"Glad to meet you, Terry, but I have one question. How can you Brits drink your beer at room temperature? Back at the homestead we drink it cold." Slaughter offered a toothy grin and a firm hand shake.

"Don't mind him, Terry. He has the tact of a medicine ball," Maggie said.

"Ah, you chaps are refreshing. In Vietnam, John, certain allowances are made. We Brits actually drink our beer quite cold. As a matter of fact, when you gentlemen have finished here and have had a chance to freshen up a bit, I insist that you dine with me at the Caravelle at seven. I'll send my car for you. Will you join me?"

"Is a pig pork?"

Maggie looked down in embarrassment. Wilder just laughed. "What John's trying to say, Terry, is that we'd be delighted to come. He also says 'thank you.'"

"Splendid then. Here's my card. Call me when you're ready. My driver will pick you up at the Herky Hilton. That will be your quarters while on base at Tan Son Nhut. I think you will find it … interesting."

Wilder scratched his head. "My imagination is already working overtime. We're looking forward to dinner, Terry, and thanks for helping Maggie." He turned to her and placed both hands gently on her shoulders. "Everything will be fine, Red. Go relax with a hot bath and a nap. I'll call after John and I get squared away. Okay?" He kissed her cheek.

"Okay."

Wilder winked at McAlester and picked up his bag. "John, let's go check out the fancy digs our hosts have prepared for us."

"No room at the inn, I'll bet. If we have to sleep in the barn, I got dibs on the manger." They waved to Maggie and McAlester and walked to the Air Force processing line.

"Quite a pair, that," McAlester said, watching the two men walk away. "John is a colorful fellow, isn't he?"

"That's an understatement." She missed them already.

"Bill appears to be a fine chap. I can see that you fancy him quite bit." A fatherly smile.

"I love him."

They wove their way through the narrow streets of Saigon on their way to the Caravelle Hotel. The roads were congested with mopeds, bicycles, and hop-tacs, which were three wheeled motor scooters with makeshift seats on the back for passengers. A poor man's taxi would have been the proper term in some countries, but in Saigon, it was a major mode of transportation. An occasional Puegeot and Mercedes added to the congestion, throw backs to French colonial rule long since past. Diesel fumes combined with different smells from the open air markets and open sewers to create an acrid odor that accosted the senses. The sights and sounds of Saigon were a world apart from those of Washington.

"How do these people survive in this?" Maggie asked as the car made its way through the mass of vehicles and humanity.

"Does appear a bit unorganized, doesn't it?" McAlester said. "Actually, it's quite logical if you think about it. The person with the loudest horn and the largest set of—balls?—as you say, has the right-of-way. Just takes a while to get used to it."

Maggie was fascinated and her eyes took in everything around her. "Is it safe to walk the streets?"

"That's a matter of opinion and depends on a large measure on who you are. As a young American woman, I would not go out without an escort. There are areas where you obviously can't go, but we'll tell you all about that when you get your in-briefing tomorrow. Suffice it to say, my dear, that one must keep one's guard up at all times."

"I'll remember that."

"I must also caution you not to believe everything you hear, even from official sources."

She looked at him. "What do you mean?"

"Let me explain… "

The blue Air Force school bus stopped in front of the billeting office. The white concrete building was covered with a green tin roof.

A sign over the main door read *Herky Hilton*. The driver swung the door open, and the sweating passengers filed off the bus and into the melting heat. They were blasted with cold air from the air conditioner above the door when they entered the building.

"Sure am glad I brought my ear muffs," Slaughter said, noticing the beer machine just inside the building. Reaching into his pocket for change, he walked straight for it. "At least it's cool in here."

"Could be worse, John. We could be living in a bunker in a forward fire base. Being an Air Force weenie has its advantages." Wilder looked around the hallway. "Concrete building with almost no windows. Wonder what they're trying to tell us?"

"Go to your home, prisoners," Slaughter said, taking two beers from the machine and handing one to Wilder. "Survival training at Fairchild."

"Don't remind me."

"Let's get this shit over with and grab a shower. I smell like last week's scraps."

The sergeant behind the desk was prepared for the onslaught of junior officers coming through the door. Paperwork and room keys were pre-arranged on the counter. Everyone paired off with roommates and shuffled down the hall to the quarters that they would call *home* for the next twelve months.

Wilder opened the door and stepped inside. The room was sparse but functional. There was a metal bunk bed, two dressers, and a closet. The Sears air conditioner was wheezing and chugging on borrowed time, but considering the heat wave outside, it was holding its own. There were no decorations other than a black and white picture of President Nixon hanging on a nail.

"Puke green walls and military issue brown floor tile. Where's Julia What's-Her-Face when you need her? Not even a bathroom. Common head and showers down the hall. I gotta give up my housing allowance for this hovel? I'm complaining to the landlord."

"What are you complaining about now? There's beer down the hall, and it's only ten cents a can. Besides, you're not next to the elevator. By the way, since you took the manger, I claim the bottom bunk." Tossing his duffel bag into the corner, Wilder took off his shirt and shoes and dropped onto the bed. He finished his beer and lay back with his hands behind his head. "O'Club is just down the street. Not all that bad."

"There ain't no elevator." Slaughter picked up the information packet on the dresser and thumbed through it. "Looks like an in-processing schedule. Says we gotta be at the personnel office at 0800 tomorrow. We fly on day two."

"Well, at least they're not wasting time." Wilder propped himself up on one elbow. "Anything in there about an intelligence briefing?" He was anxious to make his contacts.

Slaughter scanned the document. "Yeah. Intel and in-country briefing at 1500 today. Bring your ID card, assignment orders, blah, blah. Lieutenant Ber—" His words froze in his throat.

"What's wrong with you? Swallow your tongue again?"

Slaughter looked at him. "Berwick."

"What?" Wilder swung his feet over and sat on the side of his bed. "Can't be." The two men stared at each other.

"One way to find out." Slaughter picked up the phone and dialed the four digit extension listed on the brochure.

"Wing Intel. Berwick here."

Slaughter listened carefully to the voice on the other end of the line. He looked at Wilder and slowly hung up the phone. "It's him, Bill."

"Are you sure?"

"As sure as I'm looking at your mug."

"Well, this is a new twist. I wonder what he's doing here." Wilder's thoughts ran the gamut.

"You're going to find out soon enough."

Wilder lay back on the bed and looked at the springs on the bunk over him. "Nothing we can do now. May as well relax for a while before show-and-tell." He closed his eyes. Berwick would have to wait.

"Roger, that." Slaughter went for another beer.

"... You'll become intimately familiar with Saigon, but the city is only a small part of the enigma that is South Vietnam. What goes on in the field is the important thing. Maggie, I know of your feelings concerning this war, but you must set them aside here. It's up to us to print the truth, be it good or bad. I must tell you, however, that the truth is not always forthcoming, unfortunately."

"I don't understand, Terry. Doesn't MACV cooperate with the press?"

"Not always, my dear. MACV is responsible for giving us information daily on events that happen in the field. To that end they have directed the Joint United States Public Affairs Office, or JUSPAO, to do the briefings. The relationship between the press and the chaps at JUSPAO is, shall we say, less than cooperative.

"Often there is confusion at the briefings, contrived or otherwise, and official reports are frequently inaccurate or incomplete. Vietcong losses are often overstated, while American losses are downplayed. We quite often don't know whether to believe the information or not." McAlester mopped his brow, despite the air conditioned Land Rover. "The briefings are presented each day at five in the afternoon. We have come to call them the Five O'clock Follies. You'll see your first one this afternoon."

Maggie was incredulous. "Are you saying that the public affairs people, or whatever you call them, aren't telling the truth?"

"In a manner of speaking, yes. JUSPAO often sanitizes its briefings to make the Americans look better than they are." He sensed her anxiety but pressed ahead. "Maggie, it's been that way since the press first covered combat. I can't completely fault those chaps that give the briefings. After all, the Vietcong and North Vietnamese have representatives there too. We mustn't give them valuable information, must we?"

She stared at him in disbelief. "Are you saying that there are enemy agents at those briefings?"

"Indeed, my dear. They're everywhere. The Follies are only part of it. That's why we have people, along with the other agencies, in the field getting their information first hand. It's up to us, Maggie—you and me—to put that information together and get it to the public without giving aid and comfort to the enemy. Our task is a formidable one, and we must be vigilant and use sources where we find them. But we also must be weary of the enemy we cannot see. They are not all Oriental. This is an unconventional war, and unconventional rules apply."

"Damn!" Maggie looked straight ahead, her preconceived notions crumbling around her.

"Quite."

CHAPTER 5

"Lieutenant Berwick's at lunch. He won't be back for another thirty minutes," the staff sergeant said, standing at attention.

"I'll wait in his office."

"But he—"

"No buts." Wilder was polite but firm. "And please don't tell him I'm here. It's a surprise."

"Yes, sir." The sergeant went about his business. He was in the last month of his tour, and he just wanted to keep his nose clean and go home. What difference would it make anyway if one zero waited on another? *They can all have this place*, he thought.

"I'll wait in the briefing room," Slaughter said. "If you need any help, just scream."

"Right." Wilder went into Berwick's office and closed the door.

"Why do I think the war just escalated?" Slaughter said aloud, heading for the briefing room.

Minutes later Berwick opened the door and stepped into his office. He dropped his hat to the floor and froze. "… Wilder!"

"Hello, Berwick." Wilder looked at him deadpan. "Heard you

were here and thought I'd drop by." He sat calmly behind Berwick's desk.

"Uh, what *are* you doing here?"

"Been assigned to the C-130 squadron."

Berwick was visibly nervous, but he had no choice but to face his nemesis. "I'm, uh, working with the intelligence people here."

Wilder stared at him.

Berwick took a step back. "Look, Bill, I don't want any trouble. About what happened between you and me a few years ago ... let's put it behind us, okay? Things have changed for me, and I have no fight with you. We've had our—"

"One question. You were anti-everything at the Institute. What the hell are you doing here in an Air Force uniform?" Wilder sat perfectly still, his eyes boring into Berwick's

Berwick was beginning to perspire despite the cold air in the office. "When I left Lexington, I went to the University of Vermont. I thought school would protect me, but I got a draft notice just before graduation. I decided to join the Air Force and go into the intelligence field because I didn't want to wind up in a fox hole or in some remote fire base with Charlie shooting at me. Figured that this would be the easiest way out. I—"

"Daddy couldn't get you out of it?" Wilder was caustic.

"He wouldn't discuss it. Said he'd done his turn, and now it was mine." Berwick rubbed his palms against his thighs.

His actions didn't go unnoticed. "Are you the only one here? I don't like the idea of basing my decisions solely on what information *you* give me."

"Uh, no. A new guy just got here. Captain Jerry Bryant. He's a former C-130 navigator on his second tour. We're in the same office. He'll be in charge."

"John and I met him already. Flew over with us."

"Slaughter's here?"

"He is."

Berwick unconsciously looked at the ceiling.

Wilder looked at the clock on the wall then back at Berwick. "Better get moving. It's time for your briefing."

Berwick picked up a folder and a stack of overhead slides from his desk and left the room without another word. Wilder followed at a distance.

Slaughter turned his head when Wilder sat down. "Interesting conversation?"

"Very."

"Good afternoon, gentlemen, and welcome to Vietnam. I'm Captain Jerry Bryant and this is Lieutenant Berwick. This is your initial in-country intelligence briefing. It will be a basic overview as you will get more specific information when you head out on your missions. We'll cover current threats to the local area by the Vietcong and North Vietnamese. But first Berwick will brief you on a special operation that has just taken place in North Vietnam. The operation itself was classified, but now that it's over, the results will soon be public knowledge." He waved Berwick to the podium and took a seat.

Berwick looked across the room. Wilder and Slaughter sat in the center of the back row, their attention focused on him. "Good afternoon, gentlemen. I'm Lieutenant Berwick." He spoke to the crowd but his eyes were on Wilder. "Yesterday, a rescue team consisting of Special Forces and Army Rangers conducted a nighttime raid on the Son Tay Prison twenty-three miles west of Hanoi. A fifty-six man assault team was dropped by helicopter into the compound in an effort to rescue a suspected number of American POW's ranging from seventy to a hundred. A CIA contact in North Vietnam provided information that the POW's may have been moved prior to the rescue attempt, but it was decided to carry out the raid anyway in the event that the prisoners were still there.

"The assault team received little resistance since they landed at night and weren't expected. The prisoners, however, were gone." Berwick looked straight at Wilder. "They had been moved earlier to a prison in Hanoi called the Hanoi Hilton.... "

It was late afternoon and the tropical heat was intense. With the briefings complete for the day, everyone wanted to cool down before work began in earnest the following morning.

"What kind of beer you got?" Slaughter sat on a bar stool at the O'Club.

"Brak Rabel," the Vietnamese bartender said. "Number one. You want?"

"Black Label?" Slaughter shook his head in disgust. "Well, there's some beers that I prefer but none I won't drink. Two *Brak Rabels*, please."

Wilder walked across the room and sat down beside him. "Quite a place, eh, John? Bunkers and sand bags everywhere."

"Yeah. And watch your step when you leave. You fall into one of those big benjo ditches, and there ain't no telling what's gonna grow out of you. There's stuff in there I ain't ever seen."

"Guess open sewers are cheaper than laying pipe." Wilder looked around the room. He saw Bryant sitting at the far end of the bar and motioned him over.

"The biggest one runs behind the kitchen. At least the cook won't have far to go to do his shopping." Slaughter picked up the red can of beer, looked at it, and made a sour face. "May your crotch rot off." He emptied the can in just a few gulps.

"Hey," Bryant said, taking a seat beside Wilder. He looked around the room. "It ain't the Ritz but it'll do." He gestured to the bartender. "Gin and tonic and two more beers for my friends." He turned to Wilder. "Hope you guys got something useful from the briefing today. Most of that stuff is sanitized, but you'll get more specific info when you show up for your missions." Bryant hesitated for a moment but decided to say it anyway. "Berwick told me about your prior run-in with him in school. Guess I should have given the briefing, but I didn't have time to prepare as I just got here with you."

"No big deal," Wilder said. It was time to change the subject. "Guess all of us are flying together day after tomorrow. Mission number 005."

"Yes, we are. This is my second tour. I was a crew dog the first time around, but now I'm a desk jockey. I'm going along to get a feel for things and because this mission is a special one. Can't say anything in here obviously, but I think you guys will like it."

"Are we flying with staff weenies or real people?"

"A regular crew, John. The aircraft commander is a guy named Ed Custer. Doesn't pay much attention to the rules, or so I hear, but he knows his stuff. He's an instructor pilot, and he's going to check you guys out for in-country operations. Should be an interesting mission."

"Looking forward to it," Wilder said. He held up his beer. "Here's to our first flight."

"Yep," Slaughter said, emptying another can.

"I thought I'd find you bottom-feeders in here." Maggie walked quickly across the room and wrapped her arms around Wilder's neck. She was oblivious to the leering eyes of the other men in the room.

"Hey, Red. How's the Caravelle?"

"It's pandemonium over there. You wouldn't believe it." Wilder patiently listened while Maggie went on about the goings-on with the press and their military opposites. All eyes in the room were fixed on her. Wilder was aware of the stares. As long as no one tried anything, he didn't mind. Should someone get any wrong ideas, he could easily handle it.

"Slow down, Maggie," Wilder politely interrupted. "There's plenty of time for that. How about a beer?"

"What kind?"

"Brak Rabel," Slaughter chimed in. "Tastes more like goat piss than beer, but it's the only game in town."

"Then Black Label it is." She looked around the room and noticed everyone looking at her. She unconsciously stepped closer to Wilder.

Seeing the unease in her face, he placed his hand on her shoulder to reassure her. "Maggie, I want you to meet one of the guys that came over on the plane with us. This is Jerry Bryant. He's assigned to Wing Intelligence. He's going with me and John on our first mission."

She extended her hand but didn't budge from Wilder's side. "Hello, Captain Bryant."

"Hi, Maggie. Please call me Jerry. It's rare to see such a nice lady in here. I hope we get to see you often."

"Yes, well, Bill and I will be together a lot." She withdrew her hand and backed against Wilder. She was uncomfortable now. She looked at him and said, "You're off til tomorrow, aren't you?"

"Yes, and I'm ready to go to the Caravelle for Terry's special dinner."

"Good. Let's go."

"You guys go ahead," Slaughter said, looking at his beer. "There's a steak in every can. Tell Terry that I'll take a rain check."

"I'll give him your regards, John. In the meantime, a lady has invited me to dinner. I think it'll be a step above what the cook is pulling out of the benjo ditch behind the kitchen." He slapped Slaughter on the back. "Watch out for the *Brak Rabel*. It'll kick you between the eyes."

Slaughter belched. "Catch it and paint it green."

"I don't like him." Maggie slammed the door on the Land Rover.

"Who?"

"Bryant."

"You saw the way those guys looked at you. Occidental women are a rarity in this part of the world, and when a good looking *round-eye* walks into the room, it draws attention. You have to expect it. Just don't encourage them. That's all."

"It wasn't *them*. It was *him*."

"He's no different than the rest of them, Maggie." *Change the subject.* "Anything worth looking at in the hotel? John might be interested." Being one of the few American women in a foreign land full of soldiers gave her good reason to feel uncomfortable, he thought. *Okay, she's entitled.*

"I didn't notice," she said, looking out the window in disgust.

The driver maneuvered the Land Rover through the Saigon streets like an experienced race car driver. They arrived at the Caravelle where McAlester greeted them with cocktails, French onion soup, and roast suckling pig. Dinner was exceptional and everyone enjoyed themselves. Wilder ate more than his usual. It was too good to pass up. A workout would be first on the agenda tomorrow.

The Vietnamese band hammered out more noise than music. Their attempt at *Yellow River* sounded more like *Jello Leever*, and the rest of their words were unrecognizable. The effort to Americanize the place fell short, but they made the effort.

Slaughter and Bryant were on their next round of drinks.

"Maggie's a nice girl," Bryant said. "She's working for UPI?"

"Yep. She's one of the boys." Slaughter emptied his beer and reached for another. "Her old man was the skipper on the *Ticonderoga* when Bill's brother got shot down. He and Bill's dad are good friends."

"He lost a brother?" Bryant stirred his drink with his finger.

"Yeah. He was a POW in North Vietnam." Slaughter looked at Bryant. "By the way, Berwick's briefing on the Son Tay raid went over like a fart in church. Wasn't necessary. Watch out for that bastard. He's no good." Returning to his beer, he said, "Some Russian bastard shot Little Jack in the head with his own gun." He faced Bryant. "Takes a real chicken shit asshole to do something like that, doesn't it?"

"That's the truth. Damn rotten luck." Bryant finished his drink. "What's the story on Maggie? Looks like she and Bill are pretty tight."

"Tight as green on grass. He's my best friend and he's been through hell. She's good for him. I hope they get married when we get back to the States. I'll throw a bachelor party for him that will make Attila the Hun blush. We just have to get through this bullshit first." Slaughter waved his hand at nothing in particular and at Vietnam in general. "Let's have another round."

"Okay."

After dinner McAlester bid them a good evening and retired to his quarters. In her suite Maggie patiently watched Wilder while he stared through the French doors at the expanse of the city. "A penny for your thoughts."

"We've been here one day, and already I think the American presence is a waste of time," Wilder said. "These people are just trying to make ends meet while the government screws them at every turn. I can imagine what the average slug in the rice paddies thinks. They're not much different than us; their lives are controlled by the power junkies that are trying to make a name for themselves."

"Terry calls this place an enigma. He said that we can't trust our own people to be honest with us."

He looked at her. "How's that?"

"The authorities aren't being completely straight with the press. The numbers of people killed are juggled to suit them, and they won't give us all the facts. The military calls it *body count*. I don't like it. Why can't they just be honest?"

Wilder continued to stare out the window. "There's a war going on, Maggie. I know exactly what you're talking about. Seen it before. Call it propaganda, damage control, body count, or whatever you want. It's all the same." He sat his wine glass on the table and sat beside her. "You're too honest for your own good. Just go with the flow, and report the truth as you see it. You'll be fine."

She put her hands on his face. "You're a light in this cave of darkness. You've made me so happy. I love you so much."

"I love you, too." He swept her up in his arms and carried her into the bedroom. Placing her gently onto the bed, he said, "I'll be busy for the next several days. This could be our last night together for a while."

"Don't do anything dumb, mister. I kinda like you in one piece." She pulled his face to hers. They kissed. "Make love to me."

CHAPTER 6

"Looks like everybody's here," Major Ed Custer said, looking around the room. He slumped in his chair and hung his feet over the one in front of him. "Let's get on with it."

"Gentlemen, I'm Captain Jerry Bryant, and here's what's in store for today. You're going to Da Nang and pickup North Vietnamese and Vietcong prisoners. Then you'll carry them to Con Son Island down south." He stopped to make introductions. "Major Custer, this is Bill Wilder and John Slaughter, your F-N-G's. They'll be part of your crew til they get checked out. I'll be going with you. I won't be acting as a crew member. Just freeloading."

"Fresh meat," Custer said, looking at the two pilots next to him. "Where are you guys from?"

"Franconia, Virginia."

"Denton, Texas."

They shook hands and Custer said, "Welcome to the land time forgot."

"Guess you've seen it all."

"Let's just say that if the Almighty ever decided to give the earth an enema, He'd stick it right here." He pointed to the floor, the inference to Vietnam obvious. "Anyway, most of our missions are of the trash-hauling variety, but you guys get to cut your teeth on something different for a change. This is one of the few good missions that comes along. Get to see the bad guys up close. Since we're crewed together for a while, you'll see pretty much everything. When we're done you'll be qualified in all crew positions, at least enough to fill in during an emergency. It's a good idea in case someone buys the farm along the way."

"Crap!"

"John's not up to complete sentence structure yet, but he's coming along. You'll have to be patient." Wilder patted his friend on the head. "He pulls his weight though."

"I've had two planes shot out from under me already, and it helps when you have someone to fall back on. Just a word of advice here. Watch these little zip peckers. Don't turn your back on any of them. If you have a gun keep it loaded and with you at all times."

"*If* we have a gun?" Slaughter asked.

"Yeah, *if*. Only the engineer and loadmaster normally get them. Everybody is supposed to have one, but the Air Force doesn't play by its own rules. It's bullshit but that's the way it is."

"Should've become a preacher like my old man. At least he gets to wear a six-shooter when he's saving souls." Slaughter looked around the room. "Any java in this joint?"

"We'll stop by the greasy spoon on the way to the flight line," Custer said. "The food's terrible and the coffee's so thick, you can eat it. But it'll keep you awake."

Bryant finished the briefing and gave Custer his intelligence flimsy. "Are there any questions?"

There were none.

"Then it's a wrap." Custer handed the mission folder to Slaughter. "You get to baby-sit the holy grail today, John. Bill's turn tomorrow. Let's go."

"Praise Jesus!"

They picked up their flight gear and went outside to wait for their ride to the sandbagged steel revetments that surrounded the numerous aircraft. The morning air was hot and oppressive, and their flight suits stuck to them like a second skin. Thunderstorms were already firing up. It was going to be a long day.

"We're going feet-wet up the coast. Keeps us away from small arms fire and shoulder mounted SAM's. That's Cam Ranh Bay down there. It's a major port and we have some aircraft based there. We'll fly past Qui Nhon further north. Great place to eat if you don't ask what you're eating."

"You fly whatever route you want?" Wilder asked.

"Pretty much. As long as we get the job done, we can go anyway we choose. Over water is usually the safest."

"Hey, are we getting any armed escort for these assholes?" Ronnie Gates asked from the cargo compartment.

"What do you think this is, Mr. Loadmaster? Pan Am? Of course not. You're the chief cook-and-bottle-washer back there," Custer said. "What kind of example do you expect to set for these two FNG's when all you do is complain?"

"Quit busting my chops, Mr. Ed, or I'll short-sheet your sleeping bag."

"Hey, who knows? One of those rice-eaters might be good looking, and you guys will be all alone back there." Custer winked at Wilder, who was sitting in the left seat. "Bill, I want you and John to switch seats every other leg. You guys will be qualified in both seats by the end of the week. Greenham will start you guys on the nav panel tomorrow."

"Okay. What's the story with Con Son Island? Aren't there any prisons near Da Nang?"

"Yeah, but the bad guys own most of the real estate west of the city. Con Son's a pretty rough place. When the French invaded Vietnam in the 1800's, they built a prison on Poulo Condore Island, which is about seventy-five miles off the southeast coast of the Ca Mau Peninsula in the South China Sea. When the French left, the South Vietnamese government took over the island and the prison. By that time the island was known by its Vietnamese name; Con Son. The prisoners get locked up in bamboo boxes called tiger cages. Those slobs suffer from exposure, disease, snakes, and God only knows what else.

Uncle Sam keeps sticking his nose in it, calling it inhumane treatment, but Saigon tells the embassy to butt out."

Wilder looked across the cockpit at Custer, his expression cold. "I know all about inhumane treatment."

Custer glanced at the flight engineer then at Wilder. "I've heard some stories."

Wilder gazed at the horizon for a moment, then said, "You seem to know a lot of Vietnamese history, Ed."

"Pays to know your enemy."

They flew in silence for a while, each man lost in thought. Finally, Wilder said, "Picking up the Da Nang VOR. We'll plan on starting down about twenty miles east of the runway."

"You're learning fast, Bill. Keep it high for as long as you can. Don't want to give Charlie a target. They'd love to get one of these Herks. Tell you what; plan on an assault landing based on the first three thousand feet. Remember to touch down within the first five hundred."

"Okay." Wilder positioned his seat and scanned the terrain around the airport. He could see Army helicopters firing at ground targets and smoke from ground fire in the jungle. Planning ahead was a necessity, not a luxury. Slaughter sat in the flight engineer seat, with Smitty instructing over his shoulder. Custer ran the checklist, and the crew prepared to land and pick up its unusual cargo.

Wilder taxied the C-130 to the remote parking spot on the south end of the airport. He shut down the engines while Slaughter configured the engineer's panel under Smitty's watchful eye. After opening the aft ramp and door, Gates joined the rest of the crew heading to the compound that held the prisoners.

Custer was saluted by a US Army captain and a Vietnamese major. He casually waved. "I'm Ed Custer. We're supposed to take these clowns to Con Son, I'm told. This the right place?" He gestured towards the prisoners sitting on the ramp.

"Yes, sir. I'm Captain Baxter, and this is Major Van Duc." Baxter turned towards the prisoners. "There's twenty of them. The first group is Cong and the second is NVA."

"All look the same to me. Let's get them loaded and get the hell out of here. I'm sure their buddies are around somewhere."

"They are," Baxter said. "We'll get you out of here quick." He turned to Gates. "I have two aluminum pallets. How do you want them?"

"Ten per pallet. Side by side in double rows of five and strap 'em down. The forklift will load them on the ramp, and we'll roll the pallets to the center section and lock them in place." Gates looked wearily at the prisoners. "You got these pricks tied tight?"

"Nylon cuffs on their hands and feet. The blindfolds stay on til you get to Con Son."

"No problem there."

Baxter noticed the holstered Smith and Wesson .38 revolver. "Is that the only weapon you have?"

"That's it." Gates patted the gun.

Baxter looked doubtful. "Good luck."

"Yeah."

The pallets were loaded through the rear of the airplane and secured on the rollers with mechanical locks on either side. Wilder and Slaughter watched the entire operation with skepticism. "Wonder what's going through their minds right about now?" Wilder said.

"Who gives a shit?" Slaughter replied. "If it wasn't for them, we wouldn't be here in the first place." He stood next to the pallets and studied the prisoners. "Hard to believe that these little peckers could cause so much trouble."

Bryant stepped into the cargo compartment. He looked at the prisoners then pointed at one on the front pallet. "See that one? Baxter said he was a barber in the base barber shop at Da Nang. The base commander went in for a haircut and shave. This bastard slit his throat while the colonel sat in his chair with a hot towel around his face."

Wilder stared at the small man with the black blindfold tied around his head. He clenched his fists and unconsciously stepped towards the pallet. Slaughter immediately jumped in front of him. "Let it go, Bill. This ain't the time or place, man."

"Bill," Custer called from behind him. "You're in the engineer's seat. Time to spin up." Moving forward and standing beside him,

Custer looked at the object of everyone's attention. "Welcome to the *real* war. Ain't like the crap you get from Walter Wonderful. If you don't take it in stride, it'll drive you fucking nuts. Like I said this morning, don't turn your back on them." Custer stepped around a row of prisoners. "Let's go."

They were cruising at twenty-four thousand feet along the coast. Slaughter was at the controls, and Wilder was in the engineer's seat. Custer came forward from the cargo compartment. "Not a peep out of them," he said, sitting in the right seat. He handed Slaughter a cup of coffee. "Once we get rid of these cowboys, we'll head back to Tan Son Nhut." He looked over his shoulder at Smitty, who was standing by his seat, instructing Wilder on the fuel system. "Any chance we could all crash your club tonight? I'm sick of Black Label."

Smitty grunted and stroked his handlebar mustache. "Sure. We got any kind of beer you want. You'll find all that officer's beer on the black market on Tudo Street. Black Label, huh? How can you drink that stuff? No self-respecting NCO would go near it."

"We'll just send the wild man to take care of it," Slaughter said, thumbing at Wilder over his shoulder.

"Why him?" Smitty asked.

"This yahoo is a one man killing machine. Got more black belts than a porky-pine has quills."

"That right, EL-TEE?" Smitty asked.

"Have the bruises to prove it, too." Wilder leaned back in his seat. "Speaking of which, I'm going to hit the gym first when we get back. Then I'll tag up with you guys for a few cold ones."

The static on the intercom broke through the conversation. The transmit button at someone's station was being intermittently pressed, and the noise of shouting voices was heard erratically over the headphones.

"What the hell?" Custer looked around the cockpit. Everything seemed normal. Bryant was sleeping in the top bunk, and everybody else was at his station. *Gates?* "Ron?" Custer shouted into his headset mike.

No answer.

Greenham came over the interphone. "I'll check it out." He quickly climbed down the stairs and looked around the corner into the cargo compartment. He was back on the flight deck in an instant, his face white. "They're getting loose! Gates is down, and one of the prisoners is going for the gun."

Custer was unbuckling his seat belt. "Ah, shit! Smitty, get the other—"

"I'll take care of it." Wilder jumped out of the engineer's seat and was down the stairs before anyone realized what was going on.

Slaughter calmly sipped his coffee and continued to look out the window. "Relax, guys. Everything's under control."

"What?" Custer stared at him.

"No problem. Bill's got 'em all lined up."

Custer stared at Slaughter, not comprehending the Texan's words. "I'm going back there." He unbuckled his seat belt, but his growing fear was doused when Wilder's voice came over the interphone.

"Listen, guys. Everything's okay back here. Gates is a little rattled, but he'll be fine. One of the prisoners is a little worse for wear though, and the rest are as docile as sheep."

"I'll check it out." Bryant was up in an instant. Stepping into the cargo compartment, he stood at the base of the steps and described what he saw. "You guys won't believe this. Gates is sitting on the floor rubbing his head, and the Vietnamese barber is in a heap. His face is mush, and his arm is bent in places it ain't supposed to be. My guess is that it's broken in at least two places."

"Your guess is correct," Wilder said, unloading the revolver. He looked at Bryant and keyed his mike button. "I'll stay back here til we land if that's okay with you, Ed. Gates could use the company, and you won't have any more trouble with these goons. I promise you that."

"Yeah. Good idea." Custer looked across at Slaughter, his eyes wide open. "Guess you were right, John."

"Yep." Slaughter reclined his seat and propped his feet on top of the dash, his demeanor unfazed by the entire episode.

"Damn!" Custer muttered to himself. He looked at the instruments. Fifty miles from Con Son Island. It would be time to start down soon. He looked at Slaughter and at the stairwell that led into the cargo compartment where Wilder held twenty enemy solders at bay with only his hands. *This is incredible.*

"Reckon it's time to start down," Slaughter said nonchalantly.

Custer keyed the radio. "Saigon control, this is Spare Two-Three, feet-wet to Con Son. Request descent."

"Roger, Spare Two-Three. Descend to angels five thousand. Set IFF to 5102 and squawk ident. Shore batteries are cold today. You'll go right in."

"Roger. Descending to five thousand."

The South Vietnamese soldiers were rough with the prisoners, allowing them no quarter while they shuffled towards the prison gates and the infamous tiger cages that were conspicuously out of view. The Vietcong barber that had been unfortunate enough to come up against Wilder was prodded and tormented by his captors, despite the bloody face and the painful arm that hung helplessly at his side.

Wilder silently watched the scene before him. Bryant approached and offered him a can of Coke from the crew cooler. "This place is infested with Cong, and I'm sure the word will leak out about what happened on the plane. You can bet that they'll be looking for you."

"How do you know that?"

"Seen it before. These people have a grapevine that would make Washington's pale in comparison. We have our informers too."

Wilder kept looking at the prisoners. "Well, you have one less than you used to."

"How's that?"

He looked at Bryant. "A North Vietnamese informant from the Hanoi Hilton was sacrificed to the jungle in Laos when he got the word out about my brother."

"A *quid pro quo*," Bryant said.

"Not even close."

"No?"

Wilder's eyes narrowed. "John told you about what happened to my brother. It's common knowledge."

"What does that have to do with this?" Bryant gestured towards the prisoners.

"It's not over til I get the bastard that killed him. Then you'll have your *quid pro quo*."

Bryant looked at him then at the prisoners. "Time to go."

With their human cargo delivered more or less in tact, the crew was anxious to return to Tan Son Nhut. Wilder strapped himself into the left seat, and soon the C-130 was airborne on its way home.

"… and the ARVN, along with Army reinforcements from Fire Base Alpha, defeated the enemy and drove the Vietcong intruders back into the jungle. There were one hundred and twenty-seven confirmed enemy kills and only twelve friendlies."

"How many Americans?" Maggie asked from the back of the room. She stood with her pad in her hand, writing furiously.

"Thank you, ladies and gentlemen, for your attention. This concludes today's briefing." The Army major left the room, despite the multitude of unanswered questions being thrown at him.

"Did you see that?" Maggie was incredulous. "That pompous ass just walked away and ignored everybody. Who does he think he is?" She turned to McAlester. "This isn't a news briefing. It's a damn circus! They're not telling us the truth." She threw her hands up in frustration.

"Patience, my dear." McAlester mopped his ample brow with his handkerchief. There was no air conditioning in the crowded room, and the ceiling fans were useless in the stifling heat. "Those chaps are giving us the sanitized version of what they want us to tell everyone back home. They're reluctant to give us accurate information on American casualties because they want to reflect the war in a favorable light. Remember what I said when you first got here?"

"But, Terry, how can people in Washington make decisions based on this bogus information?"

"Now you know why we call this the Follies. Remember also what I said about our field people; they supplement the information we receive here. Now it's up to us to sift through the hodgepodge and find the truth."

"It's not right."

"No, but we must attend to it. Think halcyon thoughts my dear." McAlester smiled at her. "Perhaps Bill and John will have some information for you. I suspect their day was more exciting than ours. Why don't you ring them up when they get back?"

Maggie began to relax. "Thanks for that, Terry. You're a saint." She kissed the portly Englishman on his red brow. "I may do that but first, let's get our reports on the wire."

"Let's. Then it's time for dinner. The French onion soup is absolutely superb, you know."

"Well, you guys got to see Charlie firsthand today. Not many can say that. At the rate you're going, you'll be signed off in a few days. You'll probably get your own crews soon. There's always a shortage of pilots around here, and the turnover rate is pretty high." Custer shoved his flight cap into his pocket and sat at the table. Wilder and Slaughter both pulled up chairs and sat down. The bartender brought three Black Labels.

"This ain't beer. It's toad brew." Slaughter swallowed half the can in a few gulps.

"Thought we were going to Smitty's place."

"We are, but I want to go over a few things with you first." They sat in a remote corner of the mostly empty Officer's Club. The only other patrons were two drunk Army lieutenants that were passed out at a corner table on the other side of the room, and the noise from the juke box drowned out any competition in the conversation department.

Custer looked at them and leaned over the table. "Tomorrow, we're going to Vung Tau. It's a major port city leading to Saigon." He casually looked around the room. Leaning closer, he whispered, "Listen, guys, aside from being your instructor for a few missions, I'm also the military advisor to the CIA station chief in Saigon. He wants to meet you tomorrow. I think he has some information for you, but I can't be specific."

"In Vung Tau?" Wilder asked.

"Too many eyes around here. It would be tough for us to get to the embassy in Saigon without being seen. That's all I can say for now." Custer casually leaned back in his chair. Although there was only one Vietnamese bartender, he remembered the barber from Da Nang. "Drink up. Smitty's waiting for us."

"I'll be over after I hit the gym. Hold down the fort in the meantime."

"Didn't you sweat enough today?" Custer said. "After what you did to that prisoner, I'd say that you're in pretty good shape."

"Have to keep the edge sharp," Wilder said. He finished his beer and stood. "See you guys in a little while."

"So you see, my dear, the reports go through—"

"Hello, Maggie."

Mildly startled, she turned. "Captain Bryant ... hello. What brings you here? Didn't you fly with Bill today?"

"We got back a while ago. They're still with their instructor. I decided to treat myself to a real dinner instead of the gruel they serve on the base." He looked at McAlester. "I'm Jerry Bryant. How do you do, sir?"

"Terry McAlester, Captain. Indeed a pleasure." The Englishman stood and offered a pudgy hand.

"May I buy you both a drink?"

Maggie was about to defer, but she was pre-empted by her mentor. "Why, thank you, sir. I'll have a brandy. Won't you join us?"

"Yes, thank you." Bryant sat beside Maggie and motioned to the waiter. Looking at her, he said, "What will you have, Maggie?"

"I think I'll pass. I really don't feel well." She looked at McAlester. "I don't think the soup agreed with me, Terry. If you'll excuse me, gentlemen, I think I'll have a bath and go to bed." She stood. "Besides, I'm expecting a call from Bill." Glancing briefly at Bryant then at McAlester, she said, "Good night." She picked up her purse and left the table.

Bryant watched her turn the corner, then looked at McAlester. "Left in a hurry, didn't she?"

"Poor child doesn't feel well. This heat, the food, the water, and the milieu of this city combine to make a poor combination for someone to be thrust into virtually overnight. I'm sure she'll be fine." The brandy came and the two men engaged each other in conversation. McAlester lit his customary cigar and Bryant lit a cigarette.

"Have you met her boyfriend? I assume you know of him."

"Bill Wilder. A fine chap. I met him when she arrived here."

"I came over with them."

"Really? Then this is your first exposure to Saigon?"

"Actually, this is my second tour here. I'm a staff officer this time, working in Intelligence."

"Intelligence! Well, this is a new twist, isn't it?" *A new source of information.* McAlester's face lit up like a kid's in a toy store. "I've met quite a few Americans since I've been here. From Dover, England myself. How about you, Captain Bryant?" McAlester sniffed the brandy and puffed his cigar.

"Please, call me Jerry. I'm from New England."

"Ah, I just love New England, especially in the autumn season. So many cities named after my own country." Their conversation covered everything from politics and the war to sports and personal interests. McAlester was happy to oblige his guest with answers to his questions. They spoke about Wilder, Slaughter, and Maggie.

"So she has a younger brother in the Army?"

"Unfortunately, yes. She's afraid that he'll wind up here, but she's praying for a miracle," McAlester said.

"I can understand that." The grandfather clock in the lobby struck midnight. Bryant glanced at his watch. "I've lost track of the time. This has been enjoyable, Terry, but I really must go. Being out after curfew is a bit of a problem."

"Nonsense! I'll have a UPI car take you back to the base. Your curfew doesn't apply to the press, you know."

"Thanks, Terry. You're most kind." Bryant stood and offered his hand. "Thank you for a most enjoyable conversation. Perhaps I'll drop by and have dinner with you one evening. Your remarks about the ineptness of these news briefings every afternoon doesn't surprise me. Perhaps I may have some occasional information for you and Maggie that your staff isn't privy to."

McAlester's eyes sparkled. "Splendid! That would be magnificent, sir. Of course, no one but I would know." A question in the form of a statement.

"Then consider it done. When I have something of interest, I'll come directly to you."

"Excellent." McAlester was giddy with anticipation. He was tiring of the afternoon Follies.

"Then I'll see you later. Good night, Terry."

"Good evening, Captain."

***

The bus arrived at base operations at 0500. Although the sun was on the horizon, the day was already warm. Wilder and Slaughter weren't quite awake, but that changed when Berwick walked into the briefing room.

"Good morning." Although he had to interface with Wilder, Berwick kept his distance. "I'm here to brief you on today's mission." He looked around the room. "Where's Major Custer?"

"Right here." Custer closed the door behind him and dropped into a chair. "What have you got for us?"

"Your ship number is 905 parked at hot spot six. You have forty thousand pounds of fuel, two pallets of Class C ordinance, and some Vietnamese pax. You'll off load in Vung Tau, then—"

"Do any of these rice-burners have identification?"

"They're civilians that have been cleared by the Vietnamese authorities, sir."

"Cleared, my ass. One of these days, one of those zippers is going to take out a ship, and the goddamn government won't do anything to stop it. This place is nothing more than a frigging free airline for the Vietcong." Custer was testy. "What else you got?"

"Nothing much, sir. Airport in Vung Tau is secure. No enemy action in the immediate area. Pretty much a bland mission.

"Except for the occasional bomb in the cargo compartment."

"After you drop off your pax and cargo, you just return to base. You can release seats for any passengers coming back here if you wish."

"Americans only."

Slaughter spoke up. "Do you mean to tell me that these yokals are riding around free on Uncle Sam's planes, while I bust my ass and bleed taxes to pay for it? Who's the clown running this operation anyway?"

"That's about the size of it, John. I've been asking that question forever," Custer said. "I've bitched til I'm blue in the face, but nobody listens. Just business as usual. MACV says there are *political considerations*. Don't ask me what that means. Just don't take your eyes off them for an instant. And whatever you do, if they leave any Christmas presents behind, do *not* pick them up."

"Anything else, Berwick?" Wilder asked.

"No, that's it." He could almost feel Wilder's eyes burning into him. He picked up his papers and started across the room. Stopping at the door, he turned and said, "By the way, a message came for you. Do you know a PFC Tommy McIvor?"

"What about him?" Wilder's senses were alerted at the mention of the name.

"He's coming in tomorrow on Pan Am at 1400. Going to some Army post north of Kontum in the Central Highlands. Wonders if you can meet him."

Maggie! Wilder looked at Slaughter, his face doubtful.

"You know the kid?" Custer asked.

"His family and mine are close. His old man was my brother's skipper when he got shot down. His sister is here with UPI, and he's off to one of those hell-hole fire bases. He's probably petrified. I'd like to meet him and help him get squared away. Would you mind?"

Custer nodded. He had friends in the trenches too. "Sure. Buy him a good meal and get him drunk. It'll probably be the last real chow he'll get for a while."

"Thanks, Ed." Wilder turned to Slaughter. "I wonder if Maggie knows."

"I think it would be a good idea if you went over tonight and told her." Slaughter looked at Berwick. "Got any more good news?"

"No." Berwick left the room.

"These little people make me nervous," Gates said while fondling the .357 Python revolver Wilder loaned him at the beginning of the mission. It was against regulations to carry a personal side arm, but it generally was overlooked. Wilder had managed to bring it into the country unnoticed. It had been a gift from his father. "If nothing else, this makes me feel better." Gates stroked the holster affectionately.

"Just don't shoot it at altitude unless you have to, Ron. Although we aren't that high, it could create more of a problem than it would solve."

"No sweat, Lieutenant. If they see me about to put a round into one of their little porkers, they'll calm down." In addition to two pallets of small arms ammunition and a cluster of Vietnamese, there were cages filled with chickens, pigs, and dogs, and there were bamboo baskets full of clothes, blankets, and various other belongings. The cargo compartment smelled like a barn and looked like a refugee camp. Gates waved a hand at the human cargo and said, "Might not win the war, but we'll sure as hell win their hearts and minds."

"Where have we heard that before?" Wilder looked at his watch. "We'll be starting down soon. Be careful during the off load, Ron. Keep an eye out for parting gifts."

"Just like Elvis; Return To Sender. Address Unknown." Gates walked the length of the cargo compartment, checking everything from the gazes of his sleepy passengers to the tie downs and locks on the ammunition crates. He couldn't afford to take chances.

"Spare Zero-Five, this is Vung Tau tower. Cleared to land. Wind is one-two-zero at seven knots."

"Roger, that," Custer answered. He turned to Slaughter. "Okay, John, the Feds can't help you any more. You're on your own."

"Going for a ride, boys. Hang on." Slaughter slowly retarded the throttles, allowing the speed to bleed off. The C-130 touched down, and Slaughter engaged reverse thrust. He turned off at the end of the runway and taxied towards the main ramp. "Not bad for a rookie."

"Lucky," Wilder said from the cargo compartment over the interphone.

"No respect." Slaughter taxied behind the blue Air Force *Follow Me* truck to a parking spot opposite a makeshift terminal building. He engaged the parking brake, and Custer placed the engine condition levers to stop. The engines began to wind down, and Gates opened the aft ramp and door in preparation to off load his smelly cargo.

Custer stepped onto the tarmac from the crew entrance door and looked around.

A white Volkswagen van approached and stopped in front of the plane. The passenger door opened, and the CIA station chief for Saigon climbed out. "Hi, Ed. How goes the battle?"

"Same shit, different day, Scott," Custer replied, walking towards him. "You?"

"The usual." Scott Neilson's short cropped sandy hair was glistening with perspiration, and he wiped his face with a handkerchief. A white polo shirt and tan slacks hung on his slight frame, and rivulets of sweat ran down his back. "This infernal humidity never ends." He looked at the plane. "Are they here?"

"They're in the cargo compartment watching the off loading. We're playing airline again. Pisses me off."

"Yeah. I've talked to the MACV people about this more times than I can count." He looked at Custer then at the plane. "When they're done, we'll head over to—"

"Ed, we have a problem!" Greenham shouted from the forward door. "Christmas came early. Get the EOD people out here in a hurry."

"Why does this shit happen on my watch?" Custer turned to Neilson. "You got a radio in that van?"

"I'm on it." Neilson reached through the window and grabbed the microphone. Within minutes the Explosive Ordinance Disposal team was on the way.

Custer ran to the rear of the aircraft. The passengers and cargo were gone. Other than the smell of barn animals, the aircraft was empty. Custer climbed onto the ramp and looked inside. What he saw would have been funny under different circumstances.

Slaughter lay flat on his stomach with his hand under one of the nylon troop seats. He was bathed in sweat, and the look on his face was more of embarrassment than fear. His right hand was wrapped around an inverted paper cup jammed between the locking rails and the wall of the aircraft. He was frozen in position with a sheepish look on his face. "Thought I'd clean up the pickings these cretins left behind, but I reckon they got the last laugh. I think there's a grenade in this cup. S'um bitch!"

"Hold still, John. Don't move." Wilder saw Custer come up the ramp. "Merry Christmas, Ed. Looks like we got a live one. I think the pin's out and the clip is being held by the cup. John's got a death grip on it."

Custer's eyes were glued to Slaughter's hand. "Bill, there's a white van in front of the plane. Get everyone behind it. EOD's on the way."

"Okay." Wilder looked at his friend. "See you on the flip side, John, when you get your tit out of the wringer."

"Bite my ass!"

Everyone moved quickly away from the aircraft. Only Custer and Slaughter remained on board. "Never a dull moment with you guys. What are you planning for an encore?" Custer looked at Slaughter with bemused fascination then directed his attention to the cup. "Just hold still, John. The EOD guys will be here in a minute."

"For Christ's sake, this is only my second mission in this God-forsaken country, and already I'm trying to blow myself up." Slaughter's eyes were glued to the cup. "My luck's so bad that if it was raining pussies, I'd get one with a dick in it."

"Hopefully, your luck's just changed." The EOD team climbed onto the airplane and slowly approached them. Custer stood and addressed the two men, his eyes never leaving the paper cup. "We think it's a grenade."

The grizzled Army sergeant nodded. "This is getting to be a habit. Third time this week. I sure as hell wish somebody would screen these assholes before they get on the plane. You got any pull, Major Custer?"

"Wish I did. I got half a notion to shoot one of the bastards." Custer glanced at the sergeant then back at the cup in Slaughter's hand. "Well, it's all yours."

"Yeah." Dressed in heavy pads and metal plating with a steel and plexi-glass face guard attached to his helmet, the explosives expert slowly knelt beside Slaughter. He studied the cup for several minutes before he spoke. "Okay, Lieutenant, here's the plan. We're basically going to change places." He explained the procedure step by step. "Any questions?"

"No questions," Slaughter answered, still looking at the cup.

"Here we go." The sergeant knelt beside Slaughter. It was time to leave the airplane. Custer quickly joined the rest of the crew behind the van. All eyes were glued to the plane, everyone wondering if it would explode in their faces.

After what seemed like an eternity, Slaughter came flying through the crew entrance door and made a mad dash across the ramp. "Feet, don't fail me now!" He was behind the van in an instant. Gasping for breath, he looked back at the ship and said, "Those guys got balls the size of grapefruits." He looked at Wilder. "Damn!"

"You okay?" Wilder was relieved to see his friend in one piece.

"Aside from my pride, I'm fine." Slaughter crouched behind the van, his eyes looking through the windows at the airplane. Everyone anxiously waited, expecting the worst and hoping for the best.

After several minutes, the Frankenstein-looking Army sergeant stepped off the ramp onto the tarmac. He walked slowly towards a trailer-mounted concrete and steel cylinder parked behind the airplane. His partner, similarly dressed, opened the lid. The sergeant gently lowered the paper cup and its contents into the drum-shaped container. The second team member gingerly packed small sandbags around the explosive, rendering it motionless. Slowly, the sergeant removed his hands and withdrew them from the cylinder. The steel lid was carefully closed and locked, the grenade secured.

The EOD expert removed his helmet and stared at the containment cylinder, sweat pouring from his face. He took off his bulky gloves and placed them in a storage box along with his helmet. He removed his heavy pads and threw them into the Jeep. "This job sucks." The sergeant wiped his face with a towel. "Let's get the paperwork done and get gone. I need a drink."

His partner shook his head in agreement. "Amen to that." The corporal wrote down the required information and climbed into the driver's seat. The sergeant looked at the men behind the van and gave them a thumbs-up. *One more day closer to leaving*, he thought. They drove away, towing their unfriendly cargo behind them.

"This is more fun than shooting rats at the dump," Slaughter said. He looked around and saw Neilson looking back at him. He stood and gave a weak salute. "John Slaughter at your service."

"You gave us quite a scare, John. I'm Scott Neilson, CIA station chief."

"S'um bitch! This is a hell of a way to make an entrance."

Wilder slapped Slaughter on the back. "Do me a favor, okay? Next time, just sit on your hands til someone signs for you and puts a leash on your collar."

"Deal."

"Well, now that we've had our excitement for the day, let's take a ride," Neilson said. "Ed, I'll take the crew to the mess hall on the way to my make-shift command post. The food's really good for GI chow. We'll join them later. Right now I need to talk to you guys."

***

The mood was somber and the air thick with anticipation. Wilder and Slaughter sat motionless, taking in every word Neilson uttered. Custer, although more experienced in covert operations, was on edge. The prospect of a covert Soviet killer in their midst was something unexpected.

"… and we've screened all of our informants and covert types. We don't think he's gone back to Russia, and we don't have any reason to believe he's still in the States."

"Any chance he's gone back to Hanoi?" Wilder asked, his eyes glued to the CIA chief.

"Doubtful." Neilson said. "There's no reason for it as far as we can tell. The general opinion is that he's somewhere in Saigon. It's where he can do the most damage."

Custer looked through the window at his plane in the distance. He turned to Wilder. "Saigon's a big place and he could disappear there. And he'd know if you're in-country. Remember what Bryant said about the grapevine?"

"I do," Wilder said. "Are any of our people actively looking for him?"

"Everyone is," Neilson said. "When he makes his move, we'll get him. You can count on that."

"When that times comes, he's mine." Wilder's eyes narrowed, his voice threatening.

"We're calling the shots here, Bill. Your father made that perfectly clear to you." Neilson was intimate with Wilder's situation, and he empathized with the young flyer. Nevertheless, he had to maintain control. "We have to work as a team on this and within the confines of the Agency's rules—your father's rules."

Wilder stared at him but said nothing.

Slaughter sensed the tension and changed the subject. "Scott, what's the story on Berwick? After the stunts he's pulled, he winds up in the Air Force with access to stuff we can only think about. How the hell did that pin-head get that position anyway? Have you checked him out?"

"We have and he's clean as far as we know. Why?"

Slaughter looked at Wilder then back at Neilson. "Let's just say that we don't see eye to eye with him."

"Well, he hasn't said or done anything that would lead us to believe he's a security risk. Unless you know something we don't, we don't have any reason to suspect him of anything."

Wilder faced Neilson and said, "Berwick was adamant about the war—and my brother—when we were in school. Now, a complete about face. It doesn't figure. There's something going on here, and I want to find out what it is."

"We'll keep an eye on him, but until he steps out of line, there's nothing we can do." Neilson was careful in his choice of words. "Sorry, Bill, but I have to cover all bases. Is there something else between you two I should know about?"

"I just don't trust him."

"I can live with that," Neislon said. "In this place you have to watch your back all the time. But until he trips up, we have to give him the benefit of the doubt."

"What about Bryant?" Wilder said.

"Second tour here. He was a crew member on his first hitch. Then he completed an intelligence tour in the Pentagon and volunteered to come back. Looking for a promotion I guess. He's clean."

"Okay."

Neilson pressed on. "Let's get back to the main subject. Most spies have a narrow view of their mission. They're after specific information or a specific person. Petrov, however, is on a personal vendetta to avenge his old man's death, and we know the KGB can't control him. Expect a move against you, Bill, when the opportunity presents itself. We know about the explosion at Jake's and Petrov's proclivities with women, and we should expect more of the same." Neilson's eyes dropped to the floor for a moment then returned to Wilder's stare. "We're going to separate you and John to the maximum extent we can. For starters we want you guys not to room together. Not even in the same building. Too easy a target. After Ed finishes your local checkout, you'll each get your own crew. Don't want both of you on the same ship. Two birds for the price of one. Too risky."

"Any ideas what that Russian prick might do?"

"None, John. But whatever he does, you can count on it being splashy." Neilson looked at Wilder. "I think it's safe to say that he knows how to jerk your chain, Bill, so plan your actions accordingly. He may try to get to you through your friends first, but he could go for everyone at once."

"The grenade may have been his first attempt," Wilder said.

"Possibly, but I doubt it. I've seen this before. The Vietcong are good at booby traps, and MACV gives them plenty of opportunity. I guarantee MACV will find out about this incident. Hopefully, they'll get the message this time."

"Don't count on it." Custer swatted angrily at a fly on the table.

Everyone was quiet. Finally, Neilson said, "Okay, any questions?" There were none. "Then let's close this up. If you guys need to get in touch with me, Ed will be your contact. When I get any information on Petrov, Ed will contact you right away." Neilson looked at Custer then turned to Wilder. "Bill?"

"Yeah?"

"Remember, we work as a team. No Lone Ranger stuff."

"Right." Wilder left the room without another word and began the long walk back to the flight line. He needed time to collect his thoughts.

Neilson looked at Slaughter. "Can we control him?"

"Not if he gets to Petrov first."

Neilson shook his head doubtfully. "Let's hope that doesn't happen."

"Me too," Slaughter said, "for your sake."

The MAC passenger terminal was alive with activity. The Pan Am Freedom Bird would be leaving Tan Son Nhut in a matter of hours, its cargo of happy short-timers anxiously waiting for their day in the sun, which in this case, was a flight home. The Boeing 707 was the symbol of freedom in Vietnam, and each soldier, regardless of his assignment, counted the days when he would ride her wings home.

But first it would off load the frightened young soldiers now facing their turn in the jungles of Vietnam for the first time. For young Tommy McIvor, it was a time of both excitement and fear. He didn't know what to expect. He only knew what the Army had drilled into him, what he saw in the news, and what his older sister had told him when he was still in high school. He looked around anxiously when he stepped off the plane, wondering if Wilder had gotten his message. His doubts vanished when he saw the red hair bouncing up and down and the arms waving.

"Tommy, Tommy!" Maggie shouted, running across the ramp. She wrapped her arms around her brother and hugged him with all her might, tears streaming down her face. "Tommy, I'm so happy to see you." She held onto him desperately.

"Sis!" He held his sister in his arms. "This is great! Got my big sister to meet me. I love you."

"I love you too." She stood back and looked at him. "Tommy, you've lost weight. You—"

"Take it easy, Sis. You ain't my mama. The Army just leaned me out some." A boyish smile spread across his face. "You look terrific." He looked at the scene around him. "Is Bill here?"

"Right behind you, partner." Wilder grabbed the boy's hand and shook it firmly. "Good to see you, Tom. How was your trip?" He saw the fatigue and fear in Tommy's face.

"It was too long." Tommy looked around. "What do we do now? I don't get shipped to my post til tomorrow. Guess I need to do some processing or something."

"I'll help you get squared away, Tom. Then we're going to Maggie's hotel. You'll be staying there tonight. We're going to wine and dine you before I fly you to Kontum tomorrow. John's on a mission now, but he'll meet us tonight. In the meantime you probably could use and shower and some sleep."

"Yes, sir, I sure could."

Wilder smiled and put his hand on Tommy's shoulder. "You don't have to call me sir. Besides being your friend, I'm practically your brother-in-law. Just a matter of paper work."

The words caught Maggie by surprise. She looked at him. "What are you saying?"

"I just did. Will you?"

This time the tears were happy ones. "Yes, yes, yes!" She wrapped her arms around him and buried her face in his chest. "Yes, Bill, I will."

Tommy laughed. "Well, this is one hell of a welcome to 'Nam. Came over here with a sister, and I'll go home with a brother to boot. Things are looking up already!"

The celebration at the Caravelle was lively and fun. Maggie's spirits were lifted tenfold when she saw Tommy, Bill, and John together. McAlester was the life of the party and refused to let anyone pay for a thing. Everyone did everything possible to make young McIvor feel at home. No one mentioned tomorrow, but everyone's thoughts drifted to what lay ahead. The fire bases north of Kontum were dangerous places. The body bags coming out attested to that.

On December 22 Congress prohibited the use of US combat forces or advisors in Cambodia or Laos. On paper at least, Americans were fooled. As a practical matter, however, it was business as usual. While Allied military personnel had declined to 67,700 by the end of December, American troop strength had increased to 334,600. By the end of the year, 44,245 US military personnel had been killed in Vietnam.

The carnage would continue.

CHAPTER 7

JANUARY 1971

The main supply line from North Vietnam into the South was the Ho Chi Minh Trail. It began in the panhandle of North Vietnam and wound its way through the mountainous jungles of Laos, Cambodia, and finally emptied into South Vietnam. A trip down the trail was arduous at best, but the connection of jungle roads and paths proved to be the bane of the ARVN and the Americans that supported them.

North Vietnam moved, on average, 20,000 troops per month, along with accompanying supplies, down the trail. Hmong tribesmen, recruited by the CIA, worked to cut the trail in the north, while air strikes by the Americans and South Vietnamese battered the trail in the south—all without success. Finally, in January 1971, a plan was devised to cut the trail over the border in Laos from a forward operating base near Khe Sanh. The plan called for the ARVN to cut the trail along Route 9 just over the Laotian border. Known as Operation Lam Son 719, the intrusion into Laos would be executed solely by South Vietnamese troops as Americans were forbidden by Congressional edict from engaging in combat operations in Laos or Cambodia.

"Jack, your brother-in-law is here, along with a Mr. Swanson from the FBI. I've rescheduled your meeting with the National Security

Advisor for this afternoon at three," Wilder's secretary said over the intercom.

"Send them in please. Any chance for a pot of coffee?"

"Already on the way."

"You have more pull than the President, Linda."

"I accept the compliment."

The two men walked into the room and Spencer made introductions. "Jack, this is Special Agent Jim Swanson from the FBI." He turned to the federal cop. "Jim, this is my brother-in-law."

"Pleased to meet you, Mr. Wilder." They shook hands and Swanson looked around the room. "Never thought I'd set foot in this place."

"Call me Jack." His eyes followed Swanson's. "Just a fancy cage, Jim. To tell you the truth, I'd rather be scaling a trout. Have a seat, gentlemen."

Wilder's secretary came in with coffee. "I'll hold your calls, Jack." She looked at the trio. "Enjoy it while it's hot."

"Linda is my gate keeper. Keeps me out of trouble." Turning to her, Wilder said, "This place would grind to a halt if it wasn't for you."

"Can't survive without lifer-juice." She nodded towards the coffee. "Let me know if you need anything." She closed the door, leaving the three men alone.

They engaged in idle chit-chat and enjoyed their coffee. It wasn't often that they had the chance. It was a welcome respite from the daily grind inside the DC beltway. "There's a small cabin near Jackson Hole in the Tetons," Wilder said. "Bruce and I try to spend as much time there as we can. The fishing's superb. Nothing like a mountain trout over an open fire to clear the cobwebs."

"Sounds like my kind of place, Jack," Swanson said. "When this war is over and the crazies are rounded up, maybe we can head out. I'm a fair fisherman myself, and I tie a pretty mean fly."

"Sign me up," Spencer said. "Fort Meade is getting smaller by the day. A trip to the mountains is the cure we need."

"Amen to that," Wilder said. "Well, no time like the present, gentlemen. What can I do for you?"

Spencer refilled his cup and leaned back in his seat. "Jack, as you know, the FBI pretty much handles domestic crime issues when they are designated as federal offenses. NSA doesn't get involved unless it becomes a matter of national security. Jim called me personally on this one, however, because it's ... unusual. I'll let him fill you in." Spencer looked at the FBI agent. "All yours, Jim."

Special Agent James Swanson leaned forward in his chair. "Jack, my office was called by the Baltimore police when an unusual case dropped into their lap. One of the locals at an Annapolis wharf reported his skiff missing from its slip. The police were alerted when the boat didn't turn up after a day or so. Not being a high priority crime—the theft of a small boat—it went pretty much on the back burner. A few days later a fishing boat working a few miles off shore spotted a small boat adrift. The skipper pulled along side to take it in tow, but when he saw it, he backed off."

"Why?"

Swanson glanced briefly at Spencer then turned back to Wilder. "Along with sea water, the boat was awash in blood. The skipper radioed the Coast Guard, and they were on the scene within minutes. Other than the bloody sea water, there was nothing else in the boat. Turned out to be the missing boat from the wharf. Forensics identified the blood as human, and there was a lot of it—as if a body had been drained in the boat before being thrown overboard."

"Drained? Overboard?" Wilder was on the edge of his seat.

"That's what it looks like, Jack," Spencer said. "But this is just the beginning." He looked at Swanson.

"Now it gets bizarre. The next day some beachcombers found a stuffed duffel bag on the shore not far from where the dingy was discovered. There was a body—or part of one—in it."

"*Part* of a body?"

"That's right." Swanson rubbed the back of his neck to relieve the tension. "The head, both arms, and feet were missing. Cut off with surgical precision. The body had been in the water a while, and it was impossible to identify the remains. It was a male and we guess his age to be somewhere in his twenties. That's all we know."

"Jesus Christ!" Wilder said to the ceiling. He leaned back in his chair and mulled over Swanson's words. "A mob hit?"

"Too messy. Besides, they like to make a public statement when they take someone out. Although this happened a while ago, the police have managed to keep it away from the press. This hasn't hit the papers yet," Swanson said.

"It's not only *what* happened, Jack, but *when*," Spencer said.

"What do you mean?" Wilder waited for the ax to fall.

"This whole thing happened a few days before Bill and John left for Vietnam."

"Where's the connection?" Wilder's complete attention was focused on the NSA director.

"After their plane arrived at Tan Son Nhut, one of the passengers reported that his duffel bag was missing. One bag remained after all the luggage was claimed, but there was no name on it. The military police opened it, and the kid identified everything in it to the letter. The contents were his all right, but the bag wasn't. His name was stamped on the side of his bag, but the one that came off the plane in Saigon had nothing on it." Spencer paused for a moment before continuing. "The bag with the body in it had this kid's name on it. He was at Benning the entire time this bizarre thing went down. Bottom line, Jack, is that someone—perhaps the murderer—switched bags before the flight left Dulles."

"There had to be an accomplice," Swanson said. "This person couldn't be in two places at once."

"Agreed, but why this kid and this flight? And why go through the trouble of mutilating a body to avoid an ID?" Wilder said.

"You just answered your own questions, Jack," Spencer said. "The body parts were removed specifically to prevent identification. Bill's flight was chosen to send us a message. Whoever did this has free and unlimited access to Bill and John. And I'm willing to bet my pension that the person behind all this was on that plane." The two men stared at each other, their thoughts twelve thousand miles away.

Wilder picked up the phone. "Linda, I need to send a telex to the station chief in Saigon right away."

"Okay, listen up, guys. We're getting ready to go into Khe Sanh. The field is secure, but Slaughter radioed that Charlie owns the real estate on both sides of the approach. We'll be flying through the valley between two peaks, and, based on what he said, we can expect a hot welcome. Let's get the flak jackets and helmets on. We'll land to the west, turn around on the circle at the end, and do a fast combat off load. Then we get the hell out of there and head east to Da Nang."

"Why can't we take off to the west, climb to altitude, then turn back for the coast?" Pete Perette asked from the right seat. "Why risk getting shot down twice?"

"You're being logical now, Pete. That's Laotian airspace over there, and our benevolent Uncle Sam says we can't go there. He's looking out for our bests interests, as usual," Wilder said sarcastically. "The goddamn war doesn't make any sense, and that's the short answer to your question."

In the short time Wilder had been in Vietnam, he had seen things that people back home could never fathom. The combined ineptitude of the South Vietnamese government and the Vietnamese military commanders was only exceeded by the fact that official Washington didn't have a clue about what was really going on. Because of Washington's insistence on running the war from a collective desk twelve thousand miles away, the American military had one hand tied behind its back. The Rules of Engagement imposed on the American troops by the Washington suits had given the enemy the upper hand, and the American commanders were often helpless to do anything about it.

The Vietnamese army, despite its constant training at the hands of the Americans, was incapable of winning the war on its own, and the unmitigated failure of Lam Son 719 would only serve to reinforce Wilder's opinion of the war and the inability of the United States government to get a handle on the conflict before thousands more Americans died in vain.

"That's all fine and dandy, but what happens if we get shot down?" Perette was visibly nervous. This was his first actual mission under fire.

"Cost of doing business," Wilder said. "Let's do the checklists, get the job done, and get the hell out of here."

Resigned to his fate, Perette set to work. "Okay, crew, listen up."

He read the checklists and the crew prepared for an assault landing on a three thousand foot strip of pierced steel planking. The runway began at the east edge of a plateau that extended towards the jungles just short of the Laotian border to the west. The edge of the plateau overlooked a thousand foot drop to the valley below. The northern and southern flanks of the valley were guarded by steep mountains on which the North Vietnamese had installed anti-aircraft artillery, or AAA. Flying between the mountains, the C-130's had to survive murderous enemy fire and touch down on the first five hundred feet of the short runway without catching the edge of the cliff that would plunge them into the steep canyon below. The aircraft then would have to stop within the confines of the make-shift runway, which by anyone's standards, was too short on a good day.

To add insult to injury, the Army had decided to place the ammo dump directly at the west end of the runway, and the air crews had to make it a point not to land long or to delay using the brakes. A successful landing on this strip meant performing a controlled crash. In addition to everything else, Army helicopters were parked along the left edge of the three thousand foot strip with their rotor blades hanging over the edge of the runway. Two pieces of equipment in the same place at the same time could be unhealthy, especially when one was moving at one hundred twenty knots. The crew picked up on it immediately.

"Look at that!" Fred Durkin shouted from his engineer seat. "Those fucking rotor blades are hanging over the runway. This ain't gonna work."

"I'm going fox-mike," the navigator said over the interphone. "I'll tell them to move 'em or lose 'em." Barry Sorrenson switched his selector to FM and called on the assigned secure frequency to the Army commander on the ground.

"We'll hold out here east of final approach," Wilder said. "No point in going down the chute and getting shot at, just to have to go around and play ass-over-tea-kettle trying to get out of there. Let me know what they say, Barry."

"Roger, that." Sorrenson directed his attention to the radio.

"Shit! You'd think those grunts would call in an air strike on those guns. It's like shooting ducks in a pond, and we're the ducks!" Durkin said.

"Berwick said this area was secure. No enemy activity at all." Perette squirmed in his seat. "So much for accurate intel."

"Take what that asshole says with a grain of salt," Wilder said, watching his airspeed and altitude. He didn't want to get any lower than he had to. "Nobody's going to look out for us but us. Remember that." Wilder was becoming more cynical by the day, but he knew that he couldn't allow his opinion to interfere with the safe accomplishment of his mission. He was careful to balance one against the other.

"You hit the nail on the head, skipper. Another case of the tail wagging the dog." Durkin eyed his panel. "Let me know when you're ready to close the bleed valves. The cabin pressure and outside are within five hundred feet of each other."

"When we begin our final approach, you can close 'em, Fred." Wilder looked over his shoulder at Sorrenson. "Any luck with those choppers?"

The navigator's face was a mixture of anger and disgust. "You won't believe this. The ground commander said he's a bird colonel, and he's not going to have the rotors turned. He's giving us a *direct order* to line up and land on the right side of the runway. Guy's an asshole!"

Another lifer eaten up with himself. "Okay, here's what we're going to do. Get back on the horn, Barry, and tell that prick that if he wants his mail and booze, he'll turn those rotors. He's got ten minutes. After that we're outta here, cargo and all, and he can take it up with the *Bird* back at Da Nang."

A sly smile crept across Sorrenson's face. "You got balls, man."

"Somebody's got to grab these ring-knockers by the scrotum once in a while and give them a dose of reality. Brings them back to earth." Wilder looked at the mountain peaks to the west that hid the dangerous AAA batteries that threatened their approach to the runway. "We'll hang out here for a bit. If those rotors don't get moved soon, they don't get their care packages. Period."

"You ain't gonna get promoted this way, Lieutenant," Durkin said, thankful for an aircraft commander with common sense.

"I'll take that as a compliment, Fred." The aircraft circled east of the Khe Sanh airstrip since the enemy controlled the terrain that lined the final approach. Fuel was not a problem; there was enough for three round trips, and this was only the first. Unless the ground commander complied with Wilder's demands, this would also be the last.

"I've got some activity on the FM." Sorrenson punched off the other radio monitors and keyed his mike button. "This is Spare Two-One, conform rotors are moved, over."

"*Affirmative, Spare. Request complied with and runway is open. You're cleared for your approach. Be advised that the commander wants to board your ship after you land, and that if you have to go around, you must turn immediately to the east to avoid Laotian airspace.*"

Sorrenson looked at Wilder. "Did you get that?"

"Got it and don't answer them. This is a minimum ground time mission, and we don't have time to play grab-ass." Wilder looked around the cockpit. "*Nobody* gets on this plane."

Everyone gave a thumbs-up.

"Okay, guys, let's tighten up now. We're going in."

"Bleeds coming closed." Durkin flipped the four switches on the pneumatic panel overhead. There was an instant surge of power as the bleed air demand on the engines was removed. The end result was more thrust that could be critical in stopping the airplane or making a maximum effort climb to escape enemy ground fire. "Panel secure, engineer ready." The other crew members responded in kind when their stations were secure and emergency equipment was in place.

"Burt, listen up," Wilder said over the interphone. "This is going to be a fast off load. As soon as the engines come out of max reverse, you can open the ramp and door. We'll turn around at the end and stop. As soon as we're stopped, lower the ramp and pull the locks. When that's done give us a shout. We'll goose the throttles to get the pallets moving. Give me an *all clear* as soon as they're out, then button things up. We're outta there in three minutes."

"Ready to rock, sir," the loadmaster said over the interphone. A speed off load was a dangerous maneuver. Hands and feet could be crushed in an instant. Anyone approaching the aircraft from the rear as the ramp was lowered could become road-kill before he had time to react. It wasn't uncommon for an unaware ground pounder to run up the ramp as the pallets were rolling aft. It was one of the biggest dangers in the combat off load procedure. Unfortunately, some had learned the hard way.

Burt Martin was an experienced loadmaster, and he would make sure that the locks weren't released until the aft area of the ramp was clear. He didn't want a *road-kill* notch on his revolver handle. "Just tell those assholes to stay the hell away from the rear of the plane."

"I'm on it," Sorrenson said. He would make sure that the message was transmitted and received on every available radio before and after they landed.

"Okay, guys, heads up. Here we go." Wilder lined the aircraft on final approach. "We'll keep the speed up as long as we can while in the pass. At one mile we'll hang everything out and slow to max effort speed. Everybody lock your harnesses." The C-130 approached the pass doing 250 knots, and the firestorm began. Wilder kept the plane as low as possible, hoping that the enemy would have enough sense not to fire directly at each other as he flew between them.

A shutter ran through the airplane, and all eyes, except Wilder's, were locked onto the instruments. Wilder watched the approaching runway, making sure that he didn't get too low. "Status check?"

"Everything's nominal." Durkin's reassuring voice came over the interphone.

"Secure back here," Martin said, his hand on the ramp and door control panel.

"Okay." Wilder had a death grip on the control wheel and throttles, and he could feel the shutter through the wheel in his hand. But the ship responded to his inputs, and he decided to continue his approach. *C'mon, lady, I know you can do it.* He pulled the throttles to idle and the aircraft quickly slowed. "Flaps to fifty and gear down," Wilder commanded. The indicators quickly confirmed that the wheels were down and locked. "Full flaps." The flaps extended behind the wings, and the aircraft slowed to its maximum effort approach speed.

Durkin tested the anti-skid and scanned his panel. "Good to go, sir."

"All checklists are complete," Perette added, controlled fear in his voice. He took a deep breath to calm his shaking. "Okay, Bill, do your stuff."

"Landing." Wilder's statement confirmed that the ship was now committed to the earth. When the leading edge of the runway—and the edge of the cliff—disappeared under the nose, Wilder pulled the throttles to idle and eased back on the control wheel to slow his decent rate. The main wheels made contact with the runway, and Wilder immediately stood on the brakes and pulled the throttles to maximum reverse. The aircraft shook when Wilder took it from 120 knots to zero in a matter of seconds. The aircraft stopped with room to spare.

"I'm ready," Martin shouted over the intercom.

"Clear to open," Wilder said. He taxied the aircraft around the jug handle circle at the end of the runway and stopped. "Ramp down!"

"Coming down. Locks removed, clear to unload!" Martin shouted over the noise of the engines. "Shit! These assholes are heading for the airplane. Didn't they get the word to stay the hell away?"

"Remain clear, Burt!" Wilder snapped. "I'll blow the bastards away." Wilder stood on the brakes to keep the ship from moving and pushed the throttles forward. The engines responded immediately, and the four giant fans began blowing debris behind the aircraft like a typhoon. The welcoming committee behind the plane quickly scattered, oblivious to the danger they were about to put themselves into. Wilder released the brakes and the aircraft sprang forward. The five pallets immediately rolled off the ramp and onto the ground.

"Load clear! Let's get moving!" Martin shouted into everyone's headset. "Doors coming closed."

"Reset the flaps and trim," Wilder commanded, taxiing the ship to the end of the runway.

Perette positioned the flaps and scanned the engine instruments. "Number two's running hot. I'm going to run the oil cooler to full open."

"We need that engine to get out of here. Once we're clear of the gun batteries, we'll take a look at it." Wilder aligned the airplane on the runway and stood on the brakes. "Ready?"

Durkin glanced around the cockpit to make sure everyone was seated. He gave Wilder the thumbs-up signal, and Wilder pushed the throttles forward. With the engines roaring at maximum power, he released the brakes and the ship lunged forward.

The end of the runway came fast, and Wilder pulled the nose into the air the instant the ship reached minimum flying speed. Perette raised the landing gear, and Wilder climbed the ship at its maximum rate in an attempt to avoid the deadly gunfire directed at them. Red tracers sped past the windshield, and the crew instinctively put their hands in front of their faces. The aircraft jerked from flak slamming into its side, and everyone held his breath while the plane made its way through the Valley of Death—the dubious name given to their route by the navigator.

The aircraft shook violently for several seconds then stabilized.

"We're hit!" the loadmaster shouted over the interphone. "There's a hole the size of a truck by the right troop door. We—"

"Stay strapped in!" Wilder shouted into the intercom. "Fuel leaks?"

"Negative, as far as I can tell." Martin's voice was two octaves higher than normal, and it echoed the fear he felt. "But there's holes everywhere!"

"We'll stay below ten thousand feet and keep the speed back til we can look at the damage. Durk, anything on your panel?" Wilder's eyes flashed back and forth between the altimeter and the terrain outside.

"Number three main tank is going down. We're on tank-to-engine, and the cross feeds are closed." The flight engineer quickly rattled out their fuel status and turned to the navigator with the obvious question on his face.

"Thirty minutes to Da Nang," Sorrenson said.

"If we empty that tank, we'll still have plenty of fuel. We're at twenty-three thousand pounds," Durkin said while reducing the ship's electrical load in preparation for dumping fuel.

"Okay, Durk. Hold fast til we level off and check things out. Burt?"

"Yeah?"

"How you doing, guy? Any brush fires back there?" Wilder needed information in a hurry, but he didn't want to alarm his loadmaster unnecessarily.

"No. Just lots of fucking holes! What's the plan?"

Just then the red fire warning light came on for the number three engine. "Fire on three," Perette shouted.

"Feather three and pull the fire handle," Wilder ordered, his eyes glued to the airspeed indicator. Perette and Durkin ran the emergency procedure from memory. Their eyes were glued to the red light in the fire handle, waiting—praying—that it would extinguish after the engine was shut down.

There was a collective sigh of relief when the light went out and the engine wound to a stop. The propeller feathered automatically and stood stationary.

After visually inspecting the engine from the window and satisfied that the fire was extinguished, Durkin said, "Number three prop is standing tall. Engine's secure."

"Okay. Listen up, guys. We're at nine thousand feet and clear of the gun batteries, and we'll be in Da Nang in less than twenty minutes. Pete, get on the radio and declare an emergency. Barry, crank up the HF and tell Tan Son Nhut. Tell them our status, and give intel the lowdown on the bad guys." He turned to Durkin. "Fuel's not a problem, so we can empty number three main. When that's squared away, Durk, I need you to hook up a life-line and inspect the back of the bus. Before we land, we'll have to make a flight control check too. Burt, stay put."

"I ain't going nowhere."

Wilder looked around the cockpit. "Any questions?" There were none. "Let's do it." He focused his attention on controlling the plane, while the rest of the crew scoured the ship and made preparations to land. Although the destruction in the fuselage was extensive, there was no major damage to the landing gear or flight controls. The number two engine had suffered damage by ground fire just before landing in Khe Sanh and had to be shut down enroute to Da Nang.

With only two engines running, Wilder carefully flew the airplane onto the runway and used the entire length to stop. After clearing at the end the ship fell in behind a *Follow Me* van that directed the crew to a parking spot near the command post compound.

"Shut her down and put her to bed," Wilder said after setting the parking brake. He looked around the cockpit at his weary crew. "Everybody okay?"

"I don't know what I hate the most; these zips shooting at my ass or my ex-wife's cooking," Durkin said.

"I wonder who's on our side," Sorrensen added. "Those grunts weren't any help."

"Did intel say anything to you about those guns?" Wilder asked, releasing his harness.

"*Stand by.* Seems to be their favorite phrase. Never got back to me. Probably some ground-pounder in the middle of a shift change or mid-life crisis." Sorrenson shuffled through the forward door behind the rest of the crew.

"Jesus Christ! Look at that," Perette shouted. The number three engine looked like black Swiss cheese. The cowling was completely gone, and the engine looked like it had been worked over with a giant can opener. The strut behind the engine mount was torched, and there were holes in the flaps on the rear of the wing.

"There's a lesson to be learned here, boys." The familiar Texas drawl came from behind them. Everyone turned and saw Slaughter strolling across the ramp as if he owned it. "These machines are like women. Talk nice to them, buy them a trinket once in a while, and they'll deliver the goodies. When they get bitchy, just grab hold and let them know who's in charge. They'll come around."

"Well, if it isn't Aristotle. I figured you'd be hold up in a saloon somewhere by now, John," Wilder said.

"Just a matter of time." Slaughter studied the destroyed engine. Shaking his head, he said, "Looks like Mothra ain't going anywhere for a while." He looked at Wilder. "We got out just before you came in. Didn't take any hits. Your turn in the barrel, I guess." Slaughter looked at the ship again and shook his head. "Those gomers couldn't hit a bull in the ass with a banjo most days. You're just one lucky s'um bitch!"

"Thanks, I think. What did you get from intel about this?"

"Nothing. Berwick told me that everything east of Khe Sanh was cold. Made it sound like a milk run. When I get back to Saigon, I'm gonna choke his gizzard out."

"Get in line." Wilder looked at his destroyed plane. "Sometimes, I wonder who he's working for."

"Ain't it the truth? In the meantime, I'm your ride back to the house. Load up your mob, and let's blow this pop stand."

"Right." Wilder motioned to his crew. "Let's go home, guys."

CHAPTER 8

Scott Neilson read the telex again, making sure he missed none of the bizarre details. Looking at Custer, he said, "This came in last night, Ed. I think you'll find it interesting."

Custer quickly read the message then read it again slowly to make sure his eyes weren't playing tricks. He stared at Neilson. "Is this for real?"

"As real as it gets. Jack Wilder sent the message himself."

"From the top." Custer looked at the document again. "If there's a connection between us and this duffel bag ... " He looked at Neilson. "The spooks at Langley seem pretty sure that he's here then?"

"Pretty much confirms it in my opinion. All the players are in place."

"Wilder and Slaughter. And Wilder's girlfriend. What's her name?"

"Maggie McIvor. Works for UPI out of the Saigon office for an Englishman named McAlester. A bit eccentric but harmless. Neither of them know anything about this Petrov business, and we have to make sure they don't find out. She also has a brother at Fire Base

Alpha north of Kontum. It's a safe bet that Petrov knows about him too."

"I guess there are worse places to be, but right now, I can't think of one." Custer handed the paper back to Neilson. "Why would anyone go to this much trouble? What's the point? This is the sort of stuff they do at the Lubyanka."

"Precisely. Have you met Jack Wilder?"

"Briefly."

"You know he's Bill's old man, but he's also related the NSA director. They're brothers-in-law."

"Tight club."

"More than that. They're tight with the FBI too," Neilson said. "They all put their heads together and came up with an idea that's so logical it's scary."

"I'm listening." Custer sat on the edge of the desk and waited for his boss to explain his theory.

Neilson slowly paced the floor. "Okay. Let's be the bad guys for a minute. Say that someone wants to infiltrate the military. Where would be the best place to do it? Probably not Washington. Too high profile. Why not make your entrance in a foreign country where accountability is at it's lowest? And why not Vietnam where people come and go by the hundreds every day? How difficult would it be to switch places with someone when that person was alone and in transit halfway around the world? If he could match the general physical appearance, the paperwork end would be a piece of cake for an experienced forger. And the guy probably wouldn't be working alone."

"Classic KGB," Custer said. "Finger prints, foot prints, eye color, and dental records—all gone. Brutish, but it might work."

"And no way to get a positive ID."

Custer walked to the door. "It's a new ball game, Scott."

"I'll get a list of passengers on Wilder's flight from the States. We need to reach those two immediately."

"They're on their way from Da Nang. I'll meet them at the flight line." Custer thought for a moment. "There's something else."

"What's that?"

"You mentioned Wilder's girlfriend. Petrov could make a move on her, and we all know what he does to women. We need to put a tail on her right away."

"Already done."

"I'll be in touch." Custer closed the door and was gone.

Terry McAlester mopped the perspiration from his brow. Sitting behind his desk, he sipped his tea and looked at the afternoon reports from his people in the field. The telephone rang. "McAlester here."

"Terry, this is Jerry Bryant. I hope I'm not disturbing you."

"Heavens no, Captain Bryant. I was just working on my notes. I trust you are well?"

"I'm fine."

"What can I do for you?" *A bit of information perhaps?*

"Terry, I have something that might interest you. It isn't much but you may have some insight that I'm not privy to. Perhaps I could see you, if it's convenient."

"Yes, indeed!" McAlester was on the edge of the chair, his senses alert to the possibility of an exclusive story. "Would you like me to send a car for you?"

"That won't be necessary, Terry. When would be a good time?"

"I'm at your disposal, Captain." McAlester could barely contain his excitement. "I'll be in my hotel room. Just ask for me at the desk, and the doorman will escort you."

"Around seven then?"

"Perfect," McAlester said. "I'll arrange for some refreshments."

"See you then."

McAlester hung up the phone. He looked at it as if it was a portal to another source of information that only he had access to. He smiled to himself and sipped his tea. The military people were stingy with their information on a good day, and McAlester was determined to get to the truth, regardless of the source. It was the right of the American people and their allies to know the truth, wasn't it? And who better to provide that truth than Terry Kimet McAlester, UPI's senior correspondent in Vietnam? That American soldiers were dying and reports of their deaths by their government and military leaders were intentionally misleading, was appalling to him. It was his God-given right to report the truth, wasn't it? And report the truth, he would, and it didn't matter where the information came from—as long as it was the truth—did it?

He pondered his good fortune for several minutes, then picked up the phone and dialed.

"Hello?"

"Maggie, my dear, I have splendid news. Our Captain Bryant just called. He has some information for us that apparently has not been available through MACV channels. He's on his way to the hotel now. Would you care to join us?"

Maggie wanted nothing to do with Bryant, but she also didn't want to hurt McAlester's feelings. She knew as well as anyone how perishable valuable information was, but she also didn't want to compromise herself. Despite her negative feelings towards him, Bryant was good looking, and nasty rumors always found their way to the wrong people. She didn't want to give the appearance of impropriety when it came to her dealings with other men. There had been plenty of offers from her male co-workers during her short time in Vietnam, but she loved Wilder, and she would do nothing to jeopardize that relationship. Besides, she had to dress for a private dinner date in her suite with her husband-to-be.

"Thanks, Terry. You're a dear. But I already have plans for the evening. Bill's coming for dinner, and we're going to try to call my parents. You wouldn't mind terribly if I passed, would you?" She didn't think he would.

"Not at all, my dear. You and Bill enjoy your evening together, and give my regards to your parents when you speak to them, will you?"

"I'll do that, Terry, and thanks. I'll ring you first thing in the morning for breakfast. Then we can look at what Captain Bryant has for you, okay?"

"It's settled then. Poached eggs, coffee, and bangers at eight."

"Bye." She hung up the phone and smiled to herself. *Bangers, indeed.*

Tan Son Nhut Air Base

Slaughter taxied the aircraft into the revetment, set the parking brakes, and shut down the engines. A blue Air Force panel truck pulled adjacent to the left wing and stopped. Custer climbed out of the driver's seat and leaned against the side of the vehicle.

As soon as the propellers stopped, Wilder was through the door. He gave Custer a casual salute and walked across the ramp towards him. "Hi, Ed."

"Glad you made it back in one piece. I hear you got into it with a grunt colonel." Custer chuckled. "Pretty ballsy for a young lieutenant. What were you doing up there anyway?"

"Hauling women and booze to the heathens. Is this guy making waves?"

"I'll say. He called the Tan Son Nhut command post, and he was in a tizzy." Custer watched the rest of the crew shuffle off the plane. "Is John in there?"

"Yeah, doing paperwork. He can't spell yet, so someone else has to do the writing. He just puts his paw print on it to make it legal."

Custer looked at the plane then back at Wilder. The smile disappeared. "Something's come up, and I need to see you guys right away."

"Got a hint?"

"Langley."

Slaughter watched them through the cockpit window. He could see by their looks that something was wrong. Within seconds he was out of his seat and heading across the ramp.

"How's it going, John?" Custer said.

"Passable fine, I reckon." Slaughter thumbed over his shoulder at his plane. "Look, not a scratch. Those gomers couldn't hit the floor if they fell off a bar stool."

"Lucky for you but not for Bill."

"John, we got something from Dad, and it ain't a care package," Wilder said. There was no humor in his voice.

"What's that?"

"Let's take a ride," Custer said, leaving the question unanswered. They climbed into the vehicle and sped off. The flight line pass on the window, along with the yellow flashing light on the roof, gave them uncontested access to the entire flight line. They drove past the revetments where other C-130's were in various stages of loading and unloading. Maintenance was being performed on some, while others waited silently for their crew chiefs to bring them to life in preparation for their night missions.

Custer pulled into the empty revetment at the end of the last row and stopped. There was no one around, and they wouldn't be disturbed. He shut off the engine and looked around to make sure that they were alone.

"Great place to bring a date."

"You wouldn't know what to do with it, John."

"I'm glad you guys still have a sense of humor, but I'm going to have to rain on your parade," Custer said.

"Charlie already tried."

"Well, Bill, this is going to do it. Neilson got a message from Langley, and it's gruesome to say the least." Custer told them about the mutilated body and the duffel bag, and that the CIA was certain that Petrov was in Saigon. He said nothing about the flight from Dulles. "We think he's under an assumed identity and that he's in a position where he can have direct access to either or both of you." He looked at Wilder. "We're pretty sure he knows about Maggie too, so we've assigned a detail to keep an eye on her just in case."

Wilder's fists were clenched at his side, but he didn't move. "She knows nothing about any of this."

"We'll do everything we can, Bill, to protect her, but you have to understand that, short of having agents in her room, we can't possibly watch her every second. The best thing would be for her to go back to the States. If you have any pull with her or McAlester, now's the time to use it."

Wilder took a deep breath. "If I say anything to him, he'll ask questions. Can't approach him on this."

Custer knew about Petrov's brutality towards women. He chose his words carefully. "Bill, I don't mean to get personal, but—"

"You want me to persuade her to leave the country."

"Yes." Custer hesitated, then said, "Remember what Neilson said about Petrov being splashy ... " *Get her out of here!*

"She'll smell a rat." Wilder thought for a second, then said, "I'm seeing her tonight. I'll see what I can do."

"I understand your relationship with her, Bill, but it's for her own good. Besides, she and her brother shouldn't both be here in the first place. I don't know how that happened, but I'm going to look into it."

"Thanks, Ed. I appreciate that."

"If that Bolshevik bastard gets near her, I'll kick his ass so high that he'll have to look up to shit!"

"Let's hope it doesn't come to that, John," Custer said. They sat in silence, each man thinking about this recent turn of events and how to deal with it. Two men wondered what would happen if the third got to Petrov before they did. They had their own ideas, but neither wanted to broach the subject. The third one knew *exactly* what would happen.

CHAPTER 9

"I'm worried about Tommy. I haven't heard from him since the Army sent him to the jungle. Don't they have phones there?" Maggie's lack of knowledge of military operations amused Wilder and made him love her all the more.

"Maggie, that place isn't exactly the center of the universe. No phones, but I'm sure he's fine. Just remember that no news is good news, even in your line of work."

"That's not funny." She looked helplessly at him. "Not only can't I get in touch with him, I can't report what's going on in this cursed country. MACV clams up when anyone asks questions, and I'm fed up with it. Besides that, every man in this country has his own agenda, and it's clearly in his pants. I've been propositioned by every male in this place, and it makes me sick." She buried her face in his chest, and he wrapped his arms around her. "I'm so tired of it. Why can't they just accept me as a professional woman with a job to do? Between these Neanderthals and the lack of news, I'm about to pull my hair out."

Wilder kept his thoughts to himself. He knew that she was the object of attention of every red-blooded male in Saigon, and it didn't bother him … well, maybe a little. He was no different except for the fact that she was in love with him. He wasn't worried about her being unfaithful. His main concern was her safety. "I know it's frustrating, Maggie, and you have every right to be upset. But you need to understand something; you're one of only a handful of American women in this country. On top of that you're beautiful to begin with. That combination makes you stand out in a country where most women come equipped with a bag to put over their heads."

"Ape!" she softly scolded. She hugged him.

Wilder held her and stroked her hair. "Sorry, Maggie, but it's the truth. I'd chase you too if I hadn't already caught you. Don't get too mad at these guys for coming on to you. They're lonely and a long way from home."

"Bullshit! They're horny."

"Ouch!" Wilder couldn't help smiling. "Don't pay any attention to them, Red. Remember you're the future Mrs. Ape."

"I like the sound of that." They held each other.

Wilder still had to broach the subject of her leaving, and he was careful in his choice of words. "This place is frustrating to anyone on a good day. Worse than that, it's dangerous as hell. Remember the Tet Offensive in '68? The North Vietnamese and the Cong blew this place all to hell."

"I remember it as if it was yesterday. I was protesting in Boston."

"Well, it can happen again, and I don't want you in the middle of it when it does." He held her at arm's length, and their eyes locked. "Maggie, I want you to go back to the States."

She stared at him, unable to speak. After an eternity of seconds, she found her voice. "What? … You want me to leave?" Her eyes began to mist.

He guided her to the sofa. Holding her hands, he said, "Listen, Maggie, no matter what else is going on here, this is a dangerous place. You're in the middle of a war zone, and the North Vietnamese and Vietcong don't recognize the Geneva Convention. You could be killed … or worse. Do you have any idea what they'd do to you before they killed you? You'd pray for death."

"If you're trying to frighten me, Bill Wilder, you're succeeding in spades, but I'm still here on assignment, and I'm not leaving until I finish my job." Her Irish tempter was beginning to flare.

Wilder's resolve was firm. "Think about this then; you and your brother are both in harm's way. He shouldn't be here, but he is here, and that's that. I don't know how else to say this, so I'll be blunt."

"Please do." Her face was flushed, her frustration and anger beginning to surface.

"Think about your parents, Maggie. What do you think would happen to them if either or both of you guys were killed or captured? They would be devastated. Remember what your father said about this war, and imagine how he feels about both his kids being here. We need to think about them, don't we?" It was time to soften things up a bit. "Besides, I think it would be nice to make them grandparents. What do you think?" His words and disarming smile had the desired effect.

"Oh, Bill … " Her eyes flooded and she sank in his arms.

"Maggie," he whispered, "please think about it. Our future together is at stake, along with the future of our unborn children. That's more important than anything, isn't it?"

The tears ran down her face. "Bill, I love you so much. You're right about Mom and Dad. I never considered them like this before." She pulled his face to hers and they kissed. "I thought I was more determined than this, but, within a matter of minutes, you changed everything. I'll talk to Terry tomorrow about going back to the States." She held his face in her hands. "Please stay with me tonight."

"I wouldn't think of leaving."

The knock came right on time, and McAlester opened the door with a flourish. His expected guest stood with a bottle of wine in an ice bucket. "Captain Bryant, what a splendid surprise. Do come in." McAlester stood aside and waved Bryant into the room.

"Hello, Terry. Sorry for being late, but I had to make a stop along the way. I took the liberty of bringing you a bottle of merlot. I'm not sure it will go well with the fine food that the hotel offers, but supplies are limited here." Bryant sat the bucket on the table and looked around the room. "I see that UPI takes care of its own."

"We manage, my friend." He looked at the bottle on the table.

"You are most considerate." McAlester went for a corkscrew and two glasses. "Please sit down. Dreadfully hot outside. You must be exhausted."

"It's warm." Bryant sat in a nearby chair and looked at the window. "This place is amazing, isn't it? So much going on under our noses, but no one knows a thing. I don't suppose MACV has given you anything useful."

McAlester dropped his ample mass onto the bed. "Indeed, Jerry, those chaps seem to become more bellicose every day. They regard the press as so many pains in the arse. In my time here I haven't seen much of anything that would be worthy of print since Tet of '68." He opened the wine and poured two glasses. He handed one to his guest, barely able to contain his excitement. "So, Jerry, I understand that you have some information for me?"

"I might. But first, Terry, please understand that this is between friends." Bryant leaned forward in his chair, his expression serious. "I'd like to ask you not to reveal any of this to anyone and not print anything until I can confirm the information one way or the other."

"I absolutely understand." McAlester was spring loaded, and he strained to control himself so as not to scare away this potential source of information. "And I agree. After all, nothing should be printed unless it's the truth."

"Exactly. Obviously, I can't reveal anything in advance that could hurt friendly forces. I'm sure you understand."

"Of course. Please proceed, Captain." McAlester poured them another glass of wine, his senses keen to anything Bryant had to say.

"First, a little background. There's an Army fire base camp north of Kontum. Fire Base Alpha. As you know the NVA and the Vietcong are strong in that area … "

Slaughter slammed the empty Black Label can onto the bar. "Hey, Vinh, when are you going to get some real beer in this dump? This sheep dip ain't fit for human consumption."

"No hab," the Vietnamese bartender said in broken English. "Brak Rabel number one."

"This shit's number ten for crying out loud." Slaughter looked angrily around the bar. His eyes settled on the bartender. "Bourbon."

"Okay." Vinh poured a glass of whisky over some ice and slid it across the counter.

Slaughter drank the bourbon and gazed around the smoke-filled room. *We Gotta Get Out Of This Place* was blaring from the juke box. The song had been banned by the military powers-that-be, thereby making it the number one hit in all of Vietnam among GI's. The bar was full of uniforms from the various services, particularly the Air Force and Army. Many of them were in various states of inebriation, depending their individual levels of depression. *At least you guys get a chance to get out of the bush*, Slaughter thought.

Not recognizing anyone, his thoughts returned to the intelligence briefing—or lack of it—earlier in the day, and he realized that neither Bryant nor Berwick were in the club. He had yet to see Berwick in the bar at all. He jumped off his seat and headed for the lobby, his temper rising as the alcohol took effect. He grabbed the nearest phone and dialed a number. He impatiently waited for an answer.

"Intel. Sergeant Jackson."

"John Slaughter here, looking for Lieutenant Berwick. Is he around?"

"No, sir. Left today for Hong Kong. He's on leave for two weeks. Anything I can do for you?"

"Hong Kong? What the hell's he going there for?"

"To get laid I guess."

"Is Bryant there?"

"All the zero's are gone. Want to leave a message?"

"No, thanks," Slaughter said. "Just one question though; can you tell me anything over the phone about Khe Sanh today?"

"Let's just say that there's a real estate *boom* there, especially to the east."

"Would you recommend vacationing there?"

"If I was buying an airline ticket to that place, I'd change destinations. The air traffic controllers aren't user friendly, if you get my drift," the sergeant said.

"Loud and clear."

"No missions have been scheduled in there for a while. Captain Bryant will be in tomorrow. He'll be able to answer your questions better than me."

"Know where he is?"

"He said he had to go into Saigon. Meeting with one of those asshole journalists."

Another fucking glory-hound! "Okay. Settles that. Thanks, Sarge. I'll drop by tomorrow." Slaughter hung up the phone and went back to the bar. *Damn you, Berwick!*

CHAPTER 10

Unable to sleep, Slaughter paced the floor in the cubicle that was his room, wondering what Berwick was up to. He mentally reconstructed events from the day before; of how he had been shot at while going into supposedly friendly airspace and why Wilder's plane had been almost shot down. Other than the buzzing of Army helicopters, he had heard nothing from any other aircraft going into and out of Khe Sanh all day. Aside from his and Wilder's missions, he didn't recall any other flights into that strip. Of the hundreds of ships flying all over Vietnam, why just two into this particular LZ? And why *them*? The more he thought about it, the more confused and angry he became. He wanted answers, and he was impatient to get them.

He pulled on his cleanest dirty jeans and an OD green T-shirt with *Kill A Commie For Christ* emblazoned across the chest. He slipped into his worn loafers and headed for the door.

The early morning sky was still dark as Slaughter walked the two blocks to the concrete building where his friend hung his hat. The ground was wet from the night rain, and the pungent odor of the open benjo ditches that lined the edges of the street assaulted his senses. *Fucking hole*, he thought to himself. He walked quickly, his mind churning over the shoot-out at Vietnam's version of the *OK Corral* the day before.

There is an unspoken rule that air crews follow religiously: Eat when you can and sleep when you can. Don't stand up when you can sit down, and don't sit down when you can lay down. You don't know when you'll get the chance to eat or sleep again, so do it when that chance comes, whether you want to or not. Missions went on during all hours, and crew rest went for a premium. Those off duty or just returning generally tried to keep the commotion down to a dull roar out of respect for those trying to get some rest. On this morning, however, Slaughter was like a rolling manhole cover. He had the tact of a high speed bowling ball and the strength and grit to back it up. He stormed into Wilder's building like a man on a mission, bumping into an outgoing pilot about to leave on a flight to God-knows-where.

"Hey, Animal, what are you doing up so early? Couldn't get laid last night?" Captain Tim Gallin asked while dragging his flight bag down the hall.

"Couldn't find a member of the female species worthy of my seed. Seen lover boy?"

"If you mean Wilder, he just came in. He's in the shower." Gallin stood with his hands on his hips. "What gives? You look like you could kill someone."

"Might before the day's over." Slaughter started down the hall, then stopped and looked over his shoulder. "Where you going anyway?"

"Da Nang. Why?"

"No reason. See you later."

"Yeah. You too." *Wonder what that's all about?* Gallin picked up his bag and headed out the door. He had his own survival to think of.

Rounding the corner of the shower room, Slaughter saw Wilder standing in his birthday suit under the steaming water. Less than ten feet from him was an old Vietnamese mama-san scrubbing flight suits on a washboard in a steel barrel full of hot water and an entire box of Tide. Suds were everywhere. Electric washers and dryers, courtesy of Uncle Sam, stood idle along the wall, their brand new tags still on them.

"Let me guess. You've been flying around in your red cape and boots, doing good deeds again."

Wilder looked at him. "And you've been racing the Bat-mobile, right?"

"At least the damn thing runs." Slaughter looked at the mama-san. He smiled in spite of his foul mood. She was oblivious to them. "Have you no shame, Bill?"

"Look who's talking." Wilder rinsed the soap off his face. "What are you doing here this time of night, John? Did Rosie Palm and her five sisters let you down?"

"Eat my shorts!" Slaughter glanced once more at the small woman sitting in a squatting position, her attention directed at her washboard. He looked at Wilder. "We need to talk."

"I'll be done in a bit." Wilder watched his friend abruptly leave. Sensing something wrong, he quickly rinsed away the soap and wrapped a towel around his waist. He looked at mama-san. "Thanks, ma'am. I appreciate it."

Not understanding a single word, the ancient woman mumbled something in Vietnamese and grinned at him with brown teeth stained from years of chewing betel nut. She went back to beating the life out the soap-caked flight suits, having no regard for the alien-looking white metal boxes along the wall.

Wilder slipped into a pair of cut-offs and a tank top shirt. Splashing after shave on his face, he studied Slaughter in the mirror. "Maggie asked about you." He waited for a response but got none. He picked up his coffee and faced his friend. "Okay, John, let's hear it."

Slaughter leaned against the wall and stared at Wilder. He shoved his hand into his pocket and pulled out two sheets of crumpled paper. He held them to Wilder's face. "Check it out."

"What's this?" Wilder took the papers and opened them.

"These are our flight schedules for Khe Sanh yesterday. They're all stamped and legal."

Wilder looked at the documents. "So?"

"So, of all the low-life bums in this place, why do we get to go where no man has gone before?"

Wilder looked at the papers again. "These are frag orders, John, not the Constitution." He looked at Slaughter. "What's your point?"

"My point, Great One, is that we were the only chumps to go into that hell-hole all day. Not only were we tagged, we were almost bagged, and no one else even knew about it."

"What the hell are you talking about?" Wilder's eyes narrowed. He didn't like what he was hearing. "What do you know that I don't?"

"Plenty. We weren't supposed to be there in the *first* fucking place!"

Wilder sat on the edge of the bed and looked at the papers again. "John, tell me what's going on."

Slaughter wanted to break something, but he rubbed his hands together and took a deep breath. "Listen, we've been through a lot of shit through the years."

"Tell me something I don't know."

"Remember the explosion at Jake's?" Slaughter grabbed the papers from Wilder's hand and waved them in his face. "Well, this is more of the same. Bill, we were set up."

"Keep talking." Wilder didn't move.

"I thought about it last night at the bar. I called the intel office and tried to talk to Berwick, but the NCO on duty said Berwick had split for Hong Kong on leave. Bryant was in Saigon. He also told me that all flights into Khe Sanh had been canceled for days because the bad guys owned the real estate east of the field."

Slaughter explained how he had gone to the command post and examined the original flight schedules and had learned after the fact that both he and Wilder were supposed to go to Da Nang. Fortunately, he had kept a copy of his and Wilder's original orders when he picked up Wilder's crew in Da Nang that afternoon. Somewhere prior to their intelligence briefing, the mission itinerary had been changed. Berwick had briefed them that they were going to Khe Sanh and had given them a field assessment during their pre-departure briefing. The field and the approach to it were "cold," he had said. There was no known enemy activity east of the air strip.

"Berwick lied to us, Bill. We need to go to Bryant's office. I want some answers." Slaughter slumped to the floor, the effects of alcohol and lack of sleep finally catching up to him.

Wilder read the papers again. They looked real enough, but they had somehow been altered prior to the crew's show time for the flight. He looked at Slaughter. "We have to move carefully. I think somebody's trying to kill us, and I'll give you one guess who it is."

"That Commie scum!"

"And I'll bet he has someone in the command post helping him, whether that person knows it or not. Berwick could be part of this or he could just be duped. I don't know, but we need to reach Custer and Neilson and get them up to speed on this."

"I'll get on it." Slaughter started to get up.

Wilder held up his hand. "Hold on, John. There's something else."

"What?" Slaughter dropped back to the floor.

"Maggie's going back to the States."

"Back to the States? What gives?"

"We had a serious talk last night. To make a long story short, I convinced her that Saigon wasn't safe. And if Petrov is here, and I think he is, it's more dangerous than I thought. I want her out of here."

"When's she leaving?"

"I don't know, but the sooner, the better. I want to get her out of here within a couple of days. In the meantime, we're going to pay a visit to the command post and get some answers. And if I have to go over their heads, I'll do it."

"How are we going to do this without raising suspicion?"

"Don't have to. There's an Army colonel in Khe Sanh that wants my head, and he's going to help me in my efforts. He'll prove that we were there if someone tries to deny it. Remember the rotors?"

"I do."

"I'm sure he'll move heaven and earth to accommodate me."

"I sure as hell hope so."

"Let's go." The two men left the barracks and headed for the command post complex.

"Bill, I swear I don't have any idea where these came from. The frag orders said Da Nang when I picked them up, and the clerk ran off the copies in front of me," Captain Dan Mercer, the on-duty controller, said. "I called the load section two times and verified that you were taking Class A explosives to Da Nang." He turned to Slaughter. "I did the same with you, John. Your orders were clear on this. If they were switched, it was after I put them in your folders."

Wilder stood motionless, but Slaughter paced like a nervous cat. "Who's the asshole that switched them?"

"John, a half dozen people had access these orders, including intel. What did they tell you?"

"Berwick told us we were going to Khe Sanh and that the field and approach to it were secure," Wilder said.

Mercer shook his head. "Look, guys, I'm at a loss here same as you. I don't know anything about Khe Sanh. Not trying to pass the buck, but I don't know what happened here." He scratched his head. "I'm not surprised though. This place is crawling with screw-ups." He nodded his head towards the intelligence office. "Bryant should be here in about an hour. He may be able to help you."

"He's our next stop," Wilder said. "But first I need to use your secure phone."

"Sure. You know where it is." Mercer pointed to the adjacent room. "Key's on my desk." He looked at Slaughter. "Hey, John, how about some real coffee? You look like you could use some."

Slaughter grunted and headed for the coffee urn. He poured a cup and took a drink. He grimaced. "This stuff could melt lead. Just what the doctor ordered." He turned to Mercer. "Listen, Dan, I didn't mean to bite off your head earlier. It's just that when some prick schedules my ass for target practice, I get a little sideways."

Mercer nodded. "I don't blame you, John. We're all targets in this place at some point I guess."

"But it's a little different when one of your own people sets you up."

Mercer frowned but said nothing.

Wilder relayed his story to the CIA station chief via the secure phone. "We're going to talk to Bryant now. Should have some answers soon … Yes, she's planning on leaving as soon as she can … Okay. I'll be in touch." Wilder broke the connection and hung up the phone. He rejoined Slaughter and Mercer.

"You're getting popular around here, Bill. Just got a message from the Army up north at I Corps. Seems that a Colonel Hughes from Da

Nang is on his way here to pay his respects. He asked for you specifically. What's that all about?"

"Let's just say that oil and water don't mix."

"Uh-huh."

Wilder sat to wait in Bryant's office while Slaughter paced the floor like a caged animal. Neither man spoke. Eventually, Bryant arrived. Although he didn't expect anyone, he frequently had unannounced visitors. "Hi, guys. How's it going?" Bryant sat at his desk. "What's—"

"What kind of fucking operation are you running here?" Slaughter leaned over the desk, his ham-fisted hands planted on the flat surface.

Caught off guard, Bryant leaned back in his seat and raised his hands. "Hey, relax, John. We're on the same side here. What's the problem?"

"You know goddamn well what the problem is!"

Wilder was up in an instant, his hand on Slaughter's shoulder. "Easy, John. Let's let him tell his side of the story. We'll take out our frustrations in the gym later." Wilder's face was a mixture of curiosity and anger, and he was not in the mood to be toyed with. Despite his rising temper, he remained calm.

"What's going on?" Bryant said.

Wilder dropped the flight orders on the desk. "*That's* what's going on.*" He told Bryant about the papers being switched and how, as a result, he had nearly been killed. He stood in front of Bryant's desk and stared at him. "Somewhere between the command post and this office, these orders were changed. Either Berwick's a lot smarter than I give him credit for, or you guys have been suckered by someone in this command complex." Wilder picked up the bogus flight orders and held them in the air. "How the hell do you explain this, Jerry?" He tossed the papers down and waited for an answer.

Bryant crossed his arms and stared at the documents. "The short version is I can't." He looked at Wilder. "I came in yesterday morning around six, read the SIGINT reports, and checked with Mercer. He said he had ten missions going out yesterday, but none were significant. Berwick was preparing the standard vanilla briefing for all the crews, and he didn't say anything to me about any missions to

Khe Sanh. I left shortly afterwards for MACV headquarters for the daily intel briefing."

Slaughter wasn't satisfied. "You didn't look at any of the mission set ups?"

"I'm not the one that plans these missions, John. Besides, there was no need to. There wasn't any unusual activity around Da Nang, and Khe Sanh wasn't in the picture. The only thing I've seen that could be of any interest during that time frame is the enemy activity around Kontum. Charlie and the NVA are moving down the Ho Chi Minh Trail, stockpiling munitions in the surrounding jungle. The word from MACV is that a major offensive is expected within the next few weeks. The ARVN has been reinforcing its numbers there, and we've been sending AC-130 gunships over at night to hose the place down. But nothing on Khe Sanh."

"Any word on action around Fire Base Alpha?" Wilder's thoughts went to Maggie's brother.

"No. Why?"

"I know some guys there."

Slaughter wasn't satisfied. "Well, hooray for the good guys, but that still doesn't answer the question about these damn changes to our orders. What gives?"

"What do you want me to say, John? I've no idea." Bryant reached for the papers. He examined them from top to bottom. "They look real." He looked at Slaughter then at Wilder. "I don't know what to tell you, guys, but I know that Berwick picked them up from Mercer. That's the standard operating procedure around here. Beyond that, it's a mystery to me." He dropped the papers onto the desk.

"And now that asshole has skipped town." Slaughter leaned against the door, his hands jammed into his pockets.

"He's on leave," Bryant said. "Went to Hong Kong."

"Who authorized it?" Wilder asked.

"I did. He's been here for over six months, and I didn't have any reason to deny it." Bryant glanced once more at the papers. "What would he have to gain by doing this?"

Wilder and Slaughter looked at each other, their thoughts together in a different place and time. "Let's just say that we don't see eye to eye and let it go at that," Wilder said.

"Okay, but he's done nothing wrong as far as I can tell," Bryant said.

Wilder just looked at him.

"I'll see what I can find out. In the meantime, I went to see McAlester yesterday. You know, the Englishman from UPI. Anyway, he told me that MACV is starving the newsies. They're not getting much to report."

"No news is good news here," Slaughter said.

"I guess, but they're frustrated. And when they get that way, they start making up their own stories."

"What's your point?" Wilder wasn't sure where this was going.

"My point is that they need something substantial. Otherwise, they'll start speculating, and people back home will believe what they read, true or not. I told McAlester in confidence that the Cong and NVA are massing around Kontum. I didn't give him anything classified, but he needed something to keep him honest."

Slaughter looked at the ceiling then glared at Bryant. "Who's side are you on anyway?"

"Bryant, are you crazy?" Wilder leaned forward. "If the press finds out something's going on up there, they'll go public and screw up everything. MACV knows what's happening, and they damn sure don't want those idiots to know about it if American lives are at stake. What the hell did you do that for?"

Bryant was immediately on the defensive. "Hang on, guys." He held up his hands. "I just told him to be ready when the action starts. I didn't compromise anything. I don't have any details anyway. Look, those guys need something to keep them from wondering into fantasy land, and a showdown is coming in the Central Highlands. Everyone knows—"

"No, they don't," Wilder shot back.

"I just want them to tell the truth. He gave me his word that he wouldn't publish a thing without checking with me first."

"We just got screwed." Slaughter dropped into a chair. "Those left wing tree-huggers hate the military." He kept glaring a Bryant. "So what are you going to do when they go public before they should?"

"They won't. I only talked to McAlester, and I'm telling you that he won't print anything until he gets it from me, and I'll only give him laundered information *after* it happens."

"MACV will hang you for this, Bryant, and I'll be the one to put the rope around your neck if you screw up." Wilder's eyes narrowed. "What are you getting out of this?"

"I've decided to get out of the Air Force at the end of this assignment. No future here for a navigator. There's a future in journalism, and I've decided that scoring points with someone high on that ladder won't hurt. Get my drift?"

"Yeah, I get it," Slaughter said. "I'll scratch your back if you scratch mine."

"You have a way with words, John, but essentially, that's right. But I'm not going to jeopardize our guys, and you know that."

Wilder stared at him. "A below-the-belt means to an end. You bastard! I'll be damned if you're going to threaten any American lives with this bullshit scheme of yours."

"Look, Bill, I have friends in the highlands too."

Wilder's eyes bored into him. "If you screw up, Bryant, I'll be there. You're on thin ice with this."

Bryant was getting irritated. "Give me some credit, for crying out loud. Those idiots have to be kept under control. I just want them to publish the truth. That's all. I'll be careful. You have my word."

"You bet you will."

"What about Maggie," Slaughter said. "Does she know anything about this?"

"No, she doesn't," Bryant said. "I saw McAlester alone."

"What's she going to do when she gets back to the States?"

"We didn't talk about that, John," Wilder said. "She just decided last night that she would leave." Wilder's eyes remained on Bryant. "What happens next is still up in the air."

"Maggie's leaving?" Bryant asked.

Wilder chose his words carefully. "We decided that it's too dangerous for her here. She has a younger brother up north, and the whole thing is stressful on her parents. She's going home."

"That's a good idea. What about her brother?"

Wilder's eyes burned into him. "That's none of your concern. Just find Berwick and get me some answers."

Bryant picked up the papers. "I'll see what I can do. I'll let you know when I find something."

"Call me the second you find out anything. We'll be here in minutes," Wilder said.

"Okay."

Slaughter left the room without speaking.

Bryant watched Slaughter leave. "He's a bit uncouth, isn't he?"

"Perhaps, but don't count him out. He's smarter than he looks." Wilder turned to Bryant, the malevolence still in his eyes. "And you watch yourself with McAlester." Wilder slammed the door when he left Bryant's office.

Dan Mercer held the telephone receiver in his hand. "Bill, there's an Army colonel on the other end of this line that has a pressing need to talk to you. He's calling from HQ in Da Nang. Seems that his flight got nixed. Can't imagine how." Mercer's attempt to keep from smiling failed.

Wilder took the receiver and placed his hand over the mouthpiece. He leaned towards Slaughter and whispered, "This is the guy from Khe Sanh. He's been in the bush too long, and I think he's going to ask me for a date."

"Tell the asshole to go piss up a rope."

"I'll consider your suggestion, John." Wilder placed the receiver to his ear. "Hello?"

"Lieutenant Wilder, this is Colonel Hughes calling from I Corps. I want to talk to you about your actions at Khe Sanh yesterday. I consider you insubordinate … "

Wilder again placed his hand on the receiver. "Is this being recorded, Dan?"

"Of course."

"Excellent." Wilder listened to the one-sided phone conversation for several minutes. Finally, he said, "Thank you, Colonel Hughes, for your call. You have no idea what you've done for me."

"What are you talking about?"

"You proved that I was in Khe Sanh yesterday, and your remarks about my lack of cooperation have proven that you've eaten too many C-rations. You should give them up for Lent."

"How dare you—"

"Colonel, with all due respect, you have my authorization and permission to participate in aeronautical intercourse with an automated perforated pastry. Good day, sir." Wilder placed the phone in the cradle. "And that takes care of that."

"That was beautiful," Mercer said, giving a double thumbs-up.

"What did you tell him?" Slaughter could barely contain his excitement.

Wilder patted him on the head. "John, I told him that he could go take a flying fuck at a rolling donut."

"Yeah!"

Mercer laughed. "I've heard some good ones, but that one takes the cake."

"Colonel Hughes told me to say hello to all and that he hopes you have a nice day. Later guys." Wilder headed for the door. It was time to get some much needed sleep. There wasn't anything else he could do for now.

The two pilots left the command post and headed towards their barracks. "Seems that we have two problems now," Wilder said.

"Yeah, that dipstick Berwick selling us out and Bryant kissing ass with the press. With friends like them, we sure as hell don't need any enemies."

"That's part of it, John, but what bothers me is that Berwick is being so obvious. Everything points to him."

"He's about as sharp as the leading edge of a medicine ball."

"I agree, but something tells me that there's more to it than meets the eye. I don't think Berwick is stupid or that he has the nerve to pull something like this alone."

"Well, he certainly has reason," Slaughter said. "Bryant ain't too swift either. Rubbing elbows with McAlester to make a name for himself is pretty low rent."

"True, but at least he's honest about it. Have to give him credit for that. I just hope he doesn't do something stupid and get someone killed." Wilder watched the heat waves rising off the asphalt in the early dawn. They were already soaked from the humidity, and the temperature had just begun to climb. "Hot as hell here."

"In more ways than one." It had been a long night for both of them. "Let's get some sleep. Then we'll get to the bottom of this."

CHAPTER 11

The Central Highlands of South Vietnam were strategically important to both South Vietnamese and American forces. The area was primarily occupied by the Montagnard Tribes, many of whom were friendly with Americans. They fought along side the Americans against the North Vietnamese and Vietcong. Located in the Highlands, Pleiku was the strategic center of a large US-ARVN military complex, and, as a result, the region endured heavy fighting throughout the war. Not only did the NVA and Vietcong attack the city in force on frequent occasions, they often attacked the surrounding villages, especially Kontum, where American C-130 aircraft landed around the clock, delivering supplies and ammunition to the beleaguered troops stationed there.

Daylight hours were relatively safe since the South Vietnamese Army was able to contain the enemy forces for the most part. But the Vietcong controlled the night, and it was a major victory if they could destroy a C-130 on the ground. It would, in effect, render the airfield useless until the wreckage could be removed, a task that could take days.

Kontum airport, due to its being the only avenue of re-supply and escape for the Montagnards and local villagers, drew special attention. One of the most lethal and feared weapons in the American arsenal was the AC-130 gunship. Known as Specter, the aircraft was equipped with two multi-barreled machine guns, four 20mm Vulcan multi-barreled guns, and a 40mm Bofors cannon, along with infrared sensors, low-light TV, and laser target designators. The crew could fire a continuous round of shells, interspersed with red tracers, and cover every square foot of a football field within seconds. Nothing on the surface could escape the raining devastation from the "red line in the sky."

While the Specter was devastating, the enemy was resilient. Hiding in a vast system of tunnels, they were able, to some degree, to withstand the intense aerial attacks by the Americans. When darkness fell, the Vietcong would come out of their tunnels, and the shelling of the airfield would begin.

"Okay, John, this is one way to defend against a knife attack. Remember, never take your eye off the blade. Now, attack me." They had been working in the hot gym for two hours, and they were dripping wet. Despite the heat, the exercise had worked out the kinks and made them feel human again.

"I'm gonna get you, boy!" Slaughter rushed at Wilder and thrust the rubber knife at him.

"Not today, partner." The knife came down at Wilder's face. He threw up a crossed-arm block, stopping Slaughter's forearm in mid-air. He quickly grabbed Slaughter's wrist with his right hand and, securing his grip with his left hand, stepped across Slaughter's front. Turning around, he twisted and pulled on Slaughter's arm. The knife fell to the floor, and Slaughter, caught by surprise, was forced to do a flip, landing on his back. Maintaining his grip on Slaughter's wrist, Wilder placed his foot gently on his friend's throat. "Any questions?"

"What a guy! I know you're gonna let me up," Slaughter said, his pride and body unhurt.

Wilder pulled him to his feet. "Had enough?" He slapped Slaughter on the back.

"Feel like I've been dragged through a knot hole." Slaughter wiped his face with a towel. "That's enough pounding for one day, I reckon."

Wilder laughed. "Let's hit the shower and get something to eat." They put their martial equipment into their gym bags and headed for the locker room. "When we're done stuffing our faces, let's stop by the command post and see if Bryant's turned up anything."

"Yeah."

"You still here, Mercer? You must be a glutton for punishment." Slaughter looked around the room. The activity had picked up considerably since their visit earlier in the day. "What's going on? Looks like the wolves are at the door."

"The shit's hit the fan, that's what," Mercer said, his eyes scanning the mission board on the wall.

"What's up?" Wilder asked.

"Kontum's under attack, and the friendlies are in deep *kemchee*, our guys included. The Cong have overrun several Montagnard villages, and the little people are heading to the airfield in droves. Herks are shuttling in and out as fast as they can, off loading bullets and on loading bodies."

"Is everybody getting out?" *Tommy.*

"No, Bill, and you don't want to know what Charlie's doing to those poor bastards that get left behind." Mercer's eyes were like an open book.

"What about our guys? Anyone been shot down?"

"Not yet, John, but Charlie's pressing hard. They'd love to bag a Herk on the runway. It would shut the whole operation down in a heartbeat."

"Crap!" Slaughter jammed his hands into his pockets and focused on the planning board. A large sheet of plexi-glass was attached to the wall, and a half dozen airmen were feverishly attacking it with grease pencils. On it were listed all the missions, including aircraft numbers and crews for the next twenty-four hours. "All those flights going to Kontum?"

"Yeah, and we're running every available ship and crew we have. You guys are in the line up too. Your crew rest started a while ago. Hope you haven't been hitting the sauce."

"Wouldn't say so if we did," Slaughter said.

"Bill, you're up at 0700. 0900 for you, John." Mercer wrote their names against a mission number on the board. "Each mission's running about ten hours or more." He turned to them. "Better get some sleep, guys. Might not see it again for a while."

Wilder looked down the hall towards the intelligence office. "What's Bryant have to say about all of this?"

"He got a call from MACV a couple hours ago. Those guys were just here, giving us the down-and-dirty version. Bryant's at MACV now getting the details. Should be back in a couple hours. In the meantime, we're tasked with loading every ship and digging up every available body we can."

Wilder thought out loud. "Maggie's brother is up there."

"I know."

"What's the situation at Alpha?"

"I don't know, Bill, but I'll bet they aren't sitting around drinking beer and listening to the Rolling Stones."

Wilder was pensive. "Dan, I have to go into Saigon for a while. I—"

"Sorry, Bill, but you can't."

"What do you mean?"

"Everyone's been restricted to the base."

"What?"

"Wing commander's orders. No one can leave the base, and all leaves have been canceled. Sorry, guy, but we're stuck."

Wilder thought for a moment. "Can I use your phone? I have to call the Caravelle."

"Sorry, again, Bill, but no off base calls are allowed. We can only communicate with MACV through secure channels, and they have all the lines tied up. The base operators are under strict orders."

"You mean I can't call my mama?" Slaughter said. "Charlie sticks his head up, and we have to stand in the corner. Who's side is Uncle Sam on anyway?"

"Makes you wonder." Wilder sat in a chair and looked at the planning board. "Looks like we're up to bat soon, John. May as well go back to the hooch and lay low for a while. Nothing we can do here."

"Okey-dokey."

"Dan, Bryant's checking on something for me. If he comes in with anything, get him to call me, okay? Doesn't matter what time it is. Don't worry about the crew rest thing."

"Sorry about the restrictions, guys. We're all stuck here."

"Shit happens," Slaughter said.

They walked for a while before Slaughter broke the silence. "I wonder if McAlester knows that all hell's broke loose up north? Bryant's supposed to be at MACV, but I'll bet my last pair of clean shorts that he's kissing ass with that Englishman."

"Well, more power to him if he is," Wilder said. "With the fighting in the Highlands, the cat's out of the bag anyway. I don't agree with Bryant's motives, but I can't blame him either. Nobody wants to make a career of this bullshit. This stuff's going to be all over the news in a matter of hours anyway."

They reached the barracks. "Time for some shut-eye, oh, Great One." Slaughter turned to his friend. "Listen, Bill, keep your head down. I ain't in the bad-news business." A double thumbs-up. "Later, dude."

"Yeah, and you behave yourself up there."

Walking towards his barracks, Slaughter flashed his social finger over his shoulder. "Ain't gonna happen."

Wilder was unable to sleep. He was worried about Maggie and her unsecured departure from Saigon. He lay motionless in the dark with his hands behind his head, thinking of her and Tommy. His thoughts drifted to Berwick. Why would Berwick so obviously stick his neck out to cause Wilder and Slaughter so much trouble? Was it just coincidence that Berwick was on leave when the Khe Sanh incident took place? Was he trying to escape from something? If so, what? If he was in Hong Kong, no one would be able to find him. On the other hand, he was there legally. *What's wrong with this picture?*

When the knock at the door came, Wilder just looked at the ceiling. "Yes?"

"Sergeant Cummings from the command post, sir. Sorry to wake you, but we have to alert you early." He waited for a reply. "Sir, are you awake?"

Mercer, you are a slug. "Yeah, hang on." Wilder walked across the room and opened the door. "What's up?"

"I'm sorry, sir, but one of our pilots just came down with food poisoning, and we need your crew to take his mission out." The sergeant was uncomfortable; he didn't like waking people up in the middle of the night, especially officers. "You were next on the list."

"Food poisoning?" Wilder rubbed his eyes. "Probably the rat ribs at the club last night."

"The what?"

"Nothing. Just thinking out loud." Wilder looked up and down the hall, then returned his attention to the young sergeant. "What's your first name?"

"Dave, sir."

"Okay, Dave. Give me ten minutes."

"Yes, sir." He handed Wilder a cup of coffee. "Compliments of Captain Mercer."

Wilder took the paper cup. "Thanks. Doesn't that man ever sleep?"

"He's a machine, sir." Cummings smiled and started down the hall. "I'll be in the bread truck, Captain."

"Captain?"

"Didn't you get the word? You and your sidekick just got promoted."

"Some things just slip through the cracks, I guess." Wilder smiled to himself. He showered and was ready in minutes. Adrenaline was already pumping in his veins, and he wondered what the mission would be like. He hoped that Tommy was out of danger and that Maggie would be able to get out of the country without a hitch. He felt helpless to do anything about either of them, but there was something he could do before he went to the command post.

Climbing into the blue truck, Wilder said, "Dave, how about stopping by the last barracks for a minute. I need to leave a message with a friend. It's important."

"No problem, sir." Cummings pulled away and drove around the next block, stopping in front of the corner building.

"Be back in a minute." Wilder jumped out of the truck and disap-

peared into the barracks. He knocked on Slaughter's door and waited. Nothing. He knocked again.

The voice growled. "If you ain't got indoor plumbing and long
legs, you're dead meat!" There was some muffled cursing and bang-
ing around, then the door opened. Slaughter stood nude, looking
more like a Neanderthal than a human being. "Well, you ain't pretty,
but I guess I'll allow this one time." He rubbed his eyes and looked
at his friend. "What's up?"

"Sorry, John. Couldn't sleep. I've been alerted early, and I'm on
my way to the command post. Look, I won't have a chance to check
up on Maggie. Would you—"

"Consider it done, buddy." Slaughter was instantly awake. "I'll
get word to her and make sure she's okay, even if I have to ride a
water buffalo down Tudo Street in my birthday suit."

"Looks like you're already dressed for it. We're restricted, remember?"

Slaughter waved his hand in dismissal. "Since when is there a
rule that can't be broken? What the hell they gonna do? Send me to
'Nam?"

"Right. I owe you one, John." The two men looked at each other
for a moment. They shook hands and Wilder said, "Watch your back-
side when you get to Kontum."

"Yeah. See you in hell."

"Save me a seat." Wilder turned and walked down the hall.

The command post was alive with activity. Plotters were feverishly writing on the board with their grease pencils in an effort to
keep the status updated on the dozens of aircraft flying around the
clock into and out of Kontum. Air crews were leaving for their aircraft, only to be met by other crews recently alerted to begin their
missions. The briefing rooms were packed, and every phone in the
place was ringing.

Organized chaos.

Captain Dan Mercer, having been on duty continuously for two
shifts, was going at full speed. He had a telephone receiver in each
hand and a stack of mission folders on the desk in front of him. He
nodded towards a chair when Wilder walked through the door.

Wilder sat and looked around the room. He noticed that Bryant's office was occupied and that the door was closed. A *Briefing In Progress—Do Not Enter* sign hung on the door. He patiently waited.

Finally, Mercer was off the phones. "This place is a mad house. You'd think these clowns would call each other directly. I feel like a secretary."

"You look pretty rough, Dan. Don't you ever take any time off?"

"The Air Force, in its infinite wisdom, doesn't factor that in. Maybe tomorrow." Mercer picked up the top folder on the stack. "Here's your mission setup, Bill. One of the original crew was sick and is puking his guts out. Bottom line is that you guys are going to Pleiku to pick up some Class A explosives and take them to Kontum. You'll do an engine running combat off load, pack in some Montagnards—quickly, I might add—and get the hell out of there. You'll fly back to Pleiku, drop off your pax, upload more Class A, and repeat the sequence. There will be three round trips. After that you'll refuel in Pleiku and head home."

"If we don't get shot to hell first."

The worry lines in Mercer's face said it all. "Some of our guys have been hit with small arms fire, and two planes landed in Peliku with engines out, but no one's been hurt. Two Specters just came on station, and they're hosing down the place pretty good. They'll be rotating in and out for most of the operation. Should make the bad guys stay put."

"*Most* of the operation?"

"They have to go back to reload, Bill."

"I know that, Dan, but aren't there spares to take their place?"

"No."

"Anything else we need to know about?"

Mercer looked at Wilder's mission sheet. "Uh, various mortars, rockets, and the general pain-in-the-ass VC snipers. Other than that, business as usual." He handed the packet to Wilder. "Your ship number is 009, and it's parked on Alpha row, spot one. It's in commission—so maintenance says—and it's fueled to twenty-five thousand pounds. Your engineer and loadmaster are already there." Mercer looked around then returned his attention to Wilder. "Perette and Sorrenson just walked in. Bryant will give you the specifics, Bill, as to what you can expect from the bad guys. Also, you'll be talking with the Specters on secure FM. Their tactical frequencies, along with the VHF contacts for the other C-130's and the forward air controller, are in your mission flimsy. Keep in mind that the controller on the ground is working out of a Jeep. You may not get through to him if the field is under fire. He's one of us, but he's getting ass shot at too. Just remember that nobody's looking out for you but you."

"You're just full of good news, aren't you?"

"I'm here to serve." Mercer smiled, despite his fatigue.

"I'll buy you a beer when we get back." Wilder stood and waved at his copilot and navigator.

"You bet." Mercer turned his attention to his next mission.

"Hi, guys. Glad you could make the party," Wilder said, turning to his crew.

"What's up, Kemo-Sabee?" Sorrenson asked.

The trio headed for Bryant's office. "We're headed for Kontum. The bad guys are throwing a party, and we've been invited."

"RSVP?" the co-pilot said. "Let's see what intel has to say."

They walked into Bryant's office and Sorrensen closed the door. Taking his seat, Wilder's thoughts were on a young woman in Saigon. He knew it was pointless to think about her; he had to focus on his mission. "Okay, Jerry, what do you have for us?"

CHAPTER 12

WASHINGTON, DC

As hot as it was in South Vietnam, it was cold in Franconia, Virginia. The Director of the NSA watched Walter Cronkite with mixed emotions. The news was just more of the same; body count, bombing of the North, and protesters. Disgusted, he reached out and turned off the TV.

"I'm so tired of looking at this stuff. Nothing changes, it only gets worse."

"Yeah, and as soon as the newsies get wind of what's going on in Kontum, they'll have us killing babies all over the place. Why can't they just report the facts?" Jack Wilder handed his brother-in-law a cup of coffee and picked up his own. He sat back in his recliner. "I don't know where they get their footage from, but they always seem to find the dead civilians. The bloodier, the better. Doesn't matter that the Cong slaughtered them. Just makes the Americans look bad."

"I agree with you, Jack. The media doesn't help our cause at all." He sipped his coffee. "Any word from Tom about his kids? He must be out of his skull by now."

Wilder looked at him. "I have to tell you something, in confidence of course."

"Of course."

"Word came in earlier from the Saigon station manager that Maggie's coming home. Bill convinced her to do it for her parents' sake. They don't know anything about it, so let's don't say anything just in case it gets derailed. She's going to surprise them by just showing up."

"That's the first good news I've heard in a long time. That says a lot for your son, Jack." Spencer smiled for the first time that day.

"Yes, it does. Maybe his mother and I raised him right after all." There was never a doubt. Wilder leaned back in his chair and looked at his brother-in-law.

"I know what you're going to say, Jack, and I'll tell you straight away that now's not the time. There's a serious breach of security over there, and we don't need to stir the pot. Bill's pretty level-headed, but you know what he's like when it concerns his brother. I'm sorry, Jack, but I had to say it." Spencer missed his nephew desperately, and he understood what Jack was going through. He didn't want to upset his brother-in-law, but he also didn't want to make a bad situation worse.

Wilder thought for a moment before he spoke. "You're right, Bruce, especially with what's going on in the Highlands right now. Bill's headed up there, and he needs to pay complete attention to what he's doing." He looked through the window at the falling snow. "Petrov is there somewhere, and it's just a matter of time before he makes a move. I only hope we can catch him first." He rubbed his chin. "I'm worried about all those young people."

"I know, Jack, but we have to wait."

"Yeah." Wilder rubbed his eyes. "That's the hard part."

Tan Son Nhut Air Base
Saigon

"… That's about it, guys. Charlie owns the night, but the Specters will force them to keep their heads down. Any questions?" Bryant looked around the room.

"How much does the press know?"

"They don't know anything, Bill. We've been through that already." Bryant was on the defensive.

"Just to make sure, I have some people checking." Wilder stood and headed for the door.

"What does *that* mean, Lieutenant?" Bryant shot back.

Wilder turned to him. "It means I have some people checking. By the way, the Air Force screwed up and promoted me to captain, okay?" He left without another word.

Wilder adjusted his shoulder harness and seat belt around the bulky survival vest. It was heavy and uncomfortable, but it was the one piece of equipment that no one was willing to part with. Each vest contained an emergency two-way radio, a .38 caliber revolver with twelve rounds, a compass, whistle, signal mirror, and flares. There was a first aid kit and several other items. Perhaps the most valuable item was the "rice chit." It was a cloth flag with writing in both Vietnamese and English. It stated that the bearer was an American soldier and that any one helping this soldier back to safety would be rewarded by the United States government. Wilder made sure it was in a secure place. He also had his .357 Python holstered to the pistol belt around his waist.

Fred Durkin, the flight engineer, scanned the overhead panel between the pilots. "Ship's been fueled and the crew chief gave us a clean log book. We're ready to go, skipper."

"Load's ready," Burt Martin called over the interphone.

Barry Sorrenson, the navigator, gave a thumbs-up, and the co-pilot waved his checklist, signifying his readiness.

"Okay, guys, here's the drill. We're going to Pleiku and pick up five pallets of Class A, then into Kontum. Combat off load, then uploading as many Montagnards as possible. Have to flag the seats, Burt. No time to put them down. Just pack them in and make them sit on the floor. Charlie's going to be throwing everything at us, and we don't have time for any of that coffee-tea-or-me stuff. Just get 'em in, and we're out of there. Minimum ground time."

"Gotcha." Martin was a professional, and he ignored the regulatory niceties when it came to getting shot at. "I'll get it done in four minutes—off to on."

"I'll be back there helping with the ramps," Sorrenson said. "I can keep an eye on him if anything goes wrong."

"Good idea, Barry." Wilder looked around the cockpit. "Guys, it's time to earn our pay. Any questions?"

There were none.

"Okay, Pete, let's run the Before Start checklist and get this beast off the ground."

The night sky over the Central Highlands was alive. An Arc Light strike ran from southwest to northeast just five miles west of Kontum, and the raining death from the invisible B-52's high above brought havoc, terror, and destruction to those below. Air Force and Marine F-4's bombed and strafed the countryside, while AC-130 gunships pulverized areas around the airfield itself. For their part the Vietcong used their shear mass to overrun friendly bases and occupy jungle areas around the Kontum airfield. The Cong wanted to neutralize the airfield to prevent the ARVN forces from being re-supplied with much needed ammunition. The best way to do that was to destroy a C-130 while on the runway. To that end they threw every mortar and rocket at the field the instant a plane landed, and the deluge continued until the ship was safely airborne again.

Spare Zero-Nine circled over the airfield at ten thousand feet. The crew listened carefully to the instructions from the forward air controller operating from a Jeep parked behind a concrete wall lined with sand bags.

"*Spare Zero-Nine, this is Mother. Charlie's a thousand meters north of the field. He's being pounded by the Specters, so stay out of the red tracers, guys. The area south is secured for now, but that might change. Make your approach from east to west. Turn off at the end, off load, then we'll bring out the little people. Get them loaded and take off to the east. The bad guys own the real estate to the west, so if you have to go around on your approach, make a hard climbing turn to the south. Get some altitude in a hurry. Got it?*" Although his voice was laced with fear, there was no mistaking his intent. The pilot on the ground didn't want to be in the open any more than necessary, so he made sure his instructions were clear the first time.

"Roger, Mother. We copy. We'll come in as soon as the bird on the ground lifts off," Perette transmitted. He looked at Wilder. "Christ! That guy sounds scared to death. How long does he have to be there?"

Sorrenson spoke up first. "He came in at sunset on the first Herk, and he'll leave on the last one before dawn."

"What a rotten shit detail."

"He was volunteered just you guys will be. That FAC is a C-130 pilot, and your turn's coming."

"Great."

"Hey, Burt, you ready back there?" Wilder said.

"Cocked and locked, sir. When you go to max reverse on landing, the ramp and door will come open. After we stop I'll pull the locks and give you a holler when it's time to jazz the throttles. Once the cargo is clear, we'll get the little people on and get the hell out of Dodge."

"Sounds like you're in a hurry."

"Believe me, boss, when these rice-burners start throwing shit at us, you'll know what I mean."

"Just watch yourself, Burt. One wrong move and you'll lose a foot. Barry, you'll be in place to help him with the ramps, right?"

"I'll be there."

Wilder turned to the engineer. "Durk, if something doesn't look good, sound off."

"Roger, skipper." Durkin had been a loadmaster before, and he knew the dangers involved with rolling pallets weighing thousands of pounds. "Hey, Burt?"

"Yeah?"

"You stay cool back there, and keep those big feet out of the way. Something don't work right, you yell out. No hero shit."

"Right. No hero shit."

"Pete, monitor the gunships on VHF two, and we'll both monitor guard. We'll both listen to the FAC on FM. I'll talk to him, and you keep your transmitter on the gunships. Let's keep each other out of trouble. If you see something you don't like, sing out."

"I'm on top of it." Perette checked the frequencies on all five radios and made sure the correct monitoring buttons were pulled out on each communication panel.

Both pilots looked at each other. "Let's don't miss this one, Pete."

"Amen."

The flight engineer turned off all exterior lights. The red rotating beacon, normally always on, was extinguished. The engine bleed valves were closed, allowing the engines to produce maximum thrust. Wilder would have to land the plane within the first five hundred feet or risk running off the end of the runway into the ammo dump to the west end of the airfield. He would need all the power the engines could produce to stop the airplane within the confines of the runway.

"Okay, guys, it's show time." Wilder pulled the throttles to idle and began a spiraling descent. "Flaps fifty."

"Flaps to fifty." Perette positioned the flap handle and began running the landing checklist.

Wilder allowed the airspeed to decrease to one hundred fifty knots. He increased the bank angle to forty-five degrees, and the ship began to descend in a tight turn over the field.

Passing five thousand feet, they watched while a C-130 positioned itself at the west end of the runway and ran its engines up for takeoff. *"We're outta here,"* Spare Zero-Two transmitted. The aircraft accelerated and was soon airborne. It climbed at its maximum rate and made a tight turn to the south on its way back to Pleiku.

"Keep 'em burning, guys. Contact Pleiku on tactical frequency. See you in a couple hours. Break, break, Zero-Nine, you still with me?"

"Roger, Mother. We're at angels five thousand in a left descending turn. Looking for landing clearance." Perette checked his radios again and looked towards the north at the red tracers blanketing the countryside.

"Okay, guys, you're up to bat. Wind's light and variable. Clear to land."

"The check's in the mail."

"Gear down, landing checklist," Wilder commanded, his eyes darting back and forth between the end of the runway and the airspeed indicator.

Perette placed the landing gear handle down and waited for the indicators. "Gear down and locked."

Durkin tested the anti-skid system and scanned his panel. "We're ready, chief."

"Flaps full."

Perette extended the flaps to the landing configuration. "Checklist done. We're cleared to do it."

"Right." Wilder rolled out of the turn onto final approach. His peripheral vision picked up the flashes from the small arms fire aimed at his ship, but he focused his concentration on the end of the runway. The plane slowed to its maximum effort approach speed, and Wilder unconsciously gripped the wheel and throttles tighter. Adrenaline was pumping freely now.

Saigon

The blue Air Force staff car with the two-star insignia on the front bumper rolled through the gate of Tan Son Nhut Air Base with nothing more than a salute from the sleepy military policeman manning it. The solitary driver returned the salute and puffed on his cigar. "S'um bitch," Slaughter chortled, "this is easier than falling off a log." The car wound its way through the narrow streets of Saigon until the Caravelle Hotel appeared in the distance.

Slaughter parked the car in front of the hotel and stepped out onto the street. He looked around. Despite the hour the city was alive with its garish lights and obnoxious sounds. Walking around the front of the car, he looked at the blue and silver placard attached to the bumper. "Ain't rank great?" Slaughter laughed at his own antics. He turned towards the building.

Walking through the lobby, he removed the purloined Air Force tunic and folded the coat over his arm. Taking the cigar out of his mouth, he approached the front desk. "Good evening, my pretty. I'm John Slaughter, but you can call me anytime if it pleases you. I need to speak with Miss Maggie McIvor if you would be so kind. She's a reporter with UPI, and she's a guest at this fine establishment." The young Vietnamese woman opened her mouth to speak, but Slaughter cut her off. "Nice joint you got here, lady." Looking around the room, he said, "What say you and me have a little drink later. Fine looking thing like you shouldn't be alone in a city like this." He winked at her.

The woman was an attractive mix of Vietnamese and French, and she was used to the advances of the Americans. She giggled. "You're funny." Her English was perfect. "Thank you, but my husband will be here soon. You should ask him."

Not to be out done, Slaughter said, "The more, the merrier. I should like to ask you—and your husband—to join me on the verandah for cocktails this evening." He beamed at her.

She laughed again. "But it is before sunrise, sir. Perhaps coffee instead?"

"Okay, lady, you win. I have been bested." The smile left his face. He leaned over the counter. "I have business with Miss McIvor. Would you be a gracious hostess and escort me to her room?"

She looked suspiciously at him.

"I'm serious, lady. Bill Wilder is my friend, and he asked me to make sure she's okay."

She instantly recognized the name. "Ah, yes. Bill Wilder. I understand that he and Miss McIvor are to be married."

Slaughter grinned. "You understand correctly, my lotus flower. And yours truly is going to the number one stand-in."

"The Best Man?"

"Yes. But right now I need to see her." Slaughter gestured towards the hall.

"Very well. I will be delighted to take you to her room, but I should call her first. She is sleeping."

Slaughter looked at his watch. "Yep, I reckon so. I forgot what time it was." He looked at her. "This is important." The humor was gone.

The Vietnamese woman called Maggie's room and chatted briefly. Satisfied, she hung up and said, "This way, sir."

"… Yes, yes, I know, but you've only read his dossier. I've seen his work. He's not one to be toyed with."

"You have been trained by the best, comrade, and now it is time to make your move," Petrov's handler said. "Slaughter will be on a mission, and Wilder will be exhausted when he returns. He also will be alone. That will be the time."

"*Na-shto-zhaloo-yetyes?*" Petrov snapped. What's the matter with you? He drew heavily on his cigarette. "I alone will decide when it's time to confront Wilder!" He paced in silence for several minutes. Finally, he stopped, crushed his cigarette on the floor and turned to the other man. A malevolent smile crossed his face.

"What are you going to do?" the second man said.

"I'm going to make him suffer. Before I kill him, I'm going to show him how powerless he is to protect his friends. I will destroy his spirit before I destroy his body."

"The KGB won't—"

"To hell with those pompous old men! I'll make my own decisions when it comes to Wilder." Petrov lit another cigarette. "Wilder is going to suffer, just like his brother did in that North Vietnamese prison. I know *exactly* what I'm going to do." He stormed out of the room and into the night.

Kontum
Central Highlands

The C-130 touched down at the three hundred foot marker, and Wilder immediately pulled the throttles into maximum reverse thrust. The aircraft shook violently when the propellers changed blade angle and bit into the air, causing the prop wash to reverse direction. He applied maximum braking, and the aircraft came to a halt from one hundred ten knots to zero in a matter of seconds.

"Clear on the ramp and door!" Wilder ordered. "Clearing the runway now. Reset the flaps and trim and get this thing ready to go."

Perette positioned the controls for take off and watched the brake pressure.

"Ready to pull the locks!" Martin shouted into his microphone over the din of the engines. The noise in the cargo compartment was deafening under normal circumstances, but it was unbearable with the aft ramp and door open.

"Stand by a sec," Wilder said. "We're almost in position." He maneuvered the aircraft so that he could taxi straight ahead when the pallets began to move. "Okay, pull the locks!"

"Locks pulled. Give her a kick," the loadmaster shouted.

"Rolling." Wilder released the brakes and pushed the throttles forward. The response was instantaneous, and the pallets rolled aft towards the cargo door. Within seconds the last one slid off the ramp and onto the tarmac.

"Load's clear. Stop. Help me with these ramps, Barry." The two men worked feverishly to get ready to load the Montagnards.

Wilder stopped the airplane and set the brakes. The three men in the cockpit had done their jobs. Now, they could only wait.

A rag-tag group of Montagnards, consisting of mostly women, children, and crippled old people, began to make their way from a make-shift shelter to the airplane. They carried their life's possessions in baskets on their backs, and the blast from the propellers made their journey to the aircraft more arduous yet.

"Holy shit! You gotta see this!" Sorrenson's voice was tense and full of emotion. "These people look like Holocaust survivors! I've never seen anything like it."

"We'll all look like that if we don't get the hell out of here. Hurry up!" Perette voiced the fear they all felt.

A mortar round exploded on the opposite end of the ramp from the airplane, sending dirt and debris everywhere. There was no damage to the ship, but any closer and their plans would be changed for the worse. A second mortar exploded only yards from the ammunition dump. The seconds seemed like minutes and the minutes like hours.

"The shit's hitting the fan. Hurry the hell up!" someone shouted over the interphone. It didn't matter who; the words were only an echo of everyone's thoughts. Sorrenson and Martin worked frantically to get the refugees onto the plane, but the sick and wounded could only move so fast. The crew could only curse under their breaths and wait.

Saigon

"John, what are you doing here at this time of night?" Maggie rubbed her eyes and glanced at the clock on the table. "Come in." She looked at the Vietnamese woman, who had become her friend. "You'll have to excuse him, Vandeth. He doesn't get out much."

"I think he is funny, Miss McIvor." Vandeth giggled. "I will bring coffee for you and your guest."

"Thank you." Maggie closed the door and looked at Slaughter. "What's wrong, John? Is Bill hurt?" She was visibly nervous.

"Everything's fine, Maggie. Not to worry." He gestured for her to have a seat and dropped onto a chair beside her. He looked around the room. "You news guys live high on the hog, and we shack-up with rats."

"We get by." She smiled despite her uneasiness. "John, are you sure everything's all right? Why are you here at this awful hour? Where's Bill?"

There was a knock at the door. Slaughter was there in an instant. He opened it slightly and looked out. Vandeth was there with a tray of coffee and croissants. "My mama said to beware of beautiful women bearing gifts, but I'll make an exception in your case, Lilly of the Valley." He took the tray. "*Merci*, Madame."

"*Ne Rien*," she replied. "And you are Judge Roy Bean." She smiled curtly and walked away.

What I'd give to bite into that, get a good case of lock-jaw, and be dragged to death. Slaughter sighed and closed the door with his foot. He walked to the table and sat the tray down. "How do you take your java, Maggie?"

"I'll do this, John." She picked up the carafe and poured two cups. "You pilots can't walk and chew gum at the same time. How do you like yours?"

"Raw, like my women."

She rolled her eyes. "Figures." She handed him a cup, then took her seat. "Okay, John, what's going on?"

Slaughter stirred his black coffee with his finger. Wiping his hand on his trousers, he said, "Maggie, my rich Uncle Sam would court-martial me if he knew I was here. So, mum's the word."

"I've never seen you before."

"The shit's hitting the fan in the Central Highlands. The action's hot and heavy, and the boys are flying into Kontum around the clock. Locally, everyone's restricted to the base til play time."

"Play time?"

"Mission briefing time."

"How did you get off the base?"

Slaughter flashed his What?-Me-worry? look.

"Never mind that. What kind of action, John?" She thought of her brother and her hands began to shake.

Slaughter picked up on it instantly. "The bad guys have surrounded Kontum, and the good guys are on a kick-butt mission. The boys are going in there with ammo and taking refugees out. Bill's up there now running a couple missions out of Pleiku."

Maggie sat her cup on the table and covered her face with her hands.

Slaughter took her hands in his. "Listen, Maggie, everything's fine. Bill's in and out a few times, then home. He couldn't get into Saigon tonight to be with you, and he asked me to make sure you're okay."

She looked at the night sky through the window, tears streaming down her face. "Just like that bum. He's getting his butt shot at, and all he can think about is me." She looked at Slaughter. "Why didn't he call?"

"The phones are shut down. Off limits. We can't get there from here. He came by my room on his way to the flight line and asked me to check on you and make sure your go-home arrangements are squared away. When are you leaving anyway?"

"This morning, John. My flight leaves at eight o'clock." She looked at him, and the tears began to flow. "I won't see him before I leave!"

Slaughter was caught by surprise. *Didn't expect things to happen this fast.* He had to salvage things in a hurry. He thought for a moment then said, "Maggie, it's best that you leave now. The sooner you get home, the sooner you can start planning the wedding. I'll be the keeper-of-the-faith, and I promise to keep Johnny Quest straight til we get home. Besides, think of the surprise your parents have in store for them. They'll be as happy as clams at high tide." He wasn't sure how convincing he was, but he was determined to give it his best. "And don't worry about Tommy. Bill and I are going to get his young ass out of here. Count on it."

She wiped her eyes with a napkin. "John, you are unwashed and as uncouth as they come, but you're a real friend."

"I know. If I wasn't me, I'd want to be with me! Maggie, by your going back to the States, the Wild Man will be soothed, knowing that you're safely home, rather than hold up in this dump with the bad guys out there. Pretty soon we'll all be back in the land of the big BX, and I'll hold him up while you put the ring through his nose."

She couldn't help but smile. "John, you could make a dead man laugh."

Slaughter patted the top of his head. "Guess the Animal ain't lost his touch yet." He leaned forward. "Seriously, are all your arrangements made?"

"Terry's taking me to the airport in a few hours. I'm taking a freedom bird back to the States." She leaned back in her chair and gazed pensively at the window. "Remember the flight over?"

"You kidding? I haven't been that drunk since I got here."

"I've never seen two guys as close as you and Bill are. Ever since Little Jack's funeral, I've seen you two together. It's nice to see friendship like that."

"Well, somebody's got to watch out for that problem child. Guess I'm it."

Maggie studied him for a moment. "John, when are you going to get married?"

Slaughter slapped his knee and laughed. "What? Are you kidding? The woman ain't been born yet that can slip a ring, bone, or anything else through my nose."

"I'm serious, John." She tried the stern look, but a slight smile crept onto the corners of her mouth.

"Well, one of these days, I might allow some lucky chicklet the privilege of bedding me permanently." He leaned back and smiled at the ceiling. "Yep, I'll get me a nice little spread in west Texas. I'll people it with a one-eyed, egg-sucking dog, a shotgun, the ideal woman, and settle down."

"And what, pray tell, is the *ideal woman*?" Maggie could only imagine.

Slaughter rubbed his chin and looked thoughtful. "Well, let's see.... She'll stand six feel tall in her bare feet with legs that go all the way to her neck. She won't have any vocal chords or uterus. She'll be able to burn a steak like a real Texan, and at midnight, she'll turn into a six-pack."

Oh, Lord! "I should have known."

"Hey, I got a brain storm!" Slaughter sat up straight, his eyes wide open.

"Dare I ask?" Despite his crudeness, Maggie was completely comfortable with him.

"You're gonna be stuck in that aluminum tube for a long time with nothing but processed food loaf to eat. I'm gonna get Miss Lotus Blossom to let me into the kitchen, and I'll scrape up some grub. I used to do fixin's in a hash-house back home, you know."

"John, you amaze me. If it was anybody else, I'd say it was impossible. But I don't put anything past you." Maggie clasped her hands. "Tell you what; I'll jump in the shower and get dressed while you're burning eggs. Should take about twenty minutes." She got up and walked towards the phone. "I'll give Vandeth a call. She'll let you into the kitchen."

"Great! We'll have a chow-down before you leave." Slaughter opened the door. Looking over his shoulder, he said, "Put on the face you left in the jar by the door."

"Go to hell!" Maggie laughed and threw a slipper at him. He closed the door just in time and hurried down the hall.

Kontum Airfield
Central Highlands

"The little people are in and the ramp's coming up. Let's get outta here!" Martin shouted over the interphone. "Sorrenson's moving forward."

"Tell Mother we're rolling," Wilder commanded. He released the brakes and taxied as fast as safety would allow. Another mortar exploded just yards behind them.

"There's a goddamn explosion right behind us! Shit's flying through the aft door. Get this pig off the ground!" Martin's voice had jumped an octave, but he was too busy strapping everybody down to panic.

"We're going, Burt. Just hang on. Few more seconds." Wilder looked at Perette. "Clear off to the right? We're moving out."

"Clear over here, and Mother's been alerted. Push this thing, Bill. Things are getting hot around here!" Perette scanned the darkness around the perimeter of the field. Flashes from small arms fire were everywhere, and the larger explosions were moving closer.

Wilder lined the aircraft on the runway and depressed the brakes. "Burt, tell me when the ramp's above the horizontal—"

"It is now. *Go!*"

Wilder pushed the throttles forward against the stops. The propellers bit into the air, and the airplane shook in protest. He released the brakes, and the Hercules lurched forward. Despite maximum thrust, the ship could not accelerate fast enough for him. His eyes flashed back and forth between the airspeed indicator and the runway. *C'mon, c'mon!*

"Go!" Perette shouted when the ship finally reached flying speed.

Wilder pulled back on the wheel until the nose rose into the air. The altimeter began to climb. "Gear up!"

Whump! Boom!

The aircraft lurched violently to the right, then immediately rolled left. The nose dropped through the horizon, and the airspeed began to decrease. "Number one's down!" the engineer shouted. "Part of the left wing's gone! We don't have flying speed!" Durkin flipped switches in a frantic effort to stop fuel to the flaming engine.

Despite the desperate efforts of both pilots, they were unable to control the plane. "Lock your harnesses! We're going down!" Wilder shouted. The crew locked their harnesses and braced themselves. Both Wilder and Perette had a death grip on their respective wheels. They watched helplessly as the ground rose towards them. Impact was imminent.

"Mayday, mayday!" Perette shouted into the radio. "We're hit and we're going down with all souls on board!"

"Search and Rescue enroute! Dustoff's on the way!" Watching in horror, the forward air controller on the ground was helpless to do anything. He switched to his secondary radio and transmitted on all frequencies. The calls went out to Pleiku and to the fighters flying combat air patrol overhead. The Specters, having heard the calls for help, maneuvered themselves into position without being told to do so. Within seconds they began to shower death on the airfield perimeter below. The earth exploded a thousand times when the shells hit the ground. Within seconds huge secondary explosions were set off as the Vietcong's unused mortar rounds on the ground began to ignite under the fusillade of fire from above.

Wilder squeezed the wheel until he thought it would break. The aircraft veered violently to the left due to the uneven thrust, and he pushed the rudder pedals to their stops in an attempt to keep the ship straight. He pulled the throttles to idle. "Hang on!"

The ship was out of control.

The aircraft slammed into the ground and immediately began to disintegrate. The left wing clipped a dirt mound, causing the plane to cartwheel. The fuselage broke apart, and the wings ripped off. The fuel tanks ruptured, spewing thousands of gallons of jet fuel everywhere. The ship exploded into pieces, throwing the hapless Montagnards to their deaths in the consuming inferno. The cockpit windows blew out when the nose slammed into a tree. There was no fire in the forward part of the fuselage, but the rapidly spreading fuel would soon change that. A piece of shrapnel from a broken window frame struck Wilder in the head, knocking him unconscious. What was left of the cockpit tumbled several times and finally came to rest in a rice paddy.

The roar of the explosions and intense heat from the burning jet fuel quickly brought Wilder back to consciousness. Hanging upside down in his seat by his shoulder harness, he looked through a haze of blood and pain at the conflagration around him. He looked at the right side of the cockpit. Perette was dead, his head having been severed from his body. Wilder struggled to look behind him. There was no sign of the rest of the crew. There was only a gaping hole.

The cockpit had been torn completely from the rest of the ship. In a daze, he was surrounded by fire and death, and he was helpless to do anything. There was sharp pain in his back and sides, and his head pounded. He was incoherent. Somewhere in the remote corners of his mind, he knew that he had to get out of there, but he was unable to move. The pain and shock were too much, and Bill Wilder descended into darkness.

Saigon

The shower seemed to wash away all the stress and worry that had accumulated since her arrival in Vietnam, and Maggie was grateful for it. She decided that worrying about Bill would be fruitless, and she put it out of her mind. She knew that he could take care of himself. He and John were a pair not to be taken lightly, and she knew that she had nothing to worry about.

She turned off the water and stepped out of the shower into the steamy bathroom. Wrapping herself in a towel, she began to dry her hair with another. *The House Of The Rising Sun* was playing on the Armed Forces radio station. It reminded her of Jake's honkey tonk. She promised to call him when she got back to the States. She wanted him to host her wedding reception in his place. She knew that he would insist on it. She thought about her career with UPI and of her future life with Bill Wilder. Despite the danger he was in, his only concern was for her. There was no decision to be made; he was first in her life and her career was second. She began to put on her makeup.

There was a knock on the door. "Just a minute," Maggie shouted from the bathroom. "Hold on, John. I'll be right there." She slipped into a bathrobe and walked to the door. She slid the bolt and turned the knob.

Suddenly, the door flew open, kicked inwards by the intruder's boot. Maggie fell backwards and banged her head on a chair. She fell to the floor unconscious.

Looking around to see if anyone had been alerted, Petrov quickly stepped into the room. He closed and bolted the door and propped a chair under the door knob to prevent the door from being opened from the hallway. He stood motionless and looked around the room, making sure that he was alone.

He sat a small bag on a nearby table. He then picked up Maggie's limp body and carried her to the bed. He took a pack of cigarettes from his breast pocket, lit one, and opened the bag. There were several lengths of rope, a roll of duct tape, smelling salts, a wire garrote, and a switch blade knife. He placed the items on the bed and stood back to examine what lay before him.

A sardonic smile crossed his face. But then the headache began, and his hands went to his temples. He squeezed his eyes shut in a vain attempt to force the pain away, but it only increased. He quickly went to work. He tied Maggie's hands and feet to the four corners of the bed....

Kontum
Central Highlands

The fire raged out of control, fed by the ocean of jet fuel. The bodies of the Montagnards, along with most the crew, were consumed in the flames that roared uncontrollably towards the night sky. The Specter gunships pounded the surrounding jungle with everything they had. No living thing could withstand the hell-fire that belched from the dark ships, but the damage had been done. The airfield was closed to all fixed wing aircraft, and the only things that could land were helicopters. Dozens were enroute from Peliku, including Huey Dustoff med-evacs and deadly Cobra gun ships. But for all their efforts, the Americans in the night sky could do nothing but helplessly watch the inferno below.

Wilder's head reeled as he slowly regained consciousness. He was on his back in a deep ditch, the explosions and fire a distance away. He lay motionless, not knowing who or where he was. He moaned when a wave of pain shot through his body.

"Take it easy, buddy. You got a bad bump there. Just lie still and enjoy the view. We ain't going nowhere any time soon." Wilder felt his head being lifted and a gauze bandage being wrapped around it. "You're one lucky *hombre*, partner. Charlie's having a field day with your space ship. Bagging a Herk is big business around here." The bandage now complete, the stranger gently lowered Wilder's head onto a folded field jacket. "Best way to get the bleeding to stop is for you to be still. It's gonna hurt for a while, so you may as well relax."

Despite the throbbing, Wilder was now fully alert. His eyes tried to focus in the dark, but he couldn't see a thing. "What ... where am I?"

"About a hundred meters this side of hell."

"What ... happened?" It was difficult to speak, and Wilder was confused.

"Your plane bought the farm. That simple. When it hit the ground, it broke up and the fuel ignited. The rest is history. You're one of the lucky ones, partner. The front end was thrown far enough from the gas that it didn't light up. I dragged you in here. As far as I can tell, you're the only survivor." The stranger patted him on the shoulder. "I'm sorry."

"What? I—" Wilder tried to sit up, but the pain forced him back down. "Jesus!"

"He ain't around, friend. The devil's out there. Just take it easy. There's nothing you can do, Captain Wilder, so be still and enjoy the view."

"How do you know who I am?" The pain was excruciating, and Wilder decided to take the stranger's advice. He lay motionless.

"I can't do much, but I *can* read." The stranger pointed at the name tag on Wilder's flight suit.

"Who are you?"

"Name's Keesee. Just happened to be in the neighborhood." The stranger pulled a canvas tarp over Wilder. "We can talk later. I'll give you some morphine for the pain, then you get some sleep. I'll keep an eye out for the SAR team. They'll have you out of here at first light."

"Do you have a first name?" Wilder wanted to know the person that saved his life.

"Wayne. I'm a merc, and that's all you need to know."

"Mercenary?"

Quiet laughter then silence. "... Yeah. No more questions. The less you know, the better. Now, try to sleep."

Wilder began to fade in and out. Despite the trauma of his injuries, his thoughts turned to Maggie. In his semi-conscious state, he dreamed of the two of them flying home together. His father would meet them and their lives together would begin. He wondered if Slaughter was able to see her before she left. Were they okay? Dizziness overcame him, and he drifted into darkness again.

Saigon

Slaughter sniffed the hot food. "Not bad, my boy. Not bad at all." He lifted the tray and started up the stairs. He thought about the food he'd been forced to eat since he arrived in-country and decided that an occasional trip to the Caravelle would be a good idea. He would have to put it on his to-do list. He reached the landing on Maggie's floor and started down the hall. Being the middle of the night, he decided that he would be quiet for a change.

Reaching for the door knob, he froze in his tracks. A boot print that he had not noticed before, jumped out at him. There was a crack where the boot had violently contacted the door. He placed his ear to the door and held his breath. Hearing Maggie's muffled screams, Slaughter was transformed into a raging bull. He tossed the tray aside and backed against the opposite door. Lowering his shoulder, he bellowed and charged the door with all his strength.

The door and the chair against it were no match for the stocky Texan. They shattered and splintered into pieces when Slaughter crashed through them. He tumbled through the opening, rolled, and landed on his feet. He stood motionless, his muscles as hard as his temper was hot. What he saw enraged him, and he slowly began to move forward, ready to kill.

Maggie was tied to the corners of the bed, her eyes and mouth taped over. She was nude except for her high heel shoes. Her hips were propped up with pillows, and she pulled furiously against the ropes. Her wrists were bleeding from the rope cuts.

"Your entrance was ill-timed, Slaughter. It's going to cost you your life."

Ivan Petrov stood frozen at the foot of the bed, a bottle of vodka in a one hand and a pistol in the other. He looked deranged and out of control.

"I'm gonna kill you, you stinking bastard!" Slaughter charged at Petrov like a tank, his hands out stretched, ready to destroy the man in front of him.

Petrov quickly raised the .38 revolver and fired twice. As fast as Slaughter was, he couldn't dodge the bullets flying at him. The first one hit him in the chest and the second in the head. Slaughter kept charging, but after two steps he fell unconscious to the floor.

Petrov aimed the gun at Slaughter's head and prepared to fire at point blank range, but the commotion in the hall distracted him. He fixed his gaze on Maggie. "Another time, you arrogant bitch!" He ran to the window and opened it. Stepping through it and onto the roof of the hotel entrance, he pulled a grenade out of his bag and pulled the pin. He looked at the struggling woman on the bed. "If you live through this, tell Wilder he's next." He tossed the grenade onto the bed and disappeared into the night.

The explosion blew out the windows and the wall along the hallway. Two hotel guests were killed instantly when the wall and flaming debris slammed into them.

Vandeth screamed when she saw the carnage. She ran to the hotel phone at the end of the hall and called the authorities. She didn't have the stomach to go into what remained of Maggie's room. Seeing it would be too much.

How could she tell Wilder?

Kontum

The UH-1 Huey flew low and slow over the rice paddies in the early morning haze. Staying clear of the burning wreckage of the C-130, the helicopter maneuvered to the edge of the jungle that, since dawn, had returned to the control of friendly forces. The chopper sat down on a small rise, and three Army corpsman jumped out. They ran to the foxhole that had been marked by orange smoke just minutes before.

"Glad you guys are here. This fella's in pretty bad shape," the mercenary said. "Got a bleeding head wound, and his back's riddled with shrapnel. He's the only one I found alive. The rest of those poor souls didn't have a chance."

"We have a bleeder here. Let's get moving," the first corpsman shouted, waving at his crew. The rescue team quickly opened a canvas stretcher and lifted Wilder's unconscious body onto it. "Let's get out of here," the team leader said. He looked at the mercenary. "Going with us?"

"Nope. Have to extract my pound of flesh first." The mercenary looked at the smoking wreckage. "Guess I'll have to get more than a pound." He looked at Wilder. "Keep the blue side up, fella."

"Keep your head down," the corpsman replied. The team lifted the stretcher and hurried back to the chopper. Within minutes the Dustoff rescue bird lifted into the air and turned towards Pleiku while the medics worked feverishly to save Wilder's life.

CHAPTER 13

CLARK AIR FORCE BASE
THE PHILIPPINES

The Air Force C-141 touched down on the runway and reversed its engines. The ship taxied clear at the end and made its way to the ramp in front of Base Operations. It was followed by a fire truck as a safety precaution, along with several ambulances. Once the aircraft was parked, the crew shut down the engines while the aft clamshell cargo doors opened. Ambulances backed up towards the rear of the aircraft in a line, ready to take the wounded to the hospital.

"We've got some damaged boys here," the chief flight nurse said to the doctor when he walked up the ramp to the cargo compartment. She pointed to the first one. "This one took a round in the chest and in the head. There's internal damage due to an explosion. The doctors in Saigon did a pretty good patch job on him, but he still needs work. He has a serious throat injury, but he's breathing on his own." She pointed out some of the other cases.

"I think we can take it from here," the doctor said. He turned to the team that boarded behind him. "Okay, people, let's get these patients to the hospital as quickly as possible. Make sure all the operating rooms are ready." He turned to the nurse. "Looks like everyone's stable."

The flight nurse pointed to the front end of the ship. "There's another one up there. He was the only survivor in a crash in Kontum. He and the one with the head injury here have to be isolated from the others *and* from each other."

"Why?"

"Orders from the CIA station chief in Saigon." She shrugged her shoulders. "I didn't ask any questions."

"Death and intrigue never take a holiday." The doctor shook his head. "We'll take care of it." He looked at the multitude of injured bodies. "Let's get moving, people."

The wounded were carefully loaded into the ambulances and taken to the base hospital. It was one of the few fully equipped and staffed medical facilities in the Orient, and it treated not only war wounds, but also every manner of exotic contagious disease from that part of the world. As a result many soldiers had no choice but to consider the Clark Air Force Base hospital their home away from home.

Wilder's wounds, although serious, were not life-threatening. The nasty bump on the head resulted in a mild concussion, and surgery removed the several pieces of aircraft metal lodged in his back and shoulder. Rest, physical therapy, and boredom were now the main prescription for him.

Slaughter's injuries were more serious. The bullet to the chest had caused a lung to collapse, and only the quick response of the doctors in Saigon had kept him from drowning in his own blood. Several pieces of grenade shrapnel had been removed from his back and neck, and there were internal injuries that required more surgery. The damage to his vocal chords was severe, and the doctors didn't know if he would be able to speak again. His head injury resulted in a nasty scar across the right side of his forehead. He constantly drifted in and out of consciousness, and the medical staff feared that he would slip into a coma any minute.

Aside from making lousy passengers, pilots also make lousy patients. Room confinement and bland food make for strange bed fellows, and taking orders from other people is not in their nature. The confining quarters of the hospital led to griping and complaining by all the "inmates" as they called themselves, and Wilder was no exception. His constant nagging was a comic opera to the hospital staff. He was confined to his room most of the time, and when he was out, he was under Marine escort. He didn't like it and he told his "baby-sitters" as much every chance he had.

Neither Wilder nor Slaughter had any idea that the other had been injured or that both were in the same hospital. The Marine guards assigned to each of them were under strict orders to keep that way.

Wilder was grateful for the treatment he received, but he was impatient to learn the fate of his crew. The doctors and nurses were reluctant to say anything. It wasn't their place. Besides, they really didn't know anything. They were in the livesaving business here and now, and they couldn't concern themselves about the deaths of those in another country. For those unfortunate souls, nothing could be done.

Jack Wilder stared through the small window at the torrential downpour washing over the Philippine Islands. His flight in the C-135 VIP jet from Andrews Air Force Base, Maryland, had been long and arduous, despite the creature comforts afforded him. Even though he would see his son for the first time since the young flier departed for Vietnam, the circumstances surrounding Wilder's visit couldn't be worse.

The wind and rain pushed the limits of the experienced Air Force crew, and they had to make two attempts to land before they were successful. As the aircraft made its way slowly across the sheets of water that covered the tarmac, the Air Force steward came into the Director's cabin.

"Sir, is there anything else I can get for you before you leave the aircraft?"

"No. Thank you, Lester. I'm fine." Wilder looked at the young airman. "Ever been to Vietnam?"

"No, sir. Not yet." The sergeant felt uneasy standing in front of the CIA officer.

"Let's hope you never have to." Wilder stood and walked slowly towards the front of the airplane. He placed his hand on the young airman's shoulder. "I have a son in the hospital here. He was in a crash in 'Nam. He's about your age."

"I'll pray for him, sir," the airman said, genuinely meaning it.

"I appreciate that." Wilder wearily made his way to the front of the aircraft.

At 2020 local time the VIP jet came to a stop in front of Base Operations. The air police quickly cordoned off the area around the aircraft, and the Transient Alert personnel positioned a set of portable stairs against the side of the ship. A crew member opened the forward entry door and handed Wilder an opened umbrella. Before Wilder could step through the opening and into the rain, an Air Force officer made his way up the stairs.

"Welcome to Clark, Mr. Director. I'm Colonel David Patsun, the base commander." He'd recently been informed of Wilder's arrival, but not of the reasons for it.

"Thanks, Dave. I appreciate the lack of fanfare." The men shook hands. "The fewer people that know I'm here, the better." Wilder looked through the open door. "Is the weather always this nice?" He wanted to get his mind off the purpose of his visit.

"Only when it rains, sir. I have a staff car waiting to take you to your quarters. If you'd like, I can arrange for dinner to be brought from the Officer's Club."

Wilder patted his stomach. "I'm trying to cut down, but thanks anyway. Just a shower and a short nap."

Patsun was at a loss as to why such a high ranking VIP showed up at his base without the press in tow, but he said nothing. He knew better than to question the CIA.

The men leaned into the wind and held onto the rail while they carefully negotiated the wet metal stairs. Reaching the staff car, Wilder climbed into the back seat.

"All arrangements have been made, Mr. Wilder, and no one's aware of your arrival," Patsun shouted through the rain. He saluted and moved away from the automobile.

"Thanks again, Dave. I'll stop by tomorrow for coffee and a chat." Closing the door Wilder said, "Quarters, please." The driver acknowledged with a "yes, sir" and proceeded carefully through the pouring rain. They were followed by Secret Service and military police vehicles. Wilder didn't notice. His mind was elsewhere.

His recent conversation by secure phone with Scott Neilson in

Saigon had burned in his mind for the last few days. He kept hearing the words over and over, and he wondered what, if anything, he could do to make things easier for his son, who had endured a lifetime of tragedy already. The simple truth was that he couldn't. That simple answer made things more complicated than he could ever imagine. So many things had become elliptical, and the ends didn't meet. He had to pull a lot of strings and step on dozens of toes to arrange this trip. Despite his desperate need to see his son, however, Wilder began to wonder if this face-to-face meeting was a good idea after all. But there was no other choice, was there? He had been forced into the role of the Grim Reaper, and he hated himself for it.

The knock at the door was right on schedule. "Hello, Scott," Wilder said. "Good to see you again. Come in."

Neilson entered the room, and the Secret Service agent closed the door from the hallway. "Welcome to Clark, Mr. Wilder. How was your trip?"

"Too long. I feel like I've been beaten with a rubber hose." Wilder noticed the dark circles under Neilson's eyes and motioned to a nearby chair. "Sorry, Scott. You must be a little foggy too. When did you get here?"

"Two days ago. I wanted to make sure that the staff kept Bill and John separated and that there were no loose ends."

"I appreciate that." Wilder sat on the bed. "Any unusual activity?"

"My team hasn't found anything out of the ordinary. Our boys were brought here under a John Doe alias, and there are dedicated Marine guards with them. I'm certain nobody knows they're here."

"We have to keep it that way." Wilder scanned the notes scattered across the bed. He looked at Neilson. "We rig for silent running now, Scott. As far as anybody knows, they didn't make it." He held up two pieces of paper. "Death certificates."

"I understand."

Wilder dropped the papers onto the bed and looked at his Saigon station chief. "Anything on Petrov?"

Neislon slowly shook his head. "He left his trademark equipment but nothing else. There were no prints and no one saw him."

"John did."

"Yeah, … I guess he did."

"How's he doing anyway?"

Neilson hesitated for a moment before he spoke. "John fades in and out. The doctors say he's on the edge of a coma."

"Damn!" Wilder rubbed his eyes. "How about the OSI?"

"As useless as a screen door on a submarine."

Wilder stared at the floor, resigned to the task ahead. There wasn't anything else he could do. "Now's as good a time as any."

"Yes, sir, I suppose it is." Neilson opened the door and stood aside. Jack Wilder prepared to face the toughest assignment of his career.

He stood silently, looking at his sleeping son. The Marine guards stood at rigid attention on either side of the door, trying their best not to notice what was going on. Wilder slowly walked into the room and stood next to the bed. He looked at his damaged son and struggled to fight back the bile in his gut.

Neilson leaned against the wall. He wouldn't change places with his boss for anything. He had said as much out of respect.

Wilder moved a chair close to the bed and sat. "Bill … ?" He placed his hand on the young man's shoulder. "Wake up, Bud." His father gently shook him.

After several seconds Bill moved his head and slowly opened his eyes. He looked at his father, not really seeing him. Finally, his eyes focused and he was instantly awake. He tried to push himself up, but the pain was too much. He settled back on his pillow with a painful grimace. He looked briefly at Neilson across the room, then back at his father.

"Dad!" He rubbed his forehead with the back of his hand. He was dizzy from moving too quickly. "What are you doing here?"

"I was in the neighborhood and thought I'd drop by for a beer and a handshake." Wilder was happy to see his son alive, and he realized then that coming to Clark had been the right decision after all.

"I'm glad to see you, Dad." Bill looked around the room briefly then back at is father. "But I never thought we'd meet in a place like this. A lot's happened since John and I left the States. Where is he anyway? Have you talked to him?"

"No, I haven't. " Wilder managed to evade the issue for the time being, and the two men visited as father and son for the first time in months. They comforted each other, and their being together helped Wilder gain the courage he would need to tell his son the painful truth.

Eventually, they fell into silence. Bill knew that something was wrong. His father wouldn't fly halfway around the world for no reason. It was time for Jack Wilder to put his cards on the table, and the dread of that unpleasant task showed on is face.

"Dad, you didn't play hooky to come here because I stubbed my toe. What's going on?"

Wilder looked desperately at his son. There was no other way. "Bud, there's something I have to tell you. I don't know how to else say it, so I'll just start at the beginning."

Bill stared at his father. "I'm listening."

Wilder looked briefly at Neilson then turned back to his son. "You were the only survivor from the crash in Kontum. The forward air controller that worked your flight made it out in one piece, but everyone else perished."

Bill remembered the crash and the explosion, but the rest was a blur. "Those poor bastards. God rest their souls." There was nothing he could do, except pray for them. His thoughts shifted to events prior to the crash. "What happened to Fire Base Alpha? What about Tommy?"

"Tommy's fine. He's home now."

"Was he hurt?"

"No. We got him out due to special dispensation."

"So you were able to get him out because of Maggie? John and I hoped for that."

"There were extenuating circumstances, Bud."

"What do you mean?" Despite the pain, Bill forced himself to sit up.

"I'll get to that in a minute, son. Please listen."

Bill's eyes were glued to his father.

I'd give my soul if I didn't have to do this, Wilder thought to himself.

"Bill, when you were in school, you used to read anything you could get your hands on by Ernest Hemmingway. Remember?"

"I do." The eyes didn't move.

"Do you remember his classic definition of guts?"

"He called it 'Grace under pressure.' Why?"

Wilder leaned forward, his face close to his son's. His voice was soft but firm. "Because grace under pressure is what you need right now. Listen to me, Bud. This is going to hurt, but you must be strong."

"I've about seen it all, Dad. What else is there?" Bill was perfectly still, his eyes riveted to his father's.

"Petrov made his move." Wilder watched his son visibly stiffen. *God, give me strength.* "Bill, he broke into Maggie's room at the Caravelle and tried to attack her. John knocked the door in—"

"What—"

"Please, son, let me finish." Wilder wiped away the sweat running down the side of his face with his hand. "The Vietnamese woman on duty at the front desk said that John came in the middle of the night to see Maggie. He fixed breakfast for her in the hotel kitchen so she would have something to eat before she left for the airport. When he came back to her room with the tray, he heard a commotion inside. He knocked the door down and caught Petrov red-handed."

"Was she—"

Wilder held up his hand to silence his son. "When John went after him, Petrov shot him."

Bill closed his eyes.

"Then Petrov tossed a grenade on the bed and escaped out the window." Wilder leaned over and placed both hands on his son's shoulders. "Look at me, son." Bill opened his eyes and looked at his father. "Grace under pressure, okay? Maggie was on the bed when the grenade exploded. She didn't stand a chance."

"Oh, God!" Bill rolled his eyes towards the ceiling and fell back on his pillows.

"Bud, there's more."

Bill looked at his father with red eyes.

"She was pregnant. I'm so sorry."

The silence in the room was as powerful as the raging typhoon outside. Not a word was spoken for almost an hour. Wilder patiently watched his son while Neilson quietly looked at the sheets of rain running down the window. Bill didn't move or make a sound. Neilson thought Bill was asleep, but Wilder knew better …

… Bill's mind was on a different plane. Everything that happened in his life was part of a larger plan, a plan that was part of and woven through him. The concept of *Ch'uang tzu-chi* gave him voice to words that others didn't have the courage to say, and the ability to act when others could not. His years of martial training and Zen discipline had conditioned him to accept the Infinite and to be part of it. He had studied, and accepted, the Gaia Hypotheses—the idea that the earth itself was a self-correcting, thinking organism that had its own ways of regulating the various species that populated it. He was one of the Regulators, and it was his purpose to correct an imbalance in the earth, thereby enabling it to regulate and heal itself. A *Good* had been killed by an *Evil*, and it was his responsibility in the grand scheme of things to destroy that evil and to bring stability to the entire living organism …

… Bill slowly opened his eyes. He looked at his father for a moment before he spoke. "… John?" There was little emotion in his voice.

"Both of you were evacuated here on an Air Force plane. He's badly damaged, son, and the doctors are trying to keep him from slipping into a coma. I can't go into details about his wounds, but they're extensive. The good news, if there is any, is that they are healing. His throat was badly injured though, and the doctors don't know if he'll regain his speech. I'm so sorry, Bud. I wish there was something I could do—"

"There is."

"Name it."

"Take me to see him."

Saigon

The Tan Son Nhut command post was quieter than usual. Everyone was busy at his assigned task, but the mood was somber. No one spoke unless it was necessary in the course of his work. Captain Dan Mercer and his counterparts had gone to twelve hour shifts. It afforded them a chance to get some much needed sleep while, at the same time, keeping the room staffed with a rated officer that could organize and control the bedlam within. Having been briefed by the off-going duty officer, Mercer looked at the plexi-glass status board and made a mental note of where all the missions were. He stared at the yellow line that went the length of the board across the names of the crew that went down in Kontum. Wilder's name was first on the list.

"That family has suffered more than any ten should have to."

"They were all good guys, Dan," Bryant said. "Did the others have families?"

"Not that I'm aware of."

"Just when you think you're on top of things, something like this happens." Bryant sat in a chair next to Mercer's desk. "Did anybody find out what happened to Slaughter?"

Mercer shook his head. "I don't know what to make of it. The entire base has been searched. It's like he vanished into thin air." He looked at Bryant. "It's just as well that Wilder never heard about the Caravelle. That poor girl. What a waste!" He looked at the board again. "I'll be so glad when this shit's over. This war sucks!"

"Sure as hell does."

Clark Air Force Base
Philippines

"Do you think that's a good idea?" Jack Wilder didn't. "John might not recognize your voice. He's not coherent."

Bill leaned towards his father to the extent he could. "Dad, I've lost everything. He, you, and Bruce are all the family I have left." In spite of his anger and forcefulness, tears ran down his face. "There's nothing else to lose. I have to see him. He's my only link to Petrov, and I'm his only link to life in this God-forsaken place." Bill stared his father down. "*Please ...* "

Wilder saw the hurt in his son's eyes. He didn't know what to do, but he did know that he had to do something. He looked at Neilson, now sitting beside him. Neilson nodded affirmatively. Wilder turned back to his son. "Okay, Bill. We'll go see him. But there are no promises."

"Let's go."

Wilder helped his son into his wheelchair, while Neilson told the Marine guards that they would being going to Slaughter's room. Within minutes the CIA men were making their way down the hall. Wilder didn't know what to expect, but he didn't think anything good would come of it. He did know, however, that his son had the upper hand and that the young pilot would use it to his advantage. Wilder had to be careful.

He wheeled his son into Slaughter's room and stopped beside his bed. He looked briefly at the unconscious man then left the room. It was time for the two classmates who had endured so much together to be alone.

Bill stared at his friend. His mind was flooded with the memories, both good and bad, of experiences they had shared since they met in 1965; the sweat parties, inspections, flight school, too much beer at happy hour. Their flight to Southeast Asia together brought a fleeting smile to his face. Slaughter's antics, after getting both of them in trouble on more occasions than he could remember, were pleasant memories. When he thought about their night at the *Ding How Dog* and of how they'd been set up, the smile left his face.

He looked at the tubes and wires that were plugged into his best friend, and a lump formed in his throat. "You dirt ball, why did you have to go and get yourself blown all to hell?" Bill wheeled his chair to the head of Slaughter's bed. With tears in his eyes, he said, "I owe you my life, John. I won't forget what you did for Maggie. You did your job, my friend. Now, it's my turn. But I need one more favor, buddy." He placed his mouth near Slaughter's ear. "Listen to me, John," Bill whispered, "I know you can hear me. I need to know who he is. Tell me the name of the person that did this. Do it for us, my friend. Do it for Maggie."

Slaughter was unresponsive, but Bill refused to give up. "Let's get him, John. You and me. I need that Texas stubbornness now, old buddy. Tell me who did this, and I'll get the son-of-a-bitch for the three of us. I swear it." Bill's eyes bored into his friend, sending his thoughts—his will—to the unconscious man. *Hear me, John. Hear me.*

Slaughter's eyes slowly opened. They were unfocused and rolled about randomly.

"I'm here, John. Your pain-in-the-ass sidekick. Give me a name … that's all I need. Do it for Maggie and me." Tears streamed down Bill's face. He had lost his soon-to-be wife and their unborn child. His best friend—now hanging onto life by a thread—was the only clue to an assassin that had to be destroyed. Bill Wilder was ready to strike, but he had to have a name first. "*Please*, John!"

The eyes remained unfocused, but Slaughter's mouth slowly began to move.

Bill leaned closer. *Please!*

Slowly, Slaughter pursed his lips in an effort to speak. His eyes tried to focus on the face looking down at him. "Buh, … Buh!" was all he could manage. He began to shake and his eyes watered. Finally, exhausted from the effort, his eyes rolled up into his head, and he slumped into unconsciousness.

Bill began to panic. "Dad, get in here quick!"

Wilder was in the room in an instant. "What?"

"Call the doctor! I think John's slipped over the edge."

Neilson bolted down the hallway. In less than a minute a team of doctors ran into the room. "What happened?" Dr. Koenig, the chief surgeon, asked.

"He opened his eyes and tried to speak but passed out," Bill said. "He's not responding to anything."

The doctors quickly examined Slaughter's breathing pattern and blood pressure. They looked at the screens that monitored his heart rate and vital signs. Koenig looked at Wilder and shook his head. "We'll run some quick tests and an EEG. He may have lapsed into a coma." He didn't say what he really thought.

Bill turned his wheelchair and faced the doctor. "Tell us the truth. Is he going to live?" The determination in his eyes and voice told the doctor that he wouldn't leave until he got the answer he wanted.

"I honestly don't know if he'll survive this or not. He has some serious injuries and an uphill battle in front of him. But being young and in good shape, he has a fighting chance. This coma might be a good thing for him in the short term; his body can heal without interruption. In the meantime, there isn't anything we can do but to keep him comfortable."

"Okay, here are the rules, gentlemen." Jack Wilder was taking charge now. "Nobody enters this room unless he's with one of you." He looked at each doctor in turn. "I'll give you a list of people that are allowed access to him, but no one, not even me, is to be allowed in here without one of you. The only exception is my son. Is that clear?"

"We'll double the guard and keep the hall empty," Koenig said. "We're going to twelve hour shifts now. Dr. Brown and I will alternate, and one of us will constantly check on him. No one will be allowed in here without one of us. Colonel Patsun will give us all the security we need."

Wilder looked at the two medical men. "Gentlemen, I don't mean to make your jobs more difficult than they already are, but I'm certain that his life is in danger." He nodded towards Slaughter. "There's already been an attempt on him." He pointed to Bill. "This guy is in the same boat. No attempt on him yet, but that could change. Could you perhaps put them closer together now? It might make keeping an eye on them easier."

"Consider it done," Koenig said. He looked at Bill. "We'll put you across the hall right away. The rooms on either side of both of you are empty and will remain that way. Security won't be a problem."

"Thanks, doc." Bill looked briefly at his comatose friend. He turned his chair around and wheeled himself out of the room without another word.

Koenig's eyes followed him. "These guys must be close."

"That's an understatement." Wilder followed his son into the hallway.

Bill's mind was on fire. He strained to understand how this could have happened, and he wondered if there was anything he could have done to prevent his friends from being butchered. His stomach churned when he thought of Maggie. Accepting her death would be difficult; the fact that she was gone had not really hit him yet. His best friend lay near death, and he was powerless to do anything about it. He didn't look up when his father stood beside him.

"Bud, I wish there was something I could say or do that would take the pain away. I understand what you're going through, and I want you to know that I'll stay here with you as long as you need. We'll get through this together." Wilder stood with his hand resting on his son's shoulder. The physical touch gave them each other's strength and further secured the bond between the two remaining survivors of the Wilder family. For Jack Wilder it was an admittance that his own strength came from his son and that Bill would have to carry the torch from this point on. For Bill it was support from the man that had helped him whenever he was down. Bill knew, however, that no one could help him now but himself. He would have to draw upon an inner strength and face this most difficult task alone. He was determined more than ever to do it.

Bill looked up at his father. "Dad, you have to get back to Washington. Somebody has to run the show." He looked down the empty hall. "What's next with me?"

"Let's get you back on your feet first, Bud. That's the important thing now."

"I need to get back to Vietnam." It was not a request.

"No."

"Listen, Dad, Petrov tried to kill me and failed. Think about it. If he sees me in Saigon, business as usual, he'll get reckless and try again. I'll be ready for him."

"Sorry, Bill, but I'm calling the shots on this one. Scott's going back to Saigon tonight. The plan is simple; as far as everybody else is concerned, you're both dead. Slaughter died in that explosion and you in the plane crash. We think Petrov will get sloppy when he learns that both of you are gone. In the mean time, you're staying here. You're not going to do anybody any good in a wheelchair."

"But—"

"No buts."

We'll see.

CHAPTER 14

The days turned into weeks, but for Jack Wilder, time stood still. His people in Saigon had turned up nothing, and the Vietnamese government was worse than useless during the investigation of the Caravelle explosion. Officials actually went out of their way to hinder the American investigative efforts. The CIA obviously knew the truth—or most of it—but for appearance sake, MACV and the South Vietnamese government blamed the explosion on the Vietcong. Passing the buck—right or wrong—to the bad guys was synonymous with blaming dead pilots for crashing their own planes. Government, as a bureaucratic entity, has always had the ability to point the finger at those that can't point back. MACV and the Thieu regime were no different.

Life in the Clark Air Force Base hospital had become boring and mundane. Per orders from Langley, Bill Wilder was severely restricted in his movements. With the exception of the time he was in his room, he was never without a Marine escort. Although he became friends with his guards, certain questions weren't asked. The Marines knew that he was one of the good guys, but they had no idea of his true identity. To them he was "John Doe," and he didn't make them any the wiser. He had made a complete recovery and had resumed his workouts, allowing for the fact that he couldn't leave the hospital. He continually honed his martial skills, and his Marine guards welcomed the chance to learn from him. His emotional state, however, was still in turmoil. The controlled anger below the surface had to be slaked. To that end, Wilder kept to himself, confiding in no one. His father was no exception.

Slaughter's physical wounds had healed for the most part, but the doctors had no idea if he would come out of his coma. He had not responded to any stimulus they had subjected him to, the only exception being Wilder's voice on rare occasions. The EEG brain waves had spiked several times, along with a rise in blood pressure. The doctors felt that Wilder's presence had a positive effect on the comatose pilot, and they encouraged the sessions. But it was anybody's guess as to when Slaughter would rejoin the world of the conscious.

Wilder was becoming more impatient with each passing day. Although he had spoken with his father by phone several times, no new information was passed. Slaughter's condition remained essentially unchanged, and the restrictions on Wilder's movements remained the same.

One rainy night he stood in front of the mirror and asked himself the same questions he'd asked countless times before, but the answers never came. The *Why?* began to drive him crazy. He decided then and there that he'd had enough. He walked across the hall into Slaughter's room. The Marine guards remained at their stations at the ends of the hallway, their eyes following his every move.

The two men were alone. Wilder stood beside the bed and looked at his inert friend. *If I could only read your mind,* he thought. He leaned close to Slaughter's ear. "They'll pay for this John. I swear it." He touched Slaughter's arm. "Be well, my friend. *Adios.*" He turned and left the room for the last time.

CHAPTER 15

NEWPORT, RHODE ISLAND
APRIL 1972

The mood in the Newport chapel was as somber as the foul weather outside. A cold rain fell on everything and dampened everyone's already miserable spirits. Tom and Audrey McIvor sat in the front row. Tommy sat beside his mother, and Jack Wilder sat next to Captain McIvor. Spencer was seated next to his brother-in-law. The enormous church was packed. Friends and family had come to pay their respects to the McIvor clan and to the memory of Margaret Erin McIvor. It was *deja vu* all over again for Wilder. He'd been through this himself not long ago, and the McIvors had been there for him. Now, they had lost their oldest child, and he was helpless to do anything. Just being there for his friends wasn't enough.

He thought about his son recovering from his brush with death in a hospital in an alien land halfway around the world. He wondered if Slaughter would ever come out of his coma and what effect it would have on his son if Slaughter didn't make it. The thought of it repulsed him, and he pushed it from his mind. He thought about retiring from the Agency, but he knew he couldn't until Bill and John were safely home. And there was the Petrov problem. Until the last chapter was written in that book, he would have no choice but to stay at his post. At least he could do *something* there.

He looked at Audrey. He saw the same pain in her face that he'd seen in his wife's at the Annapolis chapel just a few years earlier. *When does it end?* Wilder felt more helpless now than he had ever felt in his life.

A man in a dark suit came down the side aisle. Trying to be as unobtrusive as possible, he stepped into the pew and sat beside the NSA director. He whispered into Spencer's ear and quickly made his exit. Spencer sat mesmerized for a moment, his eyes staring straight ahead. He turned discretely towards Wilder and said, "Let's step outside. We need to talk."

Caught by surprise, Wilder was mildly annoyed. "Can't it wait, Bruce? This isn't the time—"

"No, it can't." Spencer's eyes bored into him.

Wilder stared at him, seeing the worried look. "Very well." He turned to McIvor. "Excuse me, Tom. Something's come up. I'll be right back."

McIvor nodded, his mind elsewhere. Wilder and Spencer slid to the end of the pew and quietly made their way down the side aisle to the rear door.

Stepping outside into the chilling rain, they headed for the shelter of the government limousine. The agent that had alerted Spencer earlier opened the rear door for them, careful not to look either of them in the face. He knew of the pain they had gone through, and he didn't want any part of what was coming. Wilder and Spencer climbed into the car, and the agent closed the door behind them.

Wilder mopped the rain from his face with a handkerchief and looked at Spencer. Something had to be seriously wrong for the memorial service to be interrupted by the Director of the NSA, especially when such close friends were involved. "Okay, Bruce, what's so important that we walked out on the McIvors when they need us the most?"

Spencer watched the cold sheeting rain on the windshield. "He's gone."

"What are you talking about?"

"Bill's gone. Disappeared."

Suddenly, Jack Wilder was more tired than he could ever remember. He leaned back in his seat and closed his eyes. "What do you mean *disappeared?*"

"Colonel Patsun just called from Clark. Bill's gone. No one's seen him since last night. He just vanished. The Marines and military police have combed the base, but there's no sign of him."

Wilder took a deep breath and slowly exhaled. "If Bill doesn't want to be found, looking for him will be a waste of time." *What the hell do we do now?*

CCK Air Force Base
Taiwan

The C-130 "Rotator" landed at CCK Air Force Base in Taichung, Taiwan. The weekly flight made the trip from Vietnam and the Philippines to Taiwan, where TDY crews disembarked from their turn in the "barrel" for some much needed time off at their home station. They were happy to be going home to Taiwan, where many considered themselves to be on permanent R&R. Although it was in the operating theater of the war, it was a world apart from Vietnam from a practical standpoint. Things were looser here, and the air crews enjoyed their time off after completing their mundane training on the base.

The plane taxied to its designated parking spot, and the engines were shut down. After the propellers stopped turning, the passengers began to disembark through the aft ramp. There were flight crews, maintenance personnel, and other military people making their transit around the western Pacific.

Captain Mike Whittier, on leave from Vietnam, was one of the lucky few that had some time off from the war. On the flight from the Philippines, Whittier struck up a conversation with the mechanic next to him. Sergeant Hank Swanson boasted that the night life Taipei was legendary, and he planned to take the train to Taipei as soon as he cleaned up some loose ends and got some sleep. Swanson gave Whittier a list of the "better" places to go, and Whittier promised to try every one.

After the crews went through the dog-and-pony show known as military customs, Swanson offered the young pilot a ride into Taichung where he rented a house with several mechanics and pilots. Their live-in maids, or *amahs*, always threw a welcome-home party for the guys when they returned from Vietnam, and Whittier was welcomed. He accepted the invitation.

Whittier blended right in. There were a dozen Air Force people and many local women, all prostitutes. Each member of the household had his own live-in *amah* to take care of his every need. It was a veritable paradise for bachelors, both Class A and Class B. The music was loud and the booze was plentiful. Japanese stereos blasted out music, but the neighbors didn't mind because all of them were military personnel doing the same thing. Downtown Taichung was a party town as far as the military people living there were concerned.

Beginning early in the afternoon, the party went on through the night. The morning sun found bodies sprawled everywhere, either sleeping or passed out. It would be almost noon before anyone made a move, except for Whittier.

Waving down a taxi, he climbed into the back seat. "Train station," he said. The driver, not understanding a word, nodded in the affirmative and prepared to drive off. Whittier tapped him on the shoulder and said, "Choo-choo!" He proceeded to make noises like a train.

"Okay, Joe." Pointy-Talky is common language in any culture, and it worked well here. Within seconds the taxi was on its suicide mission to the station. It raced down the narrow streets, blasting right through the intersections, opposing traffic not withstanding. Taxi drivers sat towards the middle of the seat, rather than directly behind the wheel. Their reasoning was that Buddha sat on their left side, and Buddha protected them. As a result, drivers didn't look to their left as they sped through busy intersections. If by chance a truck barreled through from their left, too bad. The law of survival was that the driver with the loudest horn and the heaviest foot had the right-of-way. Big balls ruled the road. Riding in a taxi in Taiwan was one of the most hazardous things a military person could do, combat not withstanding.

The ride was only several minutes, but it seemed like an eternity to the passenger in the back seat. Arriving at the station, Wittier gave the driver a twenty NT$ note and got out of the car. Thankful to have his feet on firm ground once again, he went to the ticket window and bought a one-way first class pass to Taipei.

He looked around the station. The place was alive with activity. There were families with anxious children, along with farmers and their animals. They, along with merchants packing their wares, waited patiently for the train to arrive. Everyone was represented, and Whittier felt at home among the Taiwanese and American travelers that were on their way to Taipei.

The train pulled into the station and slowly came to a stop. When the bell rang, the doors opened and a wave of people emptied from the cars. Everything that humanity had to offer was there. Whittier was both amused and appalled at the scene. Taiwanese in their best finery exited next to the poorest of dirt farmers with their pitiful livestock. It was a cross-section of life in the Orient.

Whittier patiently waited. The train was serviced and the first boarding call was made. Joining the crowd, he was swept into the second car. He found a seat by the window and sat down. He watched with detached amusement while people jostled for position and settled in. Within minutes the train began to pull away from the station. Whittier pulled his ball cap over his eyes, slumped into his seat, and went to sleep.

Franconia, Virginia

The Ford stopped in front of the home of the Director of the National Security Agency. Bruce Spencer and Jack Wilder climbed out of the vehicle and walked to the house in silence. They entered through the kitchen door, and Wilder sat at the table.

"I'll make coffee," Spencer said. "I'm not much of a cook, but I can brew better joe than that institutional stuff."

"Sounds good to me." Wilder undid his tie and opened his collar. He'd always been weary of uniforms, and the civilian suits were just more of the same. He rubbed his eyes in a vain effort to push the tiredness away. "We can't find him. None of our operatives know anything about him anyway." He looked at Spencer. "I think he's gone rogue on us, Bruce, and I'm afraid of what he might do. The really scary part is that I don't blame him. We haven't been forthcoming with him."

Filling the coffee maker, Spencer looked at his brother-in-law. "Don't be so hard on yourself, Jack. You've done the right thing, and you know it. Put yourself in his place. That kid's been through hell. His brother was murdered by a madman, his girl friend blown to pieces by the same person, and his best friend is hanging on by a thread, courtesy of you know who. Frankly, I'm surprised it took this long for Bill to strike out on his own. Let's give him the benefit of the doubt, okay? I think he has his marbles in one bag."

Wilder looked at the NSA chief. "Thanks, Bruce. I needed that."

At that instant the telephone rang. Spencer grabbed the wall receiver. "Yes?" His face want dark. He sat the coffee pot down and leaned against the counter, as if trying to keep from falling down.

Wilder's eyes were glued to him.

"Let's have it." Spencer's face was screwed into a knot, his eyes glued to the counter. "Is he alive? ... Now, you listen to me. You triple the damn guard, and you let nobody, and I mean *nobody*, in that room. The chief surgeon only. No exceptions. In the meantime, I'm going to arrange for an unannounced airlift. A C-9 Nightingale will arrive tomorrow. Other than the crew, he is to be the *only* patient on that plane. No passengers. Period. Understood?" Spencer slowly hung up the phone. He leaned on the counter with both hands, his head hanging down. "God, help us!"

Expecting the worse, Wilder patiently waited. Pushing the panic button would accomplish nothing.

Spencer slowly walked across the room and sat at the table. He looked at his brother-in-law. "Jack, I didn't think things could get worse. You're not going to believe this."

"Try me."

"Someone just made an attempt on John's life. Somebody gave him an injection of something—I don't know what—but it nearly exploded his heart. His vital signs were out of control by the time the doctors got to him. They got him calmed down, but it's too early to know if he'll pull through." Spencer's expression was one of helplessness. "That was Colonel Patsun. He's got the hospital in a lockdown, and the OSI is in on the act now."

Wilder pounded the table in frustration. "This is a goddamn circus. You and I both know those idiots couldn't find a hooker in a whore house with a thousand dollar bill." He stood and walked to the phone. Picking it up, he looked at Spencer. "Bruce, as far as anyone outside this room is concerned, Slaughter just died in that hospital. No one is to know his real identity, including the C-9 crew bringing him home."

"I agree, Jack." Spencer reached over and pushed the button on the coffee machine. "Nobody knew that those two boys were at Clark. As far as the Air Force is concerned, those guys were just John Doe One and John Doe Two out of 'Nam. They weren't manifested. You know what that means."

"It means that we have a leak." Wilder looked briefly out the window then at Spencer. "I need to use your secure phone, but I need your honest opinion on something first."

"We're family, Jack, and there's not much of it left. We're lucky that our positions give us the latitude to do what's needed. Just say it."

They stood in silence for a moment before Wilder spoke. "Bruce, I've dreaded the possibility of this day for years, and I've prayed that it would never come, but it's here. Bill's on his own now—a loose cannon, if you will. He's obviously out of our control, but we *do* know his basic intentions."

"And?"

"This is a difficult decision, and it doesn't come lightly. I've decided to legally transfer Bill into the black operations end of this nasty business for real. His code name is now *Ninja*. I'm going to approve the sanction of Ivan Petrov, and I'm authorizing *Ninja* to carry out the assignment. This gets Bill off the hook legally if he gets to Petrov before we do."

"Be careful with this, Jack. You know what will happen if all the I's and T's aren't dotted and crossed on an assassination mission."

"There's no other choice, Bruce." Wilder picked up the red secure phone on the counter and dialed a sequence of numbers. "Petrov has to be taken out, and no one can get close to him except *Ninja*. It's just a damned bad coincidence that *Ninja* and my son are the same person."

Spencer knew that his brother-in-law was right. There was nothing he could say. He looked at the coffee machine, waiting impatiently for it to complete its cycle. He needed something stronger, but he wouldn't do it for the sake of the man at the other end of the table. Right now that man needed all the support he could get.

Taipei, Taiwan

The dawn began to break over the mountains to the east, and already the streets were filled with the multitudes on their way to market, or merchants getting ready to peddle their wares. The pre-dawn noise grew louder as the thousands of trucks, cars, and mopeds jammed the streets. It was pretty much like any other large city; the dog-eat-dog world of commerce.

Sam Lassiter awakened to the gentle knock at the door. "Room service," the heavily accented female voice announced.

"Just a minute." Lassiter slipped into his bathrobe. He opened the door, and a Taiwanese girl, barely in her teens, bowed slightly and pushed the breakfast cart through the opening. "Come in," Lassiter said, stepping aside just in time. He couldn't help but smile at the girl's lack of timidity. She pushed the cart across the room and parked it next to the window overlooking the city. Lassiter grinned and handed her a generous tip. "Thank you for stopping by, Suzy Wong."

"*Sy chen!*" The girl giggled and hurried out of the room, closing the door behind her.

Lassiter sat at the small table and poured himself a cup of coffee. He buttered a piece of toast, leaned back in his chair, and looked across the city. He thought about the people down below him and wondered about their problems. Their biggest ones, he imagined, were how they were going to feed their families, pay the rent, and figure out how to keep more of their hard-earned money from their version of the tax man.

The Taiwanese people were governed by the Nationalist Chinese that had come from the mainland after the Communists had taken over China under Mao. That the Taiwanese didn't like their benefactors was no secret, but the military government there didn't allow for dissident behavior. Politics notwithstanding, the average guy on the street was content to concern himself with the mundane things in life like how to survive.

Lassiter pushed those thoughts from his mind and turned to more immediate things. After breakfast, he would check out of the hotel and head for the docks at Keelung. There, his plans would go into motion. He finished his coffee and toast and began to pack. Picking up the several passports on the bed, he slid them into the false bottom of his suitcase. As a trader and exporter of fine teak wood furniture from Taiwan, the local customs officials weren't overly concerned with what he took out of the country. They were mainly interested in what was imported from Hong Kong and Communist China. The Nationalists on the island were legally at war with the Communist mainland, but the local government officials were only concerned with lining their pockets. An expatriate American selling furniture was of little consequence.

Lassiter paid his bill in cash. He stepped through the front door of the hotel and into the mass of humanity. He hailed a taxi and told the driver where to take him. "Keelung," was all Lassiter had to say. The driver drove at break-neck speed to the harbor town as if his life depended on it. Arriving more or less in tact, Lassiter gladly stepped out of the care-worn Datsun and retrieved his bag. He paid the driver and walked the short distance to the harbor master's office.

Standing in front of the Hi Fat Shipping Company, Ltd., Lassiter looked around at the rusted steamers along the docks. *A person could disappear here and never be seen again*, he thought. Entering through the main door, he approached the counter where a shapely Taiwanese woman sat behind her desk reading a magazine.

"Good morning, sir. May I help you?" she said in perfect English. She liked what she saw in the American, and she slid her hands down her thighs to let him know that she was interested.

"My name's Sam Lassiter, and I wish to book space on your next ship heading to South Vietnam. I'm exporting furniture to Saigon, and I need to book passage for me and my merchandise. I know that this is late notice, but do you have anything available? I'm willing to pay whatever you ask." Lassiter smiled at the woman and ran his eyes approvingly over her body. It was obvious that she was available, and he played on her vanity to get what he wanted.

"I'm sure we can find something, Mr. Lassiter. Let me look." She ran her finger down the shipping schedule. "Yes, here we are. The *Shangri-La* sails at midnight. It will make a port call at Subic Bay, then go on to South Vietnam. Will that do?"

"Perfect," Lassiter said. He pulled out his passport and credentials, along with a roll of NT$. When she saw the money, her eyes widened. Money could by anything here. He handed her the passport and a cargo manifest. "I have one container of furniture that will arrive from Taichung this afternoon. It's listed in my name, and I'd like to have it boarded as soon as it gets here. Would you be so kind as to make the arrangements?"

"I would be delighted, Mr. Lassiter." She smiled lewdly at him.

"I don't believe I caught your name."

"Linda Wan. And I will make all arrangements for you, sir." She picked up the phone and dialed a number. Speaking in Chinese, she looked at Lassiter. She had other things on her mind. After a minute she hung up the phone and said, "Everything is arranged. Your passage in First Class is confirmed, and your container will be loaded in the forward hold as soon as it arrives. Your ticket and paperwork will be waiting for you when you board at ten this evening." She handed the documents back to him. When he reached for them, she brushed his fingers with hers. "Should you need anything else, *anything*, I'm at your disposal."

Lassiter smiled. "You've been so helpful, Miss Wan, and I'd like to thank you for you kindness. Perhaps lunch at a nearby hotel?" He wanted to maintain his anonymity, but he also didn't want her to lose face. He didn't need any problems right now.

"I'll arrange for a private room right away." Looking at him with bedroom eyes, she made a quick phone call. Within minutes they left the shipping office together.

Despite wanting to keep to himself, he found her exciting. And the stress that he had been under begged for relief. Watching her walk through the door, he realized just how much he needed a woman right now. The simple act of sex without complications would relieve the tension that had been building up over the past months.

CHAPTER 16

WASHINGTON, DC

The C-9 Nightingale touched down at Andrews Air Force Base just after midnight. The aircraft cleared the runway and taxied towards the south end of the airport, followed by a fire truck and the Security Police. Once stopped, a panel truck, similar to the catering trucks used by the airlines, pulled up to the left side of the plane opposite the cargo door. One of the two Marines in the rear of the truck activated a hydraulic lift and raised the truck bed to the same level as the aircraft floor.

Two flight nurses carried a single litter from the aircraft onto the truck. They strapped the litter securely to the metal rack mounted along the side wall and took their seats beside the patient. The second Marine lowered the truck body to its original position. The vehicle backed away from the aircraft and turned towards the main road. The truck was preceded by two military police vehicles and followed by two more. A single unmarked Ford brought up the rear.

The convoy drove through the main gate and turned onto the beltway that surrounded Washington. In less than an hour it arrived at the Bethesda Naval Hospital where the panel truck pulled into the emergency entrance. The patient was rushed inside, followed by a team of guards and the occupants of the Ford.

Jack Wilder and Bruce Spencer stood silently in the corner, watching doctors and nurses examine their patient. Monitors were connected and vital signs were taken. There had been no change in his condition since his journey began half a world away.

"The patient is stable and doesn't appear to have suffered from the trip. He's holding his own, Mr. Wilder."

"We appreciate all you've done, Dr. Koenig," Wilder said. He looked at the man entering the room. "This is Dr. Jackson. He'll be taking over this case now." The two doctors shook hands. "I expect you'll be heading back to Clark soon."

"That's correct."

"We've arranged for you and your team to spend some time here. Catch up on your sleep and see the sights. You've worked overtime on this, and I insist that you and your crew take some time off. There are some great restaurants in this town. We have you set up at the Marriott. Tab's on us." Wilder shook Koenig's hand. "I can't thank you enough for what you've done."

Koenig looked wearily at the inert body on the bed. "I haven't done anything, Mr. Wilder. That boy's done all the work. I pray that he comes out of this."

"As do we all," Spencer said.

Wilder turned to the Marine guards. "Guys, as of right now you work for me and no one else. Understood?"

The two soldiers snapped to attention. "Yes, sir," the ranking man said.

"You and your teams will have rotating shifts. Absolutely no one is to enter this room except for me, Director Spencer, Dr. Jackson, or the two nurses you see here. *No one.* If anyone else comes in here for as much as a paper cup, I'll have both of you shipped to Siberia with nothing but spam to eat, and it'll be a one-way ticket. Understood?" A smile crept onto Wilder's face, but the Marines knew that he meant business. His reputation had a long reach.

"Sir, my mama couldn't get into this room," the sergeant answered. "We'll cover this place like white on rice."

"You'll have direct phone and radio contact with me and Dr. Jackson. Whatever he needs, make sure he gets it. I'll talk with your commander and arrange for your crew's billeting. Call my number if anything comes up. Any questions?"

"No questions, sir." The guards looked around the room and familiarized themselves with the faces that they would see more often than not. They left the room and quickly briefed the rest of their team as to their duties. The squad members took their positions up and down the hallway. Their appearance intimidated the hospital staff, and that was okay with the Marines. They took their job seriously. The people with authorized access to the patient at the end of the hall were on a very short list.

It was the middle of the night at CIA headquarters. Jack Wilder sat at his desk looking into the darkness that hid the Potomac River below. It was the one place where he felt that he had some measure of control in a sometimes uncontrollable world. His agents in Moscow had turned up nothing on Ivan Petrov, and his son was God-knows-where doing God-knows-what. Wilder's only contact with his son and the fugitive spy lay comatose under heavy guard. He'd considered every conceivable option but kept coming back to the same conclusion. He didn't like his choices, but he had to do something. Doing nothing wasn't an option.

Wilder picked up the phone and pressed a button to a secure line. He turned on the speaker and dialed a number. Hearing the familiar clicks and beeps that assured an unmonitored conversation, he waited.

The telephone rang half a world away. "Neilson."

"Hello, Scott. Jack here."

"Colonel Wilder!" Neilson looked at his watch. "It's two in the morning there, sir. Why are you up and around this time of night?"

"Couldn't sleep. Truth is I have some bad news," Wilder said, looking into the darkness outside. "Slaughter didn't make it."

"What?"

"I don't know the details, but the doctors said he had a heart attack. Something to do with the drugs somebody gave him. He never came out of it."

"Jesus Christ! That kid was an ox. I'm so sorry, Jack. This is a hard one to swallow."

Wilder continued to look out the window. "The body was shipped back to the States yesterday. He'll get a full military funeral at Arlington."

"Sir, I don't know what to say." Neilson changed the subject. "The Caravelle has been combed by the Vietnamese police, and you know how inept they are. The zips aren't letting our people—"

"That doesn't matter, Scott." Wilder looked at the speaker phone. "We've learned all we're going to from that."

"Probably so, sir."

"We've found Bill."

"What? Found him? Where?"

"The important thing is that we have him on ice in a safe house in the States. He lost it when we told him about Slaughter. I don't know what we can do except to keep him under wraps and let the shrinks try to straighten him out."

"Are you keeping him local?"

"Classified."

"Does he know anything about the Caravelle incident?"

"If he does, he's not talking."

"This is one hell of a turn. I wish him well, sir. If there's anything I can do—"

"Thanks, Scott. I appreciate that."

"I'll keep digging at this end, Colonel Wilder. I'll contact you the instant I find anything."

"I'll be in touch." The line went dead. Wilder leaned back in his chair and thought about his actions over the past several days, legal or not, culminating with this phone call. He was satisfied that he had done the right thing. He closed his eyes and dozed until the sun's morning rays ushered in the start of a new day.

Taipei, Taiwan

The *Shangri-La* set sail from Keelung right on schedule. Turning south through the Formosa Straits, the ship had fair weather for the first leg of its trip to the Philippines. The name *Shangri-La* was a misnomer from the outset. The ship was long past its prime, but for Sam

Lassiter, it was perfect. He came out of his stateroom, which was not much more than a dirty closet, and leaned against the rail. The sky was dark and the sea was calm, excellent for making good time. Looking around the deck, he didn't see anyone except an occasional member of the Taiwanese crew busy at work. No one spoke English, and that was fine with him. The less contact he had with others, the better. He would take his meals in his cabin and only come out after dark. For Sam Lassiter, this was not a pleasure cruise, and the fewer people that were aware of his existence, the better.

Three days later the *Shangri-La* docked at Subic Bay to take on more fuel and additional freight. During that time Lassiter remained in his room, carefully observing the activities of the harbor personnel through his small porthole. A few passengers disembarked while others boarded, and Lassiter's trained eye saw no one that would concern him. A few extra NT$ to the ship's crew assuring his anonymity also helped.

After less than eight hours in port, the ship sailed south again and began the week long trek through the South China Sea towards the port city of Cam Ranh Bay on the southeast coast of South Vietnam. In his cabin, Sam Lassiter, importer and exporter of fine teak furniture, prepared for his arrival in South Vietnam.

Saigon

The telephone rattled in a dilapidated bar on Tudo Street. The drunk dressed in jungle fatigues sitting at the end of the bar picked up the receiver. "Yeah?"

"The second one is dead. The first one is under CIA guard somewhere. No more information available."

"*Da Syedahnya.*" Good bye. He hung up the phone and leered at the Vietnamese prostitute hanging onto him. "Let's *di-di-mao* this place, bitch. It's time to show me what you can do." The young woman, not understanding a single word, shook her head in agreement, took the offered money, and left with her high-paying customer. She had no idea that it would be her last night on earth.

***

"Are you serious? What the fuck's going on here?" Ed Custer sat his beer on the table. Despite the Vietnam heat he suddenly didn't want it anymore.

"My sentiments exactly," Neilson said. "Whoever got to Slaughter knew not only where to find him, but knew exactly what to do."

"No shit!" Custer's respect for Jack Wilder notwithstanding, he was as frustrated with the CIA as he was with MACV and the Vietnamese. "The inmates are running the asylum."

Neilson scratched his head and looked through his window at the heat waves rising off the street. "You're probably closer to the truth than you realize." He looked at Custer. "Do you want to go to the funeral? Slaughter's getting full military honors at Arlington, and I think Jack would appreciate your being there. I can make the arrangements if you want."

"Yes, I would. Thanks. There's a C-5 going to the States tonight. I'll jump on it. Emergency leave, that sort of thing." Custer hated seeing his countrymen killed for no good reason, and he hated missing their final send off just as much. "I'll go see Colonel Wilder while I'm there and offer your condolences. It's the least I can do. That poor man's been through the wringer. I'm surprised he hasn't canceled his own check by now."

"He still has Bill."

"Yeah."

CHAPTER 17

CAM RANH BAY
SOUTH VIETNAM

The *Shangri-La* jostled against its moorings. The wind and rain added insult to the already heavy humidity, but the crew was too busy to notice. Working like ants, they labored in the foul weather to empty the cargo holds. Sam Lassiter looked through the porthole for any unusual activity. Having packed his things the day before, he closely inspected the cabin to make sure nothing was left behind. He pulled the brown fedora over his gray hair, turned up his collar, and stepped out into the storm.

He carefully made his way through the bowels of the ship to the gangplank. Walking with a stoop and slight limp, he carefully crossed over the water onto the ground. A South Vietnamese official standing to the side waved him over. "Papers please," he said in Vietnamese. Lassiter handed over his passport and a copy of his shipping manifest. The official, not wanting to be in the rain any longer than necessary, gave the documents a cursory examination. Satisfied, he handed them back to Lassiter. "How long stay Vietnam?" he said in broken English.

"Two days, sir. I'm importing furniture from Taiwan and buying fine Vietnamese furniture in return. It is excellent. Very expensive."

The flattery worked. "Yes," the guard mumbled and waved him through.

"Thank you, sir." Lassiter shoved the documents into his bag and, leaning against the torrent of water, made his way to a hop-tac. Climbing into the bootleg taxi, he shouted through the wind to the driver. "Number one hotel." Any hotel would do.

The Hotel Vin was reminiscent of bygone French influence. The building was falling into disrepair, and the elder Vietnamese man behind the counter made up for the hotel's shortcomings with copious bows. "You like room?" he asked in stilted English. He slid a flimsy rice paper registration form across the counter. "Name, please?"

"Father Sean O'Malley. I'd like one night please." O'Malley signed the form and paid in advance with cash. The old man handed O'Malley a key and pointed down the hall. O'Malley nodded and walked quickly to his room.

Bolting the lock behind him, O'Malley removed his hat and coat and hung them on the hook on the back of the door. Before removing his wet collar and tunic, he carefully searched the room for cameras or listening devices. The chances of the room being bugged were slim to none, but he was not taking any chances. He removed his .357 Python revolver from its holster and tossed it onto the bed. He stripped off his wet clothes and stepped into the makeshift shower. Although it barely worked, it was a welcome change from bathing with imagination in the sink of a rusting ship. He toweled off, put on some fresh clothes, and lay across the bed. He closed his eyes and let his thoughts wonder.

His mind went into high gear. It was time for Bill Wilder to set the next part of his plan into motion.

CIA Headquarters
Langley, Virginia

"Sir, Major Custer to see you," Wilder's secretary said over the intercom.

"Please send him in, Linda." Wilder stepped from behind his

desk and welcomed Custer with a firm handshake. "Welcome home, Ed. How was your trip?"

"Long, Mr. Director. Thanks for taking the time to see me."

"I'm not much into titles, Ed. Jack works fine. Pull up a chair." Wilder motioned to the leather recliner in the corner. "Help yourself to the bar. You'll find about whatever you want."

"Thank you, sir." Custer poured himself a bourbon straight up and dropped into the chair out of exhaustion. He looked around the room for a moment then at Wilder, who sat patiently on the corner of his desk. Custer felt uncomfortable sitting in the presence of such a powerful man. He looked at the glass and took a long drink. The warm liquid felt good. "This hits the spot, sir." He looked at Wilder. "Won't you join me?"

"I'd love to, Ed, but the quacks at Bethesda won't allow it. Besides, I've had more than my share over the years. Comes with the territory." Wilder stood and looked out the window. "Thanks for coming to John's funeral."

Custer sat the empty glass on the bar. He walked to the window and stood beside Wilder. "I liked that kid. He was a good man and a good stick. Damn rotten luck. I'm sorry, sir."

"I'm sorry any of this happened. He was Bill's best friend, and he will be missed. He was like a son to Elizabeth, God rest her soul. He filled the void left by Little Jack. I'm glad she's not here to see this."

Custer wanted to say something to ease Wilder's pain, but he was at a loss for words. He decided to change the subject. "Sir, is there any word on Bill? Neilson said that he disappeared from Clark. "

Wilder looked at him. "You guys knew each other for only a short while, but he spoke highly of you. Guess you guys hit it off pretty good."

"His head's on straight, sir. My money's on him."

"That seems to be the general opinion around here."

"Yes, sir." Custer stood almost at attention in the presence of the Operations Chief. He had a profound respect for the man, more so than the position Wilder occupied.

Wilder walked to the bar and poured two bourbons. "Screw the doctors." He handed one to Custer and raised his glass. "May our troops come home soon."

"All of them." The two men touched glasses and drank.

There was a single knock at the door. Spencer walked in. Custer unconsciously stood at attention when the NSA Director entered. Spencer extended his hand. "Hello, Ed. Thanks for coming." He saw the empty glasses in their hands and said, "A salute to the good guys, I'll wager. I'll have one of those. Reload, Ed?"

"Uh, yes, sir. Thank you."

"Will you be at the service at Arlington tomorrow?"

"Yes, sir."

"Well, I'm sure John would appreciate it. Planning on staying a few days afterwards, I hope."

"Sir, may I speak freely?" Despite their relaxed demeanor, Custer still felt a little ill at ease.

"I insist," Wilder said, smiling.

"Sir, I'm a little burned out and fed up with the bullshit that's going on in Saigon, and I'd like to get away from it for a while."

"Well, you're working for me, Ed," Wilder said, "and I'm ordering you to stay and catch up on some rest. Stay as long as you want."

"I appreciate that, sir."

"Now, Ed, think carefully. Does anyone in Saigon know about this other than you and Neilson?"

"Not that I know of, sir. The only people I've spoken to besides Bill and John is Neilson. We kicked around the possibility that McAlester knew something, but we've come up empty on that."

"We've assigned other resources to cover him. We know that Bryant was giving him information about the Central Highlands, but it wasn't anything the Brit couldn't have learned on his own. A nose for news; that sort of thing. I don't think he's privy to any of this." Wilder thumbed through a folder on his desk. "We know that Bryant is trying to feather his bed with the press. He put in his paperwork to get out of the service when his tour's over. Can't blame him for that. Nothing else there."

"What about Berwick?" Custer said. "It's no secret that he and Bill don't get along. Bill doesn't talk about it."

"It involved Bill's brother when he was a prisoner in Hanoi."

"I see."

"It's beyond that now, Ed. He thinks Berwick is somehow responsible for the blast that killed his girlfriend."

Custer was almost afraid to ask but pressed ahead anyway. "Was he?"

Wilder and Spencer looked at each other. "That's being worked as I speak."

"Understood, sir." Custer knew when to shut up, and now was the time.

"Let's just say that we have a few stones left to turn over, Ed. The big thing for us now is that Bill's out of the loop. He's cooling his heels in a safe house in the middle of nowhere."

"He is?" Wilder's words came as a shock. Custer had heard nothing since the crash in Kontum. "Is he okay? Did he—"

"He's fine, Ed," Wilder said. "He's being treated for emotional problems right now."

Custer was at a loss for words.

"Bill will be all right." Wilder hated lying to the major but he had no choice. It was part of his plan.

Nothing was said about the mole in Saigon or the leak at Clark.

The small congregation stood silently in the clear air of Arlington National Cemetery, its members coming to pay final respects to a fallen comrade-in-arms. The same navy chaplain that had given the final benediction for Little Jack at Annapolis stood over the grave of Air Force Captain John Attison Slaughter. Much had happened since that day long ago, and the only two men that knew the real truth stood to the side with their bodyguards and bowed their heads while the chaplain recited the Lord's Prayer.

CHAPTER 18

SAIGON
MAY

The rain pelted the tin roofs of the shacks that proliferated the capital of South Vietnam. Despite the weather the people of Saigon went about their business because they had little choice. Bicycles jostled in the busy streets with mopeds, both competing with the occasional automobile or truck. Everyone was ankle deep in water, and any effort to protect one's self from the deluge was futile. The darkness added to the controlled pandemonium.

Perfect, Father O'Malley thought. Despite the fact that the Vietnamese were overwhelmingly Buddhists, no one gave a second thought to a bent gray-haired Catholic priest in the market buying food for the many orphaned street children. Making his way through the throng, he stopped at intervals to barter with local farmers peddling their fruits and vegetables. Carrying several small bags of food and used clothing, O'Malley worked the streets until he came to the block across from the Caravelle Hotel.

He stood silently and looked at the devastation. Although the debris had been removed and construction had begun to repair the damage, anyone could tell what had happened. What had been Maggie's room was now a gaping hole, covered with plastic. Workers had built a bamboo scaffold around the side of the building, but it would be a while before the effects of the blast were completely gone. O'Malley stared at the wreckage with rage coursing through his veins.

He saw a street urchin begging on the corner. There were many, an unfortunate result of the union of American GI's and Vietnamese women, and this one was no different than the rest. He was, however, at the right place at the right time. O'Malley made his way across the street and approached the boy. Seeing the Catholic priest approach, the child didn't know whether to stay or run. But seeing the bags of food and having no place else to go, he decided to stay.

O'Malley stopped in front of the boy and kneeled. He smiled and said, "God be with you, my child. We're going to scratch each other's back." O'Malley handed the bags of food and clothes to the young boy. "Take this to your family, son." He had no idea if the boy understood a word or not. It didn't matter anyway; the child smiled at him, grabbed the bags, and ran down the street into the darkness. "Hope I made your day, buddy," O'Malley said in a low voice. The child had unknowingly returned the favor; his location on the corner of the block opposite the hotel gave O'Malley the chance to approach unnoticed by the Vietnamese police that guarded the building. No one would think twice about a holy man giving a starving child a bite to eat. Looking in the direction of the departed orphan, O'Malley slowly stood. In less than a minute he disappeared into the alley that went behind the Caravelle.

The rain came in torrents as the night wore on. By two a.m. the only activity in the streets was an occasional moped or military vehicle on a random patrol. The city was trying to sleep.

The lobby of the Caravelle was empty. The Vietnamese woman sitting behind the counter was reading a copy of *Romeo and Juliet*. Despite the war in this country gone mad, Vandeth had found solace in something written by someone from another country long ago.

Immersed in the book, she didn't hear O'Malley come up behind her. He gently placed his hand over her mouth to keep her from screaming. "Hello, Vandeth." Momentarily frightened, the woman jumped and tried to shriek. "Shhh! It's okay. It's only me," he said in a calming voice. He slowly released her and gently turned her towards him.

Her face registered shock and surprise. She gasped and put her hands to her cheeks. "Captain Wilder? Is it you?"

He put his finger to her mouth to silence her. "Yes, Vandeth, it's me." Wilder looked around the room and motioned towards the office in the rear. "Let's step inside." Vandeth followed him into the empty room and closed the door. Seeing the anxiety in her face, he said, "Not to worry, it's only a costume." Wilder looked through the peep hole in the door. Satisfied that no one was around, he said, "I know this is a shock to you, and I'll explain everything later. But right now, Vandeth, I need your help."

The woman had tears in her eyes. "Captain Wilder, I am so sorry about what happened to Miss McIvor. She was a lovely lady, and she was my friend." She stared at Wilder, her heart filled with sorrow. "I do not understand. Why did this happen, and why are you dressed like a Catholic priest?"

"Vandeth, you are the only person I can trust right now. I need your help, and I must ask you to keep our meeting a secret. Please tell no one that you know of me. The less you know, the better." Wilder's voice conveyed the seriousness of the situation, and it didn't go unnoticed by her.

She was bewildered by his presence, but she also trusted him. She had become good friends both with him and Maggie before her death, and she was willing to do whatever he wanted. "Yes, Captain, our meeting will remain a secret." She smiled for the first time. "I'm so happy that you are alive and well, but … " Her face clouded over.

"But what?"

"I'm sorry to learn of your friend's passing. I only met him the night of the incident, and he—"

"It's okay, Vandeth. He made it out alive that night. He's out of the country now."

She lowered her head. "But Captain, my husband learned at Tan Son Nhut just today that Captain Slaughter was put to rest in your Arlington Cemetery. A Captain Mercer got a call from a Mr. Spencer in the United States. You did not know?"

Wilder stared at her in disbelief. He felt like he'd been kicked in the stomach by a mule. His legs felt numb. He slowly sat down on the chair next to him and looked at the floor. Minutes passed in silence.

Vandeth placed her hand on his shoulder. "You are cold and wet. Wait here. I will be right back." Wilder sat motionless; he hadn't heard a word. In a short time she returned with a pot of coffee and a plate of hot croissants and cheese. She placed the tray on the table beside him and said, "Please, you must eat. Save your strength." Despite her concern for him, there was nothing she could do to ease his pain. She left once more and returned with a change of clothes. "I will arrange for you to stay here in the storage room. No one except me goes there. You must rest." Her heart went out to the man sitting in front of her. He had lost everything and had nowhere to turn. She decided then and there that she would be his support. After all, she had lost a friend too, hadn't she?

Major Ed Custer stepped through the crew door of the C-141 Starlifter and into the oppressive Saigon heat. The two weeks in Washington vanished into thin air as the humidity and depression of the war hit him in the face all at once. *Home away from home*, he thought. He decided to get right to work. It made the time pass by faster and hastened his departure permanently from this God-forsaken place.

After a shower and a few hours sleep, Custer requisitioned an Air Force staff car for the trip to the American Embassy in Saigon. Military personnel passed through its gates as a matter of routine, and no one paid any attention to the comings and goings of another American military officer. Once inside he made his way to the office of the CIA station chief.

"Major Custer to see you, Mr. Neilson," the secretary said, opening the door to Neilson's office. Custer walked in and closed the door behind him.

"Hi, Scott. I just got in a few hours ago and thought I'd stop by. Any news?" Custer sat in a wicker chair and wiped the sweat from his brow.

"Same stuff, different day. Tough coming back here after being in the States, isn't it?"

"Yeah, but here I am." Custer looked at the phone on Neilson's desk. "Any calls about Wilder's status?"

"No. Still being held incommunicado. I can imagine what kind of mental shape he's in. Hell, look at what happened to his friends. It's enough to drive any man crazy."

"Almost anyone. My guess is that his old man is holding him to keep him from tearing Petrov apart."

"Assuming we could find the Russian. From what we know about Petrov, I imagine he can hold his own," Neilson said.

"You've never seen Wilder pissed. For that matter, neither have I. But I did see what he did with a bunch of bad guys that got loose in a plane once. Wasn't pretty, and he didn't even break a sweat. He's a one man killing machine."

"Do you have any idea where he is?" Neilson asked.

"No, and I didn't ask."

"Change of subject. How was the funeral?"

"I'm glad I went, but it was sad. A lot of people showed up, and there wasn't a dry eye in the place when it was over. It's a damned shame what happened to him," Custer said. "Slaughter was one of the good guys."

"Yeah."

Wilder wondered if the deaths of his friends and crew could have been prevented. The tragic events were not his fault, but he felt responsible just the same. As bad as Maggie's death had been, the loss of his best friend had dealt a severe blow to his psyche, and he struggled constantly to come to terms with it.

Vandeth kept her word and did everything she could to help him. Her husband, Vietnamese Colonel Tranh Vinh, worked at the airlift command post as a liaison, and he knew of Wilder and Slaughter. He learned of Slaughter's "death" through Mercer. Fortunately for Wilder, Vinh kept him informed through his wife without realizing it.

Neither he nor anyone else knew that his wife was keeping the young pilot under wraps in the Caravelle, and Vandeth was determined to keep it that way. She felt that she owed it to her American friends, even though two of them were dead. She gave Wilder every bit of news and information she could find. From her, he learned that

Major Custer had gone to the States for Slaughter's funeral and that he had stopped to pay his respects to Wilder's father. He was now back in Saigon.

Wilder kept himself hidden. During the day he stayed under cover, but by night he searched the streets of Saigon for any clue, however remote, that would lead him to Petrov. Inside, he knew that his efforts were in vain, but he had to do something to put out the burning fire in his gut. He began to question his self-worth, and he wondered if he would ever get the chance to even the score.

Finally, he couldn't take it anymore. Leaving the relative security of the hotel, he slipped into the night. Searching the outskirts of the city, he found a non-descript Buddhist temple. It was dark and empty, and the joss sticks burned along with candles left by the monks. Wilder looked at the statue of Buddha. Although not a Buddhist himself, he knew of the Buddhist philosophy as practiced by martial artists worldwide. He sat in the lotus position and looked at the statue. He closed his eyes and began to meditate ...

... Perseverance is the most demanding of all the tenants of *Tae-Kwon-Do*. It is the baseline and foundation of both the physical and mental conditioning that the martial artist must build upon, and it requires that he be in total control of his emotions and rise above the misery around him. Once learned, the student then becomes the master of his actions, rather than a slave to his reactions ...

... Wilder slowly opened his eyes to the first rays of the sun. He had not moved for hours, but his body and mind were fresh. The meditation reinforced his commitment to the task that awaited him. It also reaffirmed his promise to his dead friends. Their passing was difficult for him, but he knew that their deaths would not be in vain. He stood and bowed before the statue of Buddha, turned, and disappeared into the shadows before the monks began their rounds. Wilder knew what he had to do.

"Vandeth, I need some information."

"Certainly, Captain Wilder."

"Where do the embassy people go to unwind? Is there a particular bar or restaurant? A place that doesn't call attention to them?"

She was embarrassed. She lowered her eyes and said, "Many go to the lounges in the red light district."

"I'm sorry, Vandeth, but this is important. Perhaps Colonel Vinh knows of such a place."

"You may wish to start with the *Petite Rouge*. The food is excellent. Many of the correspondents from the hotel go there. " Her face reddened. "I'm sorry. It was one of Miss McIvor's favorites."

Wilder smiled at her. "No need to apologize, Vandeth. I only ask because I need to make contact with someone."

She nodded her understanding.

"I know this is difficult for you, Vandeth, but our friends were killed by someone that I believe is still here. Whoever he is, he knew their schedule and where to find them. Worst of all, I believe he knew them personally. We cannot bring them back, Vandeth, but we can stop him from doing any more killing. I'm going to find him. I can't say anymore than that. The less you know, the safer for you. Understand?"

She smiled sadly at him, tears forming in the corners of her eyes. "Make him pay for what he did."

"Count on it."

CHAPTER 19

SAIGON

It was Saturday night and the streets were alive with activity. The blaring horns of diesel trucks, automobiles, and mopeds assaulted the senses. American soldiers in their jungle fatigues mixed with the Vietnamese, and everyone was in a hurry for one reason or another.

Two intoxicated American soldiers stumbled down Tudo Street. They gaped at the women that paraded in front of the bars and bath houses that comprised this area of the city. Loud music blared through the open doors, enticing any would-be patron to enter, while merchants along the edge of the street tried to hawk their wares to the unwary.

The GI's made their way through the throng of people, moving this way and that to avoid the hawkers and beggars. They tripped around the lines of carts parked haphazardly along the street, avoiding the mopeds and occasional loud horn indicating an approaching four-wheeled *kamikaze* that was hell-bent on being king of the road.

Thinking more with their anatomy than with their brains, the two young soldiers feasted their eyes on the dozens of women that hung around the bar entrances. There were prostitutes of every shape and size, all dressed in cheap mini-skirts, hot pants, and go-go boots. Collectively, they looked and sounded like a flock of parrots.

With their eyes on the numerous women bidding for their attention, they didn't see the two "cowboys" racing their moped towards them from the rear.

One of the soldiers had a 35mm camera hanging from his shoulder. That the camera was on the side closest to the road, was a mistake for its owner. But it was perfect for the rapidly approaching thieves. The two unwary victims stopped to banter and negotiate with several women. Bent on satisfying their carnal desires, they were oblivious to what was going on behind them.

The moped driver slowed and swerved towards the soldier with the camera as if trying to avoid a collision with a bicycle. They passed the soldiers slowly, and the passenger reached out and grabbed the camera with both hands. Jerking sharply on the strap, the camera came off its owner's shoulder with ease.

"What the hell—?" The soldier spun around and watched his camera ride off into the crowd on a moped. "Hey!"

The thief laughed and waved his social finger at his victim. The bike sped through the crowd before the hapless man could collect his wits enough to give chase.

"Jesus Christ! Did you see that? That bastard stole my camera!"

"I told you not to bring it, you dumb-ass. Nothing you can do about it now." The second soldier turned his attention back to the woman closest to him. "What's your name?" The erection was talking now instead of the brain. His friend's loss was the furthest thing from his mind.

"Helen," the little woman said in broken English. "Short time, okay?"

"Okay!" her customer replied. She took him by the arm and led him towards the rundown hotel across the street where rooms were rented by the hour.

The former camera owner looked down the street. The thieves were gone. Not knowing what else to do, he just stood there. In less than a minute another "Helen" focused her attention on him. He slowly turned his head towards her, the camera now forgotten.

"Hey, Charlie, good time?"

"Uh, yeah. Sure." The pair turned and followed their friends into the hotel.

Handing out food to some children, the gray-haired priest watched the entire episode from a distance. Knowing that the "cowboys" were coming did nothing to sway him from his mission. There was nothing he could do about it anyway from where he stood. He gently patted the .357 Python under his cassock and turned his attention back to the children.

The priest slowly made his way down the street until he stood across from the *Petite Rouge* lounge. Offering used clothing to some children, he carefully watched the patrons, mostly Americans and wealthy Vietnamese, enter and leave. There was nothing unusual going on as far as he could see, but he had to start somewhere, and this place was as good as any.

Standing against the sliding metal door of one of the closed shops that lined the street, Wilder looked at his watch. It was just before midnight. Despite the hour the street was still busy with people, mostly prostitutes and street hawkers. Wilder stood in the darkness of a closed shop doorway and patiently waited. Perhaps there was nothing here, but he would wait a little longer before working his way back to the Caravelle.

He stood in the shadows, his eyes glued to the lone man coming out of the *Rouge*. It was Scott Neilson. Nothing unusual there; the place was a local watering hole for embassy people and government officials after all. Wilder watched him for a few moments and was about to dismiss him when Neilson's behavior piqued Wilder's curiosity.

Neilson crossed the street and stopped at the opposite corner. Leaning against a signpost, he lit a cigarette. He tossed the match over his left shoulder with his right hand. He casually looked up and down the street.

Okay, Neilson, what's going on? Wilder had researched Neilson, along with Custer and other operatives in the area, but he didn't know that Neilson smoked. And why did he throw a match over his left shoulder with his right hand? Wilder retreated further into the shadows and waited.

Minutes passed. Neilson turned and slowly walked down the street towards an alley away from the *Rouge*. Stopping at the next corner, he lit another smoke and tossed the match as before. Wilder made his move. He quickly went around the block from the opposite direction and approached the unlit alley from the rear. Stealth was the name of the game now, and his black cassock and rubber soled shoes served their purpose. He was all but invisible. He crept through the darkness like a cat and worked his way through the litter-filled alley, using the piles of trash as cover. Halfway down the narrow passage, he hid behind a large wooden crate under some stairs going up the side of a building. Sliding further into the shadows, he *became* the darkness.

Neilson casually looked around. Satisfied that he had not been followed, he quickly turned into the alley and stepped away from the light. Leaning against the wall in the shadows, he crushed out his cigarette and waited.

He wasn't aware of the eyes that followed his every move.

Ten minutes later a man dressed in civilian clothes and wearing a Yankees baseball cap stepped into the alley and approached him. They talked quickly and in low voices. Unable to hear the conversation, Wilder stared intently at the second man. There was something familiar about him, but what was it?

Bryant! What are you doing here? Unable to hear or get any closer, Wilder watched every move and nuance. The two men spoke quickly, as if being rushed—or afraid of being caught.

The conversation was over in less than a minute. Bryant turned and walked to the top of the alley. Satisfied that nothing unusual awaited him, he disappeared down the busy street. Neilson waited for several minutes then left in the opposite direction, passing within inches of the hidden priest.

Wilder lost no time. Staying in the darkness, he hurried to the rear of the alley and looked in both directions. A block down the street, Neilson had climbed into a pedi-cab and was preparing to leave. Wilder saw a bicycle leaning against a shop door. Seeing its owner preparing to strap a bundle to the rear rack, Wilder approached him, reached into his pocket, and pulled out a roll of American dollars. He held out the money and pointed to the bike.

Pointy-Talky at work again. The Vietnamese merchant gave Wilder a toothless grin, took the money, and waved Wilder towards the bike. The rusted machine wasn't worth the effort it would take to junk it, but right now, it was priceless. Wilder mounted the bike and followed Neilson from a distance.

The pedi-cab wound its way through the busy streets to the American Embassy and stopped a block short of its destination. Neilson paid the driver and walked the short distance to the metal gates. Both the Vietnamese and Marine guards recognized him, and the gate was open when he approached.

"Good evening, Mr. Neilson," the Marine guard said. "Late night?"

"Early morning, guys," Neilson replied, walking through the gate. He covered the short distance to the building and disappeared through the front door without looking back.

The Catholic priest watched casually while pedaling slowly down the road.

CHAPTER 20

Hiding in the Caravelle, Wilder mulled over events from the night before. He wondered how Neilson and Bryant had come to know each other. More importantly, he wondered why they met in such a secretive manner. Were they trying to hide something? Passing information? What did Neilson know that he, Wilder, didn't? It was time to get some answers, but how? He thought about Vandeth and how she had helped him. He didn't like the idea of trusting a virtual stranger, but if she wanted to betray him, she would have done it by now. He decided to take a chance—there was no other choice.

He waited until just before dawn. Certain that there was no one around, he gave the signal that he needed to make contact with her. Vandeth looked across the lobby out of the corners of her eyes. Certain that she was alone, she picked up a stack of papers and casually walked to the storage room.

Stepping into the closet, she began to arrange the papers on the shelf. After a moment Wilder whispered, "Vandeth, can you get me access to a phone? I need to call the States."

"There is a phone in the rear office," she whispered. "I can connect you through the switchboard if you wish." She stole a look at him. "I want to help—"

"Vandeth, I appreciate what you've done for me more than I can say, but I don't want to jeopardize your safety anymore. There are certain people that want me dead. If you are discovered, your life will be in danger."

"This entire city is dangerous, Captain. I am not afraid."

You have guts, lady. "I need to make a call to a number in Washington. Can you do that without calling attention to yourself?"

Vandeth smiled. "Of course. We have the press corps here, remember? They call Washington all the time."

"Perfect," Wilder said. *There's a silver lining in this dark cloud after all.* He gave her the number. "I'll wait in the storage room. If anyone comes into the lobby while the line is open, disconnect it immediately. Please be careful, Vandeth. I don't want you to call attention to yourself."

"Do not worry, my friend. I'll have you connected in a minute." She left the room, closing and locking the door behind her. Wilder looked through the peep hole into the lobby. It was empty. Satisfied, he went into the rear office and locked the door behind him. Sitting at the desk, he looked at the phone and waited. He wondered what he would say and what the reaction would be on the other end. The phone in Washington was on a secure line, and he knew that the conversation would be scrambled and recorded. That made it easier. He stroked the .357 under his shirt. Despite his lethal martial abilities, the weapon gave him an added feeling of security.

The seconds dragged. What seemed like hours was only a few minutes. Finally, the phone rang. Wilder picked it up. The female voice with the Southern accent on the other end was music to his ears. "This the operator. What city please?"

"Franconia."

"Yes?"

He gave the operator the number and waited. He heard the familiar series of clicks and buzzes that indicated the scrambler was working. Finally, the phone rang. It was answered on the second ring.

"Spencer."

Bill welcomed the familiar voice. He didn't want to shock his uncle, so he eased into the conversation. "Hey, Bruce, any chance you Washington suits could buy me a ticket home? I'd sure like a real cheeseburger and some fries."

"Jesus Christ, Almighty!" Spencer almost dropped the phone.

"No quite, but close."

"Bill? Is this really you?"

"Yep, it's me. Warts and all."

Spencer's mind was going in every direction. "Where are you, son? What's going on? We—"

"Listen, Bruce. I don't have a lot of time, and I need help."

Spencer heard the seriousness in his nephew's voice. He grabbed a pad and pen. "Okay. Talk to me, Bill."

Bill quickly filled his uncle in on the missing pieces. He briefly explained his disappearance from the hospital in the Philippines and what he had done since then. He told Spencer in general terms where he was and of the clandestine meeting between Neilson and Bryant. "… That's the down and dirty version. I need to find out what's going on with Neilson, and I need to make contact with someone I can trust. Any ideas?"

Spencer's mind was racing. "Bill, we can't use the normal safe houses in 'Nam. We have a mole in our operations there, and he could compromise you. Can you stay low for a while?"

"I can."

Spencer rubbed his forehead. *This is nuts.* "Okay, listen. Stay where you are and keep out of sight. I need to get in touch with your father. Give me your number and I'll call back in twenty-four hours."

"Negative. No numbers. I don't trust anyone here. I'll make the call."

"Okay, Bill. We'll get you some answers fast. Call back same time tomorrow."

There was silence on the line for several seconds, then Wilder said, "Word here is that John died. Is it true?" His voice was strained but calm.

"Disinformation, Bill. Let's just say that one shouldn't believe everything one hears. Bottom line is that John's alive and under our control here in the States. His condition hasn't improved, but he's definitely alive. Rest easy on that, son."

Bill looked at the ceiling. *Thank you.* "Tell Dad I'm okay. I'll call back tomorrow." He reluctantly hung up the phone; it was his only contact with sanity. He closed his eyes and said a silent prayer.

Washington, DC

Jack Wilder could barely contain himself. The news that his son was alive and well did more for him than anything since Little Jack came home for Christmas in 1965. His excitement was tempered by the fact that Bill was alone in Saigon with no one to turn to. It was Jack Wilder's job to change that. "Bruce, I think we have an out here."

"Let's hear it."

"Ed Custer."

"I thought so. He's as clean as a whistle, Jack. We've known him since his college days, and I put a tail on him while he was here. Just to make sure. He's good to go."

"A tail? And you didn't tell me?"

"No need to, Jack. Just wanted to make sure for myself. And I'm sure."

"We need to get in contact with him—outside the embassy. We can contact the Tan Son Nhut command post and give him a vanilla message. He'll know who it's from, and he can use the secure phone there to get back to us." Wilder looked out his window for a moment, then said, "Did Bill ask about John?"

"Yes, and I told him the truth."

Wilder nodded. "It's about time Bill got some good news."

CHAPTER 21

FRANCONIA, VIRGINIA
NEXT DAY

Two of the most powerful men in Washington were helpless to do anything. They sat nervously in Spencer's kitchen and waited for the red phone on the counter to ring. The minutes dragged like hours, but the men were patient—they had no other choice. The NSA Director had ordered an electronic sweep of his home hours before to preclude any listening devices from putting a damper on the anticipated call. It was standard procedure to scan the Director's home on a regular basis, but this was a special occasion. The order was given and the house was combed only a day after the regular scheduled event. No questions were asked.

Jack Wilder was edgy. He was anxious to speak with his son, but he was afraid of what he might hear. Legally, Bill was a rogue agent, and that wasn't acceptable in the CIA. Fortunately, only his father knew the truth.

Bill, of course, had no idea of his legal status, but that would change with the ringing of the phone.

"Bruce, I thought I'd seen everything, having been in the spook business for so long. But this is the most difficult situation I've ever been in. My son, for Christ's sake, my *son!* A licensed *assassin!* Elizabeth would kill me if she was here. How the hell did I ever get into this mess?" Wilder had been unable to sleep since Spencer told him of his son's call, and he began to pace the floor like a nervous cat.

"It's not your fault, Jack. You knew this could happen. You know how determined Bill is, and you know that nothing can stop him once he makes up his mind. We're all involved with this. Blame it on whatever you want, but your position here is going to help us, not hurt. It's not the cause of our problem; rather, it's the solution." Spencer knew that his words were falling on deaf ears, but, if nothing else, they made *him* feel better. "Listen, Jack. Bill sounded like his normal self to me. And when I told him about John, I could hear genuine relief in his voice. Give the kid some credit. He knows what he's doing."

Wilder stopped pacing and looked at his brother-in-law. "You're right, Bruce, but I don't like the idea that I can't control him. Worse yet, I can't accept the fact that I've allowed this to happen."

"Allowed what to happen?"

"I allowed him to get this involved, I made him an agent, and *I'm* responsible for the jam he's in."

"Hold on, Jack." Spencer held up his hand. "You didn't make him go into the Air Force any more than you made Little Jack join the Navy. And forget the POW camp. You had no more to do with that than the man in the moon. You want to blame yourself for everything. But you know what? Those boys made up their own minds without any help from anyone, and nothing you or my sister did made any difference whatsoever. 'Joss is joss,' as Bill says. They would do the exact same thing with or without your approval, and you know it. You have to accept that and stop blaming yourself for events you can't control."

"Did you go to shrink school or something?" Wilder looked sideways at his brother-in-law.

"I should have. It pays more."

At that instant the phone rang. Both men looked at it like it was a bomb. Spencer's eyes said, *Talk to your son.*

Wilder's hand shook when he put the receiver to his ear. "Wilder." He felt like putty when he heard the voice from the other side of the world.

"Dad, I hear the fishing's great this time of year in the Rockies. You guys ought to head out to Boulder. Be careful on those snowshoes though. You never could walk in them!"

"Bill?" Wilder squeezed his eyes shut. "*Jesus Christ*, son! Are you all right?"

"I'm fine, Dad." Bill's voice almost cracked. Being isolated from his family half a world away was difficult beyond description, and he craved the sound of his father's voice. "I've been out and about, Dad, but I'm hanging in there."

"Bill, for God's sake—"

"Dad, everything's fine. Listen, I don't have a lot of time, so please give me something I can grab hold of."

Wilder fought to control his emotions. He knew that his son was in a desperate situation and that he needed information in a hurry. "Listen, Bud, here's the short version." He gave Bill a quick rundown of events since his visit to the Philippines, and he explained how Slaughter came to be at Bethesda. He hesitated, knowing that his next words would affect his son for the rest of his life. "Listen carefully, Bill. This is important. As far as the Agency is concerned, as of right now, you work directly for me. Understood?"

"Yes, sir."

"As Director of Operations, I authorize you to terminate Ivan Petrov with extreme prejudice."

"I understand, sir, and I accept the assignment."

Terminate with Extreme Prejudice was a legal term used by the CIA to sanction, or kill, an individual that was deemed by the Agency to be dangerous to Americans or American interests. The assassination of undesirables had been a common practice among intelligence agencies since their inception, but within the CIA, sanctions were limited because of the severity of the act itself. As a result such actions were directed with extreme prejudice, or only with special authorization from the highest authority.

"Your contact with me is Ed Custer, but he's to know nothing of this assignment. Bill, if you find Petrov, notify me through Custer before you act."

"What about the station chief here?"

"Neilson knows nothing about this, and it stays that way. Remember, this is between you and me. As far as anyone else is concerned, Bud, you died in that plane crash."

"What?"

"Listen. There's a mole in our Asian operations." Wilder told his son about the faked death certificates and of Slaughter's being transferred secretly to Bethesda. "Only Bruce and I know about this, and it has to stay that way. If Petrov believes you're both out of the picture, he might become careless and show his hand. Then we can move against him."

"But how do I contact Custer? Are you sure he's clean?"

"Affirmative." Wilder told his son of Custer's visit to Washington and of his attendance at John's *funeral*. "Custer's been under a microscope since the attack at the Caravelle. I have no doubt about him whatsoever. I'm sending him a coded message through normal channels at Tan Son Nhut. He'll know it's from me. I need to know where you are so he can contact you."

"I'm at the Caravelle," Bill said matter-of-factly.

"What? That's the worst place you can be!"

"Actually, Dad, it's the safest place in Saigon. The hotel is crawling with Vietnamese police and reporters. No one would be crazy enough to show his face here now. I've made contact with the night manager. Her name is Vandeth, and she was a friend of Maggie's. She's been giving me sanctuary. She doesn't know anything, but she and Maggie were close, and I can trust her."

"I'll have give you license on that, Bill. You know the situation there better than I do. I'll get the message to Custer and have him contact you through her. But prep her beforehand."

"Understood."

"I'm glad you're safe, son. We've been worried sick. I feel like I've let you down—"

"Dad, you've given me all the reason I need to press on. I couldn't do this without your help. You guys just hang tough. We'll get through this. Just do me a couple favors."

"Name them."

"First, get John back on his feet."

"He's getting the best treatment available, Bud. We'll do everything we can. And the second?"

"Dad, I need you to find out what connection Neilson and Bryant have with each other."

"What do you mean?"

"They met in, shall we say, less then favorable circumstances the other night."

"Bruce gave me the short version."

"Why would a CIA station chief meet with the Wing Intelligence officer in a dark alley in the red light district of Saigon? Why couldn't they just meet in Neilson's office?"

"I don't know, Bud, unless one had information for the other that neither wanted to share with anyone else."

"Exactly."

"Interesting. I'll get my people to check it out. This McAlester guy is a newsie, and Bryant could be giving Neilson information about him."

"Do you thing McAlester is dirty?" Bill couldn't imagine it.

"No, but in this business, you don't turn your back on anyone. Sometimes black is white if you know what I mean."

"I'm learning fast, Dad."

"Say nothing to anyone, not even Custer when he contacts you. Remember what we talked about. Your assignment is yours alone. *No one* is to know."

"Yes, sir." There was a moment of silence before anyone spoke. Finally, Bill said, "Dad, thanks for being there. I love you."

"I love you too, son." Jack Wilder choked on his words.

The line went dead.

CHAPTER 22

SAIGON

The command post was alive with activity. The normally secure entrance was like a swinging saloon door in a western bar. Crews hurriedly passed though, picking up their mission kits and getting their intelligence briefings. Aircraft were being launched around the clock, and it only got busier as the day wore on. Shuffling exhausted crews in and out and matching them with aircraft that were often broken was a nearly impossible task. The pilots and navigators that ran the command post had a thankless job. Many longed for the good old days of flying all hours of the day and night.

Major Ed Custer sat in the corner watching the bedlam. Leaning the chair back on its rear legs, he regarded the organized confusion with amusement. As a field grade officer, he had been *offered* the position of command post controller several times. So far he had managed to dodge that bullet. His status as a CIA operative had nothing to do with these extra duty assignments that the Air Force encouraged, and he couldn't use his secret position in any way to thwart them. He hoped his luck would hold out a little longer. He was not a paper shuffler.

The door to the communications center opened, and a young airman poked his head out. Seeing Custer on the other side of the room, he waved a telex in the air.

"Is that my draft notice, Sam?"

"You should be so lucky, Major Custer. Sorry, but you'll have to read this in the comm center if you don't mind. It's nuts out here."

They went into the communications center and Custer closed the door. Slouching in a chair, he perused the paper. To the uninitiated, it appeared to be just another in the endless stream of useless messages from some paper mill in the Pentagon. But to Custer's trained eye, it had the force of a kicking mule. Glancing casually at the airman occupying himself with the telex machine, he read the message several times, making sure he understood every word. To anyone else the message was less than useless, but to Custer it was a map to the Noah's Ark.

"Sam?"

"Yes, sir?" Airman Woods glanced over his shoulder while organizing the reams of paper that came off the printer.

"Have you recorded this message yet?"

"Not yet, sir. Stuff's coming in as fast as I can tear it off the machine. I'll log this stuff as soon as this thing shuts off."

Custer stood in front the young airman and held up the paper. "Sam, you never saw this. Understood?"

Woods stopped what he was doing and looked at him. "Haven't seen a thing, and I have no idea what you're talking about, sir."

"I owe you one, partner." Custer walked to the shredder and ran the document through it, watching the paper turn into fuzz. He looked at Woods and said, "I wasn't here either."

"Never heard of you."

Custer left the command post, no longer concerned with the pandemonium around him. There were more urgent matters to attend to now.

Langley, Virginia

"This is what I sent to Custer." Wilder handed the document to Spencer.

The NSA Director read the message. "This is bland enough." He looked at Wilder. "I'd like to have seen the look on Custer's face when he read it."

"Knowing Custer as I do, his face said nothing, but his mind's spinning off its axis. We won't hear from him for a while. He has to make sure no one's tailing him first. He'll contact Bill through the Vietnamese woman." Wilder slowly shook his head. "She's the weak link here, and I don't like it. But Bill says he can trust her."

"If she'd wanted to give him up, she would have done it already. She and Maggie were pretty tight from what I understand."

"True enough. And she's been giving Bill sanctuary for weeks now. We have to go with Bill's judgment on this."

"What happens next?" Spencer dropped the paper on the table.

Wilder looked out his window at the forest surrounding the Potomac River. "We wait."

Saigon

Having brought food and water to her friend in hiding, Vandeth looked through the peephole of the door leading from the rear office to the main lobby. Satisfied that the room was empty, she quickly stepped through the doorway and locked the door behind her. At two o'clock in the morning, the Caravelle was mostly quiet. Thankfully, tonight was no exception. She took her seat behind the counter and reached for her copy of *Romeo and Juliet*.

Opening the book she noticed a blank piece of paper next to the ribbon marker. At first she didn't understand, then she realized that the paper itself was a message. Wilder had briefed her on the nuances of covert contact, and this had to be one. Her heart was pounding, and her eyes moved cautiously around the room. She didn't know what to expect.

"Don't be frightened, Vandeth, and don't look down." The voice was but a whisper. "I'm under the counter by your feet. I'm under a burlap sack."

Vandeth looked calm, but she was scared out of her wits. Holding the book as if reading it, she looked at her feet.

The burlap sack on the floor barely moved. A pair of eyes looked at her and winked. "I'm Custer. Do you have a message for me?"

Vandeth feigned dropping her ribbon. Leaning over to pick it up, she whispered, "Major Custer, Bill is hiding in the back room. Stay down. When I open the door, keep low and hurry in. I will lock the door behind you." She was visibly nervous, and Custer picked up on it immediately.

"Vandeth, I'm a friend," he whispered. "You have nothing to fear. Just no questions, okay?"

"As you wish, Major Custer." Although frightened, Vandeth was calmed by Custer's words. She knew that she was helping her friend, and, to that end, she was willing to do what was asked of her—without questions.

She casually got off the stool and pretended to organize some papers on the adjacent table. Looking out of the corners of her eyes, she decided that it was safe enough to move to the rear door. She quietly tapped once then twice more in succession and unlocked the door. Leaving it partially ajar, she stepped to the table and picked up the stack of papers she had been organizing. In that instant Custer slid through the opening. Vandeth placed the papers on a table just inside the small room and closed the door. In one smooth motion, she locked the door and returned to her seat. If anyone was watching, they would have been none the wiser.

Custer slowly got to his feet and looked around the room. He stood perfectly still, waiting for his eyes to adjust to the dark, knowing that he was being watched. Suddenly, there was the feel of cold steel against the back of his neck. He knew who it was.

"Hello, Ed."

"Never thought I'd be on the business end of that Python."

"Cheap insurance." The voice was close and menacing.

"Never thought I'd talk to a ghost either. I'm glad to hear your voice, Bill. I thought you were dead."

The gun was removed, replaced by a pat on the shoulder. Wilder stepped out of the shadow and into the dim light that filtered through the opaque window. "I sure as hell am glad to see you, Ed."

Custer stared at the catholic priest standing in front of him. "If you aren't a sight for sore eyes. A pope with a gun." The two men shook hands for a long time, the stress of their clandestine meeting finally over.

"Thank God for small favors," Wilder said. "I was beginning to wonder if I was going to be abandoned here."

"Everyone thinks you punched out. I don't know how you pulled this off, and I'm not asking. But for a dead guy, you look pretty good."

"Well, I got pretty banged up, and I have souvenirs to show for it." Wilder briefly thought of his crew. "I was lucky." He told Custer about his encounter with the mercenary in Kontum and of how the stranger saved his life.

"War brings out the best and worst in people, I guess." Custer motioned towards the shadows. "Let's sit. We have a lot to talk about."

"Yeah." They sat in the corner and allowed their eyes to adjust to each other.

Custer picked up where he left off. "I feel like I'm looking at an apparition. How'd you get here? I don't—"

"Relax, Ed. A lot has happened since the crash up north. Let me bring you up to speed." Wilder told Custer about his stay in the hospital at Clark and about his circuitous journey back to Saigon. Custer learned of the attempt on Slaughter's life, but Wilder left out the part about Slaughter being secretly moved to Bethesda. Nothing was said about Wilder's plans for Petrov.

Custer told Wilder about his visit to Langley. Wilder listened intently when Custer told him that Jack was holding his own. The words brought some measure of relief to the young pilot. Then Custer told him about Slaughter's funeral. Everyone, including Custer, thought Slaughter was dead.

At least John is safe, Wilder thought.

When Custer finished, Wilder said, "Bring me up to speed on operations in Saigon. Does anyone here other than you know my real status?"

"Not that I'm aware of. Your father made it clear that you and I are operating together as a solo team." Custer hesitated then said, "Listen, Bill, for the CIA operations chief to contact me directly and give me specific orders outside normal channels is pretty heady stuff.

I don't know what's going on, but I do know that we're not to work with anyone else. Can you clue me in?"

"The less you know, Ed, the better. Trust me on this. It's for your own good. Even though he's my father, he doesn't tell *me* everything either. He has things going on we'll never know about. Just go with the flow, okay?"

"Guess that will have to do."

Wilder looked at the window. "What's going on with Berwick?"

"He got back a few days after your accident. I don't know what happened between you guys, but he didn't say much about the crash. Seemed to take it in stride."

Wilder said nothing.

"He's pretty much running the intel office now. Bryant's in and out, spending much of his time with that Englishman from UPI."

"McAlester."

"That's the one. I guess he's buttering the Brit's bread for him," Custer said. "Wants to go to work for him when he leaves here."

"I saw Bryant and Neilson together the other night near the *Petite Rouge.*"

"Nothing unusual about that. A lot of embassy and news people go there."

"I didn't say *in* the *Rouge.* I said *near* it."

Custer's eyes narrowed. "I don't follow you."

"I saw them each go into an alley alone, using care not to be noticed. They met and talked for a short time, then left the same way they came. Neither wanted to be seen with the other." Wilder was digging, but he wasn't sure what he was looking for.

Custer frowned. "Not knowing anything about that, I'd say that Bryant was on a fishing expedition, trying to get some information to pass on to McAlester. What better way to get your foot in the door with the Englishman than to give him information the other reporters can't get?"

"Maybe. But what would Neilson have to gain? Why didn't they just meet in Neilson's office, or in a public place?"

"I don't know, unless Bryant doesn't want to be seen screwing off by his superiors. Berwick's been complaining that Bryant's gone a lot and that he's getting stuck with all the work."

Wilder pressed the issue. "But why does Neilson have to meet with an Air Force intelligence officer in an alley?"

"No idea." Custer shrugged.

"Does Neilson smoke?"

"No. He's a health nut. Why?"

"He was that night."

"Beats the hell out of me, Bill. Maybe the stress of this place is getting to him. It wouldn't be the first time someone cracked in that job. I'll ask him when I see him."

"Don't say anything."

"Why?"

"Let's just say there's a fly in the ointment. Less is more in this case, and we don't need to muddy the waters any more than they already are. Let the smoking thing go for now. Our main priority is to find Petrov before he kills anyone else."

"That's task number one." Custer looked around the small room. "But first I have to get you out of here. I've made arrangements through liaison with Langley to move you to a safe house out of Saigon. Your father told me about it in his message. Neilson doesn't even know about it. Once we get you established there, we can plan our next move." There was a sly smile on Custer's face.

"Okay, what's behind the grin?"

"Our safe house is on a rubber plantation that was taken over from the French by the South Vietnamese government. It's a gold mine for the corrupt officials running it, and they pay the Vietcong big bucks to leave it alone. The government is in bed with the devil."

"So, I'm hiding in a rubber tree that's owned by crooks and surrounded by bad guys. Sounds reasonable. Why am I not surprised?"

"You shouldn't be. Money is the universal language, even in this God-forsaken place."

"When are we leaving?"

"Right now."

At daybreak the morning shift trickled in, and the news people shuffled through the lobby. Vandeth politely nodded to them, but her thoughts were on the two men locked in the back room. When her replacement arrived, she excused herself and quietly unlocked the door. Stepping inside and closing the door behind her, she looked around the empty room. The locked window had been opened from the inside. There was no evidence that anyone had been there. She frowned. "May Buddha watch over you, Captain Wilder." She left the room, knowing that she would not see him again.

CHAPTER 23

Over the next few days Wilder caught up on some much needed rest without having to look over his shoulder every few minutes. Although he could hear the fighting in the distance, the piece of real estate he occupied seemed oblivious to the war going on around it. The plush surroundings of the old French plantation would be an enjoyable experience for most people under normal circumstances, but the circumstances certainly were anything but normal, and Wilder wasn't most people.

He needed to get out. But being an Occidental in an Oriental war, his ability to travel in the open was severely limited. He stood out in a crowd. After five days of isolation, he'd had enough. He impatiently waited for Custer's scheduled contact.

Custer arrived under the cover of darkness. He'd had no further contact with Langley since the initial one almost a week earlier, and he knew that Wilder was getting anxious.

Wilder sat opposite him in a small room in the rear of the mansion. "Okay, Ed, talk to me." There was no time for social amenities.

Custer leaned back in his chair and placed his hands flat on his thighs. "I haven't heard a thing from Langley since the first message, Bill." He looked nervously at the man sitting across from him.

"Look, Ed, I've been shot down and shot up. John and Maggie are dead, and I have no patience for bullshit. So, if you have anything to say, please say it."

"Yeah." Custer wiped his sweaty brow with the back of his hand. He leaned forward and rested his forearms on his knees. "Petrov's still around. Several local prostitutes have turned up dead, all with his brutal trademarks."

Wilder looked at Custer for a moment then walked to the window and stared into the darkness. "Neilson and Bryant?"

"Nothing there that I can find. I've followed Neilson and haven't seen anything unusual." Custer leaned back in his chair. "In the meantime I'm still waiting for instructions from Langley. Until it comes, we have nothing to work with." Custer chose his next words carefully. "Listen, Bill, I know what you've been through, and I wouldn't wish your luck on my worst enemy. But right now there's nothing I can do, except hope for a break with Petrov."

Wilder looked at him. "I need to get a message to Langley."

Custer nodded. "*That* I can do."

"We need to find out all we can about Berwick. I think he's in this up to his neck. He conveniently disappeared when things got hot in Kontum, and he wasn't anywhere around when he was needed."

"You know he was on leave. All signed and legal."

"Too neat," Wilder said. "His office should have been crawling with intel types when the flag went up, but it wasn't. Instead of being where he belonged, he was screwing off in Hong Kong. Bryant had to run everything."

"You really have it in for Berwick, don't you?"

"I don't trust him." Wilder walked across the room and stood in front of Custer. "Tell Langley that I need everything they have on Berwick and Neilson."

Custer looked doubtful. "Bill, I think you're on a wild goose chase here. Neilson's the Saigon station chief for crying out loud! As far as Berwick is concerned, I think your vendetta against him is more personal than logical."

Wilder stared at him. "I have my reasons, Ed. Tell them you want an answer as soon as possible." Wilder went back to the window. "I'm tired of sitting here doing nothing while Petrov's on the loose." He looked Custer. "They have twenty-fours hours. If I don't get something by then, I'm out of here."

Custer stood, wanting to end the conversation before it got out of hand. "I'll get a message out tonight. But I need a *full* twenty-four hours."

"Agreed."

Custer stood beside Wilder and watched the explosions in the distance. "I'll get *something* from Langley, one way or the other. And we'll move on it, but just give me a chance, okay? I've been in this business a little longer than you, and I know how frustrating it can be."

"Clock's ticking."

Custer turned and left the room.

CIA Headquarters
Langley, Virginia

Jack Wilder studied the telex from Tan Son Nhut. That he had more on his plate than the average chief executive officer of a multi-national corporation, was an understatement. He was responsible for overseeing operations in Europe, the Middle East, and the Soviet Union. South Africa and South America had their hot spots too, and he, through his deputy directors, had to keep himself attuned to the world's clandestine operations on a daily basis.

Aside from the Cold War between the United States and the Soviet Union, Vietnam was the dominant world problem, and it concerned him more than it should have. The fact that his only living son was directly in harm's way made him feel as if he'd lost all control. He was at a loss as to how to handle the situation in Saigon, and he had delegated the responsibility for the world's other hot spots to his underlings so that he could spend his time on keeping his son alive. Vietnam and the hunt for Petrov was becoming all-consuming, and Wilder questioned the wisdom of bringing his son into the Agency in the first place.

But it was too late to turn back the clock.

Looking at the telex again, he wondered why Custer was so adamant to get information on Berwick and Neilson. Because of his son's past experience with Berwick, Wilder understood to some degree why Bill felt the way he did. But why Neilson? And why the urgency? He knew there was a security leak in the CIA's Vietnam operation, but, until now, he and the NSA Director were the only two people alive that even suspected it. Did Bill know something that he didn't? Wilder had no way to communicate with his son to learn the answers, other than through Custer. Although he trusted the major, Wilder didn't want to show his hand just yet. But he was being backed into a corner more and more with each passing day, and he was running out of options.

He picked up the phone. "Linda?"

"Yes, Jack?"

"Please call Bruce and see if he can come over this afternoon. Something's come up, and I need to see him."

"Would you like me to clear your schedule?" Wilder's secretary knew her boss like the back of her hand.

"Yes. And tell him this is important, okay?"

"I'll take care of it right away."

Jack Wilder wasn't much for political niceties or protocol. His reputation for calling the shots the way he saw them was well known in the Agency. For him to make a request to see the head of the NSA on short notice meant that something was developing that demanded immediate attention. That the CIA Director of Operations and the Director of the NSA were brothers-in-law, allowed much of the bureaucratic red tape to be bypassed. Although that relationship irked of some of Washington's elite, Wilder couldn't care less.

Wilder's intercom buzzed. "Yes, Linda?"

"Director Spencer will be arriving by helicopter in twenty minutes. I've cleared your schedule for the rest of the day, and I'm having sandwiches and coffee sent up."

"You're a saint, you know that?" Wilder couldn't help but smile to himself. "Tell that husband of yours to take you on a long vacation, or I'll have to speak with him." .

"All compliments graciously accepted. I'll be here late if you need anything."

"Put yourself in for a raise, Linda." He turned off the intercom and leaned back in his chair. Looking at the message sitting on his desk, his thoughts took him to the time when his son was a cadet at VMI. He was fully aware of the incident between Bill and Berwick, and of the criminal charges that were set aside. The commandant, Colonel Jennings, had explained the possible ramifications to Bill after Berwick left school. But Jennings had no idea why neither Berwick nor his parents filed charges against Bill.

Only Jack Wilder knew the truth.

"Hello, Linda." Spencer walked through the door. "Here's something to liven this dungeon up a little." He placed a flower planter on the window sill.

"A Spider plant! Thank you, Mr. Director. It's lovely. I'll hang it in a little while." Wilder's secretary loved plants, especially free ones. Her office was full of them. "Jack's waiting for you, sir. You can go right in."

"Linda, you remind me of my sister." Spencer chuckled. "How many times have I asked you to call me Bruce? You know that Jack and I don't stand on formalities."

She looked over the tops of her granny glasses like a mother at a child. "With all the weight you two have on your shoulders, someone in this two-horse town has to show you *some* respect!"

"Respect? What's *that*?" He winked at her and knocked once on Wilder's door.

"Come in, Bruce."

Looking at his brother-in-law staring out the window, Spencer walked across the room and took his usual seat. He could tell by Wilder's stern expression that something was going on, and he patiently waited for him to speak.

Wilder looked out the window. "Weather man this morning said it would either rain or be sunny today. Pretty much covered all bases, didn't he?"

"I'd say so, Jack. But the weather guys aren't held accountable."

"Wish we had that option."

"Indeed." Spencer studied Wilder's face. "Do I dare try to read your mind?"

Wilder frowned. "Bruce, it's time to fish or cut bait."

Spencer walked to the side board and poured two cups of black coffee. Sitting one on Wilder's desk, he returned to his seat. He sipped the hot brew, enjoying its momentary pleasure. He looked at Wilder. "Let's have it."

"I have a tough call to make, and I need your help."

Saigon

"I don't think he's a threat anymore. The girl and his best friend are dead, and he was badly hurt. I think his father's keeping him on ice somewhere. Our people were at Slaughter's funeral but learned nothing. I think it's safe to say it's over."

"You don't know where he is?" Petrov asked.

"No."

"Whether he's alive or dead, it's not over for me until I kill all of them." Petrov's voice was dead and unfeeling.

"What does that mean?"

"Wilder's father. He and his British lackeys tortured my father and forced him to confess. It's not over until all the Wilders are in their graves."

"You can't possibly get to him," Petrov's co-conspirator insisted. "He has Secret Service people all over him."

"Perhaps. But I have the advantage."

"How so?"

"They don't know where I am, but I know where Jack Wilder is."

"Do not become careless."

Petrov closed his eyes and rubbed his temples. The headache was coming back. He lit another Marlboro and dragged on it deeply. The smoke in his lungs gave some measure of relief, but the pounding in his head only got worse.

It was time to make another trip to the red light district of Saigon.

CIA Headquarters
Langley, Virginia

"He's treading water and wants to get out. Can't blame him for that," Spencer said after reading the telex from Saigon. "This message is pretty clear on that point, especially with the twenty-four hour deadline."

"I have to do something, but I don't want to play my trump until all the cards are on the table. On the other hand, he'll drop out of sight if I don't come forward on this." Wilder ran his hands through his hair and drew in a deep breath. He looked hard at the NSA Director. "Let me run an idea by you, Bruce."

"Shoot."

"I think I should go to 'Nam and meet Bill face-to-face."

Spencer frowned. "That's the most crack-pot idea I've ever heard, Jack. What put that notion in your head?"

"I haven't gone around the bend yet, Bruce. Hear me out." Wilder knew that his brother-in-law would react that way. He was ready with an answer. "Look at the facts; no one but you, Custer, and I know that Bill's alive. He's isolated in enemy territory with no place to turn. The only person there that can help him is Custer, and even Custer doesn't know the whole story. If I try to pull Bill out before Petrov's found, he'll disappear again. If that happens, we'll really lose him. Where would that leave us?"

Spencer looked skeptical.

"Think about it, Bruce. Bill was under heavy guard at Clark, and he still managed to escape. I don't like using the word *escape*, but that's exactly what he did. He's got it in for Berwick, and there's nothing I can do about it from here. The larger problem is still Petrov, of course, but no one can find him. If Bill jumps ship, then both sides of the equation will just disappear. What then?" Wilder threw his hands into the air. "We're between a rock and a hard spot."

Spencer was still unconvinced. "I understand what you're saying, Jack, but your going to Vietnam is just too risky. Why not send a coded message to the embassy and have Custer get it to Bill?" Spencer was reaching for straws and he knew it.

"The loose cannon might be in the embassy, Bruce. We don't know who to trust there. I have to assume that the embassy's communications have been compromised. Can't take that chance." Wilder shook his head. "I just don't see any other way."

Spencer rubbed his chin hard. "If you go to Vietnam, you'll have to go in complete secrecy. And you can't meet him in that rubber plantation. You can't go anywhere near Saigon. I suggest Cam Ranh Bay. It's the least risk location I can think of."

"Agreed."

The two men looked at each other for a long time. Finally, Spencer said, "Jack, this is dangerous in more ways that you can imagine, and there must be a thousand reasons why you shouldn't do it."

"Right now, I can't think of one."

The two men worked into the night, formulating plans and arranging the details. Time was critical and they labored feverishly to set the plan into motion. Finally, it was time to act. A coded telex was sent to Custer via the Tan Son Nhut communications center, directing Custer to move *Ninja* to the air force base at Cam Ranh Bay by the most secure means possible. *Beast Master* would arrive from Washington within twenty hours. The meeting was to be kept secret at all costs, and no one at the embassy was to know anything about it.

The Ford sedan pulled onto the flight line at Andrews Air Force Base in Maryland. The car stopped on the tarmac adjacent to a set of portable stairs, and waiting Secret Service agents opened the rear doors of the vehicle. Wilder and Spencer got out and quickly walked to the waiting C-135 jet.

"Jack, get in there, get the job done, and get the hell out. And keep your head down," Spencer shouted over the whine of the engines.

"I should be back in two days. Keep the light on, Bruce." The time for talk was over. The two men shook hands, and Wilder hurried up the steps. Spencer waved and climbed back into the sedan. There was no press or fanfare, just a passenger getting on an airplane for a trip. Within minutes, the tarmac was empty once more while a lone jet turned westward and climbed into the night sky.

CHAPTER 24

HICKAM AIR FORCE BASE
HAWAII

Maintenance personnel swarmed over the aircraft the instant the engines stopped turning. On final approach for landing, the jet flew through a large flock of birds, sucking several into the intake of the number one engine. The machine sputtered, flamed out, and vibrated severely. The crew landed the plane without incident, but an engine change would be necessary before the trip could continue.

Jack Wilder was irritated, not because of the destroyed engine, but because his twenty-four hour deadline was at risk.

A staff car with a four-star flag attached to the front bumper pulled up to the base of the portable air stairs that had been positioned against the side of the aircraft. In that instant, the passenger door opened, and Wilder rushed through the opening and down the stairs. There was no time for formalities or fanfare. He needed to get to a secure phone and the communications center immediately.

"Hello, General. Jack Wilder, CIA." He quickly climbed into the car. "I apologize for my abruptness, but I'm short on time. I need to get to your comm center five minutes ago."

"No problem, sir." General Schmidt turned to his driver. "Let's head for my office, Sam, as fast as you can get us there."

"Yes, sir." The driver turned on the siren and emergency flashers and sped across the tarmac.

Schmidt turned back to his passenger. "Mr. Wilder, we'll get your engine changed as quickly as possible. The maintenance guys here are the best. Your plane's being refueled right now. Just a few hours."

"Time's something I don't have, General." Wilder looked out the window. "Sorry I can't give any details, but people's lives depend on how fast we can get that plane back into the air."

"My best team is on it, sir."

"Your people will get a medal for this."

Within minutes Jack Wilder sat alone in the communications center looking at the secure phone. He had no idea what he would say, but a message had to be sent. Fast.

Tan Son Nhut Air Force Base
Saigon

Ed Custer had been hanging around the flight line for too long, at least in his mind. The continuous noise of aircraft taking off and landing, combined with the smell of jet fuel and the pungent odors of the open sewers, made for a miserable experience. The heat and humidity were relentless, and there was no relief in sight. Finally, unable to stand it any longer, he went to his next least favorite place; the command post.

Walking into the frigid room, the sweat on his body began to cool. Putting the weather on hold, he turned his attention to the organized bedlam around him. "What's going on, Dan?"

"Trying to keep our heads above water as usual, Ed," Mercer said. He glanced at the mission board to re-assure himself that flights were running as planned. Although he'd looked at it hundreds of times and could practically recite it from memory, there was always the nagging doubt that he had missed something.

Custer casually looked at the board, his eyes scanning every planned mission within the next twelve hours. The only flight from the states was a World Airways charter bringing more hapless souls to Vietnam. He was careful not to appear overly concerned with the operation. "Would you believe it? I came in here to get some relief from the oven outside, and now I'm freezing. Got any coffee in this joint?"

Mercer nodded. "This place is a pressure cooker. We have to keep it cool to stop tempers from overheating." He motioned towards the side of the room. "There's a pot of sludge by the water cooler. Help yourself." Mercer turned his attention again to the wall board.

"Thanks." Custer made his way across the room and poured himself a cup of coffee. He knew he drank too much of the black liquid, but he couldn't afford to go to sleep right now. He was looking for something, and he hoped that it would come soon.

The door to the communications center opened, and a young airman came into the room. Looking around, he spotted Custer. "Hey, Major, got a minute?"

"Sure." Tossing his half-filled cup into the trash, Custer casually walked into the communications room and closed the door. "What's this, Rusty? A letter from my congresswoman?"

"Nothing that obscene, sir. Just Pentagon gibberish." Airman Russell Paige handed Custer a clipboard.

Custer casually read the telex. The words were bland, but the message was loud and clear. *Flight delayed indefinitely. Will advise.* He read the document once more to make sure he had missed nothing. He suddenly felt helpless. "I need to shred this, Rusty."

"Just push it through the machine, sir. There's no record."

In seconds the document was fuzz. Custer looked at his watch. "Look, I have to do something, but I'll be back. There should be another message for me soon."

"I'll take care of it, sir. Uncle Sam owns me for the next eight hours." Airman Paige turned his attention back to his printer.

"Later." Custer left the command post. He didn't like the idea of being left hanging in the air, but there was nothing he could do. He thought about trying to get to the safe house, but there was no time. Without further instructions from the man on that airplane, all he could do was wait.

He phoned the communications center from his room in the BOQ to let Paige know where he was. Airman Paige would call him immediately when anything came in for him.

The waiting was the hard part.

Hickam Air Force Base
Hawaii

Jack Wilder paced the floor in the VIP waiting room. The minutes seemed like hours. He looked at his watch again, hoping that the simple action would speed things up. The meal on the table was only half eaten, and the coffee pot had been filled twice. He thought about calling his brother-in-law in Washington, but he knew it would be pointless. If nothing else, however, it would make him feel better. He decided to make the call.

At the instant the telephone rang. "Wilder."

"Sir, General Schmidt here. Your plane's almost ready, and a staff car will pick you up in less than five minutes. By the time you board, the paperwork will be done. You're all set."

"General Schmidt, you've made my day. Thank you." Glancing at his watch, Wilder let out a sigh of relief. He pressed the button for the Hickam communications center. He gave instructions to the lieutenant on the other end, who had been waiting for Wilder's call.

"… Yes, sir. I have it, and your message will go out immediately. Have a good flight, sir."

Wilder hung up the phone, grabbed his briefcase, and hurried through the door. Within minutes he was climbing the portable stairs for the flight to Vietnam.

The steward stood in the crew entrance door. "Sir, the command post just confirmed that your message has been sent, and your designee will be notified immediately."

"Excellent." Wilder looked through the cockpit door. "May I see the aircraft commander?"

"Of course, sir." The steward stepped aside, allowing Wilder to enter the cockpit.

The pilot turned to see the senior CIA spook standing behind him. "We're just about ready to go, sir."

"I need a favor, Rudy."

"Name it, sir," Colonel Rudy Jackson replied.

"I'm short on time here. I need you to fly the most direct route possible to Cam Ranh. Do you have to refuel before we get there?"

"Yes, sir. We'll do an aerial refuel over Guam. There's a SAC unit there, and they'll send up a tanker. Next stop will be Vietnam."

"Excellent." Wilder looked at the three faces in the cockpit. "We need to get there yesterday, guys. Lives depend on it."

"Time to grab a seat, sir. We're ready to roll," the aircraft commander said. The flight engineer was busy at his panel, positioning switches to start the engines. "Crank 'em," the pilot ordered.

Wilder returned to the cabin and took a seat. There was nothing he could do now but enjoy the ride. He opened his briefcase and began to go through his papers. It would help pass the time. Within minutes, the jet was airborne.

Tan Son Nhut Air Force Base
Saigon

The knock on the door woke Custer from a restless sleep, and he was on his feet in an instant.

"Sir, Paige asked me to pick you up. He has a message for you, marked *Flash*. You need to read it immediately."

"Let's go." Closing the door behind him, Custer followed the airman to the waiting car. He was in Paige's office in minutes.

"You're the most popular guy in town," Paige said. "This just came for you." He handed Custer a folder with a single sheet inside.

Custer quickly read the document. "This is what I've been looking for, Rusty."

"Let me guess; your new assignment to the Pentagon as chief boot-licker!" Paige laughed at his own words.

"That's been reserved for you, buddy!" Custer headed for the door, but not before passing the document through the shredder. "Got a date and don't want to be late."

"We're here to serve." Paige returned to his endless paper drill.

Once outside, the smile disappeared from Custer's face. He needed a helicopter and a pilot to fly it. He had to get his partner from the safe house at the rubber plantation to Cam Ranh Bay within a matter of hours. And he had to do it without drawing any attention to himself or his passenger. Any other officer would have to go through heaven and earth to accomplish such a task, but a CIA field operative with no scruples in his pockets would have no problem. A box of frozen steaks and a unopened bottle of *Jack Daniels* wouldn't hurt either.

Bill Wilder was agitated. He hadn't heard from Custer or his father in almost twenty-four hours, and his patience was wearing thin. Although able to control his emotions, he had to *do* something to keep his sanity. Sitting in a moldy French mansion, unable to show his face to anyone, was not his idea of solving problems. The thought of Petrov running loose in the countryside while he remained out of sight, was no longer acceptable.

He looked at his watch. With less than two hours remaining in his self-imposed exile, he was no closer to learning anything. He looked out the window at the plantation guards that were there to *protect* him. Although on the CIA payroll, they were less than useless in his opinion and could tell him nothing. Time was almost up. If something didn't happen soon, he would disappear again.

Wilder could hear gunfire and explosions in the distance. The war went on around him, despite his relative isolation on the rubber plantation. Money did tend to give special dispensation when needed. That the rubber farm had not been overrun or bombed, struck him as funny in a morbid way. *Money talks and bullshit walks*, he thought to himself .

His senses picked up on a new sound. Distant at first, the noise gradually grew louder, and it was coming towards him. The *whump-whump* of rotor blades made a distinctive sound, and Wilder recognized it immediately. He pulled his black cotton mask over his face. Grabbing his Python revolver and rucksack, he slid out the door and into the night.

Hiding in the shadows, Wilder watched the ungainly machine land in the field behind the mansion. The rear door slid open, and a lone passenger hit the ground running. Keeping his head down to avoid the rotating blades, Ed Custer ran towards the house.

Wilder wasn't concerned with Custer finding him; he would allow himself to be *found* when he was ready. He wanted to check out the helicopter and its two occupants first.

The chopper pilots were worried about potential enemy ground fire, and their eyes peered through the darkness, hoping to spot any threat before it spotted them. The combination of engine noise and spinning rotors drowned out any sound an approaching stranger might make.

Wilder crept through the shadows, his black clothes blending perfectly with the night. In an instant he was inside the helicopter.

"I don't like this, man. This place gives me the creeps." The pilot nervously wiped the sweat from his eyes with his nomex glove.

"Me either," his copilot said. "And that guy in the back … who the hell is he?"

"I dunno, but I'll tell you what—"

"Hi, boys!" Wilder patted both men on the top of their helmets at the same time.

The army pilots spun their heads in surprise at the voice coming from behind them.

"Nice toy you got here," Wilder said, waving the barrel of his gun between them. "What are all those buttons?"

"Who the hell are you?" the pilot in the right seat shouted.

The smile left Wilder's face. "I'm the sole reason for your being here, friend. Just do as I ask, and you'll soon be enjoying that bottle of booze in the bag back here."

"What the—"

"We're on the same side, guys. You have to trust me on this." Wilder looked out the pilot's door window. "He should be coming out about … now."

Custer ran through the doorway and straight for the helicopter. Approaching the open troop door, he hesitated and looked over his shoulder. There was no more time. He climbed into the chopper and closed the door behind him. He moved forward to the cockpit and stuck his head between the pilots.

"Can't wait any longer. We're outta here."

"Yes, we are," the voice said from the shadows behind him.

Custer turned to see two eyes staring at him through the dim light. The black outfit made Wilder practically invisible, and the only thing that kept Custer from going for his weapon was the business end of Wilder's Python staring him in the face.

"Fifteen minutes to spare, Ed. Cutting it a little close, ain't it?"

"*Jesus*, Bill! You scared the shit out of me!" Custer shouted over the roar of the engines.

"Just keeping people honest," Wilder said, lowering the revolver. "What kept you?"

"I'll tell you about it enroute." Custer turned to the confused pilots. "Let's go."

"Strap in," the pilot shouted. He looked at his copilot. "Keep an eye out for ground fire."

"Roger, that."

"Lifting off!" The pilot in the right seat rolled on the throttle and advanced the collective. The speeding blades adjusted their pitch angle, biting into the air. The Huey rose into the night sky and turned to the east. Soon the gunship was skimming across the tree tops at maximum speed, enroute to Cam Ranh Bay.

CHAPTER 25

Located on the coast in the southeastern part of South Vietnam, Cam Ranh Bay had been an important way station for sailors and merchants as far back as Marco Polo. In 1965 the US Army Corps of Engineers engaged in massive improvements of the port, including miles of roads, installation of fuel tanks, warehouses, and cargo handling facilities. The Corps assembled a new pier that gave the port the ability to handle large ships, and the port became a major embarkation point for US military personnel and supplies. An air force base was built with a runway long enough to accommodate large military and civilian jets. The base was considered so safe by the US military that President Lyndon Johnson visited there twice.

That the base and port were considered by the Americans to be impenetrable, was unacceptable by the Vietcong. In 1969 they raided the port and damaged a hospital, a chapel, and a water tower. Because of the attack, security was subsequently tightened, and the base made more secure. The deep water port, combined with the long runway, continued to make Cam Ranh Bay, and it's air force base, a major hub throughout the war.

It was also the most secure place for *Beast Master* to come face-to-face with his rogue agent. Although Jack Wilder was anxious to see his son, he did *not* look forward to the task at hand. What the Director of Operations had to tell *Ninja* could bring down his house of cards.

The C-135 had just completed air refueling with a similar KC-135 tanker aircraft from the Strategic Air Command out of Anderson Air Force Base, Guam. Once clear of the tanker, the pilot climbed the aircraft back to its cruising altitude of 35,000 feet. Jack Wilder had always been fascinated with the idea of refueling in mid-air, and he enjoyed watching the operation from the jump seat between the two pilots. Being a government big-wig had its advantages, and this was one of Wilder's favorites. There was no room for error during mid-air refueling over the ocean. The operation was either done correctly, or it ended in disaster.

"Beautiful work, guys. Precision flying at its best."

"Thank you, sir," the pilot said. "Other than bouncing around the traffic pattern, it's the best part. Come over to the simulator next time you're around Andrews. We'll get you some stick time."

"Boy, would I like that. About all I'd do is crash it, but thanks anyway." Wilder looked at the clock on the instrument panel. It was in Zulu time, the international standard time used by pilots world wide. "How much longer?"

"About two hours, sir," the copilot said. "We'll give you a heads up about thirty minutes out if you'd like to take a nap."

"Think I'll do that." Wilder looked at the darkening horizon. It was going to be a long night. He gave the crew a thumbs-up and left the cockpit. He returned to his sleeping berth, took off his shoes, and lay on the bed. Fatigue quickly overcame him, and he was asleep in minutes.

"… so when I got you father's second message, I scrambled to get this chopper and pick you up as fast as I could." Custer told Bill about Jack Wilder's plan to see him face-to-face at Cam Ranh Air Force Base. When he was done, Custer said, "One question."

"And that would be, *Why*?"

"Uh-huh. With all the crap going on in the world, why would your dad risk his life by coming here? I wouldn't rent this real estate to my mother-in-law." Custer shook his head. "Do you know something I don't?"

"No." Wilder didn't like lying, but he wasn't really *lying*, was he? He just wasn't telling the complete truth. "His coming here is unusual, but I'm betting he has good reason. We'll find out soon enough." Wilder leaned back in the canvas jump seat and closed his eyes. "May as well nod off for a bit. Nothing else to do."

"Yeah." Custer was frustrated, considering the events of the past twenty-four hours. But he knew that Wilder was right. *What the hell!* Custer slumped back into the seat and pulled his ball cap over his eyes. Despite the noise and vibration of the helicopter, both men dozed.

Cam Ranh Bay
South Vietnam

"Roger, MAC Zero-One, wind is calm. Altimeter is three-zero-zero-two. Cleared to land. A *Follow-Me* will assist when you clear the runway," the tower controller announced into the microphone.

"*Roger, cleared to land,*" the co-pilot replied.

"What's the story on this guy?" the controller said to his assistant. He looked at the runway lights, making sure they were properly set for the weather conditions outside.

"Beats me. The flight's coming from Andrews, but it's not using the standard VIP call sign," the second controller said. "All I know is that we're supposed to park him on the remote ramp. The sky cops are going to cordon off the area and keep the ship isolated."

"We also have an inbound Huey with no flight plan. The base commander said to let it land with no questions. He was pretty clear on that point."

"And we ain't supposed to say anything." The second controller looked at his inbound flight log. "Sometimes I feel like a mushroom. Just keep me in the dark and feed me bullshit."

"Typical government operation."

Jack Wilder watched the lights of Cam Ranh city go by as the aircraft maneuvered for its final approach. His mind, however, was somewhere else. From the time he left Washington, he wondered how he would handle the problem facing him. But he was no closer to an answer now than he was at the beginning of his trip. In less than an hour, he would face his son. *What am I going to say?*

The C-135 touched down on the wet runway. Lowering the nose wheel to the ground, the pilot engaged reverse thrust and slowed the aircraft to taxi speed. Reaching the end of the two mile stretch of concrete, the crew saw the *Follow-Me* van on the taxi way, its lights flashing through the fog. The aircraft slowly turned off the runway and began playing Follow-the-Leader to the southern end of the airport.

The pilot set the parking brake and shut down the engines. He looked out the window at the transient alert crew scurrying about the aircraft. A ground crewman gave him the signal indicating that the wheel chocks were in place, and the pilot released the brakes. "Welcome to Disney Land, guys. Time for a shower and a beer."

"Doesn't look like much of a party town," the copilot said.

"Wish I could join you, fellas, but business first." Jack Wilder stood in the cockpit doorway. "Rudy, wheels are waiting to take your crew to the VIP quarters, such as they are. The chow's not bad, and the beer's cold. Let's plan on leaving in sixteen hours."

"We'll be ready when you are, Mr. Wilder," the pilot said. He looked out the window. "There are two staff cars on our left." The vehicles were a distance from each other.

Wilder noticed them through the side window. "The first one's yours. When you're done here, the driver will take you where you need to go. He's at your disposal."

"Thank you, sir, but we should be doing this for you," the copilot said. "We're not used to having this kind of attention."

"Comes with the territory, guys." *Wish I could change places with you*, Wilder thought to himself. "Enjoy your rest. See you at blast-off time." Wilder returned to his office in the rear of the airplane and closed the door behind him.

He thought about the second staff car. And the person in it. *What the hell am I going to say?*

384 • *Wayne Keesee*

A power cart and air conditioning unit were connected to the aircraft, and the servicing personnel finished their tasks. Within minutes there was no one inside the roped area that surrounded the plane—except for the lone car.

Jack Wilder looked at his radio-phone. He took in a deep breath and slowly exhaled. He pressed the transmit button. "Please send him up."

"Army Six, taxi to the hold point on the south end of the airport. You can discharge your passengers there," the ground controller said.

"*Roger.*" Reaching the designated spot, the helicopter gently touched down on the concrete.

"Thanks for the ride, guys," Wilder shouted over the noise of the rotating blades. "Time to enjoy that bottle of hooch."

Custer slid the troop door open and both men jumped onto the tarmac. Lowering their heads to avoid the spinning blades, the two CIA officers started across the concrete in the driving rain.

The plane was surrounded by military police and guard dogs. The single access area in front of the aircraft was manned by two guards, both of whom watched the approaching men carefully. Although the guards knew who they were, they were taking no chances. Their M-16's were at the ready.

"Gentlemen, I'm Captain Bill Wilder, and this is Major Ed Custer. We're expected."

The guard examined their credentials closely. He asked them specific questions and got the answers that only they would know. This particular guard knew them by sight from previous contact, but this was serious business. The passenger in the plane insisted on it. "Captain Wilder, Major Custer, you may board." The guard watched them go up the air stairs and into the waiting aircraft. Wilder closed the entrance door behind him. That was the signal for the guards to assume their positions at the base of the steps. From this point on, no one would be allowed to enter the ship. The use of deadly force was authorized.

"It's you he wants to see," Custer said. The two men looked at each other in the narrow hallway forward of the galley. "No time like the present. I'll wait here til he calls me."

"I don't think so, Ed." Wilder frowned. "You're as much of a part of this as I am. If he wants you to leave the room, he'll tell you."

"Okay, cowboy," Custer conceded. "It's your show. The inner sanctum awaits."

Although Custer stood beside him, Bill felt alone. His mind wondered back to that cold winter day when he and his friends left Dulles Airport on the first leg of their long journey to Vietnam. The last person he saw before he got on the airplane that would take him half a world away was his father. The last person he saw before being left alone in a hospital in another foreign country with a dying friend was his father. And now his father had come halfway around the world to confront a lowly operative with less experience than most soldiers in the entire country.

Why did the senior CIA official come to Vietnam? What would happen when Bill opened the door? What would they say to each other? What new intelligence would his father provide? Would Bill be court-martialed for actions? A thousand questions raced through his mind, but no answers came.

Bill opened the door and stepped into the small room. He froze when he saw the man sitting next to his father.

Tom Berwick stared back at him.

The memory of their confrontation years ago flashed through Bill's mind. He recalled Colonel Jennings' words that no charges had been filed by Berwick's parents and that the entire matter had died a quiet death. His own thoughts were that the problem with Berwick had not disappeared at all.

He stood perfectly still. Ignoring his father, Bill focused his full attention on Berwick. The air was ripe with tension, and he breathed slowly to maintain his self-control.

Jack Wilder came to the point of tears when he saw his son. If only they could be alone. He stood and extended his hand. "Bill, I—"

"What are you doing here, Berwick?" Bill snapped.

Berwick said nothing.

"Answer me, *damn* you!"

"Bill, sit down," Wilder said.

Bill glanced at his father while keeping his attention on Berwick. "What's he doing here?" He remained standing.

"*Sit down!*"

Bill looked at his father, immediately recognizing his authority. He slowly moved to the seat next to the window and sat. He returned his attention to Berwick.

"Listen to me, Bill. I've come here at great risk because you gave me no choice, and I don't have time for niceties." Wilder was speaking as a senior CIA official, rather than a father.

Bill knew that his father had answers for him, but this was beyond anything that he could have imagined. He looked at Berwick. *Why are you here?*

Jack Wilder was in a difficult situation. That his young agent had vanished without a trace and had gone on his own, was as illegal as it could get. The CIA could discipline him, but it would accomplish nothing. Bill had done the wrong thing for the right reasons, and Wilder doubted his own ability to do what his son had done.

"I'm glad you're safe, Bud. You gave all of us quite a scare." Wilder leaned forward. "I know you have a thousand questions, and I'll answer all of them in turn. But hear me out first." Wilder wanted to scream at his son and hug him at the same time. Seeing his boy alive and safe gave him a feeling of relief that he could barely contain. But he had to stay in control.

"What's going on here?" Bill continued to stare at Berwick.

"Be patient and listen." Looking briefly at Berwick and Custer, Wilder turned to his son. "When Berwick left the Institute, we worried that his parents would file assault charges against you. They would have been within their rights to do so. But they didn't do it for one very good reason. I asked them not to."

"What?"

"Berwick's father was in the Army with Colonel Jennings during Korea. They both spent time together in a North Korean POW camp. Jennings saved his life during that time, and when the incident between you two happened, I asked Jennings to intervene on your behalf. He asked Mr. Berwick to hold off filing any charges until I had a chance to talk with him, and he agreed.

"Berwick and Jennings were with the intelligence service before being captured by the North Koreans. Jennings was able to convince the Koreans that they both were just grunts. The Koreans had no idea of their real mission."

"Colonel Jennings said—"

"Hold on, son. Jennings and Berwick were part of an intelligence team that had been sent into North Korea ahead of our forces. They were captured with a squad of soldiers, which worked to their benefit. Their captors had no idea of their real purpose. If they had known, both of them would have been shot as spies. Jennings was responsible for their staying alive.

"Anyway, I contacted Mr. Berwick and we met in Washington. Although we agreed that you and Tom were entitled to your own views, we also agreed that both of you overreacted, and we attributed your behavior to youthful exuberance in lieu of common sense. Mr. Berwick said he wouldn't press any charges, and I thanked him for that. It was time to put the issue to rest and move on." Wilder paused and looked at Berwick. Turning back to his son, he said, "This man apologized to me for his remarks to you about your brother. Now, he has something to say to you."

"I don't understand." Bill was confused.

"I didn't agree with you back then, Bill, but things change," Berwick said. "My old man told me about his experience in Korea after I got home, and of how Jennings had saved his life. I had no idea that any of that had happened, and I began to see things differently that day." Berwick was nervous. "I got mixed up with the wrong crowd back then, I'll admit that. It was a tough time for all of us. My views of the war were based on other people's opinions, and I never thought about deciding for myself. Little Jack was a brave soldier, and I apologize to you for what I said about him."

Wilder wanted to keep the momentum going. "Bill, it's time to put this issue where it belongs; in the past. We all have ghosts to deal with, but there are more pressing problems now. So let's put our heads together and deal with them." Wilder anxiously waited for a reaction.

Bill looked out the small window into the night fog, his mind reeling. All his life his father had been there for him and had given him guidance and advice when it was needed. Now, his father was asking him to set aside his differences with a man that had slandered the memory of his dead brother. It was almost more than Bill could accept.

He looked at his father and saw the desperation in his eyes. As much as Bill hated Berwick, he loved his father more. Was Berwick sincere in his apology? Bill had no way of knowing, but he had no choice except to agree with his father's request. After all, his advice had sustained Bill throughout his life, and there was no reason to doubt it now.

"Well?" Wilder was on the edge of his seat. Beads of sweat formed on his brow, despite the air conditioned cabin.

Bill looked at his father then at Berwick. "This took some nerve on your part, Tom. We've both been through a lot since that time. I accept your apology, and I'm sorry for what I did. I hope this cleans the slate between us." Bill stood and extended his hand.

The two men shook hands.

"This has bothered me for a long time, Bill, and I'm glad we have this chance to meet and clear the air." Berwick was visibly relieved. He looked at Jack. "Thanks, Colonel Wilder, for your help."

"Gentlemen, you've made my day." Wilder stood and placed a hand on each man's shoulder. "Now, perhaps we can get back to the business of chasing the enemy, rather than each other."

"I'll buy that, sir." Custer had been standing in the background the entire time. It was the first time he had spoken since they entered the room. He had something on his mind, but he would wait until Berwick was gone. He had to talk to the Wilders alone.

Wilder was elated to see his son make peace with Berwick. That the two men had agreed to put their differences behind them, was a welcomed relief. He hoped that it was real. It was essential to his plan.

He went to the aft galley and returned with a carafe and four cups. "Before this party breaks up, let's have some real coffee. The steward showed me how to do this before he left with the crew. You guys are my guinea pigs." He filled the cups and passed them around.

After some small talk, Wilder said, "Gentlemen, this has been a long day for me, and I thank you for making the trip worth it." His words marked the end of their meeting. He turned to Berwick. "Tom,

I appreciate your coming. Now we can get back to finishing this job and bringing everyone home. Your staff car is waiting to take you to the BOQ, and a C-130 will be here in the morning to take you back to Saigon."

"Thank you, Mr. Wilder."

"One more thing."

"Yes, sir?"

"This meeting never took place."

"I understand, sir." Berwick turned to Bill. "A huge weight's been taken off my back, Bill, and I thank you for that."

"Long overdue." The two men shook hands again.

Berwick nodded to Custer and left the cabin.

They stood in silence. There was so much to say, but no one knew where to begin. Wilder wanted to share his innermost feelings with his son but couldn't because of Custer. For his part, Custer had been an observer on the side lines for the past half hour. It was his turn to speak up. "Gentlemen, I admit that I'm not the sharpest tool in the shed. I need to ask a question."

"Go ahead, Ed."

"With all respect, Colonel Wilder, I don't think you went through all this trouble to come to Vietnam just to mend fences between Bill and this Berwick guy. I'd like to know what's really going on here, sir."

"Me, too," Bill said.

"I'll tell you. But first I want you both to know that there are things going on that I can't discuss. Is that clear?"

Both pilots nodded.

"Berwick's affiliated with the Agency by way of his position with Air Force Intelligence. He's not CIA, and he doesn't know that either of you are either. As far as your presence is concerned, Bill, I swore Berwick to secrecy. He's not to say anything to anybody about you. As far as anyone in this country knows, you died in that crash."

"Okay, Dad, but you didn't come halfway around the world to arrange a feel-good session between him and me. Why was he here, and why did he have to see me at all? Up until a few minutes ago, the only people in Vietnam that knew that I was alive were the three of us."

"Good point. The short answer is that I need him. As Ed can confirm, there's a leak somewhere in our Asian operations, and we think it's in Saigon. Until we find our mole, we need information from sources outside the embassy, and Berwick, although he doesn't know it, will provide it for us. There are other reasons too, but that will suffice for now."

"What's wrong with Bryant? He's in charge of Wing Intelligence," Custer said.

"Nothing, except he's too friendly with McAlester. The Brit might be snooping where he doesn't belong, and we don't want to give him any ideas. At this point he's just a nuisance factor, and we don't need to involve him." Wilder pursed his lips for a moment, then said, "We're reasonably certain Petrov is still in Saigon, and we have assets looking for him right now. Bill, we're pretty sure that he thinks both you and John are both dead. In any event we need to find the leak as soon as we can. Berwick can help us with that."

"How so?"

"Classified. Sorry."

Custer intervened. "Here's an observation. If everybody, including Petrov, thinks you're dead, then he might let his guard down and do something stupid. You have the advantage here."

"Yes, until someone tells him differently," Wilder said.

Bill's eyebrows went up at his father's words. "I think I see where you're going with this. That *someone* may be our leak."

"We have a tail on Berwick too."

"Why's that, sir?" Custer said.

"Let's just say that we're watching our collective butts." Wilder leaned back in his chair and sipped his coffee.

"So there's a fox in the hen house." Custer rubbed his chin thoughtfully. "How do you plan to catch him, sir? With a babe?"

"Not with a babe, Ed, but with some bait."

"Where does that leave me? I'm non-existent right now."

"Not quite, Bud. You still have the safe house, and I want you to make use of it. At the same time, you can do your own snooping. Just keep out of sight and keep in touch with me through Ed. Stay away from the embassy. Remember, everyone there thinks you were killed in Kontum."

"But what about Neilson?"

"I have him going in a different direction," Wilder said.

"How about a sting operation," Bill said. "It could get things off dead center."

"What do you mean?"

"Think about it, Dad. We know about Petrov's proclivities towards women. Set up a sting in a local hotel and—"

"We can't do it. In the first place we can't show our presence in Saigon. And in the second place, you know what he does to women. We simply can't risk it." Wilder stood and placed his hand on his son's shoulder. "Look, Bud, I know how you feel. You've been through hell, and you're ready to strike out on your own. But you must be patient. We *will* find him. You must trust me on this. And when we do, it'll be your turn to step up to the plate."

Bill knew that his father was right. "Dad, I can see why you're top dog at Spook Central."

"I'll take that as a compliment." Wilder smiled at his son. "We have to be careful in this business, gentlemen. Sometimes, it's one step backwards after two forward. Carelessness is not a luxury we can afford." He sat back in his chair and looked at his young agents with the pride of a lion looking at his young cubs. Jack Wilder had just played an ace and won.

Custer knew that the two men wanted to be alone. "Colonel, I applaud you for pulling the wool over Washington's eyes and flying halfway around the earth to see us. I'll try to keep an eye on Bill, but the guy's like a shadow in the dark. Keep the blue side up, sir, and have a safe trip home." Custer turned to Bill. "See you outside, partner." A quick handshake with the DCO and Custer was gone.

Wilder's words were choked with emotion. "When you disappeared from Clark, I didn't know what to think. I was sure no one had gotten to you, but not knowing where you were or what you were doing nearly drove me crazy. Did you ever think about that while you were on your own?" Wilder wasn't speaking as the Director of Operations. Rather, his words were that of a desperate father.

"Dad, there wasn't a minute that I didn't think about it. But when I saw John and thought about what happened in Saigon, I just couldn't be a sitting duck. I had to leave. I'm sorry I worried you so much."

Tears ran down Wilder's face. He reached for his son and hugged him. "I love you so much, Bud. You're all I have."

Bill wrapped his arms around his father's bent shoulders. Age and the ceaseless pressure from his job had taken its toll on the old man, and Bill could feel it when he hugged him. It was only then that Bill realized how badly the man had suffered. He held his father close to him. "Dad, I love you more than anything. We'll get through this."

Father and son embraced each other. Since Little Jack's death, so much had happened, and the impact of everything hit them all at once. It had been a long time since they had seen each other, and this time together was an emotional release for both of them. It renewed their faith in each other and in their purpose for being where they were.

Wilder knew that his son would do anything to find Petrov. It was now up to him to guide his son, rather than control him. He had learned that lesson from watching the politicians in Washington try to run a war they couldn't possibly win. "Leave the war to the generals," he had told them. *To hell with the politicians.* Wilder had his own war to fight. He would dedicate himself to his son … and to finding Petrov.

"I'm glad we had this chance to meet, Dad. I never thought in my wildest dreams that things would turn out the way they have and that we would be in a place like this."

"War makes for strange bedfellows, Bud."

"You've said nothing about John. How is he?"

"No change, I'm afraid." Wilder slowly shook his head. "His physical wounds have long since healed, but the coma is the unknown variable. He's getting the best medical treatment available, believe me. We're keeping our fingers crossed."

"I wish I could do something for him."

"Get Petrov. That's what you can do for him."

"Dad, I swear I'll find him if it's the last thing I do." Bill hugged his father again and left the airplane without another word.

Jack Wilder stared at the closed door and wondered if he would ever see his son again.

CHAPTER 26

Stuck once more at the rubber plantation, Bill Wilder wasn't the least bit concerned with the war raging around him. His attention was focused on the man on the other side of the room.

Custer slumped in his chair. He let his head fall back against the cushion and closed his eyes. He sat still for a time, trying to make sense of recent events. Finally, he looked at Wilder.

"Well?"

"Your father told me what happened to his female agent in Russia and about the Air France stewardess in New York."

"That's ancient history, Ed. What's your point?" Wilder was impatient. He had languished in the rubber plantation for weeks, and he was no closer to finding Petrov now than when he left the Philippines so long ago.

Custer sat up in his chair. "Look, Bill, I don't like this any more than you do, so don't get short with me!" Custer had been in the spy business for a while and had seen his share of sorrow too. He volunteered for a second tour to Vietnam because he had nothing to go home to. His wife and son both died during childbirth several years before, and he had his own cross to bear.

Wilder instantly regretted his outburst. "I'm sorry, Ed. I guess I'm just a bit tired of being stuck in this place."

"We're all a little up tight these days." The creases on Custer's brow lessened. He looked around the room. "I'm sure this place is getting to you."

"I feel like I'm growing roots."

Custer leaned forward. "Your lady friend at the Caravelle ... "

"Vandeth?"

Custer rubbed his hands together, wanting to be somewhere else. "The police found her tied to the bed in one of the hotel rooms. She'd been tortured, raped, and killed. I'm really sorry, Bill. She was a nice lady."

"Damn you, Petrov!" Wilder squeezed his eyes shut. He dropped onto a chair and took a deep breath. He exhaled slowly and opened his eyes.

"It's possible that Petrov singled her out because she was always there. I don't mean to sound trite, Bill, but she would be a likely target because of her good looks."

"Her looks had nothing to do with it." Wilder began to pace the floor.

"How do you figure?"

"With all the prostitutes in the city, why would he pick a respectable woman whose husband is a colonel in the South Vietnamese Army?"

"First of all, we know that he hates the Vietnamese, and—"

"He picked her for a different reason, Ed."

"What's that?"

Wilder stood in front of Custer. "He wants people to know he's still around. And killing a colonel's wife tells everyone that he's in complete control. And there's something else."

"What?"

"Me."

"Explain."

Wilder walked to the window and sat on the ledge. He looked across the expanse of rubber trees in the distance. He could see the far away explosions from the fighting around An Loc. None of that meant anything to him. He turned to Custer. "What better way to bring me into the open than to kill someone close to me? And to do it in such a brutal way?"

"Assuming he knows you're alive. But how would he know about your relationship with Vandeth? She wouldn't tell him anything, would she?"

"She wouldn't have to. Everybody knew that she and Maggie were close. And Petrov knew that I was at the hotel a lot." Wilder's face clouded over. "No, Vandeth didn't say anything. She just happened to be friends with the wrong person. But someone told him about me."

"How do you figure that?"

"He knows I'm still alive and in-country, and he killed Vandeth to get my attention. And you know something?"

"What?"

"He succeeded."

"What do you mean?"

"He knows I'm alive, and there's no better place for me to get in his face than at the crime scene. I'm going to have a very public lunch with Terry McAlester."

Custer shook his head. "Not a good idea."

"Why not?"

"Forget Petrov for a minute. We have to find the leak in the Saigon operation that your father spoke of, and Berwick may be the only person that can lead us to him. If Petrov sees you, the leak may just disappear."

"Dad thinks Berwick's clean, but I don't trust him. His story about his change in attitude after his father talked to him about Korea is just too neat. I don't buy it."

"I don't think you have any choice," Custer said.

"Why not?"

"If Berwick tells anyone about you, we'll know he's the leaky faucet. But if you show your hand, then Berwick is no longer a player. The leak will simply disappear."

"Okay. I'll go along with that … for now."

"Fair enough. But for what it's worth, let's give Berwick a chance. If he rats on you, then we'll have our leak. If not, then we'll play it your way."

Wilder thought for a minute, then said, "That's fine for what it's worth, Ed, but there's one thing missing."

"What's that?"

"When I crashed in Kontum and John died in the Philippines, Berwick was in Hong Kong. How would he know that we'd been shipped to Clark? The simple answer is that he didn't."

"Shit! You're right! He had no way of knowing. That means that whoever knew you were there is the one that—" Custer stopped short, regretting his words.

"The one that killed John. You can say it." Wilder's face was as hard as stone. "*He*'s our leak. Berwick had nothing to do with that end of it. Whoever he is, he knew that we'd been sent to Clark under aliases, and that leaves Berwick out. Our leak is someone in the CIA hierarchy."

"But nobody knew you were in the Philippines," Custer said.

"Scott Neilson did."

Custer's eyes narrowed. "What are you saying, Bill?"

"He met Dad at the hospital after John and I got there."

"This is getting more confusing by the minute. What else haven't you told me?"

"Nothing. But you don't have to be a rocket scientist to see the connection. Who else besides my father and the Saigon station manager knew that John and I were at Clark? Nobody."

"This is almost too much to swallow." Custer looked doubtful. "I can't believe he's our leak. I've known Scott for a long time, Bill. Be careful with this."

"My father and uncle knew Petrov's old man for a long time too. They worked together in the Pentagon on Warsaw Pact intelligence. The guy was a Soviet plant. Things aren't always what they seem, Ed."

"I guess not. "

Saigon

Custer saluted the Marine guard and walked through the embassy gate. On the surface he was there for the daily intelligence briefing given to certain military staff officers for their commanders. It was standard practice, and he was expected. But he had his own reasons for coming to the embassy. Custer walked into the secretary's office. "Good morning, Steve. Is Scott here?"

"He's expecting you, Major Custer. Go right in."

Custer walked through the door. "Morning, Scott. How's the tennis arm?" He helped himself to a cup of coffee.

"A little sore, but not bad. Hard to play when Charlie has you surrounded." Neilson leaned back in his desk chair. "Too hot, anyway. What's up with you?"

"I'm here for the morning briefing, but from the sound of things, I don't think I really want to hear it."

"Yeah, I know what you mean. The VC and their northern brothers are putting on the full court press. The bad guys are getting killed by the thousands, but we're losing some prime real estate in the process."

"Never a dull minute around here. Any luck on Petrov?" Custer asked.

"We think he's still around because of the Caravelle incident. That case has his name all over it. Because Vandeth was an ARVN colonel's wife, the Vietnamese police are butting heads with MACV, and MACV is butting heads with us. Everybody wants answers, but I don't have anything to tell them." Neilson lit a cigarette and tossed the pack onto his desk.

"When did you start smoking, Scott? I thought you were the resident health nut around here."

"It's a wonder I don't take drugs. I picked up this nasty habit in the past few months. I guess the pressure's getting to me. I should quit."

"Anything on McAlester?"

"There's nothing there. He's been hanging around a lot with this Bryant guy from Tan Son Nhut. Bryant wants into UPI when he gets out of the Air Force. Buttering his bread, so to speak." Neilson took a long drag on his cigarette and blew the smoke slowly across the room. "Do me a favor, will you?"

"Sure."

"Get rid of these damn things." Neilson tossed the pack of Marlboros.

Custer caught them in mid-air. "You don't need these coffin nails, Scott. Who got you hooked?"

"Hell, I don't know. Everybody smokes in this mad house." Neilson poured a glass of water and drank half of it. He tossed the cigarette into the glass. "We haven't been able to uncover a thing yet. I'm afraid Petrov may strike again before he disappears."

"What I don't understand is why he's still here. He killed two of the three people we think he was after, and the third is in a loony bin somewhere in the States. I'd say his mission was over."

"I'm not so sure," Neilson said.

"What do you mean?"

Neilson frowned. "I think he'll go after Jack Wilder next."

"What?" Custer wanted to laugh. "He'd have better luck raising the *Titanic*. Petrov couldn't get near Jack Wilder if his life depended on it. The CIA has him covered like white on rice."

"Why should that make any difference to Petrov?" Neilson replied. "Look at what he's done so far."

"He's had his successes, but his luck's bound to change sooner or later."

"I hope so, but we have to assume the worst in the meantime."

Custer looked at his watch. "Gotta get going. Briefing starts in a few minutes." He looked at Neilson. "Get off those smokes, Scott. In this environment they'll kill you sooner rather than later."

"Think I'll take you advice."

For appearances, Custer stood in the briefing room and listened to the less-than-useless intelligence briefing. As soon as it was over, he headed straight for the Tan Son Nhut command post.

"Your best customer is back." Custer entered the communications center and closed the door.

Airman Woods looked up from his telex machine. "I was just going to send for you, sir. I have an info copy of a message from UPI to Washington. Doesn't concern any of our people, but I thought you'd be interested." He handed Custer a clipboard.

UPI journalist Terry McAlester found dead in his room at the Caravelle

Hotel in Saigon. Investigating authorities suspect foul play. No further information at this time. Details when available.

"Un-fucking believable!" Custer looked at Woods. "When did this come in?"

"About fifteen minutes ago, sir."

Custer read the message again. "Of all the shit going on the world! McAlester was harmless. Why would anyone want to hurt that old man?"

Woods looked at him. "You knew him, didn't you?"

"I knew who he was." Custer didn't elaborate. The less said, the better.

"I'm sorry to be the one to give you the news, sir. I'll contact you the minute any information comes through here."

"Don't let anyone else in on this, okay?"

"No problem, Major Custer."

"I'll talk to you later." Custer left the young airman to his tasks. *Things are getting out of hand,* Custer thought. It was time to go on a fishing expedition. He tapped once on Berwick's office door and walked in.

"Ed! What brings you here on a day off?" Berwick looked up from reading the daily airfield reports.

"Hi, Tom. I have a mission tomorrow night and thought I'd drop by to see if the odds are in my favor."

Berwick turned to the wall map behind him. "Bryant got the latest intel from MACV this morning. This shows what's going on." Berwick pointed to the map. "There's a lot of fighting going on in the Highlands, but the ARVN have been holding their own with help from B-52's. The gunships have been keeping Charlie and the NVA in their caves around Kontum City. Security around the field is pretty tight, but Charlie is unpredictable." He looked at Custer. "We'll have an update tomorrow night when you pick up your mission packet."

"Let's hope the news is boring." Custer sat on the corner of Berwick's desk. "By the way, how's Bryant doing with his UPI contacts?"

"Which one?"

"Terry McAlester."

"He hasn't said anything. Why?"

"You know he's trying to get on with UPI when he's done here. He hopes McAlester can help him."

"Can't blame him for that," Berwick said. "Never hurts to know somebody in the business."

"I guess not." *Wonder what Bryant has to say?* Custer headed for the door. "See you tomorrow night."

"I'll be here." Berwick returned to his airfield reports.

"Hi, Jerry. Got a minute?" Custer closed the door and grabbed a chair.

"Sure, Ed. What's up?" Bryant closed a file cabinet and sat on his desk.

"I have a flight tomorrow night, probably up north. Thought I'd touch bases and see what's going on."

"Well, it's getting hot around Da Nang, Quang Tri, and Pleiku. The VC are still playing games around Kontum."

"In other words, the usual. I'm getting too old for this shit." Custer looked at the wall map. "I understand you're getting out of the Air Force when your hitch is up."

"Yeah. There's no future in this place for a navigator. I don't need another *career broadening* assignment to Thule, Greenland."

"Desk jobs suck."

"Nothing's definite, but I've been trying to get a foot in the door with Terry McAlester. I figure he may be able to help me."

"I know of him." Custer thought about telling Bryant the bad news but decided against it. There was no need to arouse suspicion. Bryant would find out soon enough anyway. "Well, I guess I'll head back to the house and lay low for a while. Gonna be up all night tomorrow. Good luck with the Englishman."

"Thanks. See you later." Bryant returned to his file cabinet.

Custer left the command post complex and headed towards the BOQ. It was time to take a trip to a certain rubber plantation north of Saigon. He would wait until dark before he left. It was nice having Army chopper pilots in his pockets. And the ever-present bottle of *Jack Daniels* didn't hurt either.

The Huey touched down in the clearing behind the rundown

French mansion. Custer jumped from the right troop door and ran, head lowered, towards the building. He was met by his anxious partner in the doorway.

"Anything new?" Wilder asked, his hopes up.

"Somebody threw us a curve," Custer said, taking off his ball cap. "McAlester's dead."

"*What?*" Wilder's jaw went limp.

"The maids found him in his room. His throat was cut." Custer dropped onto a sofa, suddenly fatigued.

"This is unbelievable." Wilder looked out the window, his mind trying to find some sense of direction. "He wasn't a threat to anyone."

"The only thing I can think of is that he may have stumbled onto something he wasn't supposed to know."

"I'll wager that McAlester knew his killer beforehand," Wilder said.

"Sounds reasonable. The Caravelle's becoming not the place to stay. Gets unhealthy around there."

"Yeah. Who knows besides us?"

"Nobody I know of. I got an intercepted message from UPI. It pays to have a friend in the comm center."

"This has to come to an end, Ed."

"Any ideas?"

Wilder looked out the window. "No, but I can't stay here any longer."

Custer knew that he couldn't contain Wilder if he had to. He decided to go out on a limb. "I'm going to throw you a bone."

"I'm listening."

"This is illegal as hell, but I'm taking you on a mission tomorrow night. I have to go up north with some ARVN troops. I have a new crew that's TDY from Taiwan, and they won't know you from Adam. I'll just tell them that you want a look-see because you're going in the following night as forward air controller."

"I think they'll buy that."

"I'll smuggle you onto the base tonight. You can stay in my BOQ room. No one will see you, and nobody there knows you anyway. Besides, the place is nearly empty."

"Do you provide room service?" Wilder grinned, glad for the chance to get out.

"C-Rations only. You're too ugly to go to the O'Club," Custer said, thankful that Wilder had still had his sense of humor. "I'll come by the barracks and pick you up just before we go to the flight line."

"I appreciate this, Ed. Thanks."

"What are friends for? As far as this mission is concerned, we don't really have to answer to anybody. Your father is on the other side of the planet, and he has bigger fish to fry. I don't see a real problem here." Custer was trying to justify his decision to himself. It was one way he could keep tabs on Wilder until they had a chance to do some detective work.

"The only fly in the ointment is if we crash. Then it won't make any difference anyway."

"You've already filled that square, buddy. We need a stroke of good luck for a change," Custer said.

"No kidding!"

CHAPTER 27

KONTUM
SOUTH VIETNAM

To the uninitiated the skies over the Central Highlands of South Vietnam looked like a July celebration. But to the crew of Spare Five-Zero, it was anything but. A B-52 Arc Light strike raged to the west, the earth shattering with the impact of five-hundred pound iron bombs. AC-130 gunships circled to the north of Pleiku and west of Kontum, their red reign of fire hosing the earth and shredding everything in their path.

"I thought this was supposed to be a cakewalk," Steve Jaxon said. As a new co-pilot on his first trip to Vietnam, he didn't know what to expect, but he recalled the intelligence briefing at Tan Son Nhut before they left. "I think somebody missed the boat. Looks like heavy fire around the landing zone to me, but I'm not sure what I'm looking at."

"That's exactly what you're looking at," Custer replied. He was irritated at the lack of real time intelligence and of the apparent inability of the Air Force to give the crews the information they needed. "Berwick said this place was mostly secure, but it looks like they're getting the hell pounded out of them." He looked at Jaxon. "Mind the store, Steve. I'm gonna call the command post on HF and find out what the hell's going on."

"Don't count on getting anything useful from them, Ed," Wilder said over the interphone. Standing behind Custer's seat, he could see the conflagration on the ground. "Those ingrates are useless. If you tell them what you're seeing, they'll say it ain't there."

"I'm sure," Custer said, "but let's put the monkey on their back."

Jaxon flew the C-130 in a holding pattern at 10,000 feet south of the field. It was high enough to stay clear of any ground fire, yet close enough to the action to make an intelligent decision on their next course of action—command post permitting. The crew, without being told to, put on their flak jackets and steel helmets in anticipation of events to come.

"Steve, monitor the FM. It's set on the forward air controller's frequency. Let me know if he says anything. I'm on HF to those idiots in Saigon," Custer said.

"Roger, that."

"Hilda, this is Spare Five-Zero on eight-niner upper. Mission six-six bravo, over," Custer transmitted.

"Roger, Five-zero, this is Hilda. Go ahead."

"Be advised, Hilda, that we're circling overhead destination, and the field is under heavy attack. Military activity is heavy to the north and west. Any intel for us?"

"Stand by, Five-Zero. We're checking."

" 'Stand by.' That's all those screws know how to say."

"Standard inertia, Ed," Wilder said.

"Five-Zero, this is Hilda. Intel advises that enemy activity is minimal. You are directed to continue your mission. Over."

"Can you fucking believe it?" Custer said over the interphone. He didn't bother to reply to the transmission from Tan Son Nhut. He switched back to his FM receiver and turned off the HF radio. "Idiots!"

"I may be the rookie on this crew, but did I miss something here?" Jaxon was visibly irritated.

"No, you didn't, Steve," Wilder said. "Those drones at MACV couldn't find their way out of a paper bag with the end opened. Their information's always a week old, and they won't accept anything from the crews. Same shit, different day."

"No wonder we're losing this war."

"Welcome to Uncle Sam's world," Custer said. He tightened the straps on his flak jacket. "Okay, guys, here's the drill. We're going into Kontum and off load the troops in the back. Robby, watch yourself back there. Things are gonna happen fast. We get these guys out and get gone. Okay?"

"The faster the better." Robby Robinson was the loadmaster. Although experienced in the airplane, this was his first mission under hostile fire.

Custer looked over his shoulder at Wilder. "You okay with this, Bill? You've done this drill before and got boned for your efforts."

"I'm with Robby back there. Let's get it over with." Wilder sat on the bunk and strapped himself in. Although Custer was an experienced instructor pilot, Wilder felt uneasy not being at the controls. The lack of *hands-on* control was a nervousness that all pilot-passengers experienced.

"Okay, guys, let's run the check lists and get ready to land. Mike, when we pass through one thousand feet on final, turn off the bleed valves. If you see something you don't like, make some noise."

"Gotcha covered, Major," Mike Ducette said. The engineer quickly scanned his panel and set the fuel valves for landing. "I'll give you sink rate the last two hundred feet."

"Okay. Robby, as soon we touch down, open the ramp and door. You'll get the green light just before we stop. Get those zips off as fast as you can. When the last one bails out, we're outta here."

"Gotcha."

"Okay, guys, let's do it." Custer rolled the airplane out of the turn and onto final approach. He pulled the throttles to idle, allowing the airspeed to decrease. "Flaps to fifty and landing gear down." Jaxon positioned the gear handle and the three green indicators lit up. "Flaps full." When the ship slowed to its maximum effort approach speed, Custer lowered the nose and aimed for the end of the short runway.

"Landing check is complete," Jaxon said. "You're on speed." .

"Bleeds coming close," Ducette announced. He flipped four toggle switches on his overhead panel, and the engines surged with added power. "Put her in the box, skipper. Sink rate is eight hundred."

The aircraft descended at a steady rate towards the end of the runway, the crew alert for anything.

Whump! The ship shook violently and yawed to the right.

"We're hit! SAM through the tail!" Robinson screamed over the interphone.

Both pilots instinctively grabbed their control wheels in a vain attempt to save the aircraft. But the elevator had been blown apart, and the airplane was descending uncontrollably towards the earth. At one hundred feet above the jungle, Custer pulled the throttles to idle. "Lock your harnesses! We're gonna hit hard!" Custer fought for control, but the flight controls were useless.

Wilder braced his foot against the corner of the galley wall and tightened his seat belt. Memories of his last mission into Kontum flashed through his mind. His thoughts ran the gamut from the crash to the mercenary that had saved him. He thought about Maggie and John. Pushing them from his mind, he looked at the trees coming rapidly towards him. Pressing back into his seat, he readied himself for the worst.

The plane impacted the ground approximately a half mile short of the runway and began to come apart. The wings snapped off at the fuselage and tumbled wildly into the trees, spewing jet fuel everywhere. Fortunately, there was no fire in the fuselage since the center tank was empty. The body of the doomed C-130 turned sideways and tumbled. It broke into three pieces, and the ARVN troops in the cargo compartment were at the mercy of the elements. Bodies were thrown in every direction as the ship disintegrated.

The cockpit separated from the fuselage on impact and rolled through a rice paddy, tossing the crew in every direction. Custer managed to unhook his seat belt at the same instant his seat tore from the floor. Landing hard on a small earthen dike, he felt and heard the sickening snap of his arm.

Still strapped to his seat, Jaxon impacted a large boulder, killing him instantly. Ducette's seat landed on its back in another rice paddy. Although unhurt, he was dazed and didn't move for several moments. When the initial shock wore off, he looked around and saw Custer in the distance. He unlocked his harness, jumped out of his seat, and began to make his way through the muck towards his aircraft commander.

The navigator and loadmaster were both killed, along with many of the ARVN troops.

The piece of hull that surrounded Wilder finally came to rest on its front. Other than a few minor cuts and bruises, he was unhurt. His senses were shaken though, and he hung in his seat belt for several minutes before trying to move.

An eerie silence fell over the crash site. There was no explosion or fire, and once the pieces of the doomed ship came to a stop, there was no sound. For a moment Wilder wondered if he was deaf or dead. Hanging perfectly still, he listened to jungle, waiting for his eyes to focus and the ringing in his ears to stop. Then he heard distant shouts. He didn't know who they were, and he didn't to wait around to find out.

He unhooked his seat belt and dropped to his feet in the soft mud. Looking through the holes in the torn sheet metal that had been an airplane moments before, he saw people coming from the jungle towards the wreckage. Although it was dark, there was a full moon, and the light was sufficient for him to make them out.

They were Vietcong.

It was time to move.

Wilder quickly removed his flak jacket and checked the pockets of his survival vest. He instinctively reached for his holster. The .357 Python was still there, ready for use. He looked around for a first aid kit and found one on the split bulkhead to his left. He pulled it from its attachment and shoved it into a flight suit pocket. Lowering his head, he slid through a hole in the fuselage and disappeared into the darkness.

Ducette slogged his way towards Custer as fast as he could. His noisy splashing drew the attention of the Vietcong, and they began to chase him.

Custer stumbled to his feet and looked in Ducette's direction. Seeing the black pajamas of the Vietcong, he decided not to hang around. He waved at Ducette with his good arm and pointed past him.

Ducette looked in the direction that Custer was pointing. *Ah, shit!*

He ran as fast as the knee deep water would allow, but he couldn't run fast enough.

Custer ran towards the jungle, but just as he reached the trees, several Vietcong ran out of the jungle towards him. Custer stopped in his tracks, surrounded by black pajamas. He grabbed at the .38 revolver in his survival vest, but he wasn't quick enough.

The butt end of a Soviet AK-47 assault rifle struck him on the side of the head, knocking him to his knees. Stunned, Custer was unable to get up. Within seconds, he was surrounded.

Several shots rang out from behind him. Ducette fell face first in the water, dead.

The Vietcong swarmed over Custer and began to beat him savagely. Unable to defend himself, he curled into a ball and covered his face with his one good arm. The leader of the group fired a single shot into the air, and the beating stopped. They dragged Custer to his feet and bound his hands behind him with rope. He screamed in pain when they pulled on his broken arm. One of them kicked him in the groin, and Custer went down again. They pulled him up and began to push and drag him towards the edge of the jungle.

The leader approached the group. Looking at Custer, he said something and spat in his face. He then pointed in the direction of the crash, signaling his men to look for survivors. Their orders were to take no prisoners, other than Americans.

The Vietcong searched the paddies and the immediate area of the crash. They found several ARVN soldiers, many of them still alive. All of them were executed. By the time they were done, the rice paddies were red with blood, and the only American they had captured was Custer.

Wilder watched the slaughter from the edge of the jungle. Unable to do anything, he bit his tongue and suffered in silence while his friend and mentor was tortured. The Vietcong had no idea that he was there, but they would learn soon enough to their collective dismay.

Ninja disappeared into the night.

Satisfied that there were no more survivors, the leader barked out orders, and the Vietcong soldiers, along with their prisoner, began to hack their way into the jungle. The small group traveled through the night to a remote area north of the airfield. Although they were used to the jungle, they were hampered by their prisoner. Custer, injured from his beating, could barely move. Finally, the enemy soldiers tied his hands and feet together and ran a bamboo shaft between his arms and legs. Lifting the ends up, Custer hung helplessly like a side of beef between the two men holding up the ends. Mercifully, he fell unconscious. They continued through the night until they reached their base camp.

There was a small clearing next to a large rock outcropping on two sides that afforded some protection from the elements, as well as security from a rear attack. The porters dropped Custer to the ground. Hitting the jungle floor with a thud, he was dazed, in pain, and unable to move because of his bonds. The leader was sadistic. He kicked Custer in the groin and hit him on the back of the head with his AK-47. Custer passed out again. Two men dragged him into a bamboo cage and locked it with a steel bar and a rusty padlock.

The hours passed. The moon had set and, with the exception of the small fire, the night was pitch black. Everyone was asleep, including the two guards on opposite sides of the camp. The only sounds were the hisses and growls of the things that crept through the jungle.

The first guard awakened with a start, but it was too late. Before he could draw a breath, the K-bar knife silently slit his throat. The tense body went limp, and Wilder slowly lowered it to the ground. He slid back into jungle as silently as he had come.

The second sleeping guard was leaning against a tree only a few feet away, his head slumped over. He never knew what happened. One after the other, *Ninja* permanently silenced the Vietcong soldiers. The leader was the only one spared, so far.

Wilder wiped the bloody knife on the black shirt of one of his victims and slid the weapon into its sheath. He removed a leather lace from one of his flight boots and wrapped the ends around his hands. He quietly slipped into the light of the dying camp fire until he was within inches of the sleeping VC leader. *Ninja* remained perfectly still for several minutes to make certain his prey was oblivious to his presence.

Wilder stared unemotionally at the VC commander. Killing these people neither pleased nor upset him. They were the enemy in a war he didn't ask to be part of. But he was part of it and that was that. The man sleeping on the ground in front of him could easily have been one of his brother's tormentors in that North Vietnamese POW camp. For that possibility and for what he did to Custer, he would die.

Wilder looked at the bamboo cage, neither shocked nor surprised at what he saw. .

Bent over and leaning against the bamboo poles, Custer stared back at him. In spite of the pain he gave Wilder a thumbs-up. The happy expression on Custer's swollen and bloody face told Wilder all he needed to know.

Ninja turned his attention back to the sleeping Vietcong soldier. He carefully looped the garrote over the man's head and around his neck. In the next instant, Wilder pulled the leather cord as tight as he could.

The Vietnamese was instantly awake. In panic he grasped at his throat, but his frantic efforts got him nowhere. Wilder dragged the man backwards, not allowing him to gain his footing. Despite his desperate efforts, the struggling man was unable to break the hold around his neck, and within seconds he began to weaken.

Wilder kept the pressure on until the man passed out. When he began to go limp, Wilder released the garrote and dropped the body to the ground. The man had been strangled nearly to death, and he wouldn't regain consciousness for some time. Wilder turned his attention to the bamboo cage.

Custer was in serious condition. His broken arm had swollen to twice its normal size, and he had been beaten to the point that he could barely stand. He had several nasty cuts that would become infected unless he got medical treatment quickly. Wilder had to get him back to safety before his injuries became life-threatening. The two men were in a survival situation now, deep in enemy territory, and it would take all of Wilder's training and skill to save them.

Wilder pried the rusted lock with his K-bar knife, and it gave way with little resistance. He removed the steel rod and opened the door to the cage. He looked at Custer for a moment before he spoke. What he saw sickened him, and he would kill the man on the ground behind him for it. "Take it easy, Ed. Try to relax, buddy. I know it hurts, but I need to move you." He reached inside and gently hooked his arms under Custer's shoulders.

"I sure as hell am glad to see your ugly face. Thought I was a goner." Custer's voice was barely a whisper. He had been hit across the throat with a rifle butt, and his neck was swollen and bleeding. He winced when Wilder dragged him out of the cage, but he didn't complain. He was grateful to be rescued, and it showed in the painful grin on his face.

Wilder gently lowered him onto a reed mat next to the fire and slid a satchel bag under his head. Custer's breathing was labored and painful. In addition to a broken arm, he had several cracked ribs and open wounds. "My arm's useless, and I can't feel a thing."

Wilder looked him over. "Think you can walk? Your boots are by the fire."

"You kidding? I'll crawl if I have to. Help me get them on. We gotta get gone."

"All in good time, my friend. First things first." Wilder pulled the first aid kit from his flight suit pocket and opened it. He removed a bottle of disinfectant, several gauze bandages, and a roll of adhesive tape. He soaked a wad of cotton with the medicine. "Grit your teeth, Poncho. You're gonna feel this."

"Shit. After what those pricks did to me, this will be a piece of cake." Custer lay his head on the satchel and closed his eyes. He was exhausted from his ordeal, and the sting of the ointment was almost pleasurable to him.

Wilder dressed Custer's wounds to the extent he could. He gathered several bamboo sticks and tore the shirt from one of the dead Vietcong. He fashioned a makeshift splint around Custer's forearm and secured them with the dirty shirt.

Custer winced but said nothing.

"Sorry, Ed, but I have to immobilize this arm. Once we get it in a sling and get some APC's in you, the pain should ease a bit."

"Whatever you say, Nurse Nightingale, but Charlie over there's gonna wake up, and he'll be pissed when he sees your party favors. We need to get moving."

"Almost done." Wilder finished wrapping the arm. He fashioned a sling from a pair of VC pajama bottoms and carefully placed the cloth loop around Custer's injured arm. He secured the ends over his shoulder and back. "There. How does that feel?"

Custer grinned in spite of his pain. "You missed your calling, Bill. You should've been a quack."

"I'm afraid of needles." Wilder looked at the inert Vietcong soldier to make sure he wasn't regaining consciousness. "I'll get your boots. Then I'm going to tend to our host here."

"Kill the bastard!" Custer gritted his teeth when a wave of pain shot through him.

"He'll wish I had when I'm done." Wilder retrieved the boots and helped Custer put them on. Despite the cuts and swelling suffered from walking through the jungle, the boots fit reasonably well. Wilder tied them, then sat back to look at his handiwork. "Well, you won't win any beauty contests, Ed Custer, but you'll survive to buy me a beer."

"Not if we don't get out of here." Custer looked at the dark jungle.

"In a minute." Wilder dragged the last enemy soldier across the campsite and propped him against a tree in a sitting position. Gathering the rope that had been used on Custer, he tied the man's hands behind him. Wilder then tied him to the tree, making sure that there would be no possibility of escape. He spread the man's legs and staked his feet to the ground with the remaining rope. He reached into his survival vest and pulled out a chocolate bar. He opened the melted candy and rubbed it on the Vietcong's face and bare feet. Wilder then dragged the bodies of the enemy dead to the center of the campsite and piled them on top of each other in full view of their unconscious leader.

All of their throats had been cut.

Looking at the stack of bodies, Wilder said, "A few years ago some enemy soldiers tied one of our people to the ground in the jungle near the Golden Triangle. He was eaten alive." Wilder looked at Custer, his face devoid of emotion. "Now it's pay back time."

Custer stared at him, his mouth agape. "I damn sure am glad we're on the same side. That's all I can say."

"I haven't scratched the surface yet." Wilder helped Custer to his feet. "Can you walk?"

"I'll stumble along."

"Need a crutch?"

"I'll manage. Grab a couple AK's and let's move." Custer was startled by a loud squeal. "What the hell was that?"

"Rats."

"*Rats?*"   .

"They like chocolate." Wilder checked the magazine of an AK-47, ignoring the giant rodents at the edge of the campsite.

"I don't think I want to know what's going to happen. Let's get the hell out of here."

Wilder picked up two more weapons and a bandoleer of ammunition. He looked over his shoulder. Several rats the size of small dogs were cautiously making their way towards the body tied to the tree, their red eyes glowing from the embers of the dying fire. They snarled at the two men standing on the other side of the clearing, but the smell of the sweet chocolate was too strong to resist, and they cautiously moved closer.

Wilder looked at the night sky to get his directional bearings. "Let's go."

They started through the jungle. Neither man said a word when the screaming began.

CIA Headquarters
Langley, Virginia

"Jack, Scott Neilson's on the scrambler from Saigon," the DCO's secretary said.

Jack Wilder's day was already fourteen hours long. After dealing with his Moscow operations and the upcoming Nixon trip to China, he had more on his plate than ten men his age. He was about to leave for home for a well deserved steak when the call came. The Saigon operation had become personal now, and he hoped that Neilson had good news.

"Hello, Scott. How's the heat out your way?"

"Mr. Director, the outside temperature is the least of our worries. I'm afraid the news isn't good."

Wilder wasn't surprised. Nothing from Vietnam was good these days. "What is it?"

"We lost a C-130 in Kontum. Custer was the aircraft commander, and we don't know if he survived. The SAR people went in after sunrise and found some of the crew and a lot of ARVN, all dead. The Vietcong killed any survivors. The flight engineer was found shot in the back. The rest of the crew died in the crash. There's no trace of Custer."

Wilder thought he would collapse under the strain. He dropped wearily into his chair. "Who else knows about this?"

"The command post people. The mood's pretty somber there. It's the third Herk to go down in Kontum, Bill's being the first." Neilson realized that he'd chosen his words poorly. "I'm sorry, sir."

"Not your fault." Wilder's mind was racing. "Keep me posted, Scott."

"Yes, sir. I'll let you know the minute anything comes in."

Wilder hung up the phone and leaned back in his chair. He closed his eyes, overcome with fatigue. He thought about Neilson's words, *"… the third Herk to go down in Kontum, Bill's being the first."* He thought about the hundreds of missions that had gone into Kontum in the past six months. Only three had been lost, and his agents were on two of them. What were the random odds of that happening?

He picked up the phone and called downstairs.

"Moore here. What can I do for you, Mr. Wilder?" Barry Moore was the resident expert on NVA and Vietcong military movement. Located in the bowels of the CIA building, his office monitored all enemy activity in Vietnam. If anyone had an answer to Wilder's question, Moore would.

"Barry, I need a field report on Kontum for the past forty-eight hours, including enemy troop activity. Also, I need to know how many flights have gone in there in that time frame," Wilder said.

"Just a moment, sir."

Wilder waited impatiently, dreading the answer but already knowing what it would be.

"Okay, sir. The short version is that the field is surrounded by

NVA and Vietcong troops. Air strikes have been hitting the area for days, but the bad guys still own most of the real estate. We're not aware from this end of any flights into Kontum during that time. In fact, we've sent messages advising all users in-country to avoid the entire area below ten thousand feet."

"Thanks, Barry." Wilder hung up the phone, wondering what to do next. He knew there was a leak in Saigon, but where? Although he had his suspicions, he didn't want to tighten the noose just yet. He had to reach his son first.

The it hit him. With Custer out of the picture, there was no way he could reach his son at the rubber plantation, and he knew that Bill wouldn't wait indefinitely for someone to contact him. At that instant Jack Wilder felt completely helpless. His position as the Director of Operations for the CIA was less than useless. There was nothing he could do but go home and try to sleep. But sleep would be elusive.

Ninja had disappeared again.

CHAPTER 28

THE VIETNAM JUNGLE

The bright rays of the morning sun were unable to penetrate the cloud cover and the steamy jungle foliage below. As dim as the light on the ground was, it was not welcomed by the two American pilots trying to evade capture. Moving through the thick jungle by night was treacherous enough, but doing so in broad daylight was asking for trouble.

Custer wasn't doing well. Despite having his boots on, his feet bled constantly from the injuries suffered at the hands of his captors. His breathing was labored because of his swollen throat, and his arm was becoming more painful by the minute.

Wilder looked at their surroundings. They were on top of a knoll covered with thick undergrowth. From his perspective, it was the perfect place to hide and transmit their position with either of the two emergency radios they had. The immediate problem was lack of food and water. Wilder could take care of that, but he was uneasy about Custer's condition.

"I can't go any further," Custer whispered. He could barely speak now, and walking was all but impossible.

"We'll stay here and get some rest," Wilder said. He looked

around and found a clump of thick brush surrounded by elephant grass. "We'll tunnel into the bush."

"What about the rats?" Custer vividly recalled the screams from the night before.

"Neither of us smells good enough to eat. They won't bother us." Wilder pulled the thick vegetation back for several feet and stomped the grass and undergrowth down at the rear of a thicket. He looked at Custer. "I'm going to drag you backwards under the arms into our cave here. Then I'll cover our tracks. After we get some sleep, I'll find us some food and water."

"Okay... Think they're looking for us?"

"Count on it."

Custer stared at him. "You don't look scared at all. Do you have any idea what they'll do if they find us?"

"They won't find us."

"I wish I had your confidence, partner." Custer rubbed his throbbing arm.

"Trust me." Wilder's eyes scanned the jungle. He didn't want to say what he felt.

"I don't have any choice." Custer closed his eyes and leaned against a tree. Exhausted, he passed out within seconds.

Once their hiding place was secure, Wilder inventoried their supplies. The Soviet AK-47's were fully loaded. Wilder's Python was ready, and there was a full box of ammo for it. There were two .38 revolvers, each with six rounds. There were four day-night flares, eight gyro-jets, two emergency radios, two flashlights, and a half empty first aid kit. Between them they had two cans of emergency drinking water and four pemmican bars that tasted like compressed sawdust.

There were water vines, wild bread fruit, and palms that Wilder could dig to get at the palm hearts. There were also banana trees. He had to be careful, however, not to leave a trail for the Vietcong. They were masters of the jungle, and the two Americans were on their turf.

Wilder rubbed mud on his face and hands to provide some camouflage. He then removed any shiny patches from his flight suit and put them in his pockets. He did the same for his wounded friend.

Satisfied that he and Custer were safe in their hiding place, he leaned against a tree, his Python by his side. He was asleep within minutes.

National Security Agency
Ft. Mead, Maryland

The Director of the National Security Agency decided put everything on the back burner and go home. The world was going to hell in a hand basket, but he wasn't going to help it get there any more this day.

He picked up his briefcase and headed for the office door. In a short time he would kick off his shoes, sit back in his favorite chair, and enjoy a glass of twelve year-old bourbon. But at that instant, the phone rang. Irritated at the instrument for all the bad news it brought, he reluctantly picked it up. "Spencer."

"Bruce, I'm glad I caught you before you left. I need to see you."

"Where are you, Jack?"

"At the house."

"I'm on my way."

"Neighborhood's become a damn fortress," Spencer said to his driver. He looked around at the unmarked cars guarding the Wilder residence. It was depressing to see what things had come to. He got out of the car and walked quickly to the front porch.

The door opened before Spencer could ring the bell. "Thanks for coming, Bruce."

"You look tired, Jack." The rings under Wilder's eyes were darker than Spencer remembered. He followed his brother-in-law into the kitchen.

"Bad news. We have to talk." They sat at the kitchen table.

"What's going on, Jack? You look like the Grim Reaper's knocking at the door."

"Custer's plane was shot down in Kontum. Everybody's dead and Custer's missing."

"What?" Spencer stared at Wilder, dumbfounded. "This is crazy! I thought that all flights in there had been put on hold."

"They were. And get this; of the three planes shot down there, Bill was on the first, and Custer was on the last."

Spencer cocked his head. "Are you saying they were set up?"

"Looks like it, but nobody seems to know the story there." Wilder poured two whiskies.

"I know how you feel, Jack, but there's no need to drown yourself in that bottle."

"There's more," Wilder said, ignoring Spencer's warning.

"What?"

"*Ninja's* gone missing again."

The Vietnam Jungle

Bill Wilder switched off his emergency radio. While he desperately wanted to contact the rescue teams that he hoped were in the area, he wanted at all costs to avoid alerting the Vietcong. The transmissions were a calculated risk he had to take, and he hoped that the good guys received them first.

"What? What's up?" Custer awakened when Wilder prodded him. He rubbed his face with his good hand. "Did you make contact yet?"

"Not yet, but we'll get there." Wielding his K-bar, Wilder cut a length of vine and allowed the water to drain into an empty water can. He handed it to Custer. "Drink this, Ed. You won't catch anything from it. It's about the only thing around here that's pure." He handed Custer two bananas. "Eat these, then I'll give you two more APC's."

Custer was ravenous. He drank the water and ate the bananas as if it was his last meal. He took the APC's Wilder gave him then leaned back against the tree. The sleep had helped, and he felt reasonably well, considering his physical state. He looked around at his close-in hiding place and nodded approvingly. "It ain't the Ritz, but it works."

"How do you feel?"

"Tolerable."

"How about your feet?"

"They hurt."

"Well, we have to take care of basic transportation."

"Transportation?"

"Your feet. Without them, you're as good as dead." Wilder reached into a flight suit pocket and pulled out a pair of socks wrapped in a plastic bag.

"You're a walking drug store." Custer couldn't believe his eyes. "Where did you get those?"

"I liberated them from your foot locker while I was hiding in your room." Wilder winked at him and took the socks out of the plastic bag. "I'm going to remove your boots and try to dry your feet. I'll dress your wounds and put your boots back on." Wilder carefully removed Custer's boots and gently wiped the blood and sweat from his feet with a red bandanna. Although cut in several places, the bleeding had finally stopped. Wilder applied disinfectant and several gauze pads then carefully slid the clean cotton socks over Custer's feet. He wiped the insides of the boots with the bloody bandanna. Once the boots were on, he laced and tied the leather cords. Satisfied with his handiwork, he gave Custer a thumbs-up.

Custer nodded approvingly. "That feels pretty good. I could almost run a marathon in these things."

"You may have to before this expedition's over." Wilder listened to the jungle sounds and looked around. "It'll be dark soon." He looked at Custer. "You feel up to traveling?"

"I'll be ready." Although Custer knew he didn't stand a chance without Wilder, he was determined to carry his own weight.

"Let's stay close and keep quiet."

"I ain't going nowhere."

Within an hour the jungle was pitch black, the moonlight unable to penetrate the jungle canopy. Wilder looked at his compass. "Ready?"

"No time like the present."

"Let's go."

Franconia, Virginia

Jack Wilder awoke with the sun in his eyes, his head pounding from the whiskey from the night before. He'd slept on the sofa, too tired from the previous night to drag himself to bed. Sitting up, he looked around the room. His eyes focused on his brother-in-law still sleeping in the recliner in the corner of the room.

Wilder rubbed his eyes and made his way to the kitchen. Fumbling with the coffee machine, he thought about events from the previous day. Despite his own failing health, he wondered if Custer was alive. Had he been captured? If so, was he being tortured? In that instant, his mind flashed back to the prison in Hanoi where his oldest son had suffered and died.

He shook his head to clear his mind, but the quick movement only served to aggravate his headache. He wondered about Bill. Where was he? What was he doing? Was he hurt? Was he even alive? Nothing made sense anymore. There were more questions than answers, and neither he nor Spencer were any closer to those answers now than they were the night before.

Wilder sat alone at the kitchen table drinking his coffee. He was "out of airspeed and ideas," as Bill would say when there were no options left. He looked at the black liquid in his cup, hoping it would provide answers to his questions. He thought about his boys when they were young and when he was able to control events around them. *If only we could be back in those happy times …*

"I hope you feel better than you look," Spencer said, dragging Wilder back into the present. He poured himself a cup of coffee and sat across from his brother-in-law.

"Worse." Wilder rubbed his temples.

"I didn't sleep either. I wracked my brain all night trying to figure some options, and I'm coming up short. We don't have anybody in theater that we can trust on this?"

"Nobody other than Bill or Ed. I've examined this thing from every angle, Bruce, and every time I come to the same conclusion."

"What's that?"

"We have to bring them in. All of them."

Spencer shook his head in disagreement. "You do that, Jack, and your leak disappears. Look, we don't know why Custer went into Kontum, or even if he was supposed to. Let's assume someone set him up and go with that premise first."

"You were always the analyst, Bruce." Wilder scratched the stubble on his face. "Okay, let's assume that someone did set him up. How could they get away with sending him in there without anybody else knowing?"

"They did it with Bill when he went into Khe Sanh," Spencer said. "There's so much confusion over there, it would be easy."

"I'll grant you that." Wilder thought for a moment. "But whoever it is has firsthand knowledge of enemy troop movements, and he has the ability to direct missions wherever he wants."

"True, but people in the command post don't. They only set up the missions that are handed to them. The original orders come from MACV or the embassy."

"I don't think MACV is the problem, Bruce. Too much visibility. It has to be someone at a lower level. Someone that can change things at the last minute."

Spencer thought about it. "Okay. That makes sense. Someone at the local level would be low enough on the totem pole such that no one else would notice."

"That leaves Neilson, Bryant, and Berwick."

"I doubt Neilson could do it without being detected. And I thought you said Berwick was on our side."

"I do, Bruce, but my son doesn't. Don't ask me why. The kid came clean with Bill when we met in Cam Ranh. Besides, he works in intelligence. He can't set these missions up. He only briefs the crews on what's going on. Likewise with Bryant. And I think he's pretty much FIGMO. Berwick's running that office now."

They sat in silence, each man considering every possibility from different angles. However, it was up to Wilder to decide what to do since Neilson and Bill worked for him. As far as Berwick was concerned, the young captain was a non-issue in Wilder's mind. Scott Neilson had been in the *business* for years and had an excellent reputation. His record had put him in consideration for Saigon Chief-of-Station to begin with. Although not the most desirable location in the world, it was a high visibility assignment with a great deal of potential. Wilder was almost embarrassed for even thinking that Neilson could be bought. It had to be someone close to Neilson, someone that had access to everything in the embassy. That could be almost anyone. *But just suppose ...*

"Jack, I have an idea. It's a long shot, but it's so crazy, it might just work."

"I'm listening." Wilder looked over his cup.

Spencer walked across the room, collecting his thoughts. "Okay. Let's suppose for a moment that people in Saigon find out that Bill is alive and in a safe house somewhere in the States and that—"

"What?"

Spencer held up his hand. "Hold on, Jack. Hear me out." He pressed his finger against his lips for a second. "Let's say that he's being trained for another foreign duty assignment. We put the word out through official channels that the Agency is looking for volunteers to train with him in a special operations mission, and that Vietnam vets will be given a priority look-see." He waited for a reaction.

"Keep going." Wilder was intrigued.

"Give Neilson the official word and have him screen potential candidates. That will give him free reign to talk to anyone he wants to, and we'll see who or what surfaces. I think Petrov will jump at it because it will give him *carte blanche* to finish what he started, and it'll narrow the playing field because he'll secretly be in our chosen circle."

"Sounds like a long shot, Bruce. We'll have to study this in detail."

"We're pretty much out of options."

"There's just one small problem," Wilder said.

"What's that?"

"We have to find Bill first."

The Vietnam Jungle

Wilder switched on his radio and silently transmitted the emergency signal that he hoped would be picked up by search and rescue teams.

He transmitted for fifteen minutes, then switched the radio off. Packing it into his survival vest, he nudged Custer from a fitful sleep.

"God, I hurt. Got any more APC's?" Custer sat up and rubbed his face.

"Not many." Wilder rummaged through one of his pockets and pulled out a small bottle. "Take two but hold off on the rest, Ed. There's no more where they came from."

"Give me one."

Wilder handed a pill to Custer then took a compass reading. Pleiku was to the southwest, and it was the closest contact with friendly forces that Wilder knew of. Although travel would be dangerous, they couldn't stay where they were. The area was rife with enemy soldiers, and it was just a matter of time before they closed in.

"How are your feet?"

"They hurt, but I'll survive. Any luck with the radio?"

"Not yet, but I'll keep trying. They'll find us sooner or later," Wilder said. "They know we're out here."

"So does Charlie." Under different circumstances, Custer wouldn't be so concerned, but he knew his physical condition was a burden to both of them. "Look, Bill, I can't travel with any speed, and I'm just holding you back. I think you should go on your own and leave me in a good hiding place. I can wait it out."

"Ain't happening, buster." Wilder regarded him like a parent looking at a mischievous five-year old. "You may out rank me, Ed Custer, but I'm not leaving your ass here. End of subject."

"I had to ask." The relief was obvious on Custer's face. "Thanks."

"Let's choke down this designer meal. We'll move out when it gets dark." Wilder handed Custer some bananas. They ate the fruit and drank the remaining water. Wilder buried the peels in the mud and covered the ground with dead palm leaves. He stuffed the empty can in a flight suit pocket.

While waiting in silence for darkness to come, each man turned to his innermost thoughts. For a moment, they were somewhere else, each with someone he loved. Vietnam didn't exist; only their family and friends.

Their solitude was interrupted by screeching birds, and they were instantly thrust back into their hostile environment. It was time to move out. Without a word, they checked their survival vests once more and began to move into the night.

The two pilots slogged through the dense jungle at a speed slower than either would have liked. Although Custer said nothing, he was in chronic pain and was hampered by his injuries. Wilder knew that his friend wouldn't be able to travel much further, and that their moving only made matters worse. They would have to find a place to hide until they could be rescued. There was no other choice.

After several hours, they stopped to rest. Wilder dug a tunnel through some undergrowth, and the two airmen hid themselves in the bush. Wilder cut a water vine and held it over Custer's face, allowing the clear fluid to drain into his mouth. Custer relished the cool liquid. Cutting one for himself, Wilder leaned against a palm tree and drank. He looked around at the darkness.

"Ed, we can't go on. Traveling in the dark is too risky, and there are too many booby traps. Daylight's not an option either. The bad guys are everywhere." Wilder looked at the sky. "This is as good a spot as any. It's high enough for a chopper to get in, and there's a field of elephant grass to the west."

"Guess my idea wasn't so bad after all."

"Forget it. I'm not leaving you alone."

"No argument here," Custer said. He took several deep breaths, hoping to ease his pain. He looked at his aviator watch. "Two o'clock. Time to make another transmission."

"Okay, mother." Wilder pulled the emergency radio from his breast pocket. Placing the earphone in his right ear, he switched the radio on and listened. His senses came alive when he heard a voice over the guard channel.

"Spare Five-Zero, this is Rescue One, over."

Wilder could barely contain himself. "There's a Jolly Green up there looking for us."

Custer sat up but said nothing.

"Spare Five-Zero, if you read, give us a slow count to ten and back. We need to get a fix on your azimuth."

Struggling to stay calm, Wilder keyed the mike button. "Rescue One, this is Spare Five-Zero. I read you five-by-five, over."

"We've found them!" the chopper pilot shouted over the ship's interphone. With those words, the crew in the giant helicopter began to scan the jungle below. *"Roger, Spare Five-Zero, we copy. I need your authentication number, guy."*

Wilder was mildly irritated with the rescue pilot's request, but he understood the necessity of making sure they each were talking to the correct person. The enemy could listen to American radio transmissions and get a fix on their positions.

"What's your authentication number, Ed?"

Custer put his hand against his temple, unable to think through the pain. "I—I don't know. I can't remember."

Wilder had to think fast. He knew that the rescue pilot would leave the area if he suspected a hoax. He decided to take a chance. "The aircraft commander is injured. This is Bill Wilder. My authentication is one-zero-niner-zero, over."

There was a protracted silence. Finally, the chopper pilot said, *"I don't think so, Charlie. If you can't come up with something better than that—and I mean right damn now—we'll call in the fast-movers."*

"This is no *fucking* joke!" Wilder shouted into the radio. "I'm with Ed Custer, and we're the only two left of mission six-six-bravo into Kontum. The bad guys are everywhere, and you need to get our asses outta here! And I mean *right-fucking-now!*" Wilder's eyes were wild. He scanned the darkness around him, hoping that his voice didn't attract attention.

"Roger, Five-Zero, standby."

"Hurry the hell up!" Frustrated, Wilder wanted to throw the radio into the jungle but held it against his forehead instead. It was their only link to the outside world, and he clutched it tightly. He looked at Custer, barely able to make out his friend's face in the dark.

Custer's eyes were locked onto his.

"This is bullshit! They want us to *stand by!*"

"They're verifying us with Hilda," Custer replied, rubbing his broken arm. "I hope the bitch doesn't screw this one up."

"Cross your fingers."

The wait seemed like an eternity, but it was less than two minutes. *"Five-Zero, this is Rescue One. We're coming to get you, guys. Give us a five count and a gyro-jet. Once we get a visual, we'll move in."*

A wave of relief washed over Wilder. Giving Custer a thumbs up, he pressed the transmit button and counted to five and back to zero. He then pulled a gyro-jet flare from his survival vest and cocked it. Looking at Custer, Wilder held the flare out at arm's length and snapped the trigger. The flare ignited and flew straight up through the jungle canopy, lighting the sky above it.

"Five-Zero, we have a visual on your signal and are coming in. Be advised that there is enemy activity to your north, less than five hundred meters from your position. When you hear our rotors, give us vectors til we're overhead. We'll drop a penetrator. What's your medical status? Over."

"I'm okay, but Custer's a mess. I'll hook him up first, over."

"Roger, that. Hang in there, sir. We'll be there in a jiffy." In pilot-speak, a jiffy was the equivalent of a nano-second. But it was a lifetime to the desperate pilots waiting on the ground.

Holding onto the radio as if it was a lifeline, Wilder pulled his .357 Python from its holster. He quickly checked the weapon to make sure it was fully functional. He had never used it for anything except target practice, but now he was ready to kill with it.

"I see them!" Custer's eyes locked onto the red rotating beacon on the helicopter. "They're coming from the west."

"Got 'em." Wilder reached for his compass and aimed it at the sound of the helicopter. He looked at the numbers on the glowing dial and keyed the mike button on the radio. "Rescue One, we're at your two o'clock position, approximately two hundred meters. Fly heading zero-eight-zero."

"Zero-eight-zero," the chopper pilot replied, turning immediately to the new heading. *"Copy range. Keep talking, guys. Be advised Charlie's spotted us and is moving in for the intercept. Be ready to move fast."*

Wilder looked to the north. He couldn't see them but he could hear their screams. "Keep coming," he yelled into the radio. He could see the rotating beacon getting larger by the second. "Fifty meters. Turn right ten degrees."

"Ten right." The helicopter was now heading straight for them.

At that same instant, a Vietcong patrol spotted the Jolly Green rescue bird and began firing at it. Several meters to the north, a round from a Chinese rocket powered grenade launcher flew towards the chopper.

"RPG!" the paramedic shouted over the interphone. The pilot immediately pushed forward on the controls, forcing the helicopter into a dangerous dive at the trees below. The machine lurched down and to the right in an attempt to avoid the shoulder-fired missile. The projectile flew past the chopper and crashed harmlessly into the jungle behind the ship.

Two Cobra gunships were escorting the Jolly Green, one on either side. The first one fired two rockets at the spot where the RPG came through the trees. The ground erupted with several explosions when the rockets found their targets. One missile hit an enemy ammo cache, and the ground shook when the stored ammunition began to cook off.

The shock waves from the explosions hit Wilder and Custer, knocking them down. "Jesus Christ! Those bastards are right next door to us," Custer shouted.

"Let's move!" Wilder yelled. Grabbing Custer by the arm and holding the radio to his ear, he shouted, "Come back to your left a little. Twenty more meters and you're right over us. Get that damn penetrator down here! Charlie's on our ass!"

"Holding over head," the pilot transmitted. The giant helicopter stopped its forward movement and held a stationary position. "Lower away," the pilot shouted over the interphone.

The paramedic in the open door threw a switch, allowing the steel cable to unwind. The jungle penetrator slid down through the thick jungle foliage. The heavy steel base of the device was pointed so that it would punch through any vines or branches it encountered, and the fold-out arms and tie straps were locked closed to prevent any entanglement.

Wilder anxiously watched the device come down. It couldn't move fast enough for him. Looking over his shoulder, he didn't see anyone, but he could distinctly hear the Vietcong shouting as they made their way through the jungle. It was just a matter of time before they spotted the two downed pilots. Wilder prayed that he could get Custer hooked up to the penetrator before time ran out. He turned his attention back to the rescue device looming just out of reach. *Come on, come on!*

The steel shaft hit the ground with a dull thud, and Wilder immediately went to work pulling the leg bar out and unhooking the body strap. He dragged Custer across the jungle floor with strength borne from fear. He could hear the Vietcong in the distance, and the combination of their screams and the helicopter above urged him to work faster.

He forced Custer to straddle the leg bar and hug the steel cylinder. Wilder then slipped the strap over Custer's head and underneath his arms. Custer was permanently attached to the device now. If he passed out and lost his grip, the helicopter crew could still get him onboard. Satisfied that his friend was secure, Wilder shook the cable to indicate that he was ready. He keyed his radio. "Pull him up, now!"

"*Coming up!*" the pilot replied. Hearing the words and feeling the cable shake back and forth, the paramedic threw the switch. The cable began to rewind, and the penetrator began its ascent.

"Hang in there, Ed," Wilder shouted. "You'll be in the chopper in a minute. I'm right behind you, buddy." He patted Custer on the shoulder and backed away as the ungainly device and its passenger moved upwards. Custer was on his own now, and in less than a minute he would be safely on board the helicopter.

The Vietcong were moving in. Gunfire rattled the darkness, and the stinging whisper of invisible bullets was only inches away. Wilder dove to the ground and rolled behind a tree. He looked up at the chopper and saw Custer being pulled inside. *Take care, buddy*, Wilder said to himself. The VC were almost on him, and he knew that a snowball in hell stood more of a chance than he did of being rescued.

He keyed the mike button. "Get the hell out of here, and get Custer to a hospital. I'm gone."

"*We're starting back down. We'll have you out of there PDQ!*"

"Negative! Charlie's everywhere, and I'm outta here!" Wilder switched off the radio and shoved it into a pocket. The Vietcong were closing in, and Wilder was on the edge of panic. But panic wouldn't save him; only self-control and rational thinking would do that. *Take it easy, Billy boy. Don't lose it.* Releasing the safety on his Python, he slid into the darkness of the bush.

If the Cong wanted him, they would have to come and get him. But the price would be high.

"We have to go back for him, but he wants us to clear the area." The chopper pilot glanced at Custer when he was pulled into the chopper. "What's with this guy?"

"Forget it," Custer shouted. "When he says leave, he means it. He's his own rescue squad." Custer lowered his head to the floor and closed his eyes.

Ping! A round from an AK-47 hit the armor plating under the pilot's seat. The pilot keyed his mike button. *"This is Rescue One. Return to base. R-T-B now."* The giant helicopter turned to the southwest and climbed as fast as it could, followed by the Cobras. The three birds disappeared into the night sky.

Bill Wilder was alone.

CHAPTER 29

CIA HEADQUARTERS
LANGLEY, VIRGINIA

Jack Wilder and his brother-in-law had solved the world's problems over coffee a thousand times, but the real world was something different. He didn't know where his son was, and, until Bill was found, he was helpless to do anything to bring this madness to an end.

His limited supply of patience was about used up. Wilder wasn't the type of man to sit and watch helplessly. He picked up the secure phone and dialed a series of numbers.

"Station watch, Saigon," a voice on the other end said. "Alan Smith here."

"This is Jack Wilder calling from Langley. Is Neilson about?"

"Director Wilder?"

"The same."

"Sir, Mr. Neilson isn't in right now," Smith said, almost embarrassed. "He left the office a couple of hours ago. He's been putting in some long hours, and he decided to cut loose early and get some sleep. Is there anything I can do for you?"

"Listen carefully, Al. This is most important."

"Yes, sir." Al Smith was instantly alert to the man from Langley.

"I want you and a team of Marine guards to go to Neilson's residence and escort him to Tan Son Nhut Air Base. A C-141 will be waiting there. He's to board that plane under guard and leave for Andrews immediately. He's to talk to no one, and I mean *no one*. No baggage, no nothing. Is that clear?" Wilder's voice left no mistake as to his intent.

"Yes, sir. The commander of the Marine embassy guard is standing here with me. I'll take care of it right away. Mr. Neilson will be at Tan Son Nhut within the hour." Smith knew not to question the CIA Operations Chief, but his curiosity got the best of him. "Is there anything I need to know, Mr. Wilder? I mean is there anything else I can do?"

"Just get him on that plane, Al. If he asks any questions, tell him I need him immediately for a special project. That's all you know. In any event, he sees and talks to no one until he's on that plane. Understood?"

"Yes, sir."

Wilder hung up the phone and picked up his cup. He sipped the black liquid. *It's time to deal the cards.*

The Vietnam Jungle

Gunfire was heavy and Wilder couldn't run. His only hope of avoiding capture was to blend in with his surroundings. A nearby pool of stagnant water choked with reeds and covered with think green algae caught his attention. He slid silently slid into the muck. Before completely submerging himself, he broke off a reed and fashioned a long straw. Lying on his back and placing one end into his mouth, he pointed the other end upwards. He disappeared beneath the green slime, the only evidence of his existence was the hollow reed that became one of the thousands that rose around it.

The infuriated Vietcong ran through the jungle, looking in vain for the renegade American that had executed their comrades. Sound was amplified in the water, and Wilder heard the splashing when the Cong ran through the pond. Several times he thought they would find him; they nearly stepped on him more than once. But despite several near misses, Wilder remained untouched and undiscovered.

After several minutes, the noise and gunfire began to fade. The jungle gradually fell silent once more as the VC made their way south. Wilder stayed below the surface, taking no chances. He waited for several minutes, then slowly poked his head through the scum. He opened his eyes and looked around, moving his head slowly so as not to attract attention. The Vietcong were gone. He looked at the night sky. There was no sign of the rescue helicopter. He slowly lifted his Python revolver out of the muck. It was covered with slime, but the heavy coat of oil protected the weapon from the water's effects.

Satisfied that he was alone, Wilder crawled out of the muck and into a clump of bushes. He removed a plastic bag from one of his pockets and took out a dry rag. He wiped the slime from his face and cleaned the revolver to the extent he could. He repeated the procedure with his military .38 and his compass.

Wilder put the military revolver back into his survival vest and slid the Python into its holster. He looked around to get his bearings and took a compass reading. He needed to make himself scarce, and he had to avoid any more encounters with the Vietcong. He was in enough trouble already without calling any more attention to himself. He patted his revolver again for comfort and began his silent trek through the jungle.

Tan Son Nhut Air Force Base

The C-141 Starlifter rose from the runway and turned eastward. The pilot flew the plane at its maximum rate to quickly gain altitude as a precaution against enemy ground fire. The jet climbed to 33,000 feet on the first leg of its journey. It would hook up with refueling aircraft several times on its way non-stop to Washington. The aircraft commander connected the automatic pilot and tilted his seat back. It was going to be a long flight.

Scott Neilson sat on the rear bunk in the cockpit. He looked at the Marine guard sitting next to him. "May as well get some sleep, Captain. It's going to be a long ride."

"Thank you, sir, but I'm fine. I'll just keep you company if you don't mind," the Marine replied. He was careful not to say anything else.

Am I under arrest? Neilson knew that there was no point in asking questions. The Marine next to him knew less than he did. Neilson slumped in his seat and closed his eyes. The whine of the engines soon put him to sleep.

CIA Headquarters
Langley, Virginia

Jack Wilder didn't know how to react to the news. Ed Custer had been rescued. Although his injuries were extensive, they weren't life threatening. Wilder was grateful that Custer was safe, but the news that his son had been left behind nearly crushed his spirit. He felt more alone now than when his wife died. He stared at the picture on his desk. In it his wife sat beside him on the sofa, while the two boys stood behind them. It was the day that he'd been sworn in as the Director of Operations for the CIA. It was one of the happier times in his life. Since then, however, his position in the Agency had only brought him pain. But he couldn't resign now. He had to finish what he started.

Wilder had to bring his son home.

He dialed a private number at Fort Mead, Maryland. It was answered on the first ring. "Hello, Jack. What's up?"

"Custer's been rescued. He's suffered some serious injuries, but he'll recover."

"That's good news, Jack, but you didn't call just to tell me that. I can hear between the lines."

"Bill was with him in the jungle, and he's still out there." There was no other way to say it.

"My God!" The words hit Spencer like a hammer between the eyes.

"The rescue team couldn't get to him. The Vietcong were everywhere. I fear the worst."

"Stop it, Jack. Don't let your imagination run wild. It's the worst thing you can do."

"But—"

"Listen to me. That boy is one the most resourceful people I've ever known. He's in his element now, and you know that."

Wilder said nothing.

"If Custer got out with his injuries, that tells me that Bill had something to do with it. I have to think that he stayed behind for another reason." Spencer was trying to convince himself as much as his brother-in-law.

"Why would he pass up a rescue?"

"Who knows? There could be a thousand reasons. He may have stayed behind to hold off the bad guys so Custer could get out. I don't know. But I can tell you that my money's on him. You have to believe that, Jack."

"They're going back in at daybreak to look for him. I only hope to God he can hold out til then." Wilder sank in his chair, despair overcoming him.

"Jack, listen to me. We will get him out of there. Believe that!" Spencer wondered if his brother-in-law was becoming irrational. "I'm coming over. You stay put. I'll take a helicopter and be there in a few minutes." Spencer clicked off the line and dialed Wilder's secretary.

"Mr. Wilder's office," his secretary answered.

"Linda, it's Bruce Spencer. No time for small talk. Listen carefully."

"Go ahead." She sensed something wrong.

"Go into Jack's office and sit with him. Don't let him out of your sight, no matter what. Talk to him. Tell him anything and everything that's on your mind. Occupy him and don't let him be alone. I'll be there as fast as I can."

"I understand."

"Please hurry." The line went dead.

Linda didn't bother to knock.

"What's up, Linda?" Wilder looked at her with red eyes.

"Jack, I need your help in deciding what to buy my husband for his birthday." She did her best to hide her shock at his appearance. "Men know more about that stuff than I do. So, give me some ideas."

In a short time, Spencer walked unannounced into Wilder's office. "What's this? Starting the party with out me, eh?" He winked at Wilder's secretary.

"Fresh coffee's on the way." Linda left the office and closed the door.

"What's going on here, Bruce? I was born in the dark, but it wasn't yesterday." Wilder looked suspiciously at his brother-in-law.

"You and I are going to visit." Spencer sat in his leather chair.

"Visit?"

"Yes. I'm staying with you til Bill's found. I'm not leaving you alone, and that's that. Don't even think of arguing with me." Spencer would not be denied.

"Why? You think I'm smoking dope and skipping rope?" Wilder was indignant.

"No. Just upset, Jack. And justified, I might add. I'm here to support you, not baby-sit."

Wilder stared at him. Finally, he said, "I know what you're doing, Bruce, and I appreciate it." Family means everything after all.

Tan Son Nhut Command Post

Every one cheered when the news of Custer's rescue came in. Mercer was on duty when the call came from Pleiku. Hanging up the phone, he shouted the news across the room. It was the first good news since Custer's plane went down.

Berwick ran from his office. "What's all the commotion? Somebody get Jane Fonda?"

"Custer's been rescued," someone shouted.

"Shit hot! Where is he?"

"Pleiku. The doctors patched him up, and he's on his way back here now. Should land in less than an hour," Mercer said.

"What about the rest of the crew?"

The smile left Mercer's face. "They didn't make it."

"I'm going to the hospital when he gets here."

"I wouldn't do that, Tom." Mercer frowned at him.

"Why not?"

"According to the guys at Pleiku, he's pretty pissed at you. Something about being sent into a firestorm. What's he talking about?"

"Beats me." Berwick shrugged. "Kontum was secure when he went up there, but I told him that the bad guys were everywhere. He—"

"What? We had no missions to Kontum."

"Sure we did. That's what frag order said."

"What frag order? What are you talking about?"

"Look at the goddamn thing!" Berwick was irritated at Mercer's tone. He went to a corner file cabinet and pulled out the folder of the previous week's missions. Flipping through them, he found Custer's mission order. His jaw dropped when he scanned the sheet of paper.

"Well?"

"Holy shit!" Berwick stared at the document.

"Is that all you can say? *Holy shit?* Give me that." Mercer pulled the paper from Berwick's hand and carefully examined it. He looked at Berwick. "This frag order is for Pleiku, not Kontum. What the hell's going on here?"

Berwick frowned at the document. "I have no idea."

Mercer leaned close to Berwick's ear. "Your office. Now!" Mercer stormed down the hall, Berwick following in silence. They entered the empty room and Mercer slammed the door.

Mercer stood with his back to the door, his hands on his hips. "Start talking. Tell me why Custer went into Kontum. And while you're at it, tell me why you told him the field was cold? Last I heard, the bad-asses owned that real estate."

Berwick gaped at him. "Look, my info was that the field was secure but the VC were in the area. His orders—the ones I saw—were to go into Kontum with a load of ARVN troops. One trip up and back from Tan Son Nhut. That's it."

"The ARVN were expected in Pleiku. Where did you get this damn thing?" Mercer waved the document in Berwick's face.

"It was in my basket the day before the mission, like usual. In fact, Custer came in and looked it. He knew beforehand where he was going, and I told him that the area was mostly safe. VC were in the area, but gunships were holding them at bay. I got *that* information from MACV."

"Who at MACV?"

"Bryant. They brief him, and he passes the info to me. You know that. The flight orders and mission setup were in my basket when I came in the day before Custer's mission." Berwick threw up his hands in frustration. "I don't make this stuff up, Dan."

"Yeah, well, I'll tell you something, mister, and you'd better not say a damn word to anyone. For your information, Bill Wilder was on that plane too."

"What are you talking about? He's dead!" Berwick recalled their meeting in Cam Ranh. *Why was Wilder on that plane?*

"You heard me. Everybody thought he died in Kontum, but it seems that he's been hiding out somewhere. Somehow he got on Custer's flight but got left behind during the rescue. From what Custer said, Wilder saved his life. And now he's out there trying to stay alive while we stand around jerking each other off wondering how any of this happened in the first place." Mercer was beside himself. "This is a cluster-fuck of epic proportions!"

"Christ, Almighty! Wait til his father finds out."

"I wouldn't want to be a fly on the wall there when the shit hits the fan in his office." Mercer left the room without another word.

What the hell's going on? Berwick didn't know what to think. He and Custer were the only ones in Vietnam that knew Bill Wilder was alive—until now. He picked up the secure phone. "Operator, this is *immediate* priority. This is Captain Berwick, and I need a secure line to Langley, Virginia. I need to speak to Mr. Jack Wilder ... Yes, *that* Jack Wilder. I'll wait."

After a minute, a familiar voice came on the line. "Wilder here."

"Mr. Wilder, this is Captain Berwick calling from Tan Son Nhut."

Wilder looked at his watch. It was the middle of the night in Vietnam, and he wondered why Berwick would call him at all, never mind during the graveyard shift. "This must be important, Tom. What's up?"

"Sir, Ed Custer's been pulled out of the jungle."

"I know. I got the word a while ago."

"He, um, he's being flown to Tan Son Nhut, sir. He'll be here soon." There was a pregnant silence. "Is there anything you need me to do, sir?"

"No, but thanks for the call." Wilder broke the connection. There was no time for niceties. He looked at Spencer, who had been dozing before the phone woke him. "That was Berwick. They just got the word at Tan Son Nhut about Custer."

"Nothing on Bill?"

"No, but everyone now knows he's alive and in-country, and it's just a matter of time til Petrov finds out." Wilder rubbed his eyes then placed his hands flat on his desk. "I'm getting Custer out of there." Wilder didn't ask for an opinion, and none was offered. He picked up the phone and dialed the Pentagon. There would be no stops in the Philippines or anywhere else. This flight, like Neilson's, would come directly to Andrews Air Force Base.

The Vietnam Jungle

Suffering from exhaustion, Wilder slept soundly under the jungle undergrowth. His ordeal from the night before, along with the resulting lack of sleep, finally caught up with him. Despite the heat, humidity, and insects, he slept better than he had in days.

The rising heat woke him, and he slowly crept from beneath the undergrowth. He cautiously scanned his surroundings and listened to the sounds of the jungle. Other than birds and monkeys, there was silence. He checked his equipment and found everything in place. His weapons, along with his martial training, would prove unhealthy to anyone that chose to confront him. Nevertheless, there was fear in the pit of his stomach.

He pulled the radio from his vest and placed the earphone in his right ear. He listened for a signal ... anything.

Nothing.

He turned on the emergency locator transmitter, and the radio transmitted silently over the international guard frequency of 121.5. Fifteen minutes later, he switched off the device, slipped it into his pocket, and prepared to move out. Looking at his compass, he decided to move to the southwest. He had to keep his guard up and move carefully. Even if there were no Vietcong around, there were any number of booby traps.

He ate three bananas and drank from a water vine. He carefully buried the peels and rubbed mud on the exposed end of vine to hide the cut. Although traveling in daylight was dangerous, he couldn't stay where he was. The Vietcong were searching for him, and he had to make himself scarce.

Wilder cautiously made his way through the undergrowth, keeping to the shadows and avoiding open areas. He was ever mindful of the traps scattered through the jungle, especially in areas where Americans were present.

Booby traps ranged from punji sticks to grenades, mines, and other explosive devices. Punji sticks were sharp shafts of bamboo, often dipped in human feces, arranged in tight rows in tall grass or jungle undergrowth where they couldn't be seen. If the Americans were fired upon, they would retreat to the jungle or hide in the grass, where they often would fall victim to the lethal spikes. They were particularly nasty, and many troops died from the resulting infections, rather than the puncture wounds themselves.

Other traps consisted of a bullet buried straight up with its firing pin on a bamboo stub that fired when someone stepped on the bullet's tip. There was the Malay whip. It was a log with poisonous spikes tied all around it that was suspended between two trees. Held back by lines, the device would release when American soldiers hit a trip wire with their feet. The log would swing down and take out several victims at once. The use of these traps was indiscriminate, and they alienated both the locals and the Americans against the Vietcong.

Wilder traveled for several hours, finally coming to a small stream. Crouching in the bushes, he carefully examined the stream and the opposite bank. He was about to step into the water when his eyes caught the glint of a shiny object. Freezing in position, he examined the object carefully. It was one of several metal spikes that protruded from a basketball-size piece of concrete. The concrete ball was suspended by a rope and held back by another line. Wilder's eyes slowly followed the line to the edge of the bank in front of him.

It was strung across the ground between two stakes with a trigger device on one end. If Wilder tripped the line with his foot, the spiked ball would come crashing down and meet him with full force when he was in the middle of the stream. In an instant, he would be impaled on the primitive killing machine.

Wilder carefully reached out with a stick and hooked it over the line. He pulled sharply on the stick and rolled behind a tree. In seconds the ball swung across the narrow trail, its deadly spikes stabbing at the air. It swung harmlessly back and forth, finally coming to a stop in the middle of the stream.

Wilder stared at the lethal device. Looking at the steel spikes, he had to give the Vietcong a measure of respect. They were a formidable enemy, and he would be extra careful in their back yard.

He crossed the stream further down and dug into the bushes. He took out his radio and turned it on. Listening through the ear piece, Wilder transmitted on the emergency frequency. He continued for fifteen minutes. He was about to turn the radio off when he heard his call sign.

"Spare Five-Zero, this is Rescue Two, over."

Wilder's heart began to race. "Rescue Two, this is Spare Five-Zero. Where are you guys?" His eyes frantically scanned the sky, and he shrank into the bushes, afraid that enemy soldiers would hear him.

"Five-Zero, I read you five-by. Give us a count."

Wilder keyed the mike button again. "One-two-three … "

"Five-Zero, we have a bearing on you. You're at our six o'clock position. Are you aware of any enemy activity in your area?"

"Negative." Wilder could barely control his excitement. Looking around, he spotted a small clearing to his right. The grass was about waist high, perfect for a quick pickup—or an ambush. "There's a clearing on my right. I'm moving there now."

"Roger, that, Five-Zero. Authenticate to keep us legal."

"One-zero-niner-zero!" The adrenaline was pumping.

"Copy, Bill. Let us know when you see us. Be ready."

"I was born ready." Dry humor was better than none, and it helped calm Wilder's frayed nerves. He quickly made his way to the edge of the clearing while scanning the area for any enemy activity. Seeing the black dot of the helicopter coming towards him, he keyed the mike button. "You're headed right for me. I'm in the trees at the far end of the clearing."

"Roger. We have a visual on the LZ with two Cobras in tow. Give us orange smoke."

"Coming up." Wilder took a flare from his survival vest and pulled the cap off the pull-ring. He started towards the center of the field.

At that instant one of the Cobras fired an air-to-ground missile to the left of Wilder's position. The missile hit a Vietcong camp, and the hidden stockpile of weapons began to light off.

Wilder dove to the ground and pulled the Python from its holster. He looked frantically in every direction for any movement but saw nothing. The helicopter was getting closer. It was time to make his move.

He pulled the ring on the flare and tossed it towards the center of the field. In seconds, the flare came to life, filling the air with bright orange smoke and the pungent smell of burning sulfur. The helicopter pilot instantly spotted the smoke and headed straight for it.

It was also spotted by the Vietcong.

The helicopter positioned itself directly above the smoke and began to hover. *"Penetrator coming down. Enemy activity at your ten o'clock, two hundred meters. Cobras moving in."*

"Copy," was all Wilder could manage. The time for hiding was over. He was literally in a race for his life. He ran towards the helicopter with his Python in his right hand. The jungle penetrator was coming down fast, but to Wilder it hung suspended in mid-air. After an eternity of seconds the device struck the ground.

Wilder grabbed a strap and pulled it over his head and underneath his arms. "Get me outta here!" he shouted into the radio. The penetrator started up with a jerk when the helicopter began to climb. Despite his grip on the metal cylinder, Wilder was buffeted by the rotor down wash. His life was literally hanging in the balance, and he hoped the helicopter crew was having a good day.

Enemy soldiers ran across the field, firing both at him and the helicopter. Wilder shot one in the chest. Before he could fire a second round, one of the Cobras fired a burst from a M24A 20mm cannon, killing all of them instantly.

The paramedics pulled Wilder into the helicopter. He looked around frantically, not sure he was inside the aircraft. Finally, seeing the familiar American flight suits and the round eyes looking back at him, he collapsed on the deck, his heart pounding, thankful to be alive.

"Welcome aboard Lizard Air, Captain Wilder, with non-stop service to Pleiku," the paramedic shouted over the engine noise. "No long-legged stewardesses with cocktails, but at least you boarded the right flight."

Wilder held onto the man's arm. "Never thought I'd ever see you guys. I swear I'll never bad mouth helicopters again." A grin appeared through the sweat and dirt.

"Yeah, yeah, we hear that all the time." The paramedic gave the pilots a thumbs-up, and the helicopter turned towards Pleiku. "Okay, sir, just relax. I'm going to check you out and see what injuries you have." The paramedic began his examination.

"Aside from needing my weekly shower, I'm fine. Honest." Wilder sat up and looked around, glad to be alive. But his thoughts were elsewhere. "What about Custer?"

The paramedic laughed at the mud-covered man in front of him. "You're a piece of work, Captain Wilder. After what you've been through, your first concern is for your friend. You're okay in my book." He pulled a cloth from a bag and soaked it in water. "But you're a mess. I'm gonna scrub your face and see if there's anybody under all that crud."

"What about Custer?"

"I'm the guy that pulled him in. He's was pretty banged up, but he'll be fine. He's in Tan Son Nhut about now, playing grab-ass with the nurses. You must've made an impression on him."

"Huh?"

"He asked about you all the way to the base. Wanted to go back for you," the paramedic said. "You fly-boys sure look out for each other."

"Yeah, well, when your ass is in a sling, the only people you can count on is your crew."

"Ain't it the truth. Just take it easy, sir. You've more than done your job. Now, let me do mine."

Exhaustion took over, and Wilder lowered his head onto a parachute pack and closed his eyes.

The helicopter pilot radioed ahead. "Pleiku tower, this is Rescue Two. We're R-T-B with one, and he's good to go, over."

"Copy, Rescue Two. Radar contact two-seven miles northeast. Squawk two-five-one-zero and ident," the tower controller said.

"Roger." The pilot set the transponder to the new code and pressed the ident switch.

"Okay, Rescue Two. Come on home. Cleared to land on the pad. Medics standing by."

"We're on our way."

Tan Son Nhut Command Post
Saigon

Mercer dropped into his chair when the call came in, relieved that Wilder was plucked from the jungle. The controller at Pleiku confirmed by phone that Wilder had been rescued and that his injuries were minor. But along with the good news, Pleiku told Mercer that he was to say nothing to anyone about the rescue, per Wilder's request. Other than Mercer, no one was to know anything.

This is crazy, Mercer thought, but he knew that Wilder wouldn't make such a request without reason. He went to Berwick's office.

Berwick looked up from his desk, a nervous expression on his face. "What now?" After their last confrontation, he didn't know what to expect.

Mercer closed the door and stood in front of Berwick's desk. "I'll get straight to the point, Berwick. This is between you and me."

"Why not?"

"Wilder was picked up about an hour ago. He's in Pleiku, and he's okay."

"Thank God. That's great news. Have you called his father?"

"Never mind that. No one is to know that he's alive. And I mean *no one*. The only two people that know, other than Pleiku, are you and me. We're not to say anything about his existence, much less his rescue. I'm only telling you because you're aware of him already. Do you understand?"

"What about Custer? Are you going to tell him?"

"No," Mercer said with finality. He looked at the wall map of the Central Highlands. "I don't know what's going on here, but I'm going to do exactly what he wants. You say nothing to anybody, including Bryant." He looked at Berwick. "If you do, I swear I'll have you court-martialed."

"Wait a minute, Mercer." Berwick jumped up. "Where do you get off threatening me? You're the one that told me Wilder was on that plane in the first place. I had no idea about any of this til you announced it to the whole frigging world."

"You must have known that he was alive before any of this happened."

"Why do you say that?" Berwick wasn't sure how much Mercer knew, but he wasn't going to volunteer anything. "You act like this is all my fault. I didn't know he was on that plane. I'm sick and tired of being blamed for every damn thing that goes wrong around here."

Mercer stared at him. Perhaps he had come down too hard on Berwick. But how did Custer's orders get changed, and how did Wilder fit into this? There were no answers, only a stone wall. "Sorry I barked at you, Tom, but somebody's not playing straight with us, and I need to find out who it is."

"No shit." Berwick looked around the room for non-existent answers.

"From now on, no crews leave for the flight line until I see their orders. I'll be the last one to touch those documents before they launch."

"Fine with me."

Mercer left Berwick's office for the BOQ. He had been on duty for twelve hours. It was time for several drinks. Sobriety was but one of the many casualties of war.

CIA Headquarters
Langley, Virginia

Jack Wilder had not been home for days. An empty house was not a home, and Langley had become the center of his existence. For all practical purposes, it was his second home. It also helped him avoid the ghosts that haunted him when he was alone.

Showered and shaved, he felt almost human. He sat down to a breakfast that had been sent from the employee cafeteria. He was pouring a cup of coffee when his brother-in-law walked in.

"Morning, Jack." Spencer noticed his appearance. "A good night's sleep and a hot shower makes all the difference." He took the offered cup and sat in his usual chair.

"I have Linda to thank for that. She said if I didn't take a bath, she'd find gainful employment elsewhere. And speaking of employment, don't you ever go to work? You spend more time here than at the National Silly Authority."

"That place is a zoo. Besides, the coffee's better here."

"Breakfast?"

"No, thanks. I gave at the office." Spencer looked at the bank of telephones on the desk. "No word yet on Bill?"

"No, but Custer's coming non-stop as soon as he's able to travel."

"What's your reasoning?"

"I think his mission was a setup. Somebody gave him bogus information and changed his orders. Then they were changed again after Custer took off to show that Kontum was never in the plan. Has to be someone with regular access to the paperwork. Whether that person knew Bill was on that flight is unknown. I decided to bring Custer out because I fear another attempt on his life. Things are out of control over there, and bringing him back to the States is the only sure way I have of keeping him alive."

"Based on what we know, that sounds like the best course of action."

"Neilson's coming in later today. He thinks I'm putting him in charge of a special project, but, in reality, he's—"

The Pentagon hot line rang, cutting off Wilder in mid-sentence.

Spencer picked it up. "Jack Wilder's office. This is Bruce Spencer." Listening to the message from the Pentagon, he looked at Wilder and smiled. The smile turned into a grin, and he gave his brother-in-law a thumbs-up. "This is the best news I've heard in months. I'll tell him. Thanks."

"What gives?" Wilder put his fork down and looked anxiously at the man with the ear-to-ear grin. "I haven't seen that look for longer than I can remember."

"I'm going to get rid of that perpetual frown on your face, Jack. Bill's been plucked from the jungle, and he's none the worse for wear. He's on his way to Tan Son Nhut as I speak."

Wilder threw his napkin into the air and jumped to his feet. "Great God, Almighty! That's the best news I could ever hope for!" He looked at the morning sky. "You do take care of drunks, fools, and children after all!" Tears of relief washed down his face, but he didn't care. Jack Wilder had reason to live now. His son had been rescued, and it was time to bring him home.

"We need to call McIvor and give him the news," Spencer said, smiling.

"First, I want to get Bill on that plane with Custer. I want those boys home where they belong." Wilder's face beamed, and he paced the floor, waving his hands while he talked.

"Take it easy, Jack. You're going to wear out the carpet." Spencer was happy to see the relief in his brother-in-law's face.

Wilder turned to him. "When all the players are in place, I'm going to set up a team briefing on the bogus project I told you about. Neilson will head the team, or so he'll believe. At some point Bill will make his appearance, and we'll see what happens."

"Players?"

"Volunteers for this special ops mission. The word's already out in Saigon, thanks to Neilson. And I'm willing to bet a year's pay that our leak shows up. Then we'll see what crawls out from under the rocks."

"With Bill in Washington, Petrov won't have any choice but to show."

"I'm counting on it, Bruce."

"Are you going to tell Custer the truth about Slaughter?"

"Eventually."

"We have to be careful here, Jack. We have to keep a lid on Slaughter for as long as we can."

"No one will know about him except us and Bill. We'll keep it that way for now. For the time being we have to get all of our assets in one place. It will allow us to start from a known position and give us complete control. In the meantime, I want to get those boys on a plane." Wilder smiled for the first time in months.

"Let me have the privilege, Jack." Spencer picked up the phone and called the Pentagon. "General Carter, this is Bruce Spencer calling from Jack Wilder's office. I have a mission for you of the highest priority… "

PART THREE

CHAPTER 1

JUNE 4, 1972
ANDREWS AIR FORCE BASE, MARYLAND

Thunderstorms blanketed the Atlantic coast from New York to Florida, and the midnight sky was a soup of rain and fog. Visibility everywhere was nil, and air traffic at Washington National and Dulles airports was at a virtual standstill. Only aircraft equipped for low visibility approaches were making any headway along the eastern seaboard.

Andrews Air Force Base was no different. Fortunately, there weren't many military flights at this time of night, and the C-141 on final approach for runway 36R had auto-land capability. The crew was completely spent. The aircraft had flown non-stop halfway around the world with several air refuelings enroute. The pilots were grateful for small wonders such as the avionics equipment that would relieve them of the stress of trying to land the ship themselves in bad weather in their exhausted state.

"Mac One-Two, you're clear to land. Wind is calm and altimeter is two-niner-eight-zero. Runway visual range is one thousand two hundred."

"Roger, Andrews, cleared to land," the copilot said. The crew went the extra mile to make sure that everything was done and that the landing gear was down. Extreme fatigue was one of the down sides of being a long-haul Air Force pilot, and each crew member was well aware of his personal limitations. "Let's don't miss this one, guys," the co-pilot said. "I don't think I can go anymore."

"Yeah," the pilot said. "Let's land this bitch and go to bed."

"One thousand feet above the field," the co-pilot announced. All eyes were glued to the instruments, and adrenaline was flowing, despite the fatigue. The jet flew down the electronic glide path to the end of the runway. Approaching the touch down point, the throttles slowly came to idle, and the aircraft flared and touched down. The pilot then pressed the red button on the control wheel, disconnecting the auto pilot, and took over manually. He reversed the engines, and the airplane began to decelerate.

A collective sigh of relief swept through the cockpit when the pilot turned off the runway. A *Follow Me* van led the C-141 to the south end of the airport. Reaching their designated parking spot, the crew set the brakes and shut down the engines. Completing their checklists, the crew looked forward to a comfortable bed in some barracks somewhere. Their long ordeal was finally over.

For the lone CIA agent sitting on the lower bunk, however, the end of this journey signified the beginning of another. Scott Neilson unbuckled his seat belt, picked up his small bag, and began to make his way to the crew entrance door. He was irritated that the Marine officer that sat next to him during the entire flight followed him down the steps. *What's going on here?* By now he knew it was pointless to ask, however, and he tried to push the whole trip out of his mind.

Stepping through the crew door, Neilson was pelted by the rain. He looked through the dark and saw the black sedan in the distance. Standing beside the car was a man in a plain black suit. He waved to Neilson and pointed at the car. Neilson quickly made his way across the tarmac and climbed into the back of the vehicle. The Secret Service agent got in beside him and closed the door.

"Miserable night," Neilson said, looking out the window.

"Yes, sir." The agent looked straight ahead.

Neilson knew that there would be no conversation, but he had to try to find out what was going on. "Where are we going?"

"Mr. Neilson, my name is Harper, and I'm with the Secret Service. Director Wilder asked that we escort you to the Farm, sir. After you get a chance to rest, Mr. Wilder will meet with you to explain your new assignment. He did direct me to tell you that your mission in Saigon has been compromised and that you're to remain at the facility for your own safety until further notice." The agent looked straight ahead while the driver pulled onto the road and headed for the main gate.

The Farm? Compromised? Why the Secret Service? Neilson was confused, but he was too tired to press the issue. Besides, the Secret Service agent next to him didn't know anything anyway. He was just a delivery man. Neilson knew it would be pointless to ask. He leaned back in his seat and closed his eyes. Within minutes he drifted into a fitful sleep.

The black sedan, along with the one behind it, pulled out of the main gate at Andrews and began the relatively short trip to the CIA training camp. Neilson never knew that he had been in custody since he boarded his flight in Saigon the day before.

June 5

The sun was bright and the air was thick with humidity. The temperature at mid-morning was already eighty-five degrees, and Washington prepared itself for another scorcher.

Jack Wilder had been in his office for hours, waiting for the call from the Andrews command post that would tell him that his son was arriving. He studied his notes from the day before; the plans for the *mission* that, hopefully, would bring this dark episode in his life to an end. One player was safely under wraps, and he anxiously waited for the arrival of the second flight from Vietnam. This one was under his direct personal control, and he made it clear that the passengers were not to be interfered with. They would be given complete freedom of movement, after the doctors released them, to do as they wished for forty-eight hours. No exceptions. After what they had been through, they deserved it, Jack's *project* notwithstanding.

The telephone rang. Wilder looked at the flashing button on his secure line. Only a handful of people and government agencies had access to it, and the Andrews command post wasn't one of them. It was one line that he wished would go away because it only gave him bad news when he answered it. He picked up the receiver. "Wilder."

"Good morning, sir. Dr. Jackson at Bethesda."

"Hello, Doc." Wilder's ear was instantly attuned to the voice on the other end on the line, and he sat up in his chair. "To want do I owe the pleasure?" Slaughter was never far from his thoughts.

"I have some good news, Jack. Your young charger is beginning to respond. Although not focusing on anything, he's opening his eyes and talking incoherently. Nothing that makes any sense, but from a medical standpoint, he's light-years ahead of where he was when he came here, and I'm cautiously optimistic. We're keeping our fingers crossed."

Wilder leaned back in his chair, and the pain in his stomach eased. "Doc, this is great news. I can't tell you how this makes me feel. That young man is like a son to me."

"Our hopes are up, Jack. We're keeping round-the-clock surveillance on him, and I'll immediately let you know of any change. In the meantime the guards have this place wrapped up tighter than Fort Knox. Not to worry about anything here."

"You've made my day, Dr. Jackson. When this is over, we'll get that tee time I promised."

"I'll hold you to it, Jack. Talk to you later." The line went dead.

Wilder was elated. In the back of his mind he never thought Slaughter would come out of his coma, but the phone call from Bethesda gave him new hope. He had two more reasons to be excited. First, his son was coming home from Vietnam for good. Second, Wilder would have the opportunity to tell his son that his longtime friend was on his way to recovery. He smiled to himself. *This is going to be a good day.*

Although happy over the news of his son's imminent return and Slaughter's probable recovery, Jack Wilder was acutely aware that his plan to bring Petrov to the surface was rapidly approaching. It was wrought with pitfalls, and it was dangerous in the extreme. The news from Bethesda, although welcomed, added another factor to the equation. If anyone learned that Slaughter was alive, it could force Petrov underground again with the possibility that he would disappear altogether. Bill had been through a lifetime of hell, and he deserved some good news. Jack decided to tell him everything. In the meantime, he would call NSA and give the good news to his brother-in-law. He picked up the phone and pressed a button.

June 6

The Starlifter taxied to its parking spot in front of Andrews Base Operations. Custer's stretcher was carried to a waiting military ambulance. Bill Wilder accompanied him on foot. The two men were taken to Walter Reed Army hospital where they were examined extensively by Jack Wilder's personal physician. Bill was given a clean bill of health before he left Vietnam, but Custer still needed medical attention and extensive rehabilitation. He still suffered some pain, and he would be out of commission for a while. But he was stable and didn't require immediate hospitalization, and there was nothing wrong with his spirits. He was ready for some serious *down* time.

"Major Custer, a certain gentlemen in the government hierarchy asked me to give you a hall pass so you guys could disappear for a couple days, but I want to see you back here by the end of the week," the Army doctor said. "In the meantime, lay low and let those stitches heal. No running around on all fours or jumping off bar stools." The doctor smiled, knowing that his patient would probably do just the opposite. Who could blame him?

"I'll try to behave, Doc." Custer winced when he laughed.

"I'll keep him in line, sir."

"Make sure he's here by Friday, Bill." The doctor looked at both men with a fatherly smile. "Now get out of here before I have both of you committed."

"Thanks, Doctor. We'll behave." Custer looked at Wilder. "Bill, drive this chariot, will you?"

"Let's go." Wilder guided the wheelchair to the elevator and pushed the button. "Time to get the hell away from flight suits, airplanes, and Uncle Sam for a while."

"How did you arrange it? I figured the gnomes at the Pentagon would want to pick our brains first."

"They do. But having a cool old man who's a big shot has its advantages. And right now one of those advantages is that we get a hall pass. We're taking a detour, Ed. I want you to meet a friend of mine. His name's Jake Newton, and he has a world class beer joint that will bring tears to your eyes. And when it comes to 'Nam, he's been there, done that, and bought the T-shirt. He's for real, and I know you'll like him."

"I already do. Let's go."

A blue Air Force sedan was waiting for them when they came out of the hospital, courtesy of the motor pool and a phone call from Langley. Although Jack Wilder was chomping at the bit to see his two young charges, he knew they needed this time to rejoin the *world*. Their traumatic experience had taxed their physical and mental capacities to the maximum, and Wilder knew they needed time to unwind and clear their heads. After all, he'd been in their shoes before, and he knew what it was like to come home from a hostile land and need some time to cut loose. His plans would keep; not all the players had arrived yet anyway. The three most important ones were home safe, however, and that was all that mattered for now.

They turned off the main road into a dirt lot full of pot holes and pickup trucks. The place was essentially the same as it was when Wilder left for Vietnam, and for that, he was grateful. He parked close to the front door and looked at the perpetually falling down building. "The Rock of Gibraltar."

"What?"

"Let's get you inside. I'll explain then." Wilder gently helped his friend out of the car and towards the steps.

Custer looked at the building and the derelict vehicles scattered haphazardly in the lot. "What a hole!" He laughed in spite of his pain.

"Jake will appreciate your kind words. A few soda-pops and you won't feel any pain."

"I smell grease and stale beer. Where's this Jake guy?"

"Bringing up the rear, good buddy!" Newton said from behind them. "Bill, you piece of cow dung! C'mere boy!" Newton hugged him like a long lost brother, lifting him off the ground. "I sure am glad to see your mug! Welcome home, Bro!"

"Easy, Jake. You keep hugging me like that and people will start talking funny about us. It's good to see you again, my friend." Wilder nodded towards Custer. "Jake, I want you to meet someone. This broken down old screw is Ed Custer. He's one of the good guys. Kept me straight in 'Nam." He turned to Custer. "Ed, this Neanderthal is Jake Newton."

"All I can say, Ed, is if you hang out with this numb-nuts, then you're okay in my book. Let me lighten your load, partner." Newton carefully lifted the injured man and carried him through the door. He sat Custer on a cushioned chair and propped his legs on another.

"Place still looks like a hovel, Jake. That's good." Wilder looked around the room. "So, what's been going on since I left?"

"*You're* asking *me* what's going on? For crying out loud, Bill! After what you've been through, life here's been Jello." Newton turned to Custer. "Ed, Colonel Wilder told me what happened to you guys over there. Shit-on-a-shingle, man! Let me get some cold beers and hot burgers in you guys. It's the least I can do." Newton motioned to the bartender. Within seconds a bucket of beer bottles appeared.

The three men ate, drank, and talked about everything that had happened since Wilder and Slaughter left for Vietnam. They recalled happier times, but when Wilder spoke of Maggie, Custer and Newton only listened. They could see the hurt in his eyes, and they wanted to respect her memory. After a period of silence, Wilder went to the window and looked into the darkness for a long time.

The minutes turned into hours, and eventually they were the only ones in the building. The doors were locked and the outside lights were turned off. But the beer flowed, and the trio enjoyed each other's company into the wee hours. Newton told Custer about his problems with the law and about how the Wilders intervened and helped him get his life back. He also told Custer about his brush with death in a dark alley, and how Wilder appeared and gave him a new lease on life. Custer was dumbfounded when Newton finished his story. His life wasn't the only one Wilder had saved.

Wilder looked at his watch. It was five in the morning. "We've either missed our appointment big time, or we're early as hell." He looked at Custer. "That arm needs some sleep, buster. And the way you look, Jake, I don't think a cat would drag you in. Time to put this party on hold, guys."

"Only temporarily. When this gig with the bad guys is over, we're gonna pick up where we left off."

"Bad guys? What are you talking about?"

Newton looked furtively around the room. "Bill, I talked to your dad, and he's cleared me to train with you on a mission he's setting up. Time for some pay back and a chance to return a long overdue favor."

"What mission?"

"I guess you haven't heard since you just got back from gook-land, but the Colonel has something in mind. Something to do with a certain Ivan Petrov. He's arranging a reception for his players at the Farm, as he calls it."

Wilder's senses zeroed in at the mention of the Russian's name. "No, I haven't heard, but I'll find out soon enough." He looked at Custer. "You know anything about this?"

"No, I don't, but sign me up. I want to get even for this." Custer held up his injured arm.

"Pay back's coming. That I promise." Wilder looked at Newton. "Then I'll see you at the Farm, big guy." Wilder moved to help Custer but was front-ended by Newton.

"I'll take care of this breathing lump, Bill. And as for you, Ed, tell Captain Speed Brake here not to have a heavy foot. You guys have had too many brews to be tooling around the neighborhood in that military heap-mobile."

"I'll keep an eye on him."

"Thanks for the company, Jake," Wilder said. "Damn good to be home." Sitting in the driver's seat, he closed the door and started the engine. "See you at Show-and-Tell."

"I'm there, my friend. Does a body good to see you back and in one piece, old buddy. You have a home here." He slapped the top of the car and waved them off.

Wilder pulled onto the highway and began to pick up speed. Custer looked into the side mirror at the lone man disappearing in the distance. "I like that guy. Could've used him in the jungle that night."

"And he would've made a real difference. Jake's taken out more than his share of Cong."

"No doubt." Custer looked at him. "Quite a story about how you guys met in that alley."

"Yeah, well, Jake likes to talk."

They drove for a distance. Finally, Custer said, "I can't wait to hit the sack. You got a sofa I can crash on?"

"Yep. It's called a queen sized bed, and there's no one to bother you for as long as you want. We'll get some sleep, then a big breakfast—sometimes tomorrow afternoon sounds good." Wilder's eyes kept darting back and forth between the road and the rear view mirror. "Ed, did you know that five-fourths of all pilots are dyslexic?"

"What?"

"That's right. And they can read backwards too."

Custer looked at him. "What are you talking about?"

"Don't turn around." Wilder again glanced into the mirror. "That Ford behind us has been tagging along since we left Andrews yesterday."

"Are you sure?" Custer resisted the temptation to look over his shoulder.

"Nine-five-zero-bravo-mike-fox. Maryland tags. Looks like a '72 Ford Pinto. Light brown. One of the ugliest excuses for a car I've ever seen. There's a note pad in the glove compartment. Write down the tag number. We'll get someone to run it when we get to the house."

"How long have you known?" Custer scribbled down the information and shoved the piece of paper into his shirt pocket.

"I've been watching him all night. Why do you think I kept looking out the window at Jake's?"

"I don't know. I guess you just wanted to see what real trees looked like."

"Under normal circumstances, you'd be right. But we were expected. That car was parked on the far end of the lot all night." Wilder looked at Custer. "I've been there before, Ed. The difference is I'm ready this time."

"Who would know where to find us?"

"The Russians have eyes all over Washington." Wilder's expression darkened. "I can guess who's behind it too."

"Petrov's people keeping an eye on us?"

"That's my guess. And I'll bet he's being followed by one of our guys. Dad would never cut us loose without a baby-sitter."

"Standard procedure." They rode in silence, wondering about the car behind them. Approaching the exit for Franconia, the Pinto disappeared into the early morning darkness.

CHAPTER 2

JUNE 9

Jack Wilder was ready to get down to business, but all the players had yet to be assembled. Patience was of the essence now, and he was in no hurry to compromise the delicate operation that lay before him. He was relieved that his son and Custer were back home and that they could now recover uninterrupted from their ordeal. There was much to discuss with them, but he didn't want to burden them too soon. After a good night's sleep and a hot meal, the process would begin.

First, he would tell Custer the truth about Slaughter.

"Nothing to do but eat and sleep. It's best cure I can think of." Custer was on his third cup of coffee. "Thanks for letting me camp out here, Mr. Wilder."

"It's my extreme pleasure, Ed. Believe me when I say welcome home."

"Home indeed." Custer looked at the comfortable surroundings. "If it wasn't for Bill, I wouldn't be here. What he did in that Vietcong camp was something to behold. And he was willing to sacrifice his own life to get me on that helicopter." He looked across the table at the scruffy face looking back at him and raised his cup in a salute. "I owe you my life, partner. You're the bravest son-of-a-bitch I've ever known, and I'm proud to be in your debt. With your father's concurrence, I'm going to recommend you for the Medal of Honor."

Bill shrugged it off. "To hell with that, and you owe me nothing. Just doing my job, Ed. You would have done the same for me." He looked around at the familiar family kitchen. "Never thought I'd miss home so much. If I never see another jungle again, it'll be too soon." Bill rubbed his unshaven face and looked at his father. "Dad, how about boring me with some down home local news? How's folks around here?"

"Everybody's fine, Bill, and the neighbors all want me to give you their best. They want to throw a party for you when you're up to it. And I agree with Ed's idea about the Medal of Honor."

"Forget it, Dad. Not interested." Bill emptied his cup.

"Bruce is anxious to see you guys. He's in Europe but he'll be back soon. He's bringing some German beer for you two." Wilder refilled everyone's cup and sat at the table. No more beating around the bush. He knew what his son wanted to hear. "Time to get serious for a bit. There's something I have say, and it's between the three of us and no one else."

The two pilots anxiously looked at him.

"Ed, remember John's funeral?"

"Yes, sir."

"The entire thing was faked. John's alive."

"What?" Custer's eyes widened.

"He's being kept under wraps until this Petrov business is over. I'm sorry I had to lie to you, Ed, but I thought you might be tailed when you came to Washington for the funeral. You in fact were. I apologize for using you like I did, but we had to give some disinformation to those following you."

"No apology necessary, sir. This is great news. How is he?"

"The news gets better. John's been in a coma, but he's starting to come around. He's been opening his eyes and talking randomly, and the doctors say that's a good sign." Wilder winked at his son.

"Dad, are you telling me that inert dirt ball is going to become his obnoxious self again?" Bill's smile was genuine, and it pleased his father immensely.

"Hopefully."

"This is the best!" Bill looked at the ceiling. "Thank you." A lone tear ran down his face. He looked at his father, barely able to control his excitement. "Can we see him?"

"In good time, son. But first there's something else we need to talk about, and John's in the middle of it." Wilder told them of his plan that, in fact, would never take place. He then briefed them on his true intentions, which were bolder still. "That's it in a nut shell. What do you think?"

"I figured you had something going, sir, but this blows me away. It's perfect."

"Our fingers are crossed, Ed. Our people are working on the details as I speak. What do you think, Bud?"

"I'm there. Let's do it." Bill was anxious to set his father's plan in motion.

"Most of the players believe you were killed in Vietnam, and the few that do know you're alive have no idea where you are. Once everyone's in place and briefed, you'll walk into the room. Every movement and nuance will be recorded on camera. The least sign from anyone could make all the difference. If there's a fox in the hen house, we may find out then."

"Petrov might not bite."

"Entirely possible, Bud. But I suspect our mole, whoever he is, is Petrov's contact. Petrov will find out about this meeting one way or the other. Of that I'm certain. We have Neilson confined at the Farm. We told him that his position in Saigon was compromised and that we had to re-assign him. When everyone's in position, I'll bring him out. He thinks he's the kingpin in this operation, and we're not going to give him any reason to think differently. We'll see how it plays out."

"Excuse me, Mr. Wilder, but there's something else." Custer looked at Bill. "Tell him about the snoop."

"We had a baby-sitter with us from Andrews until just before we got here. Brown Ford Pinto. I got the plate number."

"Our people were on him from the beginning. It was a KGB drone."

"Then any mole at the meeting will know about me. That pretty much kills the element of surprise."

"Perhaps, Bud, but our people picked him up as soon as he left you. He had no radio, and he had not gotten to a phone yet. We're keeping him on ice for a while. In any event, no one will know what the real plan is, even after you walk into that room."

"I assume you're not locking everyone up til the meeting."

"Only Neilson. As of this minute we think he may—and I emphasize *may*—be dirty. We base that only on what you've given us, but all the indications are there. We have no proof, however, and until we do, we have to handle him with kid gloves. We're going to gauge his reaction along with the others when you walk into that room. We have to start somewhere, and all options are on the table." Wilder looked at his two charges. "Now, lets go see John."

"Gentlemen, please come in." Dr. Jackson looked over Wilder's shoulder at the two young men behind him. "Bill, Ed, welcome home from the war." Jackson shook their hands. "We're all proud of what you've done, and we're glad that you're now out of harm's way." He looked at Custer's arm. "Ed, I know the doctors that are treating you, and they're the best. You'll be one hundred percent before you know it."

"Thank you, sir."

Bill could barely control his excitement. "Doctor, I understand that your premier patient is giving the nurses a hard time."

Jackson laughed. "Well, not just yet, Bill, but I'm hoping for it soon. Would you like to see him?"

"Yes, sir, please." Bill looked uncertainly at his father then at the doctor. "Uh, can I see him alone?"

The doctor looked at Wilder and got a subtle nod. "Let's take a walk." He put his hand on Bill's shoulder, and the two men started down the hall. "Bill, I know you've looked forward to this for a long time, and I'm glad I was able to give you good news about John's condition. His physical injuries have healed, but there was some damage to his vocal cords, and his voice is gruff. And at this point he's still incoherent."

"I understand, sir. He's a gruff kind of guy anyway." His eyes were glued to the doctor's. "Will he pull out of this?"

"We hope so, but a lot of it will depend on you. We've done all we can for him, and the best therapy now is the voice of an old friend. If anyone can bring him out of this completely, it's you. So, sit with him. Talk to him. Believe me, Bill, he'll hear you and he'll respond sooner or later. But be patient. It could take an hour or it could be days before he responds."

"Yes, sir."

They walked the length of the empty corridor. The only other people in the wing, aside from the nurses, were the Marine guards standing in front of Slaughter's room.

"Gentlemen, this is Bill Wilder, Director Wilder's son. From this minute on, he is to have unlimited access to this room at any time of the day or night. And to the patient in it. Understand?"

"Yes, sir," the ranking guard said, standing at attention. He saluted. "Captain Wilder, your father has told us all about you, sir. This is a real privilege."

"The pleasure's all mine, guys. Thanks for looking out for my buddy in there." He looked at the doctor. "Can I go in now?"

"Yes, but remember what I said about being patient." Jackson squeezed his arm, assuring him that everything was all right.

"I'm in this for the long haul." Wilder nervously stepped into the room, and Jackson closed the door.

He stood at the foot of the bed and stared at the first friend he made at the Virginia Military Institute a lifetime ago. He remembered how Slaughter's descriptive language and devil-may-care attitude made the difference when many of their Brother Rats were deciding whether to stay or leave that first year. More often than not they stayed, thanks to his tension relieving antics. Wilder thought about Slaughter's humorous relationship with the local law officials in Texas when he was growing up. But mostly he thought about how his friend looked after Maggie and of how the Texan was willing to give his life to save hers. Tears flowed while he looked silently at the unconscious man.

Wilder walked slowly across the room and stood beside the bed. He remembered doing the same thing in the Philippines not long ago. Then, Slaughter was barely recognizable. Now, at least, with the exception of the angry scar on his neck, he looked like the grizzled fireplug Wilder remembered, and he was grateful for that. He picked up a chair and carefully placed it beside the bed. He sat quietly and looked at his friend for a long time.

He leaned forward so that his mouth was close to Slaughter's ear. "John, it's me, your old cell mate from school. How you doing, buddy?" Wilder was having a difficult time maintaining his composure. "You've always been one for weaseling out of work, but this takes the cake. Just lying around here freeloading, while all these pretty nurses fuss over you. What nerve! But don't you think it's about time you stepped up to the plate and paid your bill? I do. Besides, I don't have anybody to get into trouble with. So, what do you say?"

There was no response.

Wilder fell silent, wondering what to say next. Other than the steady beeps from the monitors, the room was quiet. *Come on, old friend, give me a sign.* He again leaned close to Slaughter's head. "John, if Maggie was here, she'd chew you out for being such a lazy bum. You know how she is with useless slugs like you and me. And Jake wants to know when you're going to join the party."

Nothing.

Wilder took a more serious tone. "We're getting close to Petrov, John. I know you saw him, and I need your help to catch him. Tell me who he is. Do it for Maggie. Do it for the three of us. Let's get the bastard." Wilder watched for the slightest response, but Slaughter remained inert. He waited for several minutes then stood to leave.

As he turned towards the door, something caught his eye.

Slaughter's right hand was beginning to move. He slowly raised his arm and scratched his ear. He then rubbed his face and lay his arm across his stomach. Seconds, that seemed like hours, passed by.

Wilder's heart jumped into his throat when Slaughter opened his eyes. He looked in Wilder's direction. There was no recognition at first, but soon his eyes began to focus on the man standing beside his bed. He stared at the strange face. Finally, he opened his mouth. "Uh, hmm. Who are you?"

Wilder fought to control his excitement. He touched Slaughter's shoulder. "It's me, John. It's Bill." He wasn't sure that Slaughter understood him. "I'm here with you, John, and you're going to be all right. Do you understand me?"

"Uh, okay," Slaughter said, not quite sure of what was happening. He studied Wilder for a moment with a confused look, but the confusion soon gave way to recognition. "Bill, are you all right?"

"Jesus Christ on a crutch!" Wilder almost choked when he spoke. "John, you understand me!"

"Of course I understand you." Slaughter rubbed his eyes. "S'um bitch, I'm tired. Come back later with something to eat. I'm going to bed." He closed his eyes and was asleep in less than a minute.

"Welcome back to the world, by brother." Wilder was beside himself with excitement. He could hardly wait to tell everyone the news. He ran down the hall.

"The look on your face tells me that the news is good," his father said when Bill burst into the waiting room.

"Did he wake up?" Custer asked.

"More than that!" Bill was ecstatic. "He scratched his face and looked at me. Things didn't register at first, but then he recognized me and called my name. He said he was tired and wanted to sleep, but he wants me to bring him something to eat when I come back." Bill looked at the doctor. "That's a good sign, ain't it?"

"A good sign? Bill, that's an understatement! You've just accomplished in two hours what an entire team of experts hasn't been able to do for months. This is wonderful!"

"Well done, Wild Bill," Custer said. "Good job."

"Good job, indeed. Son, you've just helped John overcome the biggest hurdle of all. You're the medicine he needs. But I have to intervene here, gentlemen." Jack Wilder looked at everyone to make sure he had their attention. "You must remember that we're the only people that know John's here or that he's alive." He looked at Bill. "Bruce knows too, but to everyone else outside this room, John is dead and buried. Is that clear?"

"Wait a minute, Dad. If we take him public, Petrov will know that he's been exposed, and it'll be easier to catch him."

"We can't do that. Everyone believes John's gone. But he's alive and he knows who Petrov is. That's our ace in the hole. If John shows at the wrong time, Petrov will simply disappear. For now we keep John under wraps, and everyone continues to believe he's in Arlington National Cemetery." Wilder's remarks were an order, not a request.

"But the clock's ticking, and we need to move on this."

"And we will, Bud. But we need John, and you're the key that will unlock his memory. Patience is what you need now."

Bill looked at his father, knowing that impatience was his enemy.

"I want you to spend as much time with John that you can before the first team briefing. Talk with him but don't rush him. He may not remember much about what happened in Saigon right now, but we need his memory of those events to pull this off. For that, Bill, you are in charge."

"Your father's right," Jackson said. "Sometimes the brain suppresses events that are traumatic, and it often takes years of therapy to bring them out. It's an internal self-defense mechanism. Although he's on the road to recovery, his brain needs time to adjust and recover. Just coax him here and there, and allow him to speak his mind. That's the best therapy possible."

"Could I stay here? I mean camp out with him? We could talk any time he wanted."

"Excellent idea," Bill's father said. "What are the chances, Dr. Jackson?"

"Consider it done. We'll set Bill up in the adjacent room. This entire corridor is empty anyway. I'll make the arrangements."

"Thanks, Doctor. I'll let the guards know what's going on." Wilder turned to his son. "Bud, your primary mission now is to bring John back to the present. You must concentrate on this. There are obvious restrictions though. You can't go wondering around the hospital or outside. You might be seen and arouse suspicion. Whenever you need to leave, we'll take you out undercover. It's essential that we keep a lid on this place." Wilder looked at Custer. "Ed, you'll stay with me in Franconia til you get back on your feet. I'll fill you and Bill in on the details of my plan in due course. In the meantime, we'll concentrate on your and John's recovery while the other players assemble for this make-believe mission." Wilder smiled at his two young agents. "It's game time, gentlemen.

CHAPTER 3

CIA HEADQUARTERS
JULY 1

The players in Jack Wilder's poker game were finally assembled. Each had arrived at a different time, and none were told about the others. Most had come from Vietnam, while others were plants. These additional agents had been briefed as to the group's real purpose, and they were there to watch the others during their training.

Everyone would be kept isolated from each other until the initial meeting. At that time they would assemble, and Jack Wilder would brief them on the nature of their mission. Once the initial indoctrination was completed, Bill would walk into the room and the game would begin.

"You've paired down your list considerably, Jack." Spencer looked at the stack of folders on the desk. "What did you use for a baseline?"

"They all are aware of what happened to Bill and John in Vietnam, and they each have relative experience in some form. All have top secret clearances. With the exception of Custer, they believe John died over there, and I'm going to keep it that way. I'm assuming for now that none of them had anything to do with it, but I believe that someone in the group is our mole. Everyone was spoken for when

Bill and John ran into problems. The only one that could have known anything is Neilson because he was in the Philippines with me. There wasn't anyone else around. Neilson knew about the attempt on John, but he was back in Saigon when it happened."

"Someone in Angeles City could have carried out the attack."

Wilder rubbed his hands together. "We have to assume that there were enemy agents there and that someone provided them information about the hospital." He looked out the window. "But I find it hard to believe that Neilson's our mole. He's been around for a long time, and I've seen him in places where he could have easily been compromised."

"True, Jack. But everyone has his price."

"A sad state."

"Well, one way or the other, we'll find out. Who's in the line up?"

"Most of the Air Force types that worked with Bill and John in Saigon are in the briefing room downstairs as I speak. Dan Mercer signed on from the command post, along with Berwick. Jerry Bryant ran the intel office there, so he's pretty much up on everything."

"What about his going to UPI?"

"Apparently, that's on hold. When McAlester turned up dead, Bryant was left high and dry. So when this mission was offered, he decided to sign up. Jake Newton's joined us too. We may have a use for his demolition experience. There are two guys from the Saigon Embassy, but Neilson didn't work with them. We have four of our Vietnamese agents, including Charlie Hoosier, to keep an eye on things and give the mission a sense of reality."

"Wasn't he in charge of POW training when Bill and John made their initial run through the Farm?"

"Yes, he was. We'll see what floats to the top when Hoosier puts this group through the wringer." Wilder looked at his watch. "Including Bill and Ed, that's thirteen people in our little parade."

"Lucky thirteen." Spencer nodded. "You're going to put them through that POW hell then?"

"Yes, once they're done here. Except for Bill, Custer, and Neilson, everyone will go through it. These guys have to be convinced that this mission is for real. I can't think of a better way to eliminate the weaker ones, unless I put them through SEAL school. And you know what Navy pukes think about the Air Force." Wilder always used the Navy as a whipping post when he needed levity to lighten the load.

"Navy wussies." Spencer headed for the door. "No time like the present, Jack."

Wilder grabbed his jacket. "Let's launch this ship." The two men left Wilder's office and headed for the elevator. Neither man said a word as they made their way through the labyrinth of the CIA building. Both were concentrating on the poker hand they were about to deal to the players patiently waiting downstairs.

They watched from behind a two-way mirror while the group filed into the room. Bill stood beside his father, studying each man with interest. Neilson was the only one not there. He was in another room and would come in with Jack Wilder. Charlie Hoosier and his Vietnamese countrymen mingled with the group so their presence wouldn't be patently obvious. Everyone took his designated seat around the oval table. There were desk mats with each man's name, along with a legal pad, a pen, and a bottle of water. A podium stood at the front of the room. The two-way mirror was at the opposite end, and the hidden ceiling cameras were focused on each man's face.

Everyone fell silent when Wilder entered the room, followed by a self-assured Scott Neilson. "Good morning, gentlemen. My name's Jack Wilder, and I'm the Director of Operations for the Central Intelligence Agency. Before we get down to business, I just want to say a few things. Many of you know each other, but I want to make sure that all of you know each other not only by name, but also by sight, sound, color, and smell. You'll be spending most of the next few months together, and your survival in the future could well depend on any one man in this room. Take a good look at every face and remember it."

The group took a collective look around the room, especially at the Vietnamese. Everyone was expressionless, as expected, but the hidden cameras were zoomed in. Wilder was careful to notice any movement or facial expression, while Bill and his uncle studied everyone from behind the mirror. The meeting was being filmed, and every frame would be poured over later by dozens of analysts.

"Okay, gentlemen, let's begin." Wilder motioned for Neilson to step forward. "This is Scott Neilson, former Chief-of-station in Saigon."

Former? Neilson briefly glanced at him but said nothing. He hadn't been told anything since his arrival at Andrews, and he had no choice now but to watch and listen.

"Scott will be the assistant team leader during your training. He will report to the team leader who is waiting in another room, and that person will report directly to me. Each of you has been screened and selected to train for a classified mission that quite possibly could make the difference in the lives of some American POW's. It's also possible that you could be killed during the course of this operation. You'll be working directly for me, and you will take your orders only from me through my designated representative in the field. No exceptions. Is that clear?"

Everyone nodded.

Assistant team leader? Neilson patiently waited.

"This mission is of the utmost secrecy, and you are not to discuss any part of it with anyone for any reason whatsoever. To do so will get you a life sentence at Club Fed in Leavenworth, or a firing squad. Is *that* clear?" Wilder waited for the words to sink in before continuing. "Gentlemen, no one outside this room, other that your team leader and the director of the National Security Agency, knows about this meeting or its purpose. It will stay that way.

"Some of you will not survive the training. There's no shame in that. This mission will require the utmost effort and endurance from everyone. Your physical and mental capabilities will be taxed to their limits and then some. The mission itself is extremely dangerous, and some of you may not make it out alive. If anyone gets left behind, there will be no rescue mission, and the government will disavow any knowledge of you or your actions."

The silence was so profound that a pin hitting the floor would sound like a hammer on an anvil.

The door opened and Spencer entered the room. He nodded at Wilder and looked at the men around the table. "Good morning, gentlemen."

"This is Director Spencer from the National Security Agency.

He's privy to everything here, and he will assist me in planning and directing this operation. You may take notes during this and subsequent briefings to refer to later, but nothing leaves this room. All materials remains here on the table. You will be searched both before entering and prior to leaving this room each time." He studied the group for a moment, then said, "Gentlemen, if any of you don't feel comfortable with what you've heard so far, or if you want to withdraw for any reason whatsoever, now's the time. There will be no repercussions, and no one will know any difference. You'll simply go to your next duty assignment outside of this agency. So, make your decision now."

No one spoke or moved.

Wilder looked at Spencer then turned his attention once again to the group. "Very well, gentlemen, let's begin. You will train for a rescue mission to one of the POW camps in North Vietnam. The particular camp in question will remain classified until just before deployment." There was a murmur in the room, and Wilder waited for the initial reaction to subside. "All of you will train with explosives and Soviet weapons, and you will learn hand-to-hand combat and survival techniques. You'll learn to speak passable Vietnamese and learn local Vietnamese customs. And last but not least, all of you will undergo extensive POW indoctrination." Wilder looked at Hoosier. "This is Charlie Hoosier. He and his team will be in charge of that part of your training. I won't go into details, but suffice it to say that Mr. Hoosier has as much reason to hate the North Vietnamese as anybody. He and his brothers will train you in how to deal with them. Listen to their counsel.

"You will train at the CIA facility in Tidewater. We call it the Farm. Your cover while you're there is that you are businessmen working on a government contract. You'll be briefed on the specifics of that this afternoon. You'll meet at a different location each day and be transferred to the Farm secretly at various times of the day or night. Once your hitch at the Farm is over, you'll be flown to Panama. There you'll undergo your POW training. That part will be the most difficult. When the POW phase is complete, the team leaders and I will make a final assessment as to who should be retained and who will be released. Then the remaining group will be evaluated during a raid on a simulated POW camp. At that point I alone will make the determination as to whether or not the mission is to proceed. Are there any questions before I bring in your team leader?"

There were none.

"Very well." Wilder pressed a button on the podium, and the door opened.

Bill Wilder walked into the room.

With the exception of Newton, Custer, and the Vietnamese, there was shock on everyone's face. Every expression was recorded on film while Jack looked on. *One or more of you is a damn good actor.*

Bill stepped to the podium and acknowledged everyone with a nod. He waited for the initial shock at his appearance to subside. Finally, he said, "I'll wager none of you expected to see me here."

No one said anything at first. Then Dan Mercer leaned forward and placed his palms on the table. "You scared the shit out of me with your Tarzan antics in the jungle, Bill. If there's such a thing as nine lives, you've certainly used eight of them. Speaking for myself, I think you should sit this one out and enjoy life."

"That goes for all of us," Bryant added. "You gave all of us quite a scare, and it's good to see you back from the dead."

There was general agreement all around.

"Thank you, gentlemen. After the party in Vietnam, you have no idea how glad I am to be here." Bill looked at his father. "After that screwing in the Oriental bush, don't I get some time off?"

Laughter broke the tension in the room.

"If it's any consolation, Bill, you don't have to go to POW school again."

"Well, that's something I guess." Bill grinned at his audience. *Which one of you is the mole?* "Gentlemen, you've had a brief overview of what some would consider an impossible mission. It's absolutely essential that you be up to the task because there won't be any second chances if you're caught. It will be intense, and it won't let up until you are either washed out *here* or return—alive—from *there*."

"We're with you, Bill," Newton shouted from the back of the room. "Give us the goods, and let's get cranking."

"Soon enough, my friend. I won't go into specifics as to why any of you were chosen for this mission, but I will say that you were picked from over a hundred highly qualified candidates. All of you have been to Vietnam. Some of you already speak some Vietnamese, and at least two of you speak Russian."

That remark caught everyone by surprise, including Jack. He kept his composure, however, and remained silent.

"It's imperative that you dedicate yourselves to preparing for this mission. American lives are at stake here. Not only will we be rescuing some of those guys, but we'll also be making a statement to the North Vietnamese. We'll be in their face in their own back yard."

Bryant raised his hand.

"Yes?"

"I don't mean to be the fly in the ointment here, Bill, but if we pull this off, what will Uncle Sam say if he has no idea about this in the first place?"

"Good question, Jerry. Do you guys remember the botched raid on the Son Tay compound in 1970? The government was behind it then, but no one knows about this one except the people in this room. If we pull it off, Uncle Sam will learn of it through private channels, go public with it, and take the credit. If we fail, no one will be the wiser."

"You know how leaky Washington is, Bill," Newton said. "If the big-mouths in the press find out about this, they'll have a field day."

"True enough." Bill looked around the room. "Understand this, guys. All of us—and I mean *all* of us—are under the microscope. If there is a leak, it will come from this room." He let the statement hang for a moment. "Your training begins at five in the morning, so I suggest you get a good night's sleep tonight." Bill moved towards the door then suddenly stopped and turned around. It was time to fire a shot across the bow. "Oh, there's one more thing, gentlemen. I have some good news. John Slaughter is alive and has made a full recovery. I thought you'd like to know."

Stunned silence.

All eyes were glued to him, including his father's. Bill knew that he had just thrown the man a curve ball. But he had to play his own hand, and this was the time and place to put his declared mortal enemy on notice. Bill looked at his father. *I'm sorry, Dad.* Seeing the shock on everyone's face, it was time to drop the bomb. "John told me about the explosion that killed my girlfriend, and he saw who did it." With that, Bill left the room and closed the door behind him.

CHAPTER 4

SAME DAY

Patience and insight are but two of the many qualities an intelligence operative must have before venturing into the unknowns of espionage. Without them, nothing in *Spookdom* is possible, and the shortness of either can cause the half-life of an operative to be shortened by a factor of one hundred percent. Once either of these qualities is lost, an operative is about as useful as a screen door on a submarine. Then the question often becomes: Is he a traitor or just plain dumb?

That was just one of the questions that ran through Jack Wilder's mind as he stared at the younger version of himself standing in front of him. *What the hell have you done?* His emotions ran the gamut between love and hate, and they collided with his professional responsibilities in how to deal with the brazen young operative in front of him. Bill had gone against a CIA directive in that he had given out critical information that the Director of Operations wanted held from everyone. Jack now wondered if his house of cards would collapse around him before his plan ever had a chance to get out of the starting gate. Further, Bill had violated a trust between father and son, and disappointment showed on his father's face. *What the hell are you thinking?* Jack glared at his son.

Bill was afraid to move. He could almost feel his ears burning from his father's thoughts. He knew that he had crossed the one line that should never be transgressed, and he mentally prepared himself for the ass-chewing of the century. He also knew that he could be thrown into the slammer until the Second Coming. He was, however, prepared to stand his ground because he believed that he was right. After all, he had his father's convictions in him, didn't he? Standing motionless, he glued his eyes onto a spot on the wall above his father's head and waited for the ax to fall.

Spencer sat in the leather chair that had become more of a comfort than his chair at home. It was his familiar port in the stormy sea of frustration and family loss that had become Jack Wilder's office. He had his own ideas and opinions about this project and the players involved, but this was neither the time nor the place to say anything, especially since this was an operation in which he had no authority whatsoever.

He did, however, have a moral obligation to both his brother-in-law and his nephew. They were his only family, and he was prepared to defend both their positions if it came to that. In the meantime, however, he would quietly watch and listen.

Jack looked at his son for a long time, wondering what to say and how to say it. He leaned forward and clasped his hands on top of his desk. *Where the hell do I begin?* He looked blankly at the wall for a minute before speaking. "Two thousand years ago, a Roman general named Iphicrates was preparing to send his army into combat, knowing that many of his troops would perish. In spite of that, however, he was able to see the big picture, and he knew that this battle would be decisive. It would win the war. He said that the needs of the many must outweigh the needs of the few—a profound statement if there ever was one. There are a lot of people in the spy business, and some will fall victim as a result of their operations. Unfortunately, it's the price that has to be paid in this dark game of cat-and-mouse.

"Bill, there are many people involved in this project, and you've just compromised more of them than you'll ever know. I have to assume that your reasons are valid, and I expect you to explain yourself when I ask you to. Your mother once told me that I should listen to other people's opinions more than I do. My response to her was that listening to other people talk about something of which they know nothing could get people killed. I also told her that, had I listened to her all those years, I'd be a four-star general by now, instead of sitting behind this goddamn desk about to squash some insolent prick that thinks he knows more than I do. I wonder how that sits with you." Jack's eyes bored into his son's.

"Sir, I—"

"Shut up! You'll speak when I tell you to and not before."

Bill stared harder at the spot on the wall.

"In all the years I've been in this business, I've never seen an operation undermined before it got off the ground like this one has been. And by my own son!" Jack Wilder was working himself up, and he knew that he had to control his temper. His blood pressure was rising, and his heart wasn't twenty-one years old any more. He leaned back in his chair and closed his eyes. He breathed deeply. After a minute he opened his eyes and calmly looked at his son. "You've gone against the rules of the Agency, and you've disregarded my personal directive. I could dismiss you right now for your actions. What you did in there could endanger the lives of other agents unknown to you, and I could lock you up and throw away the key. I hope you understand the seriousness of all this."

"Yes, sir."

"Well?" Jack wasn't in the mood to be toyed with, but he desperately hoped that his son could justify his actions. Otherwise, he would have no choice but to dismiss him.

Bill had rehearsed his answer over and over again, but standing in front of his father now, he was at a loss for words. He saw the hurt and disappointment in his father's face, and he began to wonder if he had done the right thing. Looking at the prematurely aged man behind the desk, Bill tried to put himself in his place. He couldn't.

"Sir, I understand what you've said, and you have every right to do whatever you feel necessary. I'll accept any action you elect to take. But I respectfully ask that I be allowed to explain myself before you make a decision." Bill returned his eyes to the spot on the wall and waited for an answer.

Jack was in a quandary. On the one hand, his orders were that Slaughter's condition and whereabouts be kept secret. The only other person besides the three men in the room that knew about Slaughter was Ed Custer, and Jack had told him about Slaughter himself. On the other hand, he understood his son's feelings. It was too easy to put himself in Bill's place. Jack wanted retribution for his first son's death. Bill wanted it not only for a lost brother, but also for the woman that carried his child to her grave. He regretted the verbal dressing down of his son, but his position allowed him no choice. *This goddamn job sucks!*

Bill didn't move.

"Look at me, Bud."

Their eyes met.

"Sit down." Jack's face softened. He briefly glanced at his brother-in-law for his non-verbal opinion.

Spencer nodded approvingly.

Bill sat in the chair facing his father's desk. He didn't fear his father, but he did have a healthy respect for the man that had raised him, and he didn't want to do anything to make his father's life any more difficult than it already was.

"I'm sure there's a reason for what you did, Bill, but you threw me a curve ball in there when you told everyone about John." Jack leaned back in his chair and picked up the coffee cup on the side table. He tried to make himself look relaxed.

"Sir, I—"

"Bill, forget where you are, and let's talk as father and son. Just tell me your thoughts."

Bill rolled his head to loosen the muscles in his neck. He rubbed his eyes and looked out the window. *Why us?* He wanted for the three of them to be anywhere but here, doing anything but this. He looked at his father. "Dad, I know you think I've betrayed you, and I want you to know that I would never do anything to hurt you. God knows it isn't easy for you, and I understand that. But you need to know where I'm coming from. We're both after the same guy, okay? We're just going about it differently. You look at things from the strategic level because you have to. You have things going on all over the world that demand your attention every minute of the day. But I've been in the trenches at ground level—literally—trying to catch one man. I'm on the tactical level here, so please try to see things from my position.

"I didn't ask to be dragged into this. When my brother went to Vietnam, I was just a horny high school kid, interested in nothing but girls and martial arts. Back then I couldn't find Vietnam on a map if my life depended on it. Then Little Jack was shot down and captured in some God-forsaken piece of real estate that isn't fit for man nor beast. He was tortured with other Americans that shouldn't have been there any more than him. Then some Russian bastard blew his brains out with his own gun because he had a hard-on for you. He thought you caused *his* old man's death. The frosting on the cake was when John and Maggie were blown to bits in Saigon by the same bastard that killed my brother!"

"Son, I know you're upset—"

"Dad, please let me finish. You have your ideas about catching Petrov, but you're thinking from the CIA planning level. I'm on the *ground* level, and I know he's here. And my telling the guys in that room that John is alive, will force him to make a move sooner rather than later."

"I understand how you feel, Bud, but if Petrov learns that John is alive, he'll disappear into the woodwork. If that happens, we're back to square one again."

Bill shook his head. "With all respect, Dad, I don't think so. If Petrov thinks John's alive, then he'll have to assume that John told me about the bombing. The fact of the matter is that John doesn't remember anything about that night. I've spent hours talking with him about it, but everything's a complete blank from the time he got to the hotel until now. But Petrov doesn't know that. He has to think that John told me everything. Because of that he'll have to make a move on me. I'm in his face now, and he doesn't know if I have a royal flush or a single deuce." Bill looked at his father like a fox at a rabbit. "Please, Dad, give me a chance. I've earned the right."

"Yes, you have, Bill." Jack had to admit that his son was right. His peripheral vision saw Spencer's approving gesture.

"Petrov's been handed to me on a silver platter. He'll come into my circle soon enough. Dad, your strategy has worked this far, but the ball's in my court now. Please let me run with it."

"Son-of-a-bitch!" Jack crossed is arms and leaned back in his chair. He looked at his son as if seeing him for the first time.

July 2

"I don't know what to say, Mr. Wilder. Quite frankly, I was thrown for a loop when Bill said John was alive. I sure am glad to hear it though. That guy's been through hell." Scott Neilson sat across the kitchen table from his boss. It was the first time Neilson had been to the Wilder residence, and it was the first time he had really relaxed since his arrival from Vietnam.

Jack Wilder was circumspect. "I'm just glad they're both safe. It's been quite an ordeal for both of them." He paused to collect his thoughts. "Scott, I asked you here for several reasons. To begin with I wanted to talk with you away from everybody else. Despite the security at the Farm and my office at Langley, being *here* will afford both of us a chance to relax and get to the real reason for our secrecy." Wilder wanted Neilson to feel that he was being trusted above the others. After all, Neilson would be in charge of the group during the actual training. He would also be privy to information that no one else would have.

At least that's what Neilson was supposed to think.

Wilder poured two cups of coffee and sat one in front of Neilson. Taking his seat at the opposite end of the table, he leaned back in the wooden chair and rubbed his eyes. He picked up his glasses and looked at them. "Scott, you've been with the Agency for a long time, and your record has been exemplary. Being station chief in Saigon is no small task, and I applaud the work you've done. Now, I have something to tell you in the strictest of confidence."

"Yes, sir." Neilson suspected that he was going to be briefed on some inside information that would be of paramount importance to the POW rescue mission.

"We've suspected a mole in our Saigon operations for some time, but we have no idea who it is. I asked you to come back to the States and oversee this mission because I don't want to compromise your position with respect to the operations there. I brought you back abruptly without explanation because I didn't want anyone in Saigon to have a chance to suspect anything. But now I suspect that our mole might be part of this group—"

"A mole? In Saigon? This is incredible! And you think he's here at the Farm? I'm sorry, sir, but I find this a little hard to swallow."

Neilson's response was predictable, but Wilder's face remained blank. "We're fairly certain there's a foreign operative in our midst, but we don't know where. He could be here or still in 'Nam. And there may be others associated with him, both here and there. We've had several Kontum missions sabotaged in recent months. Kontum appears to be a favorite because Bill and Custer were involved in two similar missions there. There have been others since we brought them home, but we don't know if they're related. In any event we're assuming the worst case scenario. We're going on the assumption that the mole or one of his people is part of this team."

"This is unbelievable." Neilson nervously rubbed his hands together. "What do you have in mind, sir?"

"To start with, no one on the team has any idea of this. You and I are the only ones that know about this chink in the armor. I told you, Scott, because you've ferreted out spies in some of your prior postings, and I need your help to find this one now. As far as everyone else is concerned, all the players are legitimate. Your job is to watch everyone without being obvious. You'll report any suspicious acts only to me. Don't even talk to Bill. I'll set up a time and place on a rotating basis to meet with you. We'll never be seen together at the Farm or at Langley unless it's with the rest of the group. I'll probably have you brought here under cover." Wilder paused for effect. "Scott, keep your eyes open and your ear to the ground."

"Yes, sir. I'll stay on top of it."

Wilder had made his pitch, and he saw the look he wanted on the face of the man sitting across from him. The bait had been taken and the hook set. Now, it was time to sit back and watch where the fish went with it.

CHAPTER 5

JULY 5

Jack Wilder sat at his desk at Langley and thought about the day before. The Fourth of July holiday was a welcomed respite from the madhouse that he worked in, and he took the day off. He spent the holiday with his son, brother-in-law, and Custer in Franconia, and the four men enjoyed each other's company to the exclusion of everything else. Nothing was said about Vietnam or Little Jack. Vietnam would not go away, unfortunately, but it was relegated to the back burner if only for one day. And although he was in their hearts, it was time to let Little Jack rest in peace. As for Bill, the constant ache for Maggie would not go away until his final reckoning with Petrov. That day was drawing near, however, and that thought soothed the burning in his soul.

Wilder was grateful for the small things, and spending yesterday with what remained of his family, free of the unending turmoil of the CIA, was worth more than a king's ransom. But his calm moment of introspection was about to be blown to bits.

His private line rang, and it seemed more urgent than usual. He picked up the receiver and reluctantly put it to his ear. "Wilder."

"Bad news, Dad." Bill's voice was calm but the words exploded in Jack's ear.

"John? Is he all right?" Jack was on the edge of his seat.

"John's fine. It's Neilson."

"What about him?"

"He's dead. A wire garrote." Bill waited for the words to hit home.

"*Damn!*" Jack suddenly felt exhausted. "Where?"

"In his hotel room. The maid found him and got the hotel manager. He called me since I gave him my name as point of contact for the group."

"Who else knows about this?"

"Just us and John Conway at the FBI. I used your access code to call him. He's taking charge of the investigation, and he'll keep it under wraps. No news types snooping around."

"Good." Jack thought for a moment. "Look, I need you to get everybody into martial training as scheduled. We have to make things look normal. The busier we keep everybody, the better." Jack hesitated before he hung up. "Thanks for being on top of things, Bud." He placed the receiver in its cradle and left for the elevator. The helicopter ride to the Farm would be relatively short, but it would seem like an eternity. *If it wasn't for bad luck, I wouldn't have any luck at all.*

July 6

Bill Wilder did his best to make life miserable for his teammates. He instructed them in practical hand-to-hand combat techniques, as well as how to fend off several attackers at once. He had them attack him in turn, and he easily tossed them around like rag dolls, throwing them firmly to the ground and causing a bit more pain than some thought necessary. A few claimed some prior martial training, and each tried to impress Wilder with his own prowess. But when push came to shove, none came close.

"Form a circle around me, gentlemen. Let's go for about fifteen feet across. Now's your chance to get even. Attack at will, but do it like you mean it because it damn sure ain't gonna be free!" *Let's see who's playing dumb.*

Berwick ran at him with a rubber knife. He swung the knife in an arc across Wilder's face. Wilder ducked the first arc then threw up a forearm block against Berwick's arm when he reversed his swing. Grabbing Berwick's wrist, he twisted it and jerked his arm backwards. Berwick flew rearwards and landed on his back with the knife on the floor under Wilder's foot.

At that instant Bryant charged at Wilder's back with his arms extended, reaching for the neck. Wilder's peripheral vision caught Bryant's shadow. A vicious back kick to the stomach left Bryant writhing on the ground, gasping for air.

Mercer and Newton both ran at Wilder at the same time. Despite his size, Newton knew that he stood about as much of a chance against his friend as a snowball in hell. He remembered that night in a dark alley years ago when he watched Wilder destroy a small mob of hooligans without breaking a sweat. But he was in this until the end, and he gave it his all. He and Mercer rushed at their would-be enemy. Wilder deflected one against the other, and both of them fell over Berwick and Bryant, crashing to the floor.

There was considerable moaning and swearing, but no one wanted a rematch with the man staring down at them. Wilder was amused at their discomfort. He knew that no one would really attack him, unless in anger, and no one here—at least as far as he knew—had received any *real* training before now. *Which one of you is not what you seem to be?*

Finally, after several more throws, falls, and bruised egos, the session was over. The exhausted group sat on the floor and leaned against the wall. Wilder looked at his team, satisfied that he had brought them down a notch. "Welcome to the world of Martial Arts, gentlemen. A true martial artist can kill you, and there's nothing you can do to stop him, except to get to him first. I'm not going to make experts out of any of you, but I *am* going to teach you enough to defend yourselves on the street. There isn't enough time here to go into any depth, but you will learn enough to disarm somebody should the need arise. Hopefully, you won't have to use any of this, but if you do, it will probably be one-on-one. I will tell you this though; don't go looking for a fight. Anyone looking for trouble is not as good as someone expecting it. Remember that."

The door opened and Jack Wilder walked purposefully into the room. Everyone started to get up but gladly dropped to the floor when he raised his hand. He looked briefly at his son, then at the group. The frown on his face made everyone uncomfortable. "Gentlemen, I have an unfortunate announcement. I regret to say that Scott Neilson was killed in an auto accident this morning. His taxi was hit broadside by a truck. He died instantly."

"Bloody hell!" Newton shouted. "All that shit in 'Nam he went through, just to be greased in a goddamn cab. Poor bastard!"

Everyone looked at each other, searching for something to say.

"Neilson was a professional, and he'll be sorely missed. He was a fine man and an excellent agent. Despite his death, however, this mission is still on. Things have changed on my end for now, and I have to redirect some assets and delay our timetable. You will continue with your martial training for the next several days. Then, for public appearances, you'll go about your business at home for a week before returning here. During that time each of you will leave the Washington area and go to your home of record so as not to bring suspicion on yourself. You'll reconvene in your hotel exactly seven days hence." *And the FBI will be on you like fleas on a dog.*

Bill knew before class that his father would make the announcement about Neilson, but he played along, carefully watching everyone.

"When you're done here, you'll be briefed on the changes to your schedule. The bottom line is that you will make no reference to this place or your training. Under *no* circumstances are you to discuss anything having to do with this mission, and you are to have no contact with each other after you leave here." Jack was reticent to say any more. "That's all, gentlemen." He looked at each face in front of him then turned and left the room.

"Dad, John's going bonkers in that hospital. Physically, he's completely healed, and he has all of his marbles. He just doesn't remember the explosion. Except for the growling in his voice, he's a hundred percent. But he needs to get out. Everyone knows he's alive, so there's no reason to keep him locked up anymore."

"I don't know, Bud. It's risky." Jack understood his son's reasoning, but he wasn't sure what to do.

"He's been through hell, sir, and it's time to cut him some slack. I want to go see the McIvors, and I want him to go with me. We haven't seen them since before we all went to Vietnam." Bill walked around the desk and placed his hand on his father's shoulder. "It's the right thing to do, Dad, and you know it."

Jack stood and looked up at his son. Despite Jack's height, Bill towered over him. Jack's work had consumed so much of his time that he couldn't think clearly. Hearing his son's words now, he realized that there indeed was life outside the CIA. And the McIvors were never far from his mind. Jack knew his son was thinking of them and of John, instead of himself, and for that, Jack couldn't say no.

"Please, Dad."

"Son, you have me backed against the wall, and I have no counter. Seeing the McIvors is a fine gesture, and I encourage you to take John with you. He has to be released at some point." Jack didn't want to suffer the ignominy of being the one to stop Bill and John from fulfilling their destiny, whatever that may be. But he couldn't compromise their mission either. He had to juggle his players carefully. "Of course you guys can go, but there are some obvious precautions you must make."

"Okay."

"First, you can't be anywhere near each other until both of you get away from the Washington area. That he's alive makes him a target. If Petrov sees him, he may try to kill him."

"I've thought of that," Bill said, sitting on the corner of his father's desk. "How about getting him to Andrews so he can catch a military hop to Pease in New Hampshire? I'll take the Eastern shuttle, get a rental car, and pick him up at the base."

"Everyone on your team has access to Andrews, Bud. I'll arrange for an Agency jet to get him to Pease. You take the shuttle out of DCA and get the rental. That looks innocent enough. I'll make arrangements for one of our contacts to meet John and baby-sit him til you get there. Just watch you six o'clock position. We don't want any surprises."

"Dad, this visit is long overdue. Thanks."

"You're right. It is long overdue." Jack picked up the phone and looked at his son. "Before we do any of this, let me call Tom and see if it's okay for you guys to come. He and Audrey moved to North Conway a while back, and I want to make sure your visit won't inconvenience them. It'll be an emotional time for them, but I know they'll welcome both of you with open arms." Jack dialed the number in New Hampshire from memory. He knew that the McIvors would welcome the two young pilots. Their meeting would bring the needed closure they all longed for.

July 7

Bill Wilder sat in the window seat in the emergency exit row of the DC-9. He looked out the window at the small boats on the Potomac River and wondered if the would-be sailors had any idea of what was happening in the world around them. He suspected that they didn't. *Ignorance is no excuse*, he thought, but he couldn't help but envy them a little.

He turned his attention to the flight attendants' monotonous drone that no one paid any attention to. *Fasten your seat belts. Pull down on your masks and place them over your nose and mouth ...* He wondered if the attractive young woman standing in the aisle really knew what she was doing while she absently went through the motions. He hoped so for her sake.

Wilder thought back to that night when Captain Thomas McIvor came to Washington on another Eastern Shuttle flight to be with the Wilder family when the news of Little Jack's death came. He thought it ironic that he was now doing the same thing in reverse. How he wished things were different.

The airplane lined up on the runway and began to accelerate. The nose rotated when the ship reach flying speed, and the DC-9 lifted smoothly into the air. The pilot turned to the left and began climbing the jet along the Potomac River. Wilder looked out the window at the Washington Monument and Pennsylvania Avenue. He thought about President Nixon's Inaugural Parade and of the melee he and his classmates had with the hippies at the end their march. He couldn't help but smile at the memory of the First Captain chasing a protester up a telephone pole. The smile disappeared when he recalled the uneasy feeling that came over him during the bus ride afterwards to Fort Belvoir. That was when Little Jack died. Even halfway around the world, blood was thicker than water, wasn't it?

The jet climbed to thirty-three thousand feet and began to make its way towards Boston. Wilder reclined his seat and closed his eyes. He wondered how Slaughter would be when they met. Slaughter had missed a great deal during his coma, and he still had a lot of catching up to do. The shrinks at Bethesda were miracle workers, Wilder thought, but Slaughter needed to get back into society and be with his friends. Wilder wondered what his own reaction would be when he saw the McIvors for the first time since Maggie's death. The questions weighed heavily on his mind, but there was nothing he could do about them for now.

He drifted off to sleep.

The twin-engine Falcon landed at Pease Air Force Base near Dover, New Hampshire, and taxied to Base Operations. A blue Air Force staff car approached the left side of the plane when the passenger door opened. John Slaughter stepped into the opening and looked around. The day was sunny and warm, and he stood in the doorway for a full minute and relished the feel of the sun's warmth on his face. It had been a long time since he had been outside, and he was going to enjoy it to the fullest.

A smartly dressed young woman stepped out of the staff car. Approaching the small jet, she extended her hand. "Captain Slaughter, I'm Sara Hill. I'm your contact while you're here. Welcome to Pease."

Other than the nurses at Bethesda, Slaughter had not seen a woman since he visited Maggie at the Caravelle in Saigon on that fateful night. The Bethesda nurses, although quite competent in their duties, were in the final throes of a terminal hurt-dance in the Looks Department as far as John Attison Slaughter was concerned. He looked at the woman standing on the tarmac with her hand extended and undressed her with his eyes.

"Captain … ?"

"How do, beautiful lady! You're about the finest looking thing

I've seen since I've been back to the zone of confusion." He bounded down the steps two at a time. Bowing deeply, he kissed her hand. "John Slaughter, ma'am, at your service."

"Oh! Well, thank you. I trust your flight was pleasant?" She found him disarming and liked him immediately.

"Passable fine, my dear, but it would have been perfect if you had accompanied me." Slaughter had a lot of catching up to do, and he wasn't going to miss a beat. He smiled graciously.

"Uh, thank you again." Sara looked towards the staff car then at him. "I'm to take you to the Bachelor Officer Quarters. Your room has been arranged, and the Officer's Club is nearby. Your associate will arrive this evening." She started towards the waiting car.

"Hold on there, Missy!" Slaughter wasn't about to be shut out.

Sara turned and looked at him.

"I don't mean to offend, Miss Hill, but you're the first round-eyed female thing worth looking at since I escaped from Vietnam. Please allow for that, and please allow this reprobate the pleasure of taking you to dinner tonight." He beamed at her. "As you may know I've been out of circulation for some time, and I have lot of catching up to do. I must say I find you extremely attractive, and it would be my greatest pleasure if you would join me this evening for wine, food, and song. I've had a bath and it ain't even Saturday. I've had all my shots, and I'm even wearing shoes. So, dear lady, will you please have mercy and adopt this wayward child for the evening?"

"This is the most unusual invitation I've ever had, Captain Slaughter. I accept. Thank you." She laughed and climbed into the car. "But first, we have to get you settled in."

"Works for me." Sliding in beside her, Slaughter closed the door, and the car sped towards the BOQ. Within minutes, he would be settled in his room having a beer. A short nap, a shower, a change of clothes, and he would have his first real meal outside of a hospital in months. And with a beautiful woman. *There is a god in heaven after all*, he thought.

"Be still, my beating heart!" Slaughter said when Sara walked into the room. "Miss Hill, you look good enough to eat!" He bowed and kissed her hand.

"Really? Thank you, I think. Please call me Sara." *How refreshing to meet an honest person.* "I must say that you have a way with words, John. May I call you John?"

"Lady, you may call me anything your heart desires." His eyes sparkled at her. "John works fine, but I also answer to any guttural form of expression you care to use. Now, would the lady care for a cocktail?" Slaughter slid his arm around her waist and gently urged her towards the lounge. *A snack before the feast,* he thought to himself.

"Thank you, John. I'd like that."

The evening progressed and they got to know each other. None of the obvious questions were asked, however. Each knew that the other was connected with the Agency in some fashion, but that subject was the furthest from their minds. The physical attraction between them was intense, and before the evening was over, they found themselves in Slaughter's bed.

It was a welcomed release for both of them.

Logan airport has never been user friendly, and air traffic control has yet to evolve beyond the crystal ball stage, or so the thinking goes among pilots. After twenty minutes of holding over Providence for no particular reason—the weather was clear—then delaying radar vectors on final approach, the shuttle from Washington finally was cleared to land. Getting to the gate was another adventure altogether. After holding short of intersecting runways for departing aircraft for ten minutes, the DC-9 taxied to the Eastern terminal. Getting off the airplane and to the rental car facility was an ordeal in and of itself.

Wilder finally got out of the airport and onto Route One north towards New Hampshire. Driving in the Boston environs was nothing but a mechanical stampede, and Wilder didn't want to deal with the local drivers any more than he had to. Once he passed Route 128 that ran a semi-circle around Boston, he settled back and decided to enjoy the ride. The sun had set in the west, and in less than an hour he would be at Pease.

"May I help you, sir?" the airman asked from behind his desk.

"Hi. I'm Bill Wilder, and I'm here to meet a friend. His name is

John Slaughter, and he should have pulled in sometimes this afternoon."

"Just a minute, sir. I'll check."

"Thanks." Wilder looked around the small office and wondered what it would be like to be stationed here. The area was beautiful, but the facilities on the base were vintage World War II.

The airman looked at his register. "Captain Slaughter checked in around two this afternoon. He's in room 205." The airman stood and pointed down the hall to his left. "Just go to the stairs and up one flight. Go down the hall a short distance. Room 205 is on your left. Would you like me to ring him for you?"

"No, thanks. He's expecting me. I'll just walk on up." Wilder headed down the hall and up the stairs. In less than a minute he stood in front of Slaughter's door. He was about to knock when he heard a lusty moan coming from the room. The woman, whoever she was, apparently was enjoying herself. Wilder grinned at the door. *Welcome back to the world, buddy.* He went back to the lobby.

"Is there a problem, sir?"

"My friend's indisposed for the time being. I'd like to leave a message for him, please."

"Yes, sir."

"Just tell him that once he gets his sea legs back, I'll be at the bar at the O'Club."

"Sea legs?" The airman wasn't sure he heard correctly.

"That's right. He'll understand. And tell him I'd like to meet her sometimes."

The slap on the back could only be from one person. "S'um bitch! They'll let anybody in this dump!"

Wilder turned to see Slaughter staring at him. "Well, look at what the cat dragged in. Hope your trip was pleasant."

"Oh, yeah!"

"I'm glad to see that you did your part to mix it up with the locals, John. I hope you came to attention at the proper time." Wilder motioned to the bartender for two beers.

"Oh, yeah!" Slaughter picked up the beer and took a long drink. He wiped his mouth with the back of his hand and belched. "Damn, that's good." He looked at Wilder. "Got here this afternoon, and there hasn't been a dull minute since. My handler turned out to be quite … helpful."

"I gathered that." Wilder looked casually around the room. "Does Miss Strumpet know why you're here?"

"No. She's Agency and didn't ask." Slaughter grinned. "Your dad has all bases covered. Let's get a table." Slaughter dropped a quarter into the jukebox and pushed some buttons. The music was just loud enough to drown out any conversation. They walked across the room and sat in the corner. There wasn't anyone else in the cavernous room anyway, so they didn't have to worry about being heard.

They sat in silence for several minutes, each man thinking about how he would handle the McIvors tomorrow. Wilder wondered how he would react when he saw Maggie's grave for the first time. Would he hold up? Or would he go to pieces in front of her family? Slaughter wracked his mind in a vain attempt to remember what happened that night at the Caravelle. Would the sight of her picture or her grave cue his memory? Or would he just draw a blank? He didn't know which would be worse, but he knew that he had to be strong for his friend.

And then there was the unborn child that never had a chance. How would they handle that?

"John, this is your first day out of the hospital and on your own. How are you handling it? How do you feel?"

Slaughter thought for a moment, then said, "I feel fine, Bill, but I honestly don't remember a thing about that night. I'm sorry, buddy, but when I think about for it for any length of time, I get a blue ribbon headache. I'm sure something's there, but I just can't find it. Pisses me off."

"What do you think about seeing the McIvors tomorrow? Are you up for it?"

"Are you?" The men looked at each other.

"Game, set, and match." Wilder nodded in submission. "I guess we'll find out."

"Let's don't push them, Bill. Remember, this is a courtesy call more than anything else."

"Yeah." They fell silent once more and stared at the bottles on the table as if they were genies that would provide the answers to their questions. Unfortunately, the answers would never come. Finally, Wilder said, "When we were in 'Nam, did you ever have reason to suspect Scott Neilson of complicity?"

"What?" Slaughter was non-plussed. "Neilson? What the hell does he have to do with any of this? He's in Saigon spying on zips."

Wilder leaned across the table. "John, somebody killed Neilson in his hotel room near the Farm two days ago. From the looks of things, it sounds like Petrov."

"Killed? S'um bitch!" Slaughter looked at Wilder as if seeing him for the first time. "The shit really hit the fan while I was sacked out, didn't it?"

"You have no idea."

"Well, if Petrov's behind this, then he's onto us."

"You're on the money, John. He knows you're alive, and he believes you can identify him. He's after both of us now, and he'll move heaven and earth to get to us." Wilder told Slaughter every detail of the plan he and his father had put together to flush Petrov into the open.

"S'um bitch! Count me in."

"You're the center piece, John."

CHAPTER 6

JULY 8

Wilder watched the sun rise from his BOQ room. He had been up most of the night, pacing the floor and wondering what he would say when he came face to face with the McIvors. Would he feel like a stranger imposing himself on a family that had been wracked by the loss of a child? Or would they welcome him with open arms as one of their own?

Slaughter had been up also, wondering what Captain McIvor would ask him about his daughter and her last night on this earth. What could he have done differently that might have prevented her death? Was it his fault? *Why can't I remember anything?* He paced the floor for hours, unable to come up with any answers. He finally decided to get ready to leave. There wasn't anything he could do here.

They met in the parking lot. Each man knew what the other was thinking. Wilder opened the door on the driver's side and looked over the roof at his partner. "You look like I feel. I've been up all night wondering how this is going to pan out. I hope we're doing the right thing."

"I feel pretty rough too, but we have to do this."

"No time like the present." Wilder started the engine while

Slaughter peeled back the lids on two cups of coffee. They left the base and headed north in silence.

They pulled into the driveway shortly after noon. Wilder turned off the ignition and looked at the house. Then he looked at the mountains in the distance. "I'd like to hike up there sometimes."

"When this is all over. Let's go." They climbed out of the car and approached the house.

"Hey, Dad, they're here!" Tommy McIvor shouted. He ran through the doorway to meet them. "Captain Wilder, Captain Slaughter," his eyes darted back and forth between them. "Wow! It's great to see you guys. What a surprise!" The younger McIvor, although now out of the Army and safe at home, didn't quite know how to react. He didn't know whether to come to attention or to hug the two men that had become his big brothers. It didn't matter because the decision was made for him.

"Looking good, Tommy! How are you, my friend?" Wilder gave young McIvor a bear hug. It was returned in kind.

"I'm fine, sir. Thank you." Tommy turned to Slaughter and extended his hand.

"C'mere, boy." Slaughter grabbed his hand and slapped him on the back. "You look better than ever, my young bud. A carbon copy of your old man. I'm glad to see you back at home where you belong."

"Thank you, sir."

"It's Bill and John, okay? Enough of that gung-ho stuff. That's all behind you now." Wilder grinned at him. He saw Maggie in the young man's face, and it was all he could do to contain himself.

"Bill, John!" Tom McIvor stepped into the yard. "It's so good to see you guys." A round of handshakes. He looked them over approvingly. "If you two don't beat all! From boys to men in such a short time. The commander will be glad to see you."

"Commander?" Wilder looked at Slaughter for an explanation but got only a shrug.

"Audrey. I'm retired from the Navy, and she's the skipper of this ship." He thumbed over his shoulder towards the house.

"Oh, I get it." Wilder laughed. He was immediately at ease.

"They do like to be in charge, don't they, sir?"

"Yes, they do, John. And forget the *sir* stuff. I'm the one that should be saying that to you. Name's Tom, okay?" He put his hands on their shoulders, the sparkle in his eyes saying *Welcome.* "Come on in, guys. The *commander* is looking forward to seeing you. She's been fixing up something special for this occasion."

"I'll bet Mrs. M is prettier than ever," Slaughter said.

For his part, Wilder could only think of how much Maggie looked like her mother. He steeled himself in preparation.

"Let's go inside, fellas. She's in the kitchen. I'm sure there's some cold beers around here somewhere." Walking through the open doorway, McIvor shouted, "Audrey, there are two Air Force weenies here to see you."

"This is wonderful, just wonderful! Welcome, boys." Audrey McIvor came into the living room from the kitchen. She clasped her hands together when she saw them. She hugged Wilder like only a mother could. Pulling his face down to hers, she kissed him on the forehead. "I'm so glad you're home safe, Bill. This means so much to me." There were tears in her eyes. "Johnny, you're well. I'm so happy for you." She hugged and kissed him too. She stood between them and put an arm around each of them, pulling them close. "This is such a treat! I'm tickled pink that you boys came." She nudged them towards the kitchen. "I have some fresh apple pie and homemade ice cream for you. Come and sit. Tell me all about yourselves. How's your father, Bill?" She looked at Slaughter. "How are your parents, Johnny?"

"Take it easy, Audrey. They just got here. Plenty of time for that," her husband chortled. Tom McIvor was amused at his wife and grateful to the two young men for bringing a smile to her face. He was worried that she would go to pieces, especially when she saw Wilder, but, thankfully, that didn't happen. Not yet anyway.

Audrey was on Cloud Nine, having both Wilder and Slaughter in her home at the same time. It was the first time both had visited her together and the first time for either of them in her new home. Everyone, including Tommy, sat around the table. Conversation covered everything, including the weather, Air Force careers, Tom's retirement, and Tommy's plans for college. Maggie wasn't mentioned. That subject would come up soon enough.

Dinner consisted of cheeseburgers, fries, and beer—per Slaughter's request. He'd had enough institutional food in the hospital and longed for the All-American Staple. Audrey was more than happy to accommodate him. After everyone finished, Wilder and Slaughter insisted on washing the dishes. It made them feel good to contribute something and to be part of the daily ritual of the McIvor clan, if only for a short while.

Afterwards, McIvor said, "Let's take a walk guys. There's something I want to show you." He looked at his wife. "Coming, Audrey?"

"You guys go ahead and visit. I'll stay here and busy myself. I want to mix the sauce for the steaks tomorrow." In truth, she knew what the men would be talking about, and she wasn't ready to face it yet.

"Okay. The sun will set soon, and I want these young bucks to see Mt. Washington at dusk. We'll be back in a bit." McIvor knew what was going through her mind, and he didn't want to press the issue. He turned to his two guests. "Let's hit it, fellas."

The three men hiked a short distance to the top of a hill at the edge of the forest. They stood for a while, looking at Mt. Washington in the distance. Although it was early July, the evening was cool and the visibility clear. The view was spectacular, and it made Wilder want to be *there* more than ever. "I'd like to hike it one day," he said, looking at the mountain.

McIvor was pensive. Both Wilder and Slaughter knew that he was reflecting, and they fell silent out of respect. He sat on a nearby boulder and looked at the mountains. "Maggie used to hike that mountain all the time. It was one of her favorite ways to relax, especially when she came home from school in Boston. She loved the mountains more than anything." He pointed towards the slight hill to their right. "There's a small cemetery on the other side of that rise. Maggie's buried there, facing the mountain. She would have wanted it that way."

Wilder felt like he'd been stabbed in the heart, but he just stood motionless and stared at the mountain. He had to maintain his composure, not only for Maggie's father, but also for himself. He strained to control his emotions but gave voice to them. "I miss her so much."

He looked at McIvor. "I'm so sorry that this happened, sir, but I swear to you that I will avenge her death. I can't say anymore than that."

McIvor looked sadly at him. "Bill, you're part of this family, and we love you like our own son. Maggie's at peace now, and her mother and I have come to terms with it. Audrey has her bad days, and I do what I can to comfort her. It's hard accepting the fact that Maggie's gone, but I suppose we'll get used to it. I just hope it isn't too soon."

Slaughter was uncomfortable. He walked over and stood in front of McIvor. "Sir, Maggie was the best. One of the guys, if you will. I loved her like a sister, and I have to share some of the blame for what happened—"

"Don't punish yourself, John. She thought the world of you. When she called from Saigon each week, she never failed to mention your name. And she laughed every time she talked about you. You made quite an impression on her, and I thank you for keeping her spirits up when she felt down. You did everything right, son, and Audrey and I are grateful to you for it."

Slaughter fell silent. He had been vindicated by the one person from whom it made all the difference. It was a rare time for the Texan to be out of words, and this was one of them.

"He's right, John," Wilder said. "You were willing to give your life for her, and that's about as good as it gets. You have no reason to feel ashamed." He turned back towards the mountains. A red cardinal perched itself on a branch of a nearby tree and chirped at them.

"Maggie loved cardinals," McIvor said. "They were her favorite birds. She used to come here and feed them. They seem to flock to her."

"Tom, if you don't mind, I'd like to stay here a while before I go back to the house."

"That's fine, Bill. Stay as long as you want." McIvor understood the young man's emotional pain and his need to be alone at Maggie's grave. Turning to Slaughter, he said, "Let's head back to the house, John, and have some beers. We can sit on the deck and let the bugs eat us."

"Sounds good to me, sir." Slaughter turned to Wilder. "Don't stay too long, buddy. Something might drag you away."

"Just a little while." Wilder started towards the cemetery. Slaughter and McIvor watched him for a moment before turning back towards home.

Wilder stood in front of Maggie's grave. He was overcome with emotion, and tears ran down his face when he read the inscription on the tombstone. "I love you more than life, Maggie. I swear by all that's holy that I will make him pay for this." A cardinal perched itself on the stone and chirped at him. After a moment, it took flight and turned towards the mountain.

Wilder climbed on top of a large boulder and stood facing Mt. Washington. He sat in the Lotus position and breathed deeply. It had been a long time since he last meditated. It soothed his conscience and freed his mind from the emotional baggage he carried with him every day. It would also bring him closer to Maggie than he had been since her death.

With his eyes closed, Wilder concentrated on his inner spirit, separating himself from his physical bounds. His conscious being slowly ascended to a higher plane of awareness. Oblivious to his physical surroundings, his mind became one with the spiritual elements around him. He felt Maggie's presence, and it was strong and compelling. Her spirit urged him towards the mountain.

Go there …

… Time passed. Wilder slowly opened his eyes. Sitting motionless, he stared through the darkness towards Mt. Washington. Although he couldn't see the mountain, it was in his mind's eye. Something there beckoned to him, and he couldn't force it from his thoughts. He stood and inhaled the cool mountain air. His mind was clear now. He would climb the mountain tomorrow.

By the time he got back to the house, Slaughter and McIvor had emptied several bottles of beer. Although not drunk, they weren't feeling any pain. Audrey handed a beer to Wilder and offered him a seat. Thanking her, he sat on the deck floor and looked towards Mt. Washington. "We're going up there tomorrow, John. There's something up there we need to see."

"Like what? A moose in heat?" Slaughter belched and took another drink.

"I'll know it when we see it." Wilder turned to Audrey. "Is there a place where we can get some hiking and camping equipment tomorrow?"

"There's a Bean outlet not far from here."

Wilder looked once more at the mountain, then turned away. It was time to pay attention to the emotional needs of his hosts. He looked at Slaughter then smiled at Audrey. "Mrs. McIvor, has John been boring you with his adventurous tales of good deeds and daring?"

She laughed. "As a matter of fact he has, Bill. And I must say that John has a way with words. He told us about the fun the three of you had on your flight to Vietnam and of the way he acted with the lady passenger next to him, telling her that he was a mortician. Of all things!" The smile slowly left her face. "He also told me about the tiger cages those people use on their prisoners. How awful."

Wilder knew what was really on her mind, and it was time for him to broach the subject and give Audrey the chance to openly express her heartache to him. He had known for a long time that this moment would come, but he had no idea of what he would say or how he would react. He had dreaded this moment, but now that it was here, he was thankful for it.

She looked at him, sensing his thoughts.

"Mrs. McIvor, Maggie kept us from going crazy over there. She was a saint in a den of heathens. She stood up for what she believed in. She wasn't afraid to speak her mind, and she rose to the top because of it. Terry McAlester thought very highly of her and frequently said so. She was his best journalist. You can be proud of her in every way."

Audrey looked at him with sad eyes that said, *Thank you.* She wanted to hug the young man standing in front of her—the man that would have been her son-in-law, but she didn't want to show weakness in front of her adoptive family.

"It's okay, Audrey. Bill understands." Her husband knew what she was going through.

At those words, Audrey rushed into Wilder's arms, buried her face in his chest, and cried uncontrollably.

Wilder gently held the shaking woman in his arms and stroked her hair. Now more than ever, he had to be strong, and it was one of the most difficult things that he had ever done. Audrey had lost her daughter in a war that should have never happened. And Maggie carried Audrey's grandchild to her grave. Audrey had lost a daughter *and* her unborn grandchild to a beast that he had sworn to find.

"Catch him." Audrey held onto Wilder like he was her only salvation. She sobbed pitifully.

"I promise." Wilder held the shaking woman close to him and looked at her husband.

"Do it for Maggie." Tom McIvor was stoic. He stood tall with his hand on his wife's shoulder, tears running down his face.

Patting Audrey gently on her back, Wilder looked at Slaughter and said, "We're going up tomorrow."

"Yep."

CHAPTER 7

JULY 9

They were up before daybreak, but the McIvors were sitting at the kitchen table when Wilder and Slaughter came into the room.

"Good morning, guys. Seems like everybody's up early," McIvor said.

"I hear that Mrs. M makes the best coffee in these parts, and I wanted to sneak in here before this unwashed cretin next to me got it all."

"These are civilized people, John. Behave yourself." Wilder sat at the table.

"How about some breakfast, boys?" Audrey said.

"We don't want to put you through any trouble—"

"Nonsense, Bill. Blueberry pancakes and cheddar cheese omelets will be up in a jiffy." Audrey was enjoying herself now.

"Bodacious fixings, Mrs. M. I haven't had a home-cooked meal like this since I can remember."

"Well, we're going to fix that, John," McIvor said. "The commander is pretty mean in the kitchen. You're in for a treat." He poured coffee for everyone then got up to help his wife. Keeping busy was a way to cope, and the McIvors' movements weren't lost on their guests.

Tommy came into the room. "Morning, guys."

"Tommy, my boy. What are you doing up so early? Kids your age are supposed to sleep til noon during the summer," Slaughter said. "Do you have list of chores a foot long, or are you just anxious to get my autograph?"

"Actually, I'd like to hike the mountain with you guys," Tommy said, his eyes looking around the room for approval.

"I don't think so." Audrey looked at her son.

"Why not? I've been doing it for years."

His father stepped in. "We don't mind if you hike, Tommy. You know that. But Bill and John need to do this for themselves. Just trust me on this, okay? We'll go tomorrow if you like." McIvor's voice was firm but not unkind.

The look on his father's face told Tommy all he needed to know. "Okay, but can I go to Bean's with these guys? I'd like to show them the good stuff."

"That's a good idea," Wilder said. "We need someone to show us what to avoid." He looked across the table. "How about it, John?"

"Tommy's the expert." A double thumbs-up.

"That's fine," Audrey said, content that the issue was settled. She was asserting her *commandership* as the mother hen. It gave her comfort. She returned her attention to the main event of feeding her menfolk before they started their day.

"So, Tommy, what are your plans for college?" Wilder asked.

Tommy talked about this school and that before the conversation drifted to girls and cars. He reminded Wilder and Slaughter of themselves when they were in high school. Some things never change. Everyone chatted over breakfast and coffee, and once again, the two pilots insisted on KP duty over Audrey's mild objection.

They relaxed on the deck and enjoyed the warm morning sun. Conversation revolved around the McIvors' upcoming trip to Ireland to visit the old homestead. It was time to go back to their roots and see the family they hadn't seen since before McIvor commanded the *Ticonderoga*. Moreover, it would help them close the tear in the family circle and bring peace to the McIvors once more.

"I guess we should get going. Audrey, Tom, it's been good to see you. You guys are the best. Thanks for putting up with us hooligans. Enjoy your trip to Ireland, and keep in touch."

"Thank you so much for coming, John," Audrey said. "You and Bill being here means so much to us." She looked at the mountains with melancholy eyes. "Be careful up there."

"A piece of cake, Mrs. M. And thanks for the groceries. If I keep eating like this, I'll have to get a job selling shade at the beach." Slaughter picked up the bag of sandwiches and stuffed them into his bag. He hugged Audrey and shook McIvor's hand.

"Luck to you, John. Thanks for coming," McIvor said.

Winking at them, Slaughter slung the bag over his shoulder and walked out the door. He wanted to give Wilder a moment alone with the McIvors before the two men started their journey.

They stood in silence. Finally, McIvor said, "Bill, your being here has done more good than I can say. You're family now, and you always will be. You're the son-in-law we always wanted."

"Thank you, sir." Wilder smiled sadly at Maggie's father. "I appreciate that more than you'll ever know." He turned to Audrey. "You remind me so much of my mother. I can't think of anyone I'd rather have for a mother-in-law than you."

Audrey smiled at him, too choked up to speak.

"Peace for us soon. I love you both." There was so much more to say, but Wilder didn't have the words. He hugged Audrey and shook McIvor's hand.

"Godspeed, Bill." Maggie's father hugged him with desperation, knowing that the young man would again be in harm's way.

Slaughter was waiting in the driver's seat when Wilder climbed into the car. He studied his friend for several seconds. "Pretty tough, huh?"

"Hardest thing I've ever done." Wilder looked at the mountains. "Let's go."

In spite of the rising temperature and humidity, Wilder checked his equipment to make sure his cold weather gear was in tact. The weather could change in a matter of minutes on the top of the mountain, and too many hikers had learned that lesson the hard way. Many had paid the ultimate price for their lack of preparation. Despite the popularity and relative ease in comparison with real mountain climbing, Tuckerman's Ravine was not a cake walk. Even the best hikers had to be careful when negotiating the paths and ledges at the higher elevations, especially when the rocks were wet.

They stood at the eastern base of Mt. Washington. That Wilder had to climb the mountain based on spiritual intuition, was about as dumb as it got, Slaughter thought, and he made it a point to say so. "Okay, partner, you're taking me on a goose chase, so I have to ask a question. Where did you get the idea that this rock has the answer to our problem? What's up there that's so damned important?"

"I don't know but we're going to find out." Wilder stood with his hands on his hips, looking up the slope. *Something.*

"I hope your two marbles are in one bag." Slaughter never questioned his friend's judgment, but he didn't especially share Wilder's beliefs in meditation and the spirit world either. "Let's get to it."

They chose the shortest trail up the mountain. They hiked for hours, stopping occasionally to drink water and look at the weather. Although they couldn't see the thickening clouds moving in from the west, they felt the drop in temperature as they made their way up the slope. Despite the sweat from their exertion, they both wore ball caps to keep their body heat from escaping too rapidly, and they kept their windbreakers out just in case.

The slope gradually steepened and the trail narrowed. A steady drizzle began to fall when the cloud cover moved over, forcing them to slow down. They stopped and put on their windbreakers.

"This could get nasty." Wilder looked at the darkening sky.

"Yeah, and these rocks are slicker than eel shit. If it gets much worse, we'll have to find a place to hang our hats and wait it out." For all his faults, Slaughter was cautious, and he wasn't willing to take any more chances than necessary.

Wilder wiped the rain from his face with a chamois cloth and looked at his friend. "You know, John, sometimes you actually make sense. You get the sweet end of the lollipop."

"I should. I've been getting the fuzzy end of the stick long enough. I'll just be glad when this shit's over."

"No argument here." Wilder pointed to the moss-covered granite ledge above. "Be careful up there. If you decide to take a leap for mankind, I'll have more paperwork on my hands than the federal government."

"Yeah, and be careful yourself." Slaughter shoved his canteen into its pouch and took the lead. It was his turn to chance bouncing first.

The rain came down harder, bringing their progress almost to a standstill. By the time they reached the narrow rock shelf less than fifty yards ahead, the rain was coming down in sheets, and visibility was almost nil. They dropped their gear under a rock outcropping away from the ledge and looked around.

"I think we should get a tent pitched and get into some dry clothes," Wilder said, looking at the heavy clouds. "We'll wait this out and drink Audrey's coffee."

"My mouth tastes like the floor of a New York City cab." Slaughter pulled a two-man tent out of his pack. Both men worked quickly, and within minutes, the tent was up. They changed into dry clothes and stretched out on their ponchos to relax. Wilder poured coffee into two plastic cups and handed one to Slaughter.

"I've been thinking about Berwick and how he fits into all of this," Wilder said. "Why would he volunteer for this mission? He's not the athletic type. What does he hope to gain?"

Slaughter propped himself up on one elbow and looked at him. "You told me you guys patched things up when your dad flew to 'Nam. Were you serious about that, or were you just blowing smoke?"

"A little of both, I guess. Dad has the full background on him, and he obviously knows more about him than I do, but I still feel uneasy." Wilder settled back on his poncho. "Berwick has a tail on him like everybody else, but that doesn't mean anything. I just don't know what to think."

"Well, for what it's worth, I don't trust that little ferret any more than you do." Slaughter thought for a moment. "How much of this Berwick business do Custer and Newton know?"

"They both know everything, but Custer's on the sidelines for this operation. And it's not for his lack of wanting to get involved either. Those Vietnamese pricks nearly killed him, and it's going to be a long time before he's in one piece. Kind of like you."

"At least I didn't feel any of it." Slaughter looked through the tent flap. The rain was coming down in sheets. "May as well take a nap. We ain't going anywhere for a while." He slid his pack under his head and closed his eyes. Within minutes he was snoring.

Wilder looked at his sleeping friend. He put down his cup and lay still, listening to the rain for over an hour before finally dozing.

By the time the rain ended, the sun was on the west side of the mountain, and the temperature had dropped considerably. Wilder stuck his head through the tent opening and looked around. If they were going to find anything today, they would have to get moving soon. "Rise and shine, John. It's beginning to clear, and we have to make the summit before dark." Wilder began to pack his equipment.

"Christ on a crutch! Me and Betty Boop were lining up to do the deed, and you screwed it up. So much for *that* dream." Slaughter sat up and rubbed his eyes. He looked through the flap at the breaking clouds. "Hope there's a beer at the top of this rock." He got up and began to shove his poncho into his pack.

Progress was slow because of the slippery rocks and mud, but they had to reach the top before dark. Finally, after enduring more rain, they reached the flat area just below the eastern summit. The expanse marked the end of that particular trail. The weather station sat several hundred yards ahead, accessible by a path designated with stone markers. Wilder dropped his pack to the ground, took out his canteen, and drank deeply. He handed the canteen to his partner.

"Well, we're here. This looks like a good place to set up shop and spend the night, John."

"Yep." Slaughter gulped the water and wiped his mouth with his jacket sleeve. "Only thing better than this would be a cold beer. How about it?" Not getting an answer, Slaughter looked around.

Wilder had gone ahead several yards, looking towards the summit.

Satisfied with their location, Slaughter decided to find a place to pitch a tent. There was a large boulder at the far end of the clearing with a sign on it. He walked across the ledge, taking in the view to the east. Standing in front of the boulder, he looked across the landscape at the lights around Sebago Lake in Maine. *Ain't Texas, but it'll do*, he thought. Finally, he looked at the metal sign attached to the flat face of the boulder.

Slaughter froze, his eyes glued to the words in front of him.

Wilder came down the path to the clearing. "John, where are you?" There was no answer. "John?" Still no answer. Immediately his guard was up. He scanned the horizon, his peripheral vision missing nothing. He spotted Slaughter in the distance, standing in front of a big rock. Wilder made his way across the narrow expanse. He noticed the expression on the Texan's face. "John, you look like you've seen a ghost."

Slaughter didn't move.

Wilder looked at the sign, and a cold chill ran down his spine. Something was dreadfully wrong. He stared at the sign as if it was some sort of evil talisman. The inscription burned into his mind.

In Memory Of Our Son
Jerry Allen Bryant
Lost On Tuckerman's Ravine August 4, 1954.
Your Loving Parents, Sally And Ben

"When you were alone on that hill last night, you said that Maggie came to you in a vision. She wanted to show you something." Slaughter looked at his friend. "This is it, ain't it?"

Wilder was numb. The words on the metal sign screamed in his head.

"Bill … ?"

"She never did like him. She told me that over and over again, but I just blew it off as women's intuition. I should've paid attention."

"Everybody doesn't like somebody."

"We have to get to a phone right now. I have to call to Langley, then we're heading back to North Conway. We have to get a security detail to the McIvors' house right away."

"Why?"

"Their lives could be in danger."

"Move your ass!" They ran up the trail as fast as they could, leaving their equipment behind. Within minutes they reached the parking lot near the rail station. A New Hampshire state policeman was just getting into his cruiser.

"Officer, hold up! We need your help!" Wilder ran towards him, waving his arms frantically and shouting. Reaching the policeman, Wilder explained who they were, and he gave the officer a private phone number at Langley to verify their identities. In less than three minutes they were in the cruiser, going down the mountain as fast as the narrow road would allow. At the same time a covert security team, per Wilder's request, began to make its way to the McIvor residence. It would position itself around the house, it's mission to protect the unsuspecting occupants inside.

Arriving at the state police station, Wilder and Slaughter were escorted to an empty office where they found a desk and a telephone. The officer excused himself and closed the door behind him. Wilder dialed his father's secure number in Franconia. The phone rang several times. *Come on, come on! Pick it up!*

Jack answered on the fifth ring. "Wilder."

"Dad, I don't have a lot of time, so just listen ..." Bill quickly told his father about their visit with the McIvors and what they had found at the top of Mt. Washington. He said that he had arranged for a security detail around the McIvor residence as a precaution. Town hall in North Conway would be their next stop, where they would research the death of one Jerry Allen Bryant on August 4, 1954. Bill would also attempt to locate his parents, Ben and Sally, if they were still in the area. Failing that, Jack would task John Conway at the FBI to search for the Bryants on a national scale.

"Okay, Bud, I'll get things moving on this end. But before you go, I need to call Langley and check something. Hold on." Jack pushed the hold button and dialed another number. He made his request and got the answer within seconds. He pushed the flashing button and reconnected with his son. "Here's something that might interest you, Bill. Our Captain Jerry Allen Bryant lists his home of record as North Conway, New Hampshire, and I don't think that's a common name up that way."

"*Damn!*" Bill looked at Slaughter and said into the phone, "We're on our way. I'm going to get the McIvors to Pease as fast as I can. Get a plane ready."

"It'll be there." Jack hesitated, then said, "Bud, you and John watch your backs." He felt a tightness in his chest. *Damned blood pressure!*

"We're on top of it. I'll get back to you." Wilder broke the connection and looked at Slaughter. "Get the troopers, John. I need them to pick up the McIvors and get them to Pease as soon as possible. I'll call Tom and brief him."

"Be careful what you say." Slaughter went to alert the troopers.

"For sure." Wilder dialed the number from memory.

"Hello?"

"Tom, this is Bill. Don't say anything. Just listen."

The retired navy captain listened carefully to the CIA operative on the other end of the phone while casually looking at his wife and son. They didn't notice anything unusual in his demeanor, and they paid no attention to his phone conversation. The instructions were simple; pack an overnight bag for the three of them, and wait for a state trooper named Steve Bagshaw to identify himself, along with officers Larry Hickman and Jeremy Landry. The family would be escorted to Pease where a government jet was waiting. The *Why* was never mentioned, and no questions were asked.

"… If you understand , say 'Yes.'"

"Yes."

"Get moving, sir. There's no time to waste." Wilder hung up the phone as Slaughter entered the room. "Now we need to get to town hall, but first we have to find somebody to get us in there."

"Done deal," Slaughter said. "The state police contacted a guy named Frank Vogler. He's one of the head honchos in town, and he's going to meet us there. They said he's been around these parts since dirt, and he can help us find what we're looking for."

"God, I hope so." The two men left the police barracks and raced to the town hall in North Conway, courtesy of the New Hampshire state police.

July 10
North Conway, New Hampshire
One a.m.

Being up before dawn and hiking all day up the side of a mountain in the rain, had taken a toll on the two CIA agents. Physical exhaustion was but a step away, but it was held at bay by the urgency of their mission. Fortunately, Mr. Frank Vogler, the town records clerk, was a long-time resident of North Conway, and he had known the Bryants for years. He remembered the tragic events that destroyed that family so long ago.

"Damn shame," Vogler said, his mind wondering back to that day in 1954. "I knew that boy like my own. Loved to hike the mountain with his ma and pa." He looked at his curious guests. "Yep, young Jerry fell to his death that day, and his parents never got over it. He was only ten years old when it happened. Ben got permission from the Park Service to put that metal plate on a rock at the point where the boy died. The Bryants hiked that mountain on the anniversary of Jerry's death every year for ten years." His face clouded over and he fell silent.

Wilder leaned forward in his chair, his attention captured by Vogler's every word. "Sir, I understand how difficult this is for you, but I need to know where I can find them. Do you know where they are?"

Vogler looked sadly at him and slowly shook his head. "I'm afraid that isn't possible, Mr. Wilder. They both died on the mountain on the tenth anniversary of Jerry's death." He leaned back and gazed at the ceiling, his eyes misted over. "I remember that day well. It was Tonkin day."

"What's that?" Slaughter asked, not making the connection.

Vogler continued to look at the ceiling, as if his mind was elsewhere. "That was the day the whole Vietnam thing started. That was the day the North Vietnamese shot at our boys in the Gulf of Tonkin. My son was on one of those ships. Thank God he got out safely." He wiped his eyes with a handkerchief and turned to his two guests. "You boys ever been to 'Nam?"

The two pilots looked at each other. Wilder smiled and said, "Yes, sir. We've been there." He pressed the old man politely. "Were glad your son made it home safely, sir, but we're short on time ... "

"Of course. I understand." Vogler returned his attention to the present.

"You say the Bryants died on the mountain? What happened?" Events were becoming more bizarre by the minute, and Wilder was on the edge of his seat.

"Strange, it was." Vogler scratched his head, his memory of that day brought back questions that had never been answered. "They were experienced hikers, both of them. They'd been up Tuckerman's more times that anyone else I know. Ben was a big man. Rugged type. Like hunting, fishing, and all that. Real outdoorsman. So, when he and Sally were found at the bottom of the ravine, everyone wondered how it could have happened. Her neck was broken."

"Probably slipped on the wet rocks," Slaughter said, trying to find a logical explanation. "The rain today made hiking up there treacherous."

"That's just it, Mr. Slaughter. It didn't rain that day. Was as dry as a bone. Ben was like a mountain goat. He didn't slip. But there was something else."

"What?" Wilder asked.

"All of their equipment was strewn around them, like it had been tossed over the side of the cliff. If they were wearing their packs, why would they suddenly come off and land fifty yards away? Doesn't make sense." Vogler's eyes narrowed. "There was another body next to Ben. A young man in his twenties I think. Athletic type with a dark complexion."

Wilder looked at Slaughter then back at Vogler. "Who was he?"

"No idea. Nobody was ever able to identify him."

"Dental records? Prints?" Slaughter asked.

"No. Nothing. It's as if he appeared out of nowhere." Vogler took a deep breath, his mind mulling over events of that day. He could think of nothing else to say. "I hope I've been some help, gentlemen. I'm sorry that I can't offer any more information."

Wilder looked at him as if he was the Messiah. "Mr. Vogler, you have no idea what you've done for us, and I thank, you, sir, for all your help." He looked at Slaughter. "Ten years old in 1954. That makes the age about right."

"To the day, I'll bet." Slaughter reached across the table and shook Vogler's hand. "Enjoy your son and your grandchildren, sir. You've been a tremendous help." He looked at Wider. "Let's get to Pease."

"One final request, Mr. Vogler." Wilder stood and looked at the old man.

"Anything, Mr. Wilder."

"This meeting never took place, and you've never seen us."

Vogler had no idea what was going on, but he knew enough not to ask. "I was never here."

Within minutes Wilder and Slaughter were racing to the Mt. Washington airport where a state police helicopter was waiting to take them to Pease. Within an hour, they boarded an Air Force Falcon jet for the flight to Andrews Air Force Base and another short helicopter ride to Langley.

CHAPTER 8

CIA HEADQUARTERS
LANGLEY, VIRGINIA
SEVEN A.M.

Wilder and Slaughter had been up for over twenty-four hours, and it showed in their faces. Other than the worrisome nap they got on the plane from Pease to Andrews, there was no sleep. Arriving at Langley, their day was about to begin again.

Jack hurried the two young agents into his office while Spencer poured coffee for them. Although they had already consumed enough to float a boat, they had to stay awake long enough to tell Jack what he needed to hear. "Sit down, guys, and give me the down and dirty version." The Director of Operations wanted information in naked terms right now.

"A Mr. Vogler from town hall in North Conway told us about the Bryants. The gist of it is that the Bryants met their deaths mysteriously, along with an unidentified man in his twenties. It was on the same day the Gulf of Tonkin shoot-out took place in the South China Sea. Their son's birthday was in the ball park with Bryant's." Fatigue was catching up with Bill, and he fought it as hard as he could.

Jack saw the exhaustion in their eyes, but he had to get as much information as he could. "Just a couple more questions and you guys can get some sleep. What made you hike up there in the first place? Did the McIvors send you there?"

Slaughter intervened. "Sir, with all respect, I never believed in any of that hocus-pocus stuff that Bill does, but in this case, I have to defer to a higher authority. Bill came back from meditating at Maggie's grave the night we got to the McIvors, and he said that Maggie came to him in one of his warm and fuzzy visions. She wanted to show us something on that mountain. Having seen that sign, I'm convinced she had something to do with it. We wouldn't have looked for it otherwise."

"Occasionally, John, we have to rely on the Infinite. All the intel in the world sometimes isn't as good as a hunch. I can't explain it, but it's a good thing you guys went up there." Jack looked at his exhausted young agents. "We have to convene everyone at the Farm. I'll get the word out, and we'll meet tomorrow morning at seven. That'll give you guys a chance to get some sleep."

"What about the McIvors?" Bill asked, his eyes fighting to stay open.

"They're in a safe house. No one knows where they are except Bruce and me." Jack looked at his brother-in-law. "Tell them about the social security number."

"You're not going to like this, guys," Spencer said from the back of the room. "The answer to the question is yes and no. The young man that died on Mt. Washington in 1954 didn't have a social security number. Our Jerry Bryant, on the other hand, has one. It was borrowed from another person that died in 1944, the same year Bryant—or Petrov—was born."

The two agents looked at each other, the fatigue suddenly falling away.

"Why the hell couldn't the government figure this out before?" Slaughter said. "With all the taxes we pay, you'd think these bureaucratic idiots would do their jobs."

"Welcome to Federal Ineptitude 101," Spencer said.

Jack turned to Slaughter. "John, you don't remember anything about that night in Saigon. The doctors said that you probably wouldn't, at least not right away. But they also said that something could trigger your memory and allow partial or total recall." Jack looked at his son and his brother-in-law. It was time. "John, I want to show you some pictures. I'm not going to tell you who or what they are, okay? Just look at them and tell me whatever comes to mind."

Slaughter looked around the room. "You guys are looking at me like I'm a five-hundred dollar hooker." He grinned and leaned back in his chair, crossing his arms confidently. "Let's play."

Jack opened a drawer and pulled out a manila folder. Opening it, he removed several pictures and handed them to Slaughter. "Take your time, John."

"Let's take a peek here." Slaughter picked up the first picture. It was of him and Bill when they graduated from pilot training in 1970. "You ought to look at this one, Bill. You look like a bean pole." He went through several pictures, recognizing most of them. "Survival training at Fairchild. What a hoot!" He laughed at the next several pictures.

Everybody stared at him, waiting for a reaction.

Suddenly, Slaughter fell silent, his eyes glued to the face in the last picture. He said nothing for several seconds. He alternately looked at the picture and squeezed his eyes shut. Finally, he dropped the picture on his lap, closed his eyes, and rubbed his temples. "Shit, my head hurts!"

Bill started towards him, but Spencer held up his hand. "Let him be, Bill. He has to do this on his own."

Jack watched silently from behind his desk. He had talked to the shrinks at Bethesda about the possibility of this moment taking place, and Slaughter's reaction was exactly what he was hoping for.

Slaughter opened his eyes and looked straight ahead. The confused look on his face disappeared. He looked at the picture once more then at Bill. "This is the bastard that killed Maggie."

"Okay, John. It's going to be all right now." Bill picked up the picture and studied it. He looked at his father. "This is Petrov."

Jack had seen the expression on his son's face only twice before. It was but a surface manifestation of what was going on in his mind. Bill's emotional state had evolved from fear and hate into a killing mind-set that had to be slaked. Jack knew that the time had come.

Bryant and Petrov were the same person.

July 11
7 a.m.

The team was assembled in the briefing room. The intervening days had given everyone a chance to recover from the training they had endured thus far, and everybody appeared relaxed. At least on the surface.

Jack Wilder studied the group from the other side of the one-way mirror. He turned to his son. "We've waited a long time for this day, Bill. You, John, and Ed have endured more than any men alive should ever have to go through, and Maggie made the ultimate sacrifice. I implore you now to use all your powers of self-control. You *must* stay focused for yourself, your family, and your friends."

Bill stared at the men in the other room. "Just one question."

"Yes?"

"Why can't we take him now?"

"Bud, we're ninety-nine percent sure that the man sitting at the table in there is Ivan Petrov. But we must be *absolutely* certain. If by chance it isn't him, the real Petrov will simply disappear. We can *not* take a chance." Jack nodded towards the mirror and the *Jerry Bryant* sitting at the table. "We must be positive."

Bill stared silently at the man through the glass.

"Listen, Bill, I'm not the sharpest knife in the drawer, but I'll bet my left nut that he's your man," Slaughter said. "He's the one I did battle with in Maggie's room. I'm positive of that. But your dad's right. You've preached to me about patience for years, my brother, so now it's time to step up to the plate and be an example." He squeezed Bill's arm. "We'll get the bastard. His ass is yours. When he comes to us, you can hand it to him on a plate while I run the cheering section."

Bill looked at him. A hint of a smile crossed his lips. "For the second time in your life, John, you actually make sense." He turned to his father. "What are you going to do?"

Jack smiled confidently at his son. "I'm not, Bud. You are." Jack wanted Petrov dead, rather than chance some weasel lawyer getting him off the hook on some legal technicality. Jack knew he was on thin ice with this sanction, and he had to tread softly. "Here's the plan ..."

Bill Wilder walked into the room like it was a new day, showing no sign that he was aware of anything out of the ordinary. He leaned on the podium and casually looked around. "Good morning, gentlemen, and welcome back to the inner sanctum. I trust you all had a restful break, but now it's time to get down to business. I hope everyone recovered from martial training." He grinned at them, knowing that everyone still ached. "Now, it's time to get your hiking boots on and take a little trek through the mountains. Before we head to the Panama jungles, we're going on an escape and evasion exercise in New Hampshire. You'll be broken into teams of two or three, depending on your experience level ... "

"I don't know how the hell he does it. I've never seen anyone with so much self-control." Custer watched the charade from behind the mirror.

"I've been watching him do it since he was little," Jack said. "When he sets his mind to something, there's no changing it. I hope to God it works for him now."

"He's keeping the storm in the teapot, but he's gonna pound the shit out of that murdering toad when they meet on the mountain," Slaughter said. "And I'll be there to watch."

"I'd be there with you if I could," Custer said.

"Patience, gentlemen. We're not out of the woods yet," Jack said. "We have to play this script to the letter so Petrov doesn't suspect anything. We have to give him enough rope to hang himself." The three men fell silent and watched while Bill fed the group a line of bullshit that would make a politician proud.

"... and I'll be tracking your progress the entire time. You won't know where I am, and don't try to announce your presence. Use the evasion techniques you've learned here, and make every effort to go unnoticed. Your lives will depend on your ability to go undetected by the North Vietnamese. For the purposes of this exercise, I am the North Vietnamese, and I plan to make your lives miserable if I catch you. So, don't let that happen." Bill's use of subterfuge challenged Petrov without being obvious, while pressing everyone else to do his best when they got to Mt. Washington. He knew that Petrov was formidable and highly trained in his own right, but Petrov had no idea that Bill was onto him. That fact alone would give the CIA operative maximum advantage.

Bill cast a furtive glance around the room, careful not to look directly at anyone in particular. It took all his effort to keep from staring at Petrov. *Stay cool, Billy boy,* he thought to himself. *Ch'uang tzu-chi.* He focused on his notes, not so much for the information in them, but to keep from leaping at the enemy sitting opposite him and snapping his neck like a dry twig. Finally, he looked up at the group.

"The first team up the mountain will be Mercer, Berwick, and Charlie Hoosier. Hoosier will accompany you in an advisory capacity, but he'll generally stay out of your way. He'll speak to you mostly in Vietnamese so you can learn the language as you go. The first team will start up the mountain at dawn the day after tomorrow, followed by the second team twenty-four hours later. Each team will be announced just prior to departure. Your objective is to reach the top of the mountain without being detected. If you're caught, consider yourselves dead." Bill looked each man in the face, careful not to linger on anyone in particular. Point made. "Any questions?"

Jake Newton had spent the early morning hours in Jack's office being briefed on the sting operation Bill and his father had put together, including Bryant's true identity. He was determined now more than ever to help bring Petrov down. His experience would be called upon once on the mountain, and he could hardly wait to repay the family that had dragged him from the depths of despair and helped him get his life back on track. For appearances, however, he would play the devil's advocate. He raised his hand. "Bill, why don't you send everyone in together? If one guy goes down, he'll need help, and there's safety in numbers. This is a team effort, ain't it?"

"It is that, Jake, and you have a valid point. There is safety in numbers, but we've decided to infiltrate in small teams because that offers the best chance of concealment and less chance of being caught. Once inside, we will gather forces and kick butt."

"Okay. I'll buy that." Newton tossed his hands up. "I can see why you're in charge, buddy. I guess idiocy has no bounds while genius has its limits. I should keep my mouth shut."

Everyone laughed.

"Point made, my friend. We all have something to offer. That's why we're here." Bill gave Newton a thumbs-up, the obvious meaning different from the real one. "An operation like this requires careful planning and team work, but remember the logic of *Okam's Razor* when putting this thing together: Don't get complicated when simple will do. The Vietnamese team leaders will now brief you on the details of your mission. I hope to see all of you at the top of Tuckerman's Ravine within the next several days, but not before. Good luck." Bill left the room without another word. In less than a minute he joined Slaughter, Custer, and his father in the observation room.

"What a line of hooey. You win the Christmas turkey, Bill," Slaughter said

"I second that," Custer added. "You deserve an academy award for the best bull-shitter of all time."

"That took all the self-discipline I could muster. I'm going to take him down when we get on that mountain."

Jack looked at his son with pride, anticipation, and fear. "Listen, Bill, people in this country are unknowing slaves to the biased media, while politicians and businessmen just keep screwing their secretaries, along with their constituents and employees. That's life in the land of the Big Free. *This* operation, however, is outside of their domain or anyone else's. This sanction is important for a number of reasons, but I just want you to remember two things. First, you're *Ying Bing*, a shadow warrior. You are *Ninja*. Your training has prepared you for this mission. You're acting for many people, besides your brother, Maggie, and the men in this room And no one outside this room will know about you, pass or fail. Second, you have the upper hand, but Petrov is the *agent provocateur*. He's highly trained and skilled at deception. He's also a student of Russian *Agni Kempo,* and he fights dirty—"

"I'm familiar with the form, Dad. It's more bark than bite."

Jack hesitated. He was reluctant to tell his son the rest, but there was no holding back now. Bill had to know sooner or later. "Remember what I said about there being a mole in our operation?"

"What about it?" Bill wondered where this was going since *his* target was now known.

"Neilson was that mole."

"What?" Bill's eyes narrowed. "How long have you known that? Why did you wait til now to tell me?"

"We had to be sure. You were our independent source, and you helped confirm our prior suspicions when you saw Neilson and Bryant talking with each other in that alley in Saigon. We didn't know about Bryant at that time, but there was no reason for the two of them to be together in the first place. We've had a tail on Neilson since the attempt on John's life at Clark. He said and did some things that caused us to look at him. He was sloppy and got caught. We just needed confirmation, and you provided a piece of it. Unfortunately, Petrov got to him before we did."

Bill stared through the glass at Petrov.

"Listen, Bud. Remember what you learned during your initial training at the Farm. Things aren't always what they seem, and the one that gets away is the one you don't see coming. That's all I can tell you. Trust yourself and come home to me." Jack desperately wanted to hug his son, but he remained stoic. "Godspeed." With that, Jack Wilder turned and left the room. He didn't want everyone to see his emotions welling up.

The three men fell silent. After a moment Wilder looked at his friends. "John, I'm counting on your brute strength to help me with this, and I need your expertise, Jake. The next forty-eight hours will be the final measure of our efforts. We're on deck, so let's round up this threesome and get the show on the road."

"Hold on a minute," Custer said. "I'm not much help here, and I'm not much for words either. I guess I'm the wart on everyone's back because I'm stuck in this damn chair, but I just want to say one thing."

Wilder held up his hand. "Not necessary, Ed. I hear you loud and clear, my friend, and I appreciate it." He smiled at crippled man. "Remember the rats?"

Custer cringed. "How could I forget?"

"That was just the previews. Now sit back and watch the movie." Wilder patted him on the shoulder. "He's in my element now, and this party's just beginning."

"Be careful anyway."

"In spades."

CHAPTER 9

NEW ENGLAND
SAME DAY

The sky was clear, but the weather front moving in from the west promised rain by night fall. Low stratus clouds were moving in from Vermont, and it was imperative that Wilder and his team reach the top of Mt. Washington before the summit became shrouded in fog. Time was of the essence.

The C-130 landed at Westover Air Force Base in Chicopee, Massachusetts, just before noon. The aircraft taxied to a remote area north of the runways and parked. Known affectionately by its crews as the Brown and Green Trash Machine, the camouflaged airplane had the reputation of being able to carry anything anywhere at any time and in any kind of weather. It was, in effect, an airborne bulldozer. This flight, however, carried a different type of cargo.

The aft ramp and door opened, and the loadmaster gave a thumbs-up to his passengers. Three men, dressed in black fatigues, jumped off the ramp and ran towards a waiting Huey helicopter.

Tossing his equipment bag into the helicopter, Wilder turned and gave a casual salute to the crew of the airplane that had brought them from Herndon, Virginia. He hopped into the chopper and took a seat beside Slaughter and Newton. He gave the pilot the wind-up signal and leaned back in his jump seat for the hour ride to Mt. Washington. Within seconds the Huey was airborne and headed towards New Hampshire.

Slaughter looked at him. "You sure are relaxed for someone that's getting ready to hunt another human being. I thought I was laid back, but you take the cake."

"You're right about one thing, John. There is going to be a hunt."

"Do you think he'll have others with him?"

"Count on it. Those team alignments I made are just a ruse. Petrov has no intention of going up with the others. He has his own agenda."

"Okay, wise-ass, where is he now?" Slaughter asked.

"As I speak he's headed for the same place we are, but he'll run into problems before he gets there. That will give us time to prepare our reception."

"Problems?" Newton hadn't been briefed on the details. All he knew was that he was ready to get down-and-dirty with the boys from Langley when his lethal friend gave the word.

"Bryant charted a plane to take him to the Mt. Washington airport in North Conway. But it will develop engine problems and have to land short for repairs." There was a sinister smile on Wilder's face.

"How the hell do you know that?"

"Principle of the six P's, John. Prior planning prevents piss-poor performance. Remember?"

"Heard it before."

"All we can do now is relax and enjoy the ride. May as well take a snooze." Wilder pulled his black ball cap over his eyes and leaned back in his seat.

"S'um bitch! I'll never figure this guy out," Slaughter said to Newton.

"Don't bother trying. Just be glad he's on our side."

Twenty minutes later, Slaughter looked at Wilder's equipment bag and said, "I wonder what he has in there."

"Me too, but I damn sure ain't gonna stick my hand in it to find out. Something might bite back."

"Yeah. Screw that!"

***

"We're losing oil pressure on the right engine." The charter pilot looked nervously at his instruments. "I'm going to have to set this thing down somewhere."

"We don't have time," Bryant insisted. Things had not gone well since they departed Baltimore earlier in the day. "We have to get to North Conway as soon as possible. Can't you get it fixed there?"

"Look, this is a Cessna 310, not a Lear jet," the pilot said. "It doesn't have single engine capability worth a damn. We're going to set this bird down at Hanscom Field. It's just west of Boston, and it's only a few minutes ahead. We have a charter operation there that has maintenance. They can probably fix it in less than an hour."

"We don't have an hour," Berwick said from the back seat.

"Look," the pilot shouted over the roar of the engines, "this Sky King toy is going down, with or without any help from us. So, let me do my job. Then you can do yours." He tuned his radio to the Hanscom tower frequency. "Hanscom, this is Cessna One-Two Bravo. We're ten miles south and losing oil pressure on the right engine. Request straight-in landing and emergency equipment standing by. We have three souls on board and two plus three-zero hours of fuel. Estimate landing in five minutes. Over."

"Roger, Cessna One-Two Bravo. You're cleared to land on any runway. Altimeter is two-niner-eight-three. Wind is variable at five knots. Traffic pattern is empty," the tower controller answered.

"Copy, Hanscom." The pilot quickly scanned his instruments and ran his pre-landing checklist. He pushed the blade angle levers and engine mixture controls to their full forward position, then glanced at the oil pressure gauges once more. The right gauge was approaching zero, but the engine held its own. He looked ahead and saw the runway in the distance. "We're almost there. Make sure your belts are fastened."

"Can we get another plane?" Bryant said.

"Don't know. Things are pretty busy this time of year. We'll find out after we land."

"I'll pay double." Bryant was visibly agitated now.

"I said I don't know! Just wait til we land." The pilot lined up the airplane on final approach and extended the landing gear. The wheels locked down with a thump and the flaps were lowered. The plane slowed to final approach speed. A minute later the Cessna touched down and rolled down the runway. Slowing to taxi speed, the pilot turned off the runway and shut down the right engine.

"We must hurry," Bryant said.

"We'll get this squared away as soon as we can. I think it's just a loose oil line."

"I hope so," Berwick said, looking at his watch. "We have to get to North Conway quickly."

Bryant looked back at him and slowly shook his head. It was the signal for Berwick to shut up. The less the Cessna pilot knew, the better.

They taxied to the civil terminal on the west side of the field. Shutting down the remaining engine, the pilot and his passengers deplaned. They walked across the tarmac to the fixed-base operations office.

Bryant was irritated. "Can we get another plane?"

"I'll find out what's going on. Go have a cup of coffee. I'll check with our mechanics and see what they can do. They should be able to fix it pretty quick if it's the oil line. If not, we might be able to get another ship. There are two parked over there." He pointed to the south end of the ramp. "Have to make sure they aren't spoken for. I'll be back in a few minutes." The pilot turned towards the operations office, leaving Bryant and Berwick to their own devices.

"Keep an eye on the plane," Bryant said. "We don't want to lose sight of our equipment."

"We can wait over there." Berwick pointed to an outdoor lounge area just off the flight line. "We have to look casual."

"I hope this doesn't take long." Bryant looked at his watch, willing it to slow down. His head began to ache. He reached for a pack of cigarettes. "I need a drink." The two men walked to the small restaurant adjacent to the ramp. They ordered two beers and sat down to wait.

Bryant squeezed his eyes shut, the headache becoming stronger. He lit another cigarette from the butt of the first. The inability to control events around him was driving him crazy.

"Are you okay?"

"*Stoi!*" Bryant snapped. Stop! He rubbed his temples and gritted his teeth.

Berwick just looked at him.

"I have a message for our passengers," the co-pilot said to his partner after switching back to the primary radio. He looked over his right shoulder and motioned for Wilder to come forward.

"What's up?" Wilder shouted over the noise of the beating blades above.

"I'm relaying a message from someone at Hanscom Field. Your subjects are cooling their heels at the bar while their plane's being fixed. They should be airborne in about an hour."

"Subjects?" *There's more than one?*

"Yeah. Two guys named Bryant and Berwick."

Berwick! That Wilder didn't trust Berwick was no state secret, but why were they traveling together? Was Berwick *that* stupid, or was there something else going on? "Okay, thanks." Wilder returned to his seat.

"What's up?" Slaughter asked.

"Bryant and Berwick are detoured outside Boston. Their plane won't be ready for an hour."

"Berwick? That cretin's with Bryant? They're not on the same team. What gives?"

"I don't know, John, but we're going to find out soon enough."

"Is that the same Berwick that bad-mouthed your brother before you went to 'Nam?" Newton asked.

"The same."

"I knew there was a reason I didn't like that shifty-eyed little twerp. I'm gonna make him fess up when I catch him."

"Hold on there, cowboy! That prick belongs to me."

"Don't worry, John," Wilder said. "You'll have your day in court. But first we need to find out why they're together. I don't think he's stupid enough to announce himself like that without a reason."

"What are you gonna do?" Newton asked.

"Get some answers. Then, it's party time." There was no smile on Wilder's face.

Both men stared at him but said nothing.

Bryant and Berwick abandoned their table and hurried to the edge of the tarmac where the pilot waited in a golf cart to take them to their plane.

"The oil line was leaking. That's what caused us to lose pressure."

"Then we can go?" Bryant asked.

"The mechanic's completing his engine run now. I filed a flight plan, and as soon as he's done, we're on our way."

Bryant looked at his watch. "Good." They climbed onto the golf cart and started across the ramp. Fifteen minutes later the Cessna 310 was in the air.

A man in the maintenance office watched the plane lift off and turn towards the north. He picked up the phone and dialed a number in Langley, Virginia.

"Sir," the copilot shouted over his shoulder, "your guys just left Hanscom for North Conway."

Wilder acknowledged with a thumbs-up. He looked at his watch and calculated the time it would take Bryant and Berwick to get to their destination. Satisfied that his team was ahead of schedule, he looked through the front windshield at Mt. Washington in the distance. The mountain was closer now, and they would be there in a matter of minutes. "Show time, guys. Let's get our game faces on."

The three men tied their rappelling harnesses around their waists and connected their D-rings. They checked their individual equipment then inspected each other's. There was no room for error.

Slaughter noticed some unusual packages in Wilder's opened bag. He picked one up and studied it. "What the hell is this?"

"John, ever hear of a Fisher Cat?"

"A what?"

"A Fisher Cat. They're like weasels or minks. Mean little bastards."

"What the hell does this have to do with minks? Have you gone around the bend?" Slaughter looked at the reddish-brown liquid in the plastic bag. "What is this stuff?"

"Remember how Custer cringed when I mentioned rats?"

"Yeah. So?"

"So, that bag you're holding is an invitation to dinner. Be careful with that stuff, or you'll be serving yourself up as the main course."

"You're a sick puppy." Slaughter carefully placed the bag back into the padded container then closed and latched the lid.

"Approaching the LZ now. Get ready," the copilot shouted at them. Acknowledging the copilot's remarks, Wilder opened the sliding door on the side of the chopper. He picked up the three lengths of coiled rope that were attached to the floor at the other end and waited for the signal.

The Huey slowed to a hover over the landing zone. The green light came on. "Go!" the copilot shouted.

Slaughter and Newton tossed the equipment bags. Wilder then tossed the coils of rope out the door and watched them fall to the ground. Each man grabbed a rope and connected it to the D-ring on the front of his harness. Jumping from the chopper, they quickly rappelled to the surface.

The blast from the spinning rotor blades buffeted them while they unhooked themselves from the ropes. Within seconds they were free of the helicopter and heading for the scrub brush below the wind-blown summit. The helicopter departed low over the north slope of the mountain and disappeared into the wilderness.

In less than two minutes, there was no evidence that anyone had ever been there, and there were no witnesses to their arrival. There were no tourists on the mountain since both the cog railway and the auto road had been closed by the state police for repairs.

At least that's what the tourists were supposed to think.

"Mt. Washington airport up ahead," the pilot said. "We'll be on the ground in less than five minutes." The Cessna descended and maneuvered around a hill to line up for its final approach. The pilot noticed the oil pressure on the right engine. It was holding fine. *Mission accomplished*, he thought to himself. He glanced briefly at the passenger in the right seat. "Is someone going to meet you?"

"Arrangements have been made," Bryant said, looking ahead at the field. "We'll get our gear after you shut down and be on our way. I think our bill is paid in full."

"It is." The pilot extended the landing gear and flaps and slowed the aircraft. Coming over end of the runway, he pulled the throttles to idle and the plane touched down. He braked the aircraft to taxi speed and taxied to the north end of the field within yards of a waiting white VW van. Shutting down the engines, he said, "A little late, but we finally made it. Let's get out and get your bags from the rear compartment."

Bryant was out of the plane before the propellers stopped turning, Berwick close behind him. He opened the baggage door and took out a single large bag. Disregarding the pilot, they picked up the bag by the end handles and quickly carried it to the waiting van. They tossed the bag through the opening, climbed in behind it, and closed the sliding door. They were gone in minutes.

The pilot pretended to check the oil under the right engine cowling. When the van disappeared around the bend in the road, he walked into the building next to the parking lot. Finding a phone he dialed an unlisted number.

"Yes?" said the voice from Langley.

"I'm at the Mt. Washington airport in North Conway. Bryant and Berwick left in a white VW van with New Hampshire plates. Three-two-two-bravo-mike-alpha. Driver and two passengers meeting your party. Five total. All males and appear to be in late twenties and early thirties. Departed less then a minute ago."

"Got it." The line went dead.

Jack Wilder hung up the receiver and looked at his brother-in-law. "That was our charter pilot in New Hampshire. Bryant and Berwick were met by three men in a white VW van. They're being tailed by random unmarked vehicles, but I think I know where they're going. The state police have closed the auto road to the top of the mountain, claiming a rock slide."

"What about our boys?" Spencer asked. His nephew was never far from his mind.

"The helicopter dropped them on the top of the mountain over an hour ago. Our boys are in place, Bruce."

"Are you going to tell Bill the truth about Berwick?"

"I've thought about it for a long time, Bruce. If I tell him that Berwick's working with us, he won't believe me. Bill just doesn't trust him. I can only hope that I'm right about this, and that Berwick delivers. About all we can do now is sit and wait."

"And leave the rest to Providence."

"And Lady Luck." Wilder sat in his chair and looked out the window. He rubbed his left arm continuously, the tingling getting worse by the minute. The sun would be down soon. He was prepared to wait for as long as necessary.

Mt. Washington, New Hampshire

"Of all days, the damn road's closed," Berwick said. "That sign says rock slide." Standing beside the van with Bryant, he pointed to the barricade across the road with the orange sign attached to it.

"There's no rock slide," Bryant said, looking up the side of the mountain.

"What do you mean?"

"It hasn't rained up there for days." Bryant looked at the barricade. "There's nothing wrong with the rocks around here."

"Who are they?" Berwick nodded towards the van with the three occupants. "They haven't said a word since the airport."

"They're insurance." There was urgency and impatience in Bryant's voice. Rubbing his temples, he started towards the van. The headache was almost unbearable, but there was nothing he could do about it. "We'll go up the east face. It's the quickest way up. If Wilder's not there yet, we can get a jump on him before he gets into position. But we have to assume he's up there, or he wouldn't have delayed the team deployments for two days. Let's get moving." The two men prepared to begin the last part of their journey.

They were dressed in military camouflage fatigues, and their faces were covered with grease paint. The sun was slowly sliding behind a line of clouds that marked the leading edge of a cold front moving in from Vermont. A light drizzle fell as they began their ascent up the mountain.

Bryant wondered what Wilder was planning. Did Wilder know the truth, or was he just on a fishing expedition? Did Wilder know who killed Maggie? Did Slaughter really survive? If so, where was he? Were Wilder's remarks just part of a scheme to draw him into the open? Bryant realized that by positioning himself on the mountain two days before schedule and with a different team, he ran the risk of revealing himself. But this was an assigned escape and evasion mission after all, wasn't it? Everyone was supposed to get to the top undetected, and this was but one way to do it. He was expected to seek the advantage, and he couldn't be faulted for that, could he? But above all, he wondered if Wilder knew his true identity. That was the pivotal question that would govern his movements in the wilderness for the next few days.

He wondered what Wilder would do when they finally met on the mountain.

A Piper Cherokee flew south along the east face of the mountain towing a banner advertising the *Old Man In The Mountain* at Franconia Notch, which was located several miles to the southwest. It was a favorite tourist spot in the summer and fall months in New England, but the pilot of this flight had another purpose in mind. *"Phantom, this is Bird Dog, over."*

"Go ahead, Bird Dog. I see you just to the east of our position," Wilder said into his radio.

"Roger, Phantom. Be advised that there are two groups on the east face, Bryant with one and Berwick with two. Over."

"Copy that, Bird Dog. Two crews. Out." Wilder switched off the radio and put it in his pocket. He looked at his teammates. "Our guests have arrived and are coming up the east face in two teams towards Tuckerman's."

"Anybody we know?" Slaughter asked.

"Bryant with one and Berwick with two."

"Son-of-a-bitch! You were right, Bill," Newton said. "Berwick is sour."

"It appears that way. His coming up now, rather than with his team, is a pretty good indicator." Wilder looked down the east face of the mountain. "We'll just have to see what shakes loose."

"Either way, we'll deal with it." Slaughter saw the cold expression on his friend's face. "What's the plan?"

"You guys track Berwick's team. It'll be completely dark soon, and they'll be moving slow because of the weather. Find out which side of the coin they're on. If they're bad guys, take out the two clowns, Jake. John, I want you to stay close to Berwick. Spook him all you want, but I want to confront him once and for all. After that, he's all yours."

Newton shoved a pack of cherry bombs into a thigh pouch. He took a hunting slingshot out of his equipment bag and placed it, along with a small bag of ball bearings, into the other side pouch. He looked at his companions and patted the pocket containing the slingshot. "National champion two years in a row. Bertha never misses."

Wilder nodded.

"I'll be all over Berwick like white on rice," Slaughter said. He scanned his equipment then looked again at the bags of reddish-brown liquid that Wilder was packing into his shoulder bag. "What the hell *is* that stuff?"

Wilder half smiled at him. "It's beef blood and brown gravy mix. I'm going to give our friends a bath. Then we'll see what comes to dinner."

"Shit! Those damn Fisher cats!"

Wilder smeared lampblack across his face, then pulled a black cotton watch cap over his head. Hanging his small bag over his shoulder he looked at his friends. "Gentlemen, this day has been coming for a long time, and you have license to accomplish your mission as you see fit. There are no rules."

"What about Bryant?" Newton asked.

Wilder looked down the slope of the mountain then at the darkening sky. He slowly turned to them. "We'll eliminate the cub scouts first, then I'll deal with Bryant on my own terms." He slid his K-bar knife into its sheath. "Keep your ears on and stick to the coded frequencies. Rotate them every fifteen minutes." He stared at them with piercing blue eyes. "Little Jack and Maggie are watching now. It's pay back time." With that, Bill Wilder vanished like a wraith into the forest.

Slaughter and Newton looked in silence at the spot where Wilder had stood only seconds before. Finally, Slaughter said, "I've known that man through my better years, and we've been through thick and thin together. But I've never seen him like this. I feel sorry for Petrov when they meet, and I'm being kind." He hung a coil of black nylon rope over his shoulder and picked up his rucksack.

"No shit!"

CHAPTER 10

Wilder quickly made his way down the slope, careful not to make his presence known. Although the darkness and rain slowed his progress, the weather conditions would work in his favor. It would be harder for the Russian to find him. He wanted to position himself so that he would have the maximum advantage of surprise when Petrov and his two teams arrived.

He found a thicket of bushes under a rock shelf that sat high and away from one of the main trails that wound its way to the bottom of the mountain. He wasn't sure if Petrov would come this way, but it was one of the easiest trails to follow, and Wilder figured that Petrov would want to get to the top of the mountain as quickly as possible. He moved cautiously, stepping carefully on the wet rocks and avoiding the mud that would leave tracks. He backed into the bushes, careful not to leave any evidence of his presence.

Once hidden in the undergrowth, Wilder surveyed his surroundings. He could see everything in front of his position, as well as both sides and the approach from below. The granite shelf above protected him not only from the elements, but also from approach from behind.

Satisfied that he was in the best position possible, Wilder opened his bag and spread out his equipment. He connected a holster to his pistol belt. He unwrapped the oil cloth containing his .357 Python. He examined the weapon and checked the cylinders. He slid the weapon into the holster and snapped the strap over it. There were three fast-load clips of ammunition in the attached pouch. The weapon gave him a measure of comfort, but he would only use it as a last resort. He had something else in mind.

He opened a black felt bag and took out ten round stainless steel discs. They were four inches in diameter and cut into circular blades. They were star-shaped with curved edges, and they were razor sharp. Known as *shurikens*, or Chinese throwing stars, they were a favorite weapon of martial artists. They were quiet, lethal, and extremely dangerous in the hands of an expert. Wilder had trained with them for years, and he was ready to use them this night.

He took four plastic bags of the blood-gravy mix and packed them carefully into a small pouch. He connected the pouch to his pistol belt and tied the leather strap at the bottom around his leg to keep it from bouncing. Finally, he pulled a black rubber covered wire garrote from the bag. It was two feet long with loops at each end. *Time to fight fire with fire*, he thought, looking at the wire. He carefully coiled the garrote and packed it into a sleeve pocket.

Wilder buried the empty equipment bag under a pile of rocks. He surveyed his surroundings once more then sat back to wait. After an hour, he opened a breast pocket on his fatigue shirt and pulled out two pictures. He looked at them with the help of a red penlight.

The first was of his brother. Little Jack had just graduated from carrier training in Pensacola and was standing beside an F-4 Phantom jet. It was one the happiest days in Little Jack's life. In the second picture Wilder was on the floor with Maggie standing over him, her foot on his head. It looked like she had tossed him, and she was relishing her triumph. They were both laughing.

Wilder wondered what they would be doing now if Little Jack and Maggie were alive. Would his brother and friends throw him a bachelor party to end all parties? Would John make a fool of himself, as everyone hoped? Would Maggie be planning her wedding with her mother while fussing over what color to paint the baby's room? Would he be getting cold feet?

The questions weighed heavily on Wilder's mind. He thought of the good times they'd all had together, and he smiled sadly to himself. His world had been nearly perfect until events out of his control intervened to change his life forever. What did the future have in store for him? Would he ever get his life back? He sat quietly under the shelter of the rocks for a long time, concentrating his thoughts on the questions that plagued him.

Snap! The crunch of a branch broke the night silence. Wilder immediately came to a crouched position, focusing on the sound. Sitting perfectly still, he peered through the rain and darkness, a *shuriken* in his left hand.

The beam of a flashlight moved across the ground, and Wilder could hear two distinct voices. Although he didn't speak the language, he clearly understood the occasional Russian mixed in with English. Their movement was hampered by darkness, rain, and wind, and Wilder could see the two men moving slowly up the slippery path.

"I don't think he's here, Karlov, but we still must be careful." Petrov stopped and looked around. "Let's set up a bivouac by that rock formation. We can wait out the rain there."

"*Da,*" Karlov replied. The Russian looked at the sky and pulled his windbreaker collar up. "The weather in this cursed country is worse than I remember."

"Pushkin and Melinkoff will set a trap for Wilder near the top of the ravine, using Berwick for bait. We'll take him then. But remember that he belongs to me."

"Understood, comrade Petrov. But what of this Berwick?"

"He hates Wilder for his own reasons, but that is not our concern. When I'm done with Wilder, you will eliminate Berwick. But it must look like they killed each other."

Bastards. Wilder wanted to kill them at that instant, but he forced himself not to move.

"We must sleep now," Karlov said. "I will take the first watch. Tomorrow could be a long day."

It's going to be a longer night. Summoning his patience, Wilder sat back to wait.

Newton and Slaughter followed a path along the north edge of the ravine until they came to a gully that allowed the trail to pass through. They climbed up opposite sides of the rift and faced each other from a distance of fifty yards, their positions giving them visual access in all directions. Occupying the high ground when meeting an adversary was basic to combat, and both men were certain that either Berwick or Petrov and their team of cutthroats would come this way because it was the quickest way to the summit from their position on the mountain.

Reaching the top of his side of the gully, Slaughter crouched behind a boulder the size of a Volkswagen. Surveying his surroundings, he was satisfied that he could see any movement below. He took out his radio and placed the small earphone in his ear. "Charlie, this is Bravo. In position."

"Roger, Bravo. Charlie in position opposite you. I see two lights moving up the path about one hundred meters below us. I'll get back to you." Newton put his radio into his breast pocket and pulled out his slingshot. He slid three ball bearings into the palm of his leather glove and then crouched behind a small pine tree.

Slaughter heard their voices from above. Berwick was agitated and arguing with his two accomplices. "I don't want you Russians up here. If Wilder finds us before we catch him, he'll kill me."

"Na-shto-zhaloo-yetyes?" Pushkin snapped.

"Speak English, you fool! Do you want to tell everyone who you are?"

"Very well, then, *comrade.* What's the matter with you? Do you think Petrov gives a shit about you? He doesn't. You insisted on coming because you wanted to see Wilder dead. Just remember, Wilder is his, and you *will* stay out of this. Those are his orders, *pizda!*"

"What did you call me?" Berwick took a step towards Pushkin.

The second Russian stepped between them. "He called you a *cunt* because that's what you are," Melinkoff shouted. "You're here only because Petrov is allowing it. Stop your sniveling and do as you're told."

"Damn the both of you! I'll kill Wilder myself." Berwick turned in a huff and started up the path leading through the gully. He disappeared in the darkness, the Russians watching in silence.

Finally, Pushkin said, "We must eliminate him before he exposes us. Allowing him here was a mistake."

"Wait." Melinkoff raised his hand. "I want him dead as do you, but we must not go against Petrov's orders. You know what he's like when he loses his temper. He'll kill us both as sure as we're standing in this evil place."

Pushkin stared through the darkness at the trail Berwick had taken. "That *dristui* has caused us enough problems. I'll take my chances with Petrov."

"As you wish, comrade, but you are on your own."

"This is a dangerous place. Accidents happen." Pushkin started up the path.

"Charlie, this is Bravo. Berwick's with two Russians, and he's in this up to his frigging neck. He wants Wilder dead as bad as the rest of them, and the two Reds plan to ice Berwick when it's done. Sounds like he's taken off on his own, and I think one's following him. Time to cancel the Ruskies, but remember that I get first crack at Berwick."

"*Copy that, Bravo,*" Newton said. "*Berwick's coming this way, and he's being followed. Watch yourself. I'm gonna take these Commie goons out.*"

"Roger. I'm moving." Slaughter slowly climbed down the side of the gully and hid behind a stand of pines. *Gotcha now, Berwick.*

Satisfied that they were alone on the mountain, Petrov lay on his sleeping bag under a poncho. Despite the half bottle of aspirin in his stomach, the headache remained. But he was satisfied with the knowledge that, in a matter of hours, he would destroy his sworn enemy once and for all. Wilder had no knowledge of who he really was, Petrov figured. Otherwise, Wilder would have made his move by now. Killing Wilder's older brother was like shooting fish in a barrel. In fact, it was anti-climatic. The navy pilot had been in no condition to fight, and the final confrontation with him had not been challenging. But fighting the younger brother would be different.

The Air Force pilot would die a horrible death, but not before being humiliated. He would be made to again suffer the deaths of his brother and girlfriend before he died. The thought that Bill Wilder would soon suffer the ultimate pain brought some measure of relief to the pounding in his head. With the rain gently pelting his poncho, Petrov finally dozed.

Karlov took a position along a line of boulders. It afforded him the most visibility while avoiding the wind that had picked up with the passing of the cold front. Sitting on a flat rock, he pulled the hood of his poncho over his head and lit a cigarette. He leaned against the rock behind him. Satisfied that he and Petrov were alone, he closed his eyes and thought of the woman he picked up in a local bar in the North End area of Boston the night before.

Wilder slid quietly through the darkness. He crouched low and moved with the stealth and deftness of a mountain lion. He slowly approached the Russian from the rear. Stopping behind the unwary man, Wilder settled down and took in his surroundings.

He sat perfectly still, his eyes moving in every direction. Most of the animals had been scared away by the Russians, but Wilder had to make sure where every creature was, human or otherwise, before he moved. He waited.

Melinkoff wasn't prepared for this. He didn't expect Berwick to become such a problem, and he knew that Petrov would become uncontrollable if he learned that the American had taken off on his own. Melinkoff didn't know to what to do. Should he go after Pushkin and stop him? Or should he just let Pushkin kill the American and make it look like an accident? Could he trust Pushkin to do the right thing? Melinkoff lit a cigarette and sat on a dead tree stump to think.

He didn't think long.

Newton pulled a ball bearing from the palm of his glove and couched it in the leather pouch of his slingshot. Strapping the handle brace to his forearm, he kept his eyes on the Russian. He moved slowly to within yards of the unsuspecting man. Newton knelt on one knee and leaned against a tree to steady himself. Squeezing the steel ball in its pouch, he drew a bead on the Russian and pulled the leather pouch to arm's length. The thick rubber bands stretched to their limits.

Melinkoff took one more drag on his cigarette then tossed it away. He never saw it hit the ground.

Newton released the pouch.

Thup! The steel ball hit the Russian in the left temple, passing easily through the skull and lodging in the center of the brain. He was killed instantly. He dropped to the ground, having no idea what happened.

Newton waited several minutes to be sure that the other Russian was not coming back. Finally, he came down the slope and approached the inert body. Satisfied that he was alone, he leaned over and checked for a pulse. There was none. "One more cadaver to carve on," Newton said under his breath. He looked up the trail where the first Russian had gone. Keeping the slingshot strapped to his arm, he started up the winding trail.

Wilder watched the Russian. There had been no movement and the head was slumped over. He looked at the poncho under the rock ledge. Again, no movement. Both men were sound asleep. Wilder slowly reached into a sleeve pocket and pulled out his garrote.

Keeping as close to the ground as possible, Wilder approached the Russian leaning against a rock. He crouched behind the man and slid his hands through the handles of the garrote. He twisted the cable into a loop and slowly lowered it over the sleeping man's head.

With a sharp jerk, Wilder pulled the garrote tight around the man's neck and started dragging him backwards. He moved quickly, not allowing the struggling man to kick anything loose and awaken Petrov. The Russian grasped at his throat but couldn't begin to loosen the hold. Within seconds he passed out while being pulled by the neck behind the rocks that been his refuge only seconds before.

Wilder looked over the top of a boulder at Petrov. Satisfied that the Soviet was still sleeping, Wilder returned his attention to his victim. Despite the angry welt around his neck, Karlov had only been strangled to the point of unconsciousness. Wilder removed the garrote and dragged the Russian to a nearby tree. He pulled Karlov's arms over his head and tied his hands around the tree. He then pulled the legs apart and tied them to nearby bushes. Satisfied that both Russians were still unconscious, Wilder turned his attention to the liquid mixture in his shoulder bag.

He carefully opened the first bag, holding it away from his face. The stench was almost over-powering, but the desired effect would soon be evident. Wilder slowly poured the rotting mix over the Russian's head and face. He removed the boots and socks and poured another bag of the foul liquid over the feet. Another bag was poured over the inert body for maximum exposure.

When Wilder was done he re-packed the empty bags, being careful not to leave any evidence of his presence. He looked at his handiwork, wondering how long it would take before his *guests* arrived. He looked at Petrov.

Soon …

Wilder disappeared into the darkness.

Berwick was reckless. He moved too quickly for the conditions around him, and he kept slipping in the mud and stumbling over wet leaves and rocks. He tripped over a wet tree root and tumbled headlong into a puddle. "Damn you, Wilder," he shouted to any tree that would listen. "This is all your fault." He tried in vain to wipe the mud from his face but soon gave up. He started up the trail once more, cursing and making himself known to anyone within fifty yards.

Pushkin was not far behind. It was easy to follow the stupid American. Not only could he see Berwick's tracks, but he could also hear him as clearly as if they were in the same room. Pushkin knew that he had to get to Berwick before Petrov heard him. If he didn't, it could be too late for both of them. He picked up the pace.

It never dawned on him that he would never catch up.

This is too easy, Newton thought. He watched Berwick pass by, announcing his presence every step of the way, and he knew that Pushkin was close behind. He placed another steel ball into the leather pouch of his slingshot and perched himself behind a bush so he could see the Russian coming from below.

Pushkin came up the trail, his stride longer now. He was determined to catch Berwick before he got to the top of the mountain. He pulled a silenced revolver from his shoulder holster and switched off the safety.

Newton watched every move. He saw the revolver and knew that he had to neutralize the weapon first. He couldn't risk it being fired.

Pushkin stopped when he heard Berwick thrashing over some loose rocks. Several tumbled down the hill towards him, and he easily avoided them. He raised his revolver and prepared to fire the instant Berwick's head appeared.

Berwick stopped to wipe sweat from his eyes.

Pushkin took careful aim.

Crack! The steel ball tore through the back of Pushkin's right hand, knocking the revolver free. The gun tumbled into a rock fissure and disappeared.

"Govno!" Shit! Pushkin grabbed his hand. He ducked behind the nearest boulder, cowering with fear. The steel ball had passed completely through his hand, and the open wound bled freely. Who shot him? It wasn't Berwick. Petrov? That didn't make sense. His hand throbbed, and Pushkin's confusion only added to the pain.

Newton loaded another ball bearing into the slingshot and aimed. He released the pouch, and the ball flew straight into Pushkin's right eye.

Pushkin grabbed at his face with both hands. He flew backwards and slammed into another boulder. He was dead before his body hit the ground.

Berwick never heard a thing.

"Bravo, The Commies are history. Berwick's coming to you. I'll harass him til he reaches you. Then he's all yours." Newton released the mike button. His job was done for the time being.

"Bravo copies." Slaughter uncoiled his black nylon rope. He tied a small loop in one end and pulled the rope through it, forming a larger loop. He stretched the loop across the trail and covered it with pine needles and dirt. He tossed the other end of the rope over a high tree branch and pulled the line until the slack was removed. When Berwick stepped into the loop, Slaughter would jerk the rope tight, pulling the loop around Berwick's ankle. Then Slaughter would simply haul Berwick off the ground, hanging him like a side of beef.

Simple but effective. It worked when he was in high school, playing pranks on his friends. There was no reason to change tactics now.

Unaware of Pushkin's fate—or of his own—Berwick continued up the trail. He wondered blindly in the dark, having dropped his flashlight during one of his falls. The drizzle had stopped, and the moon began to cast a dim glow on the terrain as the clouds partially cleared. Berwick could just make out the trail in front of him. Despite that, he still cursed at the top of his voice.

They circled nervously, sniffing the bloody mix that covered the human animal ahead. Nocturnal and solitary by nature, the Fishers generally avoided human contact. But the smell of blood, combined with their hunger, drove them on. They cautiously approached the still person on the ground.

There were several of them, all showing their teeth. Skittish of the human scent, they scurried about, hissing and growling. But hunger was stronger than fear, and a young Fisher Cat moved carefully towards the unconscious Russian. It was soon joined by others. When they realized that nothing was going to happen, they lost all control and pounced on the hapless man.

Karlov awoke when the first Fisher sank its teeth deep into his cheek. He screamed at the top of his lungs and thrashed violently against the ropes that held him to the ground. What followed was a repeat of the events that had taken place in the jungles of Vietnam in another lifetime. The Fishers gave their victim no quarter.

Petrov was instantly awake. He threw off the poncho and reached for his .38 revolver—Little Jack's revolver. He ran towards the screaming but stopped in his tracks when he saw them. He recoiled in terror as the Fishers tore at the suffering man's face and feet.

"*Stoi! Stoi!*" Petrov shouted at the snarling beasts, but they ignored him. He watched in horror as the weasel-like animals ripped flesh. Although wary of humans, the smell of blood and beef gravy had driven the Fishers into a frenzy, and there was no stopping them. Petrov raised his gun and emptied the cylinder at the vicious animals, killing four of them. The rest scattered in the darkness, but he knew they would be back.

Petrov grasped his ammo pouch and turned it upside down,

dumping half of the shells across the ground. He emptied the cylinder, grabbed at the loose shells at his feet, and hurriedly reloaded the weapon. Although out of sight, he could hear the Fishers snarling, and he knew that he was no match for them.

Karlov's screams were pitiful. There was only one thing Petrov could do.

He aimed at Karlov's head and fired.

Grabbing his pack, Petrov moved as fast as he could. He had to get away from the carnage. Moving up the trail through the darkness, he could hear the snarling of the Fishers as they came out of the night and resumed their macabre feast. He scrambled through the darkness, the sight of Karlov being eaten alive fresh in his mind. He had never imagined anything like it before. Who would …

… Wilder!

Petrov stopped in his tracks. He switched off his flashlight and peered into the darkness. *You inhuman bastard!* Wilder had been there and had stood over him while he slept. Thinking of what Wilder did to Karlov sent Petrov into a rage. They had been together all through KGB training, and Karlov was one of the two men that had killed the Bryants on the top of Mt. Washington. Petrov wondered if Wilder had found the other team. *This is not possible.* The headache returned with vengeance. With the revolver in his hand, he started up the mountain.

Newton followed Berwick through the darkness until they came to a thicket of pine trees. It was the perfect place to let Berwick know that he wasn't alone. Standing behind a boulder, Newton lit the fuse on a cherry bomb. He threw it up the trail where Berwick had been seconds before and quickly ducked behind the rock.

Boom! The noise from the blast caused Berwick to jump forward and fall face down. He slid down the hill over some loose stones and finally stopped when he grabbed the edge of a sharp rock protruding from the mud. "*Damn* you, Pushkin! You bastard!" Berwick scrambled to his feet and looked behind him. "Show yourself, you coward!" He pulled a .22 caliber revolver from his pocket and pointed it in the direction of the blast, waiting for Pushkin to appear. He waited in vain for what seemed like an eternity. In actuality, it was less than a minute.

Fear overcame him, and he began to run up the trail through the trees. He collided with a large branch at eye level and was knocked to the ground, losing the gun in the process. He frantically searched for the weapon but couldn't find it. Ignoring the bleeding scratches on his face, he got up and ran.

Slaughter was ready.

When Berwick stepped into the loop, Slaughter jerked sharply on the rope, pulling the loop tight around Berwick's left ankle. Berwick hit the ground with a thud, grazing his head against a rock and knocking himself unconscious.

Slaughter heaved on the rope, lifting Berwick completely off the ground. He tied the rope around another tree, leaving Berwick dangling in mid-air. Folding his arms, Slaughter stood in front of Berwick and waited. He didn't have to wait long.

The blood rushed to Berwick's head, and he regained consciousness in a matter of seconds. Bewildered and confused, he thrashed his arms in a vain effort to pull himself up. Unable to free himself, he looked frantically in every direction. His eyes locked onto a dark shape outlined by the faint moonlight. "Who are you? What the hell are you doing? Let me down!"

"Hello, Berwick. We finally meet again." The dark shape approached him, stopping less that two feet away. "You really stepped into it this time."

"Slaughter! What are *you* doing here? Cut me down now!" Berwick again grasped at the rope, but it was no use. He swung his arms at Slaughter, but Slaughter only stared at him.

"I've been following you for hours, you pond scum. I know what you're up to, and when I'm done with you, you'll beg me to slit your scrawny throat."

"What?" Berwick began to panic, but then he thought of the two Russians behind him, and he regained a measure of courage. "Look, John, I don't know what you're talking about. My team and I are just trying to get to the top. We're on a training—"

"Shut your pie hole, Berwick! I heard everything you and your

Bolshevik buddies said, and I know why you're here. Bill was right about you all along, you lying prick!"

Berwick tried in vain once more to free himself. "Then you know I'm not alone. They'll be here in a minute, and they'll tell you—"

"He was right not to trust you." Slaughter stooped down and got face-to-face with Berwick. "As far as your two buddies are concerned, my friend here just sent them to the big Kremlin in the sky." Slaughter casually pointed to the big man standing behind Berwick.

Berwick jerked his head. "Who, who are you?"

"Tom Berwick, meet Mr. Jake Newton. He's the kind gentleman that gave your two Commie pals a one way ticket to hell."

"So this is the double-crossing grease stain you told me about," Newton said, looking at Berwick. "I gave your sidekicks a present they can't return." He swung the slingshot back and forth by the pouch. "Yep, when Bertha speaks, people listen."

"You're crazy! You're both fucking crazy!" Berwick thrashed wildly, trying one last time to free himself. "When Bill gets here, he'll straighten this out."

"There's nothing to straighten out," a voice called out in the darkness.

"Who's that?" Berwick said, bile and fear rising in his throat.

"It's the first person you crossed when you wished my brother dead, and it's the last person you'll ever cross on this planet. You've hung yourself in more ways than one, Berwick, and now it's time to pay the piper." Wilder stepped from the shadows and slowly approached the dangling man.

"Bill, this is all a big mistake," Berwick pleaded. "I came up early to get a head start, and I—"

"You don't think I know why you're here? I know everything, but none if it matters now. Jake took out your two friends, and Karlov is serving up dinner for the woodland creatures."

"What? What are you—"

"I have to give you credit, Berwick. I've suspected you for a long time, but your performance on that plane in Cam Ranh almost had me convinced I was wrong. You covered your tracks pretty well, but tonight you let the cat out of the bag. You're a lying traitor, and you're going to get what's coming to you."

"Don't kill me! I can help—"

"Shut the fuck up!" Slaughter snapped.

"I just want to know one thing from you, Berwick," Wilder said. "Why did you sell us out and fall in with Petrov?"

Berwick knew he was defeated. "Look, I can't help what you think, but you have to listen to me. Bryant's threatening my family." He began to hyperventilate.

"That's pretty weak," Slaughter said, his patience growing short.

"It's the truth. Please—"

"Let's hear what Wonder Boy has to say," Wilder said. "He's at the end of his rope, so to speak. He's not going anywhere." Wilder pulled his K-bar out of its sheath and cut the rope with one swipe of the blade.

Berwick hit the ground hard. Rolling onto his back, he lay still for a moment before sitting up. He reached down and loosened the rope around his ankle. He rubbed his foot, too frightened to complain. He looked at the three men encircling him, knowing that there was no chance of escape. "Look, guys, I know what this looks like. I came with Petrov tonight because I didn't have any choice. He forced me to."

"Make your point, Berwick," Wilder said. "I'm about out of patience."

"He threatened to kill my family if I didn't help him. He knows where they are, and if I don't cooperate, he'll go after them when he's done with you." Berwick leaned over and vomited.

"And you just now decided to tell us this sob story," Slaughter said. "You didn't meet Petrov til you got to 'Nam, but you bad-mouthed Wilder's brother when we were in school. Don't tell us Petrov used mental telepathy on you. What half-baked excuse do you have for that?"

"That … that was real." Berwick wiped his mouth with the back of his hand, trying to regain his composure. "I got caught up in all that anti-war stuff back then. Bad judgment, that's all."

Wilder knelt in front of Berwick and looked into his eyes. "If what you're saying is true about your parents, why didn't you say something when we met with my father at Cam Ranh? He would have given them protection, and Petrov would never find them."

"I—I don't know. He has help." Berwick's eyes pleaded in the dim moon light.

"His *help* is in hell where they belong," Newton said.

"I ain't buying this bullshit," Slaughter said. "You've known about Petrov for a long time, and you could have turned him and prevented all of this. You're only getting religion now because your tit's in a wringer!"

Berwick sat motionless and said nothing.

Despite all the evidence, a seed of doubt remained in Wilder's mind. His gut feeling was that Berwick was just trying to save his skin, and he couldn't be faulted for that. But was the terrified man in front of him telling the truth? Wilder had to find out once and for all, and he would let Berwick's actions do the talking for him.

"Bill, I—"

"Listen, Berwick, my better judgment tells me to wring your neck right now, but I'm going to give you one last chance to redeem yourself. You're going back to Langley with Slaughter and Newton to be interrogated. You're going to tell us everything you know about Petrov and his connections. And I mean *everything*. Understand?"

"Hold on, Bill. You can't let this lying creep go like that!"

"John, this is his last chance to come clean and give us some useful information, if in fact he has any."

"But—"

"No butts, John. This is my call." Wilder turned to Berwick. "You're leaving right now. These guys will take you down the mountain tonight and transport you to Langley, so get up and get moving. And remember, Berwick, you'd better tell the truth this time, or I swear I'll kill you myself."

"Okay, whatever you say." Berwick slowly got to his feet, looking at the two menacing men on either side of him.

Wilder stepped away from Berwick and motioned for Slaughter to join him. Newton stood close to Berwick, watching him like a hawk. "Look, John, I have to give him every benefit of the doubt. I don't believe him for an instant, but if we can get some useful intel from him, it's worth it. Besides, if he screws up, we still have him." Wilder touched Slaughter's arm. "I'm counting on you to help me with this, John. Now's not the time to choke the golden goose."

Slaughter realized the truth in his friend's words. "Okay, Bill, but if that cracker so much as farts sideways, I'll toss his ass into the void." He looked over his shoulder at Berwick. "We'll get him to Langley." He looked back at Wilder. "That leaves you alone up here with Petrov."

"Yes, it does." Wilder looked at Berwick. "Game's over, Berwick. Petrov and I are alone now, and it's time for him to pay for what he's done." He stood in front of Berwick, their eyes only inches apart. "I'm going to kill him. Tonight. Do you understand that?"

Berwick looked back at him, his eyes full of fear.

Wilder looked at his companions, his face void of emotion. "Get going. If Bozo tries anything cute, terminate him."

Newton spoke up. "Bill, I know there's not a man alive that can stand up to you in a fair fight, but I don't feel right about leaving you up here alone with that bastard."

"Who said anything about a *fair* fight?" Wilder again vanished into the night.

They made their way carefully down the mountain. The ground was slippery, and the trail dropped off steeply on one side. Newton was in the lead, followed by Berwick and Slaughter. Their movement was slow but steady until the trail butted against the top of a cliff.

"Look at this," Newton said, looking over the edge. "It's a straight drop off here. We'll have to navigate this ledge to get around to the wider trail on the other side."

Slaughter motioned to Berwick to sit on the ground. "Don't move." He cautiously approached the edge. "We'll need a safety line for this. Too risky without it." The two men began planning their next move.

Berwick was forming his own plan. Watching them while they worked with a rope, he slowly raised his right trouser leg and pulled a hunting knife from a sheath strapped to his calf. He quietly moved towards the two men bent over at their task. He raised the knife and prepared to stab Slaughter in the back.

Whrrr! The razor sharp blades of the *shuriken* sliced through the night air. The martial knife struck Berwick's right shoulder horizontally, slicing the muscles to the bone.

"Aaaah!" Berwick dropped the knife and grabbed his right arm with his left hand. He dropped to the ground, screaming in pain.

"What the hell?" Slaughter jumped to his feet.

Berwick was on his left side curled in the fetal position, his right arm covered in blood. The blades were lodged in the bone near the shoulder, the muscles cut in half.

"You piece of shit!" Newton started towards Berwick.

"Wait," a voice said from the darkness. Wilder stepped from the shadows and approached the bleeding man. Standing over Berwick, he looked without feeling at the wound and at the face. He turned to Slaughter. "He's all yours."

"How did you know?" Slaughter asked.

"I didn't."

"Enough of this screwing around. Your ass is history!" Slaughter grabbed Berwick by his injured arm and jerked him to his feet. Berwick howled in pain, but Slaughter only jerked him harder. "You've been a thorn in my ass for years, and it ends now. Kiss your ass goodbye!" Slaughter dragged him towards the edge of the cliff.

"John, wait!" Berwick pleaded for his life. "Don't—"

"You cursed Little Jack when he was being tortured by that murderous filth Petrov. Then you tried to get us killed in Kontum. You lied to Wilder and his father in Cam Ranh. And for your final act, you tried to stab me in the back." Slaughter held him up by the collar of his sweatshirt until Berwick's feet were off the ground. "You're going straight to hell right now." Slaughter was in an out-of-control rage.

"Wait, John, please—" Berwick pleaded.

It was too late.

Bellowing like a bull, Slaughter lifted Berwick over his head and hurled the screaming man over the cliff into the night.

The screaming could be heard for several seconds, then nothing.

Slaughter stood on the ledge, his heart pounding in anger. "That bastard got better than he deserved."

"Yeah. That leaves only Petrov." Newton looked around. "Where's Wilder?"

They were alone.

CHAPTER 11

MT. WASHINGTON
THE MIDDLE OF THE NIGHT

The weather had taken a turn for the worse. The moon had long since disappeared, and a soaking drizzle fell across the mountain. The clouds were low and thick, and visibility was limited by the rain and fog. The events earlier in the evening had given way to silence, and the only sound was that of the rain gently striking the surface of everything below it.

Wilder sat crouched in the mouth of a small cave formed by a pile of boulders that had fallen from a ledge in some ancient time. He thought about Berwick. Why had Berwick joined forces with Petrov? Why did he try to kill Slaughter? The answers to those questions probably would never be known, but it didn't matter at this point. What was done was done.

None of these tragedies, from events beginning in 1965 to now, would have happened if it hadn't been for Petrov. The people closest to Wilder were all dead or had almost died, and Petrov was responsible for all of it. Petrov's obsession with his own father's death had to be the cause, Wilder thought. Petrov believed that Jack Wilder had been responsible for the elder Petrov's death when, in fact, the man had taken his own life. But that was another issue in another time.

Leaving the relative safety of his shelter, Wilder began the last part of his journey to the top. He would wait for Petrov near the boulder that marked the real Jerry Bryant's death. It was time to give back the name that had been taken in vain so long ago.

And to settle a long overdue score.

The headache was all-consuming, but he was too close to completing his mission to let it stop him. Despite the rain and fog, Petrov moved at a fast pace, determined to get to the top before Wilder. He wanted to arrange a surprise for the man that had fed his KGB comrade to the animals. Thinking about Karlov only made Petrov angrier and the headache more intense, but it also forced him to press harder to reach his goal.

His eyes moved slowly across the dark terrain, looking for any sign of movement or human presence. For several minutes he just watched and listened, barely breathing.

Satisfied that he was alone, Wilder crept through the darkness and hid in a thicket. He opened his bag and took out three small radio transmitters. He checked his Python and knife once more, making sure they were secured to his pistol belt. Although he had no intention of using them, he had to be prepared for all contingencies.

He took in his surroundings. Only one trail led up to the small clearing. To the right of the trail was a cliff that dropped off several hundred feet. The thicket where Wilder hid stood opposite the cliff and was bordered on three sides by a wall of granite. Next to the thicket was a trail marker leading to the top of the mountain. The boulder with the sign sat at the far end of the ledge. Petrov would have to cross the length of the open area to get to it.

Perfect.

Wilder slid two golf balls into his pocket. He picked up two radios and left the thicket to place them in different locations. The first was hidden at the base of the marker boulder, while the second was placed at the opposite end of the trail leading up to the open area from below. A third radio was left in the thicket. Each radio was tuned to a different frequency, and the volume on all three was high enough be heard over the entire area.

With a fourth radio in his pocket, Wilder looked for a place to hide and wait. He carefully negotiated the narrow ledge behind the marker boulder on the far end of the clearing. Only inches from the chasm below, he leaned against the rock to secure himself. Although in a dangerous position, it was perfect for what he had in mind.

He stopped at the edge of the narrow clearing. Peering into the darkness, he listened for anything unusual. The only sound was the wind blowing around the rock formations and over the crest of the mountain. Otherwise, all was quiet.

Petrov looked across the small open area. There was a waist high thicket backed up against a granite wall to his left. Beyond the thicket was a trail leading to the top of the mountain. The right side was an open drop to the rocks below. A large solitary boulder rested at the far end of the opening. It appeared to be a marker of some sort. Wondering if the park service had placed it there, Petrov cautiously crossed the clearing to investigate.

Approaching the boulder, Petrov saw that it protruded through the ground as part of the mountain itself. The ledge had simply weathered around it over the eons. He was about to turn away when he noticed a metal sign at eye level. He held a red penlight to the sign and began to read.

Petrov cursed under his breath. The words on the sign leaped out at him. He spun around and frantically looked into the darkness. *Wilder knows.* Petrov had been tricked, played for a fool, and he had no one to blame but himself. That Wilder had toyed with him so blatantly, made him furious. The headache raged. *Damn you, Wilder!*

The element of surprise had been lost, and he had no choice but to get off the mountain before Wilder found him. There would be another day. Petrov ran across the clearing to the trail that led to the bottom of the mountain. He had to escape.

"*Hello, Ivan. It is Ivan, isn't it?*"

Petrov froze.

"*That's Russian for John. Did you know that?*"

Petrov quickly recovered from his initial shock and scrambled behind a nearby rock. He pulled out the .38 revolver that had been the instrument of Little Jack's death. He'd been discovered now, and he had no choice but to deal with it.

There was a familiarity to the metallic voice, but Petrov couldn't be sure who it was. He waited behind the rock, his senses keen to every sound.

"Your mother was quite a woman, Ivan. Olga was her name, wasn't it?" the voice said from the thicket. *"Very popular with men, I hear."*

Petrov dropped the gun, the words causing the pain in his head to become unbearable. He pressed his hands against his temples as if trying to keep his head from exploding. In that instant he knew who the person was behind the voice. "I'm going to kill you, Wilder, you spineless dog!" Petrov screamed at the top of his voice. "You're a coward just like your brother. Show yourself, damn you!"

"I'm over here. In the bushes."

Petrov grabbed the gun and jumped from behind the rock. He fired repeatedly at the thicket until his ammunition was spent. Throwing caution to the wind, he stood in the open and quickly re-loaded the weapon. Not hearing anything, he ran into the thicket, certain that Wilder had been hit. He kicked around until he found Wilder's empty shoulder bag. But no Wilder.

"Looks like you missed me, Ivan," the voice said from under his feet.

Petrov saw the radio. "You *bastard!*" He grabbed it and threw it across the clearing into the darkness. He didn't hear it hit the rocks hundreds of feet below. Having no idea where Wilder was, Petrov crawled deeper into the thicket. He checked the revolver to make sure it was loaded then waited for Wilder's next move. Squeezing his eyes shut, he thought his head would split. He was cornered, and he had to do something fast. But what?

"Ivan ... "

"You seem to have the upper hand, Wilder, but there's no need for this. We can talk," Petrov shouted into the darkness. He would reason with Wilder and trick him into showing himself. Yes, that was what he would do.

Silence.

"Where are you?" Several minutes passed. Petrov knew he

couldn't stay where he was. He began crawling through the thicket when he again heard Wilder's voice.

"So you want to talk, do you? Tell me why you shot a helpless man in the head in that Vietnamese prison. Did your candy-ass back-stabbing KGB colonel teach you that? Or does being a coward come naturally to you?"

Petrov crouched to the ground, wondering how Wilder got to the other side of the clearing. He crawled to the edge of the thicket and looked in the direction of Wilder's voice.

"I'm sitting in the path right in front of you, Ivan. Come out and play."

"Fuck you!" Petrov jumped to his feet and ran full speed towards the lower edge of the clearing, firing his revolver at the voice. He reached the trail and stopped.

"What's wrong, Ivan? Lose your compass? I'm over here."

Petrov spun around and looked across the clearing. "How … ?" *Another radio!* Wilder's voice was coming from the boulder at the opposite side of the ledge. Petrov's anger overcame his common sense, and he walked slowly across the clearing towards the boulder, reloading his revolver for the third time. He'd gone no more than ten yards when Wilder's voice distracted him once more.

"I'm still behind you. What's wrong, Ivan? Is Olga's boy losing control again?"

"The radios are original, Wilder. I'll give you that. But I'm wise to your trick." Petrov raised his weapon. "You won't get off this mountain alive. I'm going to kill you with your brother's own gun."

"I will not fear my brother's weapon." The voice came from the marker boulder at the far end of the clearing. *"You've killed your last victim, weapon or not."* This time Wilder's voice was behind Petrov.

Petrov stood his ground, aiming into the darkness, ready to fire.

Whrrr! The *shuriken* flew across the clearing and struck Petrov in the right hand. He jerked his arm up, dropping the revolver to the ground. Petrov screamed, grabbed his hand, and dropped to his knees. Howling with pain, he pulled the blade from the wound and threw it to the ground. "Wilder, you fucking dog! You'll pay for this." Petrov grimaced, staring at his hand. "Your brother had it easy, but you're going to suffer. Quit hiding like an old *babushka*. Come out and face me like a man."

The eerie sound of the wind blowing over the barren crest of the mountain in the darkest part of the night was haunting, and it would create fear in anyone with a vivid imagination. But the only thing Petrov feared was the man he couldn't see.

"Show yourself, damn you!"

Minutes passed with only the wind answering. Petrov slowly stood, his right hand throbbing and dripping blood.

"Behind you."

Petrov turned. He gritted his teeth when he saw Wilder standing less than ten feet from him. They stared at each other in silence.

Wilder glanced at the revolver on the ground, his hand resting on the handle of the Python.

"You want to shoot me," Petrov said. "Go ahead, Wilder. I'm not armed. Shoot me like I shot your coward brother!"

Wilder wanted to empty the Python into Petrov's head, but instead he slowly moved his hand away from the weapon. He cautiously untied the strap around his leg and unbuckled the pistol belt. He tossed the belt, along with the gun, into the bushes.

Petrov watched Wilder's every move. When Wilder tossed his weapon, Petrov went for the revolver.

Pok! A golf ball struck Petrov on the forehead, knocking him backwards. His hands went to his face, and he hit the ground hard.

Wilder rushed forward and kicked the gun over the ledge. He could have killed the Russian then and there, but instead, he backed away.

Petrov slowly rose to his feet and lowered his hands. He looked at Wilder, his eyes full of hate. "I only have one regret, Wilder."

"You're going to have more than that before this night is over."

"I regret that I didn't get to rape your bitch half to death before I killed her. Slaughter was at the wrong place at the wrong time. At least he paid for his mistake with his life." Petrov was trying to provoke Wilder into rushing him, but Wilder didn't move.

"John was at the Caravelle *because* of you, Petrov. Besides, you couldn't have handled Maggie. Remember, you have to tie up your women because you're not man enough to confront them on level ground. Did Olga teach you that?" Wilder slowly moved sideways, his eyes never leaving the Russian.

"*Bastard!*" The headache was beyond acute now.

"By the way, John sends his regards."

"You'll have to do better than that, Wilder. I killed him when I killed your whore."

"Wrong-O, moose-breath!" The voice came from the south end of the clearing.

Petrov jerked his head and looked behind him.

Slaughter stood at the edge of the clearing, his hands on his hips. "Not only am I alive and kicking, you Ruskie slime ball, I took out your buddy Berwick. He thought he could fly, but guess what? He couldn't. Pushkin and Melinkoff are out of the picture too. And Karlov's at a picnic, ain't he?"

Petrov glared at Slaughter for a moment, then turned his attention back to Wilder. He ground his teeth. "I enjoyed making your brother crawl before I shot him. Now, I'm going to do the same thing to you. I've been looking forward to this for a long time, Wilder." Petrov squeezed his fists, despite the pain in his right hand.

"Not as long as I have."

The two men stared at each other, each looking for the slightest opening that would allow a lethal attack. Wilder moved laterally, watching Petrov's eyes. Aware of his physical surroundings, Wilder didn't want to trap himself between Petrov and the ledge. He wanted to have everything in front of him.

From his position, Petrov was at a disadvantage. Try as he might, he could not circle behind Wilder. When he moved, Wilder moved. Each man negotiated the terrain to the extent he could, but the movement of one was offset by the other. Each was waiting for the other to strike first.

"I've seen your work, Wilder. You toyed with them." Petrov's eyes searched for hidden weapons. "But I would have killed them."

"You paid them to make fools of themselves, otherwise they would have just kept on drinking til they passed out. No one goes into a Chinese restaurant and starts a fight with a frail old man. But that's your style, isn't it, Petrov? Make some one else do your dirty work for you. And pay them like all those men paid Olga. They did pay her, didn't they? Or did she just give it away?" Wilder smiled at Petrov, knowing that his remarks would only add fuel to an out-of-control fire. "You've wanted to fight me for years, haven't you?" Wilder glanced briefly at Slaughter then returned his attention to Petrov. "Don't worry about John. He's part of the peanut gallery. I don't need any help to kill you." Wilder held out his hands in mock surrender. "So, Ivan, what are you waiting for?"

Petrov couldn't take it any longer. He ran at Wilder with his head lowered and his hands extended.

Just as Petrov was about to grab him, Wilder jumped to the side and pressed Petrov's head down with a snapping motion of his right hand. At the same time he hooked his left hand under Petrov's upper arm and pulled up sharply.

Petrov's forward momentum was deflected downward, and he did a head-first flip, landing flat on his back. The wind was knocked out of him, and he didn't move for several seconds. Finally, he staggered to his feet and looked frantically in every direction.

Wilder was nowhere in sight.

Petrov looked at Slaughter.

Slaughter held up his hands in a beats-the-hell-out-of-me gesture. "Disappeared on you, didn't he? I hate when that happens."

At that instant a horizontal round kick clipped Petrov behind the knees. His feet flew out from underneath him, and he landed flat on his back on some loose rocks. The shock of his spine against the rocks was blinding, but the pain was overcome by rage. Cursing in Russian, he stumbled to his feet.

"You have spring in your step, Ivan. Did you learn that at the Bolshoy?"

Petrov pulled a long slender blade from a sheath strapped to his side. It was over a foot long but only a half inch wide. It was razor sharp on both edges from the tip to the handle. It was painted black and the sharp edges were not visible in the dark. "You've had your play, Wilder. Now, it's my turn."

Wilder's eyes were glued to the blade, and his hands were at the same level in case he had to block it. It wasn't something he wanted to deal with. It was a wicked looking instrument, and it commanded respect. "Tell me about the headaches, Petrov," Wilder said, watching the blade. "Do you get them when women say *no* to you? Or are they because you're not strong enough to face the fact that you're not really a man? You damn sure can't fight like one. If you could, you wouldn't need to hide behind that tooth pick."

"We'll see who can't fight!" Petrov hurled the blade at Wilder's head. The instrument of death spun vertically through the air, viciously slicing the distance between them.

Unable to see the spinning blade, Wilder dove to the ground. Ducking his head, he rolled forward on his shoulder and back, landing on his feet. The black steel blade flew just inches over his head, landing harmlessly in the brush. Wilder looked quickly to see where he was. He found himself between Petrov and the cliff.

Petrov rushed at him, launching a hitching front snap kick at Wilder's face. The tip of the boot barely missed Wilder's chin, but the left back fist did not. The blow struck Wilder squarely on the left side of his face, knocking him sideways.

Wilder quickly recovered and threw a sharp side kick to Petrov's left knee before the Russian could turn towards him.

With a sickening *crack*, Petrov's knee gave way and the left leg collapsed sideways. He fell to the ground, his left leg horribly bent as his weight fell on it.

Wilder watched him writhing in pain. "So, Petrov, this is how it ends. Damn shame you're not as good as you think you are. I was looking forward to going a few rounds."

"Doesn't matter, Wilder," Petrov said, gritting his teeth from the pain. "I got what I wanted. I destroyed your family like your father destroyed mine."

"You're going to die tonight, Petrov, but first, you're going to learn the truth. Your father killed himself in that British prison. Your KGB friends would've killed him anyway. He knew to much. But like you said, it doesn't matter. The bastard got what he deserved. There's your *quid pro quo*, Petrov, Bryant, or whatever your name is."

"Are you going to shoot me like I did your brother? Or are you too much of a boy scout for that?" Despite his pain, Petrov was still lucid. He didn't think Wilder would kill a disabled man.

"I'd like to wring your neck where you sit, you arrogant son-of-a-bitch! But there are more painful ways to kill you than a wire garrote, and I'm going to be there when the drugs take hold."

"Your CIA doesn't do that sort of thing. It's illegal in this country." Petrov was certain of that.

"Did I say anything about *this* country?" Wilder turned his back on Petrov and went to pick up his pistol belt.

Petrov reached for a derringer hidden in his belt buckle. He raised the small gun and aimed.

Crunch! A steel ball passed through the back of his hand, knocking the derringer to the ground. Petrov looked at the gaping hole in his left hand and groaned.

"Bertha never says no." Newton stepped from the shadows and stood in front of damaged Russian. "So, you're the great Ivan Petrov. You don't look so great now, Lenin."

"What are you going to do with this piece of shit?" Slaughter stared at the broken man that had caused so many to suffer.

Wilder picked up his pistol belt and strapped it around his waist. "I give you guys orders to go to the base camp, and you disobey them. I turn my back on this human scum for a second and things go to hell in a hand basket." Wilder looked at his friends. "He was going to shoot me in the back. But because you clowns can't follow simple instructions, I'm still standing. I'm glad you guys don't listen." Wilder looked at the Russian. "I've changed my mind, Petrov. Drugs would be a waste of tax money."

"What are you going to do?" Petrov's tone was venal.

Wilder looked at the man that had made his life a living hell for years. "We're going to play a game." He took the Python out of its holster and knelt behind Petrov. Cocking the hammer, Wilder spun the cylinder and placed the barrel against Petrov's temple.

"What are you doing? You, you can't do that!" Petrov began to sweat. "Wait—"

Click! The hammer fell against an empty chamber.

"What's wrong, Petrov? Isn't Russian roulette the national pastime in that vodka-soaked country of yours?"

"You ... you can't do that to me!" Petrov's voice began to crack.

"You're right, Ivan. I can't." Wilder placed the Python back into its holster. He jerked Petrov's hands behind his back and cuffed them before the Russian realized what had happened. "Now, it's time for some of your own medicine." Wilder pulled a small roll of duct tape out of his pocket and tore off two strips. Holding Petrov in a head lock, he stuffed a handkerchief into his mouth. Petrov jerked against Wilder's assault but to no avail. Wilder pressed one piece of tape securely over Petrov's mouth, the other over his eyes. Wilder then tied his feet together with a piece of parachute cord. Pulling Petrov's feet up behind him, Wilder tied the hands and feet together.

Petrov jerked violently against his restraints, but Wilder would not be stopped.

"Silence is golden." Slaughter stood with his hands on his hips.

"Looks like justice to me," Newton said.

The scourge that had caused the death and destruction of so many families lay on the ground, bound and gagged. His hands and feet were cuffed and tied behind him, a defeated man.

"You are the incarnation of Satan himself," Wilder said in a low voice. He wondered how one person could bring so much death to so many innocent people. Standing over the Russian, Wilder thought about how Little Jack had suffered at the hands of the man at his feet. He tried to imagine what thoughts were going through his brother's mind when he was being tortured. He was certain that Little Jack never lost faith and that he met his death with dignity and honor.

He thought about Maggie and how she pulled him from the pits of despair after Little Jack's death. Not only did she help him find closure when Little Jack died, she also took his place. She gave him a reason to live, and she gave him her love. That love promised them a child …

… until the excuse for a human being at his feet destroyed it all.

Wilder lashed out and kicked Petrov in the head. The blow knocked him unconscious.

"What's he—"

"Let it go, Jake," Slaughter said. "That man has suffered for years because of the filthy scum at his feet. This is closure for him. Leave him be."

"Yes, … it is." Newton fell silent.

Wilder thought about Slaughter and Custer and of how they had suffered because of Petrov. He thought about his mother and of how she despaired over Little Jack. His death destroyed her will to live, and the poor woman died of a broken heart. He thought about the personal hell his father had to endure from the loss of his wife and oldest son. Despite the crushing emotional pressure, Jack Wilder never complained. Instead, he suffered in silence while trying to keep the world together for his remaining son.

Now, on the top of Mt. Washington, all those years of suffering had finally come to a climax. Wilder looked to the east. The faint glow of a new day was on the horizon. He looked at the marker that Jerry Bryant's parents had erected in his memory. At that moment, Wilder knew that his mother, Little Jack, Maggie, and the Bryants were with him on the top of the mountain.

It was time to put their memories to rest.

"Damn your soul to *hell*, Ivan Petrov!" With the strength borne from years of hate and anger, Bill Wilder picked up the struggling Russian and tossed him over the cliff—

—into the night.

—into the void.

Retribution at last.

EPILOGUE

Over 58,000 Americans died in Vietnam before that conflict ended. Thousands more suffered in silence at home over the loss of their loved ones. That some died from grief, was an ever present reminder of their sacrifices. Those deaths were never counted. Jack and Elizabeth Wilder were but two of the silent many whose stories were never told.

The cobalt blue skies over Arlington National Cemetery were laced with the high wispy ice crystals of cirrus clouds. A refreshing breeze blew from the northwest and promised an early fall. The cool air was a welcome change from the long hot and humid summer, and it helped to lift the spirits of the small group of family and friends that stood beside the grave.

"Bill, your father was one of the finest men I've ever known," Tom McIvor said, shaking Wilder's hand. "It was a privilege and honor to call him my friend. You can stand tall because of him and your brother."

"Your parents were such wonderful people, and we're so proud of you. You and John are part of our family now, and we want to stay close." Audrey McIvor wiped away her tears and kissed Wilder on the cheek.

John Slaughter stepped forward and placed a solitary rose on the tombstone. "The Colonel was the best. He touched us all. But instead of mourning his death, let's celebrate his life and be thankful for the time we had him with us." There were tears in his eyes. "I sure as hell am gonna miss him." He stood at attention and saluted. "Colonel Wilder, you're the Man."

Jake Newton reached out and shook Wilder's hand. He was choked up and the words came hard. "I can't begin to tell you what that man meant to me, so I won't try. Your whole family ... God bless them all."

Ed Custer stood with aid of his crutches and gave a thumbs-up.

With a sad smile, Bill Wilder looked at the small group and said, "Your being here means more to me than I can tell you. Thank you so much for coming. Dad would appreciate it." He turned to the uncle standing beside him. "He suffered so much, Bruce. Sometimes I think I disappointed him."

Bruce Spencer smiled at his nephew. "Bill, you were there for him when he needed you. You were the center of his life. He saw in you all the things he could never be. You'll never know how proud he was of you and Little Jack. No, you didn't disappoint him, son. You gave him reason to live." Spencer looked at the gravestone. "Yep, I know he's as proud as a peacock."

A lone piper began to play *Amazing Grace* in honor of Colonel Jack Edward Wilder. The small crowd stood solemnly, their collective hearts going out to the sole survivor of the Wilder family.

The piper turned and slowly walked across the expanse of Arlington Cemetery, playing his mournful tune. With the fading of the music, the gathering began to break up. Soon, Wilder stood alone beside his father's grave while the others waited at a respectful distance. His uncle's words were reassuring, but they did little to soothe the ache in his heart. He reached into his pocket and pulled out a medal. He carefully wrapped the blue ribbon emblazoned with the small white stars around the disc. He slowly approached the tombstone.

"You were always there for us, Dad. You're are a hero." Wilder placed his *Medal of Honor* on top of the stone and stepped back. He said a silent prayer, stood at attention, and saluted his father's grave.

A red cardinal perched itself on the stone by the medal. It looked at him and chirped happily. After several seconds it flew northward.

Bill Wilder smiled at the small bird, turned, and walked away.

ABOUT THE AUTHOR

Wayne Keesee is a graduate of both the Virginia Military Institute and Central Michigan University. He is a former Air Force pilot with service in both Vietnam and Desert Storm. He has practiced martial arts and has a Black Belt in *Tae Kwon Do*. He is a captain for a major airline, and he enjoys hiking, mountain biking, and motorcycles. He lives in Connecticut with his family.